HIS DESIRE

Ashlee Price

TABLE OF CONTENTS

I

Book Description

5 full-length novels for readers who love their stories filled with surprise marriages, billionaire bad boys, hot daddies and steamy fairy tale romances. Escape into the world of these protective alpha males and let them entertain you all night long.

His Rock

"Lena Hunt, you'll be my wife for a week."

Being married to a celebrity may sound like a dream come true but it was never mine.
Yet by some crazy twist of fate and a reality show, here I am, wife to recently retired Olympic swimmer Riley Boyle.
Flawless physique and crazy rich.
I have to be careful though, because at the end of the week, this will all be over.
That's how the show goes.

Losing my virginity or my heart wasn't in the script.

Oh, and neither was carrying his child.
But I guess fate has a way of writing its own stories.

And it looks like my story as Mrs. Boyle is just beginning…

His Surprise Package

Am I really married to a billionaire!?
This must be some mistake.
Or is it…

Being married to a handsome, chiseled, rich hottie is every woman's dream come true.
But playing the role of Aaron Walsh's wife felt more like a nightmare.
He's my husband but why is he so ice cold?
I spend most of my time trying to figure him out.
Yet, there we were, peeling back the layers of our true intentions.
Discovering that no matter how hard we try, we can't deny our magnetic attraction.
Maybe we can be more than just married on paper.
Despite the odds stacked against us.

After all, a twist of fate brought us together.
And things are getting real between us. Fast.
Actually, this could turn out to be my favorite mistake ever.

Mr. Always & Forever

Conner Blake.
Strikingly handsome.
Chiseled chin and bedroom eyes.
He stole my story, the one that was supposed to land me on the front page.
Then, he stole my heart.

When it ended, I swore that we were through for good.
Now, seven years later, he's back.
Hotter.
Slicker.
With his kisses, he robs me of every breath and thought.
With his touches, he sweeps me away to a place where I feel safe.
When he ties me up, he knows I'm his for the taking.
It's so good, it feels like a crime.
Then again, he's the father of my child so maybe I should let him get away with it.

I could be his to keep. To have and to hold. For better or worse.
But he's not the only man in town who has me in their sights.
I feel threatened.
I feel like all I've worked so hard for could be gone.

Will he be able to protect me and my child?

Married to The Royal

Roommates by Accident. A Couple by Agreement. A Royal Match by Design.

It all started out on the wrong foot...

I showed up in her apartment almost n*ked.
She tried to kill me with a guitar.
But she needed money.
And I needed a place to hide.
We became roommates on paper.
We ended up as lovers in bed.
Now, I can't get enough of her.
And I sure as heck am not letting her go.
I will make her body submit to my reign.
I will claim her heart as my throne.

There's just one huge problem – Jess doesn't know I'm a prince, a prince whose life and kingdom are currently and seriously in danger.
Will she still stay with me when she finds out or will I lose her along with everything I've ever had?

Accidentally Into You

Enemies can make the best lovers.

Introducing Grant Donovan.
Brash. Bulging muscles. Chiseled abs. Millions in the bank.
I get to have this hottie as my protector and roommate?
Well then, welcome to Chez Donovan's to me.
"You're my responsibility," he told me.
Witnessing a murder that involved your shady boss is never a smart career move.
Now here I am in a mansion with this cocky stud who is giving me the dirtiest thoughts.
How did things get so crazy?
The police want to arrest me for a murder I didn't commit.
My boss--well, ex-boss--wants me dead.
Grant's got a secret past he's not telling me about.
And, I need help in finding a way to clear my name ASAP.

Wrong place. Wrong time. Right guy?

HIS ROCK

Chapter One
Riley

I take off my shirt before heading to the edge of the pool. The breeze blows against my sweat-coated skin. The cyan surface of the water glitters under the afternoon sunlight seeping through the glass panels of the ceiling above. The smell of chlorine drifts up to my nostrils.

As I stretch the muscles of my shoulders, my thoughts wander to my childhood, when I first started swimming. Back then, I only did it because the water felt nice. Then I started doing it for other things--for records, for medals. Still, the anticipation of being in the water remains. Each time I stand at the edge of the pool, excitement ripples through my veins. It doesn't matter if there's no one watching, if there's no one swimming in the next lane. It's always been about me and the water.

Always.

I slip my goggles over my eyes and prepare to take the plunge. But my phone rings. I almost ignore it, but then I remember I'm expecting a call.

With a frown, I backtrack to the table where I've left my phone and my water bottle. I pick up the phone and lift my goggles over my swim cap to glance at the screen.

The call is from Mickey, my stepmother. I wasn't expecting it to be her, but I guess I should have been. I'm sure she's heard about what I've done by now.

I tap the screen and hold the phone to my ear. "Mickey."

"Riley, please don't tell me you're really going to be on that stupid show."

Her disappointment travels clearly over the line. I can imagine her with her painted eyebrows bunched up in the middle of her forehead, her crimson lips in a pout and her French manicured nails tapping on the surface nearest her. She's probably at her book club, trying to pass herself off as smart even though she can hardly spell my name, or at Bergdorf Goodman, buying another pair of Jimmy Choo shoes that look just like the ones she already has just so she can have something new on her Instagram account to make her friends blush in envy, or at some fundraiser, donating some of my father's money so she won't feel so guilty about spending the rest of it.

I place my other hand on my hip. "Fine. I won't tell you."

"Why, you--" She stops to draw a deep breath, confirming my suspicion that she isn't alone. When she speaks again, she sounds calmer. "Your father isn't going to like this."

And what he thinks is all Mickey ever cares about.

"Of course not," I agree. When did he ever like anything I did?

"You're just doing this to spite us, aren't you?"

I lean on the table. "Sorry to disappoint you, Mickey, but believe it or not, I have better things to do than crush your expectations."

"Why are you doing this, then? Hmm?"

I shrug. "For fun."

She snorts.

"Also because an old friend called in a favor."

"Fine, then. Have your fun. Just don't forget your agreement with your father."

"I haven't."

Like I ever could. A man on death row does not forget the date of his upcoming execution.

"There's still a month before my birthday. Filming for the show will be over way before then."

"It better. I'm throwing you a grand birthday party."

Is that what she's worried about?

I frown. "To celebrate the beginning of the end of my life? How thoughtful."

"Oh, grow up, Riley," Mickey admonishes. "And while you're at it, why don't you grow a new pair of balls, because the ones you have seem to have withered from the chlorine."

On that insult, she ends the call.

I let it go as I put down my phone. She may be a billionaire's wife now, but once a bitch, always a bitch.

But man, I wish she didn't nag so much.

I put her words behind me as I put my goggles back on. Then I jump into the pool.

As the water swallows me whole, the rest of the world melts away. All I can see is blue. All I can feel is the cold caress against my skin. As I break the surface, my arms and legs begin to move on their own, each stroke and kick propelling me forward. I lose myself to the rhythm, to the adrenaline pumping through my veins.

This is the thrill my body craves for. This is what I've trained it for.

My hands touch marble and I turn, increasing my speed on the second lap. My muscles burn fuel. My lungs savor every gasp of air.

When my fingertips graze the cold tiles a second time, I stop and straighten up. The soles of my feet fall flat against the bottom. For a moment, I just stand there with my shoulders rising and falling, my mouth gaping as I catch my breath. Then I pull off my goggles and my cap.

I'm about to hoist myself up when I see a hand in front of me. I lift my head and see a friendly face.

"What are you doing here, Jer?" I ask him even as I grip his hand, letting him pull me out of the water which seems hesitant to let me go. Drops of water cling to my Speedo swim trunks and trickle down my leg.

Jeremiah Lawrence gives me that grin I've known since sixth grade. "Sure you don't have a clue?"

As I dry myself off, I realize I do.

"Judy sent you, didn't she?"

"Well, you know my little sister's nuts about you."

That's a mild way of putting it. And if she weren't Jerry's younger sister, I would have shaken her off a long time ago.

"And we all know you're nuts about her," I remark as I grab my water bottle.

Jerry just shrugs.

"So she's heard I'm going to be on TV?" I lift the bottle to my lips.

"Man, you've been on TV a hundred times. If that was all there was, she wouldn't be worried. But you on a reality show? And one where you have to get married to boot? What's gotten into you?"

I take a final gulp of water and set my bottle down. "You of all people should understand. Remember the deal I made with my old man?"

He nods. "You're free to swim and do what you want until you turn 28, when you have to do what your father wants, which is basically to help out in the family company and settle down with a respectable woman."

Respectable meaning someone of his choosing.

"Exactly. I'm turning 28 soon, so this is my last taste of freedom."

"I get that. But getting married?"

I sit down on a lounge chair. "It's only for a week. I'll get a divorce on the last day."

His eyes narrow. "Are you sure?"

"Positive."

He nods. "Judy will be glad to hear that."

I'm sure she will. She already thinks we're married. And the problem is, since her family and mine are close, it's a possibility. In fact, I've heard Mickey say on more than one occasion that Judy Lawrence should be my wife. Not if I can help it, though of course I can't say that to Jerry out loud.

"But you're going to pretend to be in love with your wife, right?"

"Yeah." I lift my legs up and lie down on the chair. "You know, pretend I'm caring and responsible, which is basically what I do all the time."

"If only people knew what a pompous ass you are." Jerry shakes his head. "I seriously don't know what Judy sees in you."

Me neither.

"Wait." He touches his chin. "They won't show you fucking on TV, will they?"

2

"Nah." I place my arms behind my head. "But that doesn't mean it won't happen when the cameras stop rolling. Every night."

I give him a wink.

Jerry gives another sigh. "You're just playing around like you usually do, aren't you?"

"But this time, it's with a woman who won't be able to say no to me."

"Like a woman has ever said no to Riley Boyle McAllister."

I smirk because it's true. "And I won't have to think of any consequences because we both know it's just for one week."

"God forbid you think of the consequences of your actions."

I ignore that. "Besides, it's practice."

"You mean you're practicing getting married to a woman someone else chose for you?"

"Something like that."

Jerry's eyes narrow. "You're crazy."

"You already know that."

He shrugs. "Whatever. It's your life."

Exactly. It's the last four weeks of my life, so this is my last chance to do something completely crazy, to do something fun other than swimming. To feel alive and be myself.

I draw a deep breath as I gaze at the glass ceiling.

I sure hope they find someone really interesting.

Chapter Two
Lena

The can of soda clatters as it hits the bottom of the vending machine. I scoop it out and press it against my throbbing forehead. As the ice cold metal hits my skin, I let out a sigh.

That feels good.

It's hardly noon, and already I'm having a hectic day. I've had to run to the coffee shop two blocks away--twice--to get a bunch of lattes for the cast of the sitcom that's starting filming today. I had to pick up the dry cleaning for Matt, that director who just loves to order me around. I had to make twenty-two copies of a one-hundred-fifty-page script. And then I had to spend an hour searching for Ms. Harvey's missing contact lens because she refused to do her show without it. Talk about a crazy morning.

And I still have to go to the location of Wed For A Week this afternoon because the filming for Week 3 starts today and we have to make sure everything is ready for the wedding ceremony.

I sit on the bench and open my can of soda to take a sip.

Days like this, I wonder why I chose to work behind the scenes of the entertainment industry. I could have been a book editor doing nothing but read all day. Or a graphic artist glued to my computer. I could have worked in advertising, where I'd get to wear nice clothes and have meetings with clients over free coffee, and get paid much more. But no, I aspired to be a director. That's why I've been kissing asses and working my own off as a production assistant for the past three years.

Patience, I tell myself, especially on days like this. You'll get your break, Lena. Just hang in there.

But also on days like this, I wonder how much more I can take, or if I even know what I'm doing anymore. Am I really getting anywhere? How much longer do I have to wait to have my shot at my dream, or at least get a step closer?

I rest my head against the wall. How many more cups of coffee do I have to get before they give me a chance to sit behind the camera?

"Lena!" My fellow slave, Paula, calls my name as she rushes into the room. She places her hands on her knees as she pauses to catch her breath.

I turn to her with furrowed eyebrows. What is it this time?

"Calm down, Paula," I tell her. "I don't care what they told you. It's not the end of the world."

"But it could be the end of the show," she says between gasps.

"What show?"

"Wed For A Week. The guest who's supposed to appear this week just had an accident."

My eyebrows arch as my can of soda remains suspended an inch from my lips. "You mean Riley Boyle?"

I'm pretty sure he's the celebrity guest this week. In fact, some members of the crew have been looking forward to seeing him in the "sizzling hot flesh"--the exact words of Maggie, the makeup artist. Me? I'm just curious to know if he looks as good in a suit as he does in a pair of Speedos. And maybe keen on getting an autograph for my dad, who's been a fan of his since his first Olympic gold medal.

I guess that's not happening anymore.

"Not Riley," Paula says as she straightens up. "The non-celebrity, the contestant. The one who's supposed to be his wife."

"Oh."

I can't remember her name, but I know all the winners were picked out of a horde of contestants a month before the show started.

"What happened?"

"She got into a car accident just now, while on her way to the location," Paula informs me. "They don't even know if she'll live."

"Shit."

"And the producer, Ms. Deedee, is throwing a fit."

Of course she is. This whole show was her idea, inspired by her own one-week marriage to a movie actor that ended in a ton of drama. She was the one who invited the celebrity guests and handpicked the

4

winners who would be on the show opposite them. Not to mention she's invested more than half of her alimony into this show.

If it goes down, she goes down with it.

"I'm sure she'll be able to find someone else," I say as I accompany Paula back upstairs.

I find Ms. Deedee with the rest of the crew gathered in a room. Ms. Deedee is breathing into a paper bag while the director, Kevin, speaks frantically on the phone.

I approach the producer. "Ms. Deedee, are you alright?"

She eyes the can of soda in my hand and grabs it, gulping it down. "Do I look alright to you, Linda?"

Even after all this time, she still can't get my name right. Under the circumstances, I decide to let it go.

"How can I be alright? The star of my show is missing. All because that Cynthia doesn't know how to drive. And now I even have to pay her hospital bills."

So she's not even worried that Cynthia's life is in danger, huh? I sure hope the poor woman will pull through.

I pull a sheet of tissue from the box nearby and hand it to her since she seems on the verge of tears. "I'm sure Kevin will find someone--"

"There's no time." Ms. Deedee's silver hoop earrings swing to and fro as she shakes her head. "You know we have to follow the schedule or everything will be set back. And we can't just get anyone. We've already had the wedding gown made. It has to be someone who's slender, size six, at least 5'5" and--"

Suddenly, she stops. Her wide eyes stare right at me.

My eyebrows furrow. "Ms. Deedee?"

Her hands go to my cheeks. "You."

"Me?"

"Will you be on the show?"

I blink. Is she serious?

I try to free my face from her grasp. "Very funny, Ms. Deedee. I'm sure--"

"You're perfect." She stands up and turns to the other producer. "Kevin, I found a replacement!"

My jaw drops. What? She's serious?

"Ms. Deedee, I can't be on the show." I shake my head as I wave my hands in front of my face. "I'm a production assistant."

"So you know how the show works."

"Yes, but I'm part of the crew. I work behind the camera."

"Some actors make good directors because they were in front of the camera first," Ms. Deedee points out.

I can't argue with that. Still...

"There has to be someone else who--"

"Lena." She finally gets my name right as she grips my shoulders. "Do you want to keep working in this industry?"

"Yes."

"If you do me this one favor, I promise I'll return it one day," Ms. Deedee promises.

I look into her brown eyes and see her desperate plea written all over them. How can I refuse when she's looking at me like that?

I swallow. Well, I guess I could try being in front of the camera for once. Since it's a reality show, I won't have any lines to memorize. I just have to be myself.

And marry Riley Boyle.

That makes me step back and shake my head.

Riley Boyle. A former Olympic swimmer. A celebrity. A hunk. A man. I've never even had a boyfriend or a real date. How am I supposed to be the wife of a man I've never met, and on TV no less?

"I'm sorry, Ms. Deedee, but I can't."

"Please?" She takes my hands in hers. "Do this for me? For all of us?"

I glance around the room and see all the faces looking at me expectantly, even Paula's.

Shit.

"But my family..."

"You don't live with anyone, do you?" Paula says.

I throw her a frown. Thanks, Paula.

"My job..."

"I'll tell the network about it," Kevin says. "You don't have to worry. You'll still have your job when the show is done. Or who knows? You might get a promotion."

A promotion?

Still...

"I'm not ready to get married," I say. "And call me crazy, but I think I'd like my marriage to last a lifetime, not a week."

"Think of this as a rehearsal," Ms. Deedee says. "You know, like it's not real."

"But it is," I point out.

"No. It's more like a dream that lasts for a week," Ms. Deedee says.

"You'll be with Riley Boyle," Maggie pipes in. "It's the chance of a lifetime. Think of all the women who'd kill to be in your shoes."

Including you.

"You can do it, Lena," Paula urges with a smile.

I glance around the room once more, then let out a deep sigh. It's no use. I'm outnumbered. There's no way I can win against all of them.

"Fine," I give in reluctantly. "I'll do it."

"Yes!" Ms. Deedee wraps her arms tightly around me. "Thank you, thank you, thank you."

As the rest of the people in the room cheer, my eyes dart to the ceiling.

God, I sure hope I don't regret this.

Maggie pulls my arm. "Let's get you ready."

~

Hours later, I stand in front of the mirror all dressed in white. Layers of beaded chiffon hang around my neck, creating a cowl that dips just low enough to reveal a teensy bit of cleavage. The same fabric covers my back, keeping the breeze off my spine. The rest of the gown is made of white silk flowing seamlessly all the way to the floor, concealing even the tips of my freshly pedicured toes peeking out of my sandals. Lace coats my arms all the way from my knuckles to my armpits.

Even my earrings are white--pearls shaped into flowers--and a white orchid is tucked into the strands of my hair, which have been swept up into an elegant braid, leaving just a few wisps to cascade over my painted cheeks. My eyelids have been dusted with golden shimmer as well, my eyelashes painted black and my lips glossed a light shade of pink.

Wow. I really look like a bride. I guess this is really happening.

"Wow." Paula whistles as she enters the room. "You look... stunning, Lena."

I sigh. "Do I really have to do this?"

She pats my shoulder. "You'll be fine."

I place my hands over my arms. "I feel... weird. It's like I'm dreaming, like I'm not real."

To my surprise, she pinches my arm.

"Ouch!" I yelp.

"See, you're not dreaming," Paula says. "This is all real. That's why it's called a reality show."

I sigh. "I still can't believe I let you all talk me into doing this."

"Relax." Paula grips my hand. "Just enjoy the experience."

I'm not sure I can. My nerves are already setting in, and I can hear a voice in my head starting to enumerate all the things that could go wrong.

"Just think of Riley."

Nope. I can't do that either. If I do, I'll only get more nervous. I mean, what if he doesn't like me? What if we don't get along?

Shit. I'm already thinking about him.

I shake my head and place a hand over my chest.

6

Breathe, Lena. Breathe.

"Hey." Paula squeezes my hand. "You're not alone, okay? We're here."

I look at her. She's right. No matter what happens, the crew will be there. Sure, they'll be hiding, watching me through a dozen cameras, but at least I know they're there.

I squeeze her hand in turn. "Thanks, Paula."

Just then, the door opens. This time, it's Kevin who steps in.

"Are you ready, Lena?"

Am I? No, but I know the show has to start.

I nod. He leads me out of the trailer and to the house, a beautiful two-story house with white walls and blue doors and windows. I always thought it was a charming house. I never thought I'd get to live in it, though.

I follow Kevin to the garden where the hedge maze is. The bride is supposed to enter from one end, the groom from the other, meeting in the gazebo in the middle for the ceremony. I draw a deep breath.

"You'll be fine," Kevin tells me. "And I'm just glad we can finally start filming after all the problems we've had."

I say nothing. My heart is pounding now, my thoughts swimming restlessly.

This is it. This is really it.

When the camera is shoved in my face and someone asks about my thoughts, I can barely say anything. Afterwards, someone hands me a bouquet and I grip it tightly in my fingers. I start walking but I can barely feel the ground beneath my feet. Someone is leading me through the maze but I still feel lost.

After what seems an eternity, I reach the gazebo. It's draped in white lace and colorful fresh flowers. The fake judge is standing inside.

I turn my head to find myself staring into a pair of ebony eyes. I stop in my tracks. My breath catches and my heart seems to stop as well as I stare at the man across from me.

Riley Boyle.

I've seen him on TV, in the papers, online. I knew he was a hunk.

But damn, I didn't know he'd be this hot. As my eyes go over his chiseled features, my heart starts beating again. Fast. My gaze travels over his midnight blue tuxedo, taking in his broad shoulders, his slim hips, the powerful strides of those long legs. My throat goes dry and I swallow.

There's no doubt about it. Riley Boyle looks as steamy in a suit as he does in his Speedos.

The question is: Am I going to survive living seven days right next to this living, breathing, sizzling pile of concentrated muscle and testosterone?

Chapter Three
Riley

She's mine.

I've only seen my bride for a few moments, and yet I can already tell I've got her wrapped around my finger. I've seen that expression on her face many times before--that look of awe and fascination with a gleam of unabashed desire, a glint of uncontrollable lust. She's already fallen for me hook, line and sinker.

I give her my best smile and she blushes then quickly looks away.

Shy, is she? Or is she just acting? No matter. Once the cameras stop rolling, it will just be her and me, and I'll make sure nothing will come between us. I'll have her trembling and moaning beneath me tonight.

In anticipation, excitement buzzes in my groin. My gaze travels over her breasts--not too big, so I'm sure they'll fit nicely in my hands and in my mouth--over her arms that will soon be wrapped around me, and over her hips that I can't wait to clutch between my fingers, neither too wide nor too narrow. She's got a nice figure, actually, and a beautiful face with eyes that remind me of the ocean. I even like the vibrant brown luster of her hair, which must look lovelier when it's spilling past her shoulders.

Very nice.

When they told me the woman who was supposed to be my bride was in an accident and they had to find a last-minute replacement, I was afraid I'd get stuck with someone plain, but this woman sure is pretty. I wonder where they found her.

What was her name again? Lena, I think they said.

I'm sure I'll forget it once this show is over, but I can guarantee she won't forget mine, especially not after I make her scream it a few times.

We reach the stairs of the gazebo and I offer her my hand. Her fingers tremble slightly as they rest on my palm.

She's nervous, is she? Scared? Well, she is the one getting married to a celebrity. This may only be for a week, but it's something she'll remember forever. And she may know who I am, but marrying a stranger is still a big step. I have to say I admire her courage.

The ceremony begins. Like any ceremony, it's scripted. Serious. Boring. After the judge says a few things and asks a few questions, we exchange rings and sign the papers. Then comes the exciting part. I grasp her chin and press my lips against hers. To my dismay, they remain frigid.

Well, she'll warm up to me soon enough.

After we pose for the camera, we go to another part of the garden to have our first dinner. This is all the celebration we get, a candlelit dinner for two instead of a reception attended by family and friends like married couples usually have. Our first meal as husband and wife. And strangely, our first date.

"Lena, right?" I speak first as soon as the entree--seared scallops and vegetables in white truffle oil-- has been served.

She nods as she picks up her fork carefully.

So she really is shy. And it's probably her first time in front of the camera, so she's trying not to make a mistake. That's normal. But someone should have told her not to try too hard. In my experience, the more you try not to make mistakes, the more of them you end up making.

"And just let me know if I need to give you my name," I say in hopes of lightening the mood. "In case you didn't catch it earlier."

"Oh, I did." She pokes her fork into a stick of asparagus. "I mean, I caught your name, but I already knew it before then. They... told me."

"Really?" I lean forward. "So they told you I'm Tom Hardy?"

Finally, she lifts her chin and points those bluish green eyes at me. "You're not..."

She stops as she realizes I'm kidding. I grin.

"You're Riley Boyle," she says as she gives me a hint of a charming smile. "Everyone knows that."

"And what exactly do you know about me?" I ask to coax her out of her shell. Well, I'm curious to know it, too.

"That you're a swimmer with seventeen Olympic gold medals," Lena answers as she cuts into a scallop. "Which makes you the swimmer with the second most medals in Olympic history."

"Too bad I couldn't beat Michael Phelps. I broke two of his records, though."

"Have you met him?"

"A few times."

She continues eating in silence.

And she's back in her shell. Okay. I guess I'll have to prod a little more.

"Sure you don't want to ask me any more questions?" I stack an onion, a cherry tomato and a scallop on my fork and shove them all inside my mouth. "Like how I started swimming? Why I love swimming? What's the most unforgettable part of my swimming career?"

Lena tears her gaze off her vegetables to meet mine. "Something tells me you've had too many interviews."

"And you've read most of them."

"A few," she admits. "My father's a fan of yours."

"I see." Finally, she's opening up. "What does your father do?"

"He's a doctor, but he doesn't practice anymore."

"Why not?"

"He had an accident while diving and partially lost his hearing."

I pause. "I'm sorry to hear that."

She dabs her chin with the edge of the table napkin. "It could have been worse."

An optimist, hmm? I can't say I'm one, but I don't exactly dislike them.

"So your father swims." I let my last piece of scallop dance around my bowl to gather the oil before chewing on it. "Or at least, he used to."

"Yeah."

"What about you? Do you swim?"

Lena shakes her head.

I reach for my glass of wine and take a sip. "What's your sport?"

"I'm afraid I'm not the sporty type," she answers as she cuts into another scallop and eats half. "I can ride a bike. I've gone skiing and I tried to learn a bit of football after watching Bend It Like Beckham, but that's about it. Overall, I'm not really an active, outdoorsy person."

That explains why she doesn't have much muscle on her.

"You look fit, though."

And something tells me she'd look good in a two-piece swimsuit.

"Oh, my dad insisted on a healthy diet." She lifts her fork with the asparagus on it.

I grin as I tap my fingers on my glass. "You and your dad seem close."

She gives another shake of her head. "I was actually closer to my mom."

Was, I note as I watch the asparagus disappear past her thin lips.

"She and I used to watch--"

Suddenly, Lena stops. Ah, she's remembered the cameras are still turning. Pity. I would have liked to hear what she was going to say.

"Anyway, enough about me," she says as she forces a smile. "Tell me about your family."

"I thought you didn't want to ask questions."

She shrugs.

I lean back and tap my fingers on the table. Family, huh? Not my choice of topic, either.

"Let's just say they're very busy," I tell her. "And that they don't exactly approve of me being here."

"Oh." Lena pauses in the process of cutting a cherry tomato. "Why not?"

"Does your family approve of you marrying a perfect stranger?"

Her eyes meet mine. "No. You're right. It's only natural they wouldn't approve. This is crazy, after all. We're both crazy."

"Then we're perfect for each other."

I poke my fork into the squirty tomato she can't seem to cut or pin down and lift it to her lips. She reluctantly opens them to let the vegetable in. Or is it a fruit? I can never remember.

9

Either way, I wish I could shove something else in her mouth.

She covers her mouth with the napkin after as she looks away. A blush coats her cheeks.

My eyes narrow as I take another sip of wine. Could she be a virgin? I was informed that the woman who would be my wife wasn't, but since Lena is a replacement, that's not necessarily true. In fact, the more I think about it, the more I watch her as she tries to hold on to her composure while finishing her entree, the more I'm convinced she's never had a man. That means I'll be her first.

My lips curve into a grin above the rim of my glass. I can't wait to have her blushing all over.

Finally, she finishes her scallops and vegetables. A waiter takes the empty bowls away while another sets two plates in front of us with our main course--steak and potatoes.

I set my glass down. "Ooh. That looks yummy."

Lena, however, looks a tad disappointed as she stares at the tenderloin in front of her.

"Doesn't your father approve of steak?" I ask as I cut into mine.

It's medium rare, just how I like it.

"He does, but I... let's just say I got a stomachache once from eating steak."

"Maybe it just wasn't prepared well." I pop the cut piece between my teeth. The flavor of the meat and the spices bursts into my mouth. "This one's good."

She doesn't look convinced.

"Do you want me to try yours first just to be sure?" I offer.

"No, no." That makes her pick up her knife as she shakes her head. She doesn't want me to go near her plate now, does she?

"I'm fine. You're probably right. That was probably not prepared well, and of course, this one is."

She bites the morsel of beef off her fork.

"Of course." I nod. "It wouldn't do any good to have you throwing up in bed on our wedding night."

She stops chewing. Again, her cheeks grow red. A flicker of fear crosses her eyes.

Lena's a virgin, alright. Damn, I've always wanted to tease one.

"Don't worry," I go on. "I'm sure it will be perfect."

She continues chewing but averts her gaze.

"And we'll do it however you want it. Fast. Slow."

She swallows and shifts in her seat. Ooh, did I get her panties in a twist? Or a little wet, maybe?

I know I should probably stop, but this is getting fun. Just a bit more.

"You know I'm flexible, right?"

That last bit proves to be too much. Her hand holding the fork slips, which in turn makes the potato on her plate slip, or rather, jump. It hits my wine glass and topples it over, causing a burgundy puddle on the linen and a splatter on my shirt.

"Shit." Lena gets up and clasps both hands to her mouth as I straighten the glass up.

I'm too amused by her first genuine reaction of the evening to frown at the accident.

"I'm really, really sorry," she apologizes profusely as she approaches me.

"It's alright," I tell her as I glance at my shirt.

It was my fault anyway for teasing her too much.

As the waiter cleans up the mess, Lena presses her hand to her forehead.

"This is so embarrassing."

"So? Couples are allowed to do embarrassing things in front of each other, aren't they?"

I feel her tense at the word 'couple'.

"Hey. It's fine." I pat her arm. "Better my shirt than your gown."

She takes a closer look at it. "But will the stain come off?"

"I guess you'll find out. After all, you'll be doing my laundry, won't you?"

For the first time, her lips curve into a grin. "I guess I will."

"I'll leave it to you then, Mrs. Boyle."

Her robin-egg eyes widen.

"But first, let's finish dinner." I gesture to the table. "Unless you want me to take it off now? I am wearing my swimsuit underneath."

10

"No." Lena goes back to her seat. "You don't have to."

She sits down.

"Wait. You're really wearing your swimsuit?"

"You want to see it?"

"No," she answers quickly as she picks up her fork. "So you're swimming later?"

"I usually go for a quick swim before I go to bed."

"I see."

"Care to join me?"

Lena shakes her head. "I don't think so."

Another no, huh?

"I'll just wait in... inside the house."

I bet she almost said "in the bedroom".

"And do the laundry."

"Sure."

"And get all this makeup off."

And her gown?

"I'm sure you'll look great even without it."

She shrugs as she keeps her eyes on her plate. "But you just go and swim. I mean, that's your thing. And it's not like I'm going anywhere."

She lifts her hand with the ring on it to prove her point and I chuckle.

Yup. She's not going anywhere. Except to bed. Our bed.

A shiver of delight goes down my spine in anticipation.

Maybe I'll cut my swim a bit short tonight.

~

After my swim, I go inside the bedroom and find Lena standing on a stool in her maroon pajamas, peeking into the air conditioning vent.

I place my hands on my hips. "Um, Lena, what are you doing?"

I realize my mistake in sneaking up on her too late. Startled, she takes a step back and falls off the stool. Thankfully, I manage to break her fall.

"Are you alright?" I ask her as I cradle her in my arms.

She shoves herself off me and quickly puts some distance between us. "I'm fine."

I watch her as she smooths the front of her pajamas. Pajamas? Really? Not a robe with a chemise underneath? I can even catch a glimpse of gray lace through the gap between two buttons.

Oh well. At least the buttons are large, easy to take off. And maybe this is one of those cases where the unwrapping will add some thrill to the present itself.

"You're back quickly," Lena adds.

"What were you doing?" I ask again.

She tucks strands of hair behind her ear. They're flowing freely past her shoulders now, and just as I thought, it suits her better.

"Just checking that there really aren't any cameras here."

Interesting. "And?"

"I didn't find any. Oh, and I checked the bathroom, too before I took a shower."

I thought I caught the scent of soap on her. And here I thought we could enjoy a shower together. Maybe some other time.

"Good. I'll take a shower, then."

"Okay." She turns her back to me.

I close the distance between us and wrap an arm around her waist. I brush back more strands of her hair so I can whisper in her ear.

"Unless you want me to do something else first."

Immediately, her shoulders stiffen.

11

I wrap tendrils of her hair around my finger and press them to my lips, then plant a kiss on the back of her shoulder.

"Lena..."

She breaks free of my hold and turns around with her hands in front of her.

"You're right. There is something."

But I have the feeling it's not what I'm thinking.

"We need to talk first."

My eyebrows crease. "Didn't we do that during dinner?"

"I mean talk for real."

Okay.

I sit on the edge of the bed and place my hands on my lap. "I'm all ears."

"You know I'm not the one you were supposed to marry, right?" Lena asks me.

"I heard."

"I was actually a production assistant on this show and they had me fill in for your chosen wife."

My eyebrows arch. "Really?"

"That means that I didn't ask to be here, that I didn't want to marry you."

Okay. I wasn't expecting that.

"But you are married to me now," I point out.

"Yes. But I want you to understand that I'm just doing this because I was asked to. I'm going to play along. When the camera's rolling, I'm going to play your wife and do the challenges with you and all that couple stuff..."

Couple stuff? I wonder if she thinks that includes kissing, touching, making--

"But once no one's filming, I'm going to have to ask you to keep your distance and respect my privacy."

What?

"Don't worry." She raises her hands. "You can have the bed. I'll... sleep on that chaise lounge over there." She glances at it. "I'd sleep on the couch, but I'm supposed to stay in this room with you."

I throw her a puzzled look. "Are you serious?"

"Yes. We'll just be like... roommates. Housemates. Whatever. In a week, we'll part ways, so there's really no point in getting close to each other. And no need, really. I never wanted to be here and you're just..." Lena shrugs. "I don't really know why you're here, but I don't care. You'll move on with your glorious life and forget me."

"Wow." My eyes grow wide.

Shy? Scared? No. This is the real Lena.

And fuck, I think I want her even more now.

She clasps her hands together. "So, do we understand each other?"

I nod. "Loud and clear."

"Good."

She lets out a breath of relief and grabs a pillow from the bed. I grab the other end.

"Just one thing," I say to her. "You get the bed."

"Okay."

For now. Because for sure, before this week is over, we'll both be in it. And everyone can bet we won't just be sleeping.

I head to the bathroom with a wide grin.

So Lena wants to play, does she? She wants me to break through her defenses and win her over? Fine by me. I'm just as good with endurance as I am with speed.

And by God, one way or another, I'm going to get what I want from my wife.

Like Jerry said, no woman says no to Riley Boyle McAllister.

Chapter Four
Lena

I can't believe I was able to say all that to Riley.

I slap my forehead as I rest my head on a pillow. My eyes point to the turquoise ceiling.

I'd been meaning to say that since I saw him, since before the ceremony started. I rehearsed variations of the lines in my head. I didn't have a chance to speak up, though, not with the camera rolling. Not until a few minutes ago. Even then, I nearly faltered.

I place my hand over my chest. My heart has slowed down now, back to its steady beat. Earlier, though, when Riley put his arm around me, my heart was pounding like crazy. When I felt his lips on the back of my shoulder, I couldn't breathe. I still don't know how I managed to pull away. I still don't know where I got the courage to speak. Somehow, I just opened my mouth and the words came tumbling out.

My arms fall to my sides on the bed. A sigh of relief escapes my lips.

Thank goodness I was able to get that out of the way. And thank goodness Riley seemed fine with it.

Well, he seemed surprised at first. But he didn't get mad or complain or try to argue with me. For a moment there, when he grabbed the pillow from me, I thought he was angry. But he just wanted to give me the bed, which is sweet, I guess. I wasn't expecting that. I actually thought he'd be kind of a jerk. Stuck-up. Selfish. Vain. And hard to talk to. But Riley's actually nice. Friendly. Funny. Thoughtful.

I shake my head as I wrap my arms around a pillow.

Whoa. Why am I sounding like a girl with a crush? No. I do not have a crush on Riley Boyle. I'm just pleasantly surprised, is all. And maybe impressed. And maybe...

Oh, fine. I have a crush on him. I'd be a slab of stone not to. I may be a virgin, but I still am a woman, and Riley Boyle is very much a man. Just a while ago, when he caught me in his arms, I caught the smell of sweat off him--I didn't even know swimmers could sweat--and my knees turned to mush.

It's a good thing Riley agreed not to share the bed with me or I'm sure I wouldn't be able to sleep at all. I do feel a tad guilty that he's sleeping on the chaise lounge, though.

I get up and put another pillow on it and then the comforter so he can be, well, more comfortable. Then I go back to the bed and crawl under the blanket. It's thinner, but it should be fine. I have my pajamas on, anyway. Well, they're not mine. Paula got them from the wardrobe department since I didn't have time to get my things from my apartment. But they feel snug enough. I should be able to sleep like a bug in a rug.

In fact, I'm going to do that now, I think as I let out a yawn. It's been a crazy day and I suddenly feel tired. I close my eyes, and within moments, I drift off to sleep.

~

When I wake up, the first thing I notice is the silence. Usually, the first thing I hear is Mrs. Diaz's Pomeranian next door barking at the spray bottle as she waters her plants while saying her morning prayers. Or the blender from Josie's apartment as she makes breakfast smoothies to earn extra income. Or the thuds from Nate's treadmill upstairs.

But right now, I'm hearing nothing. Weird.

Then I turn on my back and see the turquoise ceiling and understand why. I'm not at my apartment in downtown LA. I'm at a house somewhere in between Monterey and San Luis Obispo. I'm on a reality show.

With Riley Boyle.

I sit up and turn towards the chaise lounge near the window. My eyes grow wide as I find it empty.

Where is Riley? I don't hear the shower, so he must be outside. Was he unable to sleep last night? Did he decide to leave because of what I asked of him?

Now that I think of it, what I did is a little unfair to him. He came here to have a wife, after all, or at least experience what it's like to have one, to have an ordinary, married life. And of course he'd feel cheated if he couldn't get that. He has every reason to complain to Ms. Deedee, to ask to leave the show.

Shit. Why didn't I think of that before?

Panicking, I rush out of the bedroom. Each time I pass a room and see no sign of Riley, my anxiety increases.

13

Is he really gone?

Then, as I pass by the pool a second time, I see him. Of course he'd be in the pool. He must have been underwater earlier. That's why I missed him. Now he's emerging. As he grips the bars and climbs up, I find myself mesmerized.

Drops of water trickle down his skin, following the paths between well-defined muscles. They drip off his biceps. They roll down his spine, some seeping into his black Speedo trunks which cling to his firm backside and his thighs like a second skin. The rest make their way down his bulging calves and slim ankles to create a puddle around his feet.

Now, that is a body!

I swallow the lump in my throat and take in a gulp of air. Weird. Riley is the one who swam, but I'm the one out of breath.

As he turns, I hide behind a pillar on instinct--only to question it a moment after. I'm not doing anything wrong. I'm just... ogling a man. A swimmer. I'm studying a swimmer's anatomy.

Yeah, right.

I glance at the ceiling. Wait. The cameras didn't catch me spying on Riley, did they? Shit. I sure hope not.

But just in case, I try to walk inside the house as normally as I can. I go to the bathroom to wash up, then to the kitchen to put on a pot of coffee. Just as it finishes brewing, Riley walks in.

My gaze pivots towards him, but I tear it away as I realize he's still in those trunks with just the addition of a towel around his shoulders.

Put on a shirt, damn it.

Then again, he's probably showing off for the camera. I'm sure the crew is loving it.

"Good morning, honey," he greets.

Honey?

"Morning," I mutter as I pour myself a cup of coffee. "Do you drink coffee or is it just all protein shakes?"

Riley chuckles. "For the record, I don't drink protein shakes."

"Oh."

"How does that coffee taste?" he asks.

I bring the cup to my lips and take a sip. "Not bad."

Maybe a little too robust for my liking, but--

My thoughts evaporate as Riley walks towards me. At first I think he's going to take a sip from my cup, but then he places his hand on my cheek and presses our lips firmly together. Not just that. His tongue slips in between. As it brushes against mine, I feel something hotter than the cup in my hands swirl in my belly. My shoulders and knees quiver.

What the hell?

Afterwards, he whispers in my ear, "Don't forget the world's watching. We can't let them down."

I know. I haven't forgotten. And I know I agreed to play along. Still, was that kiss necessary?

"You're right," Riley says out loud. He licks his lips. "The coffee isn't bad. I think I'll have a cup."

"Okay."

As soon as my back is turned to him, I draw a deep breath. Then I set my cup down and try to keep my hands steady as I pour him one.

"You slept soundly last night," he remarks. "Then again, you must have been exhausted."

"Yeah. How about you?"

"Better than I have in ages. I think married life suits me."

Liar. I'm sure he's slept better.

Then it dawns on me that he's implying we had sex last night, which is probably what the world expects. When I turn to him, I find him with a wide grin. I give him his cup of coffee and lift mine to cover my blushing cheeks.

Damn, he's a good actor. And something tells me he's enjoying this.

I'm not, but I can't let him do all the work. And I don't want to disappoint Ms. Deedee after she picked me to be on this show.

"Isn't it too soon to say that, babe?" I ask him as I lower my cup. "Surely last night was just a warm-up."

His dark eyes grow wide. What? Did I go too far?

Then his eyes grow even darker as they narrow. "Oh, you bet."

Fresh heat tingles in my veins. Shit. I don't think I can do this after all.

Just then, I hear the front door open, then footsteps. Seconds later, I see the host of the show, Seth Sinclair, step into the kitchen. He gives Riley a pat on the shoulder as he congratulates him then shakes my hand.

"So, how are you two doing?" he asks as his teeth gleam in a perfect smile. "It looks like you've settled right in."

"We have," Riley agrees.

"And you look like you've already tried the pool," Seth tells him. "I knew you'd like that."

"It's smaller than I'm used to," Riley answers. "But it's fine."

Seth laughs.

"How about you, Lena?" he asks me. "How do you feel? Does this all still feel surreal to you?"

"Definitely," I answer. "I can hardly believe it's real."

Because it's not.

"Well, I'm sure it feels like a dream come true to be married to a celebrity," Seth says. "But yes, it's time to get more real. The honeymoon is over, and as you know, today, your challenges as man and wife begin. Are you ready?"

"Yes," Riley answers confidently.

"I hope so," I add.

Someone hands Seth a wine bucket brimming with confetti and he holds it up.

"Mr. and Mrs. Boyle, it's time for you to pick your first challenge."

I glance at Riley.

"You do it," he tells me.

I hesitate. "Sure?"

"Go on," Seth urges me.

So I dip my hand inside the bucket and lift the first cork I get my hands on. Then I hand it to Seth and he reads the tiny scroll tucked inside.

You've sworn to stick together through highs and lows.

Can you reach the top? God only knows.

I clasp a hand over my mouth as I let out a gasp. Is this challenge what I think it is?

Then someone brings Seth a pair of hiking shoes and I know I'm right.

"Today, the two of you are going for a hike," Seth announces.

I shake my head. "No way."

No fucking way. I've tried hiking before with my family and I still remember how much I hated it what with all the cuts I got and the insect bites and the aches after. Of all the challenges in that bucket, why did it have to be the hiking one?

Riley, on the other hand, looks thrilled. He grins as he puts an arm around my shoulder.

"Come on, honey. Where's your sense of adventure?"

~

This isn't adventure. This is torture. Or so I think as I follow Riley up the dusty trail.

The sun is beating down on us. I can feel the sweat sticking to my armpits and piling up between my breasts. My throat feels dry because I don't want to drink too much water because I don't want to have to pee in a bush. My feet are killing me.

And yet Riley makes it seem so easy. He's sweating too, but he's hardly out of breath. I even heard him humming a while ago.

15

It must be because he's an athlete. For him, this is just like training. It's fun. For a couch potato like me, it's hell.

"Are you alright?" Riley asks me for about the hundredth time as he stops and turns.

I sit on a nearby rock. "I don't think I can take any more of this."

And I'm not acting. I really am fucking tired.

Besides, this is pointless. We get to the top and then what? We'll just have to climb back down.

"Yes, you can," he encourages me.

I shake my head. "You go ahead. I'll wait here."

Riley shakes his head in turn. "I'm not going without you. Even if that means I have to carry you."

My eyebrows arch. Is he serious? Well, he looks like it.

"You don't have to do that."

"Then why don't you walk ahead of me? That way, you can set the pace. And I can push you from behind if you need it."

I frown. "We'll never get there."

"Yes, we will as long as we keep moving."

"It's too far."

"Nothing is ever too far. And something is only far when you're not walking towards it."

I narrow my eyes at him. "Wow. You could write a book on motivation."

Riley chuckles. "If you can still make fun of me, you have enough energy to walk."

He grabs my arm and pulls me to my feet.

"I'm not making fun of you," I tell him. "I really am amazed at how you athletes manage to train so hard and push yourselves to the limit. Why?"

"Because we're masochists," he kids.

I pout.

He takes a towel out of his backpack and wipes the sweat off my forehead. "Well, I don't know why other athletes do it, but for me, I do it because I can't imagine not doing it, because I know no other way to feel alive."

My eyebrows crease. "You feel alive when you're killing yourself?"

He shrugs and gives another chuckle. "All I know is that there's nothing like the thrill of pursuing a goal like your life depended on it, nothing like the joy of surpassing your former self and triumphing over your own doubts."

"But you can do that when you're doing other things, too, like when you're making a movie or--"

"But in sports, especially in individual sports, it's all up to you. And sometimes, just a small amount of extra effort can make a world of difference."

I say nothing. I think I understand what he's saying, but I really don't think I can go on.

"Come on." Riley pulls my arm. "You're not a quitter, are you? And I'm definitely not quitting on you."

I lift my head to meet his gaze. My breath catches.

He means it. He really means it. And somehow, I can't turn away. An athlete's determination is a dangerous thing. It's powerful. Contagious. Before I know it, my body is moving forward again.

"That's it," Riley praises my effort. "One step at a time."

I take another step. I guess it's amazing what you can do when someone believes in you. My dad usually just let me give up. If I didn't want to do something, he didn't force me. Same with my mom. And yet Riley's not letting up.

I guess I'll do my best to continue. For him.

"I sure hope we get to the top soon."

~

When we do, I'm even more tired and sweaty, and I'm aching all over. But the cool breeze sweeping through my hair and caressing my cheeks gives me some relief. The spectacular view washes some of my exhaustion away. I commit it to memory since I don't have my camera with me.

Then there's that feeling Riley talked about--the feeling of reaching your goal, of accomplishing something you never thought possible.

I feel that now. And yes, I have to admit it's pretty amazing.

"You're smiling," Riley observes out loud.

I glance at him. "Well, we reached the top, didn't we?"

He pats my shoulder. "You should be proud of yourself. I'm proud of you."

The smile he sends my way makes my heart speed up again.

"Thanks," I tell him. "I wouldn't have been able to do it without you."

"But you will next time," Riley assures me. "You're stronger than you were before."

Am I? I don't know. But I do know this. I won't ever forget this sense of accomplishment.

Or this beautiful sunset.

When Riley grabs my hand, I don't jerk it away. I just let his fingers entwine with mine. Warmth, blazing orange just like the sky, bursts in my chest. My head naturally falls against his arm.

I guess some things are worth almost killing yourself for.

Chapter Five
Riley

I'm dying to hold her.

Yesterday, for the first time, Lena didn't flinch when I touched her. She didn't pull away. She even placed her head against me. Damn, I wanted to kiss her then. Harder than I ever have. I wanted to push her down on the dirt, tear her clothes off her and make her mine. I didn't even know there was such a beastly urge in me.

But I didn't. My sensible self prevailed over my sensual and I simply stood there holding her hand. I couldn't have her first time be on top of some dusty rocks, after all.

All the way down, I thought of all the ways to hold her, to take her, to make her moan and scream my name. But when we got back to the house, I saw her bruises and listened to her complaints of pain. I bandaged her cuts and even rubbed her sore shoulders. Then she fell asleep. I couldn't bring myself to wake her.

This morning, for sure, I'll have my chance. After all that happened yesterday, I'm sure Lena won't resist.

But when I come back to the bedroom after my swim, she's no longer in bed. Instead, I hear the shower running. The door to the bathroom is locked.

I frown as I stare at the knob. So she's still scared of me?

It doesn't matter. I sit on the bed and wait. Patiently.

After what seems like an eternity, I hear the knob turn. Lena comes out of the bathroom wearing a striped shirt and a jumper dress that reaches down to her knees. Bunches of her wet hair cascade down on the towel around her shoulders.

"Oh." She stops in her tracks when she sees me. "Did I keep you waiting? I'm sorry."

Damn right she did. But no more.

I stand in front of her and take her hand. "How are you feeling?"

To my dismay, she pulls her hand away. "Better. My muscles are still feeling a little sore, though." She pats the sides of her thighs.

"And your wounds?" I grab her arm to take a look.

"They've healed."

She's right. The bruises have begun to fade. And the cut seems to have closed.

"What about the one on your knee?" I ask her.

Lena glances at it. "I think it's--"

"Let me check."

I pull her towards the bed so she can sit on its edge. Then I lift the hem of her dress to take a look at her scraped knee. It, too, looks better.

But then, checking her wounds was just an excuse.

I press my lips against the fresh skin.

"Riley, what are you doing?" Lena attempts to cover her knee.

But I push the denim back, brushing my lips against the inside of her thigh. She laughs.

"That tickles."

She grabs my shoulders and pushes me off. I get off my knee and lean over her. Losing her balance, she falls on top of the bed. Her wide eyes stare up at me.

"Riley?"

I can see fear in them, but I can also catch a hint of something else. Excitement? Desire?

I lower my face to hers, hoping to kiss her so I can find out. But as soon as I close my eyes, I hear a door open. Lena pushes me away.

"Seth must be here," she says, getting off the bed.

I frown. Another foiled attempt? My patience is running out.

Still, I put on a smile as I follow Lena to the living room to meet Seth. This time, I get to choose the challenge, to pick a toothbrush from a huge mug. I pick the red one and Seth reads the note attached to it.

Two become one and sometimes three
Time for something cute and cuddly.

My eyebrows crease. Cute and cuddly? A stuffed toy?

"Come to the front yard in five minutes," Seth says.

After he's gone, I look at Lena. "What does it mean?"

She just grins. "I won't tell you so it's a surprise."

Of course she knows what it is. Doesn't she know everything about this show?

As for me, it seems to be another test of patience. Really? All this suspense is killing me.

Finally, Seth calls. Lena and I go to the front yard where a large basket is waiting. Lena runs to it and opens it.

"A puppy!" She holds up the dog inside.

"This is Rufus," Seth says. "He's a three-month-old Golden Retriever and he'll be in your care until this evening."

My eyebrows rise. What?

"Good luck." Seth waves as he walks away.

I place my hands on my hips and let out a sigh.

"What's wrong?" Lena throws me a puzzled look. "Don't tell me you're more of a cat person."

"I'm not. But I'm not a dog person either."

There were several dogs at the house where I grew up, but none of them were mine.

"Really?" She cradles the puppy in her arms.

"You clearly love dogs."

"There was always one at home when I was growing up," she tells me. "My favorite was a Border Collie named Sasha, but Golden Retrievers are adorable too."

She walks towards me and offers me the puppy. "Here."

I lift my hands as I take a step back. "It's okay. You can have her."

"Him," Lena corrects me. "His name is Rufus, remember? And we're both supposed to take care of him for a day. That's the challenge. How are you supposed to help me take care of him if you won't even hold him?"

I cross my arms over my chest.

"What?" Lena brushes the puppy's paw against my arm. "Don't tell me you're scared of one cute little puppy?"

"I'm not scared."

I just don't like taking care of things.

"Come on, Riley," she speaks in a child's voice. "Don't you want to hold me?"

Oh, I do want to hold her. Not the puppy, though.

"You know you want to," she chants.

I glance at the puppy and then back at Lena. Now both of them are looking at me with the same eyes. To hell with it.

"Fine." I stretch out my arms.

Lena puts the puppy in them. "There you go."

I lift the puppy up. "He's heavier than he looks."

"Yup. He's going to be a big boy." She pats the puppy's head. "Aren't you, Rufus?"

I frown. How can she warm up so instantly to this mutt and still feel uncomfortable around me? How come she's so nice to him when he hasn't done anything?

"Alright. Now you hold him."

I hand Rufus back to Lena, but as soon as she has her hands around him, I hear a trickling sound. Something warm hits my stomach and when I glance down, I realize the puppy has peed. On me.

Fuck.

Lena puts Rufus down on the ground and laughs.

I put my hands on my hips. "Oh, so you find this funny, do you?"

"Sorry," she says. "It's just that this is like that scene in those movies, you know, where the baby or the puppy always pees on the person it doesn't like. I didn't know it could happen in real life."

19

I tap my foot on the grass. "Well, now you do."

"Sorry." She straightens up. "But you're going to take a shower anyway, aren't you?"

My eyes narrow. "So you're not even going to get mad at the dog?"

"Oh, come on. He didn't mean to do that."

"Didn't you just say--?"

"It was an accident. Or maybe his way of warming up to you."

"Very funny."

She pats my shoulder. "He's just a puppy, after all."

Just a puppy, huh? I glance at Rufus, who's busy sniffing a potted plant. Something tells me this one's going to be a real troublemaker.

~

And I'm right.

All morning long, it's just been one 'accident' after another. I swear this puppy isn't house-trained. And in between, it's a string of disasters with him chewing on one thing and then another. Why, he nearly even chewed on my two-thousand-dollar goggles.

"Still think he's just a puppy?" I ask Lena as she picks up her drool-covered, tattered hair tie from the floor.

She shrugs. "What do you want me to say? That he's a monster? A pesky pest? A golden-furred devil sent to test the limits of your patience?"

"All of that sounds good to me."

Lena frowns. "He's a baby, Riley. He doesn't know what's wrong and right yet. And even if he did, he wouldn't piss you off on purpose. You know why not? Because he's a dog."

I know he's a dog. That's why it annoys me that Lena is treating him like a human. Why is she taking the dog's side and not mine? Why am I the bad guy?

"I mean look at him," Lena adds as she glances at the puppy, who's nestled between her feet.

Again.

That's the worst part of all. The dog keeps hanging around Lena. It keeps following her around, trying to get her attention--and succeeding. Even earlier, when it finally took a nap, it did it on Lena's lap. It's as if the damned mutt is trying to tell me, with that innocent, self-pitying look that he's giving me right now, that Lena belongs to him.

I meet the look with my own narrowed gaze.

Oh, those puppy dog eyes don't fool me. I know that beneath those floppy ears, you--

Suddenly, Rufus gets up. He lumbers towards the table in the corner and tries to squeeze himself beneath it. He manages it, too, so that only his tail is left sticking out. It almost looks like the table has a tail.

"Aww." Lena lets out a sigh.

I nearly laugh at the sight, but then I realize that for the first time, Rufus has left Lena alone.

Lena and I can finally be alone.

I grab her arm and lead her to the bedroom.

"Riley?" Lena questions me with wide eyes.

I hold a finger to my lips. "You don't want to wake the dog, do you?"

That puts a lid on her protests until we reach the bedroom. I close the door behind me and lift my hand to cradle her jaw.

My eyes hold hers. "Let's pick up where we left off this morning, shall we?"

Lena blinks. "What?"

I press my cheek against hers so that I can whisper into her ear. "I didn't tell you, but yesterday, when you were standing on the top of that hill with me, bathed in the glow of the sunset, you were so beautiful."

Her cheek grows warm. I brush my lips against it.

"I wanted to do this then."

I bring my mouth to hers, but her palms flatten against my chest and she pushes me away.

"You're kidding, right?" She gives a nervous laugh. "I mean, I was all a mess and covered in sweat and--"

"Which made me want to mess you up and make you sweat even more." The words go past my lips before I can think.

The blue green eyes in front of me grow wide.

They really remind me of the ocean, of the pool, of the water pulling me in.

I keep those eyes on me as my hand slides to her chin and holds it in place. I stare right into them until I get too close. By then, I can feel her hot breath on my face. My eyelids drop along with my lower lip, ready to capture hers.

But then I hear a whine behind me, followed by claws scratching the door.

Fuck.

"Rufus," Lena says as she pulls away.

She tries to go past me towards the door, but I wrap my arm around her waist.

"Lena." I pull her towards me.

"Riley?"

"Just leave him," I tell her as I plant a kiss below her ear, as I let my fingers entwine with hers.

The puppy whines louder.

"But I can't." Lena shakes her head. "We can't do that."

My patience snaps. I push her towards the bed. The edge of the mattress collides with the back of her knees and she falls on top of it. I push her shoulders down. My eyes bore into hers.

"No more buts. No more excuses."

I grip her chin and my mouth descends to muffle whatever protests she has left. Still, she pushes me away.

"We had a deal, remember?" Lena glares. "You know I didn't ask for this."

The look of disappointment in her eyes sobers me up as much as her words. I move away with a sigh.

She runs out the door. I catch a glimpse of her picking the puppy up over my shoulder before it closes.

I run my hands through my hair in frustration. What was I doing? What was I thinking? Lena's right. We had a deal. But for a moment there, I lost it. I lost control. And because of that, we're back where we started. No. We're even further back.

Maybe I should just leave her alone.

~

That is exactly what I do the rest of the day, but then, as the afternoon grows late, I hear a scream.

"Rufus!"

I run out of the house and spot Lena just as she jumps into the pool. I hold my arm over my face as the water splashes.

When I lower it, I see Lena and Rufus both in the water. Rufus seems to be doing just fine, paddling with his small paws and keeping his head above the surface. Lena, on the other hand, is frantically waving her hands around.

She said she doesn't swim, but she didn't say she didn't know how to.

Shit.

I take off my shirt and dive into the pool. I grab Lena first, wrapping my arm around her chest. Then I seize Rufus and bring them both towards the shallow end. Once there, I place the puppy on the tiles. He gives his fur a shake and drops of water fly in various directions.

I ignore that as I turn my attention to Lena. "Are you alright?"

She nods as she catches her breath.

I let out a sigh of relief. "You didn't tell me you didn't know how to swim."

"How could I? It would be like telling a world-class chef I don't know how to cook an egg."

"And you still jumped into the pool."

"Well, I had to save Rufus."

"And risk your own life?" I shake my head. "I don't know if I should call you brave or stupid. Besides, I don't think he needed saving."

I glance at the puppy, who's now rolling over the grass as if nothing happened.

"Yeah. Probably not," Lena agrees. She turns to me. "Anyway, thank you for saving my life."

I look into her eyes. "I couldn't very well let you drown."

"Yeah. That wouldn't make a very nice headline--'Olympic Swimmer Lets Wife Drown'."

I grimace. "Not nice at all."

"I guess your swimming skills aren't just for show."

My eyes narrow.

"Just kidding." Lena pats my arm. "Seriously, though, thank you for coming to my rescue. I guess I can really count on you when the going gets tough."

Her eyes glimmer as her thin lips curve into a smile. Again, they call out to me. The urge to kiss her roars in my chest.

But this time, I hold myself back. I'm not going to make the same mistake I made earlier. In fact, I'm not going to touch her or kiss her again, not even if she's willing, not even if she looks like she wants me to. I'll only do it if she asks.

"I'm sorry about earlier," I tell her. "I should have kept my end of the deal."

Lena shakes her head. "Well, you saved my life, so I think I can forgive you for that. Besides, I know you didn't mean it."

My eyebrows arch. "I didn't?"

"You haven't been yourself all day. I think it's mostly Rufus's fault."

I narrow my eyes at her. "Are you finally admitting that Rufus is guilty of something?"

"I'm only saying Rufus was driving you nuts," she says.

"I won't deny that."

"Do you really dislike dogs that much?"

Before I can answer, I feel something warm against my ear. I turn my head and feel a small tongue against my cheek.

"It seems as if Rufus likes you, though," Lena remarks.

He does seem like he can't stop licking me.

"Okay, okay. I get it." I push him gently away. "You're just a playful little puppy."

Annoying as he's been, I guess he's done something good by jumping into the pool and making Lena jump after him, which gave me a chance to save her and get back in her good graces.

She grabs Rufus. "You little rascal. Why did you have to jump into the pool, huh? You're just like Riley, aren't you? You can't resist the water."

My eyebrows rise. "Like me?"

"If you wanted a bath, you could have just told me." Lena cuddles the puppy. "But no, you had to go for a swim, didn't you? Didn't you? And look how you got us all wet."

She looks silly as she continues to talk to the puppy like a baby, and yet I can't take my eyes off her. Or keep myself from smiling.

I guess I can't leave her alone. I'll just have to make her come to me, then. I still have five more days.

I wonder what tomorrow's challenge will be. It can't be harder than taking care of a puppy, right?

Chapter Six
Lena

"This can't be happening," I complain again after Seth has left as I glance at the metal ring around my right hand, which is attached to the one around Riley's left.

Yup. We're handcuffed. To each other. For eight hours.

"Seems like it is."

Riley lifts his cuffed hand. Mine goes up as well.

I shake my head. "I can't believe we have to go through this. Even married couples don't get cuffed to each other."

He shrugs. "Maybe they should."

"And to make things worse, we even have to do ten things together or for each other."

"Well, Seth did have a point. The challenge would be pointless and the show would be boring if we could just sit next to each other and watch TV all day."

I sit back against the couch with a sigh. "So what are we going to do?"

"We could swim," Riley suggests. "After all, I'm still in my trunks."

That's true. I was just about to make coffee and he was just about to go for his morning swim. Thank goodness I was wise enough to go to the bathroom first, though I didn't even have time to take a shower.

"I don't think we can swim," I say as I tear my gaze away from his Speedos.

Why does he have to look so hot in them?

"Why not? You surely won't drown while you're cuffed to me."

"Can you even swim if your wrist is attached to mine?" I ask him.

Riley shrugs. "I guess we'll find out."

"No." I shake my head. "Besides, you may be in your swim trunks, but I'm still in my pajamas. I'm not going to swim in these."

"You could change."

"Nope. I don't think I can."

He rests his head against the back of the couch as he gives an exasperated sigh. "I can't believe I can't swim this morning. I get so restless when I don't start the day in the pool. I've got to stretch these muscles, you know."

I try not to gape as he flexes his arm. Yup. I know you've got amazing muscles.

"Then maybe we can just exercise," I suggest. "That should be more manageable."

Riley doesn't look satisfied with that, but he shrugs. "I guess we can try."

We head to the exercise room. It's a struggle at first. We end up bumping into each other and I almost twist my arm. But then we figure out that instead of standing side by side, we should stand in front of each other. Even then, it's still hard to move, especially since Riley is taller than me, but we manage to pull off some stretches and even a few jumping jacks.

One task completed. Nine to go.

"Well, that wasn't so bad," I say to Riley as we sit on the mat after our little workout with handcuffs. "That could even become a thing."

He snorts. "Only for people who don't really want to exercise but want to believe they're doing it."

I frown because I used to be one of those.

He wipes the sweat off his forehead. "Now I want to swim even more."

And I want to take a shower. But we can't take one together. Of course not.

I sweep my hair out of my face to at least keep my cheeks cool but the strands fall back.

"This is so unfair. At least you have your left hand cuffed so you can do things with your right hand. I can't do anything at all. I can't even comb my hair."

"Want me to do it for you?" Riley offers.

Well, there's an idea.

I nod. "Okay."

~

But maybe not a good one, I think as I feel Riley's fingertips graze my scalp while gathering up strands of my hair.

It's not only that I have to keep my right hand up as he tries to fix it. There's just something weird about having someone else comb my hair for me.

"Am I doing this wrong?" Riley asks behind me. "Because you've been scowling at the mirror."

I look at my reflection and realize he's right.

"I'm just not used to this, I guess," I tell him.

"Didn't your mother used to do it?"

I pause to think. Well, yes, I suppose she used to comb my hair and tie it and even braid it. But she stopped doing it long before she left.

"That was a long time ago," I say.

"When did she pass away?" Riley asks.

My eyebrows arch. "Oh, no. She's not... dead. She just... I just haven't seen her... in a very, very long time."

"Oh." He stops brushing my hair. "I'm so sorry. I just thought... Anyway, I'm sorry."

I shrug. "It's okay."

I guess she might as well be dead anyway.

"My mother passed away when I was eight," Riley confides as he continues brushing.

"Oh." That's something I've never heard about him before. Strange. "I'm sorry to hear that. I'm sure she would have loved to see you swim and get those medals."

He falls silent. I frown.

Shit. Did I say too much?

I try to disregard the awkward silence and shake off the weird sensation of his hands in my hair as he keeps fixing it. Finally, he stops. I check my reflection and see that he's tied my hair in a ponytail. He missed a few strands, but overall, it's fine.

"Thanks," I tell him as I get the brush from him. "That feels better. Sure you don't want a career in hairdressing?"

He snorts. "I only did a decent job because you have nice hair."

I try not to blush at the compliment.

"Do you want me to comb your hair, too?" I ask him. "Though I guess that will still count for one task."

"I'm fine."

To prove his point, he gives his head a shake. His dark strands of hair bounce off his forehead.

Okay.

"Then what should we do?"

"I still want to swim."

I sigh. "You don't give up, do you?"

"I have an idea. Why don't I go into the pool? Just immerse myself in the water. And you can just sit on the edge."

"You call that swimming?"

"Well, no, but..." Riley scratches his chin.

"I don't think we can do that," I tell him. "We have to do something together or for each other."

He sighs. "I guess you're right."

The look of dismay on his face nearly breaks my heart.

"But maybe we can sit by the pool," I suggest to cheer him up.

He turns to me with creased eyebrows. "Does that count?"

I'm not sure.

"Or we can clean the pool," I say. "That would definitely count."

"And you'll let me take a dip after?" Riley asks hopefully.

"Fine," I say. "But you have to promise not to get me wet."

~

Well, Riley didn't exactly keep his promise since my arm's drenched and so is the sleeve of my pajama top. But at least my clothes are mostly dry. Riley, on the other hand, is dripping wet, and since he can't dry himself off with just one hand, I have to help him.

"Maybe I shouldn't have let you go into the water," I say as I hold one end of the towel while keeping my gaze off his chest.

I can still feel it beneath my hands and the cotton, though, as I help him dry off, and it's all I can do to keep myself from blushing.

I really shouldn't have let him get wet at all.

"Well, maybe this counts as task number four," Riley says. "I mean, you are doing it for me."

He's right. That's the consolation.

"I guess."

Four down. Six to go.

He grabs the towel from my hand. "That should be enough."

I'm relieved to hear it, especially as I watch him dry off his thighs and legs on his own. I definitely don't want to go there.

Still, I wonder why he's being so considerate of me when just yesterday he was being so aggressive, even pushing me down on the bed. Since then, he hasn't made another move. He's not even trying to tease me. And to think that this is actually a perfect opportunity for him since we're handcuffed and all and I literally can't get away from him. What made him change his mind?

Wait. I'm not disappointed, am I?

"There," Riley says as he finishes drying his feet. "I should be dry enough to get inside the house. Then I can change and we can have something to eat. I'm starving."

Now that he's mentioned it, I am hungry, too. Well, we haven't really had anything to eat today.

"Yeah, I guess we should try to fix--" I stop as I realize something. "Did you say change?"

~

Yup, he's changing.

And here I am facing the wall and desperately trying not to look over my shoulder as he constantly tugs at my arm and I hear the rustle of fabric behind me.

Whatever you do, Lena, don't look.

I can't stop my imagination from running, though, or from painting a picture of his naked body--I mean, he has to be completely naked at one point, right? Thank goodness it isn't detailed. Well, I wouldn't know how to draw that part of him because I've never seen it, never seen one, for that matter, except on the internet, though something tells me his is fairly large and--

"Done." Riley's voice nearly makes me jump.

I draw a deep breath and turn around slowly. My eyes grow wide as they rest on his bare chest.

I tear them away. "I thought you said you were going to put on clothes."

"I'm wearing pants."

Yes, I can see that. Wait. Where am I looking?

"I can't put a shirt on," Riley adds, raising his handcuffed hand.

Right. Of course he can't. Well, I guess a pair of pants is better than wet Speedos.

"Let's just go to the kitchen." I tug on his arm. "And see what we can whip up with just one pair of mismatched hands."

~

Sandwiches. That's what we manage to finish making an hour later.

They were the easiest to make. Well, actually, I wanted to just put something in the microwave, but Riley wouldn't hear of it. So sandwiches.

I say easiest, but they were still a struggle. I couldn't chop stuff, so Riley had to do all that. And boy, did he take his time. I had a feeling he couldn't cook since I've been doing all the cooking, but I don't even think he's ever chopped vegetables in his life. I kept holding my breath, scared that he'd cut his finger off.

25

Thankfully, that didn't happen. Then we assembled the sandwiches one ingredient at a time. And juiced some oranges for our drink. More accurately, I put the oranges into the machine and Riley pressed the juice out of them. Then I poured them into glasses.

But preparing food was the easy part. Eating it is even more of a challenge. We have to take turns picking up our sandwiches and biting them. Each time, they fall apart a little more. Needless to say, we end up making a mess.

"I think my plate ate more than me," I say as I glance down at it.

"You think so, too?"

At least my stomach's not grumbling anymore.

I reach for my glass of juice with my left hand and take a sip. "At least we did three more things-- making sandwiches, juicing and eating. That's seven things we did together with handcuffs on."

"So three more," Riley says. "What next?"

"I think we should take things easy. What about a movie? We can't watch a movie all day, but we can watch one. That counts for one thing."

He shrugs. "Okay."

~

Riley doesn't look okay, though. He gives another yawn as I turn off the TV as the credits of Taxi Driver begin to roll.

I turn to him with a frown. "You didn't like the movie, did you?"

"No. I did," he argues. "It's just..."

"Boring?"

"A bit much. And maybe a bit depressing and ugly."

My eyebrows arch. "But that's the point of the movie. It's supposed to make you suffer and cringe. It's intense. That's why this movie is so good."

He shrugs.

"This movie is one of the best American films of all time, and that's not just according to me," I go on. "The story is good. The acting. And the shots. This is one of Scorsese's finest. Someday, I want to make a movie just like it."

He gives me a look of surprise. "You want to make a movie?"

Didn't I tell him that?

"Yeah." I nod as I turn my gaze back to the empty screen. "I want to be a director."

"Wow. You really like movies, don't you?"

"Maybe as much as you love swimming," I answer. "I used to watch them with... I used to watch them all the time."

"No wonder you didn't have time to do sports."

"It was easier," I admit. "Plus I learned so much from every movie as opposed to playing just one sport."

"Ouch."

"But I admire your dedication," I add. "Who knows? I might make a film about you someday."

Riley snorts. "No thanks." He stretches his arms, taking my right arm with him. "I think far too many people know too much about me already."

"Do they?"

"Plus I don't think you can find an actor who can swim as fast as me."

"Show-off," I tease him. "He doesn't actually have to swim as fast as you, you know. He just has to look like it, which is easy."

He frowns. "Anyway, enough about movies. We still have two tasks left to complete the challenge."

He's right. "What do you have in mind?"

Riley gets off the couch and I follow him to the baby grand piano in the corner.

"Do you play?" he asks me.

"My sister used to," I answer.

His eyes grow wide. "You have a sister?"

I nod. "She's older than me. She taught me a few pieces."

Though I can only remember one, I think.

"What do you know?" Riley asks as he pulls out the chair.

Wait. We're playing? Riley knows how to play?

I sit beside him. "Blue Danube."

"Really?" He lifts the cover off the keys. "That's easy."

He starts to play but stops after the cuff hits one of the keys by mistake.

"Why don't you and I play together?" he suggests. "You can play with your left hand and I'll play with my right."

"Okay."

I guess that makes sense. Actually, it might just be the perfect arrangement.

"You start," Riley says.

I position my free hand over the keys and begin to press them. I get the third one wrong on the first try, but on the second my fingers remember which keys to press. Then Riley takes over, playing with his right hand.

Our hands take turns, then play together. One by one, the notes fill the air, creating a melody that I nod my head along to. We're playing so well together that I almost forget my right hand is cuffed, and when it's over I stare at the keys in awe.

"I can't believe we just did that," I say out loud.

"Yes, we did," Riley agrees. "And very well, too. I'd clap if I could."

I look at him. "Who taught you play?"

"A tutor taught me the basics," he answers. "I learned the harder pieces by myself."

"And here I thought all you could do was swim," I tease him.

"And here I thought you didn't have any talents," he teases me back.

I frown but let it go.

He holds his left hand over the keys. "Shall we try that again?"

~

We try that two more times before Riley tries to teach me a new piece--Fur Elise. Afterwards, we head to the bedroom to do our last task--taking a nap together.

When Riley first suggests it, I think it's easy enough. We just have to lie on the bed and close our eyes, right? Now that we're in bed, though, I can't seem to set myself at ease.

Even if I close my eyes, I'm aware of Riley lying next to me. I can hear his shallow breathing. I can pick up the scent of his bare skin. Weird. I've been beside him all day. I should be used to his presence by now. I didn't even mind it anymore when we were playing the piano. But now, as much as I try not to mind it, it bothers me.

Maybe we should try something else.

I'm about to suggest that, but as I turn my head, I find him already asleep. At least, he looks like it. His eyes are closed, and for the first time I notice how thick his eyelashes are. I notice, too, that his hair is not all black--there seem to be some dark brown strands mixed in--and that his skin is incredibly smooth.

He really is so handsome.

I lift my left hand to touch his cheek but stop. I shake my head.

What am I doing? I should just let him sleep. And I should sleep, too, not fantasize about Riley.

On impulse, I turn on my side away from him. The next thing I know Riley's body presses against mine.

"Whoa," he says.

Shit. How could I have forgotten about the handcuffs?

I lie on my back only to find my face inches from Riley's. I can feel the warmth of his breath on my cheek. His gaze holds mine captive and my heart begins to pound.

What the hell am I doing?

My thoughts begin to evaporate as I stare into those dark eyes. I can't move. I can't breathe. When his searing gaze proves too much, my eyelids fall. My lips quiver.

I wait for his to press against them. Instead, I feel Riley move away.

"You should be more careful," he tells me. "Anyway, the cuffs won't be on for much longer."

My eyes slowly open and stare at the ceiling.

He didn't kiss me? Why? Since the wedding ceremony, he's been kissing me once a day and trying to more often than that. Yet, today, he hasn't. He hasn't even tried, even though God knows he's had far more chances today than before, like just now.

Why? Doesn't he want me anymore?

If so, that's good, right? That's the deal.

Then why does my chest suddenly ache so much? I don't understand it at all.

Chapter Seven
Riley

"I understand," I answer Bertha, the dance instructor in front of me who's in charge of helping me and Lena do the challenge for our fourth day--get dancing lessons and dance in front of a live audience by the end of the day.

What I don't understand is why Lena is acting aloof. Is this some pattern? Like one day she and I have some sort of magic and the next, we're acting like strangers? Or did I do something to make her mad again?

I rattle my brains for an answer but can't come up with one. What did I do? Don't tell me she's still mad about me dissing one of her favorite movies. But that was before we played the piano together, which I think was pretty amazing. She was smiling then, too. So when did she start frowning?

Not during dinner. Or maybe I was too hungry to notice after having only had sandwiches for lunch and finally managing to swim to my heart's content. After that, she went to bed and I took a shower. When I got out, she was asleep.

Before I went for my swim, then? I can't really remember what Lena did right after the handcuffs were removed. And the last thing we did with them on was take a nap. And she can't have been upset then. Why, when I was staring down at her, she looked like she wanted me to kiss her.

And damn, it took all I had not to. Yes, she might have looked willing, but like I said, I'm not taking any more chances. When I kiss her, when I take her, it will be after she asks me to.

So what did I do wrong?

I can't seem to figure it out, so I decide to ask her as we continue practicing the steps of our rumba routine.

"Is everything alright?"

"Yeah," Lena answers quickly.

Too quickly. She didn't even think about it.

"Sure?" I ask her as I turn her around. "Because you seem to be a little on edge."

"Well, dancing isn't really my thing," she answers as she does another spin.

I pull her back. "I mean you're too tense... around me, like you're scared of me."

"Me? Scared?"

I shrug as I let her go so she can do her own steps. "It just seems like you want to run away from me."

Lena stops. "I'm the one who's trying to run away?"

She gives a sarcastic laugh.

My eyebrows furrow. What's that supposed to mean?

"Stop! Stop!" Bertha claps her hands. "What is going on?"

"Nothing," Lena and I answer at the same time.

"We're just talking," I add.

Bertha sighs. "Well, you should be dancing. Whatever it is you need to tell each other, say it through your body movements. I can assure you your message will get across."

I nod. Lena says nothing.

Bertha walks away and snaps her fingers. "From the top."

The music plays again. Lena and I start executing our steps. This time, we don't say a word to each other.

I can still notice that she's tense, though, especially when she's in my arms. And I must be thinking of it too much because my focus slips away and my coordination suffers. My hand lands on top of her breast instead of just below it, and as I jerk it off, I mess up the next step. Lena stops. The music stops a moment later and Bertha gives a loud sigh.

"I'm sorry," I tell Lena. "I didn't mean that."

She says nothing, her back still turned to me.

"What is happening here?" Bertha approaches us with a scowl and her hands on her hips. "Both of you know what to do and yet your minds are somewhere else. Do you want to dance or not?"

I don't answer. I never wanted to dance in the first place. It's not my thing, either. But it's the challenge, so I'm making the most of it. Lena's not even trying.

Bertha glances at the clock on the wall. "We only have a few hours left, you know. If you keep doing this, you'll be disappointing everyone--your audience, me, yourselves. Don't you want to make everyone drop their jaws when you dance, to applaud when you're done? I assure you it's an amazing feeling."

Still, Lena looks uninterested.

Bertha sighs. "Alright, we'll try again. We'll--"

"I need a break," Lena finally speaks.

She walks towards the door.

Again, Bertha glances at the clock. "Now?"

Lena's already at the door.

I chase after her and manage to grab her arm before she slips out.

"Lena, what's wrong?"

"I said I need a break." She jerks her arm away. "Now."

And she leaves.

Behind me, Bertha clicks her tongue disapprovingly. "You know, you can't keep dancing like this. She can't keep doing this. She'll--"

"She said she just needs a break," I say to Bertha as I turn towards her. I draw a deep breath. "She'll be fine."

At least, I hope so.

~

But when rehearsal resumes, Lena is still the same. Her movements are still stiff, mechanical almost. And the mistakes pile on. As the hours tick by, I can sense Bertha's impatience, her frustration. Her sighs grow deeper. Her heel keeps tapping the wood. Those disgruntled clicks of her sharp tongue grow more frequent.

Finally, she snaps.

"This is terrible! Terrible!" She marches towards Lena. "Are you even paying attention? Are you even thinking?"

Lena just looks away.

I turn to her. "Bertha, there's no need to--"

"You can't keep covering for her mistakes," Bertha cuts me off. "Rumba is a dance done by two. If only one is dancing, it won't work."

Unfortunately, I can't argue with that.

"Now, Riley and I will do it once," she goes on. "You watch and see how it's done."

Lena retreats to the corner.

The music starts all over again, and this time Bertha and I take the floor. She's good. I have to admit it. It's all I can do to keep up. But somehow, I manage. No. She manages it. It's as if she's dragging me along, drawing my performance out of me.

When we're done, I'm out of breath for the first time. As I pause to catch it, Bertha applauds.

"That is how it's done, Lena," she says.

Still, I don't hear a word from her. I turn my head. My eyes grow wide as they meet hers.

Why does she look like she's about to cry?

Again, she rushes to the door.

"Lena!" I call after her.

"Let her go," Bertha tells me. "If she doesn't want to dance, we can't force her. And I'd rather she not dance then put on a quarter-assed performance."

I ignore Bertha and walk to the door.

"Oh, to hell with it." Bertha's heels stomp on the wood. "Fine. Both of you walk out. I'm walking out, too. I don't care about the pay. I'm done. The two of you have wasted enough of my time."

She marches out the other door. I leave the room and look for Lena. I find her sitting on the bench outside the restrooms, her shoulders slumped.

She lifts her head to look at me, then turns away quickly. Her hand covers half her face to ward off my gaze.

But I keep it on her as I sit beside her.

"Lena..."

"What are you doing here? Shouldn't you be dancing with Bertha? The two of you should just do the dance. You look better together."

I frown. Is this what it's all about?

"Don't tell me you're jealous."

She neither confirms or denies it.

"Bertha is just our instructor. You--"

"I don't know, okay? But I know I can't dance like her." Lena shakes her head. "I can't even dance at all."

"Yes, you can." I almost put a hand on her shoulder but stop so as not to make her uncomfortable. "If only you tried. You're not even trying, Lena. Even I can see that."

"So sue me."

"This is not like you."

"You don't know me."

I sigh. "Maybe not that well, but I know you're no quitter. You climbed that mountain on Day One, remember? You didn't give up even though you wanted to. And I didn't give up on you then and I'm not giving up on you now."

Lena snorts. "Yeah, right."

My eyebrows furrow at another sarcastic remark. What is she being bitter about?

I grip her arm. "Lena, if there's something wrong, you should just tell me."

"I don't know, okay?" She pulls her arm away and finally faces me. "I don't know if there's something wrong... or what's right and what's wrong. I'm just... so confused right now."

And so am I. I'm glad she's decided to tell me how she feels, but I still don't understand.

"What about?"

"I don't know," she speaks louder. "I don't know what's real and what's not. I don't know what I'm supposed to do or what you want me to do."

My eyebrows arch. "What I want you to do?"

"One minute, you're like my best friend and the next, I don't know you. You don't really care about me, do you?"

Is that what she thinks? Is that why she's acting like this?

"Just leave me alone already," Lena goes on. "Just--"

The rest of her words vanish as my lips press against hers. My hand caresses her cheek beneath a curtain of hair.

I know I said I wouldn't kiss her unless she asked, but I can't stand seeing her like this. Just this once, I'll kiss her because she seems to want me to, because she needs me to.

And I need to. I can't just let her drown in her silly fears.

When the kiss is over, Lena looks into my eyes. There are still tears brimming in her ears, but they're clearer now. The fog of fear and suffering has begun to fade.

I stroke her cheek. "What I want you to do, Lena, is to dance with me. Not for Bertha. Not for the audience. But so you and I can have fun."

I get off the bench and pull her arm.

"Dance for me. Because I won't dance for anyone else but you."

Lena wipes her tears and snorts. "I wish I could, but you know I can't dance."

"Like I said, you haven't even tried." I pull her to her feet. "Once you try, I know you can do it."

"But Bertha--"

"Forget about Bertha." I touch Lena's cheek. "She's given up on us already anyway."

Her eyebrows arch. "Really?"

"We don't need her. We already know the steps. We can sure as hell dance without her. And we will."

Lena still looks hesitant, so I grasp her chin and force her to look into my eyes.

31

"You're not in this alone, Lena. You have me. And you can bet I won't let you fail."

For a moment, she remains silent. Then she finally nods.

"Okay. I'll... just follow your lead, I guess."

I smile. "Exactly."

~

When the curtains on the stage rise and the music starts to play, I start to move. I can feel the members of the audience staring. I know the camera's out there rolling. But I focus on Lena.

I can hardly take my eyes off her anyway. Just like it was at our wedding, her hair is swept up. A touch of makeup shows off her elegant bone structure. Her frilly red dress drapes diagonally over her thighs and ends below one knee. Cut-outs on the side above her waist reveal smooth skin for me to put my hands on.

And do I put my hands on them. I clutch her tightly each time she dances next to me. I let my fingers glide over her arms, her thighs as the dance requires. As I promised, I lead her through the routine. And just as Bertha dragged me along while I was dancing with her, Lena moves with me. She falls into step beside me. She's no longer stiff now. She's trying her best. And succeeding like I thought she would. She surrenders and I carry her away.

When the music ends, we both take a moment to catch our breaths. Then I pull her into my arms as the audience bursts into applause.

"I knew you could do it," I whisper in her ear with pride in my voice.

"We did it," Lena answers with the smile I've been waiting to see. "We make a great team."

I smile back at her before turning towards the still cheering crowd. I spot Bertha in it, and even she seems happy. And why shouldn't she be? Lena and I gave it our all. We owned the stage.

And as I look into her eyes once more as the curtains fall, I wonder if there's anything we can't do.

Chapter Eight
Lena

"You can't do that," I scold Riley as I glance at the peppers on the chopping board.

He gives me a puzzled look. "Can't do what?"

I take the kitchen knife from him and then place another pepper on the chopping board.

"You have to cut vegetables the same size or they won't cook evenly." I cut the pepper into even quarters to demonstrate. "See. Like that."

He shrugs. "Fine."

He takes the knife back and continues cutting the peppers as I've taught him.

I nod. "That's better."

For today's challenge, Riley and I have to cook and host a dinner for four guests. Already, the chicken, which I've brined and rubbed with herbs and spices, is roasting in the oven. I've finished making the chocolate mousse for dessert, too, which only leaves the two side dishes for Riley to make. I wonder if he'll finish in time, though.

"So you have seventeen gold medals, you know how to play the piano and how to dance, but you don't know how to cook?" I tease him.

He frowns. "No one taught me."

Really? Then that means he must have grown up rich.

"How have you been surviving, then? Let me guess. You have your own personal chef."

"I did," Riley admits. "He worked hand in hand with my nutritionist."

I let out a whistle. "Wow. Athletes really take their health seriously, don't they?"

"Our health is everything. Our bodies are our weapons, our greatest treasures."

I nod. "But you were referring to your chef and nutritionist in the past tense. Don't they work for you anymore?"

"I've already retired, remember?"

Yes, I do remember hearing about that. I can't recall the reason, though. He's still young. And he definitely looks fit. More importantly, when he spoke just now, I could hear a tinge of frustration, of regret in his voice. It's almost like he was forced to retire.

I want to ask him why, but he looks serious enough already. I don't want to put him in a bad mood.

"And I guess your girlfriends have cooked for you, too," I say instead.

"Never had one."

My eyebrows arch. What?

No way. There's no way someone as hot and accomplished and popular as Riley Boyle has never had a girlfriend.

"Like hell I'll believe that," I tell him as I cross my arms over my chest. "I bet you've had a hundred."

"I've been with a lot of women," Riley confesses. "But I've never committed to anyone. I didn't have that luxury."

Oh. Right. Of course he can't be a virgin like me. What was I thinking?

And why do I suddenly feel jealous?

It's just like how I felt yesterday when I was watching Riley and Bertha dancing with so much passion. I couldn't help but wish he was looking at me and not her with that look of hunger in his eyes. I couldn't help but wish he was holding me, just me.

And now I'm getting jealous of women I don't even know? I frown. I'm turning into a monster, and I don't like it.

"But don't worry." Riley turns to me with a tender look in his eyes. "You're the only woman for me now."

Heat burns in my cheeks. What's up with that surprise attack?

It's just acting, of course. I know it. He can't possibly mean it.

Can he?

"Just keep your eyes on your vegetables," I tell him as I look away. "You don't want to lose a finger, do you? And pick up the pace a little. Even if you can't set a record chopping vegetables, surely you can do it faster. Our guests will arrive before we know it."

Riley grins as he gives me a mock salute. "Yes, ma'am."

~

Our guests arrive at six. They're two married couples--Ashley and Eric, who were on Wed For A Week two years ago and ended up becoming a real couple, and Candace and Sean, who have been married for ten years and have two kids at home.

As the guys have their wine out on the patio, the women help me set the table.

"So how's it like being married to a celebrity?" Ashley asks me as she pours gravy into the boats.

"I was a bit star-struck at first," I admit. "But I guess the more I got to know Riley, the more I forgot about him being a celebrity and the more I remembered he's just a man."

"A very good-looking man," Candace says as she grabs the forks and spoons. "But don't tell Sean that."

I give her a look of surprise. "Aren't you in love with him?"

"Of course I am. I love him to bits. But hey, the fact that we're married doesn't mean we can't find other guys attractive, right?"

Ashley glances around the kitchen. "This house is so much nicer than the one Eric and I lived in. But hey, I'm not complaining. I loved that green house. I mean, it's where Eric and I fell in love."

She gives a dreamy sigh. In love? I wonder how that feels.

"Sean and I fell in love at a summer camp," Candace says. "We were both counselors there."

"And was it love at first sight?" Ashley asks eagerly.

"I think so," Candace answers with a sheepish grin. "But we didn't know it until later. Like we were already in love with each other before we knew it. Crazy, right?"

"Love works in crazy ways," Ashley agrees. "Don't you think so, Lena?"

I want to say that I don't know because I've never been in love. Instead, I say, "Yup. Crazy."

Ashley giggles.

"So, Candace, you've been married ten years, right?" I ask her. "What's your secret?"

"Oh, we still fight. A lot. Over little things that don't make sense. But we just don't give up on each other."

I pause, remembering the two occasions Riley said he wouldn't give up on me. Wait. Why am I remembering that now?

"We're just there for each other," Candace goes on. "We do what we can for each other, even if it's just little things like cutting nails..."

"He cuts your nails?" Ashley's eyes grow wide. "Oh, that's sweet."

"And the kids, I think, really help keep us together."

"How old are your kids?" I ask curiously.

"Eight and five." Candace takes her phone from her pocket. "Actually, I have a picture."

Ashley and I look over her shoulders to see it--a photo of an eight-year-old boy in a baseball uniform and a five-year-old girl with pigtails and a lollipop.

"They're adorable," Ashley remarks.

"They are... in pictures." Candace puts her phone away. "In real life, they're much more challenging. But hey, I love them to bits."

"Eric and I want to have children soon," Ashley says.

I fall silent. How did this conversation suddenly turn awkward?

"Oh, right." Candace places a hand on my arm as she notices my discomfort. "You and Riley are getting divorced when the week is over, right? So I guess that means no kids."

Ashley shrugs. "Unless they become a real married couple like Eric and I."

I doubt that's going to happen. In fact, I know it's not. I've known it from the beginning. Why, then, am I feeling sad right now?

"I'm sure Riley's kids will look gorgeous," Ashley adds.

That I'm sure of.

"But what if they find out Lena's pregnant after the show?" Candace asks. "I mean, what if she gets pregnant during the show?"

"Not gonna happen." Ashley shakes her head. "It's in the contract that you have to use protection."

Candace nods. "I see." Then she nudges my arm and lowers her voice. "So have you... used protection?"

"Yes, of course," I lie with a blush.

"Then again, who's to blame you if you get carried away?" Ashley winks.

"Or if the two of you decide to get naughty?" Candace adds.

My cheeks burn even more but I hold a finger to my lips. "Shh."

They laugh.

I find myself joining in. I've never really had girlfriends before. Well, there's my sister, but I don't think we've ever had a conversation about sex. Same with Paula. So this is what it feels like.

"Then again, maybe you shouldn't," Candace gets serious again. "You're already going to be heartbroken when the week's over, right?"

"I was," Ashley admits. "Which is why I was so thrilled when Eric called."

"Do you think you'll be able to forget him?" Candace asks me.

I don't answer.

Will I? Can I?

"Oh, but let's not be so dreary." Candace rubs my shoulder. "Tonight is supposed to be a celebration."

"She's right." Ashley pours herself a glass of wine. "Let's just savor the moment while it lasts."

She pours wine for Candace and me as well before lifting her glass.

"To making the most of crazy moments."

"Cheers!" Candace raises her glass.

I lift mine as I force a smile.

They clink in the air before we lift them to our lips. We drain them and set them down on the dining table.

Candace rubs her hands. "Let's call the boys for dinner, shall we?"

~

I try to enjoy dinner, but my thoughts are already riled up. I manage to force smiles and laughs and eat my food without any accidents and even engage in small talk, but inside my head, the wheels keep turning. The questions keep coming.

Will Riley and I really pretend we never knew each other when this is over? Can I do that? I said I'd do that, right? So why am I having such a hard time thinking about it now? Why do I feel afraid?

It's not just fear. There's also... envy.

I wish I could be like Ashley and Candace. They both look so happy, so radiant because they've found their one true love, their Westley, their Noah, their Oliver Barrett IV. I wish I had the future they have. I wish that Riley would look at me the way Eric and Sean look at them.

Well, he has done that, but it's just for show.

For the first time, I wish I was one of the lucky ones. I wish I had a love that's real.

But I don't. As Ashley and Candace said, when this week is over, this game that Riley and I are playing, this farce will be over, too.

"Lena?" Riley's voice breaks into my thoughts as I put away the dishes after dinner. "Is something wrong?"

"No." I carry the dishes to the sink. "Why?"

"You just seem quiet."

I put the dishes down in the sink. "Maybe I'm just too busy watching those four. They're fun to watch, after all. It's like I'm watching a movie, a romantic comedy."

"They are nice," Riley agrees. "I don't really have a lot of friends, just one who's more like a brother to me, so it was nice talking to Sean and Eric."

I turn to him with a puzzled look. "You don't have a lot of friends?"

That's something else I find hard to believe.

"Fans and rivals and critics I've got a lot of," he says. "Friends? Not really."

"Well, I guess being a celebrity, you have to be careful who you trust."

I hold a glass under the tap and open it.

Riley grabs my wrist. "Are you sure you're okay? You know you can tell me if something's bothering you, right?"

I meet his gaze. There he goes again giving me that look that makes me feel weak at the knees. But he's given me that look from the beginning, right? So why does it affect me differently now?

"Hey," Candace interrupts as she enters the room.

I pull my hand away from Riley's and close the tap.

"Oops." Candace places a hand over her mouth. "I'm so sorry for barging in like that."

"It's okay," I tell her. "Do you need anything?"

"Well, I think before we leave, we should play a game," she answers. "You know, like a couples' game night."

I turn to Riley. "What do you think?"

He nods. "Yeah, sure. What are we playing?"

~

For the next hour, we play classic charades. And no surprise, I guess all the movies right, even the ones Riley is bad at acting out, like Monty Python and the Holy Grail and Casablanca. Thanks to that, Riley and I win. We exchange triumphant high-fives and he gives me a peck on the cheek.

The game distracted me, and I even admit I had fun. Now that it's over, though, and our guests are leaving, I'm beginning to feel uneasy again. Still, I force a smile as I say my goodbyes to Ashley and Candace.

"Hey." Ashley places her arm over my shoulder as we walk to the front door. "I owe you an apology."

My eyebrows furrow. "For what?"

"For misjudging you," she confesses. "Actually, when I heard about Wed For A Week Celebrity Edition, I thought the 'regular' men and women were all just these people who were after their fifteen minutes of fame or just bragging rights. I thought the women would be just all annoying, shallow fan girls. But you proved me wrong. It seems like you really see Riley as a man. And I can see that you've really put your heart on the line just like I did, that you really care for him. That you love him."

Love him? I shake my head.

"I think there's a mistake, Ashley. I don't--"

She doesn't let me finish. "I know you don't want to admit it. It's scary to think you can fall for someone so easily, especially someone who you know might soon be out of your reach. But there's no shame in it. When you lose to your heart, it isn't really a defeat."

I find myself unable to answer.

Ashley squeezes my shoulder. "Just like I said earlier, savor it while it lasts. Who knows? It may just last forever. If it happened to me, it can happen to you."

"Thanks," I manage to say with a weak smile.

She pats my shoulder before running off to join the rest. As I wave at them, Riley stands by my side and takes my hand in his. Immediately, I feel a warmth in my palm that spreads up my arm towards my chest. As I glance at him, my heart skips a beat.

So this is... love? Already?

Unbelievable. Then again, the more I think about it, the more I realize that what I feel for Riley is more than just a crush. After all, I feel happy around him. I want to make him happy. I want to kiss him. I want him for my own. I imagine a future with him.

I want a future with him. A real one.

Is this why I was confused before? Because I was trying to deny it? Was my head a mess yesterday because I was trying to fight my own feelings?

My gaze goes to the ring on my finger.

But so what? I'm the only one who feels this way. Riley and I aren't married. Riley doesn't belong to me. He's just playing along. He's just playing. Period.

So I can't be serious. Maybe it's too late, but I can still keep this hole in my heart from getting bigger. I can still save some of it for me.

There's two days left. In those two days, I can't let myself fall for Riley any more than I have. Or I may not have a heart left.

I may not survive.

Chapter Nine
Riley

"So we're supposed to survive being cooped up in this room with no electricity for a day for our final challenge?" I rest my head against the back of the couch. "That's easy enough. Right, Lena?"

Lena doesn't answer. She's just sitting on the couch with her knees pressed to her chest. Even before Seth arrived, she already seemed to be in a bad mood. And I can see circles under her eyes that suggest she's either been crying or didn't sleep well last night.

I guess it's her off day. Again. Then again, even last night, I could already sense that something was bothering her.

I wonder what it is this time.

"Hey." I move closer to her. "Are you okay?"

She nods.

I sigh. "Wrong question. I know you're not okay. So what's the matter?"

She shakes her head. "I'm fine."

Really? Are we going to go through this again?

"Lena, I know--"

"I'm just not feeling well," she cuts me off.

My eyebrows arch in concern. I reach out to touch her forehead.

"Did you--?"

"Don't touch me." She slaps my hand away.

I lift my hands.

She glances at me, then rests her chin between her knees. "Sorry. I'm... really just not feeling well."

"Should we ask for a doctor?"

"No."

"Do you want me to ask for some medicine? I know we're supposed to stay in here, but--"

"I already took some," Lena says.

"Okay." I nod. "I guess you'll want to rest. You can do that. I'll... find something to do by myself."

I glance at the shelf against the wall. It's filled with books and board games.

"Thanks," she mutters.

She turns on her side away from me and leans on the back of the couch. I frown. Can she really sleep like that?

Unable to resist, I place my hands on her shoulders and pull her towards me, intending to have her sleep on my lap. But Lena pulls away.

"What are you doing?" she asks with a glare.

"Just trying to help you rest better."

"Well, I didn't ask for your help," she snaps.

My gaze narrows. Why is she being so difficult?

"Well, it doesn't matter, because I'm supposed to take care of you. I'm your husband, remember?"

Or has she forgotten that we're supposed to be married?

"I remember," Lena says. "How can I forget?"

Where is this spite coming from?

"But even married couples get tired of each other."

My eyebrows arch. "So you're already tired of me? After five days?"

"You're just that exhausting," she says with a sigh. "I can't wait for this week to be over."

Her words hurt more than I expect. So she's picking a fight, is she? After all we've been through, all we've done together, she wants nothing more to do with me. She's the one casting me aside? Unbelievable.

"Fine." I move away from her. "If that's how you want this to end, have it your way."

"Fine," she grumbles as she goes back to her end of the couch.

I let out a sigh as my eyes wander to the closed door to the room.

This is going to be a long day.

By afternoon, I can't take it anymore. Being in a locked room with no TV or gadgets? I can deal with that. But being in a locked room with no gadgets and with a person who won't talk to me for some reason I can't even fully comprehend? It's so frustrating it's maddening.

"Lena, can we just at least play some board games?" I ask her. "I don't know about you, but I'm bored as hell and I'm about to go nuts."

She doesn't answer.

I sigh. "Look, I know you've decided you hate me. I'm not asking you to change your mind. I'm just asking you to have mercy and play with me. I don't mind if you beat me. And you might feel better."

Lena glances at me. "If I win, will you leave me alone until tomorrow?"

I raise my hands. "I promise."

"Fine."

She gets off the couch and kneels on one side of the coffee table.

I walk to the shelf. "But if I win, you have to kiss me."

I can imagine the frown on her face even though I'm not looking.

"Just kidding," I say as I grab the Monopoly set. "If I win, you'll have to make that chocolate mousse from last night for me again."

I meet her narrowed gaze as I turn around.

"But I thought you're not supposed to eat too much sweets," she says.

I shrug. "It wasn't that sweet. That's why I liked it. Besides, it's not like I'm competing again. I can eat whatever I want now."

Lena nods. "Okay. If you win."

I grin at the spark of competitiveness in her eyes as I set the board game down on the table. Ah. Finally, a better version of the feisty Lena.

"I will."

I don't, though. Physical activities are my forte. Board games are Lena's. Although she lost the game of chess, she won Monopoly and then Scrabble, so she wins.

"I won!" she announces as she gets on her feet.

Talk about gloating. I almost want to hurl the Scrabble board at the wall. But I draw a deep breath before standing.

"You're right," I tell Lena as I go around the table to offer her my hand. "You won."

She reluctantly shakes my hand. I grip hers and look into her eyes.

"As promised, I'm not going to bother you anymore. From now on, I'll pretend you don't exist so that tomorrow, when we part ways, it will be easier for me to forget you. Not that it was ever going to be difficult."

Her eyes grow wide. They stay on me as her mouth opens silently. Then she pulls her hand away and runs out of the room. She's free to do that now that it's nearly evening.

I can leave the room now, too, but I don't. I'm done chasing after her. I just sit down on the couch and let out a heavy sigh.

I can't believe I lost. And it's not just this afternoon. I've lost the whole game. In the end, I wasn't able to make Lena mine.

And somehow, this defeat tastes more bitter than all the ones I've tasted before.

Fuck.

Chapter Ten
Lena

What the fuck am I doing?

I bury my face in my arms as I sit by the edge of the pool.

I was the one who decided to stay away from Riley, the one who asked him to leave me alone, the one who first hurled all those hateful words at him just so he wouldn't come closer because if he did, I knew I would fall for him even more. Yet here I am at a loss. I came out the winner of those board games, yet I feel more lost than ever.

Just the memory of that icy look in Riley's eyes makes me want to cringe. Those words he said still weigh heavily on my chest, threatening to split it open.

How could he say he'll forget me so easily? Wasn't he the one who said he wouldn't give up on me?

Fuck, it hurts. More than I can say. I thought that was what I wanted to hear. I thought I wanted everything to end like this. But I was wrong.

I don't want him to forget me, to hate me. Maybe it was too much to hope for him to love me, but I definitely don't want him to hate me. I don't want things to end this way.

By trying to keep myself from getting hurt, I just ended up hurting even more. I'm such a fool. But then, I already was a fool for falling for someone I can't have. This is almost like Thorn Birds. I knew it would end badly, but I still couldn't help myself.

Stupid Lena.

As I sit alternating between sobbing and chastising myself, the sky above me grows dark. The wind takes on a chill. I should probably go inside, but just as I'm about to, Riley appears in his shirt and swimming trunks.

Just the sight of him makes my heart want to fly out of my aching chest.

I open my mouth to say something but Riley walks past me as if I'm not there. Right. He's not here for me. He's here to swim.

My chest aches even more. I clutch it as I turn to gaze at his broad back.

I have a sudden urge to cling to it. If I'm already a fool anyway, I may as well embrace my role. If this story isn't ending well, then I may as well squeeze what happy memories I can from it. I may not be able to prevent the pain, but I can prevent the regret.

Ashley's right. I should savor this while it lasts.

Those words spur me to my feet and forward. I grab the back of his shirt and grip it with trembling hands.

"What?" Riley's voice is as cold as the stare he sends me over his shoulder. "I thought you wanted nothing to do with me anymore."

"I'm sorry." I look into his eyes. "I didn't mean to say those things."

"You didn't?"

"And I'm sorry for acting like a jerk all day, for being selfish, for being stupid." I shake my head. "I just... panicked."

"Panicked?" Riley turns to face me.

"Tomorrow, you'll be gone. We'll part ways. We won't be a couple anymore. I got scared." I rub my arm. "I still am scared of what's going to happen to me afterwards."

"What's going to happen to you?"

"But I'm not going to run away anymore," I go on. "I'm not going to throw these last few hours away." I meet his gaze. "I want to be with you."

Those dark eyes opposite mine widen slightly, but Riley says nothing.

I look away with a sigh. "I can understand if you hate me now. If--"

The swimming cap and the pair of goggles in Riley's hand fall to the floor. In the next moment, he grasps my chin and tilts it up so I'm gazing back into his eyes. They're narrowed now. Scorching.

"Oh, what am I going to do with you?"

I swallow. "Kiss me? Help me seize what's left of this crazy adventure?"

His thin lips curve into a grin. "I thought you'd never ask."

The next thing I know his lips are on mine. His hand moves to the back of my neck, the other gripping my hip to keep me from falling as he pushes me back with his mouth. His tongue slips past my lips.

My body trembles. My heart pounds and warmth erupts in my chest. Then heat. It flows through my veins all the way down to my toes, melting the silly fears swimming in my gut and unleashing a hunger I never knew I had.

I cling to Riley's shirt as I let my tongue dance with his. My blunt nails scrape the muscles of his abdomen through the cotton. Longing to touch them, I let my hands wander beneath his shirt. His warm flesh quivers beneath my fingertips and he groans.

I grip the hem of his shirt and pull it up to his armpits. He sets me down on the lounge chair before taking it the rest of the way off and casting it aside. His playful eyes hold mine.

"And here I thought I was the impatient one."

I can't retort because Riley's lips have mine trapped again. As his tongue wrestles mine, his hand travels up from my hip. My skin tingles from his touch. My nipples stiffen against the cups of my bra.

When his thumb brushes against one of them, I gasp into his mouth. Riley pulls away and nibbles along my jawline as he rubs the peak of my breast through its cotton prison. Then he sets it free as he plants a kiss on my neck. As he holds it between his fingers, a moan escapes me along with the heat between my legs.

He pulls off my shirt and takes off my bra. I feel the cool air on my blushing skin and the hard wood beneath me.

When he kisses me again, I wrap my hands around his neck. His hand pries my legs open and slips between them, rubbing me through layers of fabric. The friction feels good, sending more heat through my veins. It gathers in the place that he's rubbing, making it melt. At the same time, though, I feel like those layers are in the way and I wish they would melt as well so that I could feel bare pleasure.

Just after I think that, Riley's hands grip the elastic waistbands of my pants and my underwear. He pulls them down at the same time and I lift my hips so that they can slide down my thighs, past my knees and off my ankles.

Afterwards, his dark eyes wander from my shoulders down to my feet. I look away in embarrassment and cross my arms over my breasts. Even then, I can feel the intensity of his gaze burning my skin. I can hardly breathe.

I suddenly remember that there may be a camera around the pool and I pull my knees up.

Riley puts his hands on them. "What's wrong, Lena? Don't tell me you're being shy now."

"The camera," I whisper as he licks my ear.

He pulls away. "So do you want me to stop?"

My head shakes before I can consider it. "No."

I don't want him to stop. Not now. I don't know what I'll do if he does.

"Don't worry." His lips brush against my cheek. "They won't air any sexual content. They're not stupid."

I know. Even so...

Wait. The fact that they won't air it doesn't mean they can't see it. Someone must be watching right now.

"And we're not doing anything wrong." Riley holds my gaze as he tucks strands of hair behind my ear. "We're supposed to be married, remember?"

I manage to nod.

"Don't think of anyone else, of anything else," he asks--no, demands as his eyes stare deep into mine. "This is something that belongs to only you and me."

He captures my lower lip between his, tugging on it before dragging his lips across my cheek to my ear.

"Now, part your legs for me."

I shiver as I obey. My trembling knees fall apart and his hand slides between them, all the way down until his fingers brush against the place that's hot and wet and wanting. A finger slips in and I moan. My toes curl into the wood before my legs slowly stretch out.

41

I grip the edges of the chair as Riley licks my ear and moves his finger in and out. I feel more heat ooze out of me. He adds another finger and my moans spill freely into the air. My eyes squeeze shut.

His mouth keeps mine occupied once more as he pulls his fingers out. I whimper and then gasp as I feel them brush somewhere higher.

My eyes open wide.

What was that?

He finds that nub again, stroking it this time, and I grow weak. I pull my mouth away to force more air into my lungs. My eyelids drop as I throw my head back.

Riley kisses my neck as he teases that nub. My skin blushes all over. My body trembles. I grip his arm.

"Riley!" I cry out as a wave of intense pleasure washes over me.

It robs me of breath and sends ripples all the way down to my toes. Then it slowly recedes. Riley's hand withdraws as well.

I'm still feeling a bit numb, still trying to figure out what just happened, when Riley's arms wrap around me. Before I know it, he's carrying me to the pool.

"Riley, what are you doing?" I ask in alarm.

He answers by going into the water with me in his arms. I feel it splash against my skin.

He puts me down and my feet touch the tiles. I shiver from the cold but he sends warmth flowing through my body again with a kiss. He pushes me towards the edge and I feel the marble behind me.

"Put your elbows up over the edge," Riley orders as he grabs my hips and gives me a push.

I obey even though I don't know what he's trying to do. I trust that he knows.

"Now, grip the edge."

As I do that, his hands slide beneath my thighs. Then one of them disappears. When it returns, I feel something else against my skin. Something hard and thick.

My fingers tighten around marble.

"Relax," Riley tells me as his hand cups one of my breasts. "Everything will be alright."

I try to do that as I stare up at the night sky. My mouth opens to draw in gulps of air.

Slowly, I feel him enter me. Something stings momentarily but the pain fades quickly and all I'm left with is a feeling of being stretched, of being filled, of the heat of Riley's body melding with my own.

Then he stops, but only for a moment before he grips my thighs with both hands and begins thrusting rapidly. My body jerks. I close my eyes as I surrender it to him.

He pauses to suck on one of my breasts and kiss my lips. Then he pounds into me again. I want to wrap my arms around him, but I have to grip the marble or I'll fall. My fingers begin to ache. My elbows scrape the stone.

Suddenly, Riley's hands climb up my back. He pulls me into the water, against him. Then he grips my backside as he continues moving. My face falls against his shoulder as I cling to him. My nails dig into his back.

He moves even faster and I begin to moan against his skin. This pleasure is a bit different from what I experienced earlier. That one was sharp, too intense. This one seems to be gradually mounting, causing a buzz in my veins and making my head spin.

A particularly hard thrust sends me over the edge. I cry out. Riley trembles as his fingers bite into my skin. His cock quivers inside me as he grunts. Then he falls still and silent.

I rest my head against his chest as I catch my breath. He pulls out and puts me down, but my legs won't sustain me so I end up leaning on him. He lifts me in his arms and carries me to the side of the pool. Then he sits on the stairs and sets me down on his lap.

"Are you alright?" he asks me after a few seconds.

I nod, then lift my head to meet his gaze. My lips curve into a smile.

"It was amazing."

Riley grins. "I'm glad you think so."

As I rest my head against his strong chest again, I feel his heart beat against my ear. Maybe it's because of that sound, or maybe my mind is still muddled, turned to mush by all the pleasure I've just experienced. But somehow, I hear myself whispering what my heart has been screaming out loud.

"I love you."

Chapter Eleven
Riley

Lena's words still weigh on my mind as I give her swimming lessons the next morning--her final request, since we're free to do whatever we want on our last day.

It was just a whisper, and yet I heard it. Maybe Lena didn't think so, because she hasn't repeated it since, nor has she acted differently after. If anything, she's back to the caring, independent and sometimes feisty Lena I know, the one from before yesterday.

Maybe she didn't mean that confession? Just like she didn't mean it yesterday when she said she was tired of me and wanted nothing more to do with me. Maybe it was just the sex talking. Maybe she just got carried away.

But no. Something tells me she meant it. I've heard the words before, after all. I know how they sound when the one saying them is only doing so to please, to get something in return, like a kitten purring so it can be petted.

Lena didn't say them like that. In fact, I've never heard anyone say the words quite the way she did. That's why it's bothering me.

Yes, I wanted her to fall into my trap. I wanted to make her mine. But to make her say those words? That wasn't part of my plan.

"Hey," her voice jolts me out of my thoughts and I turn to her.

She's still gripping the kickboard like I told her, her legs still moving up and down along the water's surface.

"Now you're the one being quiet."

She's right. It's not like me.

I place my hands on my hips beneath the water. "Well, now you know how I felt yesterday."

Lena frowns. "So this is revenge?"

I shake my head. "No. Sulking isn't my thing."

"Not even after you lose a race?"

I shrug. "I just take a cold shower, punch the wall a few times, go to bed and train harder the next day. Sulking won't change things, after all, and it definitely won't make you better."

She nods. "I'll keep that in mind."

I place my hands between her chest and her stomach and push her up, then lift her knees. "For now, keep in mind that you have to keep your body straight. If not, your feet will sink. That's why you're kicking too much. Kicking is for moving forward, not for keeping yourself afloat."

"Yes, sir."

I wonder how she can be so calm today after what we did in this very same pool last night. We were just like this--her body afloat, my feet firmly planted on the tiles as I tried to keep her from sinking while I carved myself into her body. Just the thought of it, just the sight of her in a two-piece swimsuit, just the feel of her skin beneath my palm is enough to make my cock stir in my trunks, raring for another go. But I step back.

She manages to keep her body straight and afloat for a few seconds. Then she starts to sink again. She kicks frantically then she stops kicking altogether. Her feet drop to the bottom and she lets out a sigh.

"I'm tired," she complains as she rests her cheek against the kickboard.

"Then rest." I pat her shoulder. "You deserve it. I'll just go for a swim."

I pull my goggles over my eyes and am off before Lena can say a word. My body sinks below the water then aligns with it. My legs propel me forward. My arms rise and fall, paving a path in the water which the rest of my body follows.

As usual, the water washes my worries away. The tension in my muscles uncoils. The heat that spreads through them like wildfire sets every cell ablaze, and when it's gone my body feels renewed.

In a way, swimming is like having sex, I guess. It's a workout. It sends adrenaline pumping through your veins and leaves you sweating, grunting and gasping for breath. In the end, you're spent but you feel refreshed, left with a lingering satisfaction unlike any other.

"You're really good at swimming," Lena says when I go back to her. "In fact, I can say it comes naturally to you."

"As natural as breathing," I agree as I push my goggles up.

"So why quit?"

I wipe the excess water off my face with my palm.

It's not the first time I've been asked that question. When I first announced my retirement, everyone was spouting it.

"Because I've reached my peak and I've done everything I can with swimming," I give Lena the same answer I gave them.

"Bull. What about Phelps?"

That's exactly the reaction I got from a few of the journalists, too.

"And even if that was the case, so what? You love swimming. I can see that. You have a right to do it for as long as you like."

"I never said I'd stop swimming. I'll just stop doing it competitively."

Lena shakes her head. "That's like saying you're just going to keep breathing and not living. It's not the same."

I glance at her. When did she begin to understand me so well?

I sigh. "It's not that simple."

She questions me with creased eyebrows. "Why not?"

Because I promised my father I'd be the son he wanted once I turned twenty-eight. Because as the heir to a billion-dollar fortune, I was never free to begin with. Because life is fucking unfair.

But I don't tell her any of that. I've already accepted my fate.

"It's just not."

Lena moves closer to me. Her narrowed eyes peer into mine.

"You're not dying, are you?"

I give her a puzzled look. "What?"

She looks away. "That's the only reason I can think of to explain why you're quitting. I mean, swimming is your life. Giving it up would be like dying. So maybe you're already dying."

"I'm not dying," I tell her.

"Then why give it up?" Lena sighs. "I just don't understand. You keep telling me not to give up on little things, yet you're giving up on what seems like the most important thing in the world to you. I know you must have a reason. I just hope that you're doing this for yourself and not for anyone else."

I frown.

She notices it. "Sorry. I'm going to shut up now."

I, too, fall silent, her words still ringing in my head. I thought I'd resigned myself to my fate. Why, then, do I feel irritated now?

Lena pats my shoulder. "Just promise me you'll be happy."

I don't know if I can.

"Oh, and one more thing. You know what's going to happen later, right?"

I shrug. "Pretty much."

"They'll give you the divorce papers and then you'll sign. Then we'll have dinner, our last dinner, which will be romantic just like our first and hopefully not as disastrous."

I grin at the memory.

"And afterwards, you'll hand me the papers, too. The end."

I scratch the back of my head. "Yeah. I think they said something like that."

"Well, I just wanted to ask you, no matter what, can you just try not to get serious? Just keep things light, you know. Because I don't want to cry."

She already looks like she's about to.

"Can you do that?" she asks me. "I know we're getting divorced, but can we just end this on a happy note? Can we just be the happiest soon-to-be divorced couple ever?"

I nod. "Okay. I'll see what I can do."

Lena smiles. "Thanks."

I told her that, but now that the divorce papers are in front of me, I find myself wavering.

After all, before I came on this show, I already had everything planned. I'd make my wife fall for me, have as much fun as I could with her, and then when the show was over, I'd just sign the divorce papers and leave without saying a word.

That was how I always ended things. In the morning, before the woman I'd bedded the night before woke up, I'd just leave without a word. And then it would be over.

Goodbyes are just so tedious.

So why should I go through that routine just because Lena asked me to?

I glance at the first page of the document on the table, frowning as I see her name.

Lena Hunt. Just a week ago, I didn't know her. I definitely didn't expect her. Now, I don't know how to get rid of her.

Part of me thinks I owe her a goodbye like the one she asked for. Another part doesn't want to say it at all. She'd definitely make a better wife than Judy or some spoiled, snobbish heiress whose pastime is to match the right dress with the right shoes or argue with her friends about whose nose job looks the best. At least, I'd be happier with that.

But I can't marry her. So I might as well say goodbye.

Or should I?

I tap my fingers on the table. The golden band on one of them glistens.

Didn't I pay for this ring? In the end, it's supposed to be auctioned and the proceeds will go to charity. Same with Lena's. With hers, though, she can choose whether or not to keep it.

What if she gives it up? Can she still keep herself from crying? Or what if she decides to keep it? What do I say to her then? Can I still keep things light then? Can I still leave her then? What if things get messy and complicated?

I shake my head. I don't want to risk it. I came on this reality show to have fun, not to deal with drama, although I'm sure that's exactly what the producers want. But I have enough of that to deal with in my real life.

Yes, Lena will be hurt, especially if the words she said to me are true. But then she'll be hurt whatever happens. Wasn't that why she was crying the other day? Because she was already hurting? Because she knew it would just get worse? She knew this was coming.

We both did.

Maybe if I just leave, it will even do her some good. She won't have to fake as many smiles for me and she won't be tempted to cry. She won't have to make a mess of herself in front of everyone. It will be a swift, decisive end, one that will crush all her hopes and make her forget about me more easily. She'll be able to move on, just like all those women I've walked out on before.

I owe her that much.

My mind made up, I sign the paper in front of me. Then I glance at the crew member who's watching.

"Call your director or your producer or whoever is in charge of this show," I tell him.

He goes. When he comes back, he's with a petite woman in a striped black and white dress. As she pushes her sunglasses up on top of her blonde hair, I realize she's the one I spoke to before the wedding ceremony.

She turns to the cameraman, who puts down his camera and stands next to me.

"Is something wrong, Mr. Boyle?"

"You're the producer, right?" I ask her.

What was her name again? I can't remember.

She nods. "Delia Jasper-Boyd, although everyone calls me Deedee."

Right.

"I've signed the papers," I tell her. "Not that it was necessary."

"Ah, but it is for the show," Deedee says.

"Yes, for the show. The one I'm done playing my part in."

"Yes, you're right. After dinner and--"

"I think I didn't make myself clear." I stand up so I'm towering over her and hold her gaze. "I'm leaving. Now."

Her eyes grow wide. Her jaw drops. Then she glances at the table as she fidgets with her golden watch. "But--"

"I agreed to be here because I owed Dan a favor. You know Dan, right? I believe he's one of the top network executives now."

"Yes."

"He used to be a producer in the sports department. He was a fan and in some ways, a friend. He asked me to be on this show because he said you needed an athlete. And so I came. But I think I've done enough now." I touch my chin. "Or should I just tell him myself?"

Deedee shakes her head. "No, that's..."

Just then, the door opens again. This time, a man with gray hair and glasses enters. Deedee looks relieved to see him.

"I'm Kevin Rothers, the director," he introduces himself to me before turning to Deedee. "What's going on here?"

"Mr. Boyle wants to leave now," Deedee informs him. "But if he does, the dinner will go to waste and we'll lack material for the final episode of the show. You do know it's the one people watch the most, right?"

"I want to leave," I repeat as I face the director. "I got married and I've done everything you asked, all the stupid challenges, without complaint. Now, I want to go. And I don't know if you've followed my career, Mr. Rothers, but when I say I'm done, I'm done."

He says nothing.

"He's threatening to call Dan if we don't let him go now," Deedee says to him.

Kevin sighs. "You've signed the papers?"

"Yes."

"And the ring?"

I take it off my finger and hand it to him. "You want me to take the suit off, too?"

He shakes his head. "You can mail it or keep it."

"I'll send it back. Now, can I go?"

He nods.

"What?" Deedee sounds horrified.

"The show will be fine," Kevin assures her.

She doesn't look convinced, but I no longer care. I slip my hands into my pockets and walk to the door.

"At least say something to the camera," Deedee pleads. "Something for Lena."

The camera turns on and points at my face.

I sigh. Fine. I'll do this last thing.

"It was fun while it lasted," I say. "But we both knew it would end. Just give up on me, Lena."

With that, I turn to the door and walk out of the room.

That's it. Just walk out. Calmly.

I'm used to this. After a race, I don't talk to my competitors or smile for the camera. Regardless of the results, of all the cameras flashing in my face, I walk to the showers without paying anyone else any heed. It's the same after a press conference. Once it's done, I walk to my car with my earphones on to drown out all the questions that I don't care to answer.

This is how I do things. This is how it's supposed to be.

Chapter Twelve
Lena

Four weeks later...

"I wasn't even supposed to be here." The woman on the screen speaks with a quivering voice as she wipes the mascara-stained tears from her cheek. "I never expected any of this. I never expected the love..."

"Or the pain," I finish the line softly before turning the TV off.

A tear trickles down my own cheek and I quickly wipe it off with the back of my hand.

Why? Why does my heart continue to break even though it's been a month?

I thought it had started to heal. After crying my heart out in the show's conclusion even though I'd told myself I wouldn't shed a single tear, I thought I was done sobbing. But in the days that followed, days the network gave me time to rest and recover, I ended up watching sappy movies in bed and crying over every single one while gorging on vanilla ice cream and potato chips. I almost didn't want to go back to work, but I did, wearing sunglasses to hide my puffy eyes. It turned out to be a good thing because work was as hectic as ever and it distracted me from the pain I was feeling. I thought that pain had finally started to evaporate along with my tears. I could smile again and even fake a laugh. I could eat and sleep again. I felt human again. I was starting to live again.

Or so I thought until the episodes I filmed with Riley started to air. At first I tried to ignore them, even though everyone else was talking about them. I've been working on the show, but I didn't realize just how popular it was until everyone saw me on it. Even my sister saw it, and then I had to explain everything to her because she got mad that I hadn't told her about it in the first place.

I tried not to pay attention to the show, but I got sucked in anyway. I started watching. I must be some particularly stupid kind of masochist. Now it's over. The final episode has just finished airing and here I am--a mess. Again.

It's like my heart is shattering all over again.

So this is what it feels like to be run over by a bus. Twice. Somehow, it seems worse than dying.

My phone rings. I don't pick it up at first because I don't trust myself to talk. But it rings a second time. I seize it off the coffee table and glance at the screen.

Ollie.

Shit. My sister must have watched this episode too.

I answer the call because I know she'll get mad at me later if I don't.

"Lena?"

"Yup, I'm still alive," I tell her. Even though I feel the life flowing out of me from an unseen gaping hole.

"Good. Because I need you to tell me where that bastard is so I can kill him."

The rage in her voice takes me by surprise. I can tell she has her jaw clenched and maybe even a fist.

Kill him? I never even thought of that.

I sit back. "Don't bother. He's already dead to me."

"Is that why you sound like you're about to cry?"

I don't answer at once. So she's noticed, huh? But of course she would. She knows me so well.

And the strange thing is, now that she's mentioned it, I feel like crying even more.

I draw a deep breath. "Don't people cry over the dead?"

"Only if the person who died was good to them."

My throat hurts from the effort of trying to hold back tears.

But he was good to me. He was... amazing. That's why it's so hard for me to let him go, even though he was the first to let go.

"I... thought he cared about me."

"Yes, we all thought that. He had us all hoping. But he crushed all those hopes, didn't he? He threw you away like some toy he didn't want to play with anymore..."

I close my eyes as my sister's words pierce me like knives.

"He didn't even have the decency to say goodbye. Isn't that why you were a mess?"

Yes. That did hurt. I was already bracing myself for the goodbye, and when I realized I wasn't even going to get that, I just started breaking down.

And I'm breaking down all over again.

My voice quivers as my tears fall. "I'm such a fool, aren't I?"

That's the hardest part of all to swallow. I should have been smarter. I knew it was a stupid show. I knew none of it was real. I knew it wouldn't last. Still, I hoped and I believed. Still, I loved.

My sister sighs. Her voice softens. "Well, you've never been in love before. Very few first loves end happily. Yours just happened to be on TV."

I sniff as I look around for the box of tissues. "So now everyone is laughing at me."

"I'm not. I don't think anyone is. My friend just sent me a text that she cried over that last episode."

I pull out a few sheets from the box and blow my nose. "So everyone feels sorry for me?"

"They're sympathizing with you. They think Riley Boyle is a jerk, which is the truth."

Yes, he is, I silently agree as I blow my nose again. But why don't I feel happy to hear it? Why can't I bring myself to hate him?

"Just forget about him," Ollie urges. "A jerk like him isn't worth crying over."

And still the tears continue to fall.

"You'll get through this," she goes on. "You may be new to romance, but you're not new to heartbreak."

My eyebrows arch. What is she talking about?

"Remember when Mom left? You cried buckets then, too."

Right. I did. I cried for nights after that.

"I remember how I tried desperately to comfort you. Dad wanted to, but he couldn't stand to see you crying, so I was the one who did it instead. I sang you songs. I played games with you and let you borrow my toys. I fixed your hair. But none of those worked. You remember what did?"

"Ice cream," I answer.

"Vanilla ice cream," she seconds.

Ever since then, it's the only junk food my Dad allows.

"I've already had tubs of that."

"Well, have some more. You've never been the kind of person to gain weight easily anyway. And if you do gain a few pounds, so what? Just jog it off."

I glance at the fridge on the far corner. "Maybe I will get another tub tomorrow."

"That's my girl. But don't forget to eat other stuff, too, okay?" Ollie sighs. "I wish I could go over there and take care of you, but I have my own babies to take care of now."

"I know."

"And Dad."

"Did he see the show?" I ask her.

"Nope. Dad doesn't really like watching TV. He says it's exhausting reading subtitles."

"I understand."

Well, that's good, because I don't know how he'd react if he'd seen me on the show. And I don't know what I'd say to him.

"I have to go," my sister says. "But not before you promise me you'll take care of yourself."

Bossy as ever.

"I will," I promise her.

"And that you won't try anything stupid."

I frown. "I think I've had enough stupidity to last me a lifetime."

"And that you'll tell me the next time you fall in love with someone. Just me. Not the whole world."

I sigh. "I don't think I'll ever fall in love again."

"Stop that. You can't give up on love just because the first man who happened to steal your heart turned out to be a complete jerk. Pity, though. I thought Riley Boyle was a keeper. Dad liked him, too."

"I know."

I was supposed to get an autograph for Dad, but I didn't have that chance.

"You'll find someone better," Ollie assures me. "Someone who'll treat you the way you're supposed to be treated. With love, care and respect."

"Whatever." Right now, I can't bring myself to believe it. "Anything else?"

"Get that tub of vanilla ice cream."

I grin. "Yes, ma'am."

"Love you."

"Love you too."

The call ends and I put down my phone beside me. My gaze goes to the empty TV screen. As I remember the last image on it, my chest tightens again, but I close my eyes and draw a deep breath. It still hurts, but that call from my sister is just what I need to keep myself together.

I push the tissue box away. No more tears.

I'm strong. I'll get through this.

I get off the couch and walk to the kitchen.

And tomorrow, I'll get myself more ice cream.

~

I reach for the handle of the fridge the same moment someone else does. I pull my hand away and stare into deep brown orbs, like pools of molten chocolate, set beneath bushy eyebrows atop a slightly humped nose. A pair of thin lips surrounded by a thin beard curve into a smile.

"I'm sorry," the man in front of me says as he steps back. "Go ahead."

"No." I shake my head. "You first."

I'm in no rush. I can wait.

His eyebrows furrow. "Wait. Haven't I seen you somewhere before?"

Uh-oh. I forgot I wasn't wearing my sunglasses or my cap.

I shrug. "Maybe someone who looks like me. I'm pretty average, after all."

"No." He touches his chin. "It is you. You're Lena from Wed For A Week. The one with Riley Boyle."

Shit. He saw that?

I quickly glance around to see if anyone heard him. Thankfully, there's no one. Even so, it's time for me to leave before someone else recognizes me.

"You know what? I'll go ahead."

I grab the handle of the fridge and open it.

"Let me." He takes the handle from my hand. "It's the least I can do."

I send him a frown. "What? For a girl who's just been dumped on national TV?"

"For an amazing woman who didn't deserve to be used," he answers.

The words take me by surprise, and surprisingly touch my frail heart. I tuck strands of hair behind my ear as I turn to face him.

"Thank you."

He shakes his head as he closes the door. "For what? For telling the truth? To be honest, it makes me sick when men treat women like that. It ruins things for the rest of us, you know. A jerk screws with one woman's heart and then she shuts it and deprives all the honest guys of their chance."

My eyebrows crease. "So you're one of the good guys?"

He shrugs. "I'm more of an Ashley Wilkes than a Rhett Butler."

My eyes grow wide. "You like movies?"

"I've watched a few," he answers.

Including Gone with the Wind, one of my favorites. I wonder what else he's seen. Wait. He likes movies and he watches reality shows on TV. He's not gay, is he?

"What's your favorite?" I ask him.

He rubs his nape. "Oh, there are too many."

"Name one."

"First Blood."

Okay. That's probably the manliest choice I can think of.

"You look confused," he remarks.

I shake my head. "I'm just... wondering why a guy who likes John Rambo would watch a reality show about relationships."

"Oh, that." He scratches the back of his head. "My twelve-year-old niece was staying at the house last night because her parents were on their anniversary date. She was watching and I just ended up glancing at the screen."

Something tells me he did more than glance, but I don't press the issue.

"She's also the reason I'm getting ice cream," he adds.

"Oh. Did she ask you to buy some?"

"No. She finished my stash."

I chuckle.

Just then, a woman in her fifties barges between us to get ice cream. We step back to give her room and wait until she's gone.

"Well, she wants her ice cream badly," the guy comments after.

I don't even know his name.

"Yeah."

"Would you like to go somewhere else for ice cream? Maybe an ice cream parlor? After a movie?"

My gaze narrows. "Are you asking me out?"

"It's better to eat ice cream with someone else than to eat it alone, right?" he answers.

Well, that's true, but...

"And I know this great comedy that just came out. They say it can make anyone laugh. Why don't we go and check if that even applies to broken-hearted people?"

"Like me?"

"You're not the only one nursing a broken heart."

My eyebrows rise. He's broken-hearted, too?

"Don't worry," he tells me. "I'm not trying to hit on you or something. I just want to be a friend. Looks like you need one."

I have to admit I do. But can I trust him? Isn't it too soon for me to be putting my faith in men again, to hang out with one?

But then his words come back to me--the one about bad guys robbing good guys of their chances. And also Ollie's words about not giving up on love and finding someone better.

Is it really too soon? Hasn't it been a month?

Wait. It's not like I'm getting a new boyfriend. He did just say he wants to be my friend.

Besides, I can't imagine Ashley Wilkes hitting on a woman.

"Well?" he asks.

I touch my cheek. "I just have a big problem."

"What?"

"I don't know your name."

He smiles as he offers his hand. "Aaron."

I shake his hand.

"Shall we go and find ourselves a teeny bit of happiness?" he asks.

I give him a smile. "Sounds good."

~

So far, everything's been good. The movie. Dinner--because Aaron insisted we have something besides ice cream in our stomachs. The huge bowl of vanilla cream topped with marshmallows and drizzled with chocolate and caramel syrup that I just finished. Even Aaron's not so bad. True, he's not as tall as Riley, or as muscular. I can see his belly bulging beneath his shirt. But he is nice. Maybe that's what I should go for--nice and not hot.

"Thank you," I tell Aaron as we walk out of the parlor. "The ice cream was great."

He pats his tummy. "Yeah, it was."

"And not just the ice cream," I add. "Thanks for everything."

I turn my head to give him a smile, but to my surprise, he leans forward. His hand grips my arm. His lips press against mine.

My eyes grow wide. Earlier, when he wiped some syrup off my chin with his thumb and then licked it, I let that go. But this?

I pull away and cover my mouth. "Aaron, what are you doing?"

He gives me a mischievous grin. "I thought you wanted to thank me."

What?

"And I've been wanting to do that since I saw you."

"But--"

"My ex-girlfriend, I broke up with her because she wouldn't let me do anything. Said she took a fucking vow or something." Aaron snorts. "She was just a fucking tease."

My hand falls from my mouth as I look at him in horror. What's going on? Who is this man in front of me? Mr. Hyde?

"But you're not like that, are you?" His grip on my arm tightens and I wince. "I saw you on TV. You gave that pretty boy a good time and--"

"Let me go," I cut him off as I try to wrench my arm free. "You're hurting me."

He grasps my chin and forces me to look into his eyes, now clouded with lust. "Don't worry. I'll treat you better than he did."

I glare at him as I slap his hand away. "You're not going to treat me at all. I'm done with you."

I pull my arm but he won't let go.

"I said let me--"

I don't finish because a motorcycle engine roars through the air. I turn my head to see it coming. Fast. It seems to be going straight for Aaron and he realizes it, too, so he releases my arm and steps back. As he does, he stumbles on the steps of the parlor and falls.

The motorcycle turns and leaves. I seize the opportunity I'm given and hail a cab.

"Lena!" Aaron shouts.

I ignore him and get inside the cab. As it drives off, I catch a glimpse of Aaron in the rearview mirror, angrily kicking a trash bin.

Good guy my ass. He was a villain all along. A jerk just like Riley. No. He's even worse.

I slap my forehead.

Oh, Lena, how stupid can you get?

I thought I'd learned my lesson, but it seems I still have a lot to learn when it comes to men. I made another mistake by trusting one just because he looked nice and he knew about movies, and I almost paid dearly for it. Thank goodness he got impatient and showed me his true colors before it was too late.

I let out a sigh of relief as I relax against the backseat.

It's good that I managed to get rid of Aaron, but I know I wouldn't have if not for that crazy motorcycle. Whether he was just fooling around or he was really trying to help me, that motorcycle driver saved me.

I wonder who he was.

Chapter Thirteen
Riley

What was Lena thinking?

I throw my helmet to the ground before walking up the marble stairs to the front door. I push them open and walk down the hall in long strides. My pounding footsteps bounce off the glass walls.

I couldn't believe it was her at first, not when I spotted her from across the street as I was about to enter my friend's bar. I didn't want to. But then I never did forget how she looks. There was no way I could mistake that lustrous brown hair, that face, that body for anyone else's.

Just at the sight of her, memories of our time together on the show began flooding back. Excitement sparked in my veins and I almost found myself walking to her. Then I saw who she was with.

She'd already found someone new. Unbelievable.

Yes, I thought that might happen. I thought I wanted it to happen. But seeing her with another man, I just felt irritated beyond words. My hands clenched into fists on their own, trembling with frustration.

How could she find another man so easily or be with another man so soon when she said she loved me?

When they kissed, I almost punched someone. My blood was boiling so fiercely that I could barely contain it. I could barely stand watching. But then they started fighting. Lena started struggling. I just had to do something.

My body moved before I could think. I was back on my motorcycle before I knew it. And I very nearly killed that asshole.

I still want to.

Even now, even though the drive home should have cooled my head, my fists are still shaking, my temper still simmering.

Who does that piece of shit think he is? How dare he lay his hands on something that's mine?

"You're home early," a voice breaks into my thoughts.

I stop as I realize that my father, Harold McAllister II, is in the great room. His back is turned to me as he sits in his favorite chair facing the window, but he must have heard me coming. A glass of cognac sits between the fingers of his right hand.

"So are you," I remark.

He's usually out until past midnight, attending conferences or holding meetings with partners who live on the other side of the globe.

"I'm not as young as I used to be," he says as he lifts his glass to his lips. "I can't always work late hours."

I know what he's saying. It's not sympathy he's asking for. Nor is he complaining about his age. He's as fit as a horse and looks well below forty. He's reminding me of the promise I made to him, the promise that I'd help him run the family company.

"Don't worry," I tell him. "I haven't forgotten our agreement. I'll show up for work the day after tomorrow."

The day after my 28th birthday.

"Good. And speaking of tomorrow, Mickey has invited a few important guests."

Of course she has. When has she ever passed up an opportunity to show off? "I'm well aware of it."

"Some of them have been doing business with me for quite some time. It is important that you gain their respect and confidence."

So my work starts tomorrow, huh?

"I understand."

I walk towards the grand staircase.

"Also, Mickey and I have talked about your marriage," he adds.

I stop in my tracks and frown. "And?"

"We think Judy will make the best wife for you."

"You mean she thinks so," I say through gritted teeth.

"I agree with her," he tells me. "The Lawrences and McAllisters have a long history of friendship. It's time we become family."

I turn towards him. "I thought you were considering others."

"Of course, but we both decided that Judy is the best choice."

"And what I think does not matter. Am I not even allowed to choose from a pool of candidates?"

"Judy is the best candidate," my father repeats. "Why settle for anyone but the best?"

My fist tightens. "And if I say no?"

"You can't," he answers. "You promised."

Right. I did. For nearly two decades of freedom, I accepted a lifelong prison sentence. And now it's time for me to serve that sentence.

I knew this day would come. I braced myself for it. But now that it's here, I can feel its crushing weight. I can barely breathe.

"Tell me," I ask him. "Now that I'll be using the McAllister name once more, are you going to start thinking of me as your son? Or will I be just an employee, a pawn in your plans?"

He doesn't answer, but his silence tells me what I need to know.

I nod. "Then there's no more point talking."

I go up the stairs two at a time. When I reach my room, I slam the door behind me like a rebellious teenager. But it's no use. I'm not a teenager anymore and there's no point in rebelling. I'm doomed to this life in my father's shadow. And the only person who could have made it all bearable will never be a part of it.

~

"Now, now, don't look so glum." Jeremiah hands me a glass of scotch as he finds me in the balcony. "This is a birthday party, right? Not a funeral."

"It may as well be," I say as I take a sip from the glass.

Even though it's my birthday, I don't feel like celebrating at all. I've made polite conversation with my father's 'important guests' and put on fake smiles. I've been on my best behavior. But celebrate? Do I have a reason to?

Jerry places a hand on my shoulder and squeezes it. "I know you're not used to dwelling in the corporate world, but you'll be fine. You just have to do as your father tells you and learn from him. That's what I've been doing."

"That's what I'm afraid of."

"Don't worry. No matter how much you mess up, he won't fire you. He can't."

I give the ice cubes in my glass a gentle swirl. "There are worse things than getting fired."

Jerry sighs. "You're just determined to sulk, aren't you? That's weird. I don't think I've ever seen you sulk before."

"I'm not sulking." I lift the glass to my lips once more.

"Is it because of that woman? What was her name again? Lena?"

My shoulders immediately tense at the sound of her name.

"Wasn't it all just a game to you?"

I lower my glass. "I said I'm not sulking. I don't sulk. I'm just... contemplating what lies ahead."

"I see." Jerry takes a sip from his own glass. "Speaking of what lies ahead, I heard my mother and yours--"

"She's not my mother."

"...your stepmother, that is, talking earlier. It seems we'll be brothers-in-law soon."

I turn to him. "You sound happy."

"About having you as a brother-in-law?" He shrugs. "I guess it could have been someone worse."

My eyebrows crease. "You sound like you're the one I'm marrying."

He laughs and puts his arm around me. "Well, I guess it's sort of like that, isn't it? You marrying my sister, marrying into my family."

"Isn't it the other way around?"

He pats my shoulder. "Besides which, I've always thought about you as a little brother, the brother I never had."

So have I. So there was no need for us to be brothers-in-law. But I guess there's nothing I can do about that now.

I sigh. "I'm not sure I want to be related to someone like you."

"Oh, don't be like that." He pats my shoulder harder.

I gaze into the distance. "Does Judy know?"

"No," Jerry answers. "But I'm sure when she finds out, she'll--"

"There you are," Judy's voice rings through the air as she approaches.

"Speaking of the angel," Jerry whispers to me before turning to face her. "Hey."

She turns to me. "I knew I'd find you."

I force a grin. "Don't you always?"

She smiles, then casts a meaningful glance in Jerry's direction.

"And I'm off," Jerry says. "I need another drink."

Of course he's leaving. One look from Judy and he wags his tail. If he wasn't my best friend, I'd punch him. Or maybe I should anyway, just to make him come to his senses.

"What were you two talking about?" Judy asks me as soon as Jerry is gone.

"Nothing." I swallow the remaining contents of my glass.

She leans on the railing. "Enjoying your birthday so far, I hope?"

I don't answer as I set my glass down.

"You know, you never did say if you liked my dress."

She runs her fingers over the blue velvet, down from the beaded neckline, between her breasts, past her belly and over to the slit that reveals her thigh.

"It looks great," I tell her.

And yet I can't help but think it would look better on Lena.

Lena. She just pops into my head at the most unexpected times.

"Really?" Judy's face lights up.

She gives a whirl.

"It took me weeks to decide on this."

Weeks that she could have spent doing something else, like learning how to cook, maybe, or at least how to behave correctly. It puzzles me, really, how Jeremiah's such a good man when his sister has so many screws loose. And yet everyone seems to adore her.

She runs her hands through her auburn hair. "You know, I watched that show you said you'd be on. Only because you were on it."

I should have known she would. Wait. Did that show air this week?

"I was worried, you know," Judy goes on. "I was almost convinced you were a real couple."

She was?

"But then it was all just a game to you, right? That was clear in the last episode." She shakes her head. "Ah, but that girl looked so heartbroken. She really fell for you. Then again, who wouldn't? I almost feel sorry for her."

I say nothing as I stare at my empty glass. I wish it was full again.

Judy clings to my arm. "But she was stupid, right? There was no way she could keep you. I mean, you're not just Riley Boyle. You're Riley Boyle McAllister. And she's a nobody. How could she hope to be with you?"

My jaw clenches.

Judy strokes my arm. "She should have known she didn't stand a chance. Ah, but she fell in love anyway."

I narrow my eyes at her. What does she know of love?

"Or was that just acting?" Judy touches her chin. "Maybe she wanted to show off her skills so she could become a celebrity herself after--"

"Lena's not like... that," I blurt out.

I couldn't keep quiet any longer, but at least I managed to change the last part of my sentence.

Not like you.

Still, Judy gazes up at me with wide, confused eyes.

I draw a deep breath. "Sorry. I'm just--"

The phone in my pocket rings.

Ah. Perfect timing.

I fish it out and glance at the number on the screen.

"Excuse me," I tell Judy. "I have to get this."

Actually I have no idea who's calling, but the fact is I'd rather talk to an insurance salesman than Judy right now.

"Riley Boyle," I say as I answer the call.

I'm still not used to adding the McAllister.

"Mr. Boyle, this is Dan Thurman."

"Dan." My eyebrows rise.

The network executive. The one who asked me to be on Wed For A Week.

"Is this a good time?" he asks.

"Yes. Why?"

I hear him draw a deep breath. "There's something important I need to tell you."

Chapter Fourteen
Lena

"I can't tell you enough how happy I am with the ratings of the show," Ms. Deedee gushes as she squeezes my hands. "Why, they're the highest we've ever had."

I manage a sheepish grin.

"And here I thought it would be a disaster." She lets my hands go and holds one palm against her cheek. "I mean it started and ended awfully, what with that accident--Cynthia's all better now, by the way-- and how Riley walked out. And I thought you two would be bad together because both of you knew it wasn't real, but people are saying you have real chemistry and they love how honest you are and..."

I shift my gaze to the wall behind her as I stop listening.

Does she really need to tell me all this? Well, I understand that she's happy, and as the 'lead actress' of the program I should be happy, too. But the fact is I wasn't acting. And whatever I've gained, be it popularity or praise or sympathy, I lost more.

Can't Ms. Deedee be sensitive even just this once?

Finally, she ceases her monologue, another producer having called her attention. I watch her go, then let out a sigh as I lean against the wall.

Seriously, I don't know if I can stand another person talking about the show.

"Hey." Paula walks towards me. "Are you okay?"

"Just tired," I answer. "And a bit overwhelmed."

"Yeah." She nods. "I can hear quite a number of people talking about the show. All good things, of course."

I shake my head. "I don't care. I just want to forget about it, to forget I was ever on it."

Paula leans on the wall beside me.

"I understand. To all of us, it's a show. To you, it's your life. It's your heart. And Riley broke it. Of course you'd want to forget about it, but that's hard when everyone's talking about it."

"Now I know how celebrity couples feel after breaking up."

She shrugs. "Well, you technically are a celebrity now."

I ignore her. "They must have wanted to move on, but they couldn't because the world wouldn't."

Paula places a hand on my shoulder. "Don't worry, Lena. I'm sure all this will pass. Give it time. In the meantime, just hang in there."

I rest my head against the wall. "I just wish it would hurry up."

She pats my shoulder but says nothing.

"Lena?" I hear Kevin's voice from one end of the corridor.

I straighten up. "Yes?"

"Dan wants to see you," Kevin informs me.

My eyebrows arch. "Dan?"

Which one? The one from the editing department? The reporter? The cast member from the sitcom?

"Danny Thurman," Kevin answers.

It takes me a moment to recognize the name. When I do, my eyes grow wide.

"You mean the Head of Marketing?"

"Exactly. Do you know where his office is?"

I shake my head. I've never been there, or anywhere above the fourth floor.

"Fifth floor," Kevin tells me. "He's expecting you."

I nod, then turn to Paula with a puzzled look.

She shrugs. "Sorry. I don't know what's going on, either."

Okay.

She takes my hand and squeezes it. "Good luck."

I look at her. Does that mean I'm in trouble? Why does she look so scared? It's making me feel nervous.

I draw a deep breath. I have no reason to be nervous. The show was a success and I didn't do anything wrong.

Did I?

I try to think as I ride the elevator to the fifth floor. All I can think is that it must have something to do with the show. Did I say something I wasn't supposed to? Did I violate the contract? Wait. Did they find out that Riley and I had unprotected sex?

Finally, the elevator stops. The doors open and I step out. I find myself in a carpeted corridor lined with doors, all looking identical, much like a hotel hallway.

So this is what the fifth floor looks like.

I stop in front of the door that has Dan's name on it. It's partly open so I peek in and find his secretary busy in front of the computer. She stops typing and arches her eyebrows at me.

"Yes?"

"I'm Lena Hunt." I lift the ID hanging from my neck. "I'm here to see--"

"He's expecting you." The secretary glances at the shut door. "Just go right in."

That's what she says, but I still knock.

"Come in," a man's voice says.

I enter the room and find a stocky man in his mid-forties seated behind his desk. He seems to be going through some documents, but he lifts his head and peers at me through his glasses.

"I'm Le--"

"I know who you are." He gestures to one of the chairs in front of his desk. "Please sit down."

I occupy the one on my right and wait for him to speak.

When he takes off his glasses and clasps his hands on top of his desk, I hold my breath. Whatever this is, it's serious.

"Lena, I'm sorry to tell you that there's a problem with the show," Dan finally says.

My gaze drops to the chair across me. It's just as I thought.

"Well, not with the show. More accurately, something bad happened on the show. Well, not something bad. More of a mix-up."

I look at him for clarification.

He rubs his temples and sighs. "I should just tell you."

Yes, he should.

"You're still married."

My eyebrows arch. What?

"You and Riley Boyle are still married," Dan explains.

My jaw drops as I get to my feet.

"No way. That's not possible. He signed the divorce papers and so did I."

"Yes, but as it turns out, the divorce papers were fake," Dan says as he tucks his hands beneath his chin.

Fake? I shake my head as I look at him in disbelief.

"It seems they got the ones they used from the set of a soap opera."

No fucking way. So all this time, I've been married to Riley Boyle?

"Mr. Boyle has already been informed," Dan says.

"And?"

"He says he wants to see you," Dan continues. "I'm sure this worries him as much as it worries you. He probably already has legitimate divorce papers ready. You'll just have to sign."

"Oh." My gaze falls to the floor.

Where is this tinge of disappointment coming from?

"Can't he just send them?" I ask.

Dan shrugs. "Maybe he wants both of you to sign them in front of a lawyer to make sure nothing goes wrong this time."

I nod. "That makes sense."

But that means I'll have to see Riley again. Can I do that?

My fingers curl into fists at my side as I take a deep breath. Yes, I can. I can't stay married to him, after all. I have to end this once and for all. Besides, I'm not the one who can't stand seeing him. He was the one who left me, who walked out on the show. Ironically, he's the one who now has to say goodbye to my face.

I almost grin at the thought.

"Everything's understood, then?" Dan asks me.

I nod. "I'm sorry for... reacting so wildly."

And making a fool of myself.

He shakes his head. "I'm the one who's supposed to apologize. And I would like to offer my apology in behalf of the network."

"It's not your fault," I tell him. "Wait. Do Ms. Deedee and Kevin know?"

"Not yet. It was the director, Frank, I was talking to."

I nod.

"As for your reaction, it was only to be expected," he says. "Anyone would be livid finding out they're married to someone by accident, although Riley did seem calm. Then again, he's not the type to have his feathers easily ruffled. It must be a result of all those years of competing in the pool."

Indeed, I can't imagine him freaking out over anything.

"Did you know I wrote a lot of stories about him?" Dan sits back. "Or that I was the one who asked him to be on the show?"

My eyebrows rise again. "You did?"

"I used to be in sports journalism, so I watched a lot of his competitions. And once you watch Riley swim a few times, you become a fan. He does it so well, after all. It's too bad he's retired."

"Do you know why?" I ask curiously. "He wouldn't tell me."

Dan shakes his head. "I'm afraid not. I expect we'll find out soon enough."

I nod.

"Anyway, he said he'll send a car to pick you up at the front gate by six. That's when you get off work, right?"

I give another nod.

He offers me his hand. "I sure hope everything turns out fine."

I give him a hopeful smile. "Same here."

~

A shiny black BMW is waiting for me when I get out of work. A man wearing glasses, a navy blue suit and a black baseball cap opens the back door for me and I enter. All through the ride, he says nothing, his eyes fixed on the road. I sit as still as I can, fidgeting nervously with the edges of my cardigan, my hair and the keychain of my backpack.

I try to think of what I'm going to say to Riley. How exactly do you act towards the person who you thought dumped and divorced you?

Do I put on a smile and pretend I'm alright? Do I act like I don't care anymore? Do I cry and ask him why he left me? Do I lose my temper with him?

I guess that depends on how he treats me. If he ignores me and pretends he doesn't know me anymore, then I'll give him the cold shoulder. But if he apologizes with that tender gaze of his...

I shake my head and the strands of hair wrapped around my finger come undone.

Seriously, I don't know what I'll do if he acts like he did at the house, all sweet and caring. After all, we're still married.

Riley and I are still married.

All day long, I've been struggling to believe it. Weren't we supposed to be a married couple for just a week? Wasn't it supposed to be just this dream that we both woke up from?

I draw a deep breath. There's no use torturing myself with my own thoughts. I should just cross the bridge when I get there.

I glance out the window.

Whenever that is.

After a while, the scenery outside changes. The buildings give way to palm trees, then houses, small ones at first, then large ones.

My eyes grow wide. Isn't this the neighborhood where Hollywood stars live? Where billionaires live?

Don't tell me Riley is a billionaire. Then again, he must be fairly rich from all the cash he won in competitions and all his endorsements. Also, only wealthy people send a car and driver when they want to see somebody.

Finally the car pulls into a driveway past a pair of huge cast-iron gates. When I step out, I find myself staring at a mansion. Light from huge chandeliers spills through the glass walls, illuminating wood and marble. The fountains, one on either side of the front doors, are lit as well, the colors changing every few seconds.

This is where Riley lives? Isn't this house too big for just one person?

Just then, the front door opens and Riley emerges in a midnight blue dress shirt and slate gray pants held by a black leather belt. His dark hair is neatly combed back, but the top three buttons of his shirt are undone. I have to force my gaze away from the patch of skin exposed there and look instead into his ebony eyes, which narrow as his thin lips form a smile.

My stomach flips.

Shit.

"Lena," he greets me as he walks down the marble stairs.

So he's acting like we're old friends, huh? Should I act the same?

"Hello," I manage as I tuck a strand of hair behind my ear.

His gaze travels from my jeans up my shirt to my face. "You look great."

So much for acting like old friends.

"You too." I meet his gaze for just a second before glancing at the house behind him. "And your house looks... amazing."

"Nah." He shrugs. "I prefer our house. I mean, the house we lived in. Without the cameras, of course."

I tense, drawing a deep breath as I try to keep the memories from flooding back.

Don't think about them, Lena. Don't remember...

"How are you?" Riley asks me.

"Okay," I answer nonchalantly. "Busy."

"I know."

My eyebrows go up. What does that mean?

"I mean, you must be a celebrity now," he adds. "You must have a lot of admirers."

I frown. What's up with his attitude all of a sudden?

I want to answer back, but I decide not to pick a fight. This is probably our last meeting, so there's no point arguing.

I go straight to the point. "Danny Thurman spoke to me. He said--"

"I know what he said," Riley cuts me off.

Okay. "So you know... about the... mistake?"

He says nothing.

"That's why I'm here," I tell him. "To make things right."

Riley nods and starts walking up the stairs. "Come with me."

I follow him inside the house, down a corridor lined with glass walls, to a great room with all sorts of expensive looking works of art and furniture, and then up a staircase.

Through it all, Riley says nothing.

Is he mad at me? What did I do?

At the top of the staircase, he turns to the room on the left, then suddenly grabs my hand.

Before I can say anything, he opens the door and leads me inside. As my gaze wanders around, I realize I'm in an office. The walls are lined with shelves and a large desk sits in the middle. Maybe this is where we'll sign the papers?

But then I see the man and woman seated on the leather couch to the right of the desk, the man seemingly in his fifties and the woman in her forties. As they turn their heads to stare at me, I realize that the man looks like an older version of Riley with the same dark hair and eyes.

A lump forms in my throat.

Is this man Riley's father? And the woman with the strawberry blonde hair and those brown eyes scrutinizing me beneath almost non-existent eyebrows his mother?

The plaques on the shelf say 'Harold McAllister', though. Wait. The Harold McAllister? That billionaire business tycoon?

What the hell is going on?

Riley steps forward and pulls me beside him. Then he speaks.

"Dad, Mickey, this is Lena, my wife."

Chapter Fifteen
Riley

Mickey's loud gasp fills the room as she gets to her feet. My father stays seated. His eyes narrow slightly at me as his fingers tighten around his glass of cognac.

"Explain," he orders.

I tell him about how the documents got mixed up and how the judge turned out to be a pastor. He listens silently, seemingly frozen in his seat. In contrast, Mickey restlessly paces the room with an expression of horror and dismay. When she can't keep quiet any longer, she grips my shoulders.

"Riley, you can't do this."

"I already have," I tell her.

"But this is a mistake. You said so yourself. There's no reason for us to... to..."

"Adhere to it?" I finish.

"To stick to it," she says.

She probably doesn't know what 'adhere' means.

When I say nothing more, she turns to her husband and wails, "Harry, this is unacceptable. You can't just let this happen."

"It's already happened," I point out.

Mickey glares at me like I'm a speck of dirt on her Chanel sunglasses.

"So you're going to stand by this decision even if you know it was an error on the part of the staff?" my father asks.

"Yes," I answer.

Beside me, Lena, who seems to have been petrified since we entered the room, finally moves. She pulls her hand away and steps forward.

"I'm sorry. There's been some--"

"Lena." My father silences her with one look. "That's your name?"

She swallows and nods.

"Can you leave us alone for just a moment?"

I place my hand on Lena's shoulder and she gives another nod.

"S... sure."

She walks to the door. As soon as she's out, Mickey starts complaining again.

"You can't seriously be thinking of keeping her as your wife," she says. "And you're out of your mind if you think your father and I are going to let you."

I ignore her and look at my father. He takes a sip from his glass.

Mickey sits beside him and places a hand on his arm. "Harold, we've already talked about this. And I've already talked to Louisa, too. Surely--"

He holds his hand up and she shuts her mouth with a scowl.

"You really want to have that woman as your wife?" he asks me.

"Yes," I answer without hesitation.

I'd rather have her than Judy. No question.

"Even though she's a nobody? Even though people will say she's not a suitable wife for you?"

"They're not going to be married to her," I say. "I am."

"So you're prepared to stand by her? You can only defend her so much, you know. You won't be able to protect her from everything."

"I will," I assure him with fists at my side.

He falls silent.

Mickey glances at me, then at her husband's serious expression, then shakes her head in dismay. "Harold, surely you don't think--"

"I will allow it," my father says.

Mickey gasps. I find myself breathing a sigh of relief.

"Consider this the one whim I will indulge as your father," he goes on. "The one fault I will overlook."

My eyes grow wide. Does this mean that my words the other night had an effect on him after all?

"But no more," he adds. "Is it understood?"

I nod. "I understand perfectly."

He lifts his glass to his lips for another sip. I take that as the sign that I'm dismissed and leave the room. I find Lena sitting on one of the chairs outside, her eyebrows furrowed in worry. When she sees me, she stands up.

"What was that about?"

"You heard what I said." I approach her. "You are my wife."

"No. That was a mistake."

"A mistake is only a mistake if you regret it, if you decide it's wrong," I tell her. "And I happen to think it's not."

Lena shakes her head as she glares at me. "What is this? Is this all still part of your game, your fun? Haven't you had enough? Haven't you done enough?"

"The game is over, Lena." I grab her hand. "This is real."

She pulls her hand away and steps back. "I don't even know you. Aren't you Riley Boyle? Then why did you call Harold McAllister 'Dad'?"

She glances at the door.

I sigh. "Harold McAllister is my father. Boyle was my mother's maiden name. I used it because my father didn't approve of me swimming and also because I didn't want people to know who I was. I didn't want anyone making things easy for me, and I didn't want anyone questioning my victories, my achievements."

Lena nods. "So you're a McAllister."

"Yes. That's why I retired--to help my father run the family company."

Her eyes grow wide. "And your mother is fine with that?"

"Make no mistake," I answer. "That woman in there isn't my mother. Her name is Mickey. She is my stepmother, my father's second wife."

She touches her chin. "I see."

"Now you know who I really am."

"That doesn't change anything, though." Lena shakes her head. "If anything, it gives me more reason not to stay married to you. I won't."

My eyes narrow. "You have no choice. I'm not giving you a divorce."

"You already gave me one before," she points out.

"And it didn't work. So maybe this is fate."

"Fate?" She gives another shake of her head. "Don't give me that bullshit."

I just grin. "Just accept it, Lena."

"No way. I'll... I'll sue."

"You think you can win against a McAllister?"

She glares at me, then her bunched eyebrows break up and arch. "Wait. If your real name is Riley McAllister and not Riley Boyle, then our marriage contract isn't valid."

"Technically, I still am Riley Boyle. Both are legally acceptable. And even if they weren't, you can't nullify a marriage contract just because one of the names is wrong. If that was the case, a lot of marriages would be over before they even began."

"Ours was never supposed to begin."

I touch her cheek. "You are my wife, Lena, whether you like it or not."

"So you're saying you're forcing me to be your wife?"

"You married me of your own free will," I remind her. "You signed the papers with your own hand."

"Because I was asked to! You know that. And because I was told we'd get a divorce."

I grab her arm. "Why are you fighting me on this? You were fine being my wife at the house."

"Because I had to be."

"Admit it. You didn't want a divorce, because you were in love with me."

She doesn't answer.

My temper rises. Why? Why is Lena resisting so much? I thought she'd be happy that we're married for real. Isn't this what she wanted? Why is she pushing me away now when she was the one throwing herself at me? Has she really forgotten about me?

Well, she can't get rid of me that easily.

I grasp her chin and press my lips forcefully against hers. I tighten my grip on her wrist as I push my tongue into her mouth.

She gasps for air as she pulls away. Then she covers her mouth with her arm as she turns her back to me.

"Maybe I did love you," Lena says softly. "But not anymore. Not after you left me just like that. Maybe you're the first man I gave my heart to, I gave my whole self to. But you threw those away, didn't you? So now you have no right to say you still own them or take them back."

She turns to look me in the eye.

"I fell for you once. I'm never falling for you again."

The words make my chest tighten. My hands clench into fists.

So this is how she wants to play it? She thinks I'm being mean to her? Fine. If it's a fight she wants, that's what I'll give her.

"You're right," I tell her. "You don't know me, Lena. That man who you lived with at that house, who told you all the words you needed to hear, who tried to cheer you up when you were sulking, who was patient and gentle with you, that's not me. I'm not that kind."

I place my hand beneath her jaw and gaze icily into her blue eyes. "I'm Riley Boyle McAllister and you are my wife. Whether you like it or not, you are mine."

I let her go, then turn around.

"And you will stay here until you've learned your place."

Chapter Sixteen
Lena

This mansion isn't a house. It's a prison, a gilded cage.

I let out a sigh as I flatten my palm against the pane of a window in the library. My gaze scours the trimmed grass and the well-tended flower beds of the lawn below.

It's been three days since I came here, three days that I've been a prisoner. After half a dozen failed attempts at escaping on my second day, one of which almost ended in a sprained ankle, I've given up. I've stopped trying to contact the cops and my family, too. They won't be able to help me anyway, and I've decided I don't want to worry Ollie or my father. After all, this is my mess to sort out.

I don't have any communication with the outside world at all now. The last thing I got was a letter from the network accepting my resignation, which I didn't even tender. I guess Riley arranged that, just as he arranged to have my things brought over from my apartment and had someone buy everything else I needed. At least, that's what his assistant, Margo, said. I haven't seen Riley since that argument we had. I've been told he's busy with work, but I have a feeling he's avoiding me as well.

This room is the only thing that makes my captivity bearable. Aside from being filled with countless books, it has a copy of nearly every film ever made from the 50s to the early 70s, including some foreign gems.

I approach one of the shelves and pull out the container of the disk for Seven Samurai, one of my favorite films from Japan. That one was made back in 1954.

As I run my fingers over the black and white image on the cover, I wonder whose collection this is. Riley's father? Grandfather? Grandmother?

I still don't know anything about them. I've seen portraits on walls, but that's all. Even the maids won't tell me anything. They barely talk to me.

I put the container back on the shelf. It's such a shame that no one seems to watch these movies, even though there's a movie theater downstairs. Maybe I'll watch them all just to pass the time. And who knows? Maybe when I'm done, I won't feel so alone.

There are only two other things that I like about this mansion--the food, which is always good, and the kennels. I discovered them just this morning while wandering in the far south of the gardens. There are seven dogs in them--three German Shepherds, two Rottweilers, one Belgian Malinois and one Neapolitan Mastiff. They haven't warmed up to me yet, so I've made it one of my goals while staying here to win them over.

I glance at the clock on the wall.

Maybe I'll go and visit them again now. They might be a little less aggressive after having had their afternoon naps. And maybe I'll pass by the kitchen to get treats to bribe them with. Sure, they're supposed to be fearsome guard dogs, but even they deserve to get spoiled every now and then.

I go downstairs with those plans in mind, but they all evaporate as soon as I see a woman sitting on the red couch in the great room doing something on her phone. She looks like she's my age, well, maybe two or three years younger. Her wavy auburn hair flows past her shoulders over her pink chiffon blouse. White pants clad her crossed legs and open-toed ruby red shoes sheath her small feet.

Is she Riley's sister? Does Riley have a sister? Stepsister?

She looks up. When her brown eyes first meet mine, they grow wide, then momentarily narrow with a glint of--is that annoyance?--then light up as she smiles. The dimples on her cheeks show.

"You must be Lena," she says as she stands up. "I'm Judy. Judy Lawrence."

She offers me her hand and I stare at it while shaking it.

"My family and the McAllisters are good friends. You could say my older brother, Jerry, is Riley's best friend," Judy adds.

"Oh." I give her a smile.

I remember Riley saying something about a best friend.

"So you know Riley well."

"Yeah." She shrugs. "But not as well as you. You're his wife, right?"

So she's heard.

I sit on the couch. "Actually, that's not exactly true."

Maybe it's because I haven't spoken to anyone in the past three days. Maybe it's because I'm in desperate need of a friend or an ally and Judy seems the most promising candidate. Whatever the reason, I find myself telling Judy everything--especially about how the divorce papers we signed on the show were fake and how Riley is refusing to give me a real divorce even though I don't want to be married to him anymore.

"Wow." Judy looks at me with wide eyes after I'm done. "So that's what happened, huh?"

"That's what happened," I agree with a sigh.

She shakes her head. "I didn't know Riley could be so mean. He's always been so sweet and kind."

My eyebrows arch. But didn't he say this was the real him? Was he lying?

Judy sits back and sighs. "It must suck being married to someone you hate."

"Well, I don't hate him, but--"

"And to be held prisoner in such a large house," she goes on as she puts a hand on her forehead. "I'd die of boredom."

Boredom is one of my lesser problems, actually.

She sits up and turns to me. "You know, you shouldn't accept this. You should demand your freedom. You should stand up to Riley."

I roll my eyes. "Believe me, Judy. I've tried. He won't listen."

"Well, try harder."

I look at her. "What exactly is it you suggest I do?"

"Threaten him," she answers. "Turn the tables around. Let him know who's boss."

"Threaten him?" I give her a puzzled look. "With what?"

"Say if he doesn't let you go, you'll kill yourself."

My eyes grow wide at the macabre suggestion.

"I don't think I can go that far."

"It's just a threat. You don't have to follow through with it."

I shrug. "Then he won't believe me."

"Hmm." Judy touches her chin. Then she lifts her finger. "I know. Say you won't have sex with him anymore."

Wow. This girl is full of crazy ideas.

"But we're not having sex in the first place," I say as I suppress a blush.

"You're not?"

I look away as I scratch my cheek. "Maybe threatening him is not a good idea."

"But there must be something we can do," Judy says. "I mean, we can't just let men do what they want. Even though we're women, we're just as strong as they are, if not stronger. You know, sometimes I think they're just scared of that. They don't want to accept that we're stronger than they are so, they do everything to make us look weak and make us do things. They're just a bunch of stupid cowards."

I glance at the woman beside me in surprise. Now she's making sense. I guess she's not just a spoiled rich girl.

"You're absolutely right," I tell her as I nod. "We can't just let men do whatever they want."

She places her hand over mine. "Hey, what if I help you escape? I think I can do that."

"You can?"

Judy nods.

Well, I guess she can, since she can come and go here as she pleases. And since she's rich and her parents are friends with the McAllisters.

"But won't Riley get mad at you?" I ask her.

She holds a finger to her lips. "Not if he doesn't know about it."

Right.

"Well, what do you think?"

I shake my head. "I wish I could, but escaping is useless as long as I'm Riley's wife on paper. I realize that now."

"Oh." She scratches her chin. "If only there was a way to make him sign divorce papers."

"If only," I mutter.

Judy sighs. "I'm sorry I can't help you."

"But you have helped me." I place my hand over hers. "Just having someone to talk to is a big help."

"Really?" Her face lights up.

Can it be that she doesn't have friends, either?

I nod.

"Are you saying we're friends?" she asks me eagerly.

I shrug. "I guess."

She grabs my hands. "Then we should do something together, something to celebrate our friendship."

I glance around. "Um, I'm grounded, remember?"

She frowns as her shoulders slump. "Oh, right."

Then she stands up. "But we can still celebrate here, right? I know there's plenty of good wines in the cellar."

"Wine?" I give her a look of surprise.

"Yeah. We'll drink to our friendship."

My gaze drops as I scratch my neck. "I'm not exactly a wine drinker. Or any kind of a drinker, for that matter. I mean, I sometimes have a bit of wine with dinner, but--"

"Oh, come on." Judy pulls my arms. "You're still allowed to have fun, right?"

"Yes," I answer. "But I don't think drinking is a good idea."

She shrugs. "Isn't that what makes it fun? Besides, you're already being punished even though you did nothing wrong, so you might as well do something bad, something rebellious and mischievous."

I have to admit she has a point.

"Drink your worries away," Judy urges. "Let loose. Let Riley know that he can keep you locked up here but he can't chain your spirit."

I nod. "I like the sound of that."

"So do I." She tugs my arm. "So, shall we go get the party started?"

I grin. "Why not?"

Judy's right. I may be a prisoner here, but even prisoners can have fun. Besides, it's not like I'm going to cause a ruckus or turn the place upside down. I'm just going to get a little drunk.

Chapter Seventeen
Riley

Lena's drunk.

I know it the moment I step into the dining room.

Not only do I see the empty bottle of Chardonnay on the table and the half-filled glass in Lena's fingers. I can also see the alcohol in her cheeks, redder than usual, and in the gloss of her eyes that are threatening to disappear beneath her eyelids.

And here I thought she didn't drink.

With a frown, I walk over to her and snatch the glass in her hands away.

"Hey," she protests with a slur.

But it's too late. I'm already gulping down what's left of the wine.

Lena scowls. "That was my wine."

I set down the empty glass. "I think you've had quite enough."

She snorts. "So not only am I not allowed to go outside or make a call, I'm not allowed to drink, either?"

"I didn't say that," I tell her. "Drinking is fine as long as you don't go beyond your limits. Clearly, you don't know yours."

She laughs. "But I only drank one bottle."

I glance at it. I bet her limit is a glass.

"How did you even find that bottle of wine?"

She grins and holds an unsteady finger to her lips. "It's a secret."

I let out a sigh, then go over to her and grab her arm. "Come on. I'm taking you to your room."

"Don't touch me." She pulls her arm away and gets on her feet, staggering a little. "Who do you think you are, huh? You think you're so hot? Or so awesome?"

"I'm your husband," I remind her.

She laughs. "You're just a jerk and a coward."

I draw a deep breath as I let go of the insult. "You're drunk."

"So?" She leans on the table as she loses her balance.

I step forward to try and help her but she just pokes her finger at my chest.

"What do you care? You don't care. So don't pretend that you do. You're good at pretending. I know you are. But I'm not falling for it anymore. I told you. I'm not falling for you anymore."

I glance at her feet. "You are going to fall soon, though, if you don't let me help you to your room."

"I'm not going to do what you say anymore." Lena shakes her head. "I may be a woman, but I have my own mind. I'm my own person. I deserve respect."

I narrow my eyes at her. How can she talk about respect when she's so drunk she can't speak clearly or stand upright?

"You can take away my freedom but you can't take away my soul," she goes on. "I'm going to do whatever it is I want from now on."

I frown. "Are you saying you're going to be an alcoholic from now on? That you're not just refusing to act as my wife but that you're not going to behave at all?"

"Exactly," she answers with a grin. "Why should I behave?"

"Because you're an adult."

She laughs.

I usually love her laughter, but seriously, I'm getting annoyed. This conversation is getting frustrating. And exhausting. I'm already tired enough from work. I don't want to deal with this right now.

I grab her arm once more. "Let's go upstairs."

"What are you going to do, huh?" Lena sneers as she looks up at me. "Are you going to punish me for being a bad girl? Are you going to lock me up in my room, Mr. Riley Boyle McAllister?"

My jaw clenches. Is she tempting me?

God knows I've been aching to touch her since she came to live here, and now that she's looking at me with those eyes...

They narrow as she gives me a wicked grin. "You can't do anything, can you?"

That's it. I've held back long enough.

I place my hand on the back of her head and bring my lips to hers. I ignore her small whimper and push my tongue inside her mouth, tasting more of the fruity, earthy hints of the alcohol she's just been indulging herself in.

Lena squirms. Her arm struggles against my hold as she places a hand on my chest, trying to push me away. But she's too weak. Instead, she ends up clutching my shirt as she loses her balance again.

That's what she gets for drinking more than she can handle.

And this is what she gets for provoking me.

I push her down on top of the table and kiss her harder. The empty bottle falls. She fights me a little more, though half-heartedly, and then her moans of protests turn into sounds of pleasure. The arms trying to push me away wrap around me. Her hands travel across my back. When her tongue pushes mine back, heat travels all the way to my groin and my cock hardens inside my boxers.

Fuck. I haven't had a woman since I left her, and now all my pent-up frustration is fueling the desire that's burning through my veins. I don't think I could hold back even if I wanted to.

I move my mouth to Lena's neck as I slip my hand beneath her shirt. She gasps for air. My fingers crawl towards her breasts. They brush against the edge of her bra and I push it up so that my palm can cup her breast instead. She moans as her nipple stiffens against my skin.

I nibble on her neck and shoulder as I play with the nub. Her nails pierce cotton and dig into my back.

I lower my head to take her other breast into my mouth after peeling her shirt up. Her hands move to the back of my head.

I circle her nipple with my tongue as I keep the other one trapped between my fingers. She shivers. I suck on one breast as I rub the peak of the other and her fingers pull on my hair. Her gasps and moans spill into the air.

As I move even lower, I catch the scent of her arousal and it makes my nostrils flare. My cock rages against its cotton confines.

I pull her pants and underwear off and bury my head between her legs. I rub my tongue against her clit and drag it down to the folds of her drenched opening, tracing them before plunging in between. She lets out a cry as her nails rake my scalp.

I ignore the sting as I lap up the sweet nectar oozing out of her. My cock leaks in response. Then I travel back up and capture her lips with her taste still on my tongue. She moans.

Maybe it's because she's drunk, but she's moaning more loudly, more freely. Her hands grip my shoulders.

As I kiss her, I unfasten my belt and pull down the zipper of my pants. I take my aching cock out of my boxers and break the kiss so I can grip her thighs. I pull them towards the edge of the table and position myself between them, then enter her as slowly as I can.

Lena holds my gaze at first, but as I continue to push inside her, she closes her eyes and throws her head to the side. Her nails scrape the surface of the table.

I stop once I'm halfway in, then pull out and enter her with one thrust. She throws her head back against the wood.

I clench my jaw as I begin moving in her tight, velvety passage. I guess that tightness means she hasn't been with anyone else, and the thought sends fresh ripples of excitement through my veins. But damn, she's incredibly tight.

Eventually, the passage loosens as it gets flooded with warmth. I begin pounding into Lena and the table rocks. The empty bottle rolls away.

Suddenly, she grabs my tie as she lifts her head. She pulls my face towards hers, her mouth engaging mine in a passionate kiss.

I wonder if this is another effect of her being drunk. If so, it might not be all that bad.

Just as abruptly as Lena started the kiss, she pulls away. Her arms cling to me as her body shivers. Her head falls back as she lets out a cry.

I pause as she tightens around me and rides the throes of her orgasm. Then she drops to the table once more. I continue moving in and out of her, managing a few more thrusts before my muscles begin to coil. I bury myself deep inside her as my cock erupts. My body trembles.

Afterwards, I stay still as I catch my breath. Lena continues to gasp beneath me. After I pull out, she lifts her legs onto the table and rolls onto her side. When I'm done fixing my clothes, I realize she's asleep.

I let out a sigh. I guess this is what I get for fucking someone who's drunk. Then again, I'm starting to get sleepy, too.

I manage to stay awake long enough to carry her and her clothes up to her room. I set her down on the bed and pull the sheets up to her chin. Then I brush the strands of hair pasted to her cheeks and plant a kiss on her forehead.

Lena doesn't move. Her eyes remain closed as she breathes softly.

She looks so good and innocent, in sharp contrast to how reckless and defiant she was a short while ago. Then again, maybe that was just the effect of the alcohol. It's the first time she got drunk, after all.

I glance at the bedside table.

Maybe I should have something ready for her first hangover.

Chapter Eighteen
Lena

I wake up with a throbbing headache, an uneasy stomach and the feeling of something wet between my legs, all of which remind me of the things I shouldn't have done last night.

I shouldn't have drunk too much wine. And I shouldn't have had sex with Riley. Wasn't I supposed to be mad at him?

I turn on my side and hug a pillow.

That's when I see the flower on the bedside table--a single red rose--along with a bottle of water and a box of over-the-counter pain relievers.

I wonder who left them. Riley? I don't remember him carrying me to bed, but I can't imagine anyone else would have, especially since I'm still half naked. I don't even remember what happened before that clearly, though I do remember him kissing me and pushing me down on the dining table.

At the memory, I blush and bury my face in the pillow.

How could I have let that happen? How could I have let Riley do that?

Even as remorse gnaws at me, though, I can't help but feel just a little bit happy. At least Riley finally paid me some attention. He even talked to me, though I don't remember the conversation all that well. And the fact that he carried me to bed and left all this on the bedside table lets me know that he still cares for me, even just a little bit.

My lips curve into a smile. I'm a fool, I know, getting giddy over such a simple gesture. And I'm a liar, telling him I'll never fall for him again when I'm not sure if I ever stopped. Even now, with just a tiny show of kindness from Riley, my heart is beating fast, my chest swelling with hope.

What am I? A child? A pet?

I lie on my back and stare at the ceiling.

Whatever. I have a good feeling about this. I have a feeling things are about to change. Yes, I'm still mad at Riley for keeping me here at the mansion, but I'm beginning to wonder why I was so against this marriage in the first place. Isn't this what I wanted? Wasn't this the ending I was hoping for back when I was on the show? A real marriage.

True, the circumstances that led to this are not what I hoped, and the fact that Riley isn't just Riley Boyle complicates things a bit. But I'm still married to the first man I fell in love with. It can't be that bad, right?

But does he love you? a voice in my head asks. He broke your heart, remember?

Yes, I remember. But what if he left me just like that for the same reason he gave up on swimming-- because someone else asked him to? What if he really didn't want to?

And yes, that was a TV show and Riley was just playing at being my husband. But it doesn't mean everything wasn't real or serious. If what I felt for him was serious, maybe what we had can last, too.

I glance at the rose on the bedside table.

He may try to be mean and intimidating, but I know the sweet Riley, the one I knew back on the show, is in there somewhere. And this rose is proof of it.

I reach for it and brush its soft petals against my chin before bringing it to my nose. The sweet scent drifts into my nostrils and I close my eyes to savor it.

Ah. I just love the smell of roses.

Or so I think until I feel my stomach churn. Quickly, I get out of bed and run to the bathroom. I manage to get to the toilet in time and hold my hair back with one hand as I spew out the foul-tasting contents of my stomach. I swear I'm never going drinking again. After flushing the toilet I wash my face and brush my teeth. As I stare at the mirror, the blue eyes staring back narrow in puzzlement.

A wave of nausea washes over me again. I drop my toothbrush and head to the toilet just as my stomach lurches.

~

"How are you feeling?" Riley asks as he sits on the edge of the bed that I can barely get out of.

"Tired," I answer. "I threw up a few times this morning, so yeah, I feel a bit weak."

He glances at the cloche on the dining cart. "Did you eat?"

I nod.

He lifts the cloche and his eyebrows crease. "What is that?"

"Rice with peanut butter and cheese," I answer.

He throws his puzzled look at me. "What?"

I shrug. "The soup that the kitchen sent me made me throw up even more, and for some reason I was craving for rice. And peanut butter. And cheese."

His eyebrows rise. "All in the same dish?"

I nod. "I couldn't finish the whole thing, though."

Riley grabs the spoon and tastes the dish. He grimaces. "I'm surprised this isn't making you throw up more."

I give another shrug. I hadn't tried the combination before either, but somehow I just thought of it and somehow it just works. Who knows? I may be on to a new recipe.

He covers the dish with the cloche. "And how's your head?"

"Feels a little heavy but it doesn't hurt anymore," I answer as I sink further into the pillow.

"Did you drink the pain relievers?"

"No. I'd just throw it up anyway and when I was done throwing up, my head wasn't hurting so much."

Riley nods. "So you feel fine now?"

"Pretty much," I answer. "But I'm never getting drunk again."

"Good." He stands up. "While I like the fact that you're more into sex when you're drunk, I prefer a sober partner."

My eyes grow wide at the remark. I blush and look away.

Wait. I was more into sex? What does that mean?

"Why did you drink that whole bottle of wine in the first place?" Riley asks.

"I didn't drink the whole bottle," I argue.

Judy and I had a few glasses each. Maybe she even had more because I was drinking so slowly.

"Yeah, yeah." He doesn't believe me. "So why?"

I think of mentioning Judy but don't. I don't want to get her into trouble.

"Why not? I'm bored here locked up in your castle."

Riley sighs. "If only you promised you wouldn't..."

He stops then shakes his head. "We'll talk again about this tomorrow. For now, you should rest."

I frown because I'm curious to hear what he was going to say, but then I nod.

"Okay. I should be back on my feet tomorrow."

~

But I'm not. In the middle of the night, I wake up to throw up again. Same thing a few moments after I wake up in the morning.

As I flush the toilet, I stare at the swirling water in confusion.

Why am I still throwing up? Shouldn't the alcohol be out of my system by now?

When it's still happening the next day, Riley calls for a doctor.

Dr. Henrick asks me a dozen questions and then has the nurse with him collect samples to run a few tests. The day after, he returns with results.

"I've found out what's ailing you, Mrs. McAllister," he says.

I glance at Riley, who's standing beside me. He looks just as nervous as I am. I reach for his hand and draw a deep breath.

"So do I have a tumor or something?" I ask the doctor. "Some terminal disease?"

"Lena," Riley scolds me.

"No," Dr. Henrick answers. "But you could say it's something you'll have to live with for the rest of your life."

The corners of my mouth droop. I'll be throwing up every day for a lifetime?

"Just cut the suspense already, doctor," Riley demands. "What's going on with my wife?"

The doctor nods.

"Mr. McAllister and Mrs. McAllister..." he glances at me. "You are expecting a child."

My jaw drops and I lean forward. "What?"

Dr. Henrick smiles at me. "You're pregnant, Lena."

Chapter Nineteen
Riley

Lena's pregnant.

The news keeps flashing through my mind even though I'm in the office, which is probably why I don't remember what happened in that meeting that just ended a few minutes ago.

I rest my elbows on top of my desk and clasp my hands in front of my face.

I can't believe it. I definitely didn't see it coming. I thought she was using contraceptives while the show was filming because that was stated in the contract. Apparently, with all the last-minute chaos, Lena didn't think of it. And I didn't even consider it when I took her in the pool that first time.

I bury my face in my hands. Now what?

I don't know what to feel. Yes, I'm glad that Lena doesn't have a serious disease. It could have been worse. But I can't bring myself to celebrate her pregnancy. It's not that I don't want it. Well, I don't know. It's more like I'm not ready.

A lot of things are happening in my life right now. I'm still learning the ropes in running this behemoth company. Lena and I are just settling into our marriage. I can't deal with this right now. And I don't even feel like trying.

"Was that first meeting that bad?" Jerry's voice jolts me out of my thoughts as he enters the room.

I put my hands down on my desk and sigh. "To be honest, I don't remember much of it."

He laughs. "I know. I probably forget half of what's said at half the meetings I go to. The other half? I wasn't listening in the first place."

He sits on the leather couch in front of my desk and grabs the newspaper from the coffee table.

"Anything new?" he asks.

"What do you mean?"

"With you and Lena," he says.

I narrow my eyes at him. Does he have mental telepathy or something?

"You know, Judy went to your house a few days ago," Jerry says. "She says she met Lena."

My eyebrows arch. "She did?"

"Yeah. Apparently they're friends now."

"Really?" I get out of my chair and walk towards the couch.

I understand why Lena would want Judy as a friend. She's lonely, after all. And she did say she didn't have friends. But Judy? Lena's not exactly like the dozens of friends she has. Besides, Lena is my wife. Why would Judy want to be friends with her? Is she over me already?

"What?" Jerry notices my puzzled silence.

"Nothing," I answer as I sit on the couch.

Maybe I'm reading too much into it. At any rate, I don't want to think about it. I've got a lot on my mind right now.

"I'm just surprised because Lena didn't mention it."

Jerry shrugs. "Maybe she didn't feel a need to tell you."

"Or maybe it's because she hasn't been feeling well." I rest my head against the back of the couch.

Jerry puts down the newspaper and turns to me. "What's wrong with her?"

I draw a deep breath. "She's pregnant."

"What?" His eyes grow wide. "You're fucking kidding, right?"

I shake my head.

He faces the coffee table. "Unbelievable."

"I know."

"You've only been married for like a week, right?"

"We were married on the show, remember?"

"Right." He touches his chin. "And you had sex with her then. Wait. You didn't use protection."

"I thought she did."

"Fuck." He runs his hand through his hair. "Women can be so wily, can't they?"

I say nothing.

Jerry turns to me. "Does Mickey know?"

I shake my head. "I told the doctor not to tell anyone yet, not until I've figured out how I feel about this."

"Oh. So what? Are you considering asking Lena to get rid of the baby?"

"No." I lift my back off the couch and lean on my elbows. "We're keeping the baby no matter what. It's just... It's a bit overwhelming."

"Of course it is."

"Something tells me I should be happy, but I just don't know what I'm going to do. I've already got a lot on my plate."

"I know." Jerry pats my shoulder. "How does Lena feel?"

I shrug. "After the doctor gave the news, I left the room. I haven't seen her since."

"I see."

"She's probably expecting something from me, but I don't know what."

"It's fine." Jerry gives my shoulder another pat. "I'm sure you'll figure it all out. For now, just let it sink in. Try to get a grip on it. The rest will come to you."

"You think?"

He shrugs. "Hey, I've never been a father so I'm no expert."

I give him a puzzled look. "Why is that again?"

"Because I don't want to be tied down. You used to feel the same."

A part of me still does, but I've known for some time that marriage was inevitable.

Jerry stands up and puts his hands in his pocket. "Anyway, don't think about it too much. Sometimes the more you try to chase after an answer, the more it eludes you."

That makes sense. Just like before. Whenever I consciously tried to beat a record, I usually couldn't.

"Thanks," I tell him.

I get off the couch as well and walk to my desk.

The answer will come to me. It always does. For now, I'll focus on work or I might get into trouble with my dad. I'll think about Lena later.

~

When I come home from work, she's waiting for me outside my bedroom.

Great.

"You sure you should be out of bed?" I ask her.

Lena nods. "Dr. Henrick gave me some stuff for the morning sickness, so I feel better now."

And she looks better. Her skin has more color now.

"That's good." I grab the door knob. "I'm sorry, though. I'm a bit tired--"

She places her hand over mine. "I want to talk about the baby."

Her gaze tells me she won't take no for an answer, so I let out a sigh.

"Fine."

I open the door and let her inside my room. Afterwards, I close the door behind her and sit on the chair by the bed.

"What about it?"

"Are you still mad at me for not being on the pill?" Lena asks.

"No."

There's no point to that now.

"But you're unhappy about me being pregnant? About us having a baby?"

"I don't know, Lena," I tell her. "This is all a bit sudden. Frankly, it's too much to take. You know I've got enough to worry about."

Her eyes narrow. Her hands grip her hips.

"Oh, so you want me to do all the worrying? You think your life is the only one being... inconvenienced?"

"I didn't say that."

"I'm the one carrying this baby, Riley." She places a hand over her tummy. "If you think you're frazzled and overwhelmed, I'm on the verge of keeling over. If you think you're confused, I'm losing my mind. I'm falling apart here."

"So what do you want me to do, huh?" I get on my feet. "Keep you together? Hold you in my arms and tell you everything's alright? Well, I can't do that, Lena. I can't right now. Honestly, I don't know if everything's alright or if everything's going to be alright."

For a moment, Lena falls still and silent. Her gaze falls to the floor.

Then she nods.

"Okay," she speaks softly. "If you want to go through this alone, fine."

I let out a sigh of exasperation because that's not what I said, but I'm too tired to argue further.

"But I can't. Let me go to my sister. I want to see her." She lifts her head to throw me a pleading gaze. "I need her."

I don't answer.

"If you're worried I might run away, don't. I know what it's like to have a broken family and I don't want that for my child. I'll only be gone a few days. And I'll leave my sister's address and phone number in case you want to check on me."

I turn towards the window because I can't stand that look in her eyes any longer.

"And I won't make a scene or anything. I just want to see my family. Please."

"Go," I answer.

I was planning to end her prison sentence anyway.

"Thank you."

She walks to the door and leaves the room. I place my hand on my forehead and sigh.

Who knows? Maybe when she comes back, I'll know how to feel about the baby.

Chapter Twenty
Lena

"You're having a baby?" The stuffed purple bunny falls from my sister's hand as she stares at me with wide eyes.

I pick it up from the rug. "You heard it right."

Ollie clasps both hands over her mouth as she gasps. Then she wraps her arms around me.

"Oh my God. Oh my God. My little sister's having a baby."

I pat her back. "You seem more thrilled than I am."

She sits beside me and throws me a puzzled look. "And why aren't you thrilled, hmm? Because you're not married?"

I scratch my chin. "Well, actually, I am."

I explain the circumstances to her and she gives another gasp.

"So you're married to Riley Boyle?"

"Riley Boyle McAllister," I correct.

"You're Mrs. McAllister?"

I shrug.

"Wow." Ollie shakes her head in disbelief. "So you cried on TV for nothing."

"Well, I wouldn't say nothing. He did leave me. We haven't even talked about that."

"But he won't give you a divorce?"

I shake my head.

"I'm pretty sure he won't give you one now that you're pregnant with his child," my sister says. Then she looks at me suspiciously. "It is his child, right?"

I frown. "Who else's would it be?"

"Right." She nods. "I forgot you're my little virgin-until-ten-minutes-ago sister who didn't even bother going out on dates. I mean, who would have thought after seeing you so passionate on the show?"

"Ollie..."

Did she really have to bring that up?

"Sorry," she mutters.

I sigh. "I don't know about him not divorcing me now, though. He doesn't seem happy about the baby."

"What? Why not?"

I give another shrug.

Ollie sits back. "He really is a jerk, isn't he? What? Did he blame you for getting pregnant?"

"He said I should have been on the pill."

"Well, you should have told him he should have worn a condom." She shakes her head. "You know, I don't get it. Why is it up to us women to take these birth control precautions? We should be ones to keep track of our periods. We should know when we're ovulating. We should take the pills or the injections and then when we don't want to have babies anymore we should get ourselves sterilized. And what do the men do, huh? All they do is stick their dicks inside us. They don't even appreciate all the hardship we go through at childbirth."

I raise my eyebrows at her. "Um, are we still talking about me, or...?"

"Sorry." Ollie tucks a strand of hair behind her ear. "I got carried away. Anyway, Lena sweetheart, it's not your fault you got pregnant, no matter what your husband says. You can't make a baby without a sperm. Besides, I'm sure he enjoyed the process, so he shouldn't complain about the result."

I hug the stuffed toy in my arms and sigh. "Yeah. It's unfair."

"Damn right."

I rest my head against the back of the couch and stare at the ceiling. "I just don't understand why he's making even more of a fuss out of this than I am. I mean, I'm the one who's giving birth, right?"

"My poor sister." Ollie holds my hand. "Men are like that, though. You think we women are the ones who deal all the drama, but they're the ones who don't want to be upstaged. They want everything to be about them."

"Well, this pregnancy isn't about him. And I don't want to think about him anymore. I have me to think about."

"You're right." Ollie touches my cheek. "You have to think of yourself more now because it's not just about you. You're living, breathing for two people now."

I look at my belly. Right now, it looks the same and it doesn't feel any different, but I know, I know there's another person growing inside me.

"How are you feeling?" my sister asks me.

I place a hand on my tummy. "I still pretty much can't believe this is happening."

"Yeah. It's surreal."

"I'm a little bit excited knowing I won't be alone anymore."

"Oh, Lena, you're never alone." Ollie strokes my hair. "Though I do understand what you mean."

"But more than that, I'm scared." I look into her eyes. "What if I'm not ready to be a mother? What if I'm bad at it?"

Ollie places her hand on my cheek. "Well, no one is ever ready to be completely responsible for the life of another person, but you have to be. And as for being bad at it, I know you won't. You can't, because you're an amazing person."

The corners of my lips curve up into a faint smile.

"And because you're my little sister." She pinches my cheek.

"Ow." I rub it.

Until now, she still likes to do that.

She gives me an encouraging smile. "If I can do it, so can you."

~

Can I? I wonder as I stare at the row of framed pictures in my sister's living room.

Most of them are pictures of her and her two kids taken at special occasions, on trips or just at home, some with her husband. In all of them, they're all smiling.

I pick up the picture where they're at the beach and run my thumb over Ollie's smiling face.

I know she hasn't always had it easy. Even she complains about being a mother sometimes, even though she's always been good at everything. And I know it was hard for her to give up her dream of being a lawyer just so she could raise her kids.

And yet I can tell she's doing a great job. I can see how much her kids love her. I can even see that Vince appreciates what she does. More than anything, I can tell she's happy being a mother. She can complain all she wants, but she's having fun and she's got it all under control.

Can I do that? Can I be like her?

I put the picture back. As I do, my gaze goes to another. This one is a picture of her, Dad and me taken on a skiing trip before she got married. My mother was long gone by then, and it was just the three of us. Three peas in a pod.

I wonder where she is now. Does she still think of her daughters? Yes, a part of me is still disappointed in her, but another part just wants to see her, just wants to understand why she left. Maybe if I did, I'd make a better mother.

But what if I end up like her? What if I end up making mistakes I can't atone for?

"Lena." My father's voice jolts me out of my thoughts.

I turn to him with a smile. "Hey, Dad."

He, too, smiles as he sees the picture in my hand. Then he starts signing.

That's a lovely picture.

I sign back. I know.

I put the picture back.

He pats my shoulder.

Olivia says you got married on TV to Riley Boyle, that swimmer.

I nod. Yes, that swimmer.

He touches my tummy. And you're having a baby?

Yes. It's true.

He smiles. Are you happy?

I pause. It's such a simple question, and yet it almost brings tears to my eyes.

I swallow the lump in my throat before I give him my answer. I'm okay.

He nods and places his arm around me. I rest my head on his shoulder.

It's strange. My father said far less than Ollie and yet I feel as if he's told me so much. And right now, as his arm holds me tight, I can almost feel him lending me his strength.

I squeeze his hand and lift my head to look into his eyes.

I'll be okay, Dad.

I know that being a mother isn't going to be easy, especially with Riley acting so selfish and immature. But if he's going to be that way, then I'll just have to grow up even more. I have to be stronger. And I'm going to be, just like my father became stronger for Ollie and me. My baby, my child is counting on me.

If my Dad could do it, if Ollie can do it, so can I. So will I.

I give my Dad a smile.

No more tears. No more fears. Riley or no Riley, I'm going to face motherhood head on. I'm going to be the best mother I can be.

As soon as I get home, I'm going to do everything I can to get ready.

~

That's what I had in mind, but when I get back to the mansion, the first person I see is Mickey. She stands up from her chair in the great room and places a hand on her hip as she greets me with a scowl.

"You're back. I thought you were gone for good."

I put on a smile as I shake my head. "Oh no. I just went to visit my family."

"You mean your ordinary family?"

I narrow my eyes at the veiled insult. I wonder if she's from a rich family like the McAllisters. Something tells me no. If that's the case, shouldn't she be kinder to me? Or does she resent me because I remind her of who she used to be, of things she'd rather forget?

Still, I decide to let it go. Mickey may be a bitch, but she's still my stepmother-in-law.

"I'm going to my room." I head to the stairs.

"Your room?" Mickey snorts. "You think this is your house?"

So she won't let it go, huh?

I turn around to face her with a sigh. "Mickey--"

"Don't say my name." She points a finger at me as she comes closer. "You shouldn't be here. You shouldn't have come back."

"I'm Riley's wife," I remind her.

"Only by mistake."

I'm sure Riley's father sometimes thinks it was a mistake to marry you, I want to say, but I don't.

Instead, I say, "What's done is done. We just have to accept it."

She has to accept it.

"Well, I won't," Mickey sneers. "I won't accept you as part of this family and I sure as hell won't let you take over this house."

"I'm not--"

"You think you're so smart, don't you?" she goes on as she towers over me, her finger in my face. "You think you can fool everyone by looking so sweet and innocent, but not me. I know exactly the kind of bitch, the kind of leech you are."

I shake my head. "I'm not like you, Mickey."

I say the words without thinking and I regret them as soon as they're out, but it's too late. Her eyeballs are already on the verge of popping out of their sockets. Her nostrils are the size of pennies. Her lips quiver in anger.

Shit.

"Mickey--"

"How dare you!"

She lifts her hand to strike me. If I wasn't pregnant I would just take the blow, but as it is, my body moves on its own to evade the slap.

But not the table behind me.

As I lose my balance, my side crashes into it and I wince in pain. The one-legged table topples and in the next moment I hear glass shatter as a red puddle stains the floor.

Chapter Twenty-One
Riley

I stare at the burgundy carpet as I rest my elbows on my knees, sinking into my thoughts in the empty conference room.

My first meeting of the afternoon is already over and the next one doesn't start for another hour. I should probably use this time to take a power nap in my office or get myself coffee or go through those documents Margot sent me so that I can leave a little earlier. Instead, I just find myself zoning out.

I still haven't figured out how to deal with Lena's pregnancy after all.

I tap my feet anxiously on the floor.

What am I supposed to do?

"There you are." I hear Judy's voice and look up to see her walking towards me in a green dress.

My eyebrows furrow. "What are you doing here?"

"I came to see Jerry. He told me that you're still out of sorts."

"He said that?"

"You do look like you're not yourself. I know. I've been around you for so long I can tell what mood you're in with just a glance."

I can't tell if that's admirable or creepy.

She pulls out a chair and sits down. "What's wrong? You know you can tell me. Is it about Lena?"

So Jerry hasn't told her yet. That's impressive.

"I thought you and Lena were friends," I tell her.

"Yeah, I guess." Judy shrugs. "She's important to you, so she's important to me."

I knew it.

She gets out of the chair and moves closer to me.

"But you're far more important." She leans over me and grips the back of my chair so that my head is trapped between her arms. Her breasts are nearly spilling out of her top right before my eyes. "So if anything is going on between the two of you, I want you to know I'm on your side. You can count on me for anything."

She touches my cheek and strokes it.

Just as I thought, she hasn't given up on me. Should I have chosen her instead? Maybe if I had--

"Mr. McAllister." Margot barges through the door.

Above me, Judy frowns. I ignore her and lean my head to the side to glance at my assistant.

"What is it?"

"Your stepmother called," she informs me.

My eyebrows arch. Mickey? What does she want this time?

Judy finally gets out of my face. I move my chair closer to the table and begin to gather my papers.

"There's been an emergency," Margot adds.

"What?" I ask with little interest.

By now, I know all too well that not all Mickey's 'emergencies' are life-and-death situations. Once, it was just a matter of something stuck in her teeth that she couldn't get out.

"She said your wife had an accident at home."

The papers slip between my fingers as I grow still.

Lena's home? And she had an accident?

My eyes grow wide. In the next moment, I'm out of my chair. In a few minutes, I'm out of the building.

~

When I get to Lena's room, Mickey is standing outside wearing an agonized expression. She opens her mouth to say something as I approach but I ignore her and go straight inside the room. I close the door behind me and rush to the bed where Lena is sitting.

"Are you alright?" I ask her.

She looks at me in surprise. "Riley..."

"What happened?" I glance at the bruise on her arm and the bandage on her leg.

"I'm okay." Lena covers the bruise with her hand. "I just suddenly got dizzy while Mickey and I were talking and crashed into a table. It's my fault, really."

"And the baby?" I glance at her stomach.

"The baby is completely fine," she answers. "Mickey already knows about it, though. The doctor--"

She doesn't finish because I wrap my arms around her. Tight. My heart pounds against her chest.

All the way here, I thought it would escape. It simply wouldn't sit still in its cage, not when I kept thinking that something bad could have happened to Lena. Or to the baby.

My baby.

I've been such a fool worrying about it. What's there to worry about? What's there to fear? Lena is my wife and she's carrying my baby. That's all there is to it.

They're both mine and I always take care of what is mine.

"Riley," Lena protests as she taps my arm.

I realize I've been smothering her and let go. My hand touches her cheek.

"Are you sure you and the baby are alright?"

She nods. "The hourglass with the red stuff in it broke so it looked like there was a lot of blood. But the only real blood is from this cut on my leg which I got from one of the glass shards." She looks at it. "No harm done really."

I kneel on the carpet and take a look at it. Then I wrap my hands around her leg and press my lips to the Band-Aid.

"Riley," Lena gasps. "What are you doing?"

"I haven't been a good husband to you, Lena," I answer as I look into her teal eyes. "I've been unfair to you and our baby."

Her eyes grow wide.

"Yes, our baby," I repeat. "I put this baby in you and I will take care of it. And you."

I lower my face to plant another kiss on her leg, but she cups my cheeks.

"I know you will," she tells me. "And that's not what I'm asking. I don't want you to treat us like we're your obligations, or worse, burdens or chains. I just want you to let us be a part of your life."

I take her hand and kiss her palm. "And you are."

I drag my lips across her soft skin all the way to her fingertips, then part them and lick one of her fingers. Then I close my lips and suck.

Lena pulls them away with a gasp.

I turn my attention back to her leg and brush my lips against her skin. I drag them all the way up to her knee and lightly suck on that part of her.

She laughs. "That tickles."

I ignore it and move even further up. I push back the hem of her skirt so I can nibble on the inside of her thigh.

She grabs my shoulders. "Mickey's outside," she reminds me.

"So?" I give her thigh a long lick and she trembles. "She knows better than to come in while I'm here."

I continue on until I reach Lena's cotton panties. I part her thighs and press my lips firmly against the front.

"Riley!" she admonishes. "What are you doing?"

"What I should be doing," I answer. "Taking good care of my wife."

I push my tongue against the cotton. Lena gasps. Her nails bite my shoulders.

"But that's--"

"You liked it last time," I remind her.

That succeeds in silencing her. When I give her another lick through the cotton, she gasps once more and falls on top of the bed.

I keep licking the cotton and it gets wetter, both from my saliva and the juices leaking out of her. The sweet scent drifts to my nostrils.

Lena moans. Her thighs tremble around me as her fingers tug at my hair. My cock quivers in my boxers.

I lift my head and look at her. She's not drunk, but she may as well be with her cheeks flushed and her eyes glossed over.

They close as I capture her lips. My hands squeeze her breasts through layers of fabric as my tongue entangles with hers. I feel their peaks stiffening against my palms.

I kiss her jaw next, and the side of her neck as I reach beneath her to find the zipper of her dress and the hooks of her bra. I undo them both and slip the bra straps off her shoulders so her breasts can spill freely, their stiff rosy peaks stretching out to me.

I take one between my lips as I slip my hand beneath her skirt and her wet panties. I suck on her breast as I dip my finger into her moist heat.

Lena throws her head back as she squirms. Her arms drop to her sides, hands clutching the sheets.

I suck on her other breast as I put in another finger. I move them both in and out slowly, careful not to go in too deeply.

I don't want to hurt her. Regardless of how my cock is straining against my pants, aching to be freed, I must keep myself in control.

She's not just a body meant for my satisfaction like those women before. She's the vessel for my child.

I withdraw my fingers and move my head lower to her belly. There, I plant a reverent kiss.

Lena strokes my hair.

"Our baby," she whispers. "I was able to hear its heartbeat just a while ago when Dr. Henrick and his friend, Dr. Stanley, were here. I wish you could have heard it."

I press my ear against her belly. "I don't hear anything."

"Of course not. Our baby is still tiny so you need a machine."

I shrug. "Next time, then."

I kiss her belly once more before I pull off her soaked panties and take off my belt.

"Did the doctor say the baby can hear us?"

Lena shakes her head. "No. Why?"

"Because we're about to make some noise," I say as I finally free my cock from its prison.

I grip her thighs and enter her slowly. She gasps.

"Tell me if I'm hurting you," I tell her hoarsely as I fill her inch by inch.

"I'm fine," she gasps out.

Still, she squeezes her eyes shut and throws her head to the side.

Finally, I'm completely inside her. I let out the breath I've been holding and begin moving slowly. Lena moves her hips.

"Faster," she says.

I chuckle. Here I am trying to be careful and there she goes making demands on me.

"Yes, ma'am."

I move faster, lifting my head so I don't see her stomach. It's still small, but I can't help but imagine the baby in there. I know what we're doing is fine. The doctor would prohibit Lena from having sex if it wasn't. But I can't help but worry.

My thoughts vanish, though, as Lena tightens around me. Her body arches. The back of her head digs into the sheets as she clutches them between her fingers. A cry escapes from her lips and fills the air.

I manage a few more thrusts into her tight passage before my own desire overwhelms me. With a groan, I pull out and spill my seed on her dress. When I finish, I lie down beside her as I catch my breath.

Lena sits up and looks at her dress. She frowns.

"Sorry," I mutter as I put my spent cock back in my boxers. "I was worried it would be bad for you if I came inside you."

She glances at me. "Then maybe next time you'll use a condom?"

I nod. "Noted."

She lies back down. I take her hand in mine and lift it to my lips, which curve into a smile as I realize that she said 'next time'. My smile turns into a frown, though, when I see the bruise on her arm again.

I kiss it.

"Ouch," Lena complains. "That spot is still tender to the touch."

"Sorry." I let go of her arm. "When did you return, by the way?"

"Just this afternoon."

"I didn't think you'd be back so soon."

She shrugs. "I'm not running away anymore."

She did say that before, but something in the way she says it now fills my chest with warmth.

"What did your family say?" I ask her.

"Oh, they're thrilled. My sister especially. You'd think she was the one having the baby."

"And your father?"

"I have his support. As always."

I nod. "I still haven't given him my autograph."

"Yup."

I prop my head on my elbow and look at her. "And what were you and Mickey talking about?"

Lena shrugs. "Nothing much. She was just surprised to see me."

Chapter Twenty-Two
Lena

Well, that was a surprise, I think as I take a walk through the gardens.

A soft breeze blows against the leaves and stalks of the flowers, making them dance. I run my fingers through the quivering petals.

On my way back home, I was determined to change a few things, mostly with myself. But what do you know? Riley changed. Yesterday, he was finally back to the Riley I'm used to, the one I knew. The one who wouldn't let me give up the climb or stumble during the dance.

The one I fell in love with.

And he's finally decided to be a father, to be a good husband. He even lifted my prison sentence and said I can leave the house to do anything I like, to buy anything I want. I even have my own driver, and I can take one of the maids with me.

I haven't gone out yet, but maybe when Judy comes--I wonder what she's doing--I'll ask her to go out with me. Or maybe I'll pass by my old workplace sometime.

I close my eyes and breathe in the air.

Ah, freedom. And to think all it took was a little accident.

I glance at the bruise on my arm, which has already turned brown from purple. Maybe I should thank Mickey.

Speaking of my stepmother-in-law, I see her walking towards me in gray yoga pants and a matching crop top. Maybe she just finished her yoga session?

I wonder what Mickey wants with me now. Well, she has a smile on her face, so maybe this conversation will be a friendly one. Maybe she'll be nicer to me now.

I cross my fingers behind my back as I return her smile. "Hello."

"Lena darling." She gives me a kiss on the cheek.

Darling?

"How are you?" She takes both my hands in hers and steps back to look at me. "How are your wounds? How's the baby?"

"I'm fine."

She hooks my arm in hers as we continue walking. "I really am so sorry about what happened yesterday."

"It's alright. No harm done."

"I'm glad. If anything bad happened to you or the baby, Riley would have killed me."

I throw a narrowed glance at her. So she's relieved because of that?

"But I didn't even push you, right? I mean, you just fell."

Is she really apologizing?

"Though I'm sorry for the things I said before that. I'm glad you didn't tell Riley about them. But then I didn't tell Riley what you told me either, because, you know, it was a woman-to-woman conversation, so I think we're even."

I take it back. She isn't any nicer at all.

She puts her hand over mine. "Anyway, none of that would have happened if I'd known you were pregnant. I would have welcomed you back with open arms."

Um-hmm.

"Well, Riley and I wanted to keep it to ourselves for just a few days," I tell her. "We knew everyone would find out eventually. I mean, it's not exactly something we can hide--"

"True," Mickey agrees as she looks at me. "Even now, you already look a bit, you know, plumper."

I purse my lips. Wow. My stepmother-in-law really has a way with words.

I remember all the stories I've heard about mothers-in-law, about them being total bitches with the lone mission of making life miserable for their daughters-in-law. Plus all the fairy tales about wicked stepmothers. I suppose stepmothers-in-law must be the worst of all.

"Anyway," Mickey goes on. "I've told Harold about the baby."

My eyebrows arch. "You did?"

I should have known she would.

"And he seemed happy to hear it," she says. "But of course he would be. There's another McAllister, an addition to the family, someone to fill this home with love and laughter."

I give a faint smile. Well, those words are actually nice.

"Needless to say, I'm happy, too. In fact, I think this deserves a celebration."

"Really?"

She lets my arm go and claps as she stands in front of me. "A grand celebration. A party."

"Oh." I was imagining more of a family dinner. We haven't had one of those yet.

Mickey touches my shoulder. "And as my apology to you for what happened yesterday, I am going to plan it all. You just leave it to me."

Something tells me that's not much of an atonement. In fact, it seems like I'm doing Mickey a favor. If I agree, that is.

"I'm not sure," I tell her. "Shouldn't we keep this among ourselves first?"

"Nonsense." Mickey shakes her head. "It's the kind of news you should shout to the rest of the world."

I wonder if there's any news she doesn't feel like shouting to the rest of the world.

"But isn't it too early for a baby shower?" I argue. "I'm only a few weeks along."

"This isn't a baby shower, silly." She waves off my concern. "This is like the party for welcoming you into our family, since you haven't had that yet, and at the same time announcing that there will be a new addition to the family."

I nod. "I see."

But I'm still reluctant about throwing a lavish party. Knowing Mickey, there will be plenty of guests, none of whom I'll know unless I've seen them on TV. In fact, I'm pretty sure most of them will be her friends. I'll just feel left out.

I touch my arm. "Maybe I'll ask Riley first. It's his baby, too."

"Nonsense." Mickey gives me a look of dismay. "Yes, it is his baby, too, but you are the mother. You will be the star of this party. You deserve it. We women are allowed few joys in life. You should seize this one and make the most of it."

I force a grin. "But I--"

"Are you telling me you'll be asking for Riley's opinion on everything for the rest of your life?"

"No, but--"

"Let me tell you a secret, Lena." Mickey holds my hand. "If you want something badly enough, your man won't be able to resist you."

Okay. It's not the motherly advice I was expecting, but I guess I'll take it.

The problem is, I don't even know if I do want this party.

I draw a deep breath. "How many people will be there?"

"Fifty at least," Mickey answers. "Just close friends, business acquaintances and a few members of the media."

My eyes grow wide. "Media?"

"Darling, you worked in TV. You've been on TV. You shouldn't have a problem with this."

She's right. Even so, I'm not sure I want to be in front of the camera again.

"No media," I tell Mickey.

She pouts.

"No media and fifty people maximum."

Mickey sighs. "Fine. It is your party."

"Then okay, I'll let you plan it."

She gives a wide smile. "Oh, you just wait. I'll throw you the grandest party ever."

Which is exactly what I'm afraid of.

~

"Maybe I should have said no," I tell Riley that night when he emerges from the pool at the end of his evening swim.

I try not to look at the glistening beads of water trickling down his chest.

"We don't need a party, right?"

"You know it's not too late to change your mind," Riley tells me as he dries his hair.

"I think it is. Mickey said she already had the invitations printed and ordered the flowers."

Riley chuckles. "Well, parties are her thing."

I sigh as I lie back on the lounge chair. "I'm afraid I'll just feel left out. Fifty guests is still a lot."

He sits beside me. "Then why did you say yes?"

I shrug. "Because I'm a fool."

"No, you're not."

"Because Mickey's persistent."

Riley nods. "That I believe."

"And because I guess I want to get along with her. She is your stepmother. She's living here with us. I don't want her to hate me."

He touches my cheek. "Oh, Lena, you can't make everyone love you. It's not up to you. It's up to them."

"I'm not asking her to love me," I answer. "I just want her to accept me. If she can't have me as her stepdaughter-in-law, then can't she have me as a friend? I know this is a big house where there's plenty of room for everyone to hide and avoid each other, but I don't want that happening, you know. Can't we all just get along?"

Riley laughs. "You're probably the first one who wants that."

"Sure your mother didn't want it, too?"

He falls silent.

I place my hand over his. "Sorry. I didn't mean to bring her up."

He shakes his head. "It's fine. You're right. I'm sure she would have wanted it."

I just nod.

"Does that mean you're going to try to win over my father, too?" Riley asks me.

I shrug. "If I can."

He chuckles. "Good luck with that."

"Anyone can be won over," I add.

"Oh, really?" Riley's gaze narrows at me. Then he touches my cheek. "Well, with that attitude, I'm sure you'll be just fine at the party. After all, it's just a small party, right?"

Chapter Twenty-Three
Riley

Small party my ass.

There are about a hundred people in this guest house, most of whom I don't recognize, though I can tell they're all members of the upper class judging from the watches glistening on the men's wrists and the gems on the women's necks and ears. Plus they're all wearing fake smiles and holding their shoulders in that all-important manner.

I can even see the flashes of some cameras--not phones but professional ones, which means there are members of the media present. I don't mind. I'm used to them. But Lena does.

She's been tense and trembling beside me, which is a pity because she looks stunning in her mint green layered lace dress. Her hair is swept in a bun at her nape with some strands braided over her head. Pure gold teardrop earrings dangle from her ears, giving off the same sheen as the golden band on her finger, the one I finally got her as a replacement for the one on the show.

After all, if this party is to introduce her as Mrs. Riley McAllister, then she should look the part.

I squeeze her hand. "Relax, Lena. Everything will be fine."

"Easy for you to say. You're not the one they're staring at or talking about."

I have noticed guests ogling her, and some not in a nice way. I've heard them murmuring, too.

"Well, it is your party," I point out.

"Are you sure it's not hers?" She glances in Mickey's direction.

She's clad in a royal blue jumpsuit with a V-neck that goes all the way down to her waist and cut sleeves that reach the floor. Her large diamond earrings glitter as she throws her head back laughing at what someone just said.

"Well, she does look like she's having fun," I agree.

Lena pouts. "I'm never believing another word she says. She said there would only be fifty guests but there's obviously more than that."

"Obviously."

"And she agreed there would be no members of the media but there are."

"I'm sure she has her reasons," I say. "Mainly that she wants to show off. Didn't I tell you that's her favorite thing to do?"

"No."

"Well, now you know."

"Thanks for the warning," Lena mutters sarcastically. "Seriously, your stepmother is just... nasty."

She lifts her fists and clenches them like she wants to either punch or strangle Mickey.

I chuckle because I feel the same way most of the time. "I guess this means all thoughts of getting along are going out the window."

"Sorry." She puts her fists down. "I know she's your stepmother."

I shake my head. "Oh, please don't stop on my account."

Lena lets out a sigh. "I don't even know anyone here."

How could she?

"Even I don't--"

I stop as I see a familiar face headed in my direction. My lips curve into a grin.

"Hey." I greet Jerry with a handshake. "I didn't know you were coming."

"Oh, you know I don't miss Mickey's parties," he answers before turning to Lena. "You must be Mrs. Riley Boyle McAllister."

"Please call me Lena," she says.

Jerry offers her his hand. "I'm Jeremiah Lawrence. You can call me Jerry."

Lena's eyes grow wide. "You're Riley's friend?"

He touches his chin. "I think I am. At least I was last time I checked."

I snort.

"And you're Judy's brother," Lena adds. She glances around. "Is she with you?"

"Nope. Sorry, but she couldn't make it."

"Oh."

I find it strange that she didn't come. Like Jerry, she usually doesn't miss Mickey's parties. But I don't press the issue. I don't think she and Lena should be friends anyway.

"You really are more stunning in person than on TV," Jeremiah tells Lena with a smile.

Lena blushes.

I send Jerry a frown. "Watch it, Lawrence."

He quickly puts his hands up. "Just paying the lady a compliment. You know I like to do that."

"Not this lady," I warn him as I put my arm around Lena.

He steps back. "Okay. Okay. I'll go find another lady to work my charms on."

"You do that," I tell him.

He leaves. Lena rubs my arm. "Hey. It's alright. He was just playing around."

"I know," I say. "Don't worry. He's fine. This is how we usually are."

"Oh."

On second thought, I'm not sure. I've never been in a serious relationship before, so we've never been in this exact situation. But I'm sure he's fine.

Lena and I head for the refreshments table but Mickey intercepts us on the way.

She grabs Lena's hand. "Come with me."

She pulls Lena away. Lena throws me a puzzled glance over her shoulder, but I just shrug as I follow the two women. They stop at the landing of the stairs.

Mickey claps her hands. "Everyone, your attention please."

Silence falls over the room.

Lena tenses. I move closer to her and whisper in her ear.

"Just breathe."

She draws a deep breath.

"Everyone, I want you to meet the person who I'm throwing this party for," Mickey says. "My stepdaughter-in-law, or let's just call her my daughter-in-law, shall we? Lena McAllister, the newest member of our family."

The crowd breaks into faint applause.

"Oh wait." Mickey puts a hand on her hip. "That's not right."

She glances at Lena. "Lena, would you like to tell them, or should I?"

Lena shakes her head. She looks too nervous to answer.

"Very well then." Mickey turns back to the crowd. "Everyone, Riley and Lena are expecting. That means the McAllister family is about to get even bigger."

Gasps and cheers erupt from the crowd. Cameras flash. Lena forces a smile.

Mickey pushes her forward. "Why don't you say a few words to our friends?"

"What?" Lena looks at her in horror.

I take Lena's hand and squeeze it. "You can do this."

But she doesn't look encouraged in the least. She just stands there, stiff as a board. Her mouth is open but no words come out. The crowd waits.

"Just say something," Mickey urges.

"I... I..." is all Lena manages to say.

The crowd begins to murmur. I frown and place my arm over her.

"What my wife would like to say is that she wants to thank everyone for coming," I say.

I squeeze Lena's shoulder as I glance at her.

"Yes, thank you," she repeats. "And thank you to Minnie, I mean Mickey..."

The crowd laughs.

"For planning this party," Lena continues nervously. "And to Riley's father, Ha... Ha..."

"Harold," Mickey supplies before I can. "Harold McAllister."

"Harold," Lena repeats. "Thank you."

Afterwards, she runs off. I follow her.

"Ladies and gentlemen, Lena McAllister," Mickey says behind me.

The crowd applauds again and some of them approach me to congratulate me but I ignore them as I go after Lena.

"Lena!"

She doesn't slow down.

"You're not supposed to be running!" I shout after her.

Still, she runs. The only time she stops is when she bumps into a guest, a woman in her fifties. The glass in her hand tilts and the champagne spills on her beaded white dress.

Lena gasps at the same time the woman does. The rest of the people around them follow.

I frown as I realize who she just bumped into--Carol Crewson, the senator's wife.

Fuck.

"I'm sorry," Lena mumbles before running off again.

"What the hell?" Carol's dismayed gaze follows her. "What kind of an apology is that? Come back here and clean up this mess!"

"In behalf of my wife, I apologize," I tell Carol as I hand her my handkerchief.

She looks at me. "Riley, what kind of woman is your wife? Doesn't she even have manners?"

"She's--"

"We're so sorry, Carol," Mickey says as she joins us. "Why don't you come with me and I'll help you clean up. I'll even lend you a new dress and pay you for that one."

"Thank you, Mickey."

She ushers Carol away from the crowd. I glance around for a sign of Lena as I ignore the whispers and the questions around me.

Where did she go?

Chapter Twenty-Four
Lena

The flushing of the toilet sounds like music to my ears. I lean against the tiled wall and let out a sigh of relief.

For a moment there, I thought I'd end up embarrassing myself in front of everyone. I knew being pregnant meant I'd have a bladder with a mind of its own, but I had no idea how bad it could get until I was standing in front of that crowd with my knees trembling and my nerves out of control. Why did Mickey have to ask me to make a speech?

I cringe and slap my forehead as I remember it.

How could I have messed up so badly? I've never had a fear of public speaking, so how could I have messed up Mickey's name? How could I have forgotten Harold's? Is this the 'pregnancy brain' that I've been reading about?

My back slides down the wall as I slump towards the floor.

Now everyone will think I'm a stuttering fool. And that's not even the worst of it. That woman I bumped into whose drink I spilled--I recognized her. She's probably someone important. And she sounded like she wanted to kill me.

I bury my face in my arms.

I may have avoided wetting myself in public, but I sure didn't avoid embarrassing myself. I still caused a disaster. How can I face Mickey, Harold and everyone after this? How can I face Riley?

"Lena, are you there?" I hear his voice from beyond the bathroom door.

I don't answer.

The knob rattles. "Lena, if you're in there, please answer me."

"Go away," I tell him. "I'm not going back to that stupid party."

"And I'm not going to make you," he says. "I just want to make sure you're alright."

I drop my hands to my sides and rest my head against the wall. "How can I be after everything that happened? I'm a laughingstock now and everyone thinks I'm stupid. They probably even caught all my blunders on camera."

Riley says nothing. In fact, everything seems to have gone silent on the other side of the door.

I stare at it with furrowed eyebrows.

Did Riley leave? Is he disgusted with me now?

Then the knob turns. The door opens and Riley steps in. He puts a coin in his pocket and then bolts the door behind him.

My eyebrows arch. "How did you--?"

My voice trails off as he wraps his arms around me.

"It's alright," Riley whispers in my ear before lifting a hand to stroke my hair. "I don't care what everyone else says or thinks. None of that matters."

I frown. "Easy for you to say. You're a McAllister, an Olympic gold medalist, and everyone adores you. I'm a nobody."

He cups my face and looks into my eyes. His gleam in seriousness.

"You're my wife, Lena. And I'm the only one you need to please."

Riley brushes strands of hair away from my cheeks. Then he strokes them as he brings his mouth to mine.

At the touch of his lips, my whole body stops trembling. My worries vanish and the ache in my chest melts away. His tongue brushes against mine and I melt away.

I open my mouth wider as I clutch at his shirt. Our tongues, our breaths become entangled and my head begins to spin. Heat travels through my veins like a bullet train on fire.

I want him. After all the crazy stuff that happened tonight, I want to know I still have something good. And if what he said is true, then I do want to please him.

Right now, Riley is all I have.

I begin to unbutton his shirt. His fingers find the zipper at the back of my dress and pull. He pushes it off my shoulders and I stand up so I can step out of it. I undo the last button of his shirt and he shrugs it off.

He pulls me close as he deepens the kiss. My breasts press against his chest. They swell and my nipples poke against the cotton domes coating them. My fingers trace the firm muscles of his abdomen. His run over my back before resting on my bum, which he squeezes through my cotton panties before pulling me even closer.

I gasp into his mouth. His erection brushes against my thigh and I shiver.

Yes, I'm trembling again. My heart is pounding like crazy again. But this time for an entirely different reason. For an amazing reason.

I place one arm around him and reach for his cock with my other hand. My fingers wrap around the tent in his pants and begin to stroke.

He trembles as well. A growl rumbles in his throat.

The rod of flesh in my hand swells even more. The cotton barrier grows hot and damp.

I, too, feel something swelling between my legs even as desire bulges in my chest. Heat swirls in my belly and seeps out of me.

Ah, now I have wet my panties. But this wetness I don't mind at all.

Riley lets out another groan. Then he pushes my hand away. He unhooks my bra and I let it slip off my arms. He pulls my arm and leads me in front of the full length mirror.

My eyes grow wide as I stare at my almost naked reflection.

He's not thinking of fucking me in front of the mirror, is he?

I turn my head to look at him. "Riley--"

He grasps my chin and silences me with a kiss. His tongue holds mine down and all I can do is moan.

His other hand traces the curve of one of my breasts. Then his thumb rubs against my stiff nipple. My knees shake.

He lets go of my chin so both of his hands can play with my breasts. When I pull away to gasp for air, my half lidded eyes go to the mirror and I see the look of lust in them. I see my flushed cheeks and my parted, swollen lips.

Is that... really me?

Riley kisses my neck then nibbles on my shoulder as he moves one hand even lower. I hold my breath as it crawls towards my underwear. I gasp as it disappears beneath the cotton and I feel the brush of his fingertips against my nub.

My legs part. My eyes close as I throw my head back against his chest. My mouth opens but no sound comes out.

He rubs my nipple as he strums the swollen nub between my legs. It burns and the fire spreads throughout my body. My underwear gets wetter. My knees shake and my toes curl into the rug beneath my feet.

The pleasure is too much. Just too much. Before long, it overwhelms me and I grip Riley's sides as my back arches. A cry escapes from my lips and splashes on the ceiling.

Afterwards, I can barely stand so I lean against him. I open my eyes and see myself in the mirror, my skin flushed and glistening with sweat. My panties look soaked.

No. They are soaked, and not with sweat.

I don't want to look at my body anymore, so I turn around and rest my cheek against Riley's chest. Again, I feel his erection poking me.

When he lifts my chin and captures my lips once more, I take off his belt. I unzip his pants and take his hard cock out so I can wrap my fingers around it.

It feels even more amazing now that it's unclothed. The skin is smooth. The tip is slightly sticky. And it throbs against my palm as if it has a life of its own.

Riley groans and pulls away. Then he pulls me towards the sink. He grabs my hips and hoists me up on the counter. Then he pulls my panties all the way off my ankles. The cold, hard marble against my heated skin makes me shiver.

"It's cold," I complain.

"I'll warm you up soon enough," Riley promises.

In the next moment, he lifts my thighs and parts them. I lean back on my arms to keep my balance. I hold my breath as I watch his thick cock slowly disappear inside me.

Amazing. I guess that thing really does fit inside me.

As he stretches me, I open my mouth to exhale. I tear my gaze away from his cock and look into his eyes, finding them glassy just like mine.

I place my hands on the back of his neck and kiss him. He slips his tongue into my mouth just as he pushes the rest of his cock inside me in one go. Afterwards, he pauses then starts moving slowly. When he moves faster, I pull my mouth away and cling to him. My arms and legs wrap around him.

He hugs my back as he thrusts into my trembling body. My nipples rub against his chest. I press my mouth against his shoulder and moan against his skin. I taste the saltiness of his sweat.

Again, the pleasure builds. Heat from his cock spreads through my numbing thighs all the way to my toes and upwards to my belly and my chest. It buzzes in my veins.

I wonder if it's an effect of my pregnancy, but lately, the pleasure has been more intense. Or maybe my body is just more sensitive.

Before long, I'm on the brink again, and after a few more of Riley's hard thrusts, I fall over the edge. I cling to him with trembling arms as I let out a cry. My heels dig into his back.

Riley suddenly he pushes me away. I watch him as he walks to the toilet and starts stroking his cock over it.

Again, he refuses to come inside me.

In a way, it's touchingly considerate, but somehow the sight of him seeking the peak of pleasure on his own bothers me. I jump off the counter with what strength I have left, and before I can think it through, I'm on my knees on the rug in front of him.

I wrap my fingers around his cock and stroke. He jerks his hips. When I part my lips, his cock slips past, and moments later I feel his hands gripping my hair as something warm splashes against the insides of my cheeks, coats my tongue and gushes down my throat.

Okay. Once his cock stops throbbing, he pulls it out. I swallow the liquid in my mouth.

Riley touches my cheek. "Are you alright?"

I nod.

Strangely, even though I can't stand the taste of garlic, ginger, bologna or broccoli, I don't seem to find the taste of his cum disgusting at all.

He offers me some tissue and I wipe my lips.

"You didn't have to do that."

"I wanted to," I tell him. "I wanted to please you."

He pulls me to my feet, puts his arms around me and kisses the top of my head.

"Better?" he asks me.

I nod. In the past minutes, I'd forgotten what happened at the party, and even now that I remember it, I don't mind it so much anymore.

Riley's right. Why should I care about what everyone else thinks? Riley and my baby are all that matter to me.

And knowing I have them, I can rest my cheek against Riley's chest and smile.

~

In the morning, I wake up still feeling wonderful.

My back and my butt hurt a little, true, but that's not enough to make me frown. As I stretch my arms, I send a smile up to the ceiling.

Yesterday may have been a disaster, but today is going to be a great day. I know it.

Or so I think until I turn on the TV and see my face on the screen, until I hear myself struggling with my speech amid jeers in the background. But that's not the worst thing I hear. Alongside news of my marriage to Riley and my pregnancy, I hear stories--stories of me lying on Wed For A Week and deceiving the audiences by painting Riley as some jerk, of me tricking Riley into marriage, of me marrying Riley just for his money.

I place a hand over my chest as it tightens.

I guess the world isn't going to let me off that easily.

Chapter Twenty-Five
Riley

"Is it that hard to take down a story that isn't even real?" I shout into my phone. "I don't care how you do it or what it takes. Just get it done."

I end the call and throw my phone onto the leather couch then sit on it as I run my hands through my hair in frustration.

A moment later, the door to my office opens and Margot steps in.

"What?" I snap at her.

She stands where she is, holding the tablet in her hand against her chest.

"Sir, various TV networks and newspapers have been calling, asking for your comment regarding your wife--"

"Just tell them all to fuck off," I tell her as I pour myself a glass of scotch. "If they can't tell what's true from what's not, they have no business being in the media."

Margot nods, then glances at her tablet. "About the meeting in fifteen minutes..."

"I haven't forgotten."

I lift the glass to my lips. The liquid blazes down my throat.

"Yes, sir." Margot turns on her heel and leaves the room.

I finish the rest of my drink in one gulp and sit back with a sigh. What is it with today? Why can't everyone just leave Lena and me alone? Can't they come up with anything else to talk about? Don't the TV networks and newspapers have more important things to report on?

I wouldn't mind it so much if they only reported on Lena being officially married to me or Lena being pregnant. Not even if they reported on what happened at the party last night. Embarrassing as it was, Lena did nothing wrong. She was just nervous during the speech Mickey forced her to give, and she didn't mean to spill her wine on Mrs. Crewson's dress. That's easy enough to explain.

What I don't like is that they're making up lies, malicious rumors, painting Lena as a woman who's not just unfit to be my wife but unfit to be a mother, a person without any intellect, manners or morals. Why? What did she do to them?

It almost feels as if someone's orchestrating all of these fabrications. But who? Who's trying to destroy Lena? Her enemy? My enemy? An enemy of the McAllisters?

The door opens again.

"What is it this time?" I ask as I lift my head.

"Whoa." Jerry puts his hands up. "I was just dropping by to check on you."

"Oh, it's you." I place my hand on my forehead. "I thought you were Margot."

"Busy day, huh?" He walks towards me.

"Tough," I answer.

"Yeah. I can see that." He peers into my empty glass. "And I saw the news."

"That's not news. It's trash."

He sits beside me. "Unfortunately, some people can't tell the difference."

I shake my head. "There should be a special cell in jail for people who spread lies, especially on national TV."

Jerry nods. "Sounds good to me."

He glances at me.

"I don't understand why you're so pissed, though. Aren't you used to the media making up stories about you?"

"I'm used to it. Lena isn't. She didn't ask for this, and what's more, she doesn't deserve this."

Jerry says nothing.

I stand up. "You know what? I'm going to tell Margot I'm holding a press conference."

"To say what?"

"To say it's all lies."

"And you really think that's a good idea?"

I throw him a puzzled look. "What do you mean?"

"Last night, you spoke up for Lena when she was having trouble, but do you think that helped her?"

I don't answer.

"If you keep fighting her battles for her, she'll never win," Jerry tells me. "And things will just get harder and harder for Lena."

"So you're saying I should just leave things alone?"

"I'm saying you should let her handle them."

My gaze narrows. "But like I said, Lena's not used to this."

"Well, she has to get used to it," Jerry says.

I frown.

"You say she didn't ask for this, but she did marry you, and then she agreed to be your wife."

"You know what happened."

"That you forced her to be your wife? Yes, but I also know that she loves you. That's easy for anyone to see. That means she should be prepared for this."

I shake my head. "But she didn't know who I was."

"So you're saying if she knew, she wouldn't have fallen for you?"

I shrug. "I don't know. I just know she's having a tough time right now and that she's pregnant. I should do something."

"It's unfortunate that she's pregnant," Jerry says.

I narrow my eyes at him.

"I mean that this happened while she's pregnant," Jerry corrects himself. "But as your wife, she has to be strong. As a McAllister, she has to prove her worth."

"She doesn't have to prove herself to anyone," I point out. "Least of all to the world."

"But she has to be the one to stand up to them, Riley." Jerry stands up. "Like I said, it's her battle to fight, to win."

"But--"

"If you step in, you won't just make Lena look weak. You'll make her feel weak. It will seem like you have no confidence in her, or even that you're smothering her. You have to give her time and space."

I sigh. I guess I can understand what he's trying to say. You can't expect someone to stand on their own two feet unless you let them try. You can't make something grow unless you give it room.

I sit down. "Fine. I'll just step in if things get too bad."

Jerry pats my shoulder. "I doubt they will. These things usually die down if you ignore them, whereas they'll just grow bigger if you add fuel to the fire."

He's right. I shouldn't allow myself to be provoked into a fight with the media or public opinion. That's a fight I can't win. I shouldn't let it bother me this much. I shouldn't let it matter.

As for Lena, I wish I could at least be with her during these tough times, but I can't because of work. I just have to believe in her and hope that she'll be alright until this all blows over.

I clasp my hands under my chin.

Hang in there, Lena.

Chapter Twenty-Six
Lena

"Lena, is it true that you wouldn't give Riley a divorce after Wed For A Week?"

"Are you really pregnant?"

"Did you know that he was a McAllister even then?"

"Why did you cry at the end of the show? Was that just an act?"

"How's your relationship with your in-laws?"

I ignore the barrage of questions and run towards the car. As soon as I'm inside, I tell my driver, Neil, to drive back to the mansion.

I only wanted to go to a spa to relax after being stressed for days. How did these reporters find me? Did the employees at the spa rat me out?

I sigh as I sit back.

Why can't they just leave me alone? Aren't they tired of spreading rumors about me?

Frankly, I'm getting tired. Tired of crying over all the vicious lies that tear me up from the inside. Tired of telling Ollie not to mind them even though I can't help but mind them myself. Tired of reminding myself that I'm not who they think I am even though I'm beginning to question who I really am. Tired of convincing myself that this will pass and everything will be alright.

I'm tired. Can't they cut some slack for a woman who's in the first trimester of her first pregnancy?

What makes things worse is that I feel like I'm facing them all alone. Like I'm all alone. Again. Lately, Riley has been so busy with work that hasn't spent much time with me, and I don't want to play the clingy, needy wife.

But damn, I need him right now.

I need someone to get me through this hell.

When I see Judy waiting for me in the great room at the mansion, a smile immediately forms on my lips.

Well, there's someone.

"Judy." I give her a hug. "I've missed you."

"You have?" She throws me a look of surprise.

"Well, I haven't seen you since we went drinking," I tell her.

"Yeah. I got busy. But it seems I wasn't the only one. I've heard about the baby and all."

I glance at my tummy. "Yeah. I am having a baby."

"Congratulations."

"Thanks."

"I did want to congratulate you sooner, but like I said, I got busy. And then I got sick."

My eyebrows arch. "Is that why you weren't able to come to the party?"

Judy nods. "I wish I had been there, though, especially now that I know what happened."

I frown as I remember it. "Yeah. It was pretty much a disaster, but it's not as bad as the lies they're telling about me. I mean, I know I messed up at the party, but those stories that are spreading right now, that's a whole different mess, a bigger mess that they're all just making up."

"I know." She takes my hand and we sit on the couch. "I couldn't bear to listen to them. Sure, I don't know you all that well, but those stories are obviously lies. What's more, they're mean. How can they do that to you?"

I shrug. "I wish someone would ask them."

Judy looks at me with wide eyes. "You mean Riley hasn't spoken to them? He hasn't tried asking them where all these lies are coming from? He hasn't asked the media to stop spreading them?"

"I don't think so." I shake my head. "He's been so busy that we haven't really had a chance to talk about this whole fiasco."

Judy touches her chin. "I see."

I place my hand on her lap. "Wait. Can he do that?"

Judy chuckles. "He's a McAllister. Of course he can. Why, even back when he was a swimmer, whenever someone would spread rumors about him, he'd shut them down. He's not exactly the kind of man who just rolls over and takes a beating."

I nod. Judy's right. He's not.

"I wonder why he hasn't done anything this time, then."

Judy shrugs. "Maybe it's a test."

"A test?"

"Maybe he's trying to see how you can handle this--or if you can handle this--on your own."

My gaze narrows. "How can I take on the whole media, the whole world on my own? I'm just one person."

Judy scratches her chin. "Or maybe he's just busy like you said. He does have a lot of stuff to take care of."

I shrug. "Maybe."

But as his wife, shouldn't I come first? Shouldn't he be taking care of me, too, especially at a time like this? He promised he would.

"Or maybe..." Judy stops.

"Maybe what?" I ask her.

She waves her hand in front of her face. "Never mind."

"Maybe what?" I insist.

"I don't know. Maybe it's because this doesn't concern Riley. It just concerns you."

"What do you mean? Are you saying he doesn't care about me?"

I won't believe it. I know he does.

"Calm down, Lena." Judy places her hand over mine. "That's not what I'm saying at all. I'm just saying that maybe he doesn't consider this as much of a threat, so he thinks that dealing with it isn't too important."

I still don't understand what she's saying. How can this not be important when his wife who's carrying his child is suffering because of it?

"Or maybe Uncle Harold won't let him talk to the media," Judy adds. "You know he always does what his father asks."

I nod. That makes more sense.

"Then maybe I should ask him to do it for me so that I can have some peace of--"

"No," Judy tells me quickly.

I look at her. "No?"

"Do you really want to give Riley more stuff to worry about, more things to do? If this is what his father wants, do you really want him to defy his father? Do you want to come between them?"

My gaze drops to my feet.

No. I realize I don't.

"There are some things you can't ask of your husband, Lena, no matter how much you want to," Judy tells me. "You can't rely on him for everything."

She's right. Riley has enough on his plate.

I sigh. "I guess I'll just have to try harder not to mind the rumors."

After all, this is my problem.

Chapter Twenty-Seven
Riley

What is Lena's problem?

For once, I was able to get my work done early, so I rushed home. I found Lena in the library returning some movies. I put my arms around her and asked her if she wanted to have dinner with me outside, but she pushed me aside and said she was tired. Well, I understand if she really is tired, but something tells me that's not it.

"What's wrong?" I ask her.

She slips the last box in her hands into the shelf. "Nothing."

My frustration seeps in and I snort. "What's this? Are we playing cat and mouse again?"

She turns to me with a puzzled look. "What?"

"Back when we were on the show, whenever there was something bothering you, you wouldn't tell me," I remind her. "You'd just give me the cold shoulder or try to push me away. You'd say nothing was wrong, but something clearly was, and then I'd have to chase after you and wriggle the reason out of you."

Lena's jaw drops.

I put my hands on the shelf and lean over her. "Well, I won't play that game anymore. Whatever it is that's bothering you, just spit out."

I grasp her chin.

"Or do you want me to fuck you first so you can tell me when you're in a good mood?"

Her blue eyes narrow along with her lips. Then she ducks beneath one of my arms and slips away.

"I said I'm tired."

"You're tired?" I grab her arm. "I'm the one who's been working twelve hours a day."

She wrenches her arm away. "I know."

"I'm the one who's been running my father's stupid company."

Lena puts her hands on her hips. "So you're saying you're the only one doing something worthwhile? You're saying you're the only one who has a right to get tired?"

I shake my head and sigh. "I never said--"

"Well, any person can get tired, especially when she has another person growing inside her."

"Don't bring the baby into this."

She beats her hand on her chest. "Any person can get tired when all she hears every day is people talking about what a slut she is, what a no-good person she is, what a fraud she is."

So is that what this is about? I draw a deep breath.

"You're not supposed to care what everyone else thinks. I thought you agreed with me on that after the party."

"That was before I heard the lies on TV." Lena steps forward. "I don't care what people say if it's based on truth, but if it's based on lies, on the worst kind of lies--how can I stand that?"

"You know the truth, so why pay attention to the lies?"

"Because they hurt, damn it!"

I pull her into my arms. "Shh. Calm down, Lena. It's only hurting because you're letting it in. You're not supposed to, okay? Just don't mind--"

She pushes me away. "Don't mind them? They're messing with my head, with my life, with my family."

"Because you're paying attention to them. You're not supposed to. Attention is like oxygen. It will just fuel the flames."

Lena shakes her head and sneers, "Well, I'm sorry that I'm not as cold as you are."

My jaw clenches. What the hell? Wasn't she the one being cold to me? Now I'm the bad guy?

"I'm trying to help you..."

"Oh, really?" Lena crosses her arms over her chest. "Are you trying to help me? Do you even care?"

My gaze narrows. "What's that supposed to mean?"

"If you really wanted to help me, if you really cared, surely you could have done something already."

"Like what?"

She shrugs. "I don't know. Maybe get the truth out there? Maybe use your influence and your money to stop the lies from spreading?"

"So you wanted me to put an end to this?"

"Didn't you?"

"Why didn't you say so, then?"

"Why did I have to ask? You're supposed to..." She pauses to draw a deep breath then proceeds in a softer voice. "You're supposed to protect me."

"Oh, so you're playing the damsel in distress right now?"

"I'm not--"

"You want me to fight for you? To save you? To fix your problems for you?"

"I didn't--"

"I thought you could handle this on your own, Lena," I tell her. "It's not my fault if you can't."

Her lips quiver. "So I'm just supposed to deal with this alone? Well, you're right. I can't." Her gaze drops to the floor as she gives a choked sob. "I can't take this anymore."

So she's finally broken into tears, huh? But that won't work on me this time.

I can't always be the one being strong for her.

"Then give up," I tell her. "Isn't that what you're good at?"

With fists clenched, I march towards the door, ignoring Lena's sobs as they flood the library.

Chapter Twenty-Eight
Lena

"I can't believe he said that," my sister says over the phone the next morning. I can hear the disappointment in her voice clearly, and it echoes mine.

I sniff as I sink further into the sheets. I've been crying nearly all night, so I thought I'd run out of tears, but like before, hearing my sister's voice is making my eyes well up again.

"I know. That's why I wasn't able to say anything after that."

I just broke down as Riley walked away.

"So what are you going to do?" Ollie asks me. "And just so you know, giving up is fine as long as it's something you decide on your own. In fact, sometimes you have to give up on something so you can keep from losing yourself."

I shrug as I stare at the ceiling. "I don't know. I mean, my mind was already messed up by all these rumors and now I have to deal with Riley's drama, too." I wipe the tear trickling down the side of my nose. "I just don't know how much more I can take."

"Well, don't wait until you're at your limit. You're dealing with too much as it is. And you're pregnant, don't forget that. All this stress isn't good for your baby."

"I know." I place a hand on my tummy. "I do worry about my baby, but I just can't help all these emotions churning inside me."

"And you're even more emotional since you're pregnant and your hormones are raging like they're at a rock concert."

"Exactly. I can only hope that all this means my baby will be strong. I mean, he or she is already going through so much."

"I know your baby will be strong, because you are strong," Ollie tells me. "But being strong doesn't mean being numb or not fighting back, or sacrificing your own happiness to make others happy."

I say nothing because my throat is already aching, my lips quivering. Another tear trickles down my cheek.

"Thank you," I sob into the phone.

For always saying the words I need to hear. For always being there for me even when no one else is.

"Hey, are you crying again?"

I answer with a sniff.

"Stop or you're going to make me cry. Just come here already. Come home to the people who know you, who love you."

I nod. My sister's right. I need to be surrounded by my family right now. Only in their company can I remember who I really am, can I heal, can I find some measure of the peace and happiness that my baby and I need.

"Okay," I tell her. "I'll go home."

"Okay. Just have someone drive you, or take the bus or the plane. Just wear a disguise. It's too dangerous for you to be driving when your mind's a mess and you haven't been sleeping well. Plus you're pregnant."

"I know."

"Whatever you take, let me know. I'll be waiting for you. We'll be waiting for you."

I wipe my tears. "I will. Thanks."

I really can't thank her enough for being the most reliable sister in the whole world.

After I end the call, I go to the bathroom to take a shower to freshen up. Then I start packing. While I'm putting my things inside my suitcase, I hear a knock on the bedroom door.

"Lena?" It's Judy.

"Come in," I tell her.

She enters the room. As soon as she sees the suitcase on the bed, her eyes grow wide.

"You're leaving?"

"I'm just going home for a while," I tell her as I put another shirt inside the suitcase. "I need a break. I need some time away."

"I understand." She comes over to me and helps me pack. "But you're coming back, right?"

"Yeah." I go to the bathroom to get my toiletries. "I mean, I'm still Riley's wife and my child needs a father. I just need time to cool my head. I need time and space."

"Of course." Judy stands in the bathroom doorway. "How long will you be gone?"

I shrug as I grab my toothbrush. "Maybe a week. Maybe two. Maybe until my head's clear or all this has died down. I don't know."

"Does Riley know?"

I pause. "No. But I'm sure he'll understand."

Besides, he doesn't care anymore.

"So you're not even telling him you're leaving?"

I walk out of the bathroom. "I'll leave a note."

"A note could easily go missing," Judy says as she follows me. "If you want, I can tell Riley."

I turn to her. "You will?"

She nods. "Yeah. Why not? It's just a simple favor and we're friends, right?"

I smile at her. "Thank you, Judy."

Judy shakes her head. "By the way, what are you taking? Are you taking one of the cars in the garage or...?"

"I'll probably take the bus. I'm too scared to be on a plane by myself and I don't want to ask Neil to drive me all the way to Nebraska."

"Won't people recognize you, though?"

I squeeze my bag of toiletries inside my suitcase. "I'll wear a disguise. I have my sunglasses and I can wear a cap."

"Or you can wear a scarf," Judy suggests. "You know, like the ones women wear over their heads in those old Hollywood movies."

"Yeah. I think I have one."

"Won't taking the bus be hard, though?" She sits on the bed. "You need to use the bathroom often, don't you? And what if you throw up?"

I pause. Come to think of it, those are valid concerns.

I shrug them off. "I don't really have a choice."

"Well, what if I give you one?"

I glance at her.

"What if I ask one of our drivers to drive you? Perry, for example. He won't mind. He's used to driving long distances."

"But--"

"And if I'm not mistaken, he's from Nebraska, too," Judy says.

"Really?"

"And I might ask him to pick up something for me in Denver on his way back."

I take a moment to consider her offer. Traveling by car would be more convenient.

"You'll still have to wear your disguise, though," Judy adds. "Even if it's just when you stop along the way."

I nod. "Yeah. I guess."

The last thing I want is for reporters to follow me all the way to my sister's house.

"So do you accept my offer?" Judy asks as she stands up.

"Alright," I give in.

After all, taking the car means I'll be safer, too.

"But I'll pay for the gas."

"No way." Judy shakes her head. "I'm giving you a completely free ride. All or nothing."

Well, if she insists.

I smile before pulling her into my arms for a hug. "Thanks, Judy. I'm really glad I have at least one friend around here."

She pats my back. "You go home and do what you have to do. Take as long as you need to take. Just leave Riley to me."

"What did you say?"

I climb back down the steps and turn to Judy. She rises from the couch.

"I said Lena isn't here anymore."

My eyes narrow. "What do you mean?"

"I mean she left. If you don't believe me, go to her room. See if her suitcase is there."

I do just that. I run up the stairs and check her room. Just as Judy says, her suitcase is missing, along with her toothbrush, her comb and her favorite pair of shoes.

No.

"I told you," Judy says behind me.

I glance at her. "Where is she?"

She approaches me with a sly grin and traces an S on the front of my shirt. "Maybe if you kiss me, I'll tell you."

She looks up at me and licks her glossed lips. Her fingers climb up my arm.

I grab her wrist and twist it. "Where's Lena?"

"Ow!" she yelps.

She pulls her hand away and rubs her wrist with a frown.

"How could you?" she wails.

Maybe if the circumstances were different, I'd feel guilty. But right now, all I can feel are impatience and frustration.

"I'll only ask one more time," I tell her. "Where is--?"

"Lena is with another man," Judy says.

My eyes grow wide. What?

"She asked me not to tell you, but fuck, you're persistent." She rubs her wrist. "I think you might have bruised my skin."

"I don't believe you," I tell her. "Lena would never cheat on me."

"Are you sure?"

I want to say yes. I refuse to think she could cheat on me when she's carrying my child, when she loves me. Then again, she hasn't told me she loves me lately. In fact, she looked like she hated me that last time we spoke.

"But where would she find another man?"

Judy shrugs. "I don't know. Online? At the mall? Lena's beautiful, you know, and you gave her a lot of money, so she's also rich. A lot of men would do anything to get their hands on that."

I suddenly remember the man who tried to get his hands on her in front of the ice cream parlor. Fuck.

"Who is he?" I demand as I step forward.

Judy hides her hands behind her. "I don't know. She didn't tell me, okay? I never saw him."

"But you're sure she left with him?"

"She said she was going to meet him and they were going to run off together. She borrowed one of our cars."

I narrow my eyes at her. "So you helped her?"

"I'm her friend, okay? You would have done the same for Jerry."

I shake my head. "Not if he was trying to cheat on his wife."

"She begged me," Judy says. "She says she was sick and tired of you. She said you didn't care about her anymore. She said she wanted a simple life. She just wanted someone who could love her and take care of her."

I nod. I see. So she really did give up on me.

But I'll be damned if I let her go with another man. Not while she's still married to me and carrying my child.

"All your cars have a tracking unit, right?" I ask Judy.

She nods. "Yes. Why? You're not going to go after her, are you?"

I walk briskly out of the room.

"Riley, she's already left you. Why try to get her back?"

"Because she's mine," I snap at her from the hall. I head to my room and sit in front of my laptop. "Now, what's the license plate number of that car?"

~

I find the car outside a bed and breakfast in a small town in Arizona. It's four in the morning so everything is quiet. There isn't even anyone at the front desk and I have to ring the bell a few times before a man in his fifties appears, glaring at me and yawning. But after I slap a few bills on the counter and give him a glare of my own, he hands me the keys to Lena's room.

Room 105.

I slip the key into the knob and open the door. I find Lena sleeping on the bed in her pale blue pajamas. She's lying on her side with a pillow under her arm. The blanket covers only her legs.

At the sight of her, a lump forms in my throat. I close the door behind me and approach the bed. She doesn't stir. Her eyelids flutter beneath a thin veil of hair.

My hands clench into fists at my sides. How can she look so innocent when she's cheating on me, the father of her child? How can she be at peace when she's on her way to leave me? How can she leave me when she said she loves me?

I bend over her and brush the wisps of her hair away from her face. The corner of her mouth twitches in a smile and my hand freezes. My chest aches.

I still remember the first time I saw her smile, although it seems so long ago. So much has happened since then. Has she truly forgotten all the moments we shared at that house? Can she run away from all the memories we've made together?

My hand hovers over hers. Maybe I can still convince her to stay. She already tried to run away from me before but I was able to win her back. Maybe if I--

My thoughts come to a stop as I notice that she's not wearing her wedding band. I glance at the bedside table and at the other table in the room but I don't see it.

Has she thrown it away? Has she truly made up her mind to throw our marriage away?

Suddenly, she stirs. She lies on her back and stretches her legs, rubbing her eyelids as she yawns. When she opens them, her blue green eyes stare right at me.

She blinks a few times. Then her eyes grow wide as she sits up.

"Riley? What are you doing here?"

I snort. "You look so shocked to see me. Why? Weren't you expecting me?"

"No." Lena's eyebrows crease. "Aren't you busy?"

"Not too busy to go after my wife."

She frowns. "So when I'm not there, you ignore me, but I leave and you come after me?"

"I wasn't--"

"Weren't you too busy to help me? To even care about the suffering I was going through?"

My jaw clenches. "Is that why you're leaving?"

"Yes," she answers.

Anger simmers in my chest.

"I can only take so much shame and suffering. I need to get away from that house, from you. I need to be with someone who cares about what I'm going through."

So Judy was right. Lena was on her way to someone.

Lena glares at me. "I don't know why you're so angry. You're the one who told me to deal with this myself. You practically sent me away."

I give her a glare of my own. "And you're scurrying off obediently? You're really that eager to get away from me?"

She looks away.

I grab her arm. "What about the baby, hmm?"

"This is what's best for the baby," she answers as she wrenches her arm away.

I glance at her tummy. "I'm not going to let you go anywhere with that baby. It's mine."

"Yours?" She snickers. "You just put it in me. That doesn't make it yours."

My temper fumes. I grasp her chin.

"I told you once and I'll say it again. That baby is mine. You are mine."

I crush her lips beneath mine. She grabs my shirt and pushes me away. Her icy gaze pierces me like daggers.

"We are not your property," Lena scoffs.

"Yes, you are," I say through gritted teeth. "And you're not getting away from me."

She snorts. "What are you going to do, huh? Lock me up again?"

My nostrils flare. "If that's what I have to do to make sure you don't leave me."

Lena shakes her head. "You are a monster. A heartless monster."

Venom drips from her words. Defiance gleams in her eyes. A knot forms in my chest.

So she hates me that much now, huh? She thinks I'm a monster?

I'll show her what a monster is.

I grab her wrists and pin them against the wall above the headboard. My eyes gaze into hers.

"You are my wife. And you're coming back with me."

She struggles to free her wrists but I hold them fast. She glares up at me.

"If I go back there and you lock me up, I'll break."

I narrow my eyes at her. "And I'd rather break you than see you in someone else's arms."

Before she can retaliate, I crush her mouth once more. I push my tongue inside her mouth. She whimpers.

I move her arms so I can hold both her wrists with just one hand. I place the other beneath her jaw and feel her pulse beneath my palm. I undo the first three buttons of her pajama top and slip my hand beneath her bra to find her nipple. She trembles.

I rub her nipple and gently twist it before letting my fingers descend. They skirt over her belly and crawl under two layers of cotton, burrowing between her legs.

At first, Lena refuses to part her trembling thighs. But as I continue to stroke her, those give way. She moans into my mouth. Her hips begin to move against my hand.

I smirk against her lips as I continue moving my slick fingers in and out of her. Then I bring them higher to circle her swollen nub.

She pulls her mouth away and gasps. I lick her warm ear and she trembles even more.

As I continue to tease that nub, I kiss her neck. My lips capture a patch of skin between her neck and shoulder and I suck hard.

She yelps. I trace the mark on her bruised skin with the tip of my tongue.

Now everyone will know she's mine.

I suck on one of her breasts next, dampening its cotton barrier.

Lena moans. The sheets rustle beneath her trembling legs.

She lets out a cry as her hips rise off the bed. Her eyes fall shut as the back of her head hits the wall. I stare at the expression of pure pleasure on her face with derision.

So her heart might have turned to stone against me, but her body is still mine, huh?

I grin. But I'm not yet satisfied.

I let her wrists go and push her down on the bed on her hands and knees. I pull her pants and underwear down until they bunch up behind her knees. Then I take my stiff cock out and ram it inside her with one thrust.

She cries out. I grip her hips and hold them up as I pound into her. The room is filled with the sound of skin slapping against skin, the creaking of the bed springs, her moans and my grunts.

When I feel the heat coiling in my balls, I grab Lena by the elbows and pull her up. I manage a few more thrusts before I bury myself deep inside her and empty my cock with a growl.

Afterwards, when my hips are no longer jerking and my body is no longer shaking, I release her arms. She falls forward on the bed. When I pull out, she collapses on her side. Her chest and shoulders heave as she pants. Her hair falls over her face. As I fix my pants, my gaze goes over her limp body and stop at the trail of white trickling down her thigh.

Just like that, I snap out of the spell I'm under. My rage, which was coiling around me like a thorny vine, vanishes. My eyes, now able to see clearly, grow wide. I sink into the chair next to me as I bury my face in my hands.

What have I done?

I stare at my hands, hands that are supposed to protect Lena and take care of her. Now they may as well be stained with blood. I bite down on my trembling lower lip as I clench them into fists on my lap.

It's all over now.

I stand up and walk towards the door.

"You can do whatever you want," I tell her without looking at her. "I'm not going to stop you anymore. If you let me know your address, I'll send a lawyer with the divorce papers. After all, that's what you've always wanted, right?"

She says nothing.

I turn the knob and walk out the door.

Chapter Thirty
Lena

A knock on the door jolts my thoughts from the past and my gaze from the window.

"Come in," I say.

It opens and Ollie enters holding a tray with a steaming mug and a plateful of pretzels. Judging from the smell, it's hot chocolate. I can catch a whiff of vanilla, too, though, and when she sets the tray down on the bedside table, I understand why. There's ice cream on top of the hot chocolate. Vanilla ice cream. My favorite.

She hands me the mug and I take it in both my hands. "Thanks."

"Feel better now?" she asks.

I nod.

I feel much better now that I'm here with her in Nebraska, here in my sister's cozy guest room. This house is by no means as big or as grand as the mansion, but I can feel the warmth emanating from its walls. I can sense the memories etched into the furniture. Now, this is a haven. A home.

"Good." My sister smiles as she touches my cheek.

I've told her everything, well, except for the sex in that room at the inn. I just said that Riley followed me but we fought and then he left. I don't know. Maybe I still find it hard to talk to Ollie about sex. Or maybe that memory is still too fresh and painful.

And I'm not talking about the physical pain, which I can no longer remember. It's not the fact that he was rough that bothers me. It's the pain that I could feel from him as we had sex. Yes, there was anger, there was lust, but there was also pain.

Riley was hurting. Even as he walked away, I could tell he was hurting.

If only he'd put his arms around me, if only he'd apologized, I would have embraced him and let him cry on my shoulder. I would have tried to take away the hurt.

Instead, he left and said we were through.

I take a spoonful of the ice cream and shove it past my lips before taking a sip of the hot chocolate. The warmth flows down my throat and seeps into my chest.

I lick my lips. "You always were good at making hot chocolate."

"Yeah." My sister nods. "Lizzie keeps telling me so. And by the way, she made this for you."

Ollie hands me a card made of paper with pink and purple hearts and a drawing of a girl that I guess is supposed to be me. In yellow crayon, only one word is scribbled--'Smile'.

And indeed, the corners of my mouth turn up.

"She's so sweet," I say.

"Yeah," Ollie agrees. "They're still sweet at this age. Just wait until they get older, though. They get all feisty and hot-tempered."

"You mean like me?" I ask her.

She ruffles my hair. "You were always a good girl. Maybe just a bit of a crybaby, which I don't think has changed."

I chuckle.

"There." She caresses my cheek. "That's what I'd like to see. The old Lena. The real Lena."

"The Lena who didn't foolishly fall for the first man she got to know," I add.

Ollie grins, but then her expression turns serious. "Do you regret it?"

I shrug as I stir my hot chocolate.

"Sorry." She touches my arm. "I shouldn't have asked that. You should stop thinking about him for now. Just focus on getting better first, on healing. Focus on yourself and then you can decide what you're going to do about him. After all, you can't make important decisions unless you can think clearly."

And I'm aware that I have important decisions to make.

"You mean I'll just think about the divorce papers when they come?" I ask her.

Ollie nods. "When they do, we'll go to my friend who's a lawyer so she can make sure everything's fair and square."

"And that the papers are real," I joke.

"Yeah. That too."

I take another sip of my hot chocolate. "Does Dad know?"

"That you're here? Yes. About the divorce? No. I was thinking we'll just tell him when everything's official."

"So he doesn't even know that Riley and I fought?"

"No," Ollie answers as she strokes my hair. "I'll leave it to you to tell him."

~

But how do I tell my father that I had a fight with my husband?

I mull over the question as I sit on the swing in the garden. It sways slowly while golden sunlight spills down through the gaps in the wooden boards above.

Strange. I've always been able to tell my father everything. Well, maybe not always. When my mom was around, she was my confidante, but after she left, I turned to Dad. I told him everything, even when I had my first period. He was always ready to listen and offer me his advice.

Yet now, I can't seem to find the words to tell him what's going on with me. Maybe because I'm still confused myself. Or maybe because I'm scared of what he'll say.

A tap on my shoulder jolts me out of my thoughts.

I turn my head and see my father standing next to the swing with a smile. I didn't even hear him coming, even though I have perfect hearing.

I pat the space next to me on the swing and he sits. He pats my thigh and begins to sign.

Are you okay, Lena?

I should have known he'd know that I'm not. That's the only time he asks this question.

I draw a deep breath. What if I say no, Dad?

He frowns. Why? What's wrong? Did you and Riley have a fight?

I grin because he's read my mind. I nod.

What about?

I shrug. We're just not getting along. He's too busy to take care of me.

And are you taking care of him?

Like I said, he's busy. I barely see him.

But when he's home, you make time for him?

Come to think of it, I don't.

I'm tired. He's tired.

My father shakes his head. That shouldn't be the case. Even if both of you are tired, one must pretend not to be, or work just a little bit harder so both of you can spend time with each other. Otherwise, the marriage will fall apart.

Yeah. It is already falling apart.

But you can still put it back together.

I look at him. I don't know, Dad. It's not just that. There's also the rumors.

You mean those silly stories?

My eyebrows arch. So my father has seen them, too?

He grasps my chin. Why must you let other people tear you and your husband apart? If you give up, they win.

I sigh. But sometimes, you just have to give up because it's too hard, right?

My father throws me an expression of disappointment as he shakes his head.

It's when things are hardest that you must not give up.

I look away because I'm at a loss for words.

He grabs my hand. You still love him, right?

I shrug. I don't know, Dad.

He points to my hand. But you're still wearing your wedding ring.

I glance at my hand. Sure enough, the golden band is still on my finger. Strange, I didn't even feel it there. I thought I removed it.

Wait. I did remove it at the inn, before my shower, and I must have forgotten that I put it back on because I was tired. But now I remember that I put it back on because I didn't know where to keep it and I didn't want to lose it. Even if Riley and I are over, I still don't want to misplace it.

I guess it's been there all this time.

The golden band glistens under the sunlight. I stroke it.

I didn't realize I was still wearing it.

But that's how it is when you love someone. It just grows on you and becomes a part of you and before you know it, you can't do without it.

He squeezes my hand.

As long as you and Riley love each other, you can make things work.

Maybe. But I'm not sure if he loves me. If he ever did. I'm not even sure if I love him anymore.

Before I can sign anything, though, my father starts again.

You know, I never told you this, but I regret giving up on your mother.

My eyes grow wide. But she gave up on you. She was the one who left.

Yes, but she came back. You and Olivia don't know it, but she did. She asked me for another chance. I didn't give it to her. I just let her go. She hurt me, yes, but I was the one who gave up on her.

My lips curve into a frown. All these years, I never knew my father felt this way.

I regret it, you know, not just because I deprived you and your sister of your mother, but because frankly, it's lonely growing old alone. I miss her more than ever. If I could take back time, I'd undo that mistake. I'd take her back in a heartbeat.

I swallow as I hold back tears.

My father touches my cheek.

People make mistakes Lena, even the ones we love, especially the ones we love. But mistakes can be lessons if we learn from them and they can make us stronger. They can make love stronger. They only remain as mistakes when you give up. Worse, they turn into regrets. But if you keep trying, if you keep loving, if you forgive, everything will work out.

I grab his hand and place it against my cheek. A fresh tear leaks out of the corner of my eye.

"Oh, Daddy..."

I wrap my arms around him and squeeze him tight. As always, he gives such good advice. Already, his words are clearing my mind and filling me with hope, giving me strength. A part of me wants to run back to Riley already and make things right, not just for our baby, but for us both.

But what if it's too late? What if he's already signed the divorce papers?

Chapter Thirty-One
Riley

I tap my fingers on my desk as I stare at the papers in front of me.

Now, this feels like deja vu. It's almost like the last day of Wed For A Week. Back then, though, the papers turned out to be fake. These ones aren't.

If I sign these papers, I'm saying Lena and I are over, and if she signs them, then we really are over.

Our marriage that should have been over long ago will be over for real. The media will have a field day.

"So you're getting a divorce for real, huh?" my father asks as he stands in front of my desk.

I forgot he was in the room.

I sit back in my chair. "I'm considering it."

He sits down. "Isn't that what you were supposed to do in the first place?"

I don't answer, but we both know he's right. And now I'm wondering if that was the mistake.

He taps his fingers on my desk. "You never did say why you didn't want to divorce her."

My eyebrows arch. "I didn't?"

I can't remember.

"No."

Why didn't I want to divorce her?

"I guess I just like her. And I felt she'd make a good wife."

"And you don't anymore?" my father asks.

I narrow my eyes at him suspiciously. We don't usually talk about personal stuff, only business stuff, so right now I can't tell what's going on in that head of his or what he's trying to do.

I just shrug.

He stands up. "Well, if you're getting a divorce, make it quick and quiet and as painless as possible."

"You make it sound like murder."

"And just because this marriage failed doesn't mean you're not getting married again," he goes on. "You had your chance. I'll give you a year and then you'll marry Judy with no more arguments or complaints."

I frown but say nothing.

He walks towards the door. "And no sulking. There's lots of work to be done."

"I understand."

Work. That's all he ever cares about.

He leaves, but the door stays open. A moment later, Jerry steps in. He comes straight to my desk and glances at the papers.

"What's this? You're really getting a divorce?"

I sigh. "My father just asked me the same thing."

"And you answered...?"

I shrug. "I'm still thinking about it."

Jerry leans on my desk. "What's there to think about? You know your marriage was a mistake."

"We have a child," I remind him.

"Who Lena seems to have ran away with. Or so Judy told me."

I say nothing.

"Is it true she left with another man?"

"I don't know," I answer.

And I don't care. It doesn't matter anyway. She left. And after what I did to her, she's not coming back.

Jerry sits in the chair my father vacated and sighs.

"I guess this is for the best."

I give him a puzzled look. "It is?"

"I'm sorry for saying this, but you're not a good match," Jerry says. "Not just because you're a McAllister and she's, well, she was a production assistant you met on a reality show, but because you're a person who cares too little and she's a person who cares too much."

I lean forward. "I care too little?"

"Not just about her. About everything. The only thing you cared a lot about was swimming. But maybe you didn't even really care about that, because you gave it up."

My eyes narrow at him. "You know I didn't give it up."

Jerry ignores me. "And then your job here at your father's company. I can see you're just doing it for the sake of, well, doing it."

"Aren't you the same?"

He chuckles. "At least I make suggestions every now and then. I try to change things up a bit and think of ways to make things easy and fun for everyone. Do you?"

I guess not.

"And let's face it, you've never cared for any of the women you've been with. And yes, we're the same in that, but I didn't marry any of those women. You did."

"I cared about Lena," I argue.

Even though she didn't think so.

"You cared about her just enough to not want someone else take her away from you," Jerry says. "But that's all, and that's not enough."

I frown.

He faces me. "If you really care about Lena, let her go and let her have some peace. Let her find happiness."

I stare at the papers on my desk. Isn't that what I said I'd do? Didn't I say I'd set her free?

I glance at Jerry. "You do realize that if this divorce goes through, I might end up married to Judy. Are you saying you want her to marry a man who doesn't care about her?"

Jerry shrugs. "She doesn't care about other people either. I'm sure the two of you will get along. And I don't care as long as she has what she wants."

I look at the papers again.

Jerry taps them. "Set her free, Riley. She's already left you."

Still, I stare.

"You know what? I'll even give her the papers myself," Jerry offers.

"You will?"

"It'll help things come to a smooth end between the two of you," he adds. "You both deserve that."

For a moment more, I stare at the papers. Then I take a deep breath and pick up my pen.

Jerry's right. This is what's best for Lena. This is what she needs, what she deserves.

I'm not going to tie her down and make her suffer any longer.

I sign my name.

"Atta boy." Jerry gathers the papers. "Now I'll go talk to the company lawyer and make sure these get to Lena."

"Thanks," I mutter.

"No problem. And hey..." He pats my shoulder. "You did the right thing."

Did I?

As I watch Jerry leave with the papers, I wonder if I did. If I did, why do I feel the same as I did on the show--like I just made a big mistake?

I sit back with a sigh.

Well, it's too late. I've signed the papers, and once Lena does, she won't be mine any longer.

It will all be over.

"Um, Mr. McAllister?" I hear Margot's voice from the other end of the door.

"Yes?"

She opens the door and peeks in. "I know you don't want to entertain calls from the media, but this one is from Danny Thurman."

I sit up. "What does Danny want?"

"Well, he was wondering if someone from the network could ask you and Lena a few questions as some kind of follow-up for the show."

"I see."

Margot shrugs. "I can tell him you said no if you like."

And she probably should. But then I remember what Lena said about me not speaking up, about me not doing something about all the rumors. This is my chance to say what's right, to clear her name. And yes, maybe it's too late, but this is my send-off gift. Maybe this way, she'll know that I did care.

"Tell him to send a reporter and maybe a cameraman," I tell Margot. "I've got some things I need to say."

Chapter Thirty-Two
Lena

"There's nothing more left to say but good night." I plant a kiss on Lizzie's forehead after pulling the covers up to her chin.

"Good night, Aunt Lena."

I leave her bed and walk towards the door.

"How long are you staying here at our house?" Lizzie asks suddenly.

I shrug.

Even after my conversation with my father, I still have a lot to think about, which is why I'm still here. I'm still waiting for clarity and maybe for a sign about what I should do next. Frankly, I don't know when I'll get it.

"Good night," I say again as I blow her another kiss. "Sweet dreams."

She yawns before turning on her side and closing her eyes.

I turn off the light, leave the room and head downstairs. I'm only halfway down, though, when I hear Ollie shouting.

"Lena!" She stands at the bottom of the stairs. "Come quick!"

I give her a puzzled look. "What?"

"Just come!"

She climbs up the steps, pulls my arms and drags me all the way to the living room. She points to the TV screen, which currently has Riley's face on it.

So Riley's on TV, huh? But what's new? Even before, he was already on TV a lot. And now that he's a businessman, it's not surprising that he makes TV appearances.

But then I hear him talking and it's not about swimming or business. It's about me.

"Lena is a good woman, maybe the best I've known," Riley says. "She didn't trick me into marrying her and she's not after my money or fame. And yes, she's carrying my child, so I suggest you all leave her alone. In fact, if I hear you say one more lie about her or bother her anymore, I'll have to make you pay for it one way or another. And trust me, the price won't be cheap."

I cover my mouth as I let out a gasp.

He finally decided to speak up and tell the media to leave me alone. He even threatened them.

He does care about me! He still does.

More than his words, though, what fills me with hope is the sight of the golden band still on his finger, which makes me remember the things my father said.

Maybe, just maybe, we can still work this out.

I run to the guest room.

"Lena?" Ollie follows me. "Where are you going?"

"I'm going to pack my things," I tell her. "And I'm going home to my husband."

~

When I arrive, Riley has just finished his late night swim. He's in his bedroom, still in his robe and his swim trunks. When he sees me, his eyes grow wide in disbelief.

"Lena? Why are you here?"

"I saw that interview you gave on TV," I tell him as I take off my scarf. "The one where you told everyone they were wrong about me."

He looks away. "Oh."

"And you know what? At the airport, someone recognized me and simply congratulated me for my pregnancy," I add. "She said she never believed those lies."

"That's good."

But he doesn't seem to be smiling.

"Anyway, I just had to come back after seeing that. I just had to let you know your message reached me."

He finally turns to me, but with furrowed eyebrows. "My message?"

"That you care about me and that you are willing to do your part to make this marriage work."

"Oh." Riley looks away again.

Why? Why doesn't he seem happy to see me?

"I've already signed the divorce papers, though. Jeremiah will--"

"It doesn't matter," I cut him off. "I didn't sign them before and I won't now."

His eyebrows arch. "You won't?"

"No." I shake my head. "Because I have a message for you, too."

I take a step closer to him.

"I love you, Riley." I lift the hand that's still wearing my wedding ring. "I always have and always will. And yes, I'm not that strong a person. Or that smart. And maybe I'm not the woman you're supposed to be with, not the woman who will make the best wife for you. But I'm not going anywhere."

I stand right in front of him and touch his cheek. "I'm never giving up on you."

Once again, his eyes grow wide. I stand on the tips of my toes to brush my lips against his parted ones. But he doesn't kiss me back. Instead, his fingers wrap around my wrist.

"But I thought you were already in love with someone else."

I shake my head again. "You're the first man I fell in love with, Riley Boyle McAllister. How could I love someone else when you already have my heart?"

Riley drops my hand. "But I can't promise you the rumors will end. There might be new ones. Other people may try to tear us apart."

"Who cares? As long as you and our child are by my side, the rest of the world can go to hell."

"I'm still going to be busy."

"I'm going to make sure we have time for each other," I promise him.

"I can't guarantee things will get easier."

"No one ever said they were going to be easy."

I don't know why he's arguing with me so much, but I'm not going to let him win.

His gaze sinks to the floor. "I might... end up hurting you again. Somehow, I can't keep calm around you. You drive me mad in many ways. What if I break you?"

I lift his chin and look into his eyes. "You can't break me, Riley. And if you do, you'll just have to put me back together again."

I place my hand against his cheek as I press my lips against his. For a moment, they remain still. Then they press back against mine as his hands grip my waist and pull me close.

My heart leaps. I've won. I've won him over.

One of Riley's hands goes to the back of my head as he deepens the kiss. His fingers tug at my hair as his tongue entwines with mine. I slip my hands beneath his robe and run my fingers over the firm muscles of his chest. My thumb brushes over his nipple.

Heat courses through my veins like a rushing river. Desire flutters restlessly in my chest and my heart begins to pound. My breasts swell. When he squeezes one of them through my clothes, I gasp into his mouth. Then I step back.

I wriggle out of my plaid jumper dress and it pools at my feet. I kick it aside along with my canvas shoes. Then I pull my pink turtleneck shirt over my head. I undo my ponytail as well and my hair tumbles past my shoulders.

Riley steps forward and touches the skin between my neck and shoulder.

"It's healed?"

I nod. "All wounds heal, Riley, if we give them time."

He looks at me tenderly as he cradles my jaw. The warmth in his eyes makes my stomach flip and sends my skin into a fever. Then he crushes my mouth beneath his--a passionate kiss that steals my breath just like the one last time. Except this time, I can tell he's not hurting. This time, it's just hunger.

And he's not the only one who's hungry.

I tug at the sash of his robe and push it off him. My hands cup his firm buttocks through the cold, slippery fabric of his swim trunks before moving to the front. The bulge in his crotch throbs against my palm.

I begin stroking him through the trunks. His palms slip beneath my bra and rub against my aching nipples. I shiver.

He plays with my nipples. I stroke his clothed cock and feel it swell against my hand. When his fingers slip past the garter of my underwear and brush against my curls, I give another shiver. I peel his trunks and wrap my fingers around his cock.

It's wet and warm just like I am. I run my thumb over the leaking tip and he makes a sound low in his throat. His thumb finds my clit and my knees quiver. I break the kiss to gasp for air.

Riley continues to stroke me and I do the same to him while gripping his arm with my other hand so I won't fall. I don't trust myself to keep standing as pleasure spreads throughout my body from his skilled fingertips. In fact, I can feel myself melting into his touch. Moans spill from my lips.

Then he stops. He takes off my bra and leads me to the bed. I take off my soaked panties and throw them aside before lying down. He takes off his swim trunks before climbing on top of me.

Again, his mouth captures mine and steals my breath, but only for a moment. Then his lips move to suck on my neck, to reverently kiss that spot that he bruised before, to suck on one of my breasts and then plant a kiss on the valley in between them. From there, his lips start a trail down to my belly button, where he plants a longer, more reverent kiss. It sends a flurry of joy into my chest.

When Riley lifts his head to meet my gaze, that joy almost bursts. His eyes are brimming with his sincere apology, with his thanks that I came back, with a plea for me to stay by his side.

I lift my hand to touch his cheek. "I love you."

And the words he whispers back after kissing my palm send my heart into a frenzy.

"I love you, Lena."

We kiss again, more tenderly this time. Then he grips my thighs. Before he can part them, though, I turn around so that I'm on my hands and knees.

"Are you sure?" Riley asks.

I hear the concern in his voice.

I nod. "I think this is better for the baby."

Besides, last time, even though he was rough, I have to admit that I still felt pleasure from this position. And I want to feel it again.

Come to think of it, this was how he took me the first time in that pool.

His hands find my hips once more. His cock enters me slowly, too slowly, and I push back. He chuckles.

"Impatient?"

"I just missed you," I say as I glance over his shoulder.

He swells inside me and I let out a moan as the rest of him enters me. Then I gasp at this wonderful sensation of being filled.

Riley is the only one who can fill me, who can complete me in this way.

He begins moving slowly and my body rocks. My knees dig into the mattress. My hands clutch the sheets. My hair falls like a veil over my cheeks. My breasts sway beneath me.

He grabs them as he keeps moving. I throw my head back and moan. Then he reaches between my legs and strokes my nub. My arms give way and my elbows hit the bed. My head crashes between them and I muffle my moans against the sheets.

It's too much. The combination of his skillful fingers teasing me and his cock plunging in and out of me at the same time is too much. My head begins to spin.

I'm on the brink of falling over when Riley suddenly withdraws both. He quickly turns me around and grips my thighs once more before pushing his cock back inside me with one thrust. Then he begins to ram into me.

I place my hands over my head and clutch the sheets as I thrash in maddening pleasure. I throw my head back and let out a cry as I fall off the peak.

I can't tell if my body is still rocking from his thrusts or my head is just spinning, but the next thing I know, I feel a gush of warmth. I open my eyes and see him above me. I reach up to pull his face to mine and kiss him as I give him a squeeze.

He pulls out and lies down beside me. Then he wraps his arms around me.

"I love you," he repeats hoarsely.

"I love you," I say back to him.

Riley pulls away and strokes my cheek. "So you didn't sign the papers, huh?"

"I didn't even get them yet," I answer.

He nods. "Right. I only signed them earlier today."

His eyes narrow at me.

"So you saw me on TV and you rushed back here?"

"Yup. I flew. It still seems safe for now."

He touches my belly as he looks at it. I place my hand over his.

"How could I not after seeing how handsome you were on TV?"

Riley chuckles.

"Or hearing you defending me, protecting me." I take his hand and entwine my fingers with his. "Or seeing that you were still wearing our wedding ring, just like I was."

He gives me a puzzled look. "But you didn't have it at the inn."

"I take it off when I take a shower, and you know, what with this pregnancy brain, I tend to forget things sometimes."

"I see."

"But maybe I won't ever take it off again. That way, I'll never forget about it or lose it. I'll wear this until I die."

Riley plants a kiss on my forehead. "Don't you go dying on me, though."

I nod. "So what made you decide to finally appear on TV?"

"I thought I'd clear your name so you could live a peaceful life after we get divorced."

"Oh."

"And also, Dan just happened to call."

My eyebrows arch. "Danny Thurman?"

Riley nods. "Actually, the network wanted an interview with both of us, something like a follow-up to that show we did. But I said I'd just seize the opportunity to say some things that needed saying. He didn't mind."

"So we're not going to get that interview anymore?" I ask him. "Because you know, I don't think I'd mind. And I want the world to see that we're happy together. But only if you like, of course."

Riley smiles as he strokes my cheek. "Why not?"

Chapter Thirty-Three
Riley

"One last question," Seth Sinclair says as he crosses his legs in his chair, which is right across from the loveseat Lena and I are in. "What is the most important thing you've learned about each other or about your relationship so far that you think will allow you both to stay together for a long time to come?"

I glance at Lena.

She squeezes my hand. "Well, for me, Riley taught me not to give up. So I won't give up on what we have. I won't give up on him. I'll keep fighting for him and with him, and we'll go through the sweetness of triumph and the bitterness of defeat together. As long as we keep moving forward, everything will work out."

She looks into my eyes and smiles. Warmth swells in my chest as I smile back.

"Wow," Seth says. "Talk about confidence. I love it. And what about you, Riley?"

"I think I just have to let Lena in, open up to her more, and at the same time, give her all I can. Having competed in swimming for so long, I was racing alone. I didn't count on anyone but myself. But now, I'm not alone. And this isn't a race. This is a journey that I'll savor with Lena."

I press her hand to my lips. The audience in the studio breaks into applause.

Seth claps as well. "Well said. And I do think the two of you will have an amazing journey, especially with your little one coming along. I'm sure all of us are rooting for you and hoping everything works out."

"Thanks, Seth," Lena says.

Seth comes over and offers her his hand. "Again, congratulations and good luck."

He shakes her hand then mine. Then he turns to the crowd.

"Ladies and gentlemen, Riley and Lena McAllister."

The audience cheers once more. Lena and I stand up. Like a beauty queen, she blows kisses and waves to the crowd until the camera stops rolling. When it does, Seth shakes our hands again.

"Thank you for coming," he says.

"Thank you for having us," Lena answers.

I lead her off the stage. A woman greets her with open arms.

"Lena!" she shouts excitedly.

"Paula!" Lena gives her a hug.

After she pulls away, she makes the introductions.

"Paula, this is Riley, though I'm sure you know that. Riley, this is Paula. She and I used to work together."

I offer her my hand. "Pleasure to meet you."

She shakes her head as she trembles in excitement. "The pleasure is all mine."

She turns back to Lena. "Ms. Deedee sends her regards. She was distraught when she found out about the mix-up and all, but now she's so happy for you. She always was one of your biggest fans."

Lena nods. "Send her my regards as well."

Other people come to greet us and talk to us. Then Lena and I walk out of the studio. I place my arm around her.

"That went well, huh?"

"I think so," Lena says. "I didn't feel that nervous this time."

I kiss the top of her head. "You did great."

She lets out a sigh. "I can't believe things are finally going well for us."

"Hey." I touch her nose. "Don't jinx it."

"Sorry. I'm just so happy."

"I'm glad," I tell her. "And yeah, I don't think anyone will give us problems anymore."

~

I take that back the moment Mickey greets us in the great room. She immediately goes for Lena and takes her hands.

"I saw your interview and you were amazing," she says.

Oh, now she thinks Lena is amazing.

"Thank you," Lena says.

Mickey glances at me. "You, too."

I don't answer.

Mickey loops her arm around Lena's as she ushers her away. "Anyway, I think we should start making plans for the baby shower. I already have some ideas. Oh, and I think we should start construction on the nursery, too."

My eyebrows crease. Don't tell me she's finally accepted Lena. Somehow, I doubt it.

"Thank you, Mickey," I hear Lena answer. "But no."

I pause. Did I hear that right?

Mickey gasps in horror. "What do you mean no?"

"No," Lena repeats. "Listen, Mickey, I respect you because you're my stepmother-in-law, and I won't try to keep you out of my life or my child's, but from now on, if there are any parties for me or for my child, I'll be the one throwing them. Also, I'll make all the decisions regarding my child, whether it be about the nursery or the first birthday or where my child goes to school."

Mickey steps back. "You're kidding, right?"

Lena shakes her head. "You run this household, but Riley and I have our own family now and we'll be the ones calling the shots about that." She glances at me. "Isn't that right, sweetheart?"

I nod. "Pretty much."

Mickey frowns. "So you're keeping me out after all."

"No, you're free to join in," Lena tells her. "But I'll be taking the lead."

Mickey still looks horrified.

Lena ignores her and stretches her arm towards me. I take it and accompany her up the stairs, leaving Mickey behind.

"Wow," I say to her. "You really stood up to her this time."

"I should have done it a long time ago."

"So you're not trying to get along with Mickey anymore? Because that sounded like a declaration of war."

"Not at all. Like I said, I want everyone to get along, but I'm not going to sacrifice my happiness or our child's for it."

I look at her. "You've changed."

Lena shrugs. "I guess I've grown stronger."

I beam with pride as I touch her cheek. "Well, you know I'll always stand by you."

"I know."

When we get to our bedroom, the one we now share, I capture her mouth in a kiss. She places her hands behind my neck and kisses me back. I'm about to lead her to the bed, but suddenly she bolts. She heads to the bathroom and after a few moments I hear her throwing up.

I frown. Not again.

Chapter Thirty-Four
Lena

"I'm fine, Riley," I assure him over the phone as I shove another spoonful of vanilla ice cream inside my mouth. "The doctor says this is perfectly normal."

Of course it sucks that I'm having morning sickness again, but at least I know it's nothing serious and that it will pass.

"If you say so," he says.

"The doctor said so," I repeat. "Now, go back to work before your dad gets mad."

"Yes, ma'am."

"I love you."

"I love you, too."

I hang up with a smile, put the phone down on the pillow beside me, and continue eating my ice cream. My gaze darts to the TV screen across from me. My Fair Lady is still on pause.

Lately, this has been my routine--staying in bed watching movies and eating nearly all day, whether I'm feeling fine or not. I just... feel lazy. And maybe after all the hell I've been through, I'm just treating myself to some much-needed and much-deserved relaxation.

I know, though, that I can't stay in bed forever. The doctor didn't even prescribe bed rest for me. And I don't want to become bigger than an elephant. Maybe if I'm feeling well tomorrow, I'll leave the house.

I'm still a celebrity so I might still have to wear a disguise, but at least people are back to saying nice things about me. It really is such a relief. I know I said I wouldn't mind what other people think or say about me, but that is so much easier to do when they're saying good things, telling true stories instead of vicious lies.

Besides, I need to do some shopping, even though I don't know whether I'm having a boy or a girl yet. Frankly, I don't care which as long as the baby is healthy and happy. That's why I can't begin planning for the baby shower. But there are still things I can buy for the nursery.

And I know exactly where to buy them.

~

"Thank you." I give the cashier a smile as I slip my credit card back into my wallet.

"Thank you and have a good day," she says.

I follow Sam, the maid who's accompanying me, out of the chic baby store. It's maybe the most expensive and the most stylish in Beverly Hills, the place where Hollywood stars pick up stuff for their bundles of joy. Nearly a dozen paper bags swing from Sam's arms.

I stop just before the door, though, when something else catches my eye--checkered bandana baby bibs that I didn't see the first time I made my rounds. I think I need one of those. Plus they look so sophisticated I simply have to take a look.

"Go ahead, Sam," I tell the maid. "You can put those in the car and wait for me."

"Yes, ma'am."

She leaves the store.

I take a closer look at the bibs and decide to get at least five of them. They're unisex anyway. I pay for them in cash and walk out of the store with another paper bag.

Outside, I stop to put my change in my wallet and check my phone. But then something else catches my attention--a woman in her mid-50s walking towards me.

She's wearing a glamorous pair of sunglasses along with an oversized floral shirt and Capri pants, and yet something about her strikes me as familiar. An actress? No. Her sunglasses may look expensive, but the rest of her clothes aren't. Plus no actress would wear a wristband that says 'I Love Hollywood' or toenails with polka dots and--

That train of thought screeches to a halt as I realize why the woman looks familiar. My heart stops as I remember where I've seen that wristband and those toenails. And those rosebud earrings.

I lift my own sunglasses to the top of my head and stare at the woman in front of me with narrowed eyes.

"Mom?"

~

"So you're saying you just happened to be walking around the area, hoping to catch a glimpse of a Hollywood celebrity?" I ask my mother as I sit across from her at the Victorian-styled cafe just a few feet away from the baby store.

She nods as she takes a sip of her blueberry frappe. "Exactly."

I shake my head in disbelief as I tap my fingers on the table.

Unbelievable. I never thought I'd see my mother again. Yet here she is sitting right in front of me drinking a frappe like it's the most natural thing in the world.

Now that her sunglasses are out of the way, I can see her face more clearly. There are wrinkles around her eyes now and I can see strands of silver mixed in with the browns on top of her head, but it's her, alright. Even after all these years, I can still remember her gray eyes twinkling as she laughed with me on the couch while we watched comedy movies. I can still remember those rosebud earrings that she said she'd give me one day but never did.

And I don't know what to say. Over the years, there have been many times when I imagined meeting her again. A few scenarios popped into my head with their own scripts. Was there one where we met at a cafe? I don't know. At any rate, I've forgotten the lines.

I lift my own frappe--honeydew and kiwi--from the table and bring the straw between my lips.

What do you say to the person who left you when she was the one person you thought would never leave?

A part of me is still disappointed in her, but strangely, I don't feel any anger or resentment. Maybe it's because it's been too long. Maybe it's because of what my dad told me. Or maybe it's because now that I'm a wife and soon to be a mother, I feel like I can sympathize with her more. Whatever the reason, I'm just surprised to see her. And maybe relieved that she seems fine. Maybe glad even.

"How have you been?" I ask her.

"Good," she answers as she puts down her glass. Then she sighs. "You know what? You're a big girl now, so I'm not going to lie to you. I told myself I'm not going to do that anymore. I'm not good. I haven't been for a while."

I take another sip of my frappe then put down my glass as well. "What do you mean? Are you sick?"

She chuckles and shakes her head. "No. I'm fine. I've never been sickly."

Come to think of it, I don't remember her ever being sick.

"What I mean is that ever since I left you, you and your father and your sister, I haven't been the same. I don't think I've ever been happy."

I purse my lips.

"Do you know why I left?" she asks me.

"Dad said you went with another man," I answer. "Well, he didn't say it right away, but he told me eventually."

She nods. "I left because your father was always busy with his work and I was getting tired just being at home and looking after you and your sister. Don't get me wrong. I love you both to bits. But I felt like I had lost myself, you know. I felt like a mother was all I had become, and I was starting to wonder if that was all I was going to be. I missed the fun and the dreams I used to have. I wanted to go on an adventure."

She puts her hand over mine. "You may not understand now, but you will one day."

I think I already do, but I say nothing.

"Then I met this man and he just made me feel like I was Francesca in Bridges of Madison County, you know, and I thought, well, Francesca never got her happy ending. But maybe I can. Maybe it's not too late for me."

I nod because I remember the movie. It was one of my favorites, too, and one of those sappy movies that I watched after Riley left me.

"That's what I thought," my mother continues. "But I was wrong. He wasn't my soul mate. I already had my soul mate. And why should I crave for an adventure when I was already embarking on the greatest journey with my children? When I realized my mistake, I spoke to your father and asked him for another chance."

"I know."

Her eyebrows arch. "You know?"

"Dad told me."

"Oh." She puts her hand over her chest as she sits back. "Then you know he refused?"

I nod.

"I made another mistake then. I didn't fight harder to take back the things I had. I just left because I didn't want to hurt your father any more than I had. I told myself I'd made a stupid mistake and now I'd have to pay for it for the rest of my life. I resigned myself to a life alone, thinking I'd be just fine." She shakes her head. "But I haven't been fine again. Yes, I've survived. I've gone here and there. And maybe I even did have a small adventure elsewhere. But I've always been lost."

I can see the sadness in her eyes that are glistening with tears. I can hear the misery in her voice even though she's trying to keep it from trembling.

She has paid the price for her mistake.

"You could have come and talked to me," I tell her. "When you left, I was the most devastated. And you know, I couldn't bring myself to resent you even though Ollie did."

She grabs a tissue and sniffs. "I knew Ollie would. She was always smart. She probably understood that I made a mistake and I made it willingly. Besides, she was always close to your father so I knew she'd resent me for hurting him."

"I hate that you hurt Dad, too," I say. "But I couldn't hate you. Yes, you left and I didn't understand why, but more than that, I remember the times when you were there, the happy times we shared."

She reaches across the table to stroke my cheek. "I remember them, too, sweetheart. And I wanted to go to you, even get you. But your father told me to stay away, and I thought that was best. Later on, when I wanted to see you again, I didn't know where you were anymore. But I've been searching all this time."

I look at her with wide eyes. "So our meeting isn't an accident?"

She shakes her head. "No. Ever since I found out you were married to Riley McAllister and someone told me where he lived, I've been hanging around here, hoping to catch a glimpse of you. I can't just walk up to your door, after all. I thought you'd come to that store to buy your baby supplies." She glances at the baby store that I was just in. "And I've been here every day."

My eyes grow even wider. "Wow. Every day?"

My mother nods. "That's how badly I wanted to see you."

"Oh, Mom." I squeeze her hand as I feel tears threatening to well up inside me.

What if I hadn't come to the store today? Or at all? Then I never would have seen her.

"Oh, don't cry," she tells me as she puts on a smile. "You're pregnant, remember? You're not supposed to be crying so much, even though you feel like it all the time."

I chuckle.

"That's better." She pats my cheek just like she used to do.

I grab her hand and flatten her palm against my face. "I miss you, Mom."

"I miss you, too, darling."

I squeeze her hand. "Daddy misses you, too, you know."

Her eyebrows arch. "He does?"

I nod. "And I'm sure Ollie does, too, even though she always acts so tough and all."

My mother chuckles.

"You know, I think it's because of her that I didn't end up resenting you. I mean, she was always there, so I never got to wish that you were."

My mother smiles. "I guess I owe Ollie a lot. How is she?"

"She's a mother now, too, and she's doing great. Dad's fine, too. He can't hear that well anymore because he had a diving accident, so he uses sign language..."

My mother gives me a look of horror. "He can't?"

"But he's fine otherwise, just a bit lonely. Like I said, he misses you, too."

My mother sighs. "It is hard growing old alone."

I lean forward. "You know, I can take you to them if you like."

"Really?" Joy flickers in her eyes, but then she shakes her head. "Maybe not now. I'm not ready. Somehow, I knew I could face you and talk to you, but I don't know if I can face them yet. Well, I thought I could, but now that it's possible, I... I guess I'm just a bit scared."

Of course she would be.

"I understand," I tell her.

Now what?

Suddenly, an idea comes to me.

"Mom, why don't you stay with me in the meantime?"

Her eyebrows rise. "With you?"

"Yes. When I give birth, I'll make sure to call Dad and Ollie. You can see them again then. And you'll have had plenty of time to prepare by then. We can celebrate the moment together, and who knows, we might just come together as a family again."

She smiles. "That sounds wonderful."

"In the meantime, you can stay with me," I add. "You know pregnancy inside and out because you were pregnant with me once. I need your advice and your help. Can you give me that?"

She brushes strands of hair from my cheek. "How can I refuse? I haven't been there for you for so long."

"You can be here for me when I need you the most."

My mother strokes my cheek tenderly. Her smile widens even though she looks like she's about to cry. "Then I will be."

"So your mom is staying here?" I ask Lena as I get into bed.

She moves closer to me and snuggles against my shoulder. "Yes. You don't mind, do you?"

"Of course not." I put my arm around her. "She's your mother."

Lena sighs. "I still can't believe I bumped into her just like that. I never thought I'd see her again."

I rub her shoulder. "Yeah. Fate has a weird way of making people meet, right?"

"In our case, it wasn't fate, though. She was just waiting for me, just waiting in one place hoping I'd show up. I don't think I could have done that."

"Where was she before that?"

"I don't know. She said she's been here and there, just trying to get by. She left her home, so she wasn't hoping to find or make a new one. She just went wherever the wind took her."

"Sounds like a carefree life."

Lena shakes her head. "You mean a lonely life. You know, I've always thought dandelions were pretty drifting in the wind. Now, I think maybe they're sad because they've left the only place they've ever known and who knows if they'll find a new one or even survive until they get there?"

I lean back so my head sinks further into the pillow. "I'm pretty sure dandelions don't have feelings."

She rests her head on the crook of my shoulder and places a hand on my chest. "But my mom does. All this time, she's been living in regret. And the strange thing is, so has my Dad."

"Then why don't they both just be together?"

"My mom says she'll wait a bit more, you know, prepare herself."

My eyebrows furrow. "For what? I thought your dad isn't mad at her anymore."

"But my mother still feels guilty. Maybe she needs to forgive herself first."

I nod. "You have a point."

"Anyway, I'm grateful that my mom agreed to stay here. I think she showed up at just the perfect time. It helps to have someone who went through exactly what I'm going through."

"Yeah. Mickey can't help you with that even if she wants to. I think that's why she's trying to 'help' in other ways."

Lena turns to me. "I've been wondering about that. So she really never had children."

"She wanted to. She and my father tried. But she just couldn't have any."

"I see." She nods. "Maybe that's why she's bitter."

I shrug then pat her hand. "Anyway, I'm glad your mother's around. Now, you have someone to count on when I'm not around."

"Yeah."

"Especially since I'm not going to be around for the next two days," I add.

Her eyebrows furrow. "Where are you going?"

"My first business trip," I answer. "It's just in Vancouver, though."

Lena sighs. "Here come the business trips."

"Hey." I squeeze her shoulder. "You know I won't cheat on you while I'm away, right? And I promise I'll always come home to you."

Her lips curve into a smile. "Then I promise I'll always be here waiting."

~

"I believe your dad's waiting downstairs," Jerry says as he enters the room.

I shut down my laptop.

"I know. I'll be just a minute."

He approaches my desk. "Sure you've got everything packed? It is your first business trip."

"But hardly my first trip," I remind him. "I'm used to going all over the world."

"Yeah. And I guess business trips are pretty much the same as swimming competitions. You know, you have to put yourself out there, try to leave a mark. And sometimes you even get to hit the pool."

I put my laptop in its case. "It's not what I'm bringing or what I'll be doing there that I'm worried about. It's about what I'm leaving behind."

"You mean who you're leaving behind." Jerry sits down. "And to think you and Lena were this close to getting a divorce. You even signed the papers."

"I know."

"And yet, now you're inseparable. Well, not inseparable, because you're clearly going on a business trip and she's staying here, but the two of you are damned close. You remind me of those high school couples I'm so sick of, you know, the ones who I yell at to get a room."

I zip my case. "Lena and I are not like that."

"Fine. Fine." He taps his fingers on my desk. "You're just like newlyweds."

"Technically, we are newlyweds," I point out.

Although it seems like forever since we've been married.

"Did you ever even go on your honeymoon? Or does being on the show count as your honeymoon?"

"No." I grab a few more things from my desk drawer. "But Lena and I will surely go somewhere before the baby is born."

He nods. "Yeah, because once the baby's born, you know, Lena won't have any more time for you."

"I doubt it," I tell him. "And don't sound like you know all about it. You don't have kids."

"You don't have to remind me. I'm well aware of how quiet it is when I wake up in the morning. Oh, unless the woman I slept with lives next door to a pet shop."

I close my drawer and grab my laptop case. "I'm going. Can you promise me you'll help Lena out while I'm gone? You know, if there's an emergency or if she needs anything. She has a checkup scheduled for tomorrow morning."

"Yeah. Sure."

"Her mother's with her right now, so--"

"Really?"

"--she's in good hands. But you know, just help her out if she asks."

Jerry gives me a thumbs-up sign. "Don't worry. Just focus on your trip and your business. I'll hold the fort for you and everything will be just fine."

Chapter Thirty-Six
Lena

"Everything looks fine," Dr. Stanley informs me as she leaves my side. "You're having a perfectly normal pregnancy."

I smile as I wipe the gel off my stomach with the tissue paper the nurse hands me and then pull down my shirt. My mother helps me get off the examination table.

"Hear that, Mom?" I ask her.

"Well, I already knew you were doing fine," she says.

"It must be nice to have your mother with you," Dr. Stanley tells me. "Next to me, she's probably the person you can ask the most questions."

"It is nice," I agree as I sit on one of the chairs in front of her desk.

"And I feel like I'm pregnant all over again," my mother adds.

Dr. Stanley grins. "Well, I sure hope both of you will have an amazing journey. I'll do my best to ensure it's smooth sailing, but Lena, you have to take care of yourself."

I nod. "I know."

"Take your vitamins. Watch what you eat. You don't want to gain too much weight."

I've already gained more than I should.

"Get plenty of rest, but also, get some exercise."

I nod. "I will, Doctor."

Just then, another nurse peers in. "Dr. Stanley, we need you in Room 3."

"I'll be right there." Dr. Stanley stands up. "Sorry. Duty calls."

"I understand."

She leaves in a rush, probably to assist some woman who's about to give birth. After paying and discussing my next appointment with the receptionist, my mother and I leave as well.

"Well, you heard the doctor," my mother says once we're outside the clinic. "You should get some exercise."

"Yup." I nod with a smile. "And I know exactly how to get it."

~

"Are you sure you can wear all those clothes in the next seven months?" my mother asks as she glances at the shopping bags that are occupying the whole table next to us at the restaurant.

I shrug. "I just couldn't choose which one I liked, so I got them all."

"Must be nice being a billionaire's wife," she mutters.

"Shh." I hold a finger to my lips.

She leans forward. "Shouldn't you have a bodyguard or something?"

"Well, Neil knows how to shoot, I think."

My mother's eyebrows arch, but she says nothing. Just then, our orders arrive--roasted prawns for me and a vegetable quiche for my mom.

"Hmm."

I close my eyes as I suck the aroma of the food into my nostrils. My mouth waters.

"That smells wonderful."

These days, I divide food smells into just two categories--those that make me puke and those that make me want to eat for a whole day.

"Well, seafood is good for you," my mother says. "But you shouldn't eat too much food in general. Remember what the doctor said."

"I know."

It's just that when I get hungry, I get really hungry.

I grab my table napkin and put it on my lap. My mother stands up.

"I'll just go to the restroom."

"Okay." I nod. "Mind if I eat ahead?"

She gives a wave. "Dig in."

As she leaves, I start eating. I tell myself I'll just eat one and then wait for my mom to come back. But then I end up eating two and then three.

I glance in the direction of the restroom as I wipe my lips. What is taking Mom so long?

When three more minutes pass and she still doesn't come back, I leave the table to go check on her.

I knock on the bathroom door. "Mom?"

When no one answers, I grip the knob. Strange. It's open.

Even stranger, though, is that the bathroom's empty.

I look around and see a door leading to the kitchen. Did she go there? But why would she?

Suddenly, my phone rings. An unknown number flashes on the screen.

Maybe it's my mom?

I answer the call and press the phone against my ear. "Mom?"

"I have your mom," says the voice at the other end of the line. It sounds like a man's voice, though I can't be sure since the person seems to be using some kind of voice modifier.

I clasp my hand over my mouth as I let out a gasp but force myself to calm down. "Where is she?"

"Oh, don't worry. You can get her back if you do as I say."

I glance around, then step inside the bathroom. I lock the door.

"What do you want?"

"A quarter of a million dollars," the caller answers.

Two hundred fifty thousand. Okay, I believe there's that much in Riley's safe at home. Of course, Riley will be pissed when he finds out it's missing, but... well, I won't think about that right now.

"I'll give you the money," I say as I grip the phone with a trembling hand. "Just don't hurt my mom."

"I won't," he promises.

But I can't trust him.

"Where do we meet?"

"I'll send you the address. Be there at seven."

"Okay."

"And don't bring anyone. Not the cops. Not anyone. Or your mother will die."

I nod. "I understand."

"And don't tell your husband."

My eyebrows arch. Don't tell my husband? Not bring him? That means this caller knows Riley isn't here. Who is he?

"I'll be waiting," he says before the line dies.

I sit on the toilet because my knees feel weak. I bury my face in my hands. I can't really describe what I'm feeling right now. I'm just overwhelmed with fear and worry and frustration.

But I can't let my emotions take control of me. And I can't cry.

I stand up and square my shoulders like a soldier preparing for battle.

I have to do what I have to do.

~

While I'm packing the money--two hundred fifty thousand dollars is a lot more money than I thought--into a backpack, Judy walks into the bedroom.

"Shit," the curse leaves my lips as I try to hide the money to no avail.

I've been caught red-handed.

What is Judy doing here? And why the hell didn't I lock the door?

She clasps her hand over her mouth as she gives me a look of horror.

"Are you doing what I think you're doing?"

"What do you think I'm doing?" I ask her.

She closes the door behind her and locks it, then approaches the bed.

"Are you stealing? Are you going to gamble that away?"

"No," I tell her as I put another wad of bills inside the backpack.

Well, yes, I'm stealing--well, borrowing--but I'm not gambling.

"You know, if you're going to an auction, you don't have to bring cash."

"I'm not buying something at an auction," I sigh.

Seriously, I can't deal with this right now. If only I could just make her leave...

"Wait." Judy sits on the edge of the bed. "Is this ransom money? Has someone been kidnapped?"

Finally, she understands.

"Yes," I answer.

I realize that maybe I should have lied, but then again, I've never been a good liar. Besides, the caller didn't say I can't tell anyone, just that I can't tell Riley.

"Who?" Judy asks eagerly.

"My mother."

Judy gives another gasp. "I didn't even know you had a mother."

I narrow my eyes at her.

"I mean that your mother was around," she corrects herself.

"Well, she was," I tell her as I throw in another wad of cash. "But now, she isn't."

Judy touches her chin. "Shouldn't we call the cops?"

I open my mouth but she comes up with the answer before me.

"Oh, right. You can't call the cops. He'll kill your mother."

My eyebrows arch. He?

"What makes you think it's a he?" I ask her curiously.

Judy shrugs. "Aren't kidnappers usually men?"

I, too, shrug. Are they?

I continue packing the money because it doesn't matter.

"Don't worry," she tells me. "I won't tell Riley. I promise."

Now where did I hear that before?

"I feel really bad that I told him where you went last time, you know," Judy continues.

So she was the one who told Riley?

"But Riley hit me, so I had no choice," she adds.

"It's okay," I say as I grab another wad.

She gets another and tosses it into my backpack. "So you're meeting with the kidnapper and then you'll give him the money in exchange for your mother?"

"I guess that's usually how kidnap-for-ransom situations go."

She gives another shrug. "It seems simple enough."

I try not to throw an annoyed glance in her direction. She can say that because she's not involved, because it's not someone she cares about who's been abducted.

"Good thing you have the two hundred fifty grand," Judy adds.

I pause. I never said the ransom was two hundred and fifty grand, did I?

I slowly lift my head to meet her gaze. "How do you know? That the kidnapper asked for two hundred fifty grand?"

"Oh." She gives me a look of surprise, then grins. "Well, you said it just a while ago, Lena."

I'm pretty sure I didn't. I may have pregnancy brain and forget a lot of things, but I know I didn't tell her the amount.

"Besides..." Judy picks up another wad of bills and runs them through her fingertips. "I know what two hundred fifty grand looks like. I've got a lot of cash, too, you know."

I know. Still, I doubt she'd know how much money I had just from looking at it. Even a bank teller needs a machine for that. And Judy can't even see all of it because some of it's already in my backpack.

She's lying. I know it. Then how does she know how much the ransom is? She wouldn't know unless-

-

"So when are you meeting?" Judy asks me.

"Tonight," I answer as I step away from the bed. "Excuse me. I just need to go to the bathroom."

"Sure."

I go to the bathroom and lock myself in. I lean against the wall and draw a deep breath to calm myself down. I can't keep my thoughts from swimming restlessly in my head, though, not now that my mind's been rattled.

Okay, let's think. Judy knew the kidnapper was a he. That could have been a guess, but since she knows exactly how much the ransom is, I'm guessing she also knows who the kidnapper is. She might even have hired the kidnapper. She certainly has the capacity, though I didn't think she'd have the brains.

But why would she do it? Isn't she my friend?

The more I think about it, though, the more I think not. Actually, she's only been around at the most opportune times. It's almost like she plans when to appear. Just like now.

What if she's been planning something all along? What if she's just pretending to be my friend? Come to think of it, I don't know her well. I just became friends with her because, well, there wasn't anyone else. That's why I trusted her so easily.

But should I have?

Right now, my instincts are screaming that Judy can't be trusted. What's more, they're telling me that this kidnap-for-ransom thing isn't going to go smoothly. They don't always, after all. If Judy is behind it, she doesn't need money, which would explain why the caller asked for a relatively small amount--and which means she's after something else.

I don't know what, but my gut is telling me there's danger ahead and the voice in my head is shouting for me to be ready.

But what should I do? Should I call the cops after all? No. The kidnapper has my mom. Should I call Riley, then? No. That's too risky as well. The best I can do is try to leave him a clue so just in case he comes back and I'm not here, he'll know I'm in trouble and he'll help me. Or at least, if something bad happens to me, the cops will know where to start looking for answers.

But how?

Judy knocks on the door. "Lena, are you okay?"

"Yeah, I'm fine," I tell her as I look around.

I can't leave a note out in the open because Judy might see it, and if I'm right and she's involved, then she'll just get rid of it. But if it's hidden, how will Riley find it?

Suddenly, my eyes fall on the soap dish and I remember something.

Last week, I bought a soap that I didn't like, a purple one. I didn't throw it away, but I told Riley I didn't like it.

I search the bathroom drawers for it now, and when I find it, I etch a message into one side using my nail file. Then I replace the white soap on the dish with the purple bar, making sure the side I wrote on is facing the dish so no one else will see it except Riley. Hopefully, when he sees the soap, he'll think it's odd that it's there and lift it and then he'll read my message.

It's still risky, I know, but it's worth a try.

"Lena?" Judy knocks on the door again. "Are you okay?"

I open the door and step out.

"Yup. I was just trying to trim my nose hairs because my nose is itchy."

Judy grimaces. "Ew."

"Did you pack the rest?" I ask her as I go back to the bed.

"No."

The rest of the bills are still on the sheets.

"You need a bigger bag," she says.

I draw a deep breath and nod.

Relax, Lena. Don't let her know you suspect her of anything.

"You're right," I tell her with a smile. "Will you help me find one?"

"Sure," she says.

I watch her as she heads to the closet.

I'm still hoping I'm wrong about Judy, but if not, I swear she's going to pay for all this. But first, I have to get my mom back.

~

I show up at the specified address before seven. A man wearing a mask asks if I have the money. Then he makes me go inside a car and blindfolds me. After a while, I'm pulled out of the car and led somewhere. I can't tell where.

Then the floor starts to rock beneath me.

Am I on a boat? The salty scent in the air and the roar of an engine confirms it.

I almost throw up because of all the rocking but manage not to. Finally, the boat stops. When my blindfold is removed, I find myself staring into darkness, but as my eyes adjust, I see the trees around me. I hear the rolling of the ocean waves.

Am I on an island?

Then I see the glow of a flashlight. It comes closer and I see my mother, who tries to speak through her gag. Her hands seem to be tied behind her. I'm about to run to her when the light shines on the person standing next to her. My jaw drops as my eyes grow wide.

"Jerry?"

So it wasn't Judy's plot after all. She's just an accomplice. Her brother, Jeremiah, is the mastermind. No wonder it felt like Judy knew him. And it makes more sense.

On second thought, it doesn't make any sense at all.

"Why are you doing this?" I ask Jerry. "Is this some game? Some joke?"

"I'm afraid not," he answers. "You see, I've been trying to get you out of the picture for a while. You never were supposed to be in it, after all."

My eyebrows furrow. "What do you mean?"

"You should never have met Riley, and you should have stayed away from him. You see, Riley is supposed to marry Judy. And when you're gone, he will. And then my sister will finally be happy."

My eyebrows arch. So he's doing this for his sister? And she's in love with Riley?

Well, she did say she was a childhood friend. And if she's in love with Riley, that explains why she said she'd help me escape when we first met, and why she encouraged me to leave and maybe even mentioned to Riley that I was meeting another man.

She was never my friend. She was always my rival.

Wait. Did Jerry say "when I'm gone"?

"So it's not money you need," I tell him. "It's me."

"Well, you can never have enough money," Jerry says. "And I need Riley's safe empty."

So he knew there was that much in Riley's safe? Of course he did. They're best friends. At least, they're supposed to be.

"But yes, it's you who's the problem," he adds.

I swallow the lump in my throat as I lift my chin. "So you're going to kill me?"

My mother shakes her head and protests through her gag. Her eyes are wide with fear.

"No," Jerry answers.

I feel a tinge of relief.

"I'm just going to leave you here to die."

That relief vanishes in an instant.

"You're going to leave me here on this island?"

"Yes," he says.

"And you think no one will rescue us?"

"This island belongs to the Lawrences. No one comes here and no boats pass by here."

Shit.

"And you're sure Riley won't find out? Are you sure you'll get away with this?"

Jerry grins. "I know I will, because I have this."

He takes out an envelope from the bag hanging from his shoulder and gets some papers out of it. My eyes grow wide as I recognize them.

Divorce papers. With Riley's signature.

They're the ones he was supposed to send me.

Jerry holds the sheets in front of me. "Now, sign or your mother dies."

He shows the gun tucked into his belt.

"You can either be stranded here with your mother or stranded here without her, but either way, you won't escape."

And if I sign, Riley will think I left him, especially since I took the money from his safe. He'll believe whatever story Jerry and Judy tell him. He's known them a long time, after all. He trusts them.

And he won't come after me.

My heart sinks at the realization, taking half the blood in my face with it. My knees fall onto the sand.

"Well, what will your choice be, Lena?" Jerry asks me as he holds the pen in front of my face.

I have no choice. Like he said, I'm doomed either way.

But I can't just let him kill my mother. At least, if I sign, there'll be two of us on this island. And we can die peacefully together.

I take the pen with a trembling hand and sign.

Chapter Thirty-Seven
Riley

Lena wants a divorce? This is the news that greets me when I come home early from my business trip?

I came straight home, too, hoping to see Lena sooner and feel the warmth of her body against mine, only to find the house empty. Not only is she gone, but her suitcase is missing, along with some of the things she bought for the baby that are supposed to be in the nursery. Her mother, too.

I called her phone but couldn't reach her, so I called Jerry, hoping he might know. I did tell him to watch over Lena. And that's when I learned the news.

Lena wants a divorce.

No. That's not right. Lena and I are divorced.

That is what the papers in front of me right now are telling me. After all, they still have my signature from two weeks ago, and now they have Lena's too. Jerry brought them over along with Lena's ring.

I stare at the golden band as it glistens on top of my desk.

Why would she want a divorce? Why now?

"I'm afraid she didn't say why, but I think her mother helped her decide," Jerry tells me.

Her mother? Didn't Lena say she regretted leaving her husband? Why would she make Lena commit the same mistake?

"Also, I think you should know that she got money from safe," Jerry adds. "About a quarter of a million dollars, I believe."

I check the safe behind me, and sure enough, most of the cash is missing. My jaw clenches.

"It doesn't make sense." I bang the door of the safe. "If Lena wants money, she knows she can have all of mine as long as she's married to me."

Jerry shrugs. "Who knows what she'll do with the money?"

I whirl around and grab the front of his shirt. "Why did you let her sign these papers? You had them the whole time, didn't you? Why did you even have them?"

"Because you gave them to me." He pushes my hand away and smooths the front of his shirt. "I never got around to disposing of them."

I narrow my eyes at him. "And you just gave them to her when she asked?"

"You said to help her if she asked. She asked. I helped her."

My fist leaves my side and flies towards Jerry's jaw. He stops it in midair.

"Calm down, Riley. I'm not the bad guy here. I'm just the messenger."

For a moment, I keep pushing my fist against his palm. My shoulders tremble in anger. My teeth grind together. Then I pull away. My gaze drops to the floor.

"What exactly did Lena ask for?" I ask softly.

"She said she wanted a divorce. She asked me if I still had the papers. She begged me to let her have them, to let her sign them. So I did. You know how weak I am against women who beg, right?"

Like hell I'll believe all that bullshit.

And yet, what can I do? The papers are here and they're signed. And Lena's gone.

For good.

I leave the office and go to the bedroom I share--shared--with Lena. As I lie on the bed, I can still smell her scent on the sheets.

How could she just leave? And without telling me why? Without saying goodbye?

The door opens. I hear footsteps approaching, and moments later, Judy's face hovers over mine.

"Oh, Riley, I'm so sorry about--"

I push her away with one arm and sit up. "Go away, Judy. I'm not in the mood to deal with you right now."

"I know you're hurting." She clings to my arm. "But I'm not going anywhere. Unlike Lena, I'll never leave your side."

I ignore her and go to the bathroom.

"Riley!"

I shut the door behind me and go to the sink. I rest my hands on the marble counter.

Even her toothbrush is gone and her bag of toiletries. Even her--

My thoughts stop as I see the soap on the dish.

Wasn't that one supposed to be white? Isn't this the soap Lena didn't like? Why is it here then?

I pick it up. My eyebrows furrow as I feel some dents beneath my fingers. I turn the soap over and my eyes grow wide as I read the words etched into the bar.

They have Mom. Must go. Love u.

I read the message again, this time with creased eyebrows as the wheels in my head turn.

What does she mean 'They have Mom'? Does this mean her mother was abducted? Is that why she needs the money? That doesn't explain the signed divorce papers, though.

Plus she said she loves me. So why would she ask for a divorce?

It doesn't make sense. Nor does the fact that this message was etched in soap. Why? Why not just leave a regular note?

I try to put myself in her shoes. I would leave a note unless I was worried that someone would steal that note.

She was trying to hide this message from someone, someone who was here in this very house. But who?

The door opens and Judy enters.

"Riley, come on. We're friends, aren't we?" She stands beside me and puts one arm around my waist. "You know you can count on me for anything. Anything at all."

I frown. I'm about to pull away from her again, but my gaze falls on her reflection and I notice the pair of earrings she's wearing--dangling golden teardrop earrings.

I grip Judy's shoulders. "Aren't those Lena's earrings?"

The way her eyes widen tells me they are.

"No," she says as she steps back.

"Don't lie," I warn her through gritted teeth.

"Fine," Judy says as she touches one of them. "They're hers, but I asked for them since they're pretty and she doesn't wear them."

"She wore them once."

Again, Judy's eyes grow wide. Right. She doesn't know because she wasn't at that party.

I grab her arm. "Why do you have them?"

"She gave them to me as a souvenir right before she left," Judy says.

Ah. So Judy was here. And yet Lena didn't trust Judy with the note. She didn't tell Judy about the abduction, even though she confided in Judy before about leaving.

I thought they were friends, and yet, all of a sudden, she decided not to trust Judy. In fact, she seemed to be hiding the facts from Judy, which tells me that Judy knows something about all this.

I grab Judy by the collar of her shirt and pin her against the wall.

"Where's Lena?"

Chapter Thirty-Eight
Lena

I wrap my arms around me as a harsh breeze blows from the sea. I can hear it howling past my ear as it threatens to blow my scarf away. Above me, I can see the clouds gathering, turning dark. I see a bolt of lightning in the distance.

A storm is brewing.

Shit.

I glance back at the temporary shelter my mom and I made out of sticks. We were able to make a fire, too, so we weren't too cold last night. Somehow, we survived. But this storm could easily blow our shack away, and all our firewood, maybe even the few trees growing on the island. Worse, the water could sweep it all away and my mom and me with it.

I stare at the shoreline, now closer than before. Already, the tide is rising.

Mom and I survived for one night. But are we going to die today?

My mother squeezes my shoulders.

"Don't worry, sweetheart. I'm sure help will come soon."

I'm not. Why should Riley come and save me when I'm no longer his wife? Unless he saw the note. But he's probably still in Vancouver. That means we have to survive for at least one more day.

My mother's chin rests on my shoulder. "I'm sorry."

"What for?"

"If not for me, you wouldn't be here. I'm the one who got myself abducted."

"You just went to the restroom," I remind her.

"But if I never came to live with you, then maybe--"

"Jerry would have abducted Ollie or Lizzie or Devon. Or Daddy. He just picked you because you were close."

"In that case, I'm glad he picked me. I deserve to suffer more than any of them."

I turn to her. "Mom, you've suffered enough. You don't deserve this. And it's not your fault. It's mine. Marrying Riley turned out to be a mistake after all."

She touches my cheek. "Oh, darling. This is not your fault. All that you did was love, and that is never a bad thing."

"Then how come we're here, being punished for it?"

I glance at my belly.

"Worse, my innocent child is being punished for it."

"Hush." She holds my face in both her hands. "Don't say that. Don't give up now."

I glance at the sky. "But the storm..."

"Storms are created and vanish in an instant," my mother says. "This may yet disappear."

"And if it doesn't?"

"Then we'll get ready. You know, when I said I had a bit of an adventure, I meant that I lived for some time in the Amazon, helping some researchers."

My eyebrows arch. "Really?"

She nods. "I picked up a few survival skills."

So that's why she was able to make that shack and the fire so easily last night.

My lips curve into a smile. "I'm glad you're here, Mom."

She smiles back then grabs my hand. "Come on. Let's get ready."

~

We manage to make a stronger shelter, but it's no use once the storm hits. The wind blows and the water rises. Our shack gets blown down and swept away.

"Mom!" I cling to my mother as the wind threatens to blow us away like a pair of leaves.

She hugs me tight as the water pools around our ankles. "Don't worry. I'll never let you go."

I bury my head in her shoulder as I shiver against the cold. My chest tightens with fear.

Is this the end?

Suddenly, I see a branch flying towards us from the corner of my eye. My mother and I duck in time but the branch gets caught on my scarf and yanks it off. As I grip it to keep it from flying, the wind wrenches me from my mother's arms.

"Lena!"

The wind carries me away and my vision blurs. My head spins and I feel like throwing up. Then suddenly, I'm falling. My feet hit water and then it swallows me.

I flail around and kick but then remember what Riley taught me. I try to calm myself down and swim. I manage to get to the surface, but a big wave washes over me and knocks me under again. After the third time it happens, my arms and legs are too tired. They're numb and feel like they'll fall off.

I don't want to give up, but I can't move anymore. I feel myself slowly sinking and I clutch my belly. I'm sorry, my child. I'm sorry I couldn't be a mother to you.

Then I close my eyes as I surrender to the water, to the cold. My chest and my head hurt and my breath is leaving me, but I struggle to find some measure of peace. I picture Riley's face in my head and smile.

Goodbye, Riley.

My thoughts begin to blur. My whole body aches.

Is this how it feels to die?

The last thing I know is the sound of someone calling my name before I give in to the nothingness.

Chapter Thirty-Nine
Riley

"Lena!"

I shout her name once more above the tossing waves. Then I draw a deep breath and plunge into the water.

That's when I see her. Falling like a rock to the bottom.

No.

I swim to her as fast as I can. I grip her waist and wrap her cold arm above my shoulder. As I swim back to the surface, I keep praying.

Please, if there's a God out there, don't take my wife and child away from me.

It seems an eternity before I reach the surface, an eternity wherein I try not to think of the worst. Through the raging waves, I try to look for the boat.

"Riley!" Someone waves from it.

I swim towards it. The current pushes me back and Lena's weight drags me down. Raindrops splatter on my face like bullets. But there's no way I'm going to lose against the water.

Summoning every ounce of strength I have in my muscles, I swim against the current, against the waves. My legs propel me forward.

Come on. Come on. Faster.

This is more important than any race I've ever been in. This is a race to save my family.

I swim even faster, pushing myself to the limit. My lungs hurt from gasping for air. My legs begin to ache and feel like they're falling apart. I ignore all that and keep swimming.

Eventually, I reach the boat. Someone pulls me and Lena aboard.

"Lena!" her mother shouts.

My body aches all over. Still, I pull myself up and crawl towards her, holding her hand as the paramedic with me gives her CPR.

"Lena, please!" her mother wails.

I squeeze Lena's hand and speak against her ear. "Don't you dare give up on me, Lena."

When she still hasn't responded after a few seconds, though, I feel myself starting to give up. Then, just when I think all hope is lost, she gasps. She lifts her head to throw up the water she swallowed, then coughs.

I let out a sigh of relief as I hold her in my arms. Thank God.

"Everything's alright now, Lena," I promise her as I rub her back and arms to keep her warm. "Everything's alright."

~

"Your wife is going to be alright," Dr. Madison assures me as she steps into the waiting room.

I let go of the breath I've been holding as I stand up and run a hand through my hair in relief.

"And the baby?" I ask hopefully.

"The tests don't show any abnormalities or adverse effects," Dr. Madison says. "Heartbeat is good, too."

I put my hand over my chest as I exhale. "Thank goodness."

"They're both fine because they were rescued just in time," the doctor adds. "A moment longer and they might not have made it."

I nod. I know. That's why I was putting everything I had on the line to beat the clock. And I did. Again.

And this time, the exhilaration I feel is even greater than all those times I won a race, because this time the reward isn't a medal. It's the lives of my wife and child.

I give the doctor a smile. "Thank you, Doctor."

"I wasn't the one who saved her," she says.

She glances at her chart. "Also, Janet Hunt is doing fine. She's your mother-in-law, right?"

I nod.

"She seems to have sprained her ankle, but otherwise she's okay. We're just running a few more tests to make sure."

"I understand."

Dr. Madison walks off.

"Can I see Lena now?" I call after her.

She turns. "Yes. Yes, of course."

~

The hospital room is a lot quieter than the hallway outside. The only sound is from the machines attached to Lena. She's sleeping on the bed, her hair fanned around her head. Her breath fogs the mask on her face.

I plant a kiss on her forehead but she doesn't stir.

That's fine. She must be exhausted after all she's just been through.

I glance at her belly and then at the machine. I can see the lines going up and down. Just as Dr. Madison said, the baby seems to be doing fine.

They're both fighters. Survivors.

"How are they?" My father's voice jolts me out of my thoughts.

I glance over my shoulder to see him standing behind me with a bouquet of flowers.

"They'll be fine," I answer. "Are you supposed to be here? I thought you were still in Vancouver."

"There was no point in me staying after you'd left." He approaches the bed and stands beside me. "Then of course I heard about what happened."

"From who?" I ask him curiously.

"Conrad Lawrence."

Jerry and Judy's father.

I draw a deep breath. "What did he say exactly?"

"That you punched Jerry."

"That I did," I admit.

"That you've had them thrown in jail."

"That I did, too. For kidnapping."

"Conrad was begging me to ask you to withdraw the charges," my father says. "He wants you to drop the case."

I touch my chin. "And what did you say?"

"That I won't forgive anyone who tries to harm a McAllister."

I turn to him with wide eyes. That wasn't the answer I was expecting.

"I know I haven't been a father to you," he says. "But you are my son, and Lena and your unborn baby are family."

I sigh. "We're already divorced, though."

"So?" My father shrugs. "Just marry her again."

My eyebrows arch. Really?

He places a hand on my shoulder. "Frankly, I never wanted you to marry Judy. She was the worst choice. I was hoping that if I told you that you had to marry her, it would motivate you to find someone better. And you have. Someone far better."

My eyebrows furrow. "You're messing with me, right?"

"No." My father shakes his head. "You know, I never told you, but your mother didn't want to marry me."

"What?"

"She was supposed to marry someone else, but I fell in love with her, so I spoke to her father and made a deal with him. And so our marriage was arranged. She hated me at first, but, ah, she learned to love me. And we were happy."

"I don't understand," I tell him. "I appreciate that you've told me this, but what does your marriage to my mother have to do with my marriage to Lena?"

"I wanted you to find your own bride and win her over," my father says.

137

"By saying I should marry someone else?"

"Like I said, I knew you didn't want to marry Judy. So I knew you'd find someone else."

I shake my head as I slip my hands into my pockets. "You are so weird."

"Even when you were thinking of divorcing Lena, I was trying to discourage you by dangling the prospect of marrying Judy."

My gaze narrows. That's what he was doing?

"If you didn't want me to divorce Lena, you should have just said so. Then I wouldn't have signed those stupid papers."

"Ah, but where's the fun in that?"

"Fun?"

"The most valuable lessons in life are the ones you learn on your own. Not the ones someone else teaches you."

I shrug. "Is there also a lesson I'm supposed to learn from being forced to help you run the company?"

"Yes," my father answers. "Hard work. Well, hard work on behalf of others. I know you worked hard at swimming, but that was for yourself. And I wanted you to learn the basics of running a company so that you could start your own if you wanted."

Unbelievable.

"Also, I thought it would be good if you tried some other things besides swimming. I didn't want your life to pass you by."

"So you forced me to settle down?"

"I forced you to start living," he says.

"I was living."

"Maybe." He shrugs. "But you were missing out on a lot, too."

I sigh. "Fine. You did everything that was best for me. You're a great father."

"It was your mother who made me promise, you know. As she was dying, she didn't ask me to take care of you. She asked me to help you make the most out of life, to realize the most important thing in life. And it seems you finally have."

"Okay." I take a moment to digest everything he just told me. "I have just one question."

"What?"

"Why did you marry Mickey?"

"That's a secret," he answers.

I frown.

He pats my shoulder. "Don't let Lena go. Don't let anyone take her away from you."

I nod. "Don't worry, Dad. I won't."

~

As soon as Lena wakes up, I sit on her bed and take her hand in mine. She lifts her other hand to touch my cheek.

"Riley," she whispers my name. "I thought I'd never see you again."

I frown. "I thought so, too."

I kiss her hand.

"I thought I'd lost you."

"But you didn't," Lena tells me. "You found my message, didn't you?"

"The one on the soap?"

"I think I might just like that purple soap after all."

I chuckle.

"And you saved me," she says. "You came after me like I knew you would. I didn't give up hoping, you know, and you didn't give up on me."

I squeeze her hand. "Didn't we promise we wouldn't give up on each other no matter what?"

She smiles, but then her features twist in concern.

"How's the baby?"

"The baby's good."

"And my mother?"

"She's fine, too. Everything's fine."

Lena nods and smiles again. "It's all thanks to you."

She squeezes my hand back and our fingers entwine. That's when I remember she's not wearing her wedding ring.

We're no longer wed. But like my father said, it doesn't matter.

"I did lose you, though," I tell Lena.

Her eyebrows furrow. "What do you mean?"

"The divorce," I say.

"Oh."

"We're not married anymore."

"Right."

"If you don't want to marry me again, I'd understand," I tell her. "You've been through a lot since you married me. But if you don't mind, I still want you as my wife. In fact, you're all I want as my wife."

Lena's blue eyes narrow. "Are you proposing, Riley Boyle McAllister?"

"I don't have an engagement ring, but..." I go down on one knee by the bed. "Lena Hunt, I don't believe I asked you this before..."

"You didn't."

"Will you marry me? For real and for good?"

Her eyes dance as she chuckles. Then she nods.

"Yes, I will."

Chapter Forty
Lena

Three months later...

"I now pronounce you husband and wife," the pastor says. "You may now kiss the bride."

The crowd behind me erupts into applause and then cheers louder as Riley's lips press against mine. Afterwards, he plants a kiss on my forehead before putting his arm around my shoulder. I rest my head against his and smile at our well-wishers.

I can see tears in the eyes of my mother, father and Ollie, all sitting in the front row. After what happened to my mom and me, my mom found the strength to face my dad. She didn't want to have any more regrets. And now they've reunited and are both living with Riley and me.

Mickey seems to be crying, too, though I don't know if it's for real. Beside her, Harold is beaming with pride. When our eyes meet, he gives me a nod. I nod in turn.

I see other familiar faces--Ms. Deedee, Paula, Maggie, Danny, Ashley and Eric, Candace and Sean. I was the one who sent the invitations this time, so these are people I know, people who I know are genuinely happy for me.

Although none of them are as completely happy as I am.

I place one hand on my belly, now very obviously home to a baby boy, and my other hand in Riley's. These are my treasures, the most important people in my life. They are what make this day truly special.

With them, I can say I'm the luckiest bride in the world.

~

"So do you like this wedding better than our last one?" Riley asks me when we're all alone in our bedroom.

"Definitely," I answer as I take off my earrings. "After all, this time, I'm surrounded by family and friends."

"You look as radiant today as you did during our first wedding, though," Riley says.

I snort. "Yeah right."

I glance down at my stomach, which is already the size of a beach ball.

One thing I can say, though--I love the gown I'm wearing now as much as I loved the first. It's a white ball gown with puffed sleeves made of lace embroidered with white flowers and a high waist marked with a sash of crystals. All the layers of chiffon make me feel like I'm floating on a cloud.

Now if only I can take it off.

I walk over to my husband. "Riley, darling, do you think you can help me?"

"Sure, wife."

He pops the buttons at the back of my gown and pulls the zipper down past my waist. He doesn't let me go afterward, though. Instead, he slips his arms into my gown. His hands cup my breasts, which are bare since the bodice has a bra built into it.

They've grown bigger and more sensitive lately, so when his fingers rub my nipples, I let out a moan. Heat swirls in my breasts and travels down between my legs.

"One thing I didn't like about our first wedding," Riley says against my neck, "is that we didn't get our wedding night."

I nod. "Yeah, I remember."

"That's not happening this time."

He turns me around and kisses me. His hand caresses my neck as he slips his tongue inside my mouth.

I place my hands against his bare chest, his buttons already done, and move them down so I can trace the quivering muscles of his abdomen. I'd like to go beyond that, too, but I can't because my stomach's in the way. I frown.

Riley chuckles.

"Do you want me that much?" he asks.

"Yes," I answer without hesitating.

He lies down on the bed and crooks a finger at me. "Come here."

I step out of my gown so that I'm in just my panties and climb onto the bed on fours. I straddle his waist and pull his face to mine for a kiss. Then I move lower and shift my legs between his, positioning my head just above his crotch.

He's already taken off his belt, so I just unbutton and unzip his pants. He lifts his hips so I can pull his boxers down. His hard cock springs free.

It never fails to fascinate me.

I take a good look at it before licking the tip. I gather the bittersweet salty substance leaking there with the tip of my tongue. Riley lets out a hiss and his thighs tremble.

I lick the rest of his cock and slowly take it inside my mouth. I fit as much of it as I can while keeping my teeth from grazing the sensitive skin. Then I start moving my head up and down.

Riley lets out a sound between a growl and a moan. His fingers tug at my hair.

I curl my lips, close my eyes and move faster. I'd like to keep at it, but giving a blow job when you're five months pregnant isn't easy, so I decide to stop and let another part of me eat him up.

I take my panties off and position my hips on top of Riley's cock. I lower them slowly so his cock enters me inch by inch. As it does, I take deep breaths. When he's completely inside me, I gasp.

He really is huge.

I take a moment to catch my breath, then I grip his shoulders, lean forward and start moving my hips. I moan as his cock rubs against a sweet spot inside me.

Riley does nothing. He just watches me intently with his arms at his sides. Yet that in itself is sexy.

As I lean back to try a different angle, I feel his gaze on my breasts, which are bouncing as I move. I can feel my stomach wobbling as well, but I ignore it. I throw my head back and close my eyes as I savor the pleasure coursing through my veins. Moans and gasps escape from my lips.

I'm close. I can feel it.

I jerk my hips even faster, as fast as I comfortably can. I can feel the strands of my hair escaping their pins and cascading down my neck one wisp at a time.

Then I try something I've never done before. I cup my breasts and play with my nipples. I hear Riley grunt. He still stays still, though. Watching. Waiting.

But my body can't wait any longer. It gives in to the pleasure, trembling as it squeezes Riley's cock. He gives a groan. A cry escapes from my throat.

When it's over, I climb off Riley and lie down beside him. I have no strength left. Riley shifts to his side, kisses my cheek and gives me a mischievous grin.

"My turn."

He turns me on my side so that my back is pressed to his chest. I can feel his wet cock poking my lower back.

It enters me slowly as his hands grip my swollen breasts. I've barely caught my breath when it flees again.

He grasps my chin and turns my face towards his so we can kiss. Then he reaches between my legs and strokes my clit as he starts jerking his hips.

I clutch the pillow beneath my head, my other hand gripping his as he rocks my body with his thrusts. The bed creaks.

Even though I just came, the flames under my skin keep burning. His fingers keep strumming my clit. His cock moves in and out of me, rubbing against spots that make me see stars.

I squeeze my eyes shut and let out a cry as I come undone once more. Riley manages a few more thrusts into my trembling body and then gives a particularly hard one. I feel his warmth burst inside me.

He pulls out and I hear him panting just like me.

I stay still for a few more moments because I simply can't move. Then I turn towards him. He faces me and kisses my forehead.

"Are you alright?" he asks.

Lately, he asks that after each time we have sex.

"I'm fine," I answer.

Riley smiles.

I touch his cheek. "Thank you."

"For what?"

"For everything," I say.

His eyebrows crease. "I haven't even given you my wedding present yet."

My eyes grow wide. "I have a wedding present? Aside from you?"

Riley nods and touches my nose. "You know my father has allowed me to acquire new businesses?"

"Yes."

"Well, I recently bought a company."

"What kind?"

"A movie production company," he answers.

I place my hand over my mouth as I gasp. "No way."

"Yes way." He strokes my cheek. "And you'll be one of the producers."

"Really?" I can feel my face lighting up.

"You'll have to wait until the baby's out before you start working, though, and even then--"

"I can still read scripts here at home," I say. "Or come up with ideas for movies."

Riley chuckles. "You really can't wait, can you?"

I shake my head then kiss him on the lips. "Thank you. This is really the best gift ever. It's my dream come true."

He frowns. "I thought I was your dream come true."

"Well, you and this company and this baby." I place a hand on my belly.

Suddenly, I feel something push against my palm. I gasp.

"Did you feel that?" I ask Riley. "He's kicking again."

Riley puts his hand on my tummy. A moment later, there's another kick. Riley smiles.

"Maybe our baby is celebrating, too."

I shrug. "Maybe. Or maybe he's swimming. You know, I have a feeling that our baby is going to be a really good swimmer."

"Like his father?" Riley asks.

"Exactly," I answer as I rub my tummy tenderly. "And I'm going to let him swim to his heart's content. And of course I'm going to be there cheering for him at every race."

"I thought you were going to make movies."

"I can do both," I say. "But I'm going to make sure he'll experience other things, too, like love."

"Are you going to find him a girl to marry?" Riley asks me.

"No." I shake my head. "I'll leave that to him. I'll just give him advice every now and then. And when he does find a girl he really loves, I'll help her out."

"You sound like you have everything planned out."

I shrug. "Well, you know, plans can go awry. I mean, look at what happened to us. But in the end, as long as you don't give up, everything works out."

"Yes." He takes my hand in his. "Look at what happened to us."

What started out as a mistake has become an amazing journey. And we've only just begun.

~*The End*~

HIS SURPRISE PACKAGE

Prologue
Aaron

"Marjorie?"

I call my sister's name a second time. When she still doesn't answer and I hear no rustle of fluffy slippers scurrying to the door, I slip my key into the knob and step inside the apartment.

Sweaters on the couch. Magazines on the coffee table. No sign of Marjorie.

Is she out?

The lights are on, though, and the whiff of Indian spices from the orange boxes in the kitchen tells me she didn't forget it's our evening of the month. The fact that they're still sitting on the counter and not in the trashcan means she's still waiting for me. So where is she?

"Marjorie, I'm sorry I'm late," I say as I walk to her bedroom. "Are you mad?"

No sign of her here, either. I do see her glasses on the bedside table, though. There are only two reasons why she'd take them off. Either she's asleep—which she isn't—or she's in the tub.

I lean outside the bathroom door.

"Marjorie?"

Still no answer. I press my ear against the door. The silence from beyond it sends bubbles of worry to the surface of my thoughts.

I knock. "Marj?"

I grip the knob and turn it. It doesn't budge. A knot forms in my throat as worry becomes fear.

"Marj!"

The knob rattles in my hand. My shoulder clashes with the wood.

Fuck. Right now, this door feels like a mountain standing in my way. Well, I won't let it.

I take a step back and raise my leg. I put all my strength into my heel as I drive it into the door just next to the knob. Its defeat resounds through the apartment in a crash.

I step inside but stop two feet away from the tub. It's filled almost to the brim, the water topped with white froth that smells like vanilla and coconut. And on one end, just beneath the faucet, ten toes stick out, each nail painted bubblegum pink.

My lungs deflate. For a moment, I can't move. Then I rush towards the tub. My knees crash against the tiles, the cold seeping through the flannel. Bubbles fly into the air as my arms plunge into the water, my hands frantically searching for something to hold on to.

When my fingers bite into a pair of slender shoulders, I lift my arms. Marjorie's body emerges from the water. Soap clings to her ebony hair that falls over her glassy eyes—empty, dull jade orbs. Her lips are bluish, her skin cold and numb. As I press her icy cheek to mine and place my hand against her neck, I feel no pulse.

My own heart stops. No!

I pull her into my arms as my mouth opens in a silent scream.

~

"Aaron!"

I don't lift my head at Hank's voice or turn my eyes towards him as I hear his footsteps approach. My shoulders still feel heavy. My hands still feel cold clenched against my chin. They still smell of vanilla and coconut.

But I doubt she does anymore. The coroner will have washed it away by now and she'll smell just like everything else in this damned hospital—of death. Another corpse waiting to be disposed of.

"Aaron." Hank's hand weighs on my back as he catches his breath. "Is Marjorie really—?"

"Lying on a cold table in the morgue?" I finish.

He squeezes my shoulder. "I'm sorry, man. I—"

"Tell me you're going to make this right." My hands clench tighter.

Hank sits beside me and sighs. "I'm a lawyer, man, not a fucking magician. I can't undo this."

I turn my head and look into his eyes. "Tell me you're going to put the man who did this behind bars."

"The man who did this?" Hank's eyebrows go up. "Aaron, I thought—"

"She didn't kill herself, Hank." My head shakes. "She would never do that."

"Hey." Hank's fingers bite into my shoulder once more. "I know this can't be easy for you. This is messed up. And I understand why you'd want to believe Marjorie didn't do this."

"She didn't do this."

"But—"

"Innocent until proven guilty. Isn't that what the law says, Hank?" I get off the bench so I can face him. "Why should Marjorie be any different? Why should it be assumed she took her own life just because I found her in a tub with no one else around?"

"Calm down, Aaron." Hank gets on his feet and raises his hands. "I'm on your side. You know I am. No one is assuming anything."

I snort.

"There may not even be any deliberate intention here," he goes on. "It could have been an accident. It happens."

I narrow my eyes at him. "An accident?"

"People drown in oceans by accident all the time. And even in tubs. Do you know someone drowns in a tub nearly every day in this country? And that's not intentional."

"This wasn't an accident."

Aaron shrugs and lifts his hands in defeat. "Fine."

I sink onto the bench and rub my temples. No way. There's no fucking way she just slipped into the water and stopped breathing or that she did it on purpose. Because if that was the case, then—

"Mr. Walsh?"

I lift my head to see a woman in scrubs walking towards me. Her mask is tucked beneath her chin. Thick glasses sit atop her nose.

"Yes?" I stand up.

"I'm Dr. Lascoe, the coroner," she introduces herself. "We found out something."

And it's important, or she wouldn't be telling me.

I glance at the paper in her hand. "What?"

"Your sister was two months pregnant."

My gaze drops to the floor. Pregnant? I did notice she was eating more than usual and that she had gained a bit of weight. I thought it was just because of all the stress from school, like she said.

Marjorie was pregnant?

I turn to Hank. "Now tell me she took her own life."

Hank shrugs and says nothing.

"I thought so."

"You think someone killed your sister?" Dr. Lascoe asks me.

I nod. My hands curl into fists at my sides. "And I think I know now who did."

~

"I'm sorry, Mr. Walsh." Judge Holden captures my gaze from behind her imposing podium. "But while there is evidence that Marjorie Walsh was murdered, I do not believe there is enough evidence here for the state to try Mr. Colby for that murder."

My jaw drops. No.

I feel like I'm back in that bathroom standing over that filled tub that has my sister's cold body in it. Numb. Helpless.

"Mr. Colby, you're free to go."

I look at the man sitting at the defendant's table. His shoulders fall as he lets out a deep sigh of relief.

Max Colby. The man who dated my sister. Who knocked her up. And who killed her.

I know he did.

144

The gavel pounds. "Court is adjourned."

Still, I stay in my seat, my gaze of icy daggers piercing into the back of my sister's murderer as his lawyer gives him a hug.

My fist tightens on my lap.

The prosecutor, a light-bearded man in his forties, turns to me. "Again, Mr. Walsh, we're sorry for your loss."

Sorry? It's not what I want to hear.

"If any new evidence turns up, I assure you, we—"

"Don't bother."

He sighs. "Mr. Walsh, I should also warn you not to take the law in your own hands. I'd hate to see you on the opposite side of the courtroom."

"Don't worry." I glance at him. "I'm not as incompetent as you are."

He replies with a look of disbelief.

Hank taps my shoulder. "We should go."

My gaze goes back to Max, following him as he exits the room. For a moment, our eyes meet. Sadness glimmers in his before he looks away. His head hangs low.

He doesn't fool me. I know he killed Marj. He may be walking away now, but one day, one way or another, I'm going to come after him and I'm going to make him pay for what he did.

He's going to wish he was behind bars, because now, there's nothing keeping me from sending him to hell myself.

Chapter One
Teri

Seven years later...

I pause halfway through the final flight of stairs and lean against the railing to catch my breath. My lungs feel on fire. My knees feel like they're wrapped in barbed wire. My feet ache, too.

I look down at my black leather flats. I should have worn my Air Max or my Keds. Then again, I didn't consider the possibility of the elevator being broken so I'd have to climb several flights of stairs.

Not that I would have had time to change. I came through the front door and Pam, my sister, shoved a box of her homemade French macaroons at my chest, saying they had to be delivered in the next hour or her client would be in trouble. She would have delivered them herself but Cody was having a stomachache and she couldn't just leave him.

What could I say? That I was tired? Pam never buys that. After all, every day, she brings Cody to school and fetches him, and in between she does the laundry, cooks the meals and bakes pastries for her business. She's the one who's tired. Me? I've been trying to find a stable full-time job, a job at an interior design firm.

Since I graduated from design school, I've applied to every firm in Pennsylvania, plus a few in Baltimore, DC and New Jersey, and I still haven't heard from most of them. I heard from one, and I went for an interview today, but I can already tell that's not going to work out. I bet they threw my application into the trash the moment I left the building.

"You're too young."

"You don't have enough experience."

"Your ideas don't sound new."

"Your designs look too plain."

That's all I hear. They won't even give me a chance to prove them wrong.

So here I am, Pam's delivery girl again. Maybe I should just apply for the job permanently. Her pastries seem to be selling well and she definitely needs the help.

But I probably wouldn't get paid. If I asked for payment, she'd ask for rent, which is only fair. I'll still end up empty-handed.

Besides, I don't think I'm cut out for delivery.

I make my way up the last few steps. Thank goodness the client only lives on the fifth floor and not on the tenth. I scan the doors lining the hallway until I spot the one that says 504. I smooth my hair just a bit and ring the doorbell.

After a few moments, the door opens and a woman with coffee brown skin, frizzy red hair and large silver hoop earrings swaying above her shoulders appears. One glance at the box I'm carrying and the corners of her full red lips turn up into a smile.

"Darling, you're a lifesaver." She turns around and grabs her purse. "My sister's arriving tonight and I promised her the best macaroons in town."

I smile and shrug. "Well, these are the best macaroons I've ever tasted."

"I know." She continues searching through the contents of her purse. "Actually, my sister was supposed to arrive tomorrow afternoon, which was why I originally told Pam to deliver these tomorrow, but all of a sudden, she calls me up and says she's already on her way. What is up with that? And so I just..."

I'm no longer listening. I don't really care why she wants the macaroons. I just want her to get them and pay for them so I can leave. How much longer is she going to go through that purse? Is her wallet really even there?

Finally, she fishes it out and hands me three twenty-dollar bills.

I look at them with arched eyebrows. "Um, do you have the exact amount? Because—"

"Oh, keep the change, sweetheart," she says. "And tell Pam I really appreciate her sending these babies right over."

I grab the bills as I hand her the box of macaroons. Okay. I get a $12 tip. Not bad.

I slip the money inside my pocket. "Thanks, Mrs. Beaty."

"Thank you. And until next time. Take care."

The door closes and she's gone.

I rub my hands together as if shaking some imaginary dust from between them. Another smooth delivery from Teri Flynn.

The only thing that wipes my grin away is the thought of taking the stairs again. But hey, it's easier going down than up. Gravity's on my side this time.

I've gone down just a few steps when my phone vibrates in my pocket. I take it out and read the message from Pam.

Were you able to deliver them? I'm going to the hospital because Cody threw up. They might keep him for the night or two. I've told Ron though he's still in Detroit. You have your keys. Don't forget to lock the front door.

I let out a sigh. Poor Cody. It seems like another case of the stomach flu.

I type my reply.

Hope Cody will get better fast. I've delivered the macaroons and am headed home. Don't worry about me.

I send the message. Well, maybe that last bit is unnecessary. She'll still worry about me anyway, even though I'm just four years younger than her, even though I'm not even her real sister. She's always been that way.

I put my phone back in my pocket and proceed down the steps. Home alone for the night, huh? What to do, what to do…

Well, I've got a bunch of Netflix shows to catch up on. Or I can finally finish embroidering that lampshade, that little project I've been working on. Or maybe tidy up the kitchen. Again.

I'm still considering all those possibilities as I take my time going down the steps. I stop in my tracks, though, as I hear a man's voice from below.

Haven't I heard that voice somewhere before?

Then I hear him give a throaty laugh and my heart stops. One glance over the railing at a head of red hair and I know who he is.

Well, I don't know exactly who he is. All I know is that once, I agreed to help a friend of mine decorate a house for a couple's anniversary party. I was invited to the party, too, as thanks, and I didn't have better plans, so I went. Everything was fine until I went to search for the bathroom after a few glasses of champagne. I found it, alright, but I found someone else inside, too, a man stroking his own dick. This man. I know because while I was standing in the doorway with my mouth gaping, he turned to me and asked me to join him. Then he laughed.

That same hoarse, throaty laugh.

Besides, he's wearing the same white suit. He must be a waiter for a catering service. Or someone's driver.

At any rate, he's definitely not someone I want to cross paths with again.

Now what? My feet start climbing back up the steps before I can come up with a plan.

Sure, I could just run quickly past him. Who's to say he'd recognize me? It's been months and he only saw me for a few seconds. I don't want to take that risk, though, because if I'm wrong and he does recognize me, I'll be in trouble. He's a fucking pervert, after all.

So what? Just keep going up so he doesn't catch up to me? But what if he lives on the tenth floor?

Back on the fifth floor, I look around for a place to hide. None. Doors are all that's on this hallway. No tables or couches to crouch beneath or behind. It's likely the same on each floor.

Should I just knock on the door to 504 again? Ask Mrs. Beaty to let me use the bathroom, maybe? She seems like a nice woman.

The quickening footsteps coming up from behind me send me into a panic. I climb up the next flight of stairs instead of racing down the hall. It's too late to turn back now.

I go up and up without glancing back. I just keep my ears open, hoping that soon the only footsteps I hear climbing the stairs will be mine. But no. He keeps following me, and when I reach the tenth floor and still hear him climbing, my heart begins to hammer in fear.

So he does live on the tenth floor, which means he can easily drag me into his apartment without anyone knowing.

Should I send Pam a text? She can't help me, though. She'll just worry, and she's got enough to worry about.

So what?

As his approaching footsteps nearly match my racing heartbeat, I look around.

Think, Teri. Think.

Maybe I can just knock on the door near the end of the hall and then hide behind the door when someone opens it. But my timing will have to be perfect. And what if that creep lives at the end of the hall? He'll still see me.

Should I just knock and ask to be let in? Maybe if I explain my situation, they'll understand. It sounds troublesome, though. And risky.

The footsteps keep coming. My heart pounds faster.

Come on. There must be something…

Suddenly, a door near me creaks open. Loud music escapes from inside, along with a woman who rushes towards the end of the hall with phone in hand. She doesn't see me.

I'm tempted to run after her, but then I realize I can still hear the music. The door the woman came from is still slightly open. And it's closer to me.

Without another thought, I seize my chance. I push the door open just a bit more and slip in. I find myself in a spacious apartment, one with a loft where people are dancing beneath the splattered lights of a dizzying disco ball. There are some people down here, too, on the couches, busy chatting, drinking and flirting.

So it is a party. Good. Maybe I can just slip out as easily as I've slipped in.

I take a peek out the door just in time to see the man I'm running away from coming down the hall.

Shit. He lives on this side? Wait. What if he's headed to this party?

I move away from the door and try to blend in with the shadows in a corner. My gaze rests on the knob as I hold my breath.

Please don't come here. Please don't come.

The moments pass. The door stays closed. I exhale.

I'm safe.

I jump, though, when I feel a tap on my shoulder. With my hand on my chest, I stare at the man in front of me wearing a striped sweater and jeans.

"Do I know you?" he asks.

Uh-oh.

I rattle my brains for an answer. Maybe I can say I delivered something? Or that I stepped inside the wrong apartment?

His thick eyebrows furrow as he glares in suspicion. I swallow.

He doesn't look stupid or forgiving, but I sure hope I'm wrong.

"I…"

"She's with me," a voice comes from behind him.

When he steps back, I see another man. Taller, with a more muscular frame. His dark hair is swept back above his wide forehead, the tips of some of the wavy tendrils hanging above broad shoulders. His eyes are dark, too, deep-set but not sunken. Together, the hair and eyes lend him the look of a savage beast, and when his thin lips pull back into a smile to reveal perfect white teeth, it's almost a snarl. Even so, my breath catches. Who would have thought a snarl could be so charming?

I am charmed—fascinated—as he walks towards me with powerful strides, like a predator about to claim its prey. I should probably run, but I don't feel fear at all. In spite of his rather wild appearance, I sense intelligence and mystery in his ebony eyes, and they pull me in. As he stands in front of me, I notice that his skin looks smooth beneath that layer of hair coating the edges of his chiseled cheeks and square chin. He may look a bit rough, but he's neat. His olive green shirt looks crisp and even expensive, the V-shaped neckline dipping low enough to give a glimpse of some curls sticking out of his chest. And I have to say that is a manly chest sitting atop sculpted abs, the muscles threatening to burst through the cotton.

He clears his throat and my eyes go back to his face. His eyebrows arch.

"Y–yes, that's right," I say as I fight off a blush. "I'm with… with him."

The man in the striped sweater turns to him with a questioning look. "Is that right, Aaron?"

Aaron, huh?

"Yup," he answers coolly before bringing his glass of whiskey to his lips.

"Well, this is new." The other man puts his hands on his hips. "It's not like you to bring a woman. Usually, you just find—"

"Don't you have other guests to see to?" Aaron pats his shoulder.

"Right." He turns towards me and offers his hand. "Pleased to meet you…"

"Teri," I say as I give him mine.

"James." He shakes my head. "But Aaron must have already told you that. Enjoy."

James wanders off and Aaron steps forward. He's even bigger standing in front of me, towering over me. I catch a whiff of spicy cologne.

"So, Teri…" He leans against the wall beside me and finishes his drink in one gulp. "Enjoying the party so far?"

He's still playing this game, huh?

Well, I can't.

"We both know I'm not with you," I tell him.

"You don't want to be?"

Again, my breath catches. My chest feels warm. Why can't I answer? I should just say no and leave. The coast should be clear by now. Is it because the answer is yes and I'm just too embarrassed to say it out loud?

He's unlike any man I've met, after all. Frankly, those have all been disappointments in varying degrees. But this man, Aaron—something tells me he doesn't know how to disappoint. This is a man who knows how to please, but he's by no means docile. No siree.

"Well, did I pass?" Aaron asks.

I give him a puzzled look. "What?"

"You've been sizing me up and ticking those boxes in your mind. Did I pass?"

Just as I thought, he's intelligent. Perceptive. Now I'm blushing.

"I wasn't—"

"It's fine. Just tell me if I passed."

Does he have to ask?

"Aaron, why did you cover for me?" I ask instead.

His back leaves the wall. In the next second, he's in front of me again. Or should I say over me? One of his arms hangs above me. His eyes look down straight into mine.

"Because you're hot," he says as his eyes wander further, down to the curves of my breasts and even lower.

I tuck my stomach in. Hot? I'm wearing a gray cardigan over a yellow blouse with copper buttons, one I've worn several times before to class and interviews. I know there's nothing special about it. Or hot. Even with the top button undone, I doubt he can see anything. And yes, I may be wearing my favorite bra, but I know my rack is still below the desired size. I've been told that before. And my stomach isn't flat. I don't work out, unless you count cleaning the house twice a week as working out. I guess my waist and hips are narrow. I've always been this way. But don't men want more curves to hold and press against?

"Is that what you want me to say?" Aaron asks with a chuckle as his gaze goes back to mine.

He's joking? Why am I almost offended?

"Or do you want me to say I'm a hero who can't resist damsels in distress?"

A hero? No. This man's not that noble.

"Tell me the truth," I answer.

With a grin, he lifts his hand to brush strands of my hair off my cheeks. His gaze holds mine as his face comes closer.

149

Is he going to kiss me?

My heart rattles in my chest in a flurry of both panic and excitement. I can't breathe.

I should probably run. But how can I when I can't even look away? I know I should fight, but those eyes, those lips... they're too much for me to resist.

My eyes close. My lips part. But instead of feeling his against them, I feel his cheek against mine as he whispers in my ear.

"It's because I was about to die of boredom at this party until you came along," he says.

My eyes fly open. So he's just amusing himself? I'm annoyed.

"Hey." He steps back. "Don't glare. You asked for the truth."

Was I glaring?

"Don't ask for something you can't handle."

I frown. "I—"

"Come." Aaron grabs my wrist. "Let's get some drinks."

He drags me off. I couldn't break free even if I wanted to. His grip is too firm. And I can't protest. Not when the music is so loud.

Finally, we reach somewhere quieter—the kitchen. Bottles of varying sizes, shapes and colors are lined up on the counter.

"What do you want to drink?" he asks.

I cock my head to one side. "Are you a bartender?"

"Do I look like one?"

No. If he works at a bar, he'd be more of the bouncer.

"I'm a businessman who likes to drink after a hard day's work," he says.

A businessman, huh? Well, he does have this presence. I can imagine him bellowing orders from the front of a conference room. But how does he keep that physique? Maybe there's a gym in his corner office?

"What about you?"

I lean on the counter. "Still waiting for a desk with my name on it."

Aaron nods. "Want me to make one for you?"

I chuckle.

"Let me make you a drink instead. So what will it be?"

I shake my head. "I shouldn't."

His eyebrows crease. "Shouldn't or won't?"

"I shouldn't even be here."

"Well, you're here now as my guest." He picks up a clean glass and drops two ice cubes into it from the bucket. "Or do you want me to tell James you're a trespasser? Mind you, his older brother's a judge, so he's paranoid about these things."

My eyes grow wide. Then I narrow them at him. "Are you threatening me?"

Aaron lifts the glass in his hand with a grin.

I sigh. "Fine. I'll make myself a drink."

I grab the glass from him and pour myself some of the Smirnoff and some Coke. I mix them together before taking a sip.

I turn to him. "Happy now?"

"Cheers." He raises his fresh glass of whiskey.

I say nothing but let my glass touch his with a soft clink.

He takes a gulp. "I was just kidding. I'm not telling James."

"Really?" My eyebrows bunch up. "Are you ever serious?"

"You'll know when I am."

The hard edge in his sentence sends a ripple of heat through me.

I bring my drink to my lips and take another sip.

"So you do drink," he remarks.

"Um, yes." I wipe my lips with the back of my hand.

"For a moment there, I thought you didn't."

"Why not?"

"Because you don't look like a girl who likes to take risks," he answers.

I frown, especially because that's something the guy who interviewed me earlier said, too.

"How is drinking taking a risk?"

Aaron shrugs. "You risk losing control, maybe doing something stupid or giving others a glimpse of your real self."

I glare. "Are you accusing me of pretending to be someone I'm not?"

He leans forward. "Aren't we all?"

I fall silent. I know what he's saying. Still…

"Who were you hiding from?" he asks after taking another gulp of whiskey. "An ex?"

"Sorry?"

"I know you're no criminal. I doubt you've ever broken a rule in your life."

He really is provoking me. "I'll have you know I played hooky a few times in high school."

"To visit the museum? To have a book signed?"

It annoys me that he got that second one right.

"And I dropped out of college," I say. "I was studying to be a teacher but I didn't finish. I realized it wasn't what I wanted."

"Good for you."

I can't tell if he's mocking me or praising me.

"But I still know you didn't come here just because of a dare or some experiment. You're not that brave."

"Hey." That stung.

"You came to this apartment because you felt you had no other choice. Am I right?"

I give him a puzzled look. "Are you a mind reader?"

"I saw the look on your face when you first stepped in. You were scared."

Unfortunately, I can't deny that.

"So, were you hiding from your ex?"

I take another sip and sigh. "Let's just say I was hiding from a creep."

"A stalker?"

"Not really."

"Want me to punch the daylights out of him?"

I glance at his fists. I bet he could do that.

"No, thanks. Contrary to what you think, I can take care of myself."

"No. You ran away."

"Some animals do that for survival."

"Only the ones that are too scared to fight."

I set my glass down and cross my arms over my chest. "Are you calling me a coward now?"

"Let me guess." Aaron leans forward. "He made a move on you and you freaked out."

"I beg your pardon."

He runs his hand through his hair. "You can't fool me, princess. You're a virgin. I know it."

My arms fall to my sides as I gasp. The nerve!

"What? Am I wearing a sign around my neck?"

"You don't have to, sweetheart."

"Don't call me sweetheart. Or princess."

But he doesn't seem unnerved in the least. He just gives me a wide grin. "So you did freak out. Just like you're freaking out now."

"I'm not…" I draw a deep breath in exasperation.

"You could have just punched him."

I look into his eyes. "I can punch you."

"Not when you look like you want me to kiss you, you can't."

I gape.

Aaron takes a step forward, challenging me.

151

I'd really like to punch him. And kiss him. Shit.

I grab my drink, finish it and set the empty glass down.

"I'm leaving."

"When you haven't punched or kissed me?"

I ignore that and square my shoulders. "Clearly, I came to the wrong apartment."

"Or you're right where you have to be."

I snort. "What is this? Are you going to preach to me about fate now?"

"No." He strokes his beard as he shakes his head. "I'm in the cargo business. Parcel deliveries. I simply believe things have a way of getting where they have to be. So do people."

"I'm not a package," I tell him.

"Well, you're certainly covered up in a lot of layers," he says as he looks down at my clothes.

I place my hand over the top button of my blouse. "Bye, Aaron."

I walk past him.

"Running away and making excuses again?" he calls after me.

I stop and glance over my shoulder. "What?"

Just then, James enters the kitchen.

"Well, there the two of you are." He nudges Aaron's shoulder, wearing a mischievous grin. "Thought you'd be in one of the bedrooms upstairs."

I resist the temptation to roll my eyes and shake his hand instead. "I'm glad I caught you, James, because I was just about to leave."

His eyes grow wide. "You're leaving?"

I nod.

"But the games are just about to begin."

My eyebrows furrow. "Games?"

"James loves games," Aaron explains. "He always has them at his parties. Sure you don't want to play? You might just be able to beat me at one of them."

I look into his narrowed eyes. Oh, he's throwing down the gauntlet, alright.

"Some of them are couple games," James says. "But there are individual games, too, and some of them have stakes."

"You might get your chance to punch me," Aaron tells me. "Or the other option. Or something even naughtier."

He winks.

"If you're capable of it."

I hate him.

"Well?" James asks hopefully as he clasps his hands. "Just play a few? After all, it's your first time here."

I glance at him and then back at Aaron.

"Fine."

I'll show him that I can take risks, too, and wipe that smirk off his face. Punching him will be just a bonus.

I walk to the counter. "Let me just get another drink first."

Aaron whistles. "Someone's stepping out of her comfort zone. Just make sure you don't get more than you can handle."

I grab the bottle of vodka by the neck as I meet his gaze. "Don't worry. I won't."

~

I'm never drinking again.

That's the thought that crosses my mind as I try to lift myself off a bean bag with one hand on the throbbing right side of my head. I taste the bitter alcohol in my mouth and I grimace.

I need to brush my teeth.

I grab my purse in one hand and my pair of shoes in the other and tiptoe across the living room, over bodies that are spread over the carpet, knocked out just as I was until a few seconds ago. I almost stumble over one but manage to regain my footing.

Thank goodness.

Once I've made it to the other side, I look around. After a moment, I remember where the bathroom is and head there.

As I pass through the dining room, I see the glasses and bottles on the table, some empty and some still half full, and the plates with leftover nachos or bones from chicken wings. There's a pile of used table napkins as well. I frown. What a mess. It almost seems like this was a party thrown by frat boys or high school girls instead of adults.

I have an urge to clean it all up but don't. Maybe if I didn't have a headache. But I do. And I really need to brush my teeth.

I proceed to the bathroom and heave another sigh of relief when I find it empty. And relatively clean. At least no one threw up in the sink or left a condom in the shower.

I set my purse down on the lid of the toilet seat and take my toothbrush and toothpaste out. As I start brushing, I stare at my reflection in the mirror.

What on earth happened to my hair? And what's that smudge on my chin?

I close my eyes and fight off the pain inside my skull as I try to remember the events of last night.

How did I end up on that bean bag, exactly?

All I can remember, though, is drinking and playing games. And more drinking. And laughing with Aaron…

At the thought of him, I pause. With toothbrush in mouth, I look under my blouse. My bra is still there. Using the mirror, I check for any marks. None other than the smudge on my chin, which seems like it's from chocolate. Finally, I dip my hand inside my panties. Nothing there.

Wait. What exactly am I checking for again?

I take out my toothbrush and spit, then gargle. Afterwards, I wipe my mouth as I lean against the wall.

I'm pretty sure nothing happened between Aaron and me. Well, I'm sure we didn't have sex. Thank goodness. I can't say for sure that we didn't kiss, though.

I trace my lower lip with my index finger. Did we?

Where is he, anyway?

After fixing myself up, I leave the bathroom and start looking for Aaron. Instead, all I find are more unconscious bodies, some snoring, some drooling. I find James, too, on a couch, hugging an empty bottle of wine with his mouth gaping wide. I find a few puddles of vomit as well. Gross.

But no Aaron.

I frown. When did he leave? Last night? How could he just leave me here?

Then again, it's not like he had an obligation to bring me home. He doesn't even know where I live.

If there's anyone I should be mad at, it's myself. I'm the one who drank way more than I could handle last night, even though Aaron warned me not to. Still, he is partly to blame since he's the one who teased and provoked me and all. And where is he now? Gone.

I'm not even sure if I got the chance to punch him.

I glance at my fist. Maybe not, or my fist would be hurting as much as my head. It's not like I could hit all that muscle without suffering any consequences.

I sigh. So I didn't punch him and I'm not sure I kissed him. Well, at least he knows now that I can let loose a little. Or a lot. And that I can make a fool of myself.

I leave the apartment with my mouth still in a pout and annoyance throbbing in my veins just as badly as the pain in my head. This time, the elevator is working. Good. I'm not sure I could go down all those flights of stairs with a hangover.

Inside the elevator, I try to cast aside my thoughts of Aaron. Who cares what he thinks? I'll probably never get to see him again. I don't have his number and I don't know where he works or lives. I don't even know his last name.

So forget him, Teri. Forget his barrel chest and his brawny arms. Forget his gorgeous bearded face and his magnetic opal eyes. Forget his deep voice and his smell of whiskey and cologne.

Forget how he made you feel dizzy and alive and free for the first time in a long time.

I slap my hand on my forehead.

How I managed to survive last night without losing my virginity I still don't know. I'm not sure I would have minded him taking it. But that would have been a mistake. Right?

Last night was a mistake, and I'm better off forgetting it. All of it. I'm going to get rid of my hangover both from the vodka and from that sexy brute of a man named Aaron.

~

After a warm bath, a long nap in my comfortable bed and a hot meal, I feel better.

Cody is still in the hospital so Pam isn't home yet either. She must have come back to get fresh clothes while I was sleeping, because I see Cody's sweater and her cardigan on one of the dining room chairs. She must have been in a hurry, too, because she didn't even have time to write a note. That's fine.

I glance at her cardigan before heading to the living room with a cup of tea.

I wonder if she knows I didn't come home last night. I guess I should be glad she doesn't. Even though I'm twenty-five, she still treats me like I'm twelve. She'll give me an earful just for sleeping over somewhere without letting her know, two if she finds out I got drunk. And if she ever learns I was with a man, I'll never hear the end of it.

I hope she doesn't find out.

Just to be sure, I'll do the laundry tomorrow and wash off any residue of alcohol still lingering on the clothes I wore last night. I'll wash some of her clothes and Cody's too, to put her in a good mood. Then she won't think I did anything wrong.

Or will she only suspect something all the more?

I sink into the couch. What am I so afraid of? I'm an adult. An adult without a job who's living with her sister, yes, but still an adult.

I let out a sigh as I sit back. My eyes dart to the pale blue ceiling.

Maybe Aaron's right. Maybe I am a coward.

Wait. Why am I still thinking of him? My head feels fine now. Sure, my memories are still a blur, but I think my blood alcohol content is back to normal now. Which means I should be done thinking about Aaron, too.

"Go burrow into someone else's thoughts, Aaron. You don't belong in mine."

That said—out loud—I sit up straight and grab the remote. Time to pick which Netflix show I should continue watching. That is, which one has a story I still remember. I don't want to have to start from the beginning.

I've just started browsing, though, when my phone rings. I dash to the kitchen counter where it's charging and answer it.

"Hello."

"Is this Ms. Teri Flynn?" an unfamiliar voice asks from the other end of the line.

I wonder who it is.

"Yes, speaking."

"This is Sharon. I'm from W.H. Clements Interiors."

My eyebrows immediately perk up. W.H. Clements? That's one of the top design firms in New Jersey, the one founded by Winona Henry-Clements, whose books I've read and whose TV shows I watched growing up. It was the first firm I applied to, my first choice. Not a day goes by that I don't hope to get a call from them. Finally, it's here.

"Hi, Sharon," I say as coolly as I can even as my fingers begin to tremble around my phone.

"You live in Ambler. Am I right?"

"Yes."

"Do you think you could come for an interview here at our Princeton office tomorrow morning at ten? We're currently looking for additional personnel and fresh ideas."

"Yeah. Sure." I resist the urge to jump up and down. "I mean yes, I will be there by ten."

"Great. Bring your portfolio and latest design."

"Of course."

"See you."

The curt phone call ends, but I remain staring at my phone, mouth gaping in awe.

This is it. This is the chance I've been waiting for. A game changer. If W.H. Clements Interiors hires me, I can finally start living my dream. Heck, I can start living. And evolving. It will be the start of the rest of my life.

If I get the job, that is.

I put down my phone and force a big smile.

No. I will get the job.

~

"I'm not quite sure you're the right fit for our firm, Teri," Sharon says in a somber tone as she goes through the photos from my portfolio, which are spread across her desk, one more time.

My heart immediately sinks along with the corners of my mouth.

"I'm afraid I don't see much creativity here." She taps her French manicured nails on one photo. "Or much of you."

The words weigh heavily on my shoulders and constrict my throat. Still, I find the courage to speak up.

"I must admit I'm still searching for my own style," I say with one hand on my chest. "But I'm open to new ideas, and I am a fast learner. Also, I can assure you that you'll find me easy to work with. I won't give you any trouble if you give me a chance. It's just that interior design is my passion. I would love nothing more than to devote my life to it just like Ms. Clements."

Sharon smiles. "I appreciate your honesty, Ms. Flynn, and I do sense your passion. I can see that you're skilled, too. I'm not saying you're not. I'm just not sure if what you have is enough, or exactly what we're looking for."

Her words feel like a boulder crushing my heart into pieces. Now I don't know what to say.

"But who knows?" She gathers my photos. "Ms. Clements may see something I'm missing."

Ah, she's dangled a thread in front of me. Whether she means it or she's just saying that because she feels sorry for me, I don't know. I give a hopeful smile just the same.

"Thank you. If you or she needs anything more from me, I'll just be a phone call away."

"Yes, we have your number. Just one more thing before you leave, though."

"Yes?" I ask eagerly.

"You say here on your application that your name is Teri Flynn. Is that right?"

I nod. "Yes. I am Teri Flynn."

"I understand that is your maiden name?"

My eyebrows rise. My maiden name? I don't follow.

"It's just that we do a background check on all our applicants before we interview them," Sharon explains. "And when we were doing yours, we discovered that you're recently married. Congratulations on that, by the way."

My jaw drops. Me, married? Now I really don't know what to say.

"If ever we do hire you, wouldn't you want us to use your married name? I understand if you haven't had time to update some of your documents, but—"

"I'm sorry." I can't hold back any longer. "Where did you say you learned I'm married?"

"Oh, we found a copy of your marriage certificate online."

What?

Sharon gives me a puzzled look. "You seem surprised. Was it something you were keeping a secret? Don't worry. We don't mind hiring married women if they're qualified."

Keeping it a secret? It's more of the fact that I'm not in on the secret. How is this even possible?

"There must be some mistake," I say as I stand up. "I've never been married."

"Really?" Sharon glances at her computer screen. "But it says right here in your file. You're married."

"To whom?" I strain my neck to look at her screen.

She answers at the same time I see the name of my supposed spouse on the document.

"Aaron F. Walsh."

I cover my mouth as I let out a gasp. My body sinks into the chair as my strength leaves me. No way.

"He is your husband, is he not?"

It can't be. How can it be? It doesn't make sense. Not at all.

I lift a finger as I turn to her. "You know what? Let me get back to you on that."

Chapter Two
Aaron

"Those shitty two-faced bastards!"

I yank the rubber band keeping my hair in place before dropping onto the leather couch in my office. The cushions creak beneath my weight. I loosen my tie as I let out a deep breath.

That meeting definitely didn't go well.

Those geezers on the board. Who do they think they are? Has their memory grown so rusty that they've forgotten who runs this company? Have they forgotten what I did to those who used to occupy the seats in that room, to those who dared to defy me?

I turn my head towards the picture on the wall behind my desk, a picture of me and the former CEO, Bran Pickett. He's in one of his trademark plaid Oxford shirts. I'm in that gray and white jumpsuit that the people in delivery still wear.

Ah. It seems like an eternity ago that I was in delivery. From there, I worked my way up to this beautiful office that occupies not just a corner but a third of the seventh floor of this sprawling building that I now own. I worked more hours than anyone else, lifted and delivered more packages than I can count until I got promoted to supervisor. Then I worked even harder, kissed a few asses that I kicked later on, and studied. That was the key.

At the same time I was coming up with codes and programs to impress my college professors, I tried to think of ways to improve the company. And one of those ideas became a hit. Bran liked it, adopted the system, and put me in charge of it, among other things. Some of the higher-ups in their fancy swiveling chairs didn't like the idea of someone climbing up the ranks so fast. Probably thought I'd eat them all up. So they schemed with some board members and had me fired. They took credit for all my hard work, too. Poor Bran couldn't do a thing. But I fought back.

I filed a lawsuit. I won. And Bran handed this company over to me. In business, the winner takes it all.

I tap the arm of the couch and grin as I recall that moment of triumph in the courtroom, the looks on the faces of those sneaky weasels who tried to put me down and take everything away from me. Of course, that was the one time the court sided with me, and my triumph was spoiled by tragedy just a few years later, but that moment—well, that was plain sweet.

"Yeah," I say out loud as I nod. "That was my moment right there."

I'm still grinning when Hank comes in.

"And here I thought you'd be in a foul mood after that squabble in the boardroom," he says as he unbuttons his jacket and sits on the armchair across from me.

I narrow my eyes at him. "Who told you?"

Hank shrugs. "I overheard a few people talking on my way here."

Of course tongues are wagging. It's not every day the boss has an outburst, which was probably heard throughout the whole floor. In fact, I pride myself on controlling my temper.

"I don't squabble."

"Wrong word." He sends a breath towards the ash blond wisps of hair hanging over his forehead, as he usually does when he's thinking, and taps his fingers on the arm of the chair. "A minor altercation, then? A dissension?"

Lawyers and their fancy words.

"I was in a foul mood," I tell him. "But then I remembered what happened the last time a bunch of old men tried to pick a fight with me."

I glance at the picture on the wall.

"Ah yes. I remember that, too."

Of course he does. He was right beside me in that fight. It was his first major case, and we both won it.

"Were we really that reckless once?"

I chuckle. "You make us sound like we're fifty. And we weren't reckless. We were bold."

"I can't remember the last time I did something so bold. Oh right, I do. It was two nights ago when I had sex with a woman behind a tree at the country club while her father was playing golf."

I frown. "How many times do I have to tell you I don't want to hear about your exploits?"

"My bad. I forgot that telling you makes you an accessory to my crimes. Not that that was a crime or that I've committed any."

"I hope not."

"What about you?" Hank leans forward. "What's the most reckless thing you've done lately?"

"You mean aside from what happened this afternoon?"

He laughs.

I touch my chin. "Actually, there is something, which reminds me. I need you to draw up some papers for me."

He gives me a questioning look. "What kind of papers?"

"Divorce papers, Hank."

He gives another laugh. "That's a good one."

So he thinks I'm joking, huh? I say nothing.

He turns serious. "Now, now, Aaron, are you saying you—?"

Just then, both doors to my office open. Instead of Holly, my auburn-haired assistant, the woman who appears is a brunette. Layers of mahogany strands frame her heart-shaped face. The shortest ones sweep diagonally over her wide forehead. Almond-shaped hazel eyes stare—no, glare—from beneath slanted eyebrows and I can see the tense line on her tapered chin from holding her lips in a pout. The lower, fuller one is sticking out.

I wonder, if I kiss those, will they finally stop pouting? But then I've never seen a woman look so alluring when she's got her panties in a twist.

"Teri." I stand up and give her a smile as I walk towards her. "I didn't think I'd see you again this soon."

She doesn't answer as she catches her breath but I can almost see the steam coming out of her nostrils.

"I'm sorry, Mr. Walsh." Holly steps forward. "I told her to wait, but—"

"It's alright, Holly," I cut her off. "She has a tendency to just walk through doors."

Teri's eyebrows arch as her lower lip drops.

"You can leave us," I add.

"Yes, sir." Holly leaves the office.

I take a step forward to get a better look at my guest. Not that I didn't get an eyeful the other day. Slender shoulders. Breasts smaller than I'd like. Supple arms. Slim waist. A bit of a curve there at the midsection, but then I never did like a woman who was all skin and bones. I feel like I'd snap them in half.

She's wearing a dress today—light peach with flowy sleeves that go all the way to her elbows and a skirt that flares out just past her knees. The V-shaped neckline shows off a bit of collarbone and maybe some cleavage if those strings of beads weren't in the way. Still, she looks more attractive, more feminine. Too bad I can tell she didn't dress up just for me.

"Drink?" I offer. "Though I don't have vodka and Coke."

She holds her white purse in front of her. "I didn't come here for a drink, Aaron."

"Yeah. After the spree you had at that party, I'm guessing you're staying away from alcohol for a while." I gesture to the couch. "Sit."

She remains where she's standing.

I shrug. "Or not."

"I won't stay long," Teri says. "I just want to hear you say you'll fix this mess."

My eyebrows go up. "Mess?"

"Yes." She clutches the straps of her purse a little tighter. "For some reason, the State of Pennsylvania thinks we're married. That's a mistake, right? Because we didn't get married. And I'm sure this misunderstanding is just as inconvenient for you as it is for me. I mean, what will your fiancée think?"

I rub my chin. "You think I'm engaged?"

Teri glances around. "Now that I've seen your office and know how rich and important you are, yes."

Her shoulders rise and fall as she exhales.

"I wish you had told me. I feel like a fool marching in here."

"Yet you did it so well."

She frowns.

"You think women would only be after me for my money?" I cross my arms over my chest as I sit on one arm of the couch.

Teri shakes her head. "That's not what I said. What I mean is that someone like you is unlikely to be single."

"Because I'm rich?"

The straps of her purse slide down to her elbow as she lifts her hands. "Can we just focus on the issue here?"

I ignore her. "You think I'd flirt with you even if I was engaged?"

Teri sighs.

Hank finally moves as he gets out of his seat. He turns to Teri.

"I think you should sit, ma'am."

"Don't call me 'ma'am'," she answers.

I stifle a chuckle as Hank glances at me.

"I'm fine," Teri adds.

"Okay." Hank nods. "I'll just—"

"Stay," I tell him before meeting Teri's gaze. "Hank is a lawyer, my lawyer."

"Oh." Teri turns to him. "In that case, maybe you can help straighten this out. After all, I'm pretty sure a law has been violated here."

"Let me just get this straight." I stand up and tuck my hands in my pockets. "You think that someone forged this document that says we're married?"

She nods. "Yes."

So she doesn't remember. Not surprising, given the state I left her in.

"Have you seen it?"

"No, but—"

"Neither have I, but I can tell you it's not forged."

Her eyebrows bunch up. "What do you mean?"

"It has your signature and mine."

"But I—" She lifts a hand, but it drops as her mouth closes.

She understands the situation. Smart girl.

The hand rises again. "Wait. Did you make me sign a marriage certificate when I was drunk?"

I put a hand on my chest. "I made you sign?"

I chuckle.

Her eyebrows bunch up all the more.

"Sweetheart, you asked to sign and then you told me to sign."

"What?" Her jaw drops. "No way."

I scratch my chin as I recall the specific circumstances. "If I remember correctly, we were playing some twisted version of truth or dare and someone asked you what your three biggest fears were and you said being covered in garbage, not accomplishing anything in your life, and spending your life alone because you expect too much of men."

"I said that?"

I nod. "Then you started talking about finding the perfect guy and how some of your friends are married already and how you're afraid you'll never get to sign your name on a marriage certificate."

Teri shakes her head. "I didn't say that."

"Then James said he'd seen one among his brother's papers. He went to get it. You held it in your hand and people started urging you to sign it. They were chanting and all. James gave you a pen and you signed. You looked proud of it, too. Then someone dared me to sign. I wasn't going to, but then you called me a coward. I said I wasn't afraid of marrying you and I signed. And someone in that crowd—I think his

159

name was Larry—just happened to be a justice of the peace and he married us and affixed his signature on the document, making it legal and binding."

Mahogany strands whip back and forth as Teri shakes her head even more. "No. No way."

"Ask Hank," I say. "He'll tell you it's valid."

"It is," Hank confirms.

Teri touches her forehead. "No. I mean there's no way all that happened."

"You can ask Larry himself," I say. "Or James. I do believe he records these games sometimes. Or someone at that party could have."

Teri falls silent. Then she sinks into the armchair as her shoulders slump in defeat. Her voice is just a whisper when she speaks.

"I'm the worst drunk, aren't I?"

"I disagree," Hank says. "You didn't commit a crime."

"I'm not sure being in jail would be any worse."

Hank starts to laugh but stops when I send a warning glance in his direction.

Teri slaps her forehead. "I can't believe I got married while I was drunk."

"At least you didn't get pregnant. I believe that's the more common complaint." I sit on the couch.

Teri looks at me questioningly.

"We didn't do anything, I swear," I tell her. "Not that I didn't want to, but there's no way I'd do that to someone so drunk. It's no fun."

"So you just let me marry you instead."

"You look like you would have preferred to get knocked up."

She rolls her eyes at me, then turns to Hank. "Are you sure it's valid? I mean, I was drunk."

Hank shrugs. "So are half the people who get married in Vegas."

Teri sighs.

"No one forced you, right?" Hank asks her. "No one held a gun to your head?"

"Ugh." She places a hand on her forehead as she sits back. Then she glares at me. "This is your fault."

"Mine?"

"Why did you sign?"

"You dared me to."

"I should never have entered that apartment." Her gaze shoots to the ceiling before piercing me again. "No. I was trying to leave and you stopped me. This is all your fault."

"It's your signature on the document," I point out.

Teri pouts.

"But don't worry," I tell her. "We took things too far, that's true. But hey, it's not the end of the world. Haven't you heard about divorce?"

Her lips straighten.

I glance at Hank. "I'm sure Hank here can get us one. You just have to sign some papers again."

"Yeah." Hank nods. "I think I can manage that, seeing as this was a mistake and all."

"A divorce?" Teri asks.

Something in her eyes tells me she's not entirely comfortable with the idea. Let me guess why. Divorce runs in the family and she doesn't want to suffer the same fate. Or maybe she thinks her chances of finding her dream guy will be ruined.

I lean forward. "Teri?"

"I…" She puts her hands on her knees. "I'm sorry, but I need to think about this. We married so rashly. I don't want us to do this rashly, too."

I nod. "I understand. Take all the time you need."

Slowly, she stands up. "I'll… I'll let you know…"

"Ask Holly for my number," I tell her. "And call me when you've made your decision. I'll be right here."

As animated as she was when she stormed into my office, she leaves dazed and confused. After the doors close, Hank lets out a laugh.

I look at him. "You've been holding that in the whole time, haven't you?"

He sits beside me on the couch. "Man, I know you get some crazy ideas sometimes, but getting married? And to a woman who didn't even know it?"

"She knew. She just forgot about it," I answer.

"I sort of get why she signed that document. But why did you? I don't believe you married her just because she dared you to, especially since you knew she was drunk and didn't mean it."

I shrug. "I couldn't just sit still and cower when she was putting herself out there."

Hank grins.

"What?" I ask him.

"You like her. Well, she doesn't look so bad. Personally, I prefer a woman with more curves, but hey, I'm not the one who married her. Plus she seems smart. And she's feisty. Maybe she's that way in bed, too."

I'd like to scold him, but I can't deny that thought has crossed my mind.

"Are you sure you didn't have sex with her?" Hank asks me.

"I didn't," I assure him. "Like I said, it's no fun doing it with someone who's drunk."

"Well, you can do it now. After all, you're married."

"We're getting a divorce," I remind him.

"I don't know." Hank gives a shrug. "Mrs. Walsh seems a tad reluctant."

I say nothing. Yes, Teri did seem reluctant, but that's only because she's still in shock. She hasn't quite swallowed the fact that she's married yet so how can she begin to digest the idea of divorce?

"What was her full name again?" Hank asks.

"Teri Flynn," I say.

Beside me, Hank freezes. I feel confused.

"What?" I ask him.

He just strokes his chin and doesn't answer.

"What?" I nudge his arm.

Hank stands up and begins to pace the room. "It's just I've heard that name before. No wonder she looked a little familiar. I thought I just saw her at a bar sometime this month, but now I remember."

I get on my feet. "Where did you hear that name before, Hank? And what did you hear?"

He stops pacing, takes out his phone and runs his finger over the screen. I wait impatiently for him to find what he's looking for.

"Well?" I walk towards him as my patience runs out.

Hank holds his phone in front of me so I can see the photo of the woman on the screen. The same hazel eyes that glared at me earlier stare back at me. Teri may look younger in the photo and her hair may look different, but it is her picture. Why does Hank have it?

"Teri Flynn," he says. "Originally Teri Colby."

"Colby?" I feel the blood drain from my face.

Hank puts his phone away. "That's right, Aaron. Teri is the sister of Max Colby."

~

So I'm married to the sister of the man who killed my sister.

It's so absurd I almost laugh out loud as I stand by the window in my apartment. Instead, I drown that urge with more whiskey, and as the liquid blazes down my throat, my sense of humor dissolves. Anger simmers in my veins.

What fucking prank of fate is this?

It's a prank, alright. And it's genius. The best. And the worst.

The fingers of my free hand curl into a fist at my side. I unclench them as I glance down.

Now that I know who Teri really is, I want to wrap my hands around her neck and squeeze the life out of her. Or snap. Either would be easy. I'd like to see the light fade from those hazel eyes the way it did from Marjorie's green ones. And then Max would finally feel how I've been feeling these past seven years.

Yes, I'll finally have my revenge.

I could ask Holly to find Teri's address for me, go over there and do it right now. But no. In order for my revenge to be complete, in order for me to be satisfied, Max has to know what I've done. And right now, I don't even know where he is. Hank and I have been looking for him for years to no avail.

I gulp down the rest of my drink before sitting down. My gaze falls on the painting of Aphrodite on the wall, which someone gave me as a present once. The hue of the goddess's hair reminds me of Teri's.

If I'm not going to kill Teri just yet, what am I going to do with her?

Maybe I should demand a divorce like Hank advised. There should be a way to get her to sign those papers. If she can get me to marry her, I can get her to divorce me. I'll bribe a judge if I have to. After all, I can't very well live with someone who shares the blood of my sister's murderer. Besides, what if she knows who I am? What if Max is using her? What if Max sent her to seduce me and then somehow twist me so I don't go after him anymore?

I shake my head. No. I'm sure Teri doesn't know. Clearly I don't know her, but my gut is telling me she's not acting on anyone's orders. If she's playing a role in some plot, she doesn't know it. Also, Hank said she got adopted. That's why her last name changed. I don't even know if she has any contact with Max now, or how long it's been since she did.

One thing I do know—older brothers don't turn their backs on their little sisters, especially not if it's just the two of them.

If Teri is in danger in any way, Max will show up. So I just have to stick around. Or better yet, I can have her call him for help.

That's it. I'll use Teri. I'll continue with this marriage on a whim and keep her as my wife. And I'll make her life hell. She'll suffer even more than Marj suffered. Then she'll call Max, and when he comes, I'll send him there as well.

I glance out the window as I picture Teri's face.

"Heaven help you for marrying me."

Chapter Three
Teri

I'm a married woman now, huh?

I let out a deep sigh as I push myself off the toilet I've been trying to clean for the past few minutes. The softness of the black chenille bathroom rug beneath my legs provides a contrast to the hard, cold tiles behind me. I wipe the beads of sweat from my forehead with a gloved hand, then pull down the mask covering half my face so I can breathe. The smell of bleach, which has overpowered the floral scents of the soap bars lined near the sink, drifts to my nostrils. I let out a shallow cough. My eyes dart to the lily pads on the shower curtain as my arms drop to my sides.

How did I get myself into a mess I can't clean up?

I still can't believe I'm married. How can I when I don't even remember it happening? I can only imagine it based on what Aaron told me. And it's not a pretty picture. Definitely not how I thought I'd get married.

Where were the flowers—the chartreuse orchids and white gardenias I always pictured gracing my wedding day? Where was the enchanting music of violins or the ribbons of chiffon and satin? Where was my charmeuse wedding gown with its train floating like a puddle across the carpet and its organza veil dancing silently with the slightest breeze? Most importantly, where was that moment when I gazed into the eyes of my groom and felt time stand still, felt the rest of the world melt away?

I had none of those. Heck, I don't even have a ring on my finger.

All I have are blurry fragments and a crystal clear document that says I'm the wife of Aaron Walsh, a man I barely know, and apparently a wealthy and powerful man.

If I close my eyes, I can still see his office with its black leather chairs, its maroon carpet with swirls of beige, his massive oak desk with its layer of glass and his modular shelves. I'd probably furnish it differently. Nonetheless, it was an office that exuded power and carried the air of serious business, just like the man who occupies it.

A CEO—one who gave his company a makeover and expanded it to what it is today, a top player in freight transport worldwide.

Cocky I can handle. Driven? Yes. Billionaire business tycoon with a drool-worthy body to boot? I'm not sure.

I slap my forehead as I let my chin drop. I guess this is what I get for having such high standards when it comes to men.

It's all the more reason for me to accept that divorce Aaron is offering. So why am I hesitating?

"Well, this is something new." Pam's voice makes me jump. "I don't think I've ever seen you this devastated from cleaning a bathroom. What? Is there a stain you weren't able to defeat? A square inch covered in mildew that you weren't able to conquer?"

I get on my feet and slip the rubber gloves off my hands before turning to her with a pout. "Very funny."

"Seriously, though…" Pam crosses her arms over her chest as she leans on the bathroom doorway. "What's bothering you? You've been in a daze since this morning—no, since Cody and I came back from the hospital last night."

I purse my lips. Of course she noticed, even though I was trying my best to put on a smile to mask the constant turmoil in my head and the heaviness in my chest. Or maybe she noticed that, too.

I want to say it's nothing, but she wouldn't believe it. And if I just tell her not to worry, she'll worry even more.

I meet her gaze. She's still waiting for an answer. I have to say something.

I walk to the sink and let out a sigh as I turn on the faucet to wash my hands. "I was just thinking about that last job interview I went to."

That's not entirely a lie. That has been weighing on my mind, too.

"Which one was this?"

"W.H. Clements."

Pam gasps. "The one you really want to get into?"

I nod. "I don't think I'm getting in, though."

Sharon made it pretty clear that I don't meet the company's standards. And after that fit I almost threw when she told me I was married, I doubt I still have a chance. They probably think I'm a complete weirdo.

"Oh, sweetie. Come here."

Pam pulls me into her arms and pats my hair. It's what she always does to comfort me.

"They can still change their minds, you know."

I doubt that.

"I'll be fine." I pat her arm and pull away so I can close the faucet. "I'm sorry I haven't been able to find a job sooner and get out of your hair."

"Stop it." Pam's hands squeeze my shoulders. "You know you're my favorite hair accessory."

I throw a weak smile at my reflection in the mirror.

Pam turns me around and cups my cheeks. "You'll find the perfect job for you. I'm sure of it. Just sit tight and wait. And clean my house in the meantime."

I chuckle.

"And deliver my pastries once in a while."

"I know."

She pats my cheek. "Just as the best pastries need ample time to bake in the oven, dreams need time to come true. But they will eventually."

I'm not sure I still believe I can be an interior designer. In fact, I'm starting to think I'm not meant to be one. But I nod.

"Thanks, Pam."

She pinches my cheeks and pulls the corners of my mouth into a smile.

"That's better."

As soon as she lets my face go, though, the corners of my mouth turn back down.

"Is that all?" Pam asks. "Sure there's nothing else bothering you?"

I guess I really can't fool her. I look away.

"What?"

I want to talk to her about Aaron. I really do. I want to ask her what I should do, whether I should agree to the divorce or not. But I can't tell her I'm married all of a sudden. She wouldn't just be shocked. She'd be disappointed in me. I'm already struggling to get a job. I don't want her to think I'm a complete failure of an adult. And I don't want to make her worry. I'm not her child. I'm her twenty-five year old younger sister.

Still, maybe there's some way to ask for her advice without telling her about my real situation.

"Well?" Pam grasps my chin and turns it towards her so I'm looking into her eyes.

I sigh as I walk past her. "Actually, there's one more thing."

"Yes?" She follows me out of the bathroom.

"You know, companies ask weird questions when they interview their applicants these days, like questions that aren't related at all to the job you're applying for."

"I've heard about that."

"Well, I did get asked a weird question. At least, I find it weird."

"What is it?"

"My thoughts on divorce," I say.

"What do you mean?" Pam asks. "Like if you would ever consider getting a divorce?"

"Would you?" I ask her.

She tucks her hand beneath her chin. "I guess I would, but only if Ron did something really bad, like he has a child with another woman or he hurts me or Cody. In short, I'd only consider divorce if our marriage was beyond repair, like if everything was already going down the drain."

I nod. "So what if, for example, you married someone by mistake. Would you consider a divorce?"

"By mistake?" Pam laughs. "You mean like if I married someone and later found out he's a fugitive, or if I went to Vegas, got drunk and woke up the next day married to some stranger I had sex with just once?"

I nearly wince at that last part. She nearly hit the bull's eye on that one, except for the fact that I didn't even have sex with Aaron. Instead, I shrug.

"Yeah, something like that."

"Well, I don't think that would ever happen to me."

She's said it.

"But if that did happen to someone, I guess they should get a divorce. There's no reason why you should suffer for the rest of your life for one wrong decision."

Right. That thought occurred to me, too.

"It's irresponsible, though. Marriage isn't a game. It shouldn't be taken lightly. I think that's one of the bad things about divorce—it makes people less responsible. Couples think they can try marriage like it's a new pair of shoes, sometimes just out of curiosity or just on a whim, and then if they don't like it, they just throw it away."

"So you don't like those couples?" I ask.

"Of course not. They're an insult to couples like me and Ron and others I know who take marriage seriously. They're the ones who give marriage a bad name."

Just as I thought. If I get divorced, people will think I'm hasty, that I can't be trusted.

"People like them, they're immature and selfish," Pam adds. "And if they can discard marriage so easily, who knows what else they can throw away without batting an eyelash?"

My gaze drops to the floor. Wow. She's really bringing on the pain. Now I feel even more apprehensive about getting a divorce. Married one day, divorced the next. It doesn't sound good at all.

Pam puts a hand on my arm. "What did you say?"

I pause, then shrug as I meet her gaze. "Pretty much the same thing but in fewer words."

She smiles. "Well, I'm sure there was no wrong or right answer. They were probably just trying to figure out how your mind works."

"Maybe."

But I need an answer. And soon.

Pam places her arm around me. "Why don't I go make us a snack? You must be hungry after cleaning and I'm—"

I don't hear the rest because my phone starts to ring. I turn my head in the direction of the sound and remember that I left it on the table outside the bathroom.

"You can go ahead to the kitchen," I tell Pam. "I'll be right there."

I run to pick up my phone. An unknown number shows on the screen.

Another job interview, maybe?

I answer the call. "Teri Flynn speaking."

"Teri Flynn?" The woman on the other end sounds surprised. "Or Teri Walsh?"

My eyebrows arch. Does the whole world know about the mistake I made now?

"I'm sorry. May I know who's calling?"

"Winona Henry-Clements."

A gasp escapes my lips. I lean against the wall as my knees wobble.

Winona Henry-Clements is calling me. Unbelievable. But why?

"This is Teri Walsh, right?" she asks. "The wife of Aaron Walsh?"

"Y-yes."

"You should have said that from the start when you came to the office and asked to meet me. I would have."

Ms. Clements would have met me? Now I'm confused.

"I don't know Aaron personally," she says. "But I do know that we always use his company when we have to ship furniture and decor to our clients or for exhibits."

"Oh."

"I wasn't aware that his wife wanted to be an interior designer. Or that he even had a wife."

I scratch the back of my head. "Well, it happened very recently. And secretly."

"I see. Well, I can understand that, and don't worry. I won't tell anyone. You're probably waiting for the right time to announce it, so I won't spoil it for you."

"Thank you," I hear myself saying.

"So you want to be an interior designer?"

"Yes."

"And you want to join my firm?"

"Yes."

"Sure you don't want to set up one of your own? Doesn't your husband want that?"

I hadn't thought of that. Well, I haven't really thought of Aaron as my husband.

"The thing is, Ms. Clements..."

"Please call me Winona."

Really?

I swallow the lump in my throat. "Winona, I'm a big fan and I want to learn from you..."

"Say no more," she cuts me off. "I've seen your designs. They lack... something, but I'm sure I can help you find that."

My eyes grow wide. "Are you saying you'll—?"

"You're hired," Winona says it plainly. "You can start next week. I'll have your office ready. And your assistant."

Office? Assistant?

"I've decided I'll make you a junior partner. I'm sure that will make your husband happy. Who knows? He might see his way to giving us some discounts, us being loyal customers and all."

I see. She's giving me a good position because I'm Aaron Walsh's wife. No. She's hiring me because I'm Aaron Walsh's wife.

"Sounds good?" Winona asks.

I open my mouth, but no words come out. This is my dream coming true, right? Why then am I not thrilled?

"Teri?"

I know. I'm not thrilled because I'm not getting this job on my own. But I'm still getting it. Or am I going to let this opportunity pass me by?

No way.

"Sounds great," I finally manage to say.

"Good. See you next week."

The call ends. I put my phone back on the table and clasp a hand over my mouth.

I'm still in awe. I never thought I'd get a call from Winona Henry-Clements herself, or that she'd offer me a job at her firm. Then again, she only did because she thinks I'm married to Aaron Walsh. What if she hears it was a mistake? What if we get divorced and she finds out?

I slap my forehead. Divorce is looking like a less and less desirable option by the minute.

So I'm staying married? How do I manage that? Will Aaron even agree to it?

My arm falls to my side as I let out a sigh. My eyes fall to my phone.

I guess it's time Aaron and I talk again.

~

I spot the midnight blue Jaguar as soon as I go around the curb at the end of the street. I glance back to make sure Pam isn't following me—I wouldn't put it past her, especially since she seemed surprised when I said I wanted to go for an evening walk. Of course she would be. I've never gone for an evening walk. I'm just glad she didn't ask to join me.

I turn my head to look straight ahead at the waiting car. Even if I squint, I can barely figure out if there's anyone inside, much less tell who it is. Except I know who's inside.

I smooth the front of my sweater before crossing the street. I draw a deep breath before tapping the passenger-side window.

The door opens. The passenger seat is empty, Aaron behind the wheel. He glances at me but doesn't smile. I slip inside.

"Hard day at work?" I ask him.

That's the only reason I can think of to explain why he seems to be in a bad mood.

He doesn't answer.

My gaze wanders over his black dress shirt. The top two buttons are undone. Black looks good on him. It brings out the color of his eyes. And it makes him seem more mysterious.

Hotter.

I swallow as I look away. Is it just me, or is it suddenly hotter in here? I'm suddenly eager to get this over with.

"You didn't have to drive—"

"I changed my mind," he cuts me off. His fingers tighten around the wheel. "I don't want a divorce."

Well, I wasn't expecting that.

"Okay." I draw a deep breath. "Well, frankly, I was thinking maybe it's better if we give this marriage a try before—"

"I'm not asking." He meets my gaze.

Those cold ebony spheres take me back. A shiver goes up my spine.

Was he always this cold? Why does he look like he hates me now?

"I'll have someone pick you up in the morning, so pack your bags," he goes on as his eyes go back to the windshield. "You'll be staying at my apartment."

My gaze drops. I didn't see that coming, either. But maybe I should have. I mean, married couples live together. That's the norm.

Wait. Are we going to be acting like a normal married couple now?

"That's all," Aaron concludes.

I look at him with wide eyes. That's all? I feel like I'm some spy who just got briefed and is now being dismissed.

Is this really the Aaron Walsh I met at that party and at his office?

I don't feel like arguing, though, not now, so I simply open the door.

"See you tomorrow."

He doesn't answer. A few moments after I get out of the car, he drives off swiftly and silently. I stand on the sidewalk with my arms over my chest as I throw a questioning glance at the crescent moon.

What on earth just happened?

Chapter Four
Aaron

"So, did she agree?" Hank asks me moments after he enters the office gym.

I don't answer at once because I'm busy taking a gulp of oxygen as I stretch my arms out on either side of the fly machine. I can feel my lungs expanding as my chest puffs out. Then I slowly let the air out as I bring my arms together again while keeping my elbows at an angle, my back straight.

"Yes." I pause when my fists are nearly touching again. "But then I didn't really give her a choice."

Hank chuckles. "I feel sorry for her already."

"Don't."

I spread my arms again, then bring them together, repeating the process a few more times as Hank goes silent. The machine creaks. I can hear whispers from the corner of the room and feel eyes watching me. They're probably the new female employees here to get an eyeful of their boss. I don't mind as long as they do their jobs.

Hank blows off the fringes of hair on his forehead as he sits on the nearby bench.

"Are you sure this is a good idea?"

I let go of the bars. I'm already at my limit anyway. Sweat trickles down the side of my face and between my pectoral muscles, seeping into my cotton shirt. My shoulders burn from the workout.

"What do you mean?" I ask Hank as I gesture for him to throw my towel at me.

He does. I catch it and wipe my face and arms.

"I mean there's no guarantee Max will suddenly show up," Hank says.

"He will."

"For all we know, he could just stay away all the more once he finds out his sister is married to you."

"He won't. He can't. He knows he owes me and I won't hesitate to collect the debt, even if it means hurting his sister."

"So Teri is a hostage?"

I slip the towel beneath my shirt. "He can think of it that way."

"If he gets the ransom note," Hank tells me. "Have you at least asked Teri if he's still alive?"

I don't answer.

"You know I've been searching for him this whole time and—"

"Well, clearly, you haven't been searching for him hard enough or I wouldn't be forced to set a trap for him!" I snap.

Silence falls over the gym. From the corner of my eye, I see a few employees scurry off in fear. In front of me, Hank sits still.

I press the wet towel against my face.

"Sorry about that," I mumble against the cotton.

"It's fine," Hank says. "You can never hold a bad temper for too long."

I put the towel down. He's right. I seem to have been in a bad mood since I found out Teri is Max's sister. Better to explode here than in a conference room.

"As long as you know I'm not the enemy here," Hank adds.

"I know," I tell him.

"I'm just worried about you, Aaron."

"I'm fine. I've already made up my mind, and I can take care of myself."

Hank raises his hands. "I bet you can." He puts them down on his knees. "Just be careful."

"Of what?"

"Women have a way of twisting men," he says. "Of making them forget who they are, their duties and priorities."

I meet his gaze squarely. "Are you saying I can't handle my wife?"

"I'm saying you're a man. Even the strongest man in the Bible was made a fool of by his wife."

My eyes narrow. "Since when do lawyers read the Bible?"

Hank chuckles.

I pat his arm. "You worry about your women. I'll worry about my wife. Well, no, I won't worry about her."

I get on my feet. "Because I already know what I'm going to do with her."

~

When I get back to my apartment, the first thing I notice is the pair of heels near the door, a sign that I'm no longer living here alone. I don't expect to see Teri, though, not when it's already nearly midnight. Yet when I get to the living room, she's there on the couch, bathing in the glow of the TV screen and wearing a lavender silk robe.

"Hello," she says softly as she gets off the couch.

I can tell she's nervous as she tucks some strands of hair behind her ear and squeezes her fingers.

What? Does she think I'm going to drag her to bed and fuck her? Not a bad idea, actually, but I'm not in the mood.

"What are you? A dog?" I scold her as I shrug off my jacket.

She gives me a confused look.

"You don't have to stay up and wait for me," I explain. "Or greet me when I come home."

"Oh, I didn't..." Teri's shoulders bunch up as she draws a deep breath. "I just thought we should talk."

I grab the bottle of whiskey and a glass from the shelf above the bar.

"About what?"

She glances around. "By the way, your apartment looks great. I wonder if—"

"About what?" I repeat as I pour myself a glass.

I don't have time to listen to her rambling.

"About our... marriage," Teri says.

"What about it?" I lift my glass to my lips.

"I don't really know what I should do." She tucks her hair behind her ear again. "How do you want to go about this?"

"Do you think married couples get a manual?"

She looks at me. "What?"

"We'll figure it out as we go."

"Right." Teri nods. "I haven't told anyone, by the way. When I moved out, I told my sister it was because of work."

I cast her a puzzled look. "You haven't told your family?"

She shakes her head. "No."

"Why not?"

"Well, I..." She fidgets with the sash of her robe. "I don't quite know how or what to tell them."

"You mean you don't want them to know you got yourself married while you were drunk?"

She doesn't answer. Bull's eye.

"Well, you have to tell them at some point," I tell her.

Especially your brother.

"Have you told your family?" she asks me.

"Got none." I take another mouthful of whiskey.

"I see." She rubs her arms. "Well, you're right. I do have to tell my family, but not right away. I'll wait until... things settle down."

Or until she's sure I won't ditch her.

I shrug. "Whatever."

I can't really force her, but I plan on convincing her eventually. I'm in no rush. I've waited seven years.

I finish my drink and leave my empty glass on the counter.

"I'm going to bed." I grab my jacket.

"Good night."

I don't answer or glance back as I walk to my room. I can sense her disappointment, though.

Good. Hopefully, tomorrow, she'll leave me alone.

169

"Good morning," Teri greets me the next day when I go to the kitchen for a glass of water.

Great. First she greets me when I come home. Now she's waiting for me to wake up.

I open the fridge. "I thought I told you to stop acting like a dog."

She shrugs. "I guess I was hoping you'd be in a better mood this morning. Coffee?"

She offers me a mug.

"I have my coffee at the office." I glance at my watch as I drink the water. "Speaking of which, I have to go."

"Right. You have to work."

At least she understands that.

"I'm starting work, too, on Monday. I forgot to tell you that."

I don't care, so I say nothing.

"I'm going to be working at W.H. Clements Interiors. You might have heard—"

"Holly will be dropping by to help you get your wedding ring today." I tap my fingers on the counter. "Choose whatever you like. She'll get mine, too."

"Oh."

Again with the disappointment.

I walk out of the kitchen.

"Aaron?" Teri calls after me.

I sigh. "What?"

"Do you think I can rearrange here a bit or—"

"No. I like the apartment the way it is."

"Right." Even more disappointment.

I walk to the front door and put on my shoes.

Let's see how long it takes before that disappointment turns to despair.

In the evening, I don't see Teri. Good. Maybe she's given up.

The next morning, though, she's in the kitchen again preparing breakfast. So much for giving up.

"Good morning," she greets me as she turns to me in her shirt, jeans and apron. "You don't have work today, do you?"

"No," I answer.

The aroma of bacon fills my nostrils and makes me hungry, but I ignore my stomach and turn away.

"Where are you going?" Teri asks.

"Biking. I do it every Sunday."

"Oh." I hear her turn off the stove. "Can I come with you?"

"No," I answer quickly.

Without giving her an explanation, I leave.

It's already early evening when I return. This time, I find Teri preparing dinner—something Italian judging from the smell of herbs and tomatoes. It smells good, too.

"Where's Ian?" I ask her. "He's the one who cooks dinner for me every Sunday."

"I told him I'd do it," Teri answers.

She brings the ladle to her lips, then stirs the pot again.

"I am your wife, after all."

"You're not a chef, though, with a decade of experience in a Michelin-starred kitchen. Are you?"

Teri looks at me with arched eyebrows. "I…"

"Never mind." I turn my back to her. "I'm not hungry anyway."

I stomp out of the kitchen.

I hear the clang of the ladle and the knob on the stove click. Then footsteps follow me to the living room.

"What is your problem?" Teri grabs my arm.

I turn to face her.

"You," I answer simply.

Her eyebrows bunch up. "What did I do?"

I shrug and lift my hands. "You're always there when I turn around."

Her eyebrows arch in surprise. "You were the one who asked me to live with you."

"Yes, but I didn't ask you to follow me around."

"I'm not—"

"Or to cook for me. Or do anything for me at all." I put my hands on my hips. "This marriage is just a business arrangement. It just happens to be convenient. That's all. It's not like either of us wants it."

Teri looks even more puzzled. "Then why didn't you just go ahead and hand me the divorce papers?"

"Like I said, this is convenient."

I turn and walk off.

Again, she grabs my arm. "What exactly am I to you?"

I glance at her. "My wife on paper. That should keep some annoying women away and show those old geezers on the board that I'm not the selfish, cold-hearted monster they think I am. Not that I care what they think."

Teri frowns. "So you're just using me?"

"And aren't you using me?" I ask her as I turn around. "Holly told me someone called Winona Clements called her. She wanted to talk to me to say that she's given you a job. It sounds like she wants me to owe her, which means she only gave you a job because of me. Am I wrong?"

Teri falls silent as her hand slides off my arm. So I'm right.

"Great." I put my hands together. "We're using each other. That's all. I don't expect you to do chores for me or care for me or whatever it is you think wives should do. As for me, don't expect me to do things for you or with you or be sweet or—"

"Why are you doing this?" she interrupts me as she meets my gaze with narrowed hazel eyes.

"What do you mean?" I ask innocently.

"You weren't like this when we first met," she answers. "You were much nicer."

Oh, that.

I grin. "That's because I was flirting with you. I wanted to fuck you, so I had to be nice, but then I didn't get the chance."

Teri's cheeks grow red. Is it anger or is it embarrassment? I don't know.

"So you were just pretending to be nice."

It's anger.

"Yeah. And this is the real me—selfish and cold-hearted and not giving a damn about you. So get used to it, sweetheart."

I march off to my bedroom.

"I hate you!" Teri shouts after me.

My lips curve into a grin. Good. That's how I want her to feel.

Or so I think until I glance over my shoulder and see her. Her chin has fallen. Tears trickle silently down her cheeks beneath curtains of her hair. Her lips are tightly pursed. Her fists tremble at her sides along with her shoulders.

My eyes grow wide.

I definitely didn't expect this. I expected she'd scream at me and hit me or throw something at me. I expected her to leave the apartment, to get wasted. But I didn't expect this.

Not this woman who right now looks like a defeated little girl with those shoulders that seem to carry the weight of the world.

Just like Marjorie looked when she was five and some other girl picked a fight with her at the playground, or when she was ten and she lost her first football match. Or when she was twelve and she found out that the guy she liked had a girlfriend.

Wave after wave of guilt washes over me. My chest constricts and I can't breathe. A lump forms in my throat.

Aaron Walsh, what have you done?

Chapter Five
Teri

I really hate him.

My nails dig into my palms as my fists crash down on the leather top of my desk. The glass swan paperweight jumps. The two pens in the metal spiral holder slide apart.

Here I am behind my lovely oval desk that still smells like varnish in this spacious office where the natural light streams in beautifully through two round windows and spills onto the teal carpet—my office. I should be beside myself in awe. I should be weeping tears of joy and praising God for whatever has led me here. I've dreamed of this moment for so long, after all. Yet I can't even bring myself to smile, not when my chest still hurts from that fight I had with Aaron.

A sigh of frustration leaves my lips as my shoulders droop.

What is his problem? He's acting like I forced him into marrying me. Wasn't he the one who told me he wasn't going to give me a divorce? And then he told me to move in—told me, not asked. I thought he wanted to give our marriage a shot. But then last night he tells me he doesn't want us to act like a married couple. What is up with that?

So what am I to him? Just a toy for his amusement? A trophy? Some kind of keepsake?

My jaw clenches. My teeth grind together as my nails rake across leather.

I really, really hate him.

"Good morning, Mrs. Walsh. I…"

I turn my head to find a woman in a pink blouse and white pants standing by the door. Her honey blonde hair is tied in a braid. Her lips, which are painted bubblegum pink, remain parted as she stops in the middle of her sentence. Her brown eyes widen.

"I'm sorry," she mumbles as she hugs her tablet to her chest. "I didn't mean to just barge in. It's just that the door was open and…" She looks away. "If this isn't a good time, I'll just…"

"It's fine." I put my hands on my lap as I give her a smile. "Please come in."

She returns my smile as she approaches my desk.

"My name is Elsa." She offers me her hand. "Ms. Clements told me that starting today, I'll be working as your assistant, Mrs. Walsh."

"Please call me Teri," I tell her as I shake her hand. "It's nice to meet you, Elsa."

She glances around the office. "Ms. Clements also said you're to spend this first week making yourself feel at home. Today, I'm supposed to give you a tour and introduce you to everyone, sort of show you the ropes. Then for the rest of the week, you're free to design your office. That's why there isn't much here yet."

That explains all the space.

I tap my fingers on my desk. "Brilliant."

"She said you can do whatever you want with it. Of course, I'm here to help."

I nod. "I appreciate that, Elsa."

She seems like a nice girl. Girl? No, woman. She's the same age as me, I think. Maybe even a year older.

"You sound like someone I can rely on," I tell her. "How long have you been working here?"

"Oh, just a couple of months. I helped my husband design the new website for the company, and afterwards I was offered a job here."

My gaze goes to the gold band on the finger of her left hand, which is similar to what I'm wearing. There was another design I wanted, actually, a textured white gold ring, but it was more expensive. Of course, Aaron could have afforded it, but I wasn't sure I should pick such a glamorous ring when we didn't even have a proper wedding ceremony. It seemed a shame.

"You're married?" I ask Elsa.

"Yes," she answers with obvious pride and joy. "Ms. Clements said you've just been married, too. Congratulations."

Instinctively, my right hand goes over my left. My lips purse as my gaze drifts away.

Congratulations? For what? For getting myself married to a man who doesn't love me, who can barely look at me, who's made it clear that I'm only his wife on paper?

"Mrs.—I mean Teri, is everything alright?" Elsa asks in concern. "You know, you can tell me if there's anything I can do for you, anything at all. I'm here to assist you in any and every way I can."

I look at her and the sincerity in her eyes takes me aback. She's kind, too kind.

"I'm fine, Elsa," I tell her.

"Are you sure?"

Now she looks hopeful. I tap my fingers on the desk as I glance at her ring, then sigh. Oh, what the heck. I may as well take her up on her offer and talk to her, one married woman to another.

"I'm still adjusting to married life, I suppose," I answer.

Elsa nods. "I see."

I look into her eyes. "Did you ever have any problem with that?"

"Oh, not at all." She smiles. "You see, Jonathan and I have been together since high school."

My eyebrows arch. Wow. I thought it was only in movies that high school sweethearts ended up together.

"I think we always knew we'd end up together," Elsa continues. "At least, I did. We just get along so well and I can't imagine being with anyone else. When we got married, it just seemed natural. It felt just like a formality, actually. I don't think anything's really changed."

As she speaks of her fairy tale romance, her eyes glisten. My chest tightens. What is this feeling? Envy?

I touch her arm and force a smile. "That's a beautiful story. I'm happy for you."

"Thanks." She places her hand over mine. "I'm sure things will work out perfectly for you. Every couple just has their own pace."

I'm not so sure.

She touches her chin. "In fact, I know quite a few people who went through the same thing you're going through now."

My eyebrows arch. "Really?"

There are other people who get married by mistake and find that staying married is an even bigger mistake?

"After the honeymoon is over and reality sets in, they feel disoriented. They start to think 'What did I get myself into?' and wonder if they shouldn't have gotten married after all."

Exactly.

"They said their husbands started to change, too. It's like they no longer felt the need to impress them so they started showing their true colors, like being lazy and insensitive."

Aaron showed his true colors, alright.

"But I think that mostly happens when you marry after being in a relationship only for a short while. If you've been with each other long enough, then you've already seen each other's true selves and learned to accept and love them."

Ouch. Could Elsa be more on point?

"Even so, I believe things can still work out," Elsa adds. "Yes, maybe the transition can be tough, but I believe everything will fall into place eventually. Nothing is impossible for two people who are in love."

In that case, Aaron and I are doomed. I don't say that, though. I just put on another smile as I squeeze Elsa's hand.

"Thank you, Elsa."

She gives an even bigger smile.

Just then, I hear a knock on the door. A man wearing a brown cap and carrying a large bouquet of red roses peers in.

"Teri Walsh?"

"Yes," I answer. I think I'm getting used to being called that now.

The man steps in. "I have some flowers for you."

"Oh." I stand up.

174

Elsa steps back so the man can deliver the flowers, which are heavier than I would have thought.

"Here. Let me help you," Elsa offers.

I hand her the bouquet and then sign the receipt. When I'm done, the delivery guy tips his hat and leaves.

I glance at the flowers and spot the small, pink envelope tucked among them.

"I guess these are from Ms. Clements," I say as I grab it.

As soon as my eyes rest on the note hidden in the envelope, though, I realize I'm wrong.

Teri,

Let's start over. I made reservations at Bistro Romano for seven. See you there.

Aaron

I blink and read the note a second time. It reads the same. Even so, I still can't believe it.

Aaron sent me flowers? And now he's asking me to dinner?

"Let me guess," Elsa says. "They're from your husband."

I don't answer as I put the note back in the envelope, but Elsa is already smiling.

"See," she says. "He's coming around."

Is he? I wonder as I sit behind my desk. He's become so unpredictable that I can't tell.

"Um, where do you want these?" Elsa asks as she lifts the bouquet in her arms.

I glance at the flowers.

Red roses. Cliché and not my favorite. Even so, I guess it's the thought that counts.

"Just borrow a vase for now," I say.

Elsa nods and leaves the room with the bouquet.

My gaze lands on the pink envelope.

Let's start over, the note said. But does Aaron mean it? Should I give him another chance?

A sigh escapes me. I guess I'll see at dinner.

~

I arrive at the restaurant a little past seven, having stopped by the apartment first to shower and change into a little black dress. I don't want to show up to the Bistro Romano in wrinkled office clothes, after all.

I've never been here before, but I've heard of it. The reviews said it had a romantic ambience, that the wine was good and the food was worth the price.

As soon as I step through the doors, I tick that first box off my list. The ambience is romantic, alright. Soft light gleams from the lamps overhead. A tall candle glows atop every table covered in white linen. The columns embraced by vines and gilded mirrors evoke the grandeur of ancient Rome, while the combination of the wooden ceiling, stone walls and brick floor make one feel welcome and cozy.

I immediately love it.

The waiter doesn't lead me to one of the tables across the floor, though. Instead, he leads me down the stairs to the wine cellar where, aside from the racks of wine bottles reflecting the golden light, I see a table just for two covered in rose petals. Aaron is already occupying one of the chairs, wearing a fancy woven pale gray shirt with no tie. The top button is undone.

He puts down his glass of wine and stands up when he sees me. Then he glances at his gold watch.

"For a moment there, I thought you wouldn't show."

"I thought I'd keep you waiting for a bit," I say.

The waiter pulls out my chair and I sit. Aaron does the same. I feel his gaze on me as the waiter pours the wine.

"You're still pissed," he says after the waiter has left.

I don't answer. Am I?

"You didn't like the roses?" Aaron picks up one of the crimson petals on the table. "I thought you would."

I shrug as I wrap my fingers around the stem of my wineglass. "You mean just as you thought I'd like being made to feel like some random prize you won in a lottery you didn't even want to join?"

Aaron's eyes narrow. "You are pissed."

I lift the glass of wine to my lips to take a sip, then smack them. "Mmm. The wine here is good."

I take another sip.

"Easy," Aaron warns. "You don't want to get drunk again."

"Why not?" I glance at him. "I've already made the worst mistake a drunk person could. What else do I have to fear?"

"Getting pregnant."

I nearly choke on the wine, then blush as I meet his gaze. Those ebony eyes seem to be smoldering as they hold mine. I swallow.

"You do know how that happens, don't you? Even though you're a virgin." He leans forward. "Or do you want me to explain? Or demonstrate?"

His fingertips brush against mine and my breath catches. I pull my hand away.

"No, thank you." I try to keep my voice from quivering as I lift my chin. "I'm well aware of it."

For a moment, he says nothing, his piercing gaze causing knots in my stomach. Then he grins.

"Just kidding." He lifts his glass to his mouth. "I would never do that to someone who was drunk, even if she was my wife."

And yet his words and the heat from his gaze just now linger in the air. I try to shake it off.

"I thought you didn't think of me as your wife."

"I never said that."

"You did."

"I didn't."

I pause to think. Fine, maybe he didn't say that exactly.

"But you acted like it," I tell him. "And actions speak louder than words."

"Which is why I invited you to dinner," Aaron says. "Let's call a truce, shall we? Enough with the open hostilities."

I open my mouth to say that he started it, but don't. It doesn't matter anyway. He's reaching out to me right now, and as unsure as I am if I should forgive him, I have to admit I can't go on hating him.

"Fine," I give in.

"Good." He raises his glass. "Shall we toast to that?"

I pick mine up and let it touch his, then take another sip. He finishes his wine. Afterwards, he glances at the waiter to let him know we're ready for our food.

Good. I'm getting hungry.

"So, how was your first day at work?" Aaron asks.

"Great," I answer. "My assistant, Elsa, is really nice. And everyone else seemed nice, too."

Well, I did notice some eyes rolling. I'm sure some people aren't happy that I got a high position so quickly when I've just started in the firm. But no one dared say it out loud.

"And the work?"

"Oh, I haven't really started yet," I say. "But I'm sure it will be fun."

Aaron taps his fingers on the table. "Why interior design?"

I shrug. "My mom gave me a dollhouse once and I just thought it was too plain so I started making it pretty. And then when I got my own room, I started working on it, too. I guess I just like making beautiful spaces."

He nods. "And where is your mother now?"

"Oh, she's..." I let out a deep breath. "My mother passed away a long time ago. So did my father."

"We're the same, then."

He did say he didn't have a family.

"But I have parents. Adoptive parents."

"And siblings?"

"I have an older sister, Pam."

"And a brother?" Aaron asks.

I pause. "Yeah. But we haven't spoken in a long time."

In fact, I can't remember the last time we spoke. I wonder how he's doing.

"Why not?"

I narrow my eyes. "What? Are you interrogating me now?"

Aaron grins. "Just getting to know my wife."

Before I can answer that, the antipasti arrives—mussels with shallots, a white wine sauce and garlic butter served with bread. My mouth waters.

I pick up my fork. "Well, here's one thing for you to know—I do love Italian food."

"I noticed."

I pop one of the mussels inside my mouth and close my eyes as I savor the explosion of flavors. Romantic ambience. Good wine. Good food. This restaurant really is everything they said it would be.

"This is really good," I say when I'm done chewing.

Aaron smiles. "Anything else you want me to know?"

"Hmm." I touch the tip of the fork to my lower lip. "Let's see."

~

"I should have known you'd drink too much," Aaron says as he closes the door to the apartment behind me.

"I'm not drunk," I tell him as I take off my shoes.

Sure, maybe I did drink one glass too many—how could I not when the wine was so good?—and I do feel a little warm and light-headed, but I still see just one of everything and I'm still standing up straight. Well, sort of.

"Easy." Aaron wraps a hand around my waist. "Let's get you to a bed this time, shall we?"

"Whoa." I push him away and lean against the wall. "I may be a virgin but you're not getting me into your bed that easily."

"I didn't say—"

"You think I don't know what you're thinking?" I raise a finger as I cut him off. "I know what couples do after they go out for dinner."

"And I already told you I don't have sex with drunk women."

I shake my head. "Except I'm not drunk."

Aaron lifts his hands. "Fine. You're not." He steps away from me. "And I'm going. To my own bed. Alone."

He turns his back to me and walks off.

I frown as I stare at his back. He's really leaving me alone just like that? Somehow, I feel disappointed.

"Thanks for dinner," I find myself saying.

He glances over his shoulder.

"And good night," I add as I look into his eyes.

For a moment, Aaron just stands there. Then the next thing I know he's walking towards me. Before I can even understand what's going on, his mouth descends on mine. I can't breathe. He sucks on my lower lip as his hand caresses my cheek. Heat swirls in my chest and gathers in the pit of my stomach.

My eyelids fall shut. My lips part and Aaron's tongue slips past. I shiver as it brushes against mine. I taste wine, and the heat from it travels all the way to the tips of my toes.

Mmm. Just as I thought, it's good wine, and it's even better from his mouth. Sweeter. Stronger. More intoxicating.

I want more.

I'm about to place my hand behind his neck as I open my mouth wider, but suddenly he pulls away.

"Good night," Aaron says as his eyes hold my wide ones. Then he walks off.

I remain standing against the wall with my mouth still gaping, my head spinning even more than before.

Did I just get my first real kiss?

Chapter Six
Aaron

I shouldn't have kissed Teri.

I scold myself as I run my hands through my hair in the shower. Drops of cold water slide down my skin, dousing the embers beneath.

I should have headed on to my room. Instead, I stopped and turned. Before I knew it, I was marching back to her.

Was it because of that black dress she had on with the strings in front that were just begging to be unlaced? Was it because of that expression of bliss that she wore all throughout dinner as she savored every course? Or maybe it was because her waist fit perfectly in my hand when I tried to keep her from falling. Or the way her eyes shimmered when she said good night.

Whatever it was, my body moved before I could think. My mouth ended up on hers.

And damn, it felt good. So good I almost didn't want to stop.

Almost.

Teri didn't want me to stop. It was clear from the look of dismay in her eyes when I did stop that she had already given in to her own desires, to me. In spite of all she said earlier, if I had continued, she wouldn't have minded it. She would even have enjoyed it, just as she enjoyed dinner.

No. She would have enjoyed it a lot more.

I would have made her enjoy it. I would have made her tremble and cry out. I would have commanded her body and consumed her soul. Just the thought of it now makes me throb.

Still, I stopped. I had to. Yes, I may have told myself I wasn't going to be outright mean to her anymore. It was getting exhausting acting like a constantly pissed drill sergeant anyway. But I haven't forgotten she's Max's sister.

The hostilities may be over, but I can still make Teri's life miserable enough for her to go crying to her brother, for him to suffer as he realizes what I've done and why.

As I turn off the shower, I grin.

I fully intend to.

~

"You're giving me a bodyguard?" Teri's hazel eyes grow wide as she finally tears them away from the laptop.

"Yes," I answer as I lean over her desk. "I stopped by just to tell you that."

Teri blinks. "Why?"

"Because you're my wife." I walk towards the window. "I have enemies, you know. And even if I didn't, you're the wife of a billionaire, a businessman, a—"

"I know who I'm married to," she cuts me off.

I turn my head and find Teri with her arms crossed over her chest, the corners of her mouth drooping in a pout.

"Then you know why I have to assign you a bodyguard," I say.

She shrugs. "I don't see you with any."

"Because I can take care of myself."

"So can I."

I shake my head. "I'm not asking for your permission."

"Why would you?" Her hands rise and then fall to her sides as she stands up. "You never asked me to marry you. You never asked if I wanted to move in with you. And you certainly never asked for permission to kiss me."

One of my eyebrows rises. Oh, she's pissed about that, is she?

I lean on the wall with one arm. "Why would I when you were begging to be kissed?"

Teri's jaw drops as her eyes grow wide. "I was not begging—"

"You were." I approach her with my hands in my pockets. "Otherwise, why didn't you push me away when I kissed you?"

"Because—"

"In fact, if I recall, you seemed disappointed when I stopped."

Her jaw clenches as she glares. Then she snorts as she turns away.

"Disappointed? You were drunk, so how would you know?"

I almost laugh. I was the one who was drunk?

"I wasn't deaf, though, and I heard you whimper," I tease.

She turns to face me. "Or you heard me groaning because you were such a lousy kisser."

Ouch.

I want to kiss her right now just to prove I'm not. Instead, I cross my arms over my chest.

"Chad will be your bodyguard and that's final," I tell her.

Teri says nothing.

"Oh, and he'll be reporting everything you do to me, too," I add. "So try not to do anything embarrassing."

She gives a gasp of horror. "You can't order someone to spy on me."

I lean over her as I grin. "I just did, honey."

Teri pouts. "You—"

She stops talking as the door opens. A woman in her fifties with anchor-shaped earrings and gold streaks in her silver hair enters the room. Her pale blue eyes grow wide as they meet mine.

"Mr. Walsh!"

She walks towards me with the briskness of a woman half her age and the composure of a British dame. My guess is she's Teri's boss.

"I'm Winona Clements, the founder of this firm," she confirms my suspicion as she takes my hand in both of hers. "It's a pleasure to meet you."

I give her a smile. "The pleasure is all mine. My wife has told me so much about you."

"Has she?" Winona glances at Teri, who's also smiling now. "Well, I can't tell you how pleased I am to have her join my firm. I'm honored, really."

I place my arm over Teri's shoulder. "And I can't tell you how grateful I am that you've given my wife a chance to show you what she can do."

"Oh, you don't have to thank me for anything." Winona waves her hand in front of her face. "Although if you insist on giving us a thirty percent discount on all our shipments, I'll gladly accept."

A shrewd and straightforward woman. No wonder she's successful.

"I'll have someone look into it," I answer.

Teri looks surprised.

"So, what brings you here?" Winona asks me. "Were you just checking on Teri, or…?"

"Yes." I squeeze Teri's shoulder. "I just wanted to see her office."

Winona glances around. "Well, I'm sure it will be lovely once she's done fixing it up."

"I'll do my best," Teri says.

"And to see her, of course, even though I just saw her this morning." I run my fingers through Teri's hair. "I just can't seem to get enough of my wife."

Teri gives me a look of disbelief.

I touch her cheek. "And you feel the same way, don't you, honey?"

Her mouth gapes. I can tell she wants to hurl more insults at me, but then she glances at her boss and she smiles.

"Yeah."

Winona clasps her hands together. "Oh, how wonderful. The two of you are just the picture of a perfect couple."

Yup. We have her fooled.

"Tell me, how did the two of you meet?"

I feel Teri tense beside me.

"Oh, we met at a party," I say. "One of my friend's parties."

"Right," Teri seconds.

It's the truth, after all.

"I saw her in a corner all by herself and I just fell in love at first sight," I add. "I knew then and there I had to have her."

Teri gives a light cough.

Winona smiles widely. "And of course, what woman could refuse Aaron Walsh?"

Teri coughs again.

I rub her back. "Are you alright, sweetie?"

"I'm fine." She places a hand around her throat. "I'm just having a hard time swallowing something."

"I'll tell Elsa to get you some water," Winona says. "And what about you, Mr. Walsh? Coffee? Tea? Something stronger?"

I lift a hand. "No, thank you. I was just about to leave."

"Oh." She looks disappointed.

I pat Teri's back. "As much as I'd like to stay by Teri's side every second of every day, I can't. Which is why I'm leaving someone else to watch over her."

Teri purses her lips.

"I'm assigning Teri a bodyguard," I tell Winona. "I hope you don't mind."

"Oh, no." The older woman shakes her head. "Not at all."

"I do," Teri speaks up. "Really, honey, I can take care of myself."

She puts on a sweet smile.

I touch her cheek. "But I'd feel better if someone was watching over you."

"I think it's a wise decision, actually," Winona adds. She meets Teri's gaze. "Your husband is a powerful man, my dear. What if someone uses you to get to him? Or against him?"

"Exactly." I cast Winona a grateful glance.

Teri lets out a sigh as her shoulders sink. She knows she can't protest now. Not against both her husband and her boss.

I kiss the top of her head. "See you later, sweetheart."

I whisper in her ear, "If you don't wipe that pout off, I'll do it myself in front of your boss."

Her shoulders grow rigid beneath my hands. When I look at her again, I find her cheeks red.

I grin as I squeeze her shoulder.

"And do get along with Chad for me."

Teri doesn't answer. I head towards the door but let Winona leave the office ahead of me. As I grasp the doorknob, I glance over my shoulder. Teri glares at me, mouthing the words "I so hate you."

I chuckle as I blow her a kiss.

Chapter Seven
Teri

Having a bodyguard is so not funny.

The corners of my lips turn down as I glance at Chad, who seems to be innocently looking at some cans of paints just like I am.

Indeed, he looks like just another customer at this hardware store. He looks like an ordinary guy, in fact. No dark sunglasses. Nothing plugged into his ear. No bulletproof vest. No gun at his hip. No weapon as far as I can see.

And he doesn't look dangerous, either. Fit? Yes. Athletic, even. He looks like a marathon runner with that dark skin and those lean muscles. But dangerous? Aaron looks like more of a bodyguard than him.

How I wish he was just another ordinary guy. But no. He's been shadowing me since yesterday, never more than three feet behind me unless I'm in the restroom or safely back at the apartment. I'm still not used to it. Even when I'm not glancing over my shoulder, I know he's there, and sometimes I can't help but feel chained or suffocated.

And Chad isn't just my bodyguard. He's a spy, too. Seriously, I don't know why I'd need someone spying on me. What does Aaron think I do when I'm out of his sight? What could I do? Spill his secrets? I don't even know them. Spend his money? He only gave me one credit card. Or does he think I'm going to run away? If I was, I would have done it already.

Besides, who tells the person you're spying on that you're spying on them? Doesn't that defeat the point? Really, Aaron could just have hired Chad and told him to watch me without me knowing. He'd still get his information—more accurate information since I wouldn't be on my guard—and I'd still be protected. Why tell me?

"Can I help you?" A salesman interrupts my thoughts.

I smile at him. "No, thanks. I can make up my own mind. I just… need to consider a few things."

"Take your time."

He walks off to assist someone else. I catch Chad eyeing him suspiciously.

I touch my chin. Wait. Is Chad supposed to keep other men away from me like I'm a concubine in Aaron's harem and he's the eunuch making sure no one else touches me or so much as looks in my direction? Now, that's funny. And also annoying. I'm not one of Aaron's belongings, and so he doesn't need to treat me like one.

I cross my arms over my chest as I approach Chad. "Would you have punched that poor guy if I actually accepted his help?"

Chad doesn't answer. Oh, right. He doesn't talk. It's weird, really. I'm well aware of his presence, but he still tries to pretend he doesn't exist.

"You have permission to talk, you know," I tell him. "No. You don't need anyone's permission. You have a right to. You're not a robot, just as I'm not some prized possession that needs watching over."

Still he says nothing.

I grab the paint fan deck hanging from the shelf.

"Which shade of green do you like better? This or this?"

Chad glances at them but says nothing.

I sigh. "What? You're not allowed to have an opinion, either? Even if I'm asking for it? Aren't you supposed to be helping me?"

He lifts his hand and points to the lighter shade of green without saying a word. Well, at least he responded.

I nod. "Yeah, I like that better, too. The darker one reminds me of artichokes and I hate artichokes. Do you like artichokes?"

This time, he doesn't give me a response.

"So you don't answer personal questions, huh? Or you can't."

No answer.

"It must suck, not being able to talk all day, being so close to me but acting like a complete stranger. If not a ghost. And constantly watching over me when I'm such a boring person. I don't know how you stay sane. I probably wouldn't be able to."

Still nothing.

I put my hands on my hips. "Did you always want to be a bodyguard, or did you actually dream of living your own life?"

When Chad still doesn't answer, I draw a deep breath.

"Fine. I give up. I feel like I'm talking to a wall here."

I walk down the aisle but stop in my tracks when I spot the man who's just entered it.

Red hair. Pierced chin. He's not wearing a white suit now, just a white shirt and jeans, but I can still tell it's him.

The wanker.

As our eyes meet, he stops too, and I see the flicker of recognition in his eyes. A knot forms in my throat.

He grins. "Hey. I think I've seen you before."

I swallow before continuing to walk as normally as I can. "I'm sorry. You must be mistaken."

"I don't think so." He grabs my arm. "I never forget a pretty face. And you look just as shocked as you did that night, too."

I try to yank my arm away, but he grips it tighter.

"Why don't you and I have dinner? I promise I won't bite—"

"The lady's with me," Chad says as he takes the pervert's hand off my arm.

He breaks into his throaty laugh. "You're kidding, right?"

Chad ushers me away.

The man keeps talking. "I'm sure I've got a bigger dick than that guy."

I roll my eyes, then glance at Chad, who doesn't seem the least bit affected.

"You know, if you punch him, I wouldn't mind it at all," I tell him.

"Fine. Walk away like you did last time," the man says. "But I'm sure we'll meet again."

Chad goes still. He takes a deep breath. Then he turns and walks towards the man. I follow him but stop as I see him twist the man's arm.

"If you ever come near her again or show your face around her, I'll break your arm off," I hear him threaten.

The man, whose face is twisted in agony, nods.

Chad lets him go, then turns to me and offers me his hand. "Let's go."

I take his hand and let him lead me to the exit. I'm still speechless from the recent turn of events, still in shock. But outside the store, just after he lets my hand go, I finally recover.

"Hey."

He turns to me and I smile.

"I like you better when you talk."

~

"Chad told me he scared off a creepy guy at the hardware store today," Aaron says as he stands in the living room.

I'm sitting on the rug with my legs crossed in a lotus position, my laptop on the coffee table in front of me right next to a pile of magazines and other sheets of paper. I look up.

"That's true. He looked cool doing it, too."

Aaron says nothing.

"Well, he looked scary at first, but then he looked really cool." I touch my chin. "You know, maybe having a bodyguard isn't so bad. I actually think Chad and I can get along."

Aaron nods. "That's good."

I watch him walk away with creased eyebrows. Is it my imagination, or did he sound just a tad disappointed?

182

I shrug as I fix my gaze back on the screen of my laptop.

At any rate, I really think Chad and I will get along better now.

~

"Here." I shove a lamp into Chad's arms, which are also weighed down by a can of paint, a coil of wire, a curtain rod and some drawer handles.

I didn't get to buy anything yesterday, so I had to come back to get my hardware supplies.

I rub the dust off my hands. "I think that's it."

"You sure?" Chad asks.

I smile. Finally, I've managed to get him to talk.

"Yeah." I nod. "With these, I can finally get started on the hard work and transform my office. You will help me, won't you?"

Chad nods.

Okay. Maybe he still doesn't talk much. But at least now I don't feel like I'm talking to a wall.

"Okay. Let's go pay for these."

I lead the way towards the cashier but stop when I realize Chad isn't following me. I turn my head and find that he's not even watching me. His gaze is directed towards an unaccompanied boy of about four or five in the opposite aisle.

The boy is on the tips of his toes, reaching for a hammer on the shelf.

My jaw drops in disbelief. Where the hell are this kids' parents? Why isn't anyone watching him? What if he—?

I'm still thinking it when it happens. The boy gets the hammer but it's too heavy and he drops it.

I clasp a hand over my mouth as I gasp, fearful that the hammer will fall on his foot. But at the last second, someone grabs him and pulls him back. The hammer clatters on the floor.

My hand falls as I let out a sigh of relief. Then my eyes grow wide as I realize it's Chad who helped the boy.

I watch as he kneels in front of the shocked boy, talking to him and making sure he's alright. As the parents come running, he steps back. The boy runs to his mother and starts crying. The father talks to Chad and then pats his shoulder. A salesman comes to check on the situation as Chad picks up the hammer and puts it back on the shelf. Then he picks up my stuff, which he put down to run and help the child.

"Wow," I say when he's next to me. "You saved that boy."

"Sorry I left you for a second," he says.

I shake my head. "You did the right thing. Maybe it's not your job, but it was the right thing to do."

Chad glances over his shoulder at the boy, who's stopped crying. His mouth gives a hint of a smile as I see the relief on his face.

My eyes narrow. "Do you have kids?"

He hesitates for a moment before answering. "One."

"A boy about his age?"

He nods.

"What's his name?"

"Wade."

I smile. "Nice name. I'm sure he's a nice kid."

"He is," Chad agrees. "He gets in trouble sometimes, too, though."

I shrug. "What kid doesn't?"

Chad just grins.

I cross my arms over my chest. "So, what's the worst trouble he's ever got himself into?"

"Hmm." Chad pauses to think. "Maybe when he reached for the cookie jar and it fell into the sink and broke."

My eyebrows arch and I shake my head. "Good thing it didn't fall on him."

"Yeah. Lucky."

"So he likes cookies?"

"Anything sweet."

"Your wife buys them or bakes them?"

"She'd like to bake them, but she says it's too hard and she can't get it done right."

"Really?" I glance at him. "You know, my sister happens to bake. She sells the stuff she bakes, too. I used to help her. I think I wrote down the tips and tricks she gave me. I can share them with you if you like."

Chad shakes his head. "You're too kind, but it's too much."

"No, it's not," I tell him. "I'm sure your wife will love it. Your son, too."

He sighs. "Mrs. Walsh…"

"Teri," I correct him. "And don't worry, I won't tell Aaron."

~

After we get back to the apartment, I make Chad wait near the front door while I go get the notebook where I scribbled Pam's baking tips. I hand it to him.

"Here you go."

He looks at the notebook. "I thought you were just giving me a copy."

"You can have mine," I press the notebook into his hand. "I don't have time to bake anymore anyway, and if I ever do get the urge, I think I know those tips by heart by now. Or I can just call my sister if I ever forget."

"Sure?"

I nod.

He puts the notebook in his pocket. "Thanks."

As he does, I notice a cut near his elbow. I'm pretty sure it wasn't there earlier today.

"What happened to your arm?" I ask him.

"Oh, it's nothing." He puts his arm behind him.

I scratch my chin. "You hurt yourself when you were trying to hang those paintings in my office, didn't you?"

"It's nothing, really," Chad says. "You don't have to concern yourself, Mrs.—"

I grab his arm. "We need to put a bandage on that."

"That's not—"

"Do you want your wife and son to worry about you? Better me than them, right?"

He finally falls silent. I grab the antiseptic spray and a Band-Aid from the bathroom cabinet.

"Something tells me you didn't really want to be a bodyguard," I say as I spray the wound. "I mean, this is a dangerous job. Well, maybe guarding me isn't, but in general it's a dangerous job. What if something bad happened to you? I'm sure you don't want to leave your son without a father, your wife without a husband."

He doesn't answer. I place the bandage over the wound.

"There. That's better."

Just then, though, the door to the apartment opens. Aaron walks in. His eyes grow wide as he sees Chad and me standing in the living room.

Chad immediately steps back. "I was about to leave, sir."

Aaron nods. After Chad leaves, he turns to me.

"What was going on here?" he asks me.

"Nothing." I shrug. "We were just talking. Is that not allowed?"

His eyes narrow. "Really?"

Aaron walks away and I'm left with my hands on my hips, puzzled.

Again, this might just be my imagination, but for a moment there, I thought I sensed a bit of tension. Was Aaron jealous?

Chapter Eight
Aaron

"I'm not jealous," I tell Teri clearly as I haul my body up the stony trail.

Above me, the sunlight drills holes into the tree canopy, creating flecks of gold on the ground. A breeze blows, cooling the sweat that has seeped into the front of my shirt.

Teri stops in front of me. Again. She bends over, leaning on her elbows as she chases after her breath.

"Then why did you fire Chad?" she asks after she's caught it.

I put a hand on my hip. "I thought you didn't want a bodyguard."

"Since when do you do what I want?" Teri opens her water bottle.

I shrug. "Say what you will, but Chad didn't lose his job because of you. He asked me to let him go."

That's true. He mumbled something about wanting to be in a less dangerous line of work because he had a young kid, and I recommended him to be a friend's driver. But I was going to let him go anyway, not because of jealousy—seriously, that's not an emotion I'm weak enough to possess—but because he wasn't making Teri's life miserable. Quite the opposite.

Besides, it's clear that she hasn't been contacting Max. Nor does she seem to have any intention of doing that.

"Did he say why?" Teri puts the lid on her water bottle.

"None of your business."

"Excuse me? I was the person he was guarding, shadowing."

"And I'm the one who asked him to do that, who paid him to do that," I point out.

Both of her hands go to her hips as she straightens up. "You are jealous."

I snort and continue hiking, going past her.

"Is that why you're punishing me?"

I stop and turn my head. "I'm punishing you?"

Teri nods. "Yes. By forcing me to go hiking with you when you've never asked me to do anything with you before and you know perfectly that I don't like the outdoors."

I tilt my head to one side. "Do I?"

Actually, I do. And yes, maybe this is some form of punishment, but not for flirting with Chad. She's had a pretty good week. I'm throwing some suffering into the mix to even things out, even if it is physical suffering.

She lets out a sigh. "So you're not punishing me?"

"Do you want me to?"

"No," she answers after a pause. "Because there's no reason for you to be jealous, although of course it's perfectly natural since I'm your wife—"

"And you're hot and smart and I'd die without you," I finish the sentence sarcastically.

Teri pouts.

Now I've gone too far. What is it with her that makes it so hard for me to rein in my temper?

I keep walking. Her footsteps trail after me.

"Fine. You're not jealous," she says. "Just mean."

"I never said I'd be nice."

She lets out another sigh.

I turn to her. "What? You want me to carry you?"

She lifts her hands as she walks past me. "Don't bother. How much further to the cabin?"

I shrug. "An hour or two."

Teri meets my gaze. "This cabin better be charming."

I grin. "I think you'll like it."

~

"Which part exactly did you think I'd like?" Teri gapes as she looks around the cabin.

The furniture is dusty. Cobwebs hang from the corners of the ceiling. There's a pile of clothes on the couch. There are books on the bed, dirty plates and empty wine bottles on the coffee table, tools on the kitchen counter, glass fragments from a broken vase on the rug in front of the fireplace. The lampshade has a gaping hole in it. The stool near the window is missing a leg and the bookcase on the wall is crooked.

Sweet. It's just as I left it.

I scratch the back of my head. "I guess I was having a bit of a party the last time I was here and I probably left in a hurry."

Teri's eyebrows arch. "You guess? Probably?"

She walks towards the couch and grabs a yellow dress from the pile.

"And I guess you weren't alone."

I shrug. "Who's jealous now?"

She pouts as she drops the dress. She picks up the lamp with the broken shade next.

"When was the last time you were here?"

"Maybe a year ago," I answer. "I've been busy."

Teri turns to me. "And it didn't occur to you to send someone here ahead of us to clean it up?"

"No. Not too many people know about this cabin, and I prefer to keep it that way."

"I see." She puts down the lamp and then grimaces as she looks at her dusty fingers. "And do you prefer to keep this cabin messy, too?"

"Fine," I say. "I'll have someone clean it up. And fix it up, too."

"When?"

I give another shrug. "Next week. Or next month. Soon."

Teri's eyebrows crease. "Are you saying we're going back down the mountain?"

"Hell, no." I pat my backpack. "I've got a hammock right here. I can sleep outside."

Her jaw drops. "What?"

"You can sleep outside, too." I glance at the closet. "There's a sleeping bag there and it should still be good."

Teri places her hands on her hips. "You want me to sleep on the cold ground?"

"In a warm sleeping bag," I correct her. "It should be soft enough."

"And what if bugs creep inside? What if a bird decides to use my face as a bathroom in the morning?"

Just as I thought, she really doesn't like the outdoors.

"Or what if you roll out of your sleeping bag and wake up covered in dirt?" I add.

She pouts.

I go over to her and pat her shoulder. "You'll be fine."

"No." Teri shakes her head. "I'm not sleeping outside."

"Then sleep here," I suggest. "You'll have a roof over your head. There's a bed…"

"You want me to sleep in the middle of this mess?"

"The way I see it, you only have two choices."

She looks around again, then sighs. "Fine. I'll clean the place up."

Well, I didn't expect that.

"Are you sure?" I ask her. "Because we just finished hiking and I'm sure you're tired and—"

"I said I'll clean the place up," Teri repeats. "Are you going to help me or not?"

"I'm sleeping outside," I tell her.

"Fine." She points to the door. "Then go outside so I can get started here."

~

Teri is still at it, I think as I turn my head to glance at the cabin from my hammock.

The lights are on and I can hear clanging and clattering from inside. I can hear music, too.

What is she doing in there? Wasn't she just going to dust a little and tidy up a bit? It's already nearly midnight and she's still working hard. Doesn't she plan on sleeping at all?

I yawn and turn on my side. Whatever. If she wants to keep being a clean freak, that's fine with me. I'm going to sleep. And tomorrow, I'm going fishing.

186

~

When I come back from fishing, I find the door to the cabin open.

"Hey, Teri!" I shout as I approach the building. "Are you hungry? I was able to catch some…"

I pause in the doorway as I gaze at the inside of the cabin, which looks completely different from yesterday. In fact, it seems like a whole new cabin. Not only is it tidy—the couch, bed, coffee table and kitchen counter are all clear—but she also fixed things up. The lamp has a new shade which looks like it's made from that yellow dress. The cases of the two pillows on the couch seem like they're made from the same material. The stool has a new leg, an old piece of firewood from the looks of it. The wine bottles have been decorated and made into candlesticks on the mantel. The bookcase is still crooked, but the books are back inside, held there by pieces of rope.

"Wow," I have to say. "You really did a number on this place."

"I guess I did." Teri beams with pride as she leans on the kitchen counter. "Once I started, I just couldn't stop working."

"I heard."

She glances at me. "So, do you have breakfast? Or should I say brunch? I'm hungry and I've already finished my snacks."

"I have fish." I lift the cooler hanging from my arm. "I was planning on grilling them outside."

"You do that," Teri says. "And then we can eat in here."

~

"That fish tasted better than I thought it would," Teri remarks later after the meal. "And here I thought you didn't know how to cook."

"I never said that, did I?" I sit back on the couch. "What's better than I ever thought it would be is this cabin."

She looks at me curiously.

"What?" I ask her.

"Nothing." She leans back as well. "I've just never seen you so impressed. With me, that is."

She glances at me.

"You're not going to change your mind about that, are you?"

I give her a puzzled look. "Why would I?"

"Because you seem to change your mind a lot. You ask me to move in and then pretend I don't exist."

"You're still not over that?"

"You yell at me and then you give me flowers. You give me a bodyguard even though I was so against it and then you take him away."

"Like I said, I didn't take him away. And can we stop talking about the past?"

Teri shrugs. "I'm just saying you like this cabin so much now, but you might hate it the next time you come here."

"I won't," I assure her. "You're a talented interior designer. That's not my opinion. It's a fact. Facts don't change."

She turns to me with creased eyebrows. "And you're saying that just because I swept the floor of this cabin, washed the dirty dishes and cleared away the cobwebs?"

"That's not all you did and you know it."

"Oh. Is this what you're referring to?" She runs her hand over one of the pillowcases. "Pretty, isn't it? The fabric is beautiful. The last woman you brought here had good taste in clothes."

I shrug. Frankly, I don't remember her, with or without her clothes.

"It's not just the pillows, either, or the lampshade," I tell her. "It's everything."

"That doesn't mean I'm a talented interior designer, though." Teri sighs as she hugs the pillow. "Cabins are easy to design. They're cozy. They have their own character built in. But houses in the city? Apartments? You have to breathe life into them. You have to give them their own sense of style, and sometimes, not everyone likes how they end up looking."

"Well, you can't please everyone."

"I can't even please a lot of people," Teri says. "Do you know that most people think my designs are too plain? Too safe? That they're not expressive or creative enough?"

"Then why did Winona Clements hire you?"

She narrows her eyes at me.

Okay. Wrong question.

"Maybe you just need more experience," I say.

She shrugs. "Maybe."

"And I'm not just talking about work experience. Maybe you have to live a little more, you know, try more things. Do more. Feel more."

Now her eyebrows are bunched up.

"What?"

"That's what you told me the first time we met, too."

"Really?"

"Yes. You told me to loosen up a little, to take more chances. And look where I ended up."

I turn to her with a grin. "Yeah, look."

And Teri does, with disbelief in her eyes. Then she shakes her head before resting it against the couch.

"Your ego is just as big as your biceps. Do you know that?"

"What? That I've got big biceps?" I lift an arm.

She sighs. "Isn't it exhausting trying to be perfect all the time?"

"Except I'm not trying."

"Seriously, where does all this confidence come from?" She yawns. "And can we talk about something else?"

"Like?"

"Anything else."

"Fine." I fold my arms behind my head and gaze up at the ceiling. "I'll talk about the woman I was here with last time. I think I remember her now. Cheryl, I think. Or was it Carrie? Something like that. I told her she was stupid to bring a dress, but then I don't think she was very bright. She was a good dancer, though, very lithe and…"

I stop talking because I feel a weight against my chest. I glance down and see a head of mahogany hair tucked just beneath my chin.

I put my hand on Teri's shoulder and shake her lightly. "Hey."

She responds with a groan.

I cradle her jaw and tilt her face towards me. Her eyelids are shut.

Great. She's asleep. Then again, I suppose that's no surprise since she barely slept last night and did so much work, not to mention the hiking yesterday. I should be surprised she even lasted this long.

My gaze falls on her lashes, which look thicker up close. The tip of her nose looks more pointed, too, and I can see the edges of her upper lip.

My thumb wanders across her smooth cheek.

How can a woman with such beautiful features—strong and delicate at the same time—have so little confidence in herself?

For a moment, I'm seized by the desire to wake Teri with a kiss, but I let that moment pass. Instead, I carry her to the bed. I could leave her on the couch, but I don't want her to wake up with any aching muscles. After all, who knows how long she'll be asleep?

As I set her down on the bed, she gives another groan, then turns on her side and curls. Her hair forms a fuzzy puddle around her head. I can almost hear her even breathing.

I drape the blanket over her shoulders and step back.

I won't be surprised if she sleeps until tomorrow morning.

188

Chapter Nine
Teri

I wake up to the caress of sunlight on my cheek. I open my eyes and see it drifting in through the window. My eyebrows crease.

It's morning already? How many hours have I been asleep?

Well, I didn't sleep straight. I woke up last night to use the bathroom, and then I lay in bed for a while, thinking. Then I fell asleep again. I must have been more tired than I thought.

I stretch my arms. Well, I'm not tired anymore. In fact, I feel refreshed.

I get out of bed, make it and head to the bathroom. As I brush my teeth, I hear bangs from outside.

Wait. Are those gunshots?

When I go out, I find Aaron with a pistol in his hand, shooting at cans lined up on a bench. His hair is tied back, his eyes completely focused on his targets. His biceps bulge where the sleeves of his shirt meet bare skin. Each time he pulls the trigger, his body jerks just a little before he recovers and aims again.

Cool and composed. And hot.

Do guys with guns always look this hot?

Finally, he finishes a magazine. As he reloads the gun, he turns his head towards me and grins. I quickly look away as I fake a yawn.

"I was wondering when you'd wake up," Aaron says.

"Well, I was tired." I stretch my neck. "But I'm feeling much better now."

"I bet."

I walk towards him. "What are you doing?"

He glances at the gun in his hand. "Shooting, obviously. This is about one of the few places I can keep myself sharp."

I look at the cans, all of which have holes in them. "You do seem sharp."

He gives a wider grin. "I'm good at everything I do."

I snort but take a step closer. "Think you can teach me?"

Aaron's eyebrows furrow. "What?"

"Teach me how to fire a gun," I tell him. "That way, I can protect myself, especially now that I no longer have a bodyguard. Weren't you the one who said I need protection?"

He shakes his head. "I'm not getting you a gun."

"Just teach me how to hold one. Let me fire a few rounds."

He says nothing.

I clasp my hands together. "Please?"

For a moment, Aaron just stares at me. Then he exhales.

"Fine. Come here."

I smile as I stand beside him. He places the gun in my hand.

"Grip it firmly, just like when you're shaking someone's hand. Not too tight." He adjusts my fingers. "And use your other hand as support."

He takes my left hand and places it beneath my right. Then he moves behind me and I can feel his body just inches away. I can smell the sweat off him. My heart races.

Okay. Maybe this wasn't such a good idea.

"Keep your arms straight." He runs his hands over my arms. "Put your left foot forward."

I do that. Slowly.

His abdomen brushes against my back and I tense. The next thing I know, his knee is between my legs.

"Wider," he commands.

His voice sends a shiver up my spine. My breath catches.

Still, I obey. Leaves rustle beneath the soles of my shoes as I slide my feet farther apart.

"That's it," Aaron commends me. "Now, bend your knees slightly. Just slightly."

I force my shaking knees to bend.

"But not your waist."

His large hands wrap around my waist. Heat swirls in my belly.

"Relax." He moves his hands to my shoulders, which now seem a mass of knots. "You're shaking."

Of course I'm shaking. I'm holding a gun for the first time and Aaron's hands are going all over me. I draw a deep breath.

"Now, keep your eyes on the target." He lowers his head to whisper in my ear. "And just—"

"I can't do this."

I hand him the gun and step back to put some distance between us.

"Okay." Aaron puts the gun down on a tree stump. "No one ever said firing a gun would be easy. Not everyone can handle the heat."

My eyes narrow. Is he toying with me?

"Especially not someone who's afraid to step out of their comfort zone," he adds.

I frown. Now I know he's making fun of me.

"Or someone who's afraid to make a mess."

My nostrils flare. My hands curl into fists and I raise them, intending to beat them on his chest, but he catches my wrists and grips them firmly.

"You just love making my blood boil, don't you?" I ask through gritted teeth.

Aaron's lips curve into a grin as he lowers his face. His eyes narrow.

"You have no clue."

My pulse races under the scorching intensity of his gaze. Those hot coals staring down at me melt my clothes away and I can feel the heat of Aaron's body against mine. I'm well aware of the smell of his sweat, of his hands holding my wrists captive. Every breath I take just fuels the fire beneath my skin and I can feel beads of my own sweat breaking out.

That gaze. It has me under a spell, commanding me to surrender.

And when Aaron lowers his face a little more, my eyes close. I feel his warm breath tickle my skin. I can smell the coffee from his mouth and I can almost taste it, so much so that my lips begin to part as if they have a life of their own.

But then it's gone. My arms crash to my sides as he lets my wrists go. As I open my eyes, I find him already walking away.

Just like he did the last time.

"I'm going to take a shower," he says before he disappears inside the cabin.

My shaky knees give way and I sit on the edge of the tree stump. My chest aches as my lungs replenish their oxygen supply and I place my hand over it. My heart hammers against my palm.

Just like last time, I'm left confused and alone.

Only this time, I'm wondering why he didn't kiss me.

~

"I should have just shot him when I had the chance," I mutter to myself as I tap my fingers on top of the ivory chest of drawers that I got for my office.

The room is fully furnished now, and beautifully so in my opinion. Plastic orchids are perched behind the brass drawer handles I've nailed to the wall, now sea foam green instead of beige. Real potted plants sit in the corners, except for the one occupied by that chic lamp I got. Pendant lights hang from the ceiling like veins. A pair of round velvet stools in raincloud gray sit in front of my desk, waiting to be occupied.

I sit on one of them as I let out a sigh.

Here I am again in my office getting pissed at my husband for acting like such a jerk even though I'm not sure what I've done to deserve it. I'm beginning to wonder if this is going to be part of my routine from now on.

My next sigh is stalled by a knock on the door.

"Come in," I say.

It opens and Elsa steps in. Today, she's wearing a royal blue blouse and white pants. Her lips are still bubblegum pink.

"Good morning," she greets me with a smile before handing me my mug of coffee. "And just allow me to say that I think your office looks amazing."

"Thank you." I hold the mug in both hands.

But then it's always easy designing for yourself.

"Ms. Clements took a peek last Saturday and she thinks so, too," Elsa adds.

My back straightens as I put my mug down on my lap. "Really?"

Elsa nods. "How was your weekend?"

I lift my mug to my lips and take a sip of coffee instead of giving her an answer.

What am I supposed to say? That it was fun except for the part where my husband refused to kiss me? Twice? Yeah, I was still half awake when he grasped my chin on the couch. I thought he'd kiss me then. I thought he didn't because he didn't want to kiss a sleeping woman. But I was definitely awake after I tried to hit him with my fists. And he looked like he wanted to kiss me then. Still, he didn't.

Being kissed without your permission is nowhere as bad as not being kissed when you expect it.

Aaron made me expect it. It's like he dangled himself in front of me and when I took the bait, he took off. What kind of man does that?

I run a finger over my lips. Was I such a bad kisser the first time that he doesn't want to do it again?

"Teri?" Elsa asks.

I let out a breath into my palm and sniff it. "I don't have bad breath, do I, Elsa?"

She shakes her head. "No. Why?"

I put my hand down on my knee. Then why does Aaron not want to kiss me again?

I know, I know. He's not in love with me. But what does love have to do with it? I'm sure he didn't love all the women he kissed or had sex with before.

Sex. The word makes me go still.

Is that what this is about? Am I sexually frustrated?

I take another sip of coffee.

That's absurd. How can I be sexually frustrated when I've never even had sex. I mean, I don't know what I'm missing, so how can I miss it? And I definitely don't want to have sex with Aaron.

Or so I think until I remember how he looked with his muscles all taut as he fired that gun. Or how I felt him breathing literally down my neck as he tried to give me that shooting lesson. Or the heat that rushed all the way down to my toes as his black eyes bore down on me.

Fine. I can imagine what I'm missing and I wouldn't mind having sex with Aaron. But clearly, the feeling isn't mutual. Maybe he wanted to sleep with me the night we first met but he no longer feels the same way after getting to know me. He doesn't even want to kiss me.

He doesn't want me. And it pisses me off. After all, what woman, what person, doesn't want to feel wanted?

Elsa clears her throat. "Are you sure there's nothing you need my help with, Teri?"

I look up at her. I've asked her for advice before. Why not again?

"Do you ever wonder what goes on in your husband's mind?"

"Sometimes," she answers. "Even though we've been together so long, I don't always know what he's thinking. Men are mysterious that way."

"And what do you do?"

"Usually, I leave him alone. He's entitled to his own thoughts. But if it really bothers me, I ask him. That's the only way to find out what a person is thinking."

I nod. She's right, I guess. But there's no way I can just go to Aaron and ask him why he won't kiss me. He'd probably just laugh at me.

"I don't mean to sound condescending or anything," Elsa continues, "but I do think communication is the key to a successful and happy marriage. You shouldn't be afraid to ask your husband what he thinks. In the same way, you should be honest and also tell him how you feel. That way, you can sort things out together."

Tell Aaron that I want to have sex with him? That sounds even worse.

"Would you like me to book a dinner at a nice restaurant for you and your husband so you can talk?" Elsa asks me.

191

I throw her a puzzled look. "Me? Invite Aaron to dinner?"

She shrugs. "Why not? I invite Jonathan to dinner sometimes. There's nothing wrong with the woman making the first move."

Maybe. But I still don't think dinner is a good idea.

"Thanks, Elsa," I say. "But maybe some other time."

"Okay. Then I'll just—"

She stops talking as my phone rings. I glance at where I've left it on my desk.

"I'll be outside if you need me," Elsa says.

As she leaves my office, I pick up my phone. My eyebrows furrow at the unknown number flashing on the screen.

Another interview, maybe? I did send tons of applications, and I haven't bothered to let them all know I already have a job.

I tap the screen and hold the phone against my ear. "Hello."

"Mrs. Walsh? This is Holly, Mr. Walsh's assistant."

Oh. "Hi, Holly."

I'll save her number for future reference.

"Mr. Walsh asked me to call you and tell you that he's attending a fundraiser on Wednesday night. He wants you to come with him."

"Me?"

But I don't like fancy parties, and I won't know anyone there. Plus, won't there be cameras? I still haven't told my family I'm married.

"I'm not sure, Holly."

"I don't think this is a request, Mrs. Walsh."

Right.

"The party is being thrown by Isabelle Gale. Have you heard of her?"

"No."

"She's a widow. Her husband was a friend of Mr. Walsh. He died of cancer a few years ago. They had no kids of their own, but she's always been devoted to children. She's throwing this party at the kids' museum to raise money for mentally and physically challenged children."

"Oh." A fancy party for a good cause, then.

"Unlike most, she doesn't let the press in to her parties. She wants people to help out of the goodness of their hearts and not just to get attention."

"I like her already."

"Then you'll be happy to meet her. Mr. Walsh will inform you of the rest of the details in person. He just wanted me to tell you now so you can get ready."

"Okay."

"That's all. Have a good day, Mrs. Walsh."

And she's gone. I put my phone down and lean against the edge of my desk.

So I guess I'm going to a fancy party with Aaron. In that case, I need a dress.

Thankfully, I know just the right person to help me pick one.

~

"Nope. Not that one, either." Pam clicks her tongue in disapproval inside the dressing room.

I run my fingers over the maroon gown I'm wearing. "Why not?"

"It's maroon," Pam says. "It's what my matron of honor wore to my wedding and it'll probably be the same color as the carpet in the ballroom."

"It's a museum, not a ballroom," I correct her.

"Then you don't want to look like a boring relic, which you will in this gown."

Boring? I study my reflection. That's not what I'm seeing. What I see is a beautiful chiffon gown that hangs off my shoulders but covers half my arms, tapers at the waist and then cascades to the floor. It's simple but elegant. And comfortable.

"I think it looks nice," I tell Pam out loud. "I like it."

"Well, I don't." She crosses her arms over her chest as she leans against the wall. "And correct me if I'm wrong, but you did bring me here to get my opinion, right?"

"Yes." I turn to her. "But I still get to make the final decision."

Pam rolls her eyes.

I sigh. "Fine. What would you have me wear?"

"This." She grabs the gold and burgundy gown hanging behind the door.

I frown as I see the thigh-high slit on the skirt and the sheer back of the bodice.

"Isn't this gown too revealing?"

Pam touches my shoulder. "Honey, you said this is a party, right?"

"A fancy party," I remind her. "Not the prom."

She snorts. "Like someone can afford a gown like this for the prom."

"I told you I'll be meeting some of the firm's old clients. I don't want to wear something too sexy."

"But you do want to get attention, don't you?" Pam asks me. "You're new to the firm. This is your chance to impress both clients and colleagues, to let them know you're not a woman to be taken lightly."

"By baring half my body?"

"Oh, come on. The back is sheer, not bare. There's only one slit, not two. And the neckline isn't plunging. It's not slutty. It's sexy."

I purse my lips.

Pam sighs. "Teri, do you want to be a wallflower at this party? Do you want your colleagues to think you're boring? Do you want clients to think you're not confident?"

"Of course not." I touch the burgundy gown. "I just…"

"What are you afraid of, hmm?"

I shrug. "I've just never been to a fancy party before and I don't want to make a fool of myself."

"Trust me." Pam grabs my hand. "You won't make a fool of yourself in this gown. You'll look gorgeous, sophisticated, ready to take on the world. And you'll make all the men drool."

My eyebrows arch. "What?"

"Come on. I'm sure there are some hot guys in your firm. Don't you think it's about time you got a boyfriend?"

I nod. "Now I get it. You just want me to wear this dress so I can get a man."

"No," Pam argues with me. "But if you do, what's wrong with that?"

I roll my eyes.

"I'm not saying wear this dress as an invitation for men to sleep with you. You won't be wearing it for them. You'll wear it for you, so you can feel sexy. And then they'll think you're sexy. What's wrong with that?"

As I glance at the gown, my thoughts turn to Aaron. Make him think I'm sexy, huh?

Essentially, what Pam is saying is that if I wear this gown, Aaron will find me desirable, irresistible. He'll want to kiss me. Or more. And I can let him.

Or not.

I can just lead him on like he led me on and then leave him hanging. It will be revenge. It will be taking the ball back in my court. It may even be more satisfying than sex.

I take the gown from Pam's hands. "Fine. I'll wear it."

Pam smiles. "Good girl."

I hold the gown in front of the mirror and grin at my reflection.

Just you wait, Aaron Walsh. Just you wait.

Chapter Ten
Aaron

I give another impatient sigh as I glance at the clock on the wall and tap my fingers on the arm of the couch.

8:03.

I told Teri to be ready at 7:45 because the party runs from seven until ten and I want to be there around eight and leave by nine and it takes about twenty minutes to get to the museum. Yet I'm still waiting for her to appear.

Maybe I should knock on her bedroom door one more time.

I'm on my way to do that when the door opens. Teri steps out into the hall in her gold and burgundy gown. At first glance, it seems like she's wearing chest armor, but as she comes closer, I see that it's intricate needlework on top of sheer fabric. I can barely see any cleavage and yet the spiral designs draw my eyes to her chest and make it look larger. The sheer fabric hugs her arms like a second skin, making them seem longer and leaner. Then there's the skirt that seamlessly flows to the floor with a slit that exposes her left leg all the way up to the thigh, about three inches above her knee.

It's stunning.

As my gaze travels back up to her face, I find her hazel eyes staring at me from under dark lashes and blushing eyelids. Her cheeks look even more defined, her lips glossed in the same hue as her skirt. Half her hair is swept back elegantly, the other half cascading, touching the top of her shoulders. Diamond earrings hang from her ears.

My breath catches and a knot forms in my throat.

She is stunning. No, not just stunning. She's sexy and sleek and glamorous, and all I want right now is to push her against the wall, mess up her hair and smear her lipstick, run my fingers across that exposed leg, and go even higher than the slit.

Instead, I clear my throat. "You took too long."

"Sorry," Teri mumbles as she clutches her golden purse.

She doesn't sound too apologetic, though. Never mind.

I offer her my hand. "Shall we go to the party?"

~

"Isabelle Gale sure knows how to throw a party, doesn't she?" Hank asks after he finds me in the upper gallery of the museum's main hall.

I gulp down some wine as I watch the crowd below. "She sure does."

My gaze travels around the hall, which I can barely recognize with all its trimmings of glass, chiffon and oversized toys painted gold. It almost looks like Santa's workshop, or what Santa's workshop would look like if it were run by King Midas—or a meticulous woman who loves all things graceful and glittery.

True to habit, Isabelle Gale is wearing another glittering gown tonight—white this time. I watch her as she makes the rounds with a glass of champagne in hand, making her guests smile and laugh. The perfect hostess. After all, she had nearly three decades of experience being a CEO's wife. A trophy wife, some called her, but Gordon always disagreed. So did I. She's just as smart as he was, as capable of doing so many things. She just never showed off.

"Are you sure she's fifty?" Hank leans on the railing. "Because she looks not a day over thirty."

I glance at him. "If you tell her that, I'm sure she'll be grateful for the compliment, but that doesn't mean she won't see through you. Word of advice—don't you even try flirting with her."

"Fine." Hank exhales. "I know how madly in love she was with her husband and how she seems to bask in the limelight now that she doesn't have to live in a man's shadow. I don't stand a chance. I don't fight losing battles."

"I know."

"You have to admire her, though, for gathering so many kindhearted and generous people."

I snort. "Most of them are only here because they want attention. Even if they can't get it from the press, they can still get it from Isabelle Gale."

Hank shrugs. "I guess."

I recognize a number of them. Businessmen. Politicians. Lawyers. Doctors. Actors. They're all dressed to the nines, all on their best behavior. They're all probably hoping to be Isabelle's next cause.

Hank nudges my arm. "Speaking of getting attention…"

My gaze falls on Teri as Isabelle talks to her. She was supposed to just head to the restroom, but on the way back, she stopped to talk to some of the children present, and they seem to have taken a liking to her, a fact which Isabelle apparently just noticed—and approves of.

"Aren't you curious to know what they're talking about?" Hank asks me.

I shrug and take another gulp of wine. "I can ask Teri later."

The two women keep talking, occasionally interrupted by the children. Then Isabelle calls one of the staff over, and moments later the music changes to something more upbeat and modern. Some of the kids run to the middle of the hall and start dancing. The crowd makes room for them. Then two of them drag a reluctant Teri into their dance, Isabelle cheering them on.

"Uh-oh," Hank remarks. "Looks like your wife is going to be the center of attention now."

One by one, I see heads turn. And yes, I know some of them are probably watching the kids in amusement just like Isabelle, but most of them have their eyes on Teri. Just like me.

How can I not look at her when she's shaking her upper body and swaying her hips like that? Her golden bodice catches the light. Her burgundy skirt flows around her legs. Her hair bounces off her shoulders. Her earrings dance with her as they glisten just like her eyes.

I didn't even know she could dance.

Well, I don't think she's that good of a dancer. I can sense some stiffness to her movements, but she is having fun, just like the children, and that makes her captivating.

And makes me want to jump off the balcony, pull her into my arms and kiss her silly so everyone knows she's mine.

But I just finish my drink and keep watching.

Beside me, Hank whistles. "Teri sure is something. Are you sure you haven't fallen for her?"

I keep my gaze on her. "Why would I?"

"Right. You're just using her. Well, when you're done using her, can I?"

I turn to him with a glare.

Hank chuckles. "Just kidding. She's all yours to do whatever you want with. I'm well aware of that. Other men might not be, though."

I see that as soon as the song ends and Teri stops dancing. As the crowd applauds and Isabelle hugs the children, men begin to flock around her.

I rush downstairs and grab Teri's hand.

"Aaron," she says my name breathlessly as she smiles. Her cheeks are still flushed. "Were you watching?"

Why? Why does she look pleased with herself? Does she have any idea how I feel?

My fingers tighten around her wrist. I intend to drag her to the exit, to bring her home at once, but the music starts playing again. This time, the passionate notes of a tango fill the air.

Tango. The one dance I'm good at.

It seems like a sign, so instead of leaving the party with Teri, I bring her back to the dance floor. So she thinks she can dance, huh? Let's see if she can keep up with me.

"Aaron?" I see the glint of fear in her hazel eyes.

I turn my back to her and pull her arms around me. I flatten her palms against my chest.

"Just follow my lead."

Before Teri can utter a word of protest, I turn around. Our faces come within inches of each other as I grab her by the waist and pull her close. The bodice of her gown rubs against my wool jacket and she gives a soft gasp.

"Put your left arm around me," I whisper in her ear as I wrap my right arm around her.

195

Her trembling hand lands on my lower back. Of course she's nervous. She was nervous when I was teaching her to fire a gun, and dancing tango is more intimate than that.

And it's about to get even more intimate.

"Higher," I tell her.

As her hand crawls up my back, I slide my right hand up her side, where her coarse bodice meets the soft, sheer fabric, up until my thumb presses against the soft curve of her breast.

Teri draws her breath in sharply. Her cheek feels hot against mine.

I pull my face away to gaze into her eyes as I continue sliding my hand up until I reach her armpit. Then I let my hand glide down the underside of her arm, past her elbow and all the way to her wrist, where I detect a racing pulse.

As my palm covers hers, Teri looks away. Her cheeks are nearly the same hue as the lower part of her gown now.

"Breathe," I say as I grip her hand. "You'll need air, because we're about to go faster."

That's all the warning I give her before I begin to move my feet. Quickly. Smoothly. Teri follows reluctantly.

"Relax," I urge her as I push and pull her along. "Move with me."

The music goes on. I lead her forward, backward, and in circles. Eventually, the stiffness of her body fades. It begins to sway and jerk to the rhythm along with mine. She surrenders and I take control.

I place my hand on Teri's belly as I move behind her and pull her arm, causing her body to tilt sideways. Then, with a jerk, I sweep her off her feet and swing her around. Before she can regain her balance, I step back. Her hand falls on my chest as she leans on me. Her leg rests against my thigh. Her lips nearly brush against mine.

With another jerk, I push her off me. Again, we dance in circles around each other, whirling. Her skirt billows around her legs like a cloud. Her hair whips across her shoulders. Then I move behind her again and lift her so I can spin her, first with one leg hooked around my waist and then with both feet off the ground.

We spin faster and faster along with the music, and at the final note I let her dip but keep my hands on her back to keep her from falling. Teri stares up at me with lips parted as she catches her breath. Her chest heaves. A sheen of sweat covers her forehead.

I meet her gaze as I, too, try to catch my breath. I hear the applause burst around us but I don't see anyone else. All I see is Teri with her flushed cheeks and her eyes glossed over with unmistakable desire. The same desire burns in my crotch and buzzes in my veins.

For a moment that seems to stretch on forever, we just stare into each other's eyes as we gasp for air. Then I lift her slowly, without breaking eye contact, until my face is hovering directly over hers.

Teri's eyes close. Our noses touch. Our breaths mingle. Her mouth is like a magnet, pulling mine ever closer. I want nothing more than to give in, but if I kiss her now, I'm afraid I might not be able to stop. So I move away and pull her to her feet.

Her eyes open. Wide. I see the confusion in them before I turn to the crowd with a smile. As the hall explodes into applause and cheers once more, Teri wrenches her hand away from mine. I glance over my shoulder to see her running up the stairs.

Where is she going?

Chapter Eleven
Teri

I wipe the sweat off my brow as I lean on the wall between the diorama of some battle and an encased pot. That's all I can make out in the darkness, which is scattered only by the moonlight streaming in through the windows—four on each side and one in the ceiling.

My body is still warm, so warm I wish I could tear off my stupid gown. Who knows? Maybe if I hadn't worn it, Aaron wouldn't have danced with me.

My hand goes over my aching chest, where my heart still seems to be dancing the tango.

Oh, why did we have to dance that?

The door creaks as it opens.

"Teri?" I hear Aaron's voice as I see his silhouette against the light in the hall.

I shake my head. "Go away."

But of course he does the opposite and steps forward.

I let out a groan as I walk to the far end of the room, far from him. My heels clatter on the floor.

"You can't just leave me alone, can you?"

The door creaks again as it closes behind Aaron.

"You're mad at me?"

I put my hands on my hips and roll my eyes. "Well, I did run away from you, didn't I? Did you think I came up here just to look at the exhibits in the dark?"

"You didn't head for the exit, though."

I throw him a look of disbelief. "And go to the apartment? Your apartment, which smells like you, where everything reminds me of you?"

His eyebrows crease. "It smells like me?"

"Ugh."

I lift my arms before letting them crash down to my sides. How can men be so dense?

"If this is because I danced with you, you were on the dance floor first," Aaron points out.

"Because the kids dragged me there."

"Yes. Three-foot-tall physically and mentally disabled kids."

My hand goes to my hip. "Are you saying I wanted to dance?"

"I'm saying you danced." He takes a few steps forward. "And I just joined you."

My eyebrows arch. "You just joined me?"

God, that almost makes me laugh.

Aaron stops walking and shrugs.

Now I do give a mocking laugh. "Aaron, you didn't just join me. You swept me up, dragged me across the floor, and spun me around in circles."

"Well, that's tango."

I ignore him. "You got me dizzy. You got me sweating and panting…"

"Are you mad at me because I made you dance the tango? You did well, though."

"No!" I raise my voice. My hand clenches into a fist. "I'm not mad at you because you made me dance like some doll. It's because… because…"

I let my voice trail off as I look away.

Aaron stands in front of me. "Because what?"

I meet his gaze. "You really have no clue, do you?"

He says nothing.

I point to the bodice of my gown. "See this gown?"

"Yeah. I've been looking at it all evening."

"Exactly. It was supposed to catch your attention. I wore it to catch your attention."

He gives me a puzzled look. "You wanted my attention?"

I shrug. "Maybe that's why I let myself get dragged onto the dance floor."

"And you did get my attention," Aaron says. "You were dancing so well I thought I'd join you. I thought you wanted me to dance with you."

"No." I shake my head. "All I wanted was to show you what you've been missing out on, what you've been shying away from."

He looks more confused. "Shying away from?"

"Yes. You've been avoiding me, avoiding kissing me at least. You make me think you're going to kiss me. You make me expect it, but you never do."

"I did."

"Only once. I'm talking about when we were on that mountain and just now, after the dance."

Aaron lets out a deep breath. "You wanted me to kiss you in front of all those people?"

I don't answer that. "You know what really pisses me off? The fact that I was supposed to make you want me, that I planned on leaving you hanging tonight like you've left me hanging, and now it's all backfired. I'm still the one wanting, hoping, left hanging in spite of this beautiful, expensive gown."

I lift the sides of my skirt and let the fabric fall.

"Maybe it's because I'm a virgin. Maybe it's because I'm a fool. But I can't win against you. And I hate it." My head shakes. "I fucking hate it."

Aaron takes another step forward as his eyes narrow. "You think I don't want you?"

"Well, you didn't kiss me," I point out. "Even though we just danced the most passionate dance ever, even though our bodies were practically melting together." I let out a sigh. "It seemed like I was the only one who danced. And they say it takes two to tango."

"It does."

Aaron grabs my hand and presses it against his crotch.

"You really think I don't want you?"

Something quivers beneath my palm. I gasp.

"Think again."

Before I can gather my thoughts, though, his hand goes to the back of my head. In the next instant, his mouth captures mine. His tongue slips in between my lips and rubs against my own.

A shiver travels down my spine and my eyelids fall shut. But the rest of my body remains still.

Why? I wanted this kiss, didn't I? I was hoping for this. Yet now that Aaron's lips are pressed to mine, I can't breathe. I'm not sure I'm ready for this.

Aaron's arm wraps around me, pulling me close. My breasts press against the front of his shirt. His tongue brushes against my palate.

My knees weaken and I cling to his back for support. My breasts feel heavy, tingling. They've come to life.

My tongue begins to move on its own, rubbing against his. The friction sends heat flowing through my veins down to my chest, my belly and all the way down to my toes before climbing halfway back up to my sex. It, too, begins to tingle.

My body has taken over. It's acting on its own. My fingers run across his back as my head moves, leaning right and left and forward as our lips and tongues clash over and over again.

Suddenly, the hand gripping my hair pulls my head back. I barely have time for a gasp of air before Aaron kisses me again, more fiercely. His tongue takes full control of mine and I whimper.

I can taste Aaron's hunger, his desire. My heart pounds in excitement.

Something swells against my abdomen. Its heat permeates layers of clothing, speaking right to my sex. It burns. It melts. My underwear gets damp. My legs shift as my balance is threatened.

His hand moves to my hip, the other to my shoulder, and we begin moving. I don't know where. I just let him guide me like I did earlier when we were dancing. It does seem like we're dancing again across the room, except this time our mouths are glued together. Except this time I feel even more dizzy, warmer and out of breath.

My back collides with the wall. The cold marble loses to the heat in my body.

Aaron's mouth leaves mine and I can finally breathe, but it doesn't go idle. My earlobe is held captive between his lips. His tongue caresses the soft flesh. It tickles and I gasp.

His hand cradles my jaw as he nibbles on the other side, down to my chin and back up to my ear. His mouth slides down to my neck. His lips graze the point where my pulse is racing before parting to suck on my skin.

I shiver. I feel like a vampire's victim, growing weak as he sucks, licks and nibbles on my neck, but it feels so good I have no will to fight. I simply grip his arm and give in.

Aaron's other hand travels up my side like it did during the dance. Like before, I hold my breath as my stomach coils in anticipation. Then I gasp as his thumb grazes the side of my breast.

Unlike earlier, his hand doesn't continue up. This time, his palm slides over my breast. I feel it even through the metal applique of my bodice and heat swirls in my chest. My nipples harden.

The hand cradling my jaw comes down. Both his hands squeeze my breasts as he continues to feast on my neck. His thumbs press down on my stiff nipples.

My sex throbs. It swells. It leaks.

Without thinking, I grind against Aaron. He grunts against my skin.

Then his mouth returns to mine. His hands abandon my breasts, one caressing my blazing cheek and the other resting on my exposed thigh.

As his palm slides up, I find myself holding my breath again. Aaron sucks on my lower lip as his hand goes higher. It crawls beneath my skirt and keeps going until it touches black lace. Then his fingers walk over the lace, right over to the middle where I feel the hottest.

Aaron's thumb presses against the moist lace and I gasp. His tongue slips back inside my mouth, keeping mine busy as he strokes me. He swallows my moans.

The friction makes my knees shake. My hands grip his shoulders as strength leaves my ankles.

When his fingers begin to delve beneath the lace, I tremble. They brush against my swollen nub and I pull my mouth away to let out a soft cry.

He kisses my ear, my neck, my shoulder as his thumb rubs against that nub of flesh. I feel it swell even more. And burn. My skin blazes. My veins roar with excitement.

It feels amazing, too amazing for words. At the same time, though, I feel an ache growing inside me. My hand grabs his to pull it lower. His fingers sink into my heat and my hips move on their own.

Our lips collide as he strokes me. I cling to his back as I feel myself drifting away.

No, not drifting. I'm being swept away until a huge wave of pleasure washes over me and I drown. I moan against Aaron's mouth as my body heats up and trembles all over. My mind turns into mush behind tightly shut eyelids. My hands clutch fistfuls of wool as my toes curl inside my shoes.

Even after Aaron's mouth and fingers leave me, I continue to feel weak. I lean against the wall, afraid I might fall. My arms drop to my sides.

So it's over, huh?

Or so I think until my eyes open and I find myself pinned down by a smoldering gaze. Aaron's eyes look darker than ever. And more dangerous. I swallow.

My eyes fall shut as he kisses me again. His hands crawl beneath my skirt, find the garter of my underwear and pull it down. The lace glides over my thighs and down to my knees where it drops to my ankles.

I clutch his shoulders and take my left foot out of my sandal to step out of it. When I do, Aaron lifts my leg. The silk falls away.

I hear a rustle as he gathers what's left of my skirt at my hip. Then I feel the same bulge that was pressing against me earlier brush against me once more.

Only this time, it's not clothed. And neither is my lower half.

By the time the wheels in my head start turning again and I realize what's going on, it's too late. The tip of Aaron's hard cock enters me and I gasp into his mouth. Then he pushes the rest inside me slowly. I feel a slight sting, but mostly I feel like I'm being stretched.

Because I am.

That part of him entering me is thick and long. I can feel it sliding into my body, carving a place for itself. It's reaching deeper and deeper.

Suddenly, Aaron stops. He pulls his mouth away from mine and I find him panting. Sweat glimmers on his forehead. Lust burns in his eyes.

"Damn, you're tight," he says hoarsely as his features clench.

My eyebrows arch. "Are you hurt?"

He laughs. The rumble of his laughter travels all the way inside my body.

Frankly, I don't know what's funny, but before I can ask, he starts moving.

His lips capture mine once more as his cock slides in and out between my legs. His fingers bite into my thigh.

The friction sets my skin on fire once more. My knees grow weak again. With just one leg on the floor, I feel unsteady. I break the kiss so I can wrap my arms around Aaron's back. I moan against his shoulder.

Again, Aaron stops, but this time only for a moment. In the next one, he lifts my other leg and hoists me up. My sandal falls to the floor and then my underwear. I wrap both legs around him and hook my ankles.

His hands grip my butt cheeks through silk as he continues with his thrusts. They grow faster, harder. I feel like I'm bouncing off him. My nails dig into his back as my breasts press against his chest.

His hips jerk as his pace becomes erratic. Then he lets out a growl through his teeth as he buries himself inside me. His hands squeeze my ass to the point of pain, eclipsed only by the heat bursting inside me.

Eventually, his hands relax. He leans against me as my back rests against the wall. His chest rises and falls as he gasps for air.

Then Aaron pulls away. My feet fall to the floor, my skirt with them. My legs still feel weak, so I keep my back to the wall. My palms rest against it, too.

As I watch Aaron fix his clothes I remember that I need to put my underwear back on. As I bend over to pick it up, I feel something ooze out of me. I quickly put my panties on to keep more of it from leaking out.

"Are you alright?" Aaron asks me.

I don't answer as I slip my feet back into my sandals. I don't know. I feel a little sore between my legs. And I'm leaking, which isn't a pleasant sensation. I feel exhausted, too, now that the excitement has faded and adrenaline is no longer coursing through my veins. Most of all, I'm still reeling from the realization that I'm no longer a virgin, that I just had sex, steamy sex with my hot husband. Am I alright?

Just as I open my mouth to say something, the door at the opposite end of the room opens. Shit. I'd forgotten we're in a museum and there's a party downstairs.

I quickly step back into the shadows and glance around for a better hiding place as a man enters the room, flashlight in hand.

He shines it on Aaron. "What the hell? You're not allowed in here."

"Really?" Aaron steps forward as he holds up an arm to shield his eyes from the bright lights. "Because I thought the privilege of seeing all the exhibits comes with attending the party."

"No," the guard says before shining his flashlight on me.

I turn my face away.

"And looking at the exhibits my ass. How can you when it's so dark in here?"

"You're right," Aaron says calmly. "We weren't looking at the exhibits."

My jaw drops as I glance at him. Wait. Is he going to admit that we just had sex? My cheeks blush. I might just die from the embarrassment.

"We were dancing," Aaron adds. "I don't know if you were watching, but my wife and I were dancing downstairs earlier. She was annoyed that she forgot a few steps, so I decided to teach her here."

The guard shakes his head. "No. I wasn't watching."

"That's a shame. Would you like to see us dance?"

My eyes grow wide. What?

"No, that's fine," the guard says.

I let out a breath of relief.

"Okay," Aaron says. "Anyway, I don't think my wife can dance anymore. Tango is pretty tiring."

He turns to me and stretches out his arm. "Isn't that right, honey?"

I walk to his side. "Yes."

That isn't a lie.

"We were about to go home, actually," Aaron tells the guard. "I was just about to go look for Isabelle and tell her that."

"She's downstairs."

"Yes, I suppose she is." Aaron puts his arm around me. "Shall we go, darling?"

I just nod.

He ushers me towards the door but stops at the doorway.

"Oh, by the way, I know we weren't supposed to be here, so how about you pretend you didn't see us?" Aaron takes a bill out of his pocket. "I don't want Isabelle or any of our friends knowing we're rule breakers."

The guard hesitates for a moment, then takes a bill.

Aaron pats him on the shoulder. "Good evening."

He leads me down the hall.

"Care for one more drink before we leave?" he asks me. "I suddenly feel thirsty."

I am, too, so I nod. "Yeah, sure."

Who knows? A glass of champagne might just help me forget what just happened.

~

It didn't. Neither did the shower after we got home. Neither did work.

Even now, four days later, I can still vividly remember what happened that night at the museum. Every single messy detail. And each time I do, my cheeks catch fire and I feel like banging my head against the wall. Instead, I settle for slapping my forehead.

Teri, you are such a fool.

Of course, having sex with one's husband isn't considered a crime. What bothers me is that I gave in. Easily. Even though I said I'd seduce Aaron and then leave him hanging like he did to me.

Well, at least I'm not hanging any longer. My curiosity and craving have both been satisfied. My problem? The fact that Aaron is acting as if nothing happened.

I thought that when he did that in front of the guard, it was just that—acting. But he's never brought it up, nor has he behaved any differently. It makes me feel as if we never had sex.

Or did he forget about it already? So soon?

It's not like I want him to suddenly be sweet and all. I don't want him to buy me presents or move into my bed or kiss me before he leaves for work or suddenly hug me when I'm cooking dinner. I just want some… acknowledgment. And maybe a little change in the way he treats me. He can't even be a teeny bit warmer? In fact, he actually feels colder than before.

I finally decide to confront him about it when he returns to the apartment after indulging his Sunday biking habit. "Hey. Is something wrong?"

Aaron shrugs. "What do you mean?"

I lean on the kitchen counter. "Well, you seem to be avoiding me. Again."

"I'm not. I've just been busy."

"Okay." I nod. "So the fact that we had sex at the museum has nothing to do with it?"

"No," he answers confidently. "Why?"

I sigh. "So are we supposed to just put it behind us?"

Aaron looks into my eyes. "Are you pregnant?"

"No."

At least, I don't think so. I hadn't even considered the possibility until now, which makes me pause. What if Aaron got me pregnant? The last thing we need in this complicated relationship is a baby.

I hold my finger up. "You know what? Next time, we should use protection. And by we, I mean you."

"What was I supposed to do? Stain your gown? Soil my tux? Make a mess on the museum floor?"

I turn away as I let out a gasp of disbelief. I don't even want to picture any of those scenarios.

"I'm just saying—"

"Fine, next time," Aaron cuts me off. "If there is a next time."

I look at him with arched eyebrows. If?

That makes my patience snap.

I walk over to him and grab the front of his shirt. "Was I that bad? Is that why you don't want to have sex with me again? Is that why you've already forgotten about the fact that we had sex?"

To my annoyance, Aaron grins. "Bad at what? Did you do anything?"

My jaw drops.

"If I remember correctly, I did all the work. You didn't do anything. Nothing special. Nothing at all."

I release his shirt as my gaze drops. My mouth continues to gape. I want to say something in my defense. But what do I say? He's right. I didn't do anything. I just... kissed him back and clung to him, which I suppose doesn't count.

My arms hang at my sides.

"Well, I am a virgin, you know," I finally tell him. "Was."

"I know."

"And it all happened so fast."

"I know."

I meet his gaze. "I can do better."

"Wow." Aaron crosses his arms over his chest. "Really?"

I frown. Now he's insulting me.

"Do you really think you can let go of yourself in bed and try new things when you can't even do it when you're on your feet?"

I don't answer. He takes my glare as a no.

"I thought so."

~

Why that arrogant, pig-headed jerk!

I hit the back of my head against the cushion of the driver's seat as I take my hands off the wheel of my car.

Who does he think he is, acting like some god? Does he really think he knows me?

Well, he doesn't. And I'll show him. I'll show him—

My thoughts screech to a halt as I hear a tap on my window. I turn my head and see Winona standing outside.

I send her a quick smile, then take a deep breath to calm myself down before stepping out of the car.

"Good morning," I greet her as I appraise her outfit.

Pearl earrings. An orange dress with puff sleeves. Fingerless gloves fashioned from periwinkle lace. Fashionable as usual.

I, on the other hand, am wearing a simple, long-sleeved black blouse and a houndstooth pencil skirt. I wasn't much in a mood to report to work today, much less wear something nice. I did add the thin red belt hastily for a touch of color, though, when I realized I was going to be meeting my first client today.

"Good morning." Winona gives me a quick hug. "Are you ready?"

I nod.

I may be a bit nervous, but I'm also excited for my first real project. Plus I need the distraction.

"Follow me."

Winona walks up the paved path towards the brick house. I follow closely behind as I take in the landscaped lawn, which also has a totem pole and a rather erotic statue of two men and a woman. I tear my gaze away with a blush.

We reach the front steps and Winona rings the doorbell. Moments later, a woman dressed in black comes to the door.

"Hi!" she greets us excitedly. "Ms. Clements, please come in."

"Oh, please call me Winona," my boss says as she gives the other woman a hug. "And this is my trusted friend who just recently joined my firm, Teri. She will be in charge of this project."

Winona turns to me.

"Teri, this is Jessica Shaw, our client."

"Hello, Teri." Jessica gives me a hug as well before stepping back. "Please come in."

I step inside the house, which is even more spacious than it looks from the outside. And beautifully furnished. I immediately get a sense of Gothic but also Victorian.

"You have a beautiful house," I say out loud.

Silently, I wonder what more she can possibly need from me.

"Thank you," Jessica says. "I quite love it even though we just bought it. And by we, I mean me and my husband, Randy."

I follow her gaze to the wedding portrait on the wall.

"We got married just weeks ago."

Winona touches my arm. "Teri here is a recent bride, too."

Jessica's eyes grow wide. "Really?"

I reluctantly brandish my ring. "Really?"

"Wow. Congratulations."

I fake a smile. "Same to you."

I step forward.

"So, are you looking to make the place more warm and romantic? Or more soft and mellow so it's ready when the baby comes?"

Winona gives me a warning glance. What did I say?

"I don't think we'll be having a baby anytime soon," Jessica says. "Randy and I are having a bit of fun."

"Of course," I say.

"And we like the house as it is. We just need help with one room."

She starts to walk off and Winona and I follow her.

"Listen to the client," Winona whispers to me as she grabs my arm. "Really listen. Not just to what they're saying. Try to understand how they feel, what they want. Know even what they're not saying."

I nod. "Right."

"And don't make assumptions."

"Yes, ma'am."

We go down the stairs to the basement, which currently has a large TV, a couch, a pair of beanbags, a wine cabinet, and what looks like an exercise and yoga area.

Well, it definitely looks different from upstairs.

"We want to make this the place where we entertain guests," Jessica says. "Friends."

I run my fingers across the back of the couch. "I see."

"We don't ever want there to be a dull moment in this room," the client goes on. "In fact, we want our friends to feel very welcome here, even more at home than they are in their own houses. I want them to feel open and free."

"Okay."

"I want this room to be thought-provoking, inspiring, maddening."

Now she's getting excited. And more difficult.

Jessica looks at me. "I'd like you to go wild. Rebellious. Naughty, even."

My eyebrows arch. Naughty?

Winona nudges my arm. "I think this is the perfect opportunity for you to try new things, to explore your skills and take your ideas as far as they can go."

I give her a puzzled look.

"Let loose, is what I'm saying," Winona says.

"Exactly," Jessica seconds. "I want everyone to let loose when they're here, to lose themselves to this room and the company and the moment."

So Winona is testing me, huh? She might have given me a job, but she still doesn't trust my skills. She wants to see if I can be bolder, be more interesting. That's fine by me.

"Do you think you can handle this?" Winona asks me.

I look around the room, glance at Jessica and nod. I'll show her what I'm truly capable of. And I'll show Winona she was right to hire me, to entrust this project to me. I'll show her I can be better.

I'll show everyone I can let loose when I want to.

"Yeah," I answer as I hold my shoulders squarely and grin. "I can do naughty."

Chapter Twelve
Aaron

"Teri?" I call out her name as I turn on the lights in the living room.

When there's no answer, fear constricts my throat.

It's just like that time. The odd emptiness in spite of the pair of shoes near the front door. The relative darkness—well, the apartment is darker this time, actually. And the forbidding silence that weighs too heavily in the air to escape notice.

Fuck.

I hold my breath as I run to the bathroom at the end of the hall. It escapes me in relief as I find the shower stall empty. Drops of water still cling to the tiles and the smell of berries still lingers. Teri was here not more than half an hour ago, but she's not here now.

Good. The question is: Where is she?

When I circle back, I find her sitting on the edge of the dining table in the dark, her face towards the window. I'm about to open my mouth to scold her, but as I turn on a lamp, I see what she has on—nothing but a pair of intersecting straps across her spine and a fringe of midnight blue lace forming a V on the small of her back. No, lower. So low I can see the beginning of the crease in her ass at the bottom-most point of the V.

I swallow, but then my eyebrows crease. What is she doing sitting in the dark? And why does she have a gown on?

I think it's a gown until she turns, not all the way but enough for me to see the lace coating her breasts and spot the hem of the outfit on her thigh.

It's not a gown. It's lingerie.

And damn, does Teri look hot in it, an opinion my cock firmly agrees with.

"Hello." Her burgundy lips curve into a smile. "I thought it was about time you came home from work. At least, that's what Holly said."

My eyebrows arch. "You called Holly."

She nods. "I hope you don't mind."

"No," I answer.

Not at all. What I do mind is that she was hiding. She deliberately made me worry. Well, now I know why, but she still gave me a scare there, one I'd rather not go through again.

"I was looking for you," I tell her.

"I know." She jumps off the edge of the table. "And now you've found me."

Yes. Now I've found her. In a blue chemise which lets me see the curves of her breasts through the lace, more clearly than I could through her gold and red gown at the party. I can even see the valley between them, exposed beneath the tiny ribbon holding the lace in place. If I just pull on that ribbon, they'll bounce free. If I just dip my hands beneath that fabric, I'll feel her bare nipples against my palms.

I'm unable to hold back a whistle. "Well, this is a surprise."

And a temptation. I wonder if Teri knows how dangerous this game she's playing is.

"It is?" She sets down the wineglass she's been holding on the table. "You probably thought I'd never wear something made of such a limited amount of fabric, did you?"

I don't answer because it's true.

She touches her shoulder. "You thought I couldn't do wild or naughty, didn't you?"

I narrow my eyes at her. "So you thought you'd prove me wrong?"

"I thought I'd show you what I'm really capable of," Teri answers as she takes a step forward. "You know, these past few days, I proved Winona and my client wrong. I was given a project where I had to transform this boring basement into a place where alcohol and ideas can run free. Oh, and I had to give it a touch of naughty. A touch of erotic. And you know what? I pulled it off. I pulled it off with impressive marks."

I tear my gaze off her breasts. "Congratulations."

"So you see, I can break out of my shell. I can do things."

I nod. "Okay."

I pull out a chair, loosen my tie and sit down.

Now Teri looks puzzled. "What are you doing?"

"You said you'd prove me wrong," I tell her as I cross my arms over my chest. "So prove me wrong. You can't do that just by wearing something sexy, you know."

Apprehension flickers in her eyes, but she holds her chin up as she flattens her palms against her abdomen. "Fine. I will."

I shrug. "I'm waiting."

For a moment, Teri just stands there. Her shoulders tremble slightly. They rise and fall as she draws a deep breath. Her eyes close and when they open again, they sport a gleam of determination.

Her hand falls away as she steps forward, walking to me slowly. She stands in front of me and I lift my head to meet her gaze.

I say nothing, though. This is her show and I'm not interrupting.

Yet.

Teri's hands grip my shoulders as she climbs onto my lap. Then she lifts one to remove the elastic band keeping my hair back. She puts it on the table and then runs her fingers through my dark strands. Her blunt nails graze against my scalp.

It feels nice. Naughty? No.

She cups my face next. Her palms press against the thin layer of hair coating my jaws and she runs her thumbs over them. My gaze dips down to her cleavage, trying to get a glimpse of her nipples.

She lifts my chin, forcing me to look into her eyes as she grabs my tie. She pulls me forward as she leans in. Her hair brushes against my cheeks and its scent of berries drifts to my nostrils. I hear the strain in her breathing and feel its warmth mingle with mine.

Her soft lips quiver as she brushes them against my own. Then they press against my mouth firmly.

I get an urge to place my hand around her neck and push my tongue inside her mouth, but I restrain myself.

I'm not saying she's bad. Just slow.

Finally, her tongue slips past my lips. It rubs against my own as she caresses my cheek. The heat travels to my crotch.

I let my tongue play with hers but I don't let it wander into her mouth. I let her tongue do the exploring. And her hands. They rest on my shoulders before sliding down to my chest and prying my arms off.

I want to wrap them around her and run my hands across her bare back and then pull her close so I can bury my face between her breasts. But I just let them drop to my sides.

Teri breaks the kiss and turns her attention to the buttons of my shirt. She pops them out one after the other but struggles with the fourth.

"Think you can go faster?" I ask her, unable to stay quiet any longer. "Because I'm getting bored."

"Shut up," she tells me as she finally releases that button and moves to the next. "Or I'll be forced to gag you."

"Really?" I give her a look of surprise. "Or you can silence me another way."

She ignores me and removes the last button. Then she pushes my shirt aside to stare at my chest. Fascination blooms in her eyes and her jaw drops.

I clear my throat. "Correct me if I'm wrong, but am I not the one supposed to be enjoy—"

Teri cuts me off with a fierce kiss. Her palms flatten against my pectoral muscles. Her fingers trace their hard edges before moving lower to press against my pack of abdominal muscles. I instinctively tighten them.

One of her fingertips follows the trail of thin hair going down from my navel and disappearing into my pants. It pauses when it touches flannel, then continues. Her hand dips between my thighs and I part them for her. Her palm presses against my crotch and my imprisoned cock throbs.

Now she's being naughty. But not naughty enough. Her hand is still moving too slowly, and there are still too many layers of fabric between her skin and mine.

I'm craving for more contact here.

I lift my hand and put it on her thigh, intent on letting it crawl up beneath her chemise. Teri slaps my wrist away and glares at me in warning.

"You didn't say I couldn't touch you," I point out.

"But last time you complained that you did all the work," Teri says. "So now, let me."

"Then do it," I challenge her.

Teri frowns, but my message goes through. She removes my belt hastily and then pops that last button out. As she pulls down the zipper, her knuckles brush against the tip of my erection and she pauses. For a moment, she stares at the small stain in front of my boxers, then she slips her hand into the slit and pulls my hard cock out.

Finally.

Again, she stares. Again, fascination shows on her face. She probably can't help it since this is her first time seeing a cock. I can't help but be amused.

"Let me guess." I cross my arms over my chest again. That way, I'll be less tempted to touch her. "You're wondering how it fit inside you."

Teri's gaze finally climbs back to my face. I can see from her expression that I'm right, but she frowns.

"Don't be so smug. I was just… studying it."

"Oh. Do you want me to give you a lesson?"

"No need," she says. "I'll… figure it out on my own."

"You mean you've never watched porn?"

Teri glares. "Just shut up."

She kneels in front of me and wraps her fingers around the base of my cock. Then she moves them up. Slowly.

"Just tell me if I'm hurting you," Teri says.

"You're hurting me," I tell her.

Her eyes grow wide. "I am?"

"My cock is swollen and you're not doing anything about it."

She frowns and moves her hand up and down. "I am doing something."

"Not enough."

Her eyes narrow. "Oh. So I'm trying your patience, am I?"

"Yes," I answer without hesitation.

Her lips curve into a grin. "Good. Then I'm succeeding at being naughty."

And annoying, I want to add, but then her thumb swipes over the head of my cock, spreading the moisture there. My breath leaves me.

Teri gives a wider grin as she keeps stroking me slowly, every now and then pressing against the head. Whenever she does, her eyes meet mine, watching for my reaction. I put my poker face on.

She wants to test my patience? Fine. I'll just have to do my best to restrain myself.

That's what I do, but it proves harder as Teri strokes my cock faster. Not to mention that I can see the tops of her breasts from here. They seem to be blushing just like her cheeks.

She's all serious now. Her grin is gone. She leans forward and plants a kiss on my stomach. Her breasts brush against my thighs.

I purse my lips. My jaw clenches.

This isn't annoying anymore. It's driving me crazy. She may be new to this. Her hand may be a little clumsy. But the fact that she's doing her best is enough to impress me. The fact that she's doing it for me makes me want her all the more.

My patience snaps. I grab Teri's wrist to take her hand off my cock. She looks up at me with questioning eyes.

"Fine. You can be naughty," I concede. "You have been naughty."

She grins.

"Do you know what happens to naughty women?"

Teri shakes her head.

"They get punished."

I stand and pull her to her feet. I push her on top of the table and lean over her.

"Aaron?"

Now her gaze is laced with fear. But I also see excitement.

I capture her lips and slip my tongue inside her mouth. She doesn't respond at first. She's probably still annoyed by the fact that our roles have been reversed. But then she gives in. Her hands go to the back of my neck.

My own work furiously to remove my tie. When it's off, I put it down temporarily so I can finally cup her breasts through the lace front of her chemise. Teri whimpers into my mouth.

My hands move to her sides and slide up until they reach her armpits. Then I take her arms off me and lift them so they're flanking her head. I continue to slide my hands up until I reach her wrists, which I pin down. Then I grab my tie quickly and wrap it around them.

Teri's mouth stops moving. When I pull away to look at her, I see the worry on her face.

She tries to yank her hands free. "What's going on? Let me go."

"Shh." I hold a finger to her quivering lips. "You're the one who has to let go. Isn't that what you said you'd do?"

Still, Teri frowns. "This is ridiculous. How can I let loose when my hands are tied?"

I give her a mischievous grin. "Ah, but you can. All you have to do is give in."

Before she can say more, I kiss her again. I pull on the tiny ribbon at the front of her chemise and it comes undone. My hands glide beneath the lace. My palms slide over her bare breasts.

Teri shivers. Her nipples stiffen against my skin.

I take the pebbly peaks between my fingers and rub them. She moans.

I keep doing that as I tear my mouth off hers and lick her ear. She turns her head to keep it from me, hiding it against her arm. I plant a kiss on her collarbone and then drag my lips to the soft valley between her breasts. Then I pull my face away so I can admire the firm mounds of flesh.

"What?" Teri asks me impatiently.

I chuckle as I meet her gaze. "What? Are you the only one allowed to stare? To study?"

She scoffs. "There's nothing to look at."

"Ah, but I disagree."

I bring my eyes back to her breasts as I squeeze them. True, they may not be that large, but they are firm and beautifully rounded and her nipples are the most alluring shade of pink.

I pinch them lightly. "I definitely disagree."

I lower my head and take one of those nipples between my lips. I give a light tug and Teri gives a loud gasp. I circle it with my tongue and she starts trembling.

I do the same with the other, getting both nipples glistening wet. Then I hold one of her breasts captive in my mouth and suck. Teri moans.

As I suck on her other breast, I let my hands wander over her thighs. They creep beneath silk and brush against more lace, as well as straps. I pull those straps down until they reach her knees, which are on the edge of the table. Then I kneel on the floor as I drag them the rest of the way down. The tiny garment slips off her ankles.

I take one of those slim ankles and press my lips to it. I pepper her legs with kisses until I reach her knees. Teri laughs as I kiss them.

So she has ticklish knees, huh? Noted.

"Stop it," she admonishes me.

I obey. I have something else in mind, after all. I grab her thighs and pull her off the table until half her body is over the edge. Then I part them as I sink to my knees again.

"Aaron?" I hear the panic in Teri's voice. "What are you—?"

The rest of her question vanishes as I move my head forward. I plant a kiss on her other pair of lips. Then I part them and slip my tongue in between those, too.

The table shakes as Teri jerks. I glance up to see only blue and her chin as her back arches. I hear her head crash down onto the wood.

Moans and gasps escape her mouth as I keep stroking her with my tongue, which becomes coated in the sweet nectar oozing out of her. I rub the nub of flesh concealed in her curls and the table shakes once more. Harder. Her heels dig into my back.

I continue teasing her for another minute as payback. Then I pull away. I get to my feet and look down at Teri as I lick my lips. She looks up at me with flushed cheeks and glossy eyes that are tearing up at the corners.

"I hate you," she tells me as her lips form a pout.

"No, you don't."

I place my hand on Teri's cheek and kiss her, giving her a taste of her own excitement as I wrap my other hand around my neglected, aching cock.

I give it a few strokes before letting it brush against her.

Teri stiffens and pulls away. I brace myself for a word of protest, but she glances at the chest of drawers near the table instead.

"Protection," she says.

I grin. "You bought a condom?"

She frowns. "Not funny."

So she anticipated that things would get this far, though I have a feeling this isn't exactly how she expected they would unfold.

I open the drawer and grab the condom.

"Just one?" I tease her as I rip the casing. "I thought you were trying to be naughty and wild."

"Shut up," Teri tells me again. "And just put it on already."

"Yes, ma'am."

I sheath myself in the rubber. Then I get back on top of Teri and grip her hips.

"Here I come."

That's all the warning I give her before pushing in. My cock slides in with one thrust.

Teri gasps. I give her only a moment to catch her breath before I start moving.

Damn, she really is tight. Even with the rubber on. Of course, I preferred it when her velvety skin was clinging to me, but she's still trying to squeeze the life out of me, so I don't complain. I just pound into her tightness, into her heat.

The table rocks. Teri throws her head back again. Her eyes squeeze shut. Her moans spill into the air.

I grunt as I pick up my pace.

Suddenly, Teri lifts her head.

"Untie me," she pleads breathlessly.

I can't spare a moment to think, so I simply pull my tie off her wrists. Her arms wrap around me.

I lift her back off the table so that she's sitting up, over the edge. Her legs envelop me just as they did last time. Her heels dig into my lower back.

I cloak my own arms around Teri as my hips jerk. She moans against my shoulder as her nails dig into my skin.

I pull on a handful of her hair and kiss her. She moans into my mouth, then pulls away to let out a cry as she shudders. Her arms and her legs tighten around me. Her sex clamps around my cock.

I manage a few more thrusts, then hold her still as I bury myself inside her. Something in my belly uncoils and my cock explodes. My entire body grows taut.

As I catch my breath and wait for the cobwebs of pleasure to fade, I feel Teri slump against my shoulder. After I pull out, she collapses on top of the table, arms at her sides. Her eyes remain closed as she pants.

I take the rubber sheath off my cock and make a knot. I wrap it in a paper towel before tossing it in the trashcan.

When I go back to the dining table, Teri is sitting in the chair I was on earlier. The ribbon in front of her chemise is back in place and the lace underwear is no longer on the floor.

"Are you alright?" I ask her as I zip myself up.

She stretches her arms out to me like a child. "Carry me to bed. I can't move."

I chuckle but carry her anyway. Her arms go around my neck. Her head rests on my still bare chest.

I bring her to the bedroom, kick the door open and set her down on the bed.

"So, was I good this time?" she asks me as I pull the sheets up to her armpits.

"No," I answer.

She frowns.

"You were wicked. Incredibly wicked."

Her lips curve into a smile. She reaches for my hand and squeezes it.

"Thanks."

Maybe it's because I didn't expect that gesture and that word of thanks. Maybe it's an aftereffect of the amazing sex we just had. But I find myself bending over and planting a kiss on her forehead.

"Good night."

I leave the room, and only when I'm back outside do I realize what I've just done—something I've never done before.

I place a hand over my mouth.

Why did I do that?

~

"What are you doing?" Hank catches me on my way to the office parking lot.

I take a deep breath and turn around. "Leaving."

"I can see that much." He stops a few feet away from me. "But why are you going to Jamaica?"

I give him a puzzled look. "How do you know where I'm going?"

"I asked Holly."

Makes sense. Still, I shake my head. "What? Are you sleeping with my secretary now?"

"No. I would never."

I shrug. Well, if Hank wanted to, he would have done it already. And if he still does, I don't think there's a problem, really, except for the fact that I know Hank is a player and Holly is the kind of woman who deserves a good guy. If she develops any kind of feelings for him, which she might if they have sex, she'll only end up getting seriously hurt.

Wait. Since when do I care about Holly's feelings? When did I ever care about any woman's feelings?

I frown as I scratch the back of my head. See. This is what I'm talking about. I don't know myself anymore.

Hank comes closer. "Aaron, I'll ask again. Why are you going to Jamaica?"

Because I need to remind myself of who I am. And who Teri is.

The enemy, or at least a weapon against the enemy. One I mustn't hesitate to use or break to exact my revenge.

"Business trip," I say out loud.

"Oh, do we have business in Jamaica now?"

I ignore him and turn towards my car.

"Bullshit," he says behind me.

I raise the middle finger of my right hand and keep walking.

Hank laughs. "You better tell me all about it when you get back."

Maybe, I think as I slip into the driver's seat of my Jaguar. Hopefully, there will be lots to tell, or at least something, because right now, more than a break, what I really need a distraction.

~

What distraction? I ask myself as I drink a third glass of tequila at a bar on Hellshire Beach in Kingston.

Yes, I've gone snorkeling and parasailing and fishing. But even amid all the thrills, I've found my thoughts turning to Teri. While gazing at fish underwater, I found myself wondering how she'd react to the same scenery. While parasailing, I wondered if I could convince Teri to try it. After all, I've convinced her to be a little wilder in bed—well, on the dining table. While on the fishing boat, I remembered the trout I caught for Teri during the time we spent at the cabin that she made all cozy and charming.

Even when I walk on the beach and see women in their skimpy swimsuits, I wonder how Teri would look in one, or think that Teri looked better in her blue chemise. I think of pushing her down on the sand and fucking her in a secluded cove with the salty breeze blowing on our hot bodies and the setting sun in the background.

I shake my head. This trip has not proved to be distracting at all.

I call the attention of the bartender. "I'll have another glass."

He promptly pours me another and puts it in front of me. I grab the glass, gulp its contents down and lick my lips.

"Hey," I hear a woman's voice behind me as I put the glass down, upside down on the bar.

In the next moment, she slips into the empty seat next to me.

"You look like you could use some company," she says.

I glance at her. She doesn't look like a local, not with her fair skin and her brown hair—chestnut brown, not mahogany brown—streaked with green. Her eyes are dark, her lips full and plummy. There's a tattoo of a hummingbird between her breasts, which are on the verge of bursting out of her yellow bikini top.

She's not bad. Maybe I can use her as a distraction.

"Do you want me to buy you a drink?" I ask her.

Her eyes narrow. "Without asking for my name?"

I turn my body towards her. "It doesn't matter, because you'll forget it by the time I'm done with you." And so will I.

Her lips form a circle. "Ooh."

Then she calls to the bartender, "Benny, give me one of those mojitos. Oh, and it's on him."

She points at me. The bartender nods.

"I see you're a regular," I remark.

"I see you're new. How long are you staying?"

"Not long."

She grins. "In that case, maybe I should skip the mojito and we should go back to your hotel already, you know, make the most of your short stay."

She leans forward so I can get an even more liberal view of her breasts and places her hand on my thigh. Her fingers give it a light squeeze. Still, I find myself hesitating, unable to summon an ounce of interest.

Why? In the past, I would have said yes right away.

"Well?" She bats her eyelashes.

I look at her breasts. Still nothing.

The fact that I don't feel interested annoys me, but I hate forcing myself to do something that I can't get anything good out of even more.

"Sorry," I tell her. "I just remembered I have something else to do."

I take out a few bills and place them on the bar. "Benny, give this lady as many drinks as she wants."

I give the woman, who still looks shocked, a final smile before getting off my stool. I'm about to walk off when she wraps her arms around me.

"You're better than any drink," she says as she presses her face against my back. "And so am I."

I sigh and glance at my left hand. Would this be easier if I hadn't taken off my wedding ring?

"I'm no longer thirsty." I pry her arms off me. "And I have to go."

I hear her mutter a curse behind me as I walk off, but I ignore her. I head to the exit and walk out onto the beach. The cool breeze blows through my hair. The soft sand sinks beneath my shoes. I gaze up at the moon, which seems to mock me with its Cheshire Cat smile.

And I lift the middle finger of my right hand.

Chapter Thirteen
Teri

"Fuck!"

The curse escapes my lips as I bump into a corner of the dining table. The collision makes waves in the bowl of hollandaise sauce I have in my hands, sending some of its contents over the edge to splatter on black velvet.

I stare at the fresh stain in disbelief.

Great. I was wearing an apron for the past two hours and nothing happened. I take it off and a dollop of creamy sauce ends up on my dress.

Note to self: Next time, don't take off the apron until you're done setting the table.

Right now, though, it's too late. The mistake has been made, the damage done, which means I have to clean up this mess and change into a new dress.

I let out an exasperated sigh as I reach for some paper towels. This dress was new, too. I picked it carefully, thinking the low neckline would be a nice homecoming treat for Aaron. That and dinner—salmon with hollandaise sauce and a side of spiced asparagus with bacon bits.

Well, at least dinner came out perfect. Almost. There's only half of the hollandaise sauce left, but I think it will be enough.

I toss the used paper towels into the trashcan and head to my room. At the doorway, I pause. The corners of my lips turn up into a smile as I remember the last time Aaron was here.

He tucked me into bed. Not that he hasn't done that before. The difference is that this time, he kissed me on the forehead. Just a simple kiss. It didn't even last more than five seconds. And yet it left my body warm. Yes, my skin was still on fire from the sex, which turned out absolutely amazing in spite of the fact that my wrists were tied during a portion of it, but this was a different kind of heat, like the warmth of a sunset. My heart was fluttering, too. Not pounding like it had been, like it wanted to escape from my chest, but fluttering, like it could just fly and take me with it.

I think I went to sleep with a smile that night. I found myself in a good mood the next day, too, which was dampened when I learned that Aaron had suddenly taken off. But what can I do? He's a businessman. He goes on business trips, sometimes on such short notice that he can't tell his wife in person before he jumps on a plane.

I walk to my closet and pick out a new dress. After going through the rack three times, I pull out the sleeveless powder blue dress with buttons in front and a knee-length hem trimmed with lace. I change into it. When I'm done, I gaze at my reflection in the mirror.

Not as sexy as the black dress, but it still looks pretty. Hopefully, Aaron will like it.

He came back this morning. I barely saw him because he was rushing to go to the office and I was rushing to get to work. I only had time to tell him I'd see him at dinner.

I glance at my watch. He should be home any minute now. Holly said he didn't have any late meetings today.

I suppress a flurry of excitement as I carry my stained dress to the laundry room. I'm about to add it to the pile when I notice that the pile is bigger than it was yesterday. And a little disorganized. As I try to fix it, I realize it's because Aaron added the clothes he used on his trip. I start to go through them, stopping when I see that one of his shirts also has a stain.

A purple stain shaped like a pair of lips.

My heart stops and sinks. Did Aaron cheat on me during his business trip?

It happens. I know. It's cliché, even. And like Winona said, no woman can resist Aaron. But he's my husband. And I thought we were finally getting along. I thought he was starting to like me.

I guess I thought wrong.

I throw the stained shirt back into the pile and stomp out of the laundry room with my forehead creased and my jaw clenched in frustration.

It wouldn't be the first time. God, I'm really such a hopeless fool when it comes to men.

A voice in my head warns me not to jump to conclusions. Maybe I'm wrong. Maybe Aaron is innocent.

Innocent? Yeah, right.

I don't think so, but I intend to be sure soon enough.

~

"How was your trip?" I ask Aaron as he takes off his shoes in the foyer.

"Good," he answers before throwing me a quizzical look. "What are you doing here?"

Just that question lets me know he's in a foul mood. I don't know why, but I'm not backing down.

I give him a puzzled look of my own. "What do you mean? I live here. Did you get amnesia during your trip?"

"I meant why are you standing there?"

"Oh, sorry." I flash a sheepish grin as I rub my neck. "I'm acting like a dog again, aren't I?"

He says nothing.

"I just missed you, I guess," I tell him with a fake smile. "I was hoping you'd call."

Aaron shakes his head. "I don't do nightly calls while I'm away."

I nod. "Okay."

He walks past me.

"I made dinner."

He stops to glance at me, then keeps walking. "I'm not hungry."

Oh no he doesn't.

I place my hands on my hips. "Are you running away from me?"

"No," he answers without looking back.

"What is this? Are we reliving my first days here at the apartment? Because you're treating me like crap just like you used to back then."

"I'm not."

"Yes, you are. You won't even look at me."

He turns and looks at me. "I'm tired, okay? I just came back from a business trip and then I worked all day."

My arms cross over my chest. "Yeah, that must have been tiring. All work and no play, right?"

His eyes narrow suspiciously. "If you have something to say, just say it."

"Fine." I put my hands back on my hips. "You cheated on me, Aaron."

His eyebrows arch. "What?"

"I saw the lipstick stain on your shirt. You were fooling around with another woman while you were on your business trip, weren't you?" I touch my chin. "Let me guess. She must have been some slim, bronze-skinned Jamaican woman who looked like a goddess in a swimsuit and had a nice laugh."

Aaron opens his mouth. For a moment, it gapes as no words come out. Then he scoffs and shakes his head.

"So what if I did?"

My jaw drops in turn. My arms drop to my sides. He's not even denying it?

My chest tightens, seemingly clenching around my heart. I didn't think it would hurt this much, but God, I feel like someone just threw me under a bus.

"I'm your wife, Aaron," I tell him with a shaky voice. Unexpected tears sting the corners of my eyes.

"On paper, yes."

My hand clenches into a fist. "So you're saying that after all this time, you still don't think of me as your wife."

"I'm saying that you're not my boss," he says. "You don't get to tell me what I can do and what I can't do."

Unbelievable.

"So I'm just supposed to stay still while you walk all over me? I'm supposed to just let you rip my heart open and watch myself bleed to death?"

Aaron snorts. "Oh, don't be so dramatic."

"I have feelings, Aaron!" I raise my voice as I beat my hand against my chest. "That's what people have. I am a person. Even if I weren't your wife, which I am, I am a person who can't help but feel things and hope for things…"

"What are you saying? That you thought after we had sex twice, I'd fall head over heels in love with you? Is that what you want? Is that what you're hoping for?"

I feel the air come out of my nose. "Fuck you."

"Fine. Hate me." He lifts his hands and let them crash to his sides. "You always have, anyway."

I do. I so hate him.

"Because just to be clear, no matter how good the sex gets, I'm never falling in love with you."

The words, clear and sharp like the edge of a knife, cut straight to my heart. Tears break free and trickle down my cheeks.

"I really, really hate you."

"Good. We understand each other's feelings."

I shake my head as more tears fall. My fists tremble.

"You can punch me if it makes you feel better," Aaron says. "You always wanted to, right?"

Maybe I should. But I doubt it would make me feel better.

"Or better yet, why don't you give your brother a call so he can come beat the crap out of me? You know, make himself useful."

"Leave my brother out of this," I tell him through gritted teeth.

"Fine." Aaron shrugs. "Keep being stubborn. Keep acting like a spoiled brat. Maybe that's why you've always been alone. And always will be."

He walks past me, back to the front door. The sound of it slamming thunders throughout the apartment.

I sink onto the couch and let the tears fall as I grip my hair in frustration. My chest aches as I struggle to breathe.

How can Aaron be so cruel? And just when I thought things were starting to good.

Ah, but that's my mistake, isn't it? I should never have hoped.

Why am I hoping? I know this marriage is an accident, a sham. I know I got myself into this mess. I know Aaron never actually wanted to marry me. But just because the sex was amazing, just because he kissed me on the forehead, I started hoping. I got carried away.

"Those things don't mean anything to him, stupid," I scold myself.

And they shouldn't mean anything to me. They shouldn't. But why? Why can't I forget them? Why, even though Aaron was such a dick and I hate him, am I the one hurting so bad?

My tear-blurred gaze falls on my phone on the coffee table. Maybe I should call Max. He doesn't have to come here and beat my jerk of a husband up. I just want to hear his voice.

But the last time we spoke, he told me not to call him again. He told me he was okay and that I shouldn't worry about him. He told me to live my life and be happy.

Easy for him to say, I think as I get off the couch to grab some tissues.

How can I be happy when I'm all alone, when I feel so alone?

Max said he left because he made a mistake, because he needed to make things right. I wonder if the mistake he made is bigger than the one I made. One thing I know for sure: I don't know how to make this right. Maybe he does?

I pick up my phone and find his name in my contacts list.

Mr. Stewey. That's what I used to call him when we were kids, what he insisted I call him. It was his favorite comic book character. I don't see that character anymore. The comic was never popular to begin with. But I still remember what he looks like—tall and lanky with patched overalls—and he still reminds me of Max.

I consider calling him for a moment, but I decide against it. I don't want to call him just to worry him. The next time I call him, it will be because I have good news.

I put my phone down and go back to my room to grab a coat. I leave my wedding ring on the bedside table.

What I need now is to forget Aaron, to forget all this. And for that, I need a few stiff drinks.

Chapter Fourteen
Aaron

The whiskey burns a trail down my throat. The empty glass lands on my desk with a thud.

"Wow. That bad, huh?" Hank asks as he walks into my office.

I don't answer. I simply reach for the bottle to pour another glass. He grabs it before I can.

"Before that, why don't you tell me why you're here and what happened in Jamaica?"

I glare at him. How dare he whisk away that whiskey bottle?

"I don't want to talk."

"Really?" He switches the bottle to his other hand like it's a ball. "In case you've forgotten, I'm a lawyer. I'm good at making people talk."

"No, I haven't forgotten that you're a lawyer," I tell him. "Or that you're my lawyer."

"All the more reason for you to talk to me."

"I could fire you, you know."

"Yes, you could. That's your prerogative."

But I don't really want to, not after all the cases he's won for me, not when I might need him to fish me out of jail and defend me if my revenge plan goes awry.

"Fine." I sigh. "I'm here because I don't want to be at my apartment, and nothing happened in Jamaica. Now give me that bottle."

He hands it to me and I pour another glass. I empty that in one gulp, too.

Hank sinks into a chair. "You and Teri had a fight, didn't you? That's why you went to Jamaica. To escape from the drama. But you came back and it's just like the episode was on pause. You got into round two and you left again, only this time, you went to the office instead of Jamaica."

I narrow my eyes at him. "What are you doing here again?"

"I came to get my coffee. You did buy me some, didn't you?"

I shake my head and sit back. "No. And Holly isn't here anymore, so she can't have known I was still here."

Hank chuckles. "You think Holly's my only source?"

My eyebrows arch.

"Just kidding. I had a feeling you'd be here."

I sit back. "Funny. Are lawyers psychic now?"

Hank leans forward. "You know, you're acting strange. Why are you being so defensive? What are you hiding?"

"Nothing."

"Right." He taps his fingers on the desk. "I guess I'll have to pry it out of you."

I shake my head. Hank doesn't give up. Then again, that's one of the things that makes him a good lawyer.

"Let's see." He blows a breath of air up towards his forehead. "Have you and Teri been fucking?"

I throw him a warning glance.

Hank shrugs. "Just answer the question."

"Yes."

He gives a triumphant grin. "Ah, I knew it. You probably had sex after you danced that sizzling tango, didn't you? Wait. Did you have sex at the museum?"

I look away. "I'm objecting to this line of questioning."

"I'll take that as a yes." Hank chuckles. "You dirty dog."

I give him another warning glance.

Hank clears his throat. "How long were you in Jamaica?"

"Two days."

"And you didn't get me any coffee?" He frowns. "You know I love Jamaican coffee."

"I was busy."

"Did you fuck anyone there? I hear the women there are really hot."

"No," I answer. "I was just enjoying the beach."

Hank looks surprised. "You didn't enjoy any women on the beach?"

"No. But Teri seems to suspect it and I didn't correct her."

"Why not?" Hank's surprise turns to perplexity.

"What's the point?"

"Okay." Hank folds his arms over his chest as he sits back. "I think I get it now. You're here because you and Teri had a fight because she thinks you cheated on her."

I shrug. "Pretty much."

Hank looks at me. "She cares for you. Otherwise, she wouldn't have thrown a fit."

I say nothing.

Hank laughs. "My God, she's fallen for you, hasn't she?"

I pause. Has she?

"You're wrong," I tell him. "She's just putting up a fuss, picking a fight. It's what women do. It doesn't mean anything."

Hank shakes his head. "You didn't see how she was looking at you after you danced, did you?"

"You mean like she wanted me to fuck her?"

"It wasn't just lust."

"Wow." I look at Hank in disbelief. "You're such an expert on women, aren't you?"

He smooths his collar. "I daresay I am."

I snort. "Teri's not in love with me."

Then again, if she is, it would explain why she's hoping for more from our marriage.

"Why are you denying it so adamantly?" Hank asks. "This is good. Teri's in love with you. You can use that. Women in love will do anything. They're vulnerable. You can have her bring Max here. You can concoct any bullshit about Max and she'll believe you. She'll take your side and even help you bring him down. And then after you get rid of Max, you can cast her aside and break her heart. Revenge will be sweeter."

Hank is right. I can go with this. I can get something out of this. So why am I annoyed? Why am I feeling reluctant?

"Oh, I get it." Hank stands up. "You're starting to care for her, too, aren't you?"

My jaw drops. "What?"

"You've slept with Teri. You haven't slept with any other woman since you married Teri, even though you must have been surrounded by dozens in Jamaica. You're upset that you're fighting…"

"I'm not upset."

"This says otherwise." He lifts the bottle of whiskey. "Wait. Did you go to Jamaica because you were avoiding her?"

"Me? Run away from a woman?"

"Why are you here, then?"

I don't answer.

Hank grins. "I rest my case."

I roll my eyes. When will I learn not to pick an argument with a lawyer?

It feels like I'm saved by the bell when Hank's phone beeps. He takes it out of his pocket. As he looks at the screen, he grins.

"Would you look at that?" he says. "Denny went to a bar without me. Traitor."

"Why don't you go?" I suggest.

I could use some peace and quiet.

Hank ignores me. "And it looks like he's found a woman. A beautiful…"

Hank stops suddenly. The grin on his face vanishes and his eyebrows furrow in concern. No, not concern. Alarm.

I get off my chair. "What's going on?"

He hides his phone behind him and gives me a sheepish grin. "Oh, nothing."

"For a lawyer, you make a very bad liar."

I grab his phone. My eyes grow wide as I see the woman on the screen. Teri. In that blue dress she had on earlier. With red cheeks, half a drink in hand and a man's arm around her shoulder.

My jaw clenches.

"Where is this?" I ask Hank.

"That tavern on Chadwick, I believe."

I give him back his phone and head towards the door.

"So you don't care about her?" Hank calls after me.

I glance over my shoulder. "I care about her not causing a scandal. She still has my last name."

"She's not wearing your ring," he points out.

I didn't notice that. Not that it matters. I put my hand on the door.

"You're going to get her?"

I roll my eyes. Why can't lawyers ever stop talking?

I turn to meet his gaze. "Just to set the record straight, if you're thinking that I'm going to let Max off the hook, that I'm going to let Teri get in my way, you're wrong."

Hank shrugs. "I'm not thinking anything."

I'd like to wipe that grin off his face with my fist. But right now, I have a drunk, cheating wife to teach a lesson to.

~

I find Teri still at the bar, laughing at the bartender. I don't know if she's still holding the same drink, but I can tell she's had enough. I've seen that look before.

"Hey." A man bars my path. He looks like the guy from the photo. "Hi, Mr. Walsh. I'm Denny, Hank's friend. He told me about... her."

He glances over his shoulder.

"I swear I didn't—"

I step past him without waiting for him to finish. I know he's not the one to blame, but I don't have the patience to listen to his excuse right now.

I grab Teri's arm. "We're leaving."

She looks at me with wide eyes, then grins. "Oh, Aaron. How nice of you to show up."

She turns to the bartender. "This man is my husband, but only on—"

I pull her off her stool. "We're leaving now."

She frowns. "But I still haven't finished my—"

I take the glass out of her hand and set it down on the bar. I take out a bill and slip it beneath the glass. Then I turn back to Teri, who's still gaping in disbelief.

"We're going home."

Teri scoffs. "So now you choose to act like my husband."

She turns on her heel and walks off.

I chase after her. "Teri."

She keeps walking past the tables.

I grab her arm. "Teri."

"Let go of me." She wrenches her arm away. "Unless you want me to make a scene right here."

No. I don't want that. I can already see a few curious glances being thrown in our direction.

Damn it.

Teri walks to the restroom. I follow her.

"You're really going to make a fool of yourself?" I ask her.

"Why not?" Teri shrugs. "I already am a fool, anyway."

The door to one of the women's restroom opens just as she approaches it. A woman comes out and Teri steps in. I push my way in with her and lock the door behind me.

Teri sighs. "What?"

"I'm not leaving without you."

218

She snorts. "You called me a dog, yet here you are following me, sticking to me like a bloodhound on a scent."

"Let's just go," I ask her. "And I'm asking nicely here."

"Oh, really? Then that would be a first. Because you never ask. And you're never nice." She pokes a finger at my chest.

I let out a deep breath. "I'm going to ask one last time."

"Then what? Are you going to drape me over your shoulder and carry me out of here?"

"That's not a bad idea," I say. "Especially since you don't seem to care about making a fool of yourself."

Fear flickers in her eyes. So she doesn't want to make a scene after all.

"Let's go, Teri." I reach for her hand.

She slaps mine away. "Don't touch me!"

"Fine." I raise my hands. "But I'm not leaving this place without you."

"Why are you trying so hard to make me leave, huh?" Teri asks me. "Is it because you're jealous? Again?"

"You're drunk," I answer.

She shrugs. "So?"

"You make stupid mistakes when you're drunk."

Teri's jaw drops, then she lets out a loud laugh. "Yeah. I know. Boy, don't I know it?"

"Good. Then let's go."

I offer her my arm. She steps back.

"No. Why should you be the only one allowed to have fun?"

"You really think getting yourself so drunk you won't remember a thing is fun? I thought you'd learned your lesson."

"Well, I thought I had a husband, too," Teri says as she leans against the wall. "I thought he was starting to like me. But it turns out I was wrong. He cheated on me with some Jamaican woman on a business trip."

"So you're cheating on me as payback?"

"Why not?" Teri gives a mischievous grin. "You're the only man I've ever slept with. How is that fair? I should sleep with at least one other man. Who knows? The sex might be better."

My temper rises. So she really was planning on cheating on me, was she?

"Uh oh. I think I made someone mad." Teri laughs. "What? Are you going to hit me now, Mr. Walsh? Have I been naughty enough for you?"

I really should slap her and bring her back to her senses, teach her a lesson. My palm is aching to do just that. And my blood is boiling. My patience has already run out.

Instead, I grab her by her cheeks and kiss her. Hard.

At first, Teri tries to fight me. She grips my wrists and tries to push them away, but she doesn't have enough strength. Besides, I know this is what she really wants.

She gives in. Her hands go to the back of my head. Her fingers run through strands of my hair as she opens her mouth and lets her tongue play with mine.

My hands move to the front of her dress. Thank goodness this one has buttons in front, because my self-control is already slipping, especially when I think that someone else could have been the one undoing those buttons tonight.

Once I have enough undone, I slip my hands inside her dress. I grope her breasts through her bra and she moans. I push the cups up and out of the way so I can rub her nipples.

Teri's hands slide down. One goes to my chest. The other reaches down to press against my crotch.

My blood rushes there. My cock throbs as it strains to feel her palm.

I really am out of patience.

I pull my mouth away from Teri's and turn her around. I plant a kiss on the back of her shoulder as I push her back lower, then start to nibble on her neck. My hands slip beneath her dress—one to caress her breast and the other to reach between her legs. My fingers stroke her beneath lace panties.

Teri gasps. A shiver goes down her back and her nails rake against the wall.

219

As I keep stroking her, I remove my belt and unzip my pants. I grab my hard cock and let it spring out of its cotton prison. I let it rub against the back of her dress a few times. Then I withdraw my wet fingers and pull her panties down to her knees. I push her even lower and lift her skirt. I grip her hip with one hand and guide my cock inside her. Raw. I don't have time for protection.

She gives a louder gasp and then a moan as I enter her inch by inch—at least until I'm halfway in. Then I shove the rest inside her with one thrust that wrings a soft cry from her throat.

She's making noises, I know. And she's not supposed to, because this is a public bathroom. But I don't care. The music outside is too loud for anyone to hear us anyway.

Besides, didn't she say she wanted to make a scene?

I start moving. Fast. I'm too pissed with her to be gentle. And she seems to be liking it. Gasps and moans continue to spill out from her lips. Her hands try to grasp the tiles on the wall. Her hips move against mine.

I reach in between her legs as I continue to pound into her. My fingers brush against her wet curls. They search for her pleasure button. And find it.

I rub the swollen nub of flesh and Teri starts shaking. I can sense my own excitement building up like a storm. Just a little longer and it will break.

But not before I break her.

I stroke Teri faster, until she throws her head back. Her hand grips my thigh.

I don't even pause to let her catch her breath. I grip both her hips again and move faster even though she's stopped moving. After a few thrusts, a groan rumbles low in my throat as I empty myself inside her.

My forehead touches her back as I take a moment to pull air back into my lungs. Then I step back. Teri's skirt falls back into place and she leans against the wall.

I wait for her to say something as I tuck my spent cock back inside my boxers and zip up my pants, but she silently pulls her panties back on.

Not so feisty now, is she?

Suddenly, her hand clasps over her mouth.

"Teri?" I ask in concern.

Instead of answering, she hunches over the toilet bowl and holds her hair back as she throws up.

I roll my eyes at the ceiling.

Great. Just great.

Chapter Fifteen
Teri

I wake up with my head throbbing, my throat dry and an unpleasant taste on my tongue. My lips curve into a frown as I stare up at the ceiling.

Great. Another hangover.

I'd rather go back to sleep and stay in bed all day. It's a Saturday, after all. But I need water and a Tylenol, so I force myself to sit up. The sheets slide off me.

As I stretch my arms, I find myself staring down at my bra. One peek under the sheets and I catch a glimpse of black lace. My eyebrows arch then furrow as I touch my chin and try to recall last night's events.

So I went to a tavern. I sat at the bar and had a few drinks—just three, actually, or more accurately, two and a half. I was flirting with a guy named Denny. And then Aaron appeared. I went to the bathroom. He followed me inside. We had sex and...

A blush coats my cheeks as I remember the sex. I slap my hands against them and shake my head. What the hell was I thinking, having sex in a public bathroom?

I try to push the images aside as I move on with my recollection. So we were in the bathroom, and I threw up. Aaron carried me out of the tavern because I could barely walk. Then I went to sleep in the car.

See. I can clearly remember what happened.

Well, up to that point, at least. I vaguely remember being in the elevator and taking off my shoes in the foyer. And I don't remember taking off my dress, though I spot it now as a pile on the floor.

Did Aaron take it off?

As I get out of bed, my gaze falls on the golden ring on the bedside table and I remember the fight Aaron and I had. I pick it up and hold it between two fingers. It glints as it catches the light.

Now what? Do I just forget Aaron cheated on me? Does the fact that we had sex and he took me home mean I don't get to be mad at him anymore? Am I still mad at him?

My head throbs and I grimace. Maybe I should save the questions for after I've had that Tylenol.

With a sigh, I slip the wedding band back on my finger, just because I don't want to leave it lying there. I grab a shirt and a clean pair of panties from my closet and drag myself to the bathroom. Then I stop by the laundry room before heading to the kitchen.

To my surprise, I see Aaron standing there.

"Good morning," he greets me as he pours a glass of water.

He hands it to me.

"I'm guessing you need this. And this."

He grabs the bottle of Tylenol on the counter, opens it and then shakes it until a pill falls into his palm. He hands it to me as well.

I pop the pill into my mouth and drink the water. The cool liquid feels nice as it goes down my throat and I can't help but give a gasp of satisfaction when I've finished it.

Aaron grins. "Better?"

I nod.

"You know, oatmeal helps, too. I can fix you a bowl."

My eyes narrow in suspicion. Why is Aaron being so nice? Isn't he supposed to be scolding me for drinking, saying "I told you so"? Isn't he mad at me for going to that bar? He seemed pretty mad last night.

I pull out a chair. "Aren't you supposed to be at work?"

"Not this morning. Saturday, remember?"

I sit down. As I do, my toe hits one of the table legs and I yelp.

First a hangover. Now a stubbed toe. This morning is really going well for me.

"Are you alright?" Aaron asks.

"No," I answer as I rub my toe. "I just stubbed my toe."

"Oh."

"And the pain reliever hasn't taken effect yet, so my head still hurts."

"Just your head?"

"And my toe."

In fact, right now, the pain in my toe feels worse.

"Anywhere else?"

I meet his gaze. I don't really get his question. Am I supposed to hurt anywhere else? He didn't hit me, did he?

"I was a little rough last night," he adds.

"Rough?"

"In the… restroom."

Now I get it. I look down between my legs. Nope. It doesn't feel sore.

"I'm fine," I say as I fight off a blush.

"Good."

He pulls out a chair and sits opposite me. I grab my glass of water and take another sip to avoid his gaze, but I can still feel it on me.

Why is he staring at me? Does he really think he hurt me? Wait. Is he feeling guilty? Is that why he's being nice to me all of a sudden?

Nice is… well, nice, but I don't want anyone feeling sorry for me.

I put my glass down. "I'm fine, Aaron. Really, I am."

He just nods.

I sigh. "Though I still am a little mad at you."

"A little?"

"I do have the right, you know. Yes, I know you don't love me. I'm not asking you to. I'm just asking for some respect, because I still am your wife, and maybe a little appreciation. I'm not asking you to live up to my expectations. I'm asking you to recognize my efforts. I am trying here to be a good wife, to get along with you, to have some kind of relationship here. You said I'm not… wild enough. I've tried to change. I put on that lingerie and I… well, you know what I did. You have no idea how hard that was for me."

"I know."

"And yet you still go and sleep with some other woman just for fun. Do you know how that makes me feel? Like all I've done is for nothing. Like no matter what I do, I'll never be enough for you."

Aaron says nothing. He just stares at me from across the table.

I draw a deep breath. "There. I've said my piece. You say yours."

"I didn't cheat on you," Aaron tells me.

My jaw drops. "What?"

"I didn't sleep with another woman," he explains. "That lipstick stain was probably from when I was trying to leave the bar and she hugged me from behind because she wanted me to stay."

I nod slowly. Well, I guess that explains why the stain was on the back of the shirt.

Relief washes over me but quickly evaporates.

"Why didn't you say so?" I ask him furiously. "Do you have any idea how hurt I was? Do you enjoy seeing me hurt? Is that it?"

"I thought it would be easier," Aaron says.

My eyebrows arch. "Easier?"

I have no clue how things would have been easier. On the contrary, he made things harder, more complicated.

"And I hated the fact that you didn't trust me. You sounded like one of those annoying, nagging wives."

I nod. "I see."

Well, I guess I am partly to blame for accusing him instead of asking.

I place my hand on my forehead. I told you not to jump to conclusions.

I draw a deep breath. "I guess it's a little hard for me to trust you when I don't really know what to expect of you."

"Which is why I think we should make some things clear," Aaron says. "Every marriage has a set of rules. I think we should make our own."

My eyebrows arch. Frankly, I've been wanting to have this conversation since day one. I guess it's better late than never.

"Okay."

"First, I won't have sex with anyone else," Aaron says. "The same applies to you."

"I wasn't really planning on having sex with a stranger," I say in my defense. "I was just... angry."

I was going to say "jealous" but I decided to change it at the last second.

"No more drinking outside," he tells me next. "I don't want you getting into trouble."

"Or making a scene. I know."

"We can have sex outside, though."

I stiffen.

"In fact, we can have sex whenever and wherever you want," Aaron adds.

I look away as a blush coats my cheeks.

"Anything else you want to add?" he asks.

"I don't like it when you ignore me, especially when I don't know why," I tell him. "So don't. If you're mad at me, tell me why. If you need some time alone, tell me."

"Okay."

"Let's talk. It doesn't have to be about everything. Let's just try to communicate with each other, try to get along. After all, we live together. Let's at least act like roommates."

Aaron nods. "So we're roommates who have sex?"

"Or sex buddies who live together."

He chuckles. "Sounds good. Shall we shake on it?"

Aaron offers me his hand and I shake it. He grins. I smile.

Sex buddies, huh? It sounds a bit weird, but it's better than strangers, or two people who are just trying to put up with each other because of some mistake. At least we'll be buddies.

More importantly, there will be sex. Amazing sex.

~

"You look like you're glowing," Pam tells me as I comb her hair.

It's a Friday night and she and Ron are going on a date, which is why she's asked me to come over and watch Cody.

"Am I?" I stare at my face in the mirror over her shoulder.

I don't really see anything different, though I do feel different. I feel... good. These past several days, Aaron and I have been getting along, and not just in bed or in the shower, though I have to say those are the best parts.

I'm doing well at work. I have a man at home. What more could I ask for?

"You're smiling," Pam teases as she turns to face me. "What's going on?"

"Nothing," I answer.

She puts a hand on her hip. "Really? You're keeping secrets from me now?"

Not now. For the past three weeks. And I still feel a little bad about it, but I don't think it's the right time yet to come clean. Maybe if things keep going well for Aaron and me?

"You know, you may not live with me anymore, but I'm still your sister," Pam tells me. "If you have a boyfriend, I have the right to know."

I narrow my eyes at her. "What makes you think I have a boyfriend?"

"Because you're glowing and smiling and being secretive."

I shake my head. "You're reading too much into things again. I'm not being secretive. And I'm only smiling because you look pretty. You're the one who's glowing, not me."

Pam smiles as she takes my hands in hers. "Aww."

"You really are."

She looks like a Greek goddess draped in her black and white dress—black on the upper right side and lower left side and white on the opposite.

"Thank you." She touches my cheek. "So you don't have a boyfriend?"

I roll my eyes. She really doesn't give up, does she?

"No. I don't have a boyfriend." Which isn't a lie.

Pam faces the mirror. "You know, you never did tell me what happened at that party."

"Nothing," I say. "I just drank, danced, met some important people."

Again, not a lie.

She smooths the front of her gown. "Did any hot guys ask you out?"

"No, but I had fun." Sort of.

Pam smiles at me. "I'm glad you did."

"Ready, honey?" Ron asks as he appears in the doorway in a red shirt, bow tie and black pants.

"Ooh," Pam purrs. "Someone looks handsome tonight."

He frowns. "Just tonight?"

She walks over to him and places her hand on his cheek. "Especially handsome tonight."

Ron smiles. "Well, you don't look so bad yourself."

"I know, right?" Pam spins.

"You look like a prom queen," Ron compliments.

Pam pouts. "I don't want to look like one of those selfish bitches."

"Sorry." Ron squeezes her hand. "I meant beauty queen."

Pam doesn't look convinced.

"My queen." Ron brings her hand to his lips.

Pam finally smiles as she touches his arm. "And you, sir, are the king of my heart."

They lean towards each other to kiss. I look away and clear my throat.

"Oops." Pam steps away from Ron and turns to me with an apologetic look. "Sorry. Forgot you were still there."

I exhale. "Clearly."

"Well, we should be going."

Pam grabs her purse and places her arm in Ron's. They go downstairs and I follow them until they get to the front door.

"Don't forget. No more sweets for Cody," Pam tells me before stepping out. "And he should be in bed by ten."

I nod. "Got it."

"If anything happens, call me."

"Nothing is going to happen," Ron says.

"Right," I agree. "So just have fun. Enjoy your evening together."

Pam takes a deep breath and smiles. "I will."

They go out the door and I close it behind them. I watch them through the glass, though. Ron wraps an arm around Pam as they walk to the car and she leans toward him. He squeezes her shoulder and she kisses him on the cheek. I hear them laughing.

I grip my chest as I feel it tighten. What is this ache?

Then I realize it's envy. I thought I was fine just getting along with Aaron and having sex with him almost every night. I thought I was happy. But now, I realize I actually want something more. I want what Pam and Ron have.

I want Aaron to love me.

I know. I told him I wasn't asking him for that. But really, every wife wants her husband to love her. And I know that Aaron and I were only married by mistake, but the more I spend time with him, the more I get to know him, the more I think we actually make a good couple.

But am I the only one thinking that? Am I the only one here falling?

Yes, I'm falling for my husband, or maybe I've fallen already. That's why I was so hurt before when he would ignore me or act coldly towards me. That's why I'm so happy now that he cares for me.

I'm happy, but it's not enough. Aaron and I are friends, but there's still a gap between us. What can I do to bridge that gap? What can I do to make him love me?

"Aunt Teri?" Cody calls from the living room.

"Coming!"

I sit beside him on the couch. He hands me the remote.

"You pick what we're watching," he says.

"Okay, but you have to be in bed by ten," I tell him. "That's what your mother said."

"And you'll tell her if I'm not?"

I ruffle his hair. "You know your mother has a nose for finding out the truth, and we don't want to get on her bad side."

"No, we don't," Cody agrees.

I flip through the channels. "Let's see. What should we watch?"

Suddenly, I stop as I catch a glimpse of Aaron's face on the screen. At first, I think it's not him, just someone who looks like him. But then I see the headline. I hear the words of the news reporter and I feel my cheeks go pale.

"Did Aaron Walsh, in fact, kill his sister?"

Chapter Sixteen
Aaron

"This is crazy."

I turn off the TV in my office and slam the remote down on the couch.

I've been seeing my face on the screen since last night, and I'm tired of it. More than that, I'm tired of all the noise—of all the lies I've been hearing and the phone outside ringing off the hook, as it has been all morning.

"Mr. Walsh?" Holly peeks in. "I have the New York Times asking for a statement."

I drop to the couch. "I don't have any. I have nothing for the press, so tell them to fuck off."

Holly glances at her notes. "I also have a Delia Marron. She says you went out with her once and you hit her. If you don't give her money, she's going to speak up about it."

I chuckle in disbelief. "She wants to get on the 'Bring Down Aaron Walsh' bandwagon? Fine by me. I don't give a damn."

Holly walks out.

Hank sits on the armchair across from me. "Who's Delia Marron?"

I shrug. "Hell if I know."

"Did you really hit her?"

I give him a warning glance.

"Listen, Aaron, I'm your lawyer. It's my job to defend you against all accusations, but I can only do that if I know all your crimes."

"As my lawyer, don't you have more important things to do right now? Like shutting up this Kylie Campden."

Kylie Campden. When I first heard that name, I thought it sounded familiar. Now I know why. Kylie Ann. That's what Marjorie used to call her. They used to hang around a lot in high school. That part of Kylie's statement is true. She said I was very protective of Marj. That's true, too. As for the part where Marj called her to say she was pregnant and that she was afraid I'd kill her? I don't know. What I do know is the lie—that Kylie saw me leaving Marjorie's apartment before I said I found her body, that I saw Kylie and I told her that if she ever told anyone she saw me there, I'd kill her, too.

Bullshit.

"Her statement won't hold up in court," Hank tells me. "You had a solid alibi for that night. You have nothing to worry about."

"So we just let her talk and ruin my reputation?"

Hank shrugs. "I could pay her to keep quiet. She's probably after money."

"Give her money for spreading lies about me?" I shake my head. "No fucking way."

"Or I could sue her for slander."

I point a finger at him. "Now you're thinking like a lawyer."

"But you know that would only make things worse, right?" Hank tells me. "If we sue her, she will be the victim and you will be the bad guy, not the other way around. And people already think you're the bad guy. The women you've slept with are painting a picture of you as a playboy who likes it rough. Your enemies will testify to the fact that you are heartless and have made threats before. Oh, and there's this."

Hank hands me his phone. The video on the screen shows me carrying Teri out of the bathroom and out of the tavern. It doesn't show her face clearly, but it shows mine.

I hand the phone back to him with a frown. "Wasn't this at least a week ago?"

"Yes. People weren't paying attention then, but they are now. They think you're an abusive husband."

I rub my temples. "So what you're saying is there's nothing I can do?"

"You can make a statement, but no one will probably believe you."

I narrow my eyes at him. "So there's nothing I can do."

"We should just let it die down," Hank says.

Easy for him to say. He's not the one whose reputation is being smashed to pieces here.

"This company has longstanding relationships with its corporate clients and partners," Hank adds. "Relationships with impeccable records. Those will remain even if some small businesses and individuals switch to UPS, which means business will still be good."

"You think?" I ask him. "You know how much I invested in this company, Hank."

"I know." He nods. "And I'm telling you one liar isn't going to bring you down."

"But you just said she has a whole army of liars with her."

"They won't bring this company down," Hank assures me. "They won't bring you down. They can't. The rumors will die down, and afterwards, you'll still be here. We'll still be here."

I'm glad he sounds so confident, but I still can't help but worry.

"So, just to be clear, you're not doing anything?"

Hank shakes his head.

I snort. "Some lawyer you are."

"Aaron, this battle isn't in a court of law. It's in a court of public opinion, and we've already lost."

I stand up and slam my hands on the table. "Because you didn't do your job! If you had found Max Colby by now, we wouldn't be in this mess."

"I tried, okay?" Hank stands up as well. "And if you hadn't been so busy fucking his sister, maybe—"

He stops as the door opens. Teri steps in.

Great.

I put my hands behind my hips as I stare at the ceiling. "What do you want, Teri?"

"I… I saw the news."

"Everyone has," I tell her.

"Is it true?"

I look at her. "That I killed my sister?"

Unbelievable.

"No," Teri answers. "I'd never think that. Is it true that your sister was murdered? Because you never told me. You never even told me you had a sister."

"Well, I've never even met your brother, either," I point out.

Her eyebrows arch. "At least I told you I have one. Not too many people know about that."

"What are you saying, Teri?" I step closer to her. "That I'm supposed to tell you everything about me?"

"But I'm your—"

"My wife," I finish the sentence for her. "I know. But do husbands tell their wives everything? No."

"I thought we were friends, too."

"Sex buddies," I correct her.

Her jaw drops. No words come out of her mouth.

"It was a long time ago, okay?" I raise my hands. "And it's not exactly something I want to remember."

"Well, clearly the world has a way of reminding us of things we'd rather forget," she mutters with a look of pain in her eyes.

My arms crash to my sides as I give her a look of disbelief. Doesn't she know I'm dealing with something serious here? And she's whining for my attention? She wants this to be about her?

Teri draws a deep breath. "I just wish you'd told me about her, Aaron."

"You want to know about my sister?" I step forward. "Fine. Marjorie Walsh was my younger sister. Four years younger. Her sign was Aquarius. I called her Marj. She was beautiful and smart and funny. And kind. She was perfect. She was my baby sister. And I loved her. I tried to give her everything. I tried to protect her. But now everyone thinks I killed her."

I grab the closest trophy on the shelf, the one I won in a marathon in high school. I throw it to the floor and it smashes to pieces.

Teri gasps as she steps back. Hank gets on his feet.

I turn around and run my hands through my hair in frustration. Now I've done it.

"What can I do to help?" Teri asks softly.

Help?

227

I shake my head and whisper under my breath, "I don't need help from her murderer's sister."

"What?" Teri comes closer.

I face her and meet her gaze. "I said I don't need your help, so just leave me alone."

"But—"

"Just go, Teri!" I point to the door. "This doesn't involve you."

For a moment, she just stands there with disbelief and pain in her hazel eyes. Then she turns and marches off. The door opens and slams shut.

I place a hand on my forehead. When I meet Hank's gaze, I raise a finger.

"Don't," I warn him.

I don't want to hear another word from him right now.

He shrugs.

The door opens again and Holly steps in. "Mr. Walsh, there's—"

She stops as she sees the golden fragments on the floor.

"Should I call... the janitor?" she asks me.

"You do that," I tell her. "At least someone will be doing his job."

I glance in Hank's direction. He shakes his head silently.

"Oh, and—"

"Holly," I interrupt her. "I'm not talking to anyone, and if you're getting tired of it too, just unplug the phone. You have my permission."

It takes her a moment to respond. "Alright, Mr. Walsh."

She steps out. I glance at Hank once more.

"You should go, too."

"Fine." He leaves.

I grab the bottle of whiskey from the shelf, pour myself a glass, and gulp the contents down.

To hell with everyone.

Chapter Seventeen
Teri

What the hell is wrong with him?

I bite down on my trembling lower lip as I stare out the car window. My fingers trap a handful of pleats as they curl into a fist.

I went to Aaron's office because I was worried about him, because I wanted to understand what he was going through, because I wanted to help him. And what did he do? He threw a trophy in front of me, shouted at me in front of his lawyer. Worst of all, he told me this whole thing had nothing to do with me and sent me away.

I flatten my palm against my forehead, between my eyebrows where I feel the veins are about to pop.

I know this happened long before Aaron met me. Seven years ago, the news said. But how can this have nothing to do with me when the man I love is clearly still suffering from it, when it's troubling him now?

Ah. I slap my forehead. But he doesn't know I love him, and clearly, he doesn't feel the same way. In fact, he was looking at me like I was some pest, some vile creature.

If I close my eyes, I can still see the anger raging in his. The frustration. At the same time, though, I can see sadness. There's a plea somewhere there, even if he can't see it himself. Even if he refuses to admit it.

I shake my head. Aaron isn't angry with me. He's angry with the unfair, cruel world that made this mess and with himself for getting caught up in it. He was only lashing out at me. He was only refusing my help because he feels helpless.

For a powerful man like him, it must suck to feel helpless. It's probably almost as bad as being accused of killing your sister.

I let out a sigh as I grip my seatbelt.

I know Aaron didn't kill Marjorie. I knew it even that first time I saw the news. Aaron may be insensitive and mean sometimes. And yes, he can shoot a gun without blinking. But I know for a fact that he's no murderer. And I became even more sure after hearing him talk about his sister. She meant the world to him.

Now I understand why he keeps bugging me about my brother. He probably thinks my brother should be at my side, just as he was at Marjorie's for as long as he could be. Maybe he's trying to bring us together because he knows that Max must miss me. Maybe he wants to talk to Max about me because that's what he would have wanted Marjorie's boyfriend or husband to do.

I grin. I can already imagine what kind of big brother he was.

"Teri?" Elsa's voice breaks into my thoughts.

"What?" I turn my head towards her.

"We're here."

She pulls into the paved driveway of a beautiful cedar and brick house. I catch the number on the mailbox at the edge of the front porch.

I draw a deep breath. I guess we're here.

Elsa places her hand over mine. "We don't have to do this now. I know you're going through... something right now. I can drive you home and tell Winona—"

"I'm fine, Elsa." I squeeze her hand. "I appreciate your concern, but really, I'm fine and work will make me feel even better."

She nods. "If you say so."

"I say so."

I take off my seatbelt and get out of the car. The breeze blows through my hair.

"What's the name of the client again?" I ask Elsa as we walk to the house.

"Annabelle Delore," Elsa answers.

I commit the name to memory as I cross the front porch. I ring the doorbell and a few moments later, I see a pair of blue eyes through the sliding peephole.

Wow. I didn't guess that that was a peephole.

"Who's there?" the female voice behind the door asks.

"Ms. Delore?" I clear my throat. "My name is Teri and I'm from W.H. Clements. I'm here with my assistant, Elsa. You called us about giving the interior of your house a makeover."

The peephole slides close. I hear a bolt unlock and the door opens.

"Come in."

As soon as Elsa and I have stepped inside, the woman closes the door. I gaze at my client for the first time.

Mid-twenties. Cornflower blue eyes—well, I already knew that. Wavy, auburn hair. Lilac cashmere sweater. Dark blue pants. A gold chain with a pendant in the shape of a...

I pause as I stare at the golden feather pendant. I'm pretty sure I've seen that somewhere recently.

Then I look at her face once more and it clicks.

I gasp. "You're Kylie Campden."

"Shh." She holds a finger to her lips, which confirms my suspicion.

"But I thought the client was Annabelle Delore," Elsa says.

"Annabelle Delore is my mother," Kylie says. "And I guess you can say she's your client. She's the one I bought this house for, the one I want it designed for. It's my gift to her, my surprise. She's always wanted a house, and well, she's just been told she has a tumor."

"I'm sorry to hear that," the words come out of my mouth automatically.

"Well, she's undergoing treatment. If it doesn't go well, I want to make some of her dreams come true before she... well, before she goes. If it does go well, I want her to live the rest of her life happily. She's already been through so much."

I nod. I understand that sentiment. What I don't understand is why is the woman standing in front of me accusing my husband of murdering his sister? She seems like a nice woman, not at all the kind to make up stories to ruin other people. It's hard to believe they're one and the same.

"I'm sorry about earlier, if I seemed weird or paranoid," Kylie adds. "It seems I've become famous overnight, and I just don't want reporters or weirdoes here."

That's another thing I don't understand. Why lie about a famous person, why go on TV if you don't want to be famous? It doesn't make sense.

"You said your name was Teri?" Kylie asks me. "Is there a problem?"

So she's noticed my apprehension.

"Is there a problem, Teri?" Elsa seconds the question. "Because if there is, I can—"

"No problem," I answer.

If they're asking me if I'm not taking this project, well, I am. And not just because I'm a professional. There's something off here, something that doesn't add up. And I intend to get to the bottom of it.

Besides, Aaron might have said he didn't need my help, but he didn't exactly forbid me to try to help him. Not that he could.

I turn to Kylie with a smile. "So, Kylie, why don't you tell me what kind of house your mother has always dreamed of coming home to?"

~

"It's perfect," Kylie says with a gasp as she finishes touring the house I've worked hard to design for the past few days.

I can hear the joy in her voice. I can see tears at the corners of her eyes.

She wipes them away. "I'm sure Mom will love this."

"I'm glad to hear it," I say. "I hope she'll be able to live here for years to come."

She turns to me with a warm smile. "How can I ever, ever thank you, Teri?"

"Well, it's my job." I shrug. "But if you really want to thank me, you can stop lying."

The joy vanishes from her eyes as they grow wide. "I don't know what you mean."

"Yes, you do," I tell her. "Kylie, my full name is Teri Walsh."

"Walsh?"

"I'm Aaron Walsh's wife. I know he didn't kill Marjorie. And so do you."

For a moment, she just stares at me with her mouth gaping. Then she sinks into the nearest chair.

I place a hand on her shoulder. "I know you're not a liar, Kylie. I know you're not a bad person."

She says nothing.

"You know what else I know? You're a good daughter, Kylie. You would do anything for your mother. Even if that means telling lies on TV."

She glances at me but says nothing.

I walk to the window. "I was wondering how you could afford a house. Or me. No offense, but I'm sure your mother's treatment is expensive."

"It is," Kylie confirms.

"And yet you are getting her treated, and I can only assume she's getting the very best that she deserves. At the same time, you've just bought this large house and had it fully furnished."

"Beautifully furnished."

I let the compliment go as I turn to face her. "Someone paid you to lie about Aaron Walsh. Am I right?"

She doesn't answer, but the fact that she's avoiding my gaze tells me what I need to know.

"I understand why you did it," I tell her. "I'm not judging you. We do crazy things for the people we love. We'd do everything for them. But that doesn't make it right."

"I don't care about doing the right thing." Kylie looks into my eyes. "All my life, my mother has done the right things. She was the best wife ever, and my dad still left her. She's been the best mother. She was a good teacher. And now look what happened. She's sick, possibly dying. She doesn't deserve this. So I don't care. I just want her to be happy for once."

I kneel in front of her and place my hand over hers. "I'm sure she's been happy all this time having a wonderful daughter like you."

She pulls her hand away and snorts. "You don't know that. You don't know what kind of daughter I've been to her. That's why I did this. I have to make it up to her before it's too late."

I stand up. "You know, if you come to Aaron, if you come clean about this and you apologize to him, he will help you. You were Marjorie's friend, after all."

"Not really," Kylie says. "I mean, I was always by her side, but that was only because I was envious of her. I wished I could be her."

"Yet she kept you by her side anyway. She became your friend, anyway. She was kind, wasn't she? Just like her brother."

Again, Kylie looks away.

"You know Aaron would never have hurt her, right?" I ask her. "She meant the world to him."

"I know," she finally admits. "I didn't lie when I said he was overprotective."

I chuckle. "I'm sure he was."

Kylie meets my gaze. "Are you sure Aaron will forgive me? Can you guarantee he'll help my mother?"

I nod as I reach for her hand. "All you did was take money from some people who wanted to bring him down. If you tell him why you did it and who you took the money from, I'm sure he'll forgive you."

"But I don't know who they are. I haven't met them. I just spoke to them over the phone and they deposited money in my account."

I squeeze her hand. "You tell Aaron what you know and he'll find them."

She stands up and starts pacing the floor. "But what if they get angry at me? What if they come after me? Or my mother?"

"Aaron will protect you," I assure her. "I promise he will."

Kylie stops and looks at me. "You love him, don't you? You think the world of him."

I touch my neck as I fight off a blush. A grin forms on my lips and I shrug.

"I guess my secret's out."

Kylie smiles, but then her lips quickly turn down. "But I'll have to tell everyone I lied, right? Everyone will know I'm a liar."

"I thought you don't care what people think," I tell her. "I thought you only cared about your mother."

She says nothing.

I squeeze her arm. "It's fine. Everyone makes mistakes. They'll forgive you eventually, and even if they don't, what matters is that you did the right thing. Trust me, it will feel better."

Kylie nods. Her lips curve into a weak smile. "You know, you're nice just like Marjorie was."

I smile in turn. "I'm glad to hear that."

"She sent me messages a few times even when she was in college, you know. She asked how I was. We were supposed to see each other and catch up the day after she died. But she... well..."

"She died."

She nods. "Do you think they'll ever catch who killed her?"

I shrug. "I hope so."

"Do you think she'll forgive me for what I did?"

I give her arm another squeeze. "If she has a big heart like you said she had, she will. I'm sure she's already forgiven you."

Kylie gives another nod, then draws a deep breath. "Do you think maybe you can not tell my mom about this? She doesn't know what I've done, and she already has a lot on her plate—"

"I won't tell," I promise her. "If I ever get to talk to her, all I'll tell her is that she's lucky to have a daughter like you."

Kylie gives a bigger smile.

I offer her my hand. "So, shall we go tell the truth?"

~

"You're now saying that Aaron Walsh didn't kill his sister?" asks the news reporter, a man in his forties who earlier said his name was Oscar.

"No," Kylie answers softly. She looks away from the camera.

"I'm sorry. What was that?"

"No." Kylie speaks louder. "I... I lied."

"You lied?" Oscar's eyes grow wide.

Kylie doesn't answer. Her hands shake as she puts them on her arms.

It's strange how people are so scared to tell the truth when they can spout a lie so easily.

Still, I can't help but feel sorry for her, especially with the reporter looking at her like she's Hester Prynne.

"So you were lying when you said Aaron Walsh was a murderer?" Oscar asks. "Ms. Campden, do you have any idea what a serious offense this is?"

And now he's trying to burn her at the stake. I can't stand it anymore, so I step forward.

"Ms. Campden made a mistake, alright? People, even the best of us, make mistakes."

Oscar glances at me. "But—"

"Even you make mistakes," I cut him off. "For example, you made a mistake when you decided to spread Ms. Campden's lie and make a story out of it without verifying the facts first. Or do you believe what anyone tells you so long as it makes a great story?"

Oscar looks at me in disbelief.

"You see, Ms. Campden lied, but isn't it your job to find out the truth? In fact, don't you owe it to your audience to tell them the truth and not just give them something juicy to nibble on, something to talk about so they can feel their lives are less mundane?"

Now he's glaring at me. "Who are you, exactly?"

"I'm Teri Walsh," I introduce myself without a second thought. "I'm the wife of Aaron Walsh."

Oscar's eyes grow wide again as I hear a murmur behind me. Then he chuckles. "Oh, I see what's happening here."

He looks at Kylie. "Ms. Campden, did Aaron Walsh pay you to say you lied? Is that why look so reluctant?" He glances at me. "Did Teri Walsh pay you?"

"I did not," I deny his accusation. "How dare you accuse me of such a thing?"

"No offense, Mrs. Walsh, but how are we supposed to believe you when you're the wife of the man being accused of murder? You're not exactly objective or credible, are you?"

I roll my eyes and scoff. "I can't believe you're accusing me of not being objective or credible. Talk about the pot calling the kettle back."

Oscar frowns, but I can sense from the way he's holding his shoulders that he's not letting up.

"So, you're saying, Mrs. Walsh, that your husband is innocent?"

"Yes."

"And you know because you were there?"

"No. I know because I know him, because I know how much he loved his sister. Even now, he still grieves."

"And I suppose you'll also deny the fact that he's an abusive husband?"

I roll up one of my sleeves. "Do I look abused?"

"No, but you look like you're very much in love with your husband, which means—"

"That I'll say anything to defend him, even when he's wrong?" I finish his sentence. "I'm his wife, not his lawyer."

"No," Oscar agrees. "But I'm guessing you'll also say he didn't hit any of those women who have claimed he was violent towards them? You do know that he slept with a lot of women—"

"I know," I cut him off. "That was before he married me. I also know that he's hot. He's rich. He's a catch. Some women can't bear the thought of a man like that casting them aside, so they make up stories. Or maybe they just want some money."

"Just to be clear, you are calling these women liars, Mrs. Walsh?"

"Why don't you ask them? Like I said, it's your job to find the truth."

Oscar nods. "Are you aware, Mrs. Walsh, that one of these women said your husband tied her up. Now, why would she make that up?"

"Maybe she didn't," I say. "But maybe she asked him to tie her up. It does make things a little bit more exciting, after all."

I hear gasps of horror, but I just shrug. What? Hasn't anyone read Fifty Shades?

Oscar turns red. Ah, he has.

He clears his throat. "So, Mrs. Walsh…"

"You know, it's sad that we look for the worst in people," I go on as I stare into the camera. "Or that we're so quick to believe in bad rumors. I find it sad that some people won't watch the news unless there's been a shooting or an earthquake that killed dozens. But fine, let's just say that's human nature. We want to see the worst in others so we can feel better about ourselves. We want to watch tragedy so we can feel lucky we're alive. We want to spread lies about others so people won't know about our dark secrets. That's fine. But go gossip about someone else. Go paint someone else as a bad guy. Because as smoky a villain as my husband would make, he's one of the good guys. As much as he looks like he could kill someone with that body of his, he's only dangerously good in bed. He was a loving brother and he's a great husband. But more than that, he's a good man."

Silence falls over the studio.

I exhale. There. I've gone ahead and said my piece.

Oscar breaks the silence first. "Mrs. Walsh, thank you for that speech, but it doesn't—"

"Aaron Walsh didn't kill Marjorie," Kylie finally speaks up.

And just when I thought she'd already evaporated.

"He would never hurt her. I only said he did because Marjorie was my friend and it felt like people had forgotten about her, like Aaron had forgotten about her. I wanted him to remember her and not to pretend she never lived. I wanted him to celebrate who she was and not be bitter about how she died. And not just him. I want the people who knew Marjorie to remember her with a smile. And I want her killer to know that he still hasn't gotten away with it. I want the right people to do their jobs and continue the fight to bring her justice."

I look at Kylie with pride. She's done even better than I thought she would. She spoke up. She owned up to her mistake. And she silenced Oscar.

He takes a few moments to recover before turning to the camera. "Well, there you have it, ladies and gentlemen. Kylie Campden and Teri Walsh…"

I stop listening to him as I turn to Kylie and grab her hand.

"Thanks," I whisper.

She shakes her head. "I couldn't have done it without you. You were the brave one."

"We both were."

She smiles and takes my hand. "Do you think what I said will be enough for your husband to forgive me?"

I squeeze Kylie's hand. "Why don't we ask him about it?"

~

Aaron returns to the apartment a few minutes past ten. I lean against the wall in the hallway, watching and waiting as he shrugs off his jacket and loosens his tie. He loosens his hair as well and when he lifts his chin, our eyes finally meet.

"Hey." His lips curve into a smile that makes my heart skip a beat.

I trace the neckline of my shirt as I throw the smile and the greeting back at him. "Hey. So, how did things go with Kylie?"

"I've told Hank to hire someone to find out who paid her. I have people watching both her and her mother. I asked Holly to do a background check on Ms. Delore's doctor and find a better one."

I nod. "It sounds like things went well."

"Thanks to you, I've been told."

His elbow rests against the wall as he stands in front of me. His hand goes to the back of his neck as his eyes look into mine.

"I also watched your interview."

I cross my arms over my chest. "You mean Kylie's interview."

"You answered more questions."

I chuckle. "I guess I did."

"And you made a speech, too."

I stick out my lower lip as I narrow my eyes at him. "Are you making fun of me?"

"No." He crosses his arms over his chest as well. "I'm admiring you."

"Really? So you're not mad at me for trying to help?"

"How could I be mad at you after you whipped that reporter's ass?"

I grin.

"Besides, you looked cute in that red blouse you were wearing. It made you seem even more feisty."

"Wow." I fidget with the front of my shirt. "I was cute and feisty at the same time?"

"You know what my favorite part of that interview was?"

I pause to think. "Um, the part where Kylie said you didn't kill your sister?"

"The part where you said you didn't mind being tied up."

I turn away and let my back rest against the wall so he doesn't see me blush. "I'm pretty sure I didn't say that."

Aaron moves in front of me and places his arm over my head. "You surprised everyone today—me most of all."

A knot forms in my throat from the intensity of his gaze.

"You were very brave."

I swallow. "Well, you tend to be brave when you're fighting for the one you love."

Those words hang in the silence that follows as Aaron's eyes pin mine down. And just when I open my mouth to take them back, thinking I've made a mistake by blurting out my feelings, Aaron's hand presses against my heated cheek. Without looking away from me, he lowers his face. My heart pounds. I can't breathe.

He strokes my cheek with his thumb before his lips cover mine. Gently. I don't think he's ever kissed me like this before. His lips feel light as cotton, and the warmth from them flows gently like a stream instead of gushing like a river, slowly but steadily spreading behind my ears, across my back, in my belly, between my legs and all the way down to my toes.

How can such a light kiss be felt all over my body? How can it deprive me of so much air that I'm already getting dizzy?

My arms fall to my sides, then grip the front of Aaron's shirt. I kiss him back. Once. Twice. Slow, lingering kisses that send shivers down my spine.

Then fast ones. His arms go around me as his mouth crashes down on mine. My hands go to the back of his neck as I surrender. My head leans back. My lips part and his tongue brushes against the roof of my mouth. It becomes entwined with mine and I moan.

Aaron's fingers slide down my back. They leave trails along my spine until they reach my waist, then they crawl beneath the hem of my shirt, climbing back up until they find the hooks of my bra.

The hooks come undone. He drags his thumbs beneath the edge of the lace until he reaches all the way to the front. I hold my breath in anticipation as they trace the curves of my breasts. They find my nipples and I pull my mouth away to let out a gasp.

Aaron buries his mouth in my neck as he plays with the stiff peaks. I rest my head against the wall as I try to catch my breath. My knees tremble. My fingers dig into his shoulders as I try to keep myself from falling.

His hands slide down to my hips once more, and suddenly, he lifts me up. I let out a yelp as I wrap my arms and legs around him.

Aaron carries me to his bedroom, where he kicks the door open and turns on one of the bedside lamps with his elbow. He climbs onto the bed and sets me down on the sheets. His eyes gaze into mine.

I reach up to touch his prickly cheek as I gaze back at him. There's lust in those onyx eyes. That's for sure. But I can also see the admiration he spoke of earlier. And appreciation. And pride.

Joy swells in my chest and I feel like my heart will explode.

So I pull his face down to mine and let some of it out through my lips. I kiss him a few times, then I stare into his eyes again and smile.

Aaron runs his fingers through my hair. "You seem happy."

"What about you? Shouldn't you be happy that your name has been cleared?"

"I am."

His mouth descends on mine for one heated kiss as he grips the hem of my shirt. Then he pulls it up and over my head until I'm only wearing the sleeves. I push them off my arms. He grabs the straps of my bra next. As he pushes them down my shoulders and arms, he leaves a trail of kisses on one all the way to my wrist. Then he takes my hand and kisses it. My heart jumps to my throat.

With the bra gone, Aaron's fingers grip the waistband of my shorts. I push his hands away. I kiss him as I unbutton his shirt and push it off his shoulders. He shrugs it off and tosses it away.

My lips curve into a grin as I admire the view of the muscles on display in front of me. Unable to resist, I put my hands on his stomach as I press my lips against his chest. My fingertips brush against each pair of hard abdominal muscle as I drag my tongue between his firm pectorals. The taste of his skin makes my head spin.

He grabs my shoulders and pushes me down on the bed. He tugs on the waistband of my shorts and I lift my hips. He pulls them down along with my underwear and throws them away.

Now I'm completely naked under him.

Aaron takes a moment to stare at me. My skin blushes all over.

"You really are beautiful," he says as his hand brushes against my breast.

I snort. "How can you call a woman beautiful when you're just looking at her breasts?"

"I'm looking at all of you."

His gaze wanders over my stomach, which I tuck in instinctively, and goes as far as between my legs. I close my thighs.

He chuckles. "Still shy?"

"And getting cold." I plant a quick kiss on his cheek.

Aaron gives another chuckle. "Then I'll do my best to warm you up."

As soon as he's said that, his mouth engulfs one of my breasts. His palm covers the other. As he sucks and squeezes, heat flows through my veins. I gasp and tremble.

He switches and then drags his lips lower, towards my navel. He traces that hole with his tongue and then draws that tongue down, lower and lower until I feel his coarse cheeks between my thighs.

I grab fistfuls of the sheets, close my eyes and draw a deep breath. By now, I know what happens next. When his tongue brushes against the bud of flesh in my patch of curls, though, I still give a sound between a loud gasp and a strangled cry. I can never brace myself enough for this sensation, or get used to it.

It's embarrassing. It's exhilarating. It's overwhelming. It's heaven.

His tongue coaxes that bud into bloom and I begin to melt. My knees rise off the mattress and my toes curl into the sheets.

He dips his fingers into the sticky sweetness oozing out of me. When he begins moving those, the two-pronged attack of his tongue and fingers causes me to throw my head back against the pillow. I grip its edges as my eyes squeeze shut. Moans tumble out of my lips.

This is madness.

Aaron continues to stroke me with his tongue and his fingers. My body feels like putty beneath them, completely under his command. Slowly but steadily, the pleasure escalates. Heat swirls in my belly and moves lower.

I grip his hair and let out a cry as my body catches fire. He moves his fingers faster and I feel myself spill around them as my back arches. My head crashes against the pillow. My arms and legs tremble.

When it's over, I vaguely feel Aaron's tongue and fingers withdraw. My knees crash down on the mattress. My arms drop to my sides. I keep my eyes closed as I catch my breath but open them when I feel the mattress bounce.

I turn my head to see Aaron standing beside the bed. He drops his pants and his boxers to his knees. His cock springs free.

I stare at it in fascination as he steps out of his clothes. Even now that I've seen it many times, it never fails to put me in awe. It's perfect. Long. Thick. Straight. Smooth. The head is just a little rosy and rounded, shaped like a mushroom.

I'm no expert on anatomy, but I do know a thing or two about art.

That is a masterpiece.

Aaron opens the drawer of the bedside table and grabs a condom. I watch as he slips it on.

I grin. How can a guy putting on a condom look so sexy?

When he's done, he puts his hands on his hips. "Done watching?"

I crook a finger at him. "Come here."

Aaron climbs onto the bed. The springs of the mattress creak beneath his weight. He settles between my legs and lifts them. I feel the rubber poking me.

Again, I brace myself. I close my eyes and hold my breath as he enters me slowly. It no longer hurts. All I get is the sensation of being full, of being filled—and now, of being one with the man I love.

Once he's completely sheathed inside me, I open my eyes and exhale. He pauses to catch his breath before bending over to capture my lips in a tender kiss, one that leaves me breathless once more.

Afterwards, he looks into my eyes again. Beneath that gaze, I end up blurting a few words again.

"I love you."

For a moment, he stays still. He doesn't laugh. He doesn't seem puzzled. He just keeps looking at me. Then he smiles.

"You really are something."

It's not what I expected to hear in return, but as he gives me another tender kiss, the tinge of disappointment in my chest vanishes.

So what if Aaron doesn't say it? I can feel it. And that is enough. Actions speak louder than words.

He pulls away, grips my thighs, and bends me over in half. A cry escapes from my throat as he begins pounding into me.

His thrusts are so hard and deep that I feel like I'm going to be torn in two. My legs ache. My back hurts. My hips burn. I ignore the pain and grip his shoulders as I writhe beneath him. I'm inching close to the edge again.

No, not inching. I'm slipping there fast.

Aaron moves even faster, and just when I wonder how much more I can take, I come undone. He stops as his body trembles with mine. His fingers bite into my thighs. My nails dig into his shoulders.

His grunts mingle with my gasps, and then there's only silence. He lets go of my legs and they fall, but he stays above me as he catches his breath. Then he pulls out. He makes a quick trip to the bathroom while I lie perfectly still. When he comes back, he lies down beside me and pulls the sheets over us both.

I snuggle against his chest as I yawn. It's been a long day, and now I'm officially exhausted.

Aaron plants a kiss on the top of my head. "Good night."

I close my eyes. "Good night."

Within moments, the sound of his heartbeat and the smell of his sweat lull me to sleep.

Chapter Eighteen
Aaron

I gaze at Teri as she sleeps beside me. Her mahogany hair fans out around her head on top of my pillow. Some wisps coat her forehead, the tips touching her eyebrows. I brush them aside.

She doesn't stir. She's sleeping soundly. I wonder what she's dreaming of behind those closed eyelids. Of me? I wonder.

I still find it hard to believe that she found out Kylie was lying all by herself. Of course she was lying, but Teri made sure of that and let everyone know it. She convinced Kylie to tell the truth. Then she said all those things about me.

The first time I watched the interview on my laptop, I was astounded, speechless. I was in shock. The second time I laughed. The third time I was in awe.

My wife really is something.

She doesn't even know me that well. She didn't know I had a sister until a few days ago. And yet she never once doubted me. She never once thought of me as a murderer, and she didn't just go on to convince the world that I wasn't. She told them all I was a good man.

I think it's the first time someone called me that. It's the first time someone ever came to my defense, actually, not counting Hank, who I'm paying to defend me.

And to think I shouted at her in my office and sent her away. Most women would have scurried off and stopped caring. Yet Teri still helped me and fought for me.

She really is something.

I know she's Max's sister, but right now, I just see an amazing woman... and I find myself smiling at the sight.

Suddenly, I hear a phone ring. It's distant but I hear it. It's coming from the room right across the hall. Teri's room.

I get out of bed and grab it but don't answer. The name on the screen says "Pam". If I'm not mistaken, that's Teri's sister. Well, her adopted sister, but I think they treat each other no differently than those who come from the same womb.

I bring the phone to my room just before it stops ringing. Teri stirs. She stretches and opens her eyes.

"Who is it?" Teri asks.

"Pam," I say as I put the phone down on the bedside table.

Teri groans. "She's been calling since yesterday."

"Why? Because she saw you on TV?"

"Yes." She rubs the sleep from her eyes. "Now that she's watched that interview, she knows I'm married. She wants to meet you."

"Why not?" I shrug after putting on a shirt. "I don't mind. In fact, I don't mind meeting your entire family."

Teri sighs. "Yeah. I guess it's about time."

~

The flight from Philly to Perrysburg, Ohio, takes about two hours. We arrive shortly after five at the Flynn residence—a two-story stone and wood house in shades of flint gray and cream. The dull facade contrasts with a front yard brimming with colorful plants and flowers.

In the midst of all those flowers, a couple wait to greet us. The man looks like he's in his late sixties, his hair nearly all gone; the woman is a decade younger, with curly red hair. Neither of them resembles Teri, but their faces light up at the sight of her. The woman gets up from her seat and starts running towards her with her arms open.

"Teri, sweetheart!"

Teri falls into her arms. "Mom."

"It feels like forever since I last saw you."

"It's only been five months, Mom," Teri corrects her. "And I've been calling."

"I know. Still…" Mrs. Flynn pulls away. "Let me look at you."

As she does, her husband comes closer.

"Hi, Dad!" Teri waves at him.

"You look like you've gained a bit of weight," Mrs. Flynn concludes as she touches her chin.

"Mom!"

"But you look good. Healthy. You have this… glow around you."

"That's what I said." Another woman comes out of the house.

Tall. Red hair. Maybe two or three years older than Teri. She must be Pam.

"When did you get here?" Teri asks her.

"Yesterday. Ron dropped Cody and me off on his way to Detroit. By the way, I also suspected it was because of sex. And as it turns out, I'm right. Again."

She places her hands on her hips and drags her gaze over me from head to toe. Then she nods.

"He looks like he's good in bed."

I grin. I like her already.

Mrs. Flynn turns to look at her. "Pamela Therese, I taught you manners, didn't I?"

Pam shrugs. "You also taught me not to get married without telling you. Did you teach Teri, too?"

"Pam!" Teri and Mrs. Flynn say at the same time.

"Fine." Pam lifts her hands. "Manners. I know. We have a guest in our presence, after all. No, wait he's part of the family, right?"

"Pam," Teri warns her again.

"We'll talk later," Pam says. "Right now, I think we need you to introduce your husband. Finally."

Teri draws a deep breath. "Mom, Dad, Pam, this is…"

"Aaron Walsh," I introduce myself as I step forward and extend my hand. "It's a pleasure to finally meet you all."

"Oh, the pleasure is ours." Mrs. Flynn gives a wide smile as she shakes my hand. "I'm Veronica Flynn, Teri's mother. You can call me Ver."

I nod. "Nice to meet you, Ver. Did you plant all these flowers?"

"Yes."

"I'm only asking because they're as lovely as you."

She smiles even wider.

"Nick," Mr. Flynn says his name as he takes my hand and gives a smaller, more fleeting smile. That's all he says.

"Nice to meet you, Nick."

"Aaron Walsh," Pam repeats my name instead of saying hers as she shakes my hand next. "Billionaire. Businessman. Former playboy. Did I forget something?"

"Good in bed," I say.

She grins.

"My husband," Teri says.

"What?" Pam pulls her hand away. "I wasn't trying to steal him."

I place my arm around Teri. "My wife is a little… possessive when it comes to me."

"Am not," Teri protests.

"Well, I would be too if I had a husband like you," Pam says.

Teri clears her throat.

"Stop it, you two," Mrs. Flynn scolds. She turns to me. "They're always like this. Arguing. It's how they get along."

"We don't always argue," Pam and Teri say at the same time.

Mrs. Flynn laughs. "Now, why don't we go in? I already have dinner ready. I made Teri's favorite— pork dumplings."

~

239

"So, what do you think of my parents?" Teri asks me as she lets me inside her old room after dinner. "I mean my adoptive parents, but yeah, that's a bit hard to say, so I just say parents. They've always treated me like their own anyway."

I don't answer at once because I'm busy imagining a younger version of her in this room—sitting by the window and gazing out at the moon, studying at the table in the corner, pinning notes on that corkboard, reading a book in bed...

"Aaron?" Teri sits on the edge of her bed.

"Your mom's a good cook," I answer as I shrug off my jacket and drape it over the back of a chair. "And she's really warm."

"Yeah, she is."

"Your dad doesn't say much, but I can tell he loves you."

Teri nods. "He's always been the quiet one."

I sit beside her and the bed creaks. I pat the mattress and narrow my eyes at her. "Are you sure it's okay for me to sleep in this bed?"

"You're not my boyfriend. You're my husband. You can't sleep by yourself in the guest room."

"Why don't we both sleep in the guest room?"

"Because that room is dusty and sad." She lies on top of her bed. "And this is my room."

"Okay."

The bed creaks again as I lie down beside her, but I ignore it. I stare up at the blue butterflies hanging from the ceiling.

"It's a nice room."

"Thank you. Like I said, I designed it myself."

"It's neater than I imagined," I say.

"Of course it's neat. It's my room."

"Of course."

A moment of silence passes.

"What about Pam?" Teri asks. "Do you like her?"

I grin. "I do. She has a strong personality and she's honest."

"You mean she's a bitch," Teri says. "But I don't mean that in a derogatory way. I mean that she's always been the tough, brave one. I've always been the... one who hides in her shell and keeps her room clean."

I look at her. "I think you're not that girl anymore. The one who hides in her shell, I mean."

She meets my gaze. "You think?"

I smile before turning my gaze back to the ceiling. "How old were you when you were adopted?"

"I was ten," Teri answers. "My parents were divorced. My mom just died. Veronica was her best friend and she took me in, said she always wanted another girl. She and Nick were actually willing to take both me and my brother, Max..."

My eyes widen slightly. That's the first time Teri has said his name.

"But Max went to my father instead. We still kept in touch, though. Then my Dad died. He came back for a while, then he went to college..."

Where he met Marjorie, put a baby in her and killed her.

"I don't know where he is now," Teri goes on. "But I miss him. He and I used to be very close. After our parents divorced and my father left, he became like my father, and then Mom got busy with work and he became like a mother to me, too. He learned how to braid just so he could braid my hair. He sold his favorite robot just so he could get me a book for my birthday."

My thoughts drift back to the only time I met Max, when Marjorie introduced him to me as her boyfriend. I hated him, of course, but he seemed like a nice man. Respectful. Caring. He made Marjorie laugh. He wiped coffee off the corner of her mouth, but he never once tried to kiss her in front of me.

Strange. I've never looked back on that memory until now.

I guess it did seem like he could do all those things Teri says he did. For the first time since Marjorie's death, I wonder: What if Max didn't kill Marj?

"Aaron?" Teri touches my arm. "Are you alright?"

"Yeah." I place my hand over hers. "I was just thinking… about Marjorie."

"Oh."

"You know, I've been thinking about what Kylie said—that I've been too focused on her death, that I've failed to remember how she lived. It's like I zoned in on the bad and forgot the good."

"You didn't forget the good." Teri turns on her side to face me and squeezes my hand. "Why don't you tell me about some of it now?"

"Hmm." I pause as I collect my memories. "She loved bubbles."

That's why she liked bubble baths.

"She used to play the guitar. She couldn't sing, though. Oh, wait. I'm only supposed to be remembering the good, right?"

"Just go on," Teri urges.

"She liked to try different kinds of food. She had a lot of friends. She had a funny sneeze."

"Funny how?"

"I can't mimic it."

"Okay."

"She was good in soccer. She liked toasting marshmallows in the fireplace and then putting them in her cocoa. She was scared of spiders." I frown. "Wait. That's bad again, right?"

"I'm scared of spiders, too," Teri says.

Right. She's scared of creepy crawlies of all shapes and sizes.

She shrugs. "There's nothing wrong with that."

I turn on my side as well. "You know, the two of you have some things in common. Apart from being scared of spiders, I mean. She liked pretty things. She was good with kids. She could dance."

Teri's eyebrows furrow. "Are you saying you married me because I'm like your sister? Because I'm telling you, that doesn't sound so…"

"I said you have some things in common," I tell her. "But you're also different."

Teri lies on her back. "Like I'm not fun and friendly?"

"Like she never wore lingerie. She didn't like being tied up."

Teri's jaw drops as she looks at me, then she laughs. "How would you know?"

I ignore her question as I climb on top of her. "And she never had sex in her childhood bedroom with her parents sleeping just down the hall."

"But I never…" Teri stops. "Oh."

"Oh, indeed."

I brush her hair aside and plant my lips on top of hers. She places her hand on my cheek and kisses me back. Her lips part and her tongue comes out. I keep it busy with mine.

I cup one of Teri's breasts through her clothes. It swells and my thumb searches for the hardened peak. When I find it, she moans into my mouth. A shudder goes through her.

As I alternate between lightly pinching and tugging at her clothed nipple, Teri reaches between my legs. Her palm rubs against my crotch and my cock hardens. She starts stroking the bulge but stops suddenly.

She pulls her mouth away from mine and glances at the door. "You did lock the door, didn't you?"

"Yes," I lie because I don't want to leave her now. Not when it's just getting good.

I kiss her again, and this time I slip my hand beneath her shirt and her bra so I can feel her breast against my palm, her nipple between my fingers. I don't want her thinking about anything but me.

I know I've succeeded when I hear another moan. Teri's hand starts moving again. She continues stroking me but then stops again.

Before I can wonder why, her fingers pop the button of my pants. They pull the zipper down and wrap around my cock. It bursts through its cotton confines and quivers against her palm.

I slide my hand down to her hip, then to her ass so my fingers can bite into a firm cheek. Then I bring it to the front and start stroking her between her legs.

Teri gives a louder moan. When I press my fingertips against her, she pulls away and gasps.

"Shh." I stop stroking her and hold a finger to my lips. "You don't want the other people in this house to hear you, do you?"

At that, her hazel eyes grow wide. For a moment, I worry that she might say we should stop. Then her lips curve into a mischievous grin as she pushes me onto my back.

"If I'm going to be quiet, I need to have something in my mouth," she says.

I grin. She really has changed.

Teri slithers towards the edge of the bed and gets off. I lift my head and find her kneeling between my legs. She wraps her fingers around my cock and strokes me a few times as I watch. Then she meets my gaze as she opens her mouth and sticks out her tongue.

A shudder goes through me as it swipes against the swollen head of my cock. Heat swirls in my balls. She holds my gaze as she drags the tip of her tongue down my quivering length and then back up.

"Oh, if your parents could see how naughty you are now," I tease her.

"You're the one who made me naughty."

Teri wraps her lips around my cock and I let out a hiss as I put my head down. I stare at the ceiling as Teri takes me inside the hot cavern of her mouth little by little, taking as much as she can. Then she sucks. My body trembles. My hands clench at my sides.

She starts moving her head back and forth as she grips the base of my cock. Her other hand cradles my sac. The friction sends fire through my veins. My nostrils flare and I breathe through my mouth.

The sound of her wet lips rubbing against my skin fills the room. Some strands of her hair tickle my thighs.

I lift myself on one elbow and place one hand on the top of Teri's head. I'd like to force her to go faster, to feel even more of that agonizing and exquisite friction from her mouth on my cock. But I can see that she's trying her best. I see the tears beading at the corners of her eyes. So I simply gather her hair to keep it out of her face and tug on it as she moves her head faster.

My leaking cock quivers as it slides in and out of her mouth. My balls grow heavy.

I push her head away. As she gives me a look that's partly confusion and partly dismay, I grab one of her arms and pull her onto the bed. I push her down on the mattress and pin her lips down with mine. I keep our mouths connected as I grab the waistband of her pants and the garter of her panties. I pull them both down.

After Teri kicks them off, I settle between her legs. I grip her hips and enter her with one thrust. She throws her head back and muffles her cry with her arm.

Her smothered cries and moans continue as I pound into her. The bed creaks, but there's nothing I can do to silence that.

I simply close my eyes and savor the sensation of being inside my wife, of being sheathed in her heat, of her moist, velvety skin clinging to me.

Suddenly, I feel her hands on my arms. My eyes open. She pulls me close.

She whispers in my ear, "I love you."

Again with those words. Like before, they awaken something inside me. Joy and pride swirl in my chest.

A part of me longs to say those words back, words I've never said before. Instead, I kiss her tenderly as I continue to move my hips.

I swallow her moans as she trembles. Her nails dig into my back. Her back arches and her breasts press against my chest.

I break the kiss so she can come up for air and manage a few more thrusts into her even tighter, hotter and wetter core before shuddering and spilling myself deep inside her. Grunts escape my lip and tumble against the sheets.

Afterwards, the room falls silent—but only until I try to get off Teri and hear a loud crack beneath my palm.

I quickly get off the bed. Teri does, too.

"Was that…?"

I put my pants back on and look under the bed. "Do you have a flashlight?"

Teri hands me one and I shine it on the underside of the bed frame. I find the crack and turn to her with a frown.

"Your bed's broken."

She gives me a look of disappointment. "Really?"

"I think it will be fine, though, as long as it doesn't take any more pressure. That means you'll have to sleep on just one side for tonight and I have to sleep in the guest room."

Teri sighs. "Can't you just sleep here? There's a sleeping bag in the attic."

So she wants me to sleep on the floor, huh? I'd really rather sleep in a bed, but she gives me that look I can't resist.

"Fine. I'll get the sleeping bag." I walk to the door.

"I can get it," she says.

I glance at her over my shoulder. "You don't have your underwear on. Or pants. You really think you should walk outside like that?"

Teri frowns. A pillow flies in my direction but I dodge it.

"Take your jacket." She throws it at me next and I catch it. "It's chilly in the attic."

I put on my jacket and leave the room. I'm on the stairs to the attic when the phone in my jacket pocket rings. I take it out and see Hank's name on the screen.

"Hey," I say as I answer the call.

"Hey," he says. "How's Teri's family?"

"Great." I continue climbing up the stairs. "Hopefully a little hard of hearing, because Teri and I just made a bit of noise."

"A bit?"

"The bed broke."

Hank laughs. "You son of a gun."

I chuckle, then turn serious as I scratch my forehead. "Hey. I was going to call you, actually. I was going to ask you something."

"What?"

"Do you think maybe the court was right, after all? Do you think maybe Max is innocent?"

Hank pauses. "You've fallen for Teri, haven't you?"

"Well, she is an amazing woman and I'm beginning to think this marriage is going to work. It was a drunken mistake on her part and I just did it on a dare, but maybe we belong together." I draw a deep breath. "I know it sounds crazy, but Teri is unlike any woman I've ever met. She makes me feel things I've never felt. For the first time since Marjorie's death, I feel alive. I feel like I want to build a future instead of continuing to live in the past. I feel—"

"Aaron," Hank cuts me off.

I rub my neck. "I know I'm rambling, but—"

"Max was the one who paid Kylie," Hank blurts out.

I pause. My forehead creases. "Are you sure? I mean, why would he do that?"

"Maybe he found out you were married to his sister and wanted her to leave you," Hank proposes. "He probably didn't expect she'd stand by your side and defend you. That must have pissed him off."

"Where would he even get that much money?"

"Who knows? Who knows what he's been up to these past few years?"

I guess it's not impossible that he could have gotten his hands on that much money.

"There's something else you need to know," Hank says. I hear him draw a deep breath. "Kylie Campden is dead."

"What?" My jaw drops. My knees weaken and I sit on the stairs. "I thought we had people watching her. I thought—"

"I don't know how it happened, either, but it happened. We shouldn't really be surprised. People who have killed before are likely to kill again."

"You think Max killed her."

"He paid her and she didn't do what she was asked to do. She failed. She betrayed him. That's motive."

I run my hands through my hair as I let out a sigh of frustration. "How's Kylie's mother?"

"She's okay. Her treatment isn't going well, though."

Which means she could die soon, too.

"You know what this means, don't you, Aaron?" Hank asks me.

I don't answer.

"It means Max killed Marjorie," he says it for me. "It means he knows you're using his sister for revenge and he's trying to take you down from afar."

I slap my forehead. I know. I know.

And most of all, it means my marriage to Teri won't work. It can't work. Marrying her was a mistake. Falling for her? An even bigger mistake. Thankfully, I can still undo both. I have to.

"Aaron?"

"I'm fine," I tell Hank. "Be at my office early. I'm going to catch the first flight out of here."

"So your hunk of a husband took off, huh?" Pam lifts her sunglasses as she glances at me.

I sit on a patio chair and set my steaming cup of coffee down on the table between us, right next to the saucer with half of Pam's sandwich, but keep my fingers around the handle.

"Yeah." I look straight ahead to where Cody and his grandfather are playing basketball. "I guess he did."

I'm still a little disappointed that Aaron left. I was shocked when he came back to the room without the sleeping bag, instead telling me that he had some urgent business to attend to and had to leave. I tried to stop him but he wouldn't let me. I stood on the front porch and watched him drive off into the night.

"What? Did he get scared Mom and Dad would give him a lecture because of all the ruckus he caused last night?"

"No." My eyes grow wide as I turn to Pam. "You heard?"

"The whole house heard. It's a good thing Cody was playing a video game on my phone and wasn't paying attention."

"Sorry."

Pam glances at me. "Are you?"

I suppress a grin. "Aaron left because of business. He is a businessman, you know."

"Don't I know it? I think I read a magazine article about him once, while I was having my hair done. They said he was the future of packaging and parcel delivery." She leans towards me. "So, how was his package? Did he deliver?"

I narrow my eyes at her even as I fight off a blush. "Very funny."

"Seriously, though…" Pam touches my arm. "How are the two of you? Is he treating you right? Not just in bed, I mean."

"Yes, he is," I answer.

Well, he has been lately, up until last night. Come to think of it, he didn't even kiss me goodbye. Then again, he did seem awfully pissed and in a hurry to leave.

"Like I said on TV, he's a good husband," I add.

"Oh, I saw that interview." Pam takes a bite out of her sandwich. "I must say I've never seen you that way before, and I felt proud." She places a hand on her chest. "I was in awe of your bravery. But of course, that was after my initial shock and dismay at finding out you got married without telling me."

I sigh. Here it comes.

I reach for her hand and squeeze it. "I'm sorry I kept it from you. I just… was afraid it was a mistake."

Her gaze narrows. "What's that supposed to mean?"

I tell her about how Aaron and I met, how we ended up married. When I'm done, Pam gasps.

"You… married him without knowing it?"

"Shh." I hold a finger to my lips. "I don't want Mom and Dad to know."

"So what story are you planning on telling them?"

"The usual story. That we met at some random place, hit it off and decided to get married."

Pam snorts. "Boring. If you're lying, you might as well make it interesting."

I roll my eyes.

"Let me get this straight. You really didn't want to marry him."

"I wasn't planning on it."

"But both of you stuck with it and somehow things worked out."

"Yeah." I nod. "That's what happened. It shows how maybe, if you stick with something long enough, it will figure itself out. If you stand by a mistake that you made instead of just shoving it under the rug and try to make the most of it, it might end up being the right thing to do."

"Oh, please. Don't give me one of your speeches."

I lift my cup to my lips.

"I'm not buying it, though," she adds as she finishes the rest of her sandwich. "It's too easy."

"Too easy?" I give her a look of disbelief. "Oh, you have no idea what we've had to go through."

"Oh, you mean you had to let him tie you up to win him over?"

I shake my head. Unbelievable.

"I'm just saying that the two of you may not know each other that well yet. Yes, you have sex. But can you say you really know him?"

I don't answer. I just take a sip of my coffee.

"I'm just saying it's too early to know that things are going to work out, especially given how you started. I mean, look at me. Ron and I dated for four years before we got married, but it was only after Cody turned three that I was convinced our marriage would last."

"Fine. Fine." I set my cup down. "I'm not saying our marriage is perfect or that it will last forever. I'm just saying that right now, things are fine. Is that bad?"

Pam sighs. "Sorry. I just have this feeling, you know, that the two of you..."

"Don't belong with each other?" I finish the sentence for her. "Do you think I'm not good enough for him? Is that what you're saying?"

"No."

I look at her. "Is it because he's a billionaire and I'm a pauper? Or is it because he's hot and I'll always be Plain Jane?"

She grabs my arm. "You're not plain. And that's not what I'm saying. All I'm saying is that the two of you are from different worlds, and couples like that, there are a lot of forces trying to tear them apart."

I narrow my eyes at her. "I'm looking at one now."

"I'm not trying to tear you two apart. On the contrary, I want you to be sure you want this marriage. I'm worried about you, Teri."

"Well, you can stop worrying about me now, Pam." I stand up. "I'm not your baby sister anymore, and you know what? I'm going to be just fine."

I stomp off towards the house.

"Are you going to ride with me tomorrow?" Pam asks after me.

I pause, then glance over my shoulder. "No. I'm going home right now to be with my husband."

~

Aaron isn't at the apartment, though. I wait for him to come home, but he doesn't. I call him but he doesn't answer. I ask Holly if there's something wrong but she just says he's busy. Too busy to talk to me, apparently.

I wait for a day, and when I can't wait any longer, I go to his office. Holly tries to keep me from going in, but I barge through the double doors anyway.

Aaron looks up from behind his desk. He looks like he hasn't slept since I last saw him. Or shaved. He has circles under his eyes and his beard looks thicker.

Worry immediately washes over me. I run to him. "Aaron..."

"Don't." He lifts a hand to stop me in my tracks. "Just don't come any closer."

My eyebrows crease. "I don't understand. What's going on? Are the board members giving you hell again? I can talk to them."

Aaron shakes his head.

"Is it a deal gone wrong? Did you lose a client? Tell me what the problem is and I'll see how I can help. I've helped you before. I'll do anything I can."

Still, Aaron says nothing. He just touches his chin and looks away.

I place my hands on his desk. "Aaron, please."

"You're the problem, Teri!"

His hands crash down on the desk as he gets to his feet and it jumps. A pen rolls over the edge. I take a step back and lift my hands.

"Okay. Just calm down, Aaron. There's no need to shout."

"You're the problem, Teri," he repeats more calmly as he looks into my eyes.

I see only dismay and sadness in his, and my chest aches. My hands drop to my thighs. A knot forms in my throat.

I swallow. "What are you saying, Aaron? What have I done?"

"Nothing." He sits down at his desk and grabs a pen, which he twirls in his fingers. "Just that after seeing the home you grew up in, after meeting your family, I've come to the conclusion that you're not the kind of wife I want."

"What?"

I can't believe what I'm hearing. It doesn't make sense.

He fidgets with the pen. "You and I are too different. You know that."

My heart sinks. Yes, I know that. I know who he is and who I am. I know what Pam told me is true. But I just don't want to believe that we can't be together.

"You knew who I was from the beginning," I tell him. "I never tried to hide it from you. I never tried to pretend I was anything else. But you married me."

"I was going to divorce you."

"Why didn't you?"

Aaron drops the pen on the desk. "Because I decided I'd have some fun."

My eyes grow wide. He said something along those lines at the party when we first met. When I asked him why he covered up for me, he said he was bored. I was amusement for him.

"And it has been fun. But you know what? Time's up." He taps his watch. "You're getting too attached to me."

My mouth gapes. My hand goes to my chest. "I'm getting too attached to you? Aaron, I've told you I love you."

"Yes. Twice." He sits back. "That was my goal and it's been achieved, so there's no reason to play this game any longer."

"This game?" I shake my head in disbelief. "What? You were just keeping me around until I told you I love you twice?"

Aaron doesn't answer or seem interested.

I go around his desk and look at him in horror. "What kind of man does that? What kind of man says he's done with a woman after asking her to introduce him to her family? No man does that."

He turns his chair to face me. "Aaron Walsh does."

I take a step back as my head reels. I place a hand on my forehead.

"I'll have Hank deliver the divorce papers."

I blink and my vision returns to normal. I still feel a little dizzy, but then again, who wouldn't be after hearing all the things I've just heard?

"So let me just get this straight." I look into Aaron's eyes as I hold back tears. "You don't love me."

"Did I ever say I did?"

"You never cared about me? It was all just a game to you?"

"Exactly. Though I must say you proved far more amusing than I could have hoped."

My chest shatters. My throat goes dry.

Aaron turns to his desk. "Like I said, Hank will give you the divorce papers. Don't worry. I'll give you a fine sum for your trouble."

That nearly makes me laugh. A fine sum for my trouble, huh? For my trouble?

"Don't bother," I tell him through gritted teeth. "You can keep your money. I don't want a single cent from you."

All I want is my heart back, but I'm not sure if there's much left of it now.

"Suit yourself."

I walk towards the door but stop after a few steps. I pull the golden band off my finger and throw it at him. It misses him but hits the portrait behind him and falls to the floor with a clatter.

"You can keep that as well." I continue walking then stop again. "Oh, and just so you know, you are the first man I've ever loved and I really wish I hadn't."

I walk past the doors of his office, leaving just as the first tear breaks free.

~

I end up crying in a church.

247

I don't know where else to go. I don't want to go back to Aaron's apartment now that I know I no longer belong there. I don't want to go to Pam's house just to hear her say she told me so. Besides, I don't know if she's back yet. And I don't have any friends. That's something that hasn't really changed.

I have nowhere else to go. So here I am in a church I've never been to before. Tears trickle silently down my cheeks as I gaze at the altar bathed in the light streaming from a stained glass window.

I don't remember the last time I prayed, but I do that now. I clasp my shaking hands together on my lap and bow my head.

Please just let the pain stop.

I don't know how to stop it. I don't know how to keep these tears from falling, how to keep my chest from feeling like it will split open. I don't know how to put myself back together again. How can I when I feel like I've been broken into a million pieces and Aaron still has some of them?

How could Aaron do this to me? All I ever did was try to be a good wife. All I ever did was love him. The hardest part is that for a moment there, I believed he loved me… and that I'm still hoping he will.

I place my hands on my forehead. Oh God, how big a fool am I?

"Teri?"

I lift my head at the sound of my name. A woman wearing a sequined pink top and a black pencil skirt stands in front of me, right at the end of the pew. I quickly wipe my tears as I realize who it is.

"Isabelle." Gale. In the flesh.

"Hey." She smiles her perfect smile.

Well, this is embarrassing. At least, I would be feeling embarrassed if I hadn't already been numbed by pain.

I sniff. "What are you doing here?"

"I dropped by to talk to the pastor about giving some kids Bible lessons."

"I see."

She's busy with her cause, as ever.

Isabelle gestures to the empty space beside me. "May I?"

I nod and move over to give her more room.

She sits beside me and I smell the scent of flowers from her hair. The diamond ring on her finger gleams as she tucks a few strands behind her ear.

"You know, there's a comfort in talking to someone you can't see. But you know what? It feels even better to talk to someone you can see."

I glance at her.

"I know that because when Gordon died, I was in dire need of comfort," she adds. "And you look the same right now."

I say nothing. I want to talk to someone. I do. I want to get this mess of feelings off my chest, get rid of the clutter in my mind. But Isabelle Gale?

She offers me a pack of tissues. "You know, I am still just another woman trying to make her way in this world. Besides, aren't we friends? Since you came to my party and all."

Isabelle Gale? My friend? It sounds hard to believe. Still, her sincere smile is hard to resist. Her warm presence is like balm to my shattered soul. And her pack of tissues is just what I need.

I pull one and blow my nose. "Thanks."

"You're welcome," she says. "And now that you've blown your nose in front of me, maybe you won't feel so shy about telling me what's going on."

I draw a deep breath. "It's about Aaron."

Isabelle sighs. "I thought so. Men. They're usually what drive us to our knees. Well, figuratively."

She pats my lap.

"So, what did he do? Or is it something he didn't do? Omission can hurt just as much as offense."

"He wants a divorce," I hear myself blurt out.

Isabelle covers her mouth as she lets out a soft gasp. "Are you sure?"

I nod. "He just told me so."

Isabelle takes my hand. "Oh, you poor thing. Did he tell you why?"

I shrug. "Just that he doesn't love me."

Isabelle's eyebrows arch. Then, to my surprise, she chuckles. She tries to suppress it, though, since we're in a church. She glances around and clears her throat.

"I'm sorry," I tell her. "But I don't see what's funny."

And I'm done amusing people without knowing it.

"Sorry. I didn't mean to laugh." She squeezes my hand. "It's just that I thought it would be something serious like he got a woman pregnant or you can't have children…"

"It is serious. At least, to me."

"Of course." Isabelle nods. "But you see, you're getting divorced not because of anything either of you did but just because of something he said."

"Well, those are pretty powerful words."

"Only if they're true."

I cast her a puzzled look. "Are you saying he's lying?"

"I'm saying that usually when people say they're not something or not doing something, they are. It's like when you say you're not worried. You only say that when you are. Or when you don't care but you do."

I have to say she has a point.

"So, you're saying he said he doesn't love me but he does?"

"Forget about what he said for a moment. Think about the things he's done."

I pause to do that. I think about the sex—sorry, God. Not just the quantity but the quality. And the meals we've shared, and him worrying about me drinking too much, and the forehead kisses. And him laughing with my family at dinner and opening up about Marjorie.

"Well?" Isabelle asks me. "Do you think he loves you or not?"

I shrug. "I might be misinterpreting things. Or he might just have been pretending."

"Or you're just making excuses. We do that when we're scared."

I say nothing.

Isabelle grasps my chin. "You know, at that party, I saw the way Aaron was looking at you. And not just when you were dancing. He was proud of you. He was happy to be with you. He definitely wasn't looking at you like a man who wasn't in love."

I snort. "That was lust, not love."

"Do you seriously believe that? Do you really think when your bodies communicate through sex, that all you get is lust? Or is there something more?"

I think back on the last times we had sex, when he looked into my eyes, when he kissed me tenderly after I told him I loved him.

I shake my head. "He's never said he loves me."

Isabelle shrugs. "That's nothing new. Most men are terrified of saying the L-word. Love is scary for them. You know why? It makes them feel weak. They don't want to see themselves as weak. But a real man sees love as strength, not weakness."

"Then Aaron's not a real man."

Isabelle exhales. "Is that what you really want to believe?"

No, I think as I look at the altar. I want to believe he loves me. Still…

"If he loves me, why did he say he doesn't?"

"Like I said, love is scary for men, especially just after they've realized it."

I fall silent. Maybe so. Maybe he's just scared. But I don't know. He didn't look scared at all when he shouted at me earlier.

Isabelle reaches for my hand again. "The way I see it, you have two options. One, you can just take his word for it, which is the easy thing to do, and give up. Sign the divorce papers. Or two, you can try to have a real talk with him. No crying. No yelling. Just talk. Make him realize what's going on. And if he still wants a divorce, fine. But at least you'll know you fought for what you believe in."

I look into her eyes.

She's right. I can't just give up because Aaron told me to. This divorce doesn't make sense. I mean, we just had sex in my childhood bedroom and he suddenly realized he doesn't love me. Why run away then? Why not just tell it to me right away?

I have to talk to him. I have to make sense of this so I can accept it. I have to ask him if...

I pause as I realize something. Aaron didn't actually say he doesn't love me, which means there's still hope. I'll have him say the words so I can move on, and if he doesn't, if he can't...

I stand up.

"Teri?"

I glance at Isabelle. "Thanks, Isabelle, but I think there's someone else I need to talk to right now."

She smiles. "Of course."

I leave the pew and start walking down the aisle towards the church entrance.

"Good luck," Isabelle tells me.

I glance over my shoulder to give her a smile. I'll thank her later. For now, I'm in a rush. My heart is pounding. My feet feel like they have wings. I wish they had wings. Then I could fly over to Aaron in an instant.

But they don't so I hop into my car. I start the engine and drive off.

I drive as fast as I can, spurred by newfound hope. I can't seem to keep calm now that I know Aaron and I can still be together.

But I must be driving too fast. A man on a bike suddenly crosses in front of me and the tires of the car screech as I step on the brakes and swerve to the side—right towards a telephone pole. Inertia propels my body forward. The seatbelt keeps me from flying into the windshield, but my forehead hits the steering wheel. The next instant, my body crashes back against the seat, knocking the breath out of my lungs. My vision blurs.

I can't talk, but the voice in my head screams for Aaron just before it goes completely silent.

Chapter Twenty
Aaron

"I take it Teri didn't receive the news so well," Hank says as he enters my office.

I rub my temples as I hunch over my desk. "What do you think?"

Saying she didn't receive the news of our divorce well is an understatement. She didn't see it coming, so she was crushed, devastated. I thought for a moment that she would keel over. When she left, she was on the verge of tears.

And that last look that she gave me still haunts me. Her words still hang over my head. They were filled with pain and disappointment but also love.

Teri really did love me. Too bad I can't love her back.

Or can't I?

In spite of everything, I was glad to see her in my office. I'm supposed to hate her, and yet I had an urge to wrap my arms around her when she started trembling, to kiss her when she said I was the first man she ever loved. I looked into her eyes and all I saw was a woman who loved me, not anyone's sister.

I acted like I didn't care, but every lie I told her tore me apart. I yelled at her, but am I really mad at her? Or am I mad at myself because I can't help how I feel, because I can't have the woman I want?

I've never felt like such a mess before.

Suddenly, the door opens. Holly steps in. One look at her and I know she has bad news.

I stand up. "What is it?"

"It's about Teri."

Just the sound of her name makes me go still. My throat goes dry.

"What happened to Teri?" Hank asks.

Holly draws a deep breath. "Mr. Walsh, Teri was in an accident."

~

"Where's my wife?" I ask the first person in white I see as soon as I arrive at the hospital. "They said she was in an accident and that she's here."

The woman leads me to the nurses' station.

"What's the name of your wife?" she asks.

"Teri Walsh."

She gets behind a computer and types. After a few seconds, she glances at me.

"Identification, please?"

I take my driver's license out of my wallet.

The woman nods. "We do have a Teri Walsh. It says here that she suffered a concussion but CT results are clear. That means there's no brain damage. Her injuries are not extensive either. She got lucky."

A breath of relief leaves me.

"You're free to see her. I believe she's in the Obstetrics Wing."

My eyebrows crease. "Obstetrics? You don't mean Orthopedics, do you?"

She looks at her screen again. "Obstetrics."

I place my hand over my mouth.

"Oh." She turns to me with arched eyebrows. "You didn't know?"

"Didn't know what?" I ask her.

"Well…" She swallows. "According to your wife's file, she's three weeks pregnant."

~

Teri's pregnant?

I lean against the corridor as I try to let that news sink in. I still haven't completely recovered from the shock of finding out I nearly lost Teri. And now I've been told she's pregnant?

She's pregnant. We're having a baby. We.

"You've changed your mind about divorcing her, haven't you?" Hank asks as he hands me a cup of coffee.

I take it. "How can I leave her when she's having a baby, our baby?"

He shrugs. "Can you stay with her knowing that her brother is a murderer?"

"Her brother," I tell Hank. "Not her."

He nods. "Oh."

"You know, when I thought I'd lost her, I felt like I was about to go mad. I don't want to lose her, Hank. Not because of an accident. Not because I'm a jerk who can't see past... the past."

"You forget that Max is around. He's killed again. He's coming for you."

"Let him come and then we can settle this, because this is between him and me. It doesn't have anything to do with Teri."

"That's not what you believed when you decided not to divorce her the first time," Hank says.

"I know. I know I tried to involve her. I tried to use her in my plot for revenge. I tried not to fall in love with her. I failed."

Hank says nothing.

"You know, I'm not even interested in revenge anymore. Nothing is going to bring back Marjorie, after all. She's gone. You know what I'm interested in? Having a family." I sigh. "You know, I think I dwelled in the past because I had nothing to look forward to. I thought I didn't have much to live for. But now I do. Teri gave me that."

"Okay."

I place my hand on Hank's shoulder. "You understand me, don't you?"

"No," he answers as he meets my gaze. "I don't understand you at all. Actually, I'm a little disappointed."

"Oh, come on."

"I think this is potentially a big mistake, but hey, I'm just your lawyer."

I squeeze his shoulder. "You're not just my lawyer."

Hank sighs. "I still think it's a mistake."

"Maybe." I shrug. "But hey, not all mistakes are bad. They're just proof that we're alive, and I want to live."

Hank nods. "Okay."

I grin and hand him the cup of coffee. Then I start running off.

"Where are you going?" Hank asks after me.

I glance over my shoulder. "To my wife."

I've already lost Marjorie. I'm not going to lose Teri, too.

~

I find Teri all alone in her room. I must be her contact person, which means her family doesn't know what happened to her yet. It's up to me to let them know, except I don't know their numbers.

That thought causes gladness to well up in my chest. I'm Teri's person.

Now, it's my turn to be hers.

I knock on the door before stepping into the room. Teri's eyes turn to mine. She can't turn her head because of the brace around her neck. Her lips curve into a smile.

"Aaron," she says my name softly, like an excited whisper.

A lump forms in my throat.

She's not mad?

I walk over to her side. "How are you?"

"Good," she says.

She doesn't look good, though. Apart from the neck brace, there's the huge bandage on her forehead. I also see the bruises on her arms as she puts her hands on her stomach.

"How's the baby?" I ask.

Teri casts me a curious glance.

252

"The doctor or nurse told me," I explain. "She said you're three weeks pregnant."

"Yeah. Who would have thought?"

I shrug. "Well, I guess it was only a matter of time at the rate we were going."

She doesn't grin at the remark. Instead, her eyes narrow.

"Is that why you're here? Because of the baby? Because if that's the only reason why—"

"I'm not just here because of the baby," I tell her as I place my hand over hers. "I'm here because I'm your husband."

"But I thought—"

"And I think I'd rather continue being your husband."

Her eyebrows arch. "But you said—"

"I said a few things back there, cruel things, things I didn't mean."

"So you're not going through with the divorce?"

"No." I shake my head and squeeze her hand. "When I heard about your accident, when I thought I was going to lose you, I realized I couldn't."

"So you changed your mind? You're only here because you're scared to lose me?"

"Because I want to keep you," I clarify my intention. "Because I want to have a family with you."

"Because I'm pregnant?"

I exhale. This wasn't as easy as I thought it would be. In fact, it's one of the hardest things I've ever done.

I draw a deep breath. "Because I love you."

Teri's hazel eyes grow wide.

"I know what I said before, but like I said, I didn't mean that. You're not just someone for me to play around with or someone to amuse me."

"Why did you keep me around, then?" Teri asks.

I shrug. "Because I was lonely."

I've never thought of that before, but now that I've said it, I realize it's true.

"I wasn't sure I'd be happy with you, but I have been." I stroke her hair. "You are unlike any woman I've ever met. Yes, you didn't want me at first, but you carved a place for yourself in my home anyway. In my life. In my heart. And now, I don't know how it can beat without you there."

For a moment, Teri says nothing. As she looks up at me, tears brim in her eyes. Eyes full of love.

I place my hand on her cheek. "I thought I never needed anyone, but you made me a mess, Teri, and you're the only one I can trust to clean it up."

Teri chuckles and puts her hand over mine.

"You mean we'll be like a real married couple? And a real family?"

I nod. That reminds me.

I take the golden band I've been carrying in my finger and hold it up. I'd go down on one knee, but then she wouldn't be able to see me, so I'll have to stand by her bed.

"Teri, will you stay by my side as my wife?" I ask her.

Her lips purse, then she smiles. Her face lights up. "I really wish I could nod right now."

I chuckle. "Just say yes."

"Yes," she says. "I will stay with you and clean up your mess."

I grin.

"Now, please give me back my ring?"

I slip it back on her finger. She lifts it up to examine it against the light. Then she reaches for my hand.

"I love you."

"I love you, too."

I plant a tender kiss on her lips. I'd like to give her a more passionate one, but that will have to wait.

After I pull away, she squeezes my hand and puts it over her belly.

"Of course, you can't feel anything yet, but…"

I press my lips to her belly. It doesn't matter if I can't feel anything yet. I know that there's another person growing inside her. My child. Our child.

"Have you told anyone?" I ask her.

"No," Teri says. "I haven't told my family about my accident, either. I don't want them to worry. But I will tell them when I'm further along. I'll tell Max first. I plan on telling him after I leave the hospital."

Of course she does. He's her brother, after all. And that means he might come and see her. That's fine. I'll protect her. I won't let Max take anyone else from me.

Teri sighs. "I still can't believe I'm pregnant."

"Neither can I," I say.

"You think it will be a boy or a girl?"

"I don't know." I shrug. "But our child will be loved."

Teri rubs her belly. "We'll need an even bigger apartment."

I nod. I guess we will. No, on second thought, I don't think that's what we need.

"You know what?" I tell her. "Why don't we buy ourselves a house?"

~

Two weeks after Teri gets discharged from the hospital, I bring her to the new house—a house of wood, stone and glass with spacious rooms and large windows sitting on acres of land.

From the very moment Teri steps inside, her face is bathed in awe. Gasps leave her lips as we go from room to room. Just watching her fills me with joy.

At the largest room on the second floor, she whirls. Her white skirt billows around her. Afterwards, she loses her balance. I catch her by the shoulders.

"Careful."

Teri leans against me and places her hand over mine. "This will be our bedroom."

That's what I thought of as well, but I let her say it. This is our house, after all, just as much hers as it is mine. Maybe even more hers, because she'll be designing it.

"Then let's mark our territory, shall we?"

"What do you m—?"

She doesn't finish, because I grasp her chin and turn her face towards me so my lips can meet hers. I push my tongue inside her mouth. She shivers against me.

Teri rests her head on my shoulder as she opens her mouth wider. Her hand goes to my nape. Her tongue mingles with mine.

I let her chin go and place my hands on her breasts. I give both mounds of flesh a squeeze before lifting her shirt.

I push her bra up and trap her nipples between my fingers. They quickly swell and harden.

A part of me swells and hardens as well, but I tell myself to be patient.

Teri doesn't seem to be. She must have felt the bulge in my crotch pressing against her back, because she reaches for it. Her fingers stroke it clumsily through my pants.

I continue playing with one of her nipples while I let my other hand slide lower. I lift her skirt so my fingers can explore what's beneath. They brush against lace and inch towards the front.

I begin to stroke her and she gasps. Her hand slides off my neck and falls to her side as she throws her head back on my shoulder.

I place the bunch of white cotton I have in my hand between her fingers.

"Hold this," I tell her.

Teri lifts her skirt. I plant my lips on her neck as I continue stroking her. My fingers slip beneath the lace and find her sensitive nub. She trembles.

I lick her ear as I tease her nipple and her nub at the same time. The hand on my crotch stops moving as she continues to tremble. Moans tumble out of her lips.

I nibble on her jaw as I abandon her engorged nub. I slip a finger inside her, letting it drown in her sweetness. Then I slip in another.

Teri whimpers and pulls my face towards hers for another kiss. I start moving my fingers. She starts moving her hips to meet my fingers. Her back grinds against my crotch.

I withdraw my fingers and push her down on the floor.

"Wait," she says. "We're doing it on the floor?"

"Well, you don't see a bed, do you?"

She looks apprehensive, so I kiss her forehead.

"Don't worry. The floor is clean. I had someone clean the whole house before bringing you here."

"I know. That's not what I'm worried about. It's just that... the floor is hard. There isn't even a carpet."

I understand what she's saying. It's hard and she's pregnant. Besides, she just had an accident.

I lie down on the floor. "You be on top, then."

This way, she won't get hurt or feel uncomfortable. I won't have to worry about pressing down on the baby, either.

Teri grins. She gets back on her feet and takes off her blouse, then her bra. I place my arms behind my head and gaze at her firm breasts. She gets rid of her skirt next, then turns around before bending over to wriggle out of her panties.

"Striptease," I say.

She just chuckles and then she straddles me. I feel her sex pulsing against my erection and even more blood rushes to my cock.

She bends over so I can see her breasts hanging from her chest. Her nipples brush against my chest as she kisses me. I try to touch them but she slaps my wrists away.

"Since I'm on top, I'm in charge," she says.

I shrug. "Fine."

I put my arms back behind my head and watch Teri as she moves between my legs. She takes off my belt and makes quick work of the button and zipper keeping my cock confined. She reaches in and frees it from my boxers.

I let out a hiss as the cold air hits my heated skin and then shudder as Teri starts stroking me with her fingers. She runs her hand up and down a few times before positioning herself on top of me.

"Are you sure you're ready?" I ask her.

"Just be quiet," she scolds me.

"Yes, ma'am."

Teri grabs the base of my cock to hold it in place. Slowly, she lowers herself on top of me, pursing her lips as she holds her breath. I breathe through my mouth as I watch her take me into her hot, wet core.

And what a sight it is.

Little by little, I disappear inside her until I'm completely in. Our bodies are connected in the deepest, most intimate way.

Teri pauses to catch her breath. Then she lifts my shirt and flattens her palms against my bare chest. I feel her weight on me as she starts moving her hips.

I don't mind. I'm enjoying the view of her breasts rocking beneath her.

Then she leans the other way and her back forms a bow as she throws her head back. Her hair cascades past her shoulders. Her breasts bounce up and down as she jerks her hips.

It's an even more magnificent sight.

My gaze lingers on her breasts but also rests on her belly. I can't help but reach out and touch it.

Teri doesn't seem to mind. She continues dancing above me, riding me with wild abandon. Moans and gasps escape from her lips.

I drag my fingers lower, past her navel and all the way to her patch of curls. I search for her nub and stroke it.

Teri lets out a cry. She keeps moving, but her movement becomes erratic. I hear her panting in between her moans.

I lift my head to catch one of her bouncing breasts in my mouth. I give it a light suck before tracing her nipple with the tip of my tongue. Then I lie back down. I grab her hips and guide her movements as I feel her faltering. I begin to move my own.

Again, she bends forward. Her hands grip my shoulders as hazel eyes stare into mine.

I hold that gaze as I thrust into her body. Teri may be on top, but I'm the one in control now, at least until she tightens around me and I start to lose control.

She trembles above me and I manage one more thrust before I finish. I hold her hips fast as my own jerk, as my cock quivers inside her and explodes.

Afterwards, Teri falls on top of me. I feel her heart hammering against my chest, which rises and falls with mine as we gasp for air. The fresh layer of sweat on her skin mingles with mine.

I give one firm cheek of her ass a playful squeeze, then push her off me. Well, halfway off. She still has one arm and one leg draped over me, her cheek against my shoulder.

I tuck myself back in. "So, you like this room?"

Teri just nods.

"You like this house?"

Another nod. Then she quickly kisses my cheek. "Thank you."

I stroke hers. "Don't thank me. As your husband, it's my duty and my pleasure to provide you with a good home."

"A wonderful home," she says as she snuggles against my chest.

I run my fingers through her hair. "Well, it's your job to make it that. Just remember what the doctor said. You're not supposed to overexert yourself."

"You mean like I just did?"

I chuckle and shake my head. "I'm serious. You need to take better care of yourself from now on."

I lift her chin so she can see how serious I am. "Promise me."

Teri's lips form a smile. "I promise."

Chapter Twenty-One
Teri

"I am taking care of myself," I say defensively to my baby as I pop a grape inside my mouth. "See, I'm eating."

So what if I'm working at the same time? I can't help it. I may have agreed to retire, but there's no way I'm just staying in bed and watching TV all day for eight months. I'd go crazy. Besides, I have a whole house to design.

I've just started on the kitchen, which I think is the most important room in the house after the bathroom, though I designed the bedroom first because I needed somewhere to sleep. I've already taken the measurements. I've sketched a floor plan. I just need to decide on a color scheme.

Hmm. How do I spice up this kitchen?

My thoughts are interrupted when the doorbell rings. I'm closer to the front door, so I walk towards it as I hear the maid rush down the stairs.

"I'll get it!"

I squint through the peephole as I place my hand on the knob. At first, I don't see much. Just some brown hair under a black hood. Then the head turns and I find myself gazing into a pair of dark brown eyes I never thought I'd see again.

"Max!"

I open the door so I can take a better look at him. His hair has grown out. A scruffy beard coats his chin. He's lost weight as well. And he looks... older, with more sunken eyes. But it's him.

"Max," I say my brother's name again before throwing myself into his arms.

Slowly, his arms wrap around me. His hand pats my back just as he used to do to whenever I felt uneasy. And just like that, I relax into his arms. I squeeze him.

"God, I missed you."

"I missed you, too."

I pull away but leave my hands on his shoulders. "Where have you been? How have you been?"

He shrugs. "Everywhere. As you can see, I managed to get by."

Yes, he did. But he doesn't feel like the Max I used to know, and that bothers me.

I touch his cheek. "Why did you leave so suddenly? Why haven't you visited me? Why wouldn't you let me call you more often?"

He looks away.

I take a deep breath. "Oh, what am I doing? You just arrived and I'm grilling you. Come inside. Please."

I take his arm and lead him inside the house.

Max lets out a whistle. "Huge house."

"Yeah. And it feels even more spacious because it's still relatively bare, but I'm working to change that. I'm a professional interior designer now, you know."

He gives me a proud smile. "Wow."

I wonder why I didn't tell him about that. It's good news, right? Or maybe I didn't feel like it was at the time, because of how I got my job.

"And you're having a baby?" He glances at my belly.

"Yes." I place my hand over it. "In less than eight months."

He nods.

"I'd put your hand on it, but there's nothing to feel yet. It's pretty early."

"It's okay."

"You know, I'm a little scared. I'm not so sure if I'm ready to be a mama, or if I'm going to be a good one, but..."

Max takes my hand. "I'm sure you'll be a great mom, Teri. Remember how you used to take such good care of your dolls?"

I grin. "Yes, I remember."

"A real baby is going to be messy, though," he adds with a frown.

"Yeah." I nod. "I know. But hey, when haven't I been able to handle a mess?"

He chuckles. It sounds just as I remember.

Max runs his fingers through my hair. "You haven't changed."

I grin. "But I have. I—"

"Mrs. Walsh?" the maid interrupts. "Would you like me to serve drinks?"

"Would you?" I ask Max.

He doesn't seem to have heard my question, though. He's looking at me with narrowed eyes, like he's seeing me for the first time.

"Max?"

"Walsh?" Max asks me. "That's your new last name?"

"Yes," I answer. "Oh, haven't you heard? You haven't seen me on TV?"

"I haven't been watching much TV."

"Oh. Well, in that case, yes, I'm married to Aaron Walsh. He's the—"

"I know who he is," Max cuts me off.

His tone has gone cold. His face has gone pale.

I cup his cheeks. "Max, what's—?"

I stop as I hear a car pull into the driveway. I get a glimpse of Aaron's Jaguar through the window.

Max steps away.

"Max?"

"You have a back door, right?"

"Yes," I say. "Through the kitchen, but you don't have—"

He runs off. I think of chasing after him because I don't understand what's going on, but just then the door opens and Aaron steps in.

"Hey," he greets me with a smile.

"Hey." I force one of my own.

But he sees past it and his eyebrows crease. "Are you alright?"

"Yeah."

I give Aaron a hug as I cast a warning glance in the maid's direction. She leaves.

"Are you sure?" Aaron asks as he touches my cheek. "You look a little... pale."

"Well, I have been working," I tell him.

He frowns.

"Just sketching and looking stuff up online."

Aaron sighs and puts an arm around me. "Well, can't you do that in bed?"

"No." I walk with him to the stairs. "I need to be in the kitchen. I have to be in the room to be able to visualize how I want it to be."

"Okay, okay."

"We do need a kitchen, you know."

"A kitchen. Not the best kitchen in the world." He gives another sigh. "Maybe I should have bought you a house after the baby's born."

"Things will be even more hectic then," I tell him.

"True."

"Um, why are you home early?"

"My meeting was cancelled. I thought I'd come home and be with my wife."

"Oh."

He has been like this lately, hanging around me, hovering around me.

"Aaron, I'm fine. Okay?"

"If you say so." He plants a kiss on my forehead and starts heading up the stairs. "I'm going to change, then I'm going to the shed to work on our baby's crib."

I cross my arms over my chest. "So that's why you came home."

He just grins.

"You know, we can just buy..."

258

But he's already gone. I sigh. Why are men running away from me today?

Then I feel my phone beep. I take it out from the pocket of my sweater. There's a message from Mr. Stewey.

Sorry I had to run. Will explain everything tonight. Midnight. Come to the old tree house west of the house. Bring your stuff.

My eyebrows bunch up.

Old tree house west of the house? This house? I haven't seen that. Then again, I haven't seen every acre of this property.

But why bring my stuff? What stuff?

I shake my head. Right now, my brother isn't making any sense. I don't have a clue what's going on. I slip my phone back into my pocket.

I guess I'll find out tonight.

~

I manage to find the tree house easily. It's painted red, after all. Well, it used to be. Now it's closer to garnet and the window has fallen off. I spot the rope ladder hanging under it, but I'd rather not risk trying it.

Wait. Max isn't exactly in the tree house, is he?

"Where are your bags?" The voice from behind me makes me jump.

I place a hand over my chest as I turn around. "Max, you startled me."

"Where are your bags?"

"Bags?"

"Where are your things? I thought I told you to pack."

I shake my head. "Max, I don't understand. You want me to leave my husband? Why?"

"Because it doesn't matter if you're carrying his baby," Max answers. "Once he finds out who you are, who I am, he's going to leave you. Worse, he might hurt you. But I won't let that happen."

I still don't understand. "What do you mean when he finds out who I am? Or who you are?"

"I'll explain. But for now, we must go." He grabs my arm.

I don't budge. "You're not making any sense. Why would he leave me? Why would he care who you are? I don't know where you've been or what you've done, but you're my brother. You're—"

"Max Colby," Aaron finishes.

I freeze.

Oh, shit.

Chapter Twenty-Two
Aaron

I thought Teri was acting suspicious. She looked surprised when I came home early, and not pleasantly surprised. She looked almost as if she didn't want to see me. After that, I caught her deep in thought a few times. Then she didn't want to cuddle in bed, said she felt warm. I took her word for it and rolled to my side of the bed. I thought I was just imagining things.

Until she got off the bed in the middle of the night and left the room.

I followed her. The moment she left the house, I knew something was wrong. I was afraid I'd catch her with another man.

Well, I have. With her brother, Max.

The sight of him immediately makes my back tense. My hands clench into fists.

Teri turns to me with wide eyes. "Aaron?"

Max stands in front of her. "Don't you even think about hurting her."

Teri puts her hand on his shoulder. "Max, Aaron won't hurt me. I don't understand why…"

She stops when her gaze meets mine. She must have seen the anger I'm trying so hard to control.

"Teri," I say through gritted teeth. "Go back to the house."

"What?"

"Don't," Max tells her. "Run to the street. My car's there."

Teri shakes her head. "I really don't understand."

"Teri!" Max shouts at her.

"I'm not going anywhere!" Teri shouts back at him. Then she glances at me. "Not until you two tell me what's going on."

"Teri," I warn her.

"Please," she begs.

I draw a deep breath. Stubborn as ever. Fine.

"Your brother killed my sister," I tell her straight, keeping my icy glare on Max.

Teri gasps.

"I did not!" Max protests.

I ignore him. "He was her boyfriend. Did you know that?"

Teri doesn't answer.

"And he got her pregnant, but when he found out, he chickened out. And so he killed her, drowned her in a bathtub."

"I didn't kill her!" Max shouts. "I loved her."

"Then why have you been running?" I ask him.

Teri glances at him. "Max?"

"I didn't kill Marjorie, Teri. Please believe me."

I snort. "Are you going to say you didn't kill Kylie, too? Even though your DNA was found at the crime scene?"

Teri's mouth gapes. "Kylie's… dead?"

Max shakes his head. "I don't even know who Kylie is."

I don't believe him. It's taking every ounce of my self-control not to send my fist flying towards his face.

"Teri, go," I tell her.

I don't want to hit her by mistake.

She doesn't move.

I glance at her. "Teri!"

"Wait." She steps forward. "You're saying this whole time, you've been thinking that my brother killed Marjorie?"

"He did," I answer.

"Then why did you marry me?"

I pause. I don't like how this conversation has suddenly turned.

"Teri..."

She shakes her head. "Why would anyone marry the sister of the man who murdered his sister? Unless..."

She lifts her head slowly to look into my eyes.

"It's revenge. You think Max took your sister away, so you thought you'd take his. You probably planned it all from the start, didn't you? It wasn't a drunken mistake on my part."

"I didn't—"

"And then what? Kill me, too? No. You could have done that already. You probably wanted me to suffer. You wanted Max to see me suffer. Isn't that why you wanted me to call him?"

I don't answer.

Teri grips her hair as she steps back. "My God, you were using me all along."

My fists unfurl. "Teri, I'll admit that was my plan..."

"You admit it?" The disappointment in her eyes weighs down on my chest.

"But it changed. You changed it because you made me love you."

Again, she shakes her head. "You don't love me."

Tears brim in her eyes. A knot forms in my throat.

"If you do, why didn't you talk to me about Max? Why are you trying to kill him now? That's why you want me to leave, isn't it? So you can kill him and get your revenge?"

"This is between us."

"Like hell it is!" Teri's shoulders tremble. "You used me, Aaron. Like it or not, you used me to get to my brother."

She stands in front of Max. "Well, I won't let you get to him."

My chest and throat burn. Teri's picking Max over me?

"So you believe him?" I ask her.

"Yes," she answers.

That one word feels like a dagger to my heart.

"You know why? Because I know him. As for you..." She shakes her head slowly. "I don't know you."

Teri turns away.

"Yes, you do, Teri. I'm your husband."

"Only on paper," she says softly as she starts walking off.

"I'm the father of your child!"

She stops, but only for a moment. Then she continues on.

I start to go after her, but Max stands in the way. He squares his shoulders and lifts his chin.

"My sister doesn't want you," he says. "She's thrown you away."

"Right," Teri agrees. She stops to glance over her shoulder. "Because you're a mess no one can fix."

She turns away and keeps walking. I fall silent as I watch her get further and further away from me past Max's shoulder. Then Max, too, turns. He chases after Teri and places his arm around her shoulder. She grips his waist and leans against him as they walk away.

I bury my fist into the nearest tree and let out an agonized roar.

~

"Should I draw up the divorce papers?" Hank asks me as he stands in front of my desk. "This is your third attempt at divorce, after all. Who knows? Third time might be the charm."

I lift my head and narrow my eyes at him.

He raises his hands. "Sorry. I'm just... trying to be your lawyer here."

I shake my head. "A lawyer isn't what I need."

"Right." He sits in front of my desk. "What do you want me to say, Aaron? That I'm sorry about how things turned out? Should I pretend I didn't warn you?"

I glare at him. "You're a lousy friend. Do you know that?"

"I did warn you," he reminds me. "I told you marrying her was a bad idea. I told you falling—"

"I know what you told me."

Hank sighs. "Okay. Now, tell me what you want me to do."

I rub my temples. "I don't know."

I can't think. My mind is still too muddled.

"Okay." Hank stands up. "Tell you what? Why don't you just leave this to me and I'll see what I can do to fix it. You know me. As a lawyer, I'm good at fixing things."

I shrug. "Do whatever you want."

"Okay."

He leaves my office. I sit back in my chair and sigh as I look up at the ceiling.

I don't care what Hank does. Nothing he can do can bring Teri back anyway. He's a lawyer, not a miracle worker.

And with her gone, I don't care about anything anymore.

Chapter Twenty-Three
Teri

"Hey." Max sits on the floor beside me and takes my hand. "Are you alright?"

No. I don't feel alright. My eyes are sore from crying. My chest feels like it's been split open. My head hurts. I haven't had a bath, haven't had a wink of sleep, haven't eaten anything. I'm tired. I stink. I'm lost. And I can't have alcohol.

No. I'm not alright.

Max squeezes my hand. "I'm sorry."

"What for?"

He shrugs. "For this."

I shake my head. "This isn't your fault. It's just some cruel trick of fate, some messed up ploy of someone up there who's bored. You didn't do anything."

"Right." He sighs as he rests his head on the edge of the bed. "I didn't do anything."

I look at him. Immediately, I see the suffering in his eyes. I place my hand on his knee.

"Max, what happened? You said you'd explain everything."

He doesn't answer. The lump on his throat moves.

I look into his eyes. "Max?"

My brother draws a deep breath. I brace myself.

"Like Aaron said, Mar…" He swallows. "Marjorie was my girlfriend. She was amazing. She was kind and smart and unafraid. She loved just about everyone and everything."

"Except spiders," I say. "I've been told she didn't like them."

Max grins and nods. "Yeah. Except spiders."

"Go on."

"We went out on a lot of dates. Some of them ended in bed."

I make a face. "I did not need to know that."

"Well, you need to know how she got pregnant, right?"

"So you did get her pregnant?"

"Yes," Max answers. "At one point, I wasn't sure, but the tests done after she… died confirmed it. That's why Aaron thinks I killed her."

My eyebrows crease. "What do you mean 'at one point'?"

He draws another deep breath. "When Marjorie told me she was pregnant with my baby, I wasn't exactly happy. I was scared."

I shrug. "Well, that's not unusual. I was scared, too. I still am scared." I touch my stomach. "Especially now."

Max squeezes my hand. "Don't worry. I'll take care of you."

I give him a grateful smile, then shake my head. "Sorry. I interrupted you. So, you were scared?"

"Yeah. Especially because I'd met her brother once."

In spite of myself, I chuckle. "Aaron is pretty scary."

"But Marjorie wasn't at all afraid. I told you she wasn't scared of anything. She was happy. She wanted me to be happy, too, but I told her I needed time to think. I was a coward and a fool. If I hadn't left her alone, if I had just pushed my doubts away, she'd still be alive."

My gaze narrows. "What do you mean?"

"I left Marjorie at her apartment. But I came back later. I wanted to talk to her since I'd already calmed down. I wanted us to talk about the baby. I have a key to her apartment. I used it. But when I got there, she wasn't alone. I heard voices coming from the bathroom. Angry voices. One was Marjorie's. The other belonged to a man. I'd never heard it before."

I simply nod as I imagine it.

"I headed to the bathroom. I was going to break up the fight but then I heard the man asking if Marjorie was sure the baby wasn't his. That made me freeze."

"I would have frozen, too," I say.

"I loved Marjorie. I thought she loved me, too. I thought I was the only man in her life. Then I find out there's someone else."

I squeeze Max's arm as I feel his pain.

"Suddenly, I wonder if I really know Marjorie. I started wondering what else she could be hiding from me. Maybe I should have confronted her then, but I just couldn't move. Actually, at that point, I couldn't hear anything anymore. It's not just my body that was frozen. It's like my mind was in a loop, too, and my senses had stopped working."

"You were in shock," I tell Max as I rub his arm.

"I snapped out of it when I saw the bathroom door move. My body just moved on its own and I ran, but instead of heading out the door, I hid in the coat closet."

My eyebrows arch. "So you saw the man who murdered Marjorie?"

"Not clearly," Max replies. "Through the slits in the door, and I only saw him from the side. He had light colored hair. Light blond. He let out this deep breath and some of it just flew off his forehead."

"So he had bangs?"

"He took off his sweater. Its sleeves were wet but not dripping. He must have wrung them out. When he did, I saw something like claw marks above his hip."

My eyes grow wide. "Claw marks?"

Max shrugs. "I don't know if they were real or tattoos, but I saw them. There were like three… strips or rips. They were gaping."

I place a hand over my mouth as I suddenly feel nauseous.

"Teri?" Max looks at me.

"I'm okay," I tell him. "My stomach just… doesn't behave so well on some days."

"Well, you haven't eaten."

"I'm not hungry. Go on."

"There's nothing left to tell," Max says. "The man left. I stayed in the coat closet for a while. I don't know how long. I don't know why. If I had left sooner, maybe Marjorie would still be alive."

"What did you do when you got out of the closet?" I ask Max.

I have a feeling I already know the answer, though.

"I went to the bathroom, took a peek and saw mostly bubbles. I tried to pull Marjorie out but I realized she was already dead. She had no pulse." Max's hands start shaking. "So I let go."

I place my hand over his.

"I let her go, Teri," Max says to me. "I just left her there. I didn't go to the bathroom to break up the fight. I didn't go to her right away to save her. And I didn't take her out of the tub. I didn't do anything."

He places his hands on top of his head as his shoulders tremble. A tear seeps out of the corner of his eye.

I wrap my arms around him. Poor Max. He's been carrying such a heavy burden these past years.

"Why didn't you tell me before?"

He meets my gaze. "And let my little sister know the brother she's been looking up to is a coward?"

I pull away. "So you haven't told anyone about this?"

"No."

"You never spoke up about the man you saw? You didn't tell Aaron?"

"You saw how he looked at me," Max says.

"But I bet he would have listened—"

"He wanted to put me in jail for killing Marjorie. He tried to."

"You were arrested?" I ask him.

Max nods.

"Because they found out you were at Marjorie's apartment the night she was killed?"

"No. They didn't know. I thought they'd find out, but they didn't."

"So why did they arrest you?"

He shrugs. "Maybe Aaron pulled some strings. Or his lawyer."

Well, he does have money.

"But the judge didn't think there was a case. She threw it out."

"And what if she'd thought there was a case?" I ask Max. "Would you still have kept your mouth shut?"

"I was prepared to pay for my crime," he answers to my dismay.

My hands go up. "What crime?"

"Not doing anything to save Marjorie."

"Then you should have told them you saw the murderer."

"And tell them I didn't do anything to stop him?" Max raises his voice.

I exhale. "So you chose to just run away?"

He falls silent.

"How does that make things right?" I ask him.

"I didn't just run away. These past few years, I've been volunteering for stuff, helping out. I haven't been doing nothing."

I nod. "So that's how you've been atoning for your sin."

"Yes."

"You know, before you atone for a sin, shouldn't you confess it first? Shouldn't you tell Aaron—?"

"I'm not telling him, Teri," Max cuts me off. "Why don't you? Who knows? He might take you back."

I let my head crash on the edge of bed.

"I'm sorry," Max mumbles.

"Take me back?" I shake my head. "I left him, remember? I'm the one supposed to take him back."

"Well, will you?" Max asks.

"After he used me?" I sigh. "You know how that feels? It feels like everything good we had was a lie."

Max sighs in turn. He takes my hand. "We'll be alright. The two of us have managed before."

I turn towards him. "Yeah. I guess it's you and me against the world again."

"And one more." Max points to my stomach.

"And one more," I agree as I look down.

Another unfortunate soul destined to suffer for the selfishness of others.

I place my hand on my stomach.

Well, not if I can help it.

~

"Do you have the papers?" I ask Hank as soon as I let him inside the motel room.

"Wow. No hello?"

I look at him in his shirt and khakis. Strange. He's Aaron's best friend. Aaron speaks of him a lot. And I've met him before. Yet I still feel like we're strangers.

Well, I guess we haven't spoken a lot. Actually, this is the first time we've been alone together.

"Just kidding," Hank says. "I have the papers—the divorce papers and the ones that say you get the property Aaron just bought and the money you asked for."

"It's not for me," I tell him. "It's for our child."

Hank nods. "Right."

He puts the papers down on the desk. "Where's Max?"

"Oh, he went out to buy some stuff."

"I see."

I step closer to him. "He didn't kill Aaron's sister, you know."

Hank shrugs. "If you say so."

He hands me a pen. I take it, but I don't sign right away. Instead, I sit down to read the papers.

Hank steps back and leans against the wall. I feel his gaze on me, though, as my eyes scan the sheets. The silence turns awkward.

I clear my throat. "You know, we've never really spoken before."

"No," he agrees. "Usually, I'm just there when you and Aaron talk and pretend I'm invisible."

"Right." I turn a page. "How is he?"

"You really want to know?"

I pause. "No."

I'm just trying to make conversation, I guess. Or I'm stalling.

"How long have you been his lawyer?" I ask him.

"Close to nine years," Hank answers.

My eyebrows arch. "That long, huh?"

"Yeah. I knew he was my soul mate the moment I laid eyes on him."

I chuckle.

"So you knew Marjorie?" I ask. "I mean, not just heard of her?"

This time, he chuckles. "Yeah. I knew the famous Marjorie."

I glance at him. "Did you think she was a saint, too?"

"A saint? No." He grabs a wisp of hair over his forehead, then blows it off. "But I guess she was—"

I'm no longer listening. My heart hammers in my chest as I turn my gaze back to the paper in front of me.

Did he just... blow his hair away from his forehead? His ash blond hair?

"Teri?" His voice makes me jump. "Are you okay?"

He moves closer to me and I feel my knees shake. I take a deep breath and force myself to calm down.

Calm down, Teri. So he has light blond hair. A lot of men do. So he has bangs. A lot of men do. So he likes to blow on them. Maybe a lot of men do.

"Teri?"

"I'm okay," I tell Hank as calmly as I can. "I just... get dizzy sometimes. Sorry if I didn't hear what you said."

"That's okay."

I wipe the sweat off my forehead.

Breathe, Teri. Calm down.

Hank frowns. "Should I turn on the air conditioner? It is quite warm in this room."

"Oh, thanks." I force a smile. "But the remote isn't working, so..."

"I got it."

Hank walks over to the air conditioner, stands on his toes and lifts an arm to reach the knob. As he does, the hem of his shirt goes up and I catch a glimpse of ink. Three lines of ink.

A gasp escapes my lips.

Fuck.

"Teri?" Hank asks.

I cover my mouth as I force myself to calm down. "You know, I feel a bit like throwing up. I think I'll go outside and get some air."

I walk to the door, but as I'm about to open it, Hank closes it.

"Teri." His voice sends a chill down my spine. "I think you and I need to talk."

Chapter Twenty-Four
Aaron

"What makes you think I want to talk to you?" I brush off Max as I walk towards my car in the parking lot.

He has some nerve showing up here where I work after all the trouble he's caused. He should leave before I can think of a reason to punch him.

"Aaron!"

I stop in my tracks and clench my jaw. My shoulders heave as I draw a deep breath.

"Aaron…"

"What?" I turn to face him with a glare.

Max lifts his hands. "Trust me, I don't want to talk to you, either. But it's important."

I notice that his hands are shaking. My jaw relaxes.

"What is it?"

"It's about Teri," Max blurts out. "She was at the motel room and now—she's not."

My eyes grow wide. I grab the front of Max's shirt.

"What do you mean?"

He swallows. "I mean that I can't find Teri. She's missing."

~

"Well, do your job and find her!" I shout into my phone before throwing it onto the couch. I rub my temples as I sit down.

How could this happen? How can Teri be missing? Why can't the cops find her? Where is she?

"No news yet?" Max asks.

I lift my head to look at him. "Why are you still here? Why are you in my office?"

"I know if anyone can find her, it's you. I want to know when she's found."

I shake my head in disbelief. "I can't believe you lost her. She's been with you only two days and you lost her."

His eyes narrow. "She's been with you for how long? Two months? And you still lost her."

My fist clenches as it itches to punch his face. He really has some nerve.

"I didn't lose her," I tell him. "You took her away from me like you took Marjorie."

"I didn't take either of them away from you."

I snort.

"I know you don't believe me, Aaron…"

"Don't call me by my first name," I warn him.

"Fine. I know you don't believe me, but I didn't kill Marjorie."

My eyes narrow. "Don't say her name, either."

"I didn't kill her," he insists.

I look away.

"I loved—"

"Just shut up!" I cut him off as I lift a finger. "Don't say a word. Don't do anything. Just sit there and be invisible. Or leave."

For a moment, Max just looks at me with his mouth gaping. Then he stands up.

"You're right," he says. "I can't just sit here and do nothing." He slaps his forehead. "God, I'm so useless. I let Marjorie slip from my fingers and now I'm letting—"

"What do you mean?" I stand up slowly.

"What?" He gives me a puzzled look.

"What do you mean you let Marjorie slip from your fingers?"

He swallows and looks away. "Nothing."

Like hell it's nothing.

I grab his shoulders and shake him. "Max, tell me."

And he does, in a quivering voice that chokes every now and then. He tells me that he was there in Marjorie's apartment the night she died. He tells me about hiding in a closet as she died.

My hands close around his neck. "You…"

"I'm sorry," Max says with tears in his eyes. "I'm so sorry. I wanted to save her. I'd give my life if it meant she could get hers back."

My hands remain on his neck.

"Sorry," Max repeats.

I let him go for Teri's sake but push him away. "You should have died instead of her."

"I know. I was willing to go to jail."

"Wait." I touch my chin. "You said you saw who killed her."

Max nods and describes him. My eyes grow wide.

"Are you sure?" I ask Max.

He nods.

Again, my fingers curl into fists. "That son of a bitch."

"You know who it is?" Max asks me.

I look at him. "Yes. And I think I know where Teri is."

I just hope I'm not too late to save her.

Chapter Twenty-Five
Teri

Come on. Come on.

I tug at the ropes binding my wrists to the back legs of the chair for what feels like the hundredth time but they still won't budge. I try to free my ankles from the front legs as well but to no avail.

I know I said I didn't mind being tied up, but this—this isn't fun at all.

I let out a groan as I look around.

I'm in a cabin. I don't know exactly where. I only know it hasn't been used in a while. I can see the cobwebs hanging at the corners. I see a rat scurrying into a hole and I nearly gag.

I'd clean it up if only I wasn't tied. Or maybe not. I don't want to do Hank any favors.

The door opens and he comes in with a steaming bowl.

"Hungry?" he asks me.

I am, but I don't say so. Who knows what's in that bowl?

"It's rabbit stew," Hank says. "Tastes like chicken."

I look away. "I'm not hungry."

"Suit yourself."

He puts the bowl down on the table—the dusty table—and then he pulls out his gun and sets it down right beside his bowl before sitting down. The sight of it is enough to make me stiffen. My throat goes dry.

What does he plan on doing with me? Is he going to kill me like he did that rabbit?

"Are you going to kill me?" I ask Hank out loud.

He laughs. "Yes."

I suppress a shudder.

"But not right away. I can't be rash this time."

"You mean unlike the time you killed Marjorie?"

He pauses, then lets out a chuckle. "You've really grown feisty, haven't you? I like feisty."

He eats another spoonful of stew.

"But you're right. I was rash that time. My jealousy, my anger, got the better of me, and next thing I knew, my hands were around her pretty little neck. And the next moment? She was no longer breathing."

This time, I'm unable to keep a shudder from crawling down my spine. Still, I try to keep myself from shaking.

"So you killed her because you were jealous? Did you love her?"

"Love? No." Hank shakes his head. "I don't do love. But I did fuck her, and I liked that. And you know what? She liked it too."

I feel like gagging again but swallow. "Why?"

"Why did I fuck her? Because she was hot."

"She was your best friend's sister," I point out.

"That's why we didn't tell him."

"But she wasn't just... a toy for you, was she? You cared about her. That's why you got so mad when you found out she was carrying my brother's child. But then, you should have expected it. He was her boyfriend, right?"

"He was useless. And a filthy coward."

My jaw clenches. "You're the one who killed an innocent girl because she didn't care for you as much as you cared for her."

"And got away with it," Hank says.

I shake my head as I look at him in disgust. "Well, if you kill me, I guarantee you won't get away with it."

Hank laughs. "I'm a lawyer, sweetheart. Did you forget? We're trained to get away with murder. Besides, I'll make it look like Max did it."

"Again?" I roll my eyes. "Isn't that getting old?"

He chuckles. "This time, Aaron will kill him for sure."

"So you plan on making him into a murderer after all he's done for you."

He turns to face me. "Really? What has he done for me?"

I take a moment to think. "Didn't he make you rich and famous?"

Again, Hank laughs. "I made me rich and famous. And you've got it wrong, honey. I'm the one who's done everything for Aaron. Without me, he'd be nothing."

"I thought the two of you were friends. You've known each other for nine years."

"Nah. We're not friends. I do stuff for him. He pays me. Sometimes, we fool around."

"That's what friends do," I tell him.

"Or at least we did until he married you."

"Oh. Poor Hank," I tease him. "You got ditched because of me."

He shakes his head and goes back to his stew. "Go ahead. Make fun of me. Have your fun now. I'll have mine later."

"You'll have fun killing me?" I ask him. "You really are sick."

"Yeah, I will," Hank says. "But before that, I'll have a different kind of fun. The same kind of fun I had with Marjorie. And Kylie."

I go still. He wouldn't.

But just the thought of it makes me speechless with fear.

He lifts the bowl to his lips then sets it down. "I'm done."

He gets off his chair and I tense. "Now for some fun."

I summon my courage so I can stall him. "So you were the one who killed Kylie, too?"

"I paid her. She didn't deliver."

"Monster," I spit out at him.

Hank grins. "Oh, you're about to find out just what kind of beast I am."

My blood runs cold.

He pulls a knife from his belt. My hands start to shake.

He approaches me with knife in hand, blade gleaming in the light. I hold my breath.

He touches the blade to my jaw and holds it against my throat.

"Such a pretty little neck."

I close my eyes. Silently, I utter a prayer to be saved.

Please don't let him do this.

Hank moves his hand lower to the front of my shirt. The sound of ripping fabric paralyzes me with fear.

No.

He cuts my shirt open, and the middle of my bra. I feel the cold air against my breasts as he gazes at them.

My skin crawls. I want to cry. I want to die.

Hank laughs. "Just as I thought, they're rather small. Maybe I should keep you for a few months. I heard they get bigger with pregnancy. And more sensitive."

My stomach churns. Tears bead at the corners of my eyes.

"And they start to leak, too. I wonder if they'll—"

A loud crash cuts off the rest of Hank's sentence and forces my eyes open. The window shatters on the floor.

Amid the rain of glass shards, I see Aaron jump in. My chest swells with relief.

He's here.

He lands on the floor and points his gun at Hank.

"Son of a bitch!"

He shoots but Hank dodges. He throws the table at Aaron, then throws the knife in his hand next.

It lands in Aaron's shoulder and he groans. I scream.

Hank jumps out the window and runs.

"Oh no, you don't." Aaron glances in my direction but then chases after Hank.

I'm about to call him back so he can untie me, but Max enters through the door.

"Max!" I say his name with a burst of relief. "You brought him, didn't you?"

He just grins.

He starts to untie me but pauses when his gaze lands on my chest.

"Did he hurt you?" he asks.

"No," I answer even as my stomach coils at the awkwardness of the situation. "He didn't have the chance."

Max finishes untying me and hands me his sweater. I put it on.

He grabs my arm. "Let's go."

"Wait." I free my arm from his grip. "We're leaving Aaron?"

"He's a big boy," Max answers. "He can take care of himself, and the cops will be here soon. My orders were to take you away from here and make sure you're safe."

And maybe I should just go. Maybe I should trust Aaron to take care of himself. But I can't just leave him.

He may have used me and hurt me, but he came to save me. He risked his own life to save me.

Besides, he's injured, I remember as I see the bloody knife on the floor. Then I see the gun, Hank's gun, next to it. I pick it up.

"Go ahead," I tell Max. "I'm not leaving without my husband."

Chapter Twenty-Six
Aaron

"You can't hide forever, Hank."

I grip my gun firmly in my hand as I put one boot in front of the other on the forest floor. I keep my eyes open for any sign of movement. I keep my ears open, too, straining to hear every sound, every rustle of a leaf, every snap of a twig.

I'm going to find that bastard if it's the last thing I do.

Suddenly, my bleeding shoulder scrapes against a branch. I wince at the pain as I put a hand over the cut.

Fuck.

In the next instant, I hear a rustle behind me. I turn to face Hank but he sends his leg flying towards me and kicks the gun out of my hand.

I'd forgotten he has a black belt in karate. Even so, there's no way I can lose a fight.

He tries to go for my shoulder. I try to punch his shitty face. One of his punches lands on my stomach but it doesn't hurt one bit.

I laugh. "Is that the best you can do?"

He responds with a kick to my groin.

"Fuck!" I curse at the pain that goes through my lower half.

Hank follows up with a kick to my face. I feel the tip of his boot against my cheek and I taste blood. But the next time he kicks, I grab his leg. I twist it and he lets out a scream of pain.

He falls to the ground. I grab the gun that is lying on top of some leaves and point it at his chest.

Slowly, Hank lifts his hands. I point the gun at his forehead.

"You're not going to kill me, are you?" he asks.

"Why not?" I glare at him. "You killed Marjorie."

"I didn't mean to."

"Bullshit." I press the barrel of the gun against his forehead. "And you were going to kill Teri, weren't you?"

"No."

"You think I'd believe you?" I scoff. "You're a lawyer."

"I'm your lawyer," he reminds me in a trembling voice. "Think of all I've done for you, Aaron. Think of where you'd be if I hadn't won that case."

"You wouldn't have won that case without me," I tell him as I press the barrel of the gun more firmly against his skin.

He closes his eyes. "Please... please..."

My jaw clenches. I want to blow his brains out. Really, I do. He's a murderer. He killed my sister and made me believe someone else had done it. He played me for a fool. Still...

"Don't, Aaron," I hear Teri's voice in the distance.

I turn my head, and in that instant, Hank sticks a branch into my shoulder. As I howl and reel back in pain, he grabs the gun from my hand and points it at my head. A gunshot thunders through the air.

The gun drops from Hank's fingers. His mouth opens in a silent scream as he grips his wounded arm.

I pull the branch out of my shoulder before picking up the gun. Once the weapon is in my hand, I glance at Teri, who's standing a few feet away holding a gun of her own. I give her a nod before pointing mine at Hank. I really should kill him.

"Aaron," Teri calls my name.

I shoot Hank in the knee and he gives a loud howl.

"That was for Marjorie," I tell him.

I leave him screaming in pain as I put my gun in its holster and walk towards Teri.

"You're just leaving him?" Teri asks me as she lowers the gun in her hands.

"Listen." I hold my palm next to my ear. "I hear a chopper coming. Hank's going to live."

"Oh."

I get the gun from her. "Thanks to you."

"To me?"

I toss the gun away. "If you hadn't shot him, I would have. In the head."

"Well, it's a good thing I did, then. This way, he'll pay for his crimes."

I nod. "And I'll make sure that even though he's the best lawyer I know, he won't get away with them this time."

Teri smiles. I pull her into my arms.

"Are you alright?" I ask her.

"Yes," she answers.

"Good."

Thank goodness. I was scared to death when I thought I'd lost her. Again.

"I love you," I whisper in her ear.

For a moment, Teri goes still. Then she puts her arms around me as well.

"I love you, too."

The words fill my chest with warmth, but then her arm presses against my shoulder and I groan.

Teri pulls away and frowns as she looks at the wound.

"Let's patch you up."

~

"How's the shoulder?" Max asks me when he comes over to the house a week later.

I glance at it. "It's okay."

It still aches sometimes and it will be a while before I can lift weights, but it's nothing I can't handle.

"Besides, this sling looks kind of cool, doesn't it?"

Max grins. "Yeah."

I nod.

He falls silent. So do I. I guess we're still not used to talking to each other. Besides, I don't know what we can talk about.

"How's Teri?" Max asks.

Ah, the one thing we have in common.

"She's good," I answer as I scratch the back of my head. "The baby's doing good, too."

"Still don't know if you're having a boy or girl?"

I shake my head. "Still don't know."

He falls silent again.

I put my hand on his shoulder. "By the way, thanks for helping me save Teri."

Max shrugs. "You mostly did the saving."

"And also, thanks for telling me the truth about what happened to Marjorie. Even if it was a bit late."

"Seven years too late," Max says. "I am so sorry I didn't tell you before. I guess I've been so... stupid."

"It's okay." I squeeze his shoulder. "Teri loves you anyway."

"Are you two talking about me?" Teri asks from the stairs. "You better not be talking about my weight."

"What weight?" I ask as I look up at her.

"Yeah," Max adds. "I don't see any... bump."

Teri laughs as she reaches the bottom of the stairs. "I'm glad to see both of you are getting along so well."

She wraps her arms around us both. "The two most important men in my life getting along. I don't know what more I can ask for."

"So you and Aaron are fine?" Max asks.

"Yeah." She turns her head to look into my eyes. "We're good. Everyone makes mistakes, after all. What's important is that you turn them into opportunities to do better, to be better."

"Well said." I plant a kiss on the top of her head.

When she lifts her chin, I grasp it and kiss her lips as well.

Max clears his throat.

"Sorry," Teri tells him after pulling away from me. "We usually don't kiss when other people are around."

"Except you're not other people," I say to Max. "You're family."

Teri gives me a grateful look, then turns back to her brother.

"We are family."

Max smiles.

"You're staying around, right?" I ask him.

"Yeah." He nods. "Even though I know she has you, I want to be there for Teri when she gives birth."

"I guess we should pick a big delivery room," Teri says.

"After all, I wasn't there for her wedding," Max adds.

"Oh." Teri touches her chin. "Actually, we didn't have a wedding ceremony."

Max's eyes grow wide. "What?"

Teri looks at me. "Are you thinking what I'm thinking?"

I nod.

A wedding ceremony? Why not?

~

The wedding ceremony takes place on the beach with only a small number of people—my most trusted friends and Teri's family—in attendance.

I stand at the makeshift altar with Max, my best man, beside me, both of us in pristine white tuxedos. He looks nervous; he's not saying a word and he keeps fidgeting with his fingers every now and then. He almost looks like the anxious groom. I, on the other hand, wear a poker face even though the excitement is threatening to burst my chest.

Strange. Teri and I have been a married couple for some time now and she's already expecting our first child. Yet I'm still excited to be wed to her.

Finally, the music starts.

Out of the tent, Pam and Cody are the first to appear, Pam in a green—no, chartreuse—gown and Cody in a miniature tuxedo of the same color. He bears the pillow containing a new pair of wedding rings, platinum gold bands Teri and I chose together.

Next comes Isabelle. I don't even know how she and Teri became such good friends. She sends me a smile that glitters as much as her gold and green gown.

Finally, Teri emerges with Veronica and Nick on each arm. The wind creates ripples in her stunning white gown and sends her veil adrift. The sunset sets her face aglow. Our eyes meet and I hold my breath.

Damn. I'm really so glad I married this woman.

I hold her gaze until she's standing just a few feet from me. She gives Veronica and Nick hugs and I shake their hands. She hugs Pam as well and then Max, who pats me on the shoulder before handing Teri over to me.

The ceremony starts. We exchange rings and vows. I'm gazing into Teri's eyes almost the entire time. Then it ends. I lift Teri's veil and kiss her against the sunset. The small crowd cheers.

In the midst of all the applause, Teri leans over to whisper in my ear. "I have something to tell you, something I said I'd tell you right after the ceremony."

"What?" I ask her.

Her face lights up with a radiant smile. "We're having twins."

Epilogue
Teri

Five years later...

"Do you think the twins will be okay?" I ask Aaron as I brush my hair in front of the dresser of the hotel room.

"Yes," he answers from the bed. "You know how much they love Isabelle."

And how much Isabelle loves them. Then again, Isabelle has always loved kids, and since she has none of her own, I'm happy to share mine with her, especially since they're such a handful these days.

The freaking fours, they say. And it's worse when you have twins, even if they are twin girls. Still, I love Jory and Rojan more than anything in the world. I can't help but miss them when I'm not with them.

Aaron gets off the bed. "Besides, didn't we say we wouldn't talk about the twins?"

I sigh. "I know, but…"

He puts his hands on my shoulders. "This is our long-awaited honeymoon, after all."

He's right. After more than five years of marriage, we're finally getting to have our honeymoon. We should enjoy it.

He lowers his head to whisper in my ear. "Come to bed."

I don't wait for Aaron to tell me twice. I put down my brush and give him my hand. He pulls me off the chair and leads me to the bed, but we don't climb onto it right away.

As we stand by the bed, Aaron cradles my face and presses his lips against mine. I kiss him back. Even after all this time, I still can't get enough of his kisses. They still send my skin burning and buzzing, make my heart flutter and my panties wet.

I place my hands on his hips and kiss him back. I part my lips and his tongue brushes against mine. I taste mint and wine.

Our tongues mingle in between gasps for air. Aaron's hands slide down to my neck and then to my shoulders, where they slip beneath my silk robe.

He pushes my robe off and the slippery sash holding it in place unravels. The garment falls to the carpet.

Aaron takes a step back. His ebony eyes narrow as they wander over my black chemise. This one is bolder than the last one I wore—completely sheer from the front and back. It almost feels like I'm not wearing anything.

I try not to blush as I give a whirl. "Do you like it?"

"I could answer that question." Aaron looks into my eyes as he places his hand beneath my jaw. "Or I could show you."

He robs me of breath with another fierce kiss. His hand goes to my breast. His thumb flicks my nipple through the sheer lace. Then he captures that stiff nub between his fingers and gently twists it.

I tear my mouth away from his and gasp. My nipples have always been one of my sensitive spots, but the added friction from the lace is sublime.

In one swift move, he slides his hand down to my hip and places his arm around me as he dips my body like he did when we were dancing tango. A cry of excitement escapes my lips.

I feel his warm breath against my bare skin just below my neck. Then his mouth finds one of my breasts and sucks it through the lace. I close my eyes as I moan. I don't know what's making me dizzier—the blood rushing to my head or Aaron's skillful mouth.

He moves his mouth to my other breast. His lips tug at my nipple before parting to let his tongue circle it. I shudder.

Just when I feel like I'm going to slip from his arms, Aaron straightens me up and kisses me again. I wait for my head to stop spinning, then reach for the sash of his robe. I give it a hard tug and it comes undone.

I step back. Now it's my turn to admire him—that defined chest, those taut abdominal muscles and the thin trail of hair in between them leading straight down to his erect cock.

Happy trail indeed.

Aaron pushes the robe off but pulls the sash. He presents it to me.

"You did say you wanted to try this again," he says.

I hesitate only for a moment, then offer him my wrists. He kisses them before binding them with the sash.

For a while, I was afraid of being tied because of what Hank did to me. But that's over now. He's rotting in jail for the crimes he committed, and I have to move on and embrace the things I like.

Once Aaron has my hands tied, he pushes my head down. I kneel on the carpet and wrap my fingers around his cock. Then I open my mouth and start to lick the length of him.

I love doing this. I love feeling his hot cock quiver against my tongue. I love knowing that I'm making him feel good. And I love the taste of him.

I drag my tongue to the tip of his cock and spread the slightly bitter yet slightly salty liquid oozing out of him across the head. His fingers grip my hair and he hisses above me.

I caress his cock with my tongue until it's all wet and glistening from my saliva, then I open my mouth to wrap my lips around him. I take him in slowly for fear of gagging. I do my best to relax my throat and hollow my cheeks.

Even so, I can only fit a few inches of him inside. When I've reached the limit, I start moving my head. I do it slowly at first as I savor the feel of his cock on my tongue. Then I go faster, knowing that's what Aaron likes.

The grunt that I hear above me confirms my suspicion. His nails rake across my scalp.

My mouth burns. My lips start to feel numb and my cheeks grow tired. Tears form at the corners of my eyes as I find it hard to breathe. Still, I continue up until Aaron pushes me away.

He pulls me to my feet and gets me on the bed. He turns me over so that I'm on my knees and elbows. Then he plants kisses along my spine through the lace. I feel his cock poke behind me as he squeezes my breasts. Then his hands slide down my sides until they reach the garter of my underwear.

Aaron pulls the moist garment down to my knees. Then he pushes two fingers in. Deep. I gasp. He moves them in and out of me slowly and I breathe through my mouth as I savor the sensation. He moves his fingers faster and my hips start moving on their own.

Slick sounds fill the room.

Suddenly, he withdraws his fingers. The tip of his cock brushes against my weeping sex. He teases me with it and lets it catch on the folds of my skin. Then he enters me slowly.

I moan all the way until his cock is completely sheathed inside me. I feel its tip press against my womb.

Aaron pauses a moment, and then he grips my hips and starts pounding into me. Skin slaps against skin. My breasts rock beneath me. My head crashes down on the bed and I bury my face against the sheets as I let out cries. The fact that my hands are tied makes me feel like I'm completely at Aaron's command, entirely his. Excitement buzzes in my veins.

Just when I'm about to go over the edge, Aaron stops and pulls out. He turns me around so that I'm facing him and captures my lips in a kiss. Then he enters me again and continues pounding into me.

I place my hands above my head and throw my head back. My body starts to tremble.

Aaron goes even faster and I'm lost. Like the sash of my robe earlier, I unravel. My back arches like a bow and my toes curl into the sheets. Tears fill my eyes as the pleasure takes over me. Soft cries spill from my quivering lips.

Aaron continues moving in and out of me a few more times, and then his fingers bite my hips as he gives a final jerk. He lodges his cock deep within me as a growl leaves his throat. His eyes fall shut as he, too, throws his head back.

I admire the sight through foggy eyes as I catch my breath. After a few moments of stillness and silence, he frees my wrists and moves away. He crashes down beside me and I roll towards him, eager to keep feeling his body against mine. My hand rests on his stomach.

Our bodies smell of sweat and sex, our skin sticky. Our hair is a mess. But this is the mess I love the most, the one I want to keep causing over and over.

"I love you," Aaron whispers as he strokes my hair.

"I love you, too," I whisper back as I smile against his skin.

He is my perfect mistake, a package sent by accident but meant entirely for me. And I am his.

We belong together, but more importantly, we belong to each other. And right now, in this perfect moment, as I gaze up at the ceiling, I can see forever.

~The End~

MR. ALWAYS & FOREVER

Prologue
Ingrid

Red.

Breath drawn, I step onto the crimson carpet and into Damien Shore's Valentine's party.

The palatial ballroom is dolled up in shades of red from top to bottom. Burgundy roses glaze the domed ceiling from which pendent Baccarat chandeliers bathe the room in a champagne glow. Scarlet silk tapestries braided with blushing lace wind up the grand pillars. High tables swathed in ruby taffeta stand against the walls lined in carmine velvet. In the middle of the room, bartenders in vermilion serve cocktails on the garnet-topped counters of the circular bar like cardinals ministering to a particularly wayward flock.

Even the crowd is in red, as prescribed by the invitation I've already surrendered to the sentry. The women are garbed in fiery couture and the men in dashing black and white tuxedos with maroon ties. All have donned cerise masks over their faces, another prescription.

With my own beaded mask in place, I make my way towards the bar. The hem of my satin gown, a take on the cheongsam but with most of the back cut out, drifts silently across the carpet. A few heads turn, some with wide grins and lipstick smiles, which I repay with my own.

I don't really know anyone at this party, though I do recognize some guests—a seasoned actress, an ex-NBA player, the on-and-off frontman of a rock band, a senator's mistress. No mask can hide the stink of fame—or infamy. As for those I don't recognize, I can only guess they're just as reputable or as wealthy, since they were all hand-picked by Damien Shore's secretary.

I may be the lone exception, having barely snagged an invitation by calling in a favor. Still, who's to tell? As long as I relax, drink, and wear a smile, no one will suspect I'm just a budding underpaid journalist in search of my first big scoop—which my instinct tells me I'll find tonight.

"Found you."

Stopping just a few feet away from the bar, I turn my head at the voice. My eyes rest on a man close to six feet tall. Tawny brown eyes peek out from a mask of red and black halves, the same shade as his side-swept hair. Even with the mask, I can tell there's a handsome face to go with the tailored dinner jacket that hangs from his broad shoulders. That square, dimpled chin below a pair of thin lips is making my heart stop.

What better way to become Lois Lane than to have my own Superman?

As he stops right in front of me, I swallow the lump in my throat. "You were looking for me?"

"Yes." He tucks his hands into his pockets, making his shoulders look even broader. "Ever since I arrived, I've been looking for the most beautiful unaccompanied woman at this party, and now I've found her."

I snort, shifting my gaze to the crowd. "You mean the only unaccompanied woman at this party, or the first one you saw to play your tricks on?"

"Or maybe just the only woman who hasn't had a drink. What can I get you?"

I glance at the bar, hesitating. Normally, I'm against men I don't know paying for anything for me, but since all the drinks are free, it should be fine.

I grin, tapping my fingers on the faux crocodile skin of my clutch purse. "Margarita."

"Good choice."

I watch him head to the bar, tucking a loose strand of hair behind my ear while I appraise the view. As he leans on the counter, I catch a glimpse of a backside chunky enough for me to take a bite out of.

Damn.

Just then, he turns, his eyes finding mine. Blushing, I look away, lips pursed.

Why the hell am I acting like a teenager with raging hormones and a first-time crush when I'm already twenty-four?

Oh, right. It's because I'm a virgin, which is practically the same thing. Still, I'm an adult, plus I'm working tonight. I should have a better grip on my emotions.

Get a hold of yourself, Ingrid. He's just a man, even if he is the hottest man you've ever met. And you're a woman, even though you're a virgin.

Touching my forehead, I frown. I am so screwed.

"Is everything okay?" my crush asks as he reappears beside me, a glass of neat whiskey in one hand and my cocktail in the other.

"Yes." I force a smile as I face him, tucking my purse under my arm.

"Here's your margarita." He hands me the salt-rimmed glass. "Blushing, just like you."

I pause, fingers around the stem of the glass. He noticed?

"And everything else in this room," he adds, lifting his glass. "Cheers."

"Cheers."

I lift my glass, set the straw aside, and take a sip, longer than usual to help me swallow my embarrassment. Afterwards, I grimace at the sourness of the cranberries and the salt-tempered bitterness of the tequila, the alcohol leaving my throat ablaze.

"Good?" my companion asks, eyebrows raised.

I nod, my expression returning to normal. "Thanks, um... What shall I call you?"

I know the masks are there for a reason and names aren't supposed to be given. Still, I have to call him something.

"Whatever you want," he answers with a mischievous grin.

Hunk comes to mind, along with Delicious, Babe Magnet and Stud.

"Clark," I blurt out instead.

For a moment, his eyes narrow, then the grin returns. "Then I shall call you Lois."

Shit. I didn't just blow my cover, did I?

"I trust you can keep my secret identity?" He winks.

"Of course." I rotate my glass and take another sip.

"So, what do you think of this party?" He tucks a hand in his pocket as he glances around the room.

"Too red."

His eyebrows furrow. "You don't like red?"

"I find it... too bold," I answer, brushing a bit of salt off the rim of my glass with my fingertips and placing it on the tip of my tongue. "And maybe a bit gruesome. It is the color of blood, after all."

His eyes travel down my gown. "And we're all sharks who get excited by the sight of it."

I cross my arms below my breasts, suddenly feeling self-conscious.

His gaze burns into them. "After all, it is the color of danger, and what is life without flirting with a bit of danger?"

Instinctively, I wrap my arms tighter around my chest, and my purse falls as a result. I hurry to pick it up, kneeling on the ground, only to find myself staring into his crotch as I lift my head.

Fuck.

I'm in danger, alright. At least, my virginity is.

Clark offers me his hand. "You don't have to kneel before me, Lois. If there's anything you want, you need only ask."

I grab it as I straighten up, forcing my wobbly knees steady.

As I try to think of something to say, my eyes fall on his ebony bow tie. "You're not wearing a red tie."

He glances at it. "Nope."

"But the invitation said..."

"To wear something red apart from the mask," he finishes the sentence. "And how do you know I'm not?"

On impulse, my eyes dart to his crotch.

He chuckles, showing me his watch with its crimson strap.

I blush. "Oh."

"Frankly, though, I don't like rules very much," he says, putting his hand away again. "And I can't say I've always followed them."

"Mr. Shore seems to like rules, though." I place my purse back under my arm. "Or so I've heard."

"You mean he likes making his own rules." He lifts his glass for another sip.

As I do the same, I narrow my eyes at him.

How much does Clark know about Damien Shore?

Just then, the music and the crowd go silent. Heads turn towards the stairs, where a man with salt-and-pepper hair and a red suit is ascending, a young woman in scarlet and diamonds on each arm. Midway, he pauses, turning to the crowd with a wide smile.

Damien Shore.

"Speaking of the devil," Clark mutters.

Casually, I flip my collar, pointing the tiny camera I bought on eBay a few days ago at the staircase.

"Good evening, beloved guests," Damien Shore starts his speech with raised arms, dark eyes peeking above red sunglasses. "And welcome to my annual Valentine's party, the grandest Valentine's party in Texas, maybe even in the US and in all the world."

The man to my left raises his glass. "Hear, hear."

"As some of you know, every night is a party for me. But tonight, as I do every year, I'm throwing this party for you so that you can all have a taste of the fun I'm having. Just don't forget my rules."

"What did I tell you?" Clark whispers in my ear.

"First, no taking off masks," Shore goes on. "Neither yours nor someone else's. Two, no throwing up on the carpet. There are plenty of bathrooms for you to use. Three, no tattling. Whatever you see or hear here, you leave here."

Yeah, right. That only confirms my suspicion that there is something wrong going on here.

"Finally, no sleeping with my household staff, not the bartenders or the maids or the guards or the horses in my stables."

The crowd erupts into laughter.

"Although kissing and groping is allowed. Whatever you do, please—and this is the most important rule—enjoy."

Applause breaks out. I stop the recording and join in, clapping.

As the applause dies down, Damien Shore continues up the stairs. Some of the men follow him, some with their women. Beside me, Clark gulps down what remains of his whiskey, disposing of the empty glass on a silver tray carried by a passing waiter.

"I'm sorry, but I have to go," he says, taking my hand and planting a kiss on it. "It was a pleasure."

My mind races.

He's leaving me already? The disappointment of my imminent abandonment stings, but that is not all. Clearly, Clark is planning on joining those other men and Damien, and clearly, they're up to something.

I have to go with them.

"Wait," I call after him as he walks off. I gulp down my cocktail and hand my empty glass to the waiter before following him, placing my arm securely in his. "It wasn't enough of a pleasure."

He grins. "Would you like to have more, then?"

I nod.

"Good."

Holding my hand, he escorts me up the long stairs. At the end of them a pair of heavy wooden doors open on an even longer, dimly lit corridor.

As my platform heels clatter on the wood and the music from the ballroom fades, my heart pounds and a voice in my head tells me I should turn back. Indeed, the wall sconces that resemble medieval torches make me feel like I'm marching into a dungeon. The paintings that hang between them, eerie paintings of torture and dark sexual encounters, lend a somber feeling to the air.

Still, I continue. Another voice is telling me that whatever story I'm looking for waits at the end of this corridor. I'm not leaving until I have it.

Finally, we reach the end.

"Are you sure about this?" Clark asks, pausing before another pair of heavy wooden doors, these lined with black velvet.

I give another nod. "Yes."

He nods at the men in black guarding the doors and they open them. We step in, my breath leaving me as I find myself in a different world entirely.

Here, in this room, just as spacious as the ballroom below but darker, naked men and women with their hands in chains and collars around their necks dance on pedestals, some around poles, some inside golden cages. Others are blindfolded and suspended from the ceilings or tied to crosses on the walls, moaning as the guests lay their hands on them. Others still are already being fucked on the tables and chairs scattered throughout the room, while some are simply being bent over and whipped, their screams of pain and pleasure filling the air.

My mouth going dry, I clutch Clark's arm tighter, suppressing the shiver that threatens to climb up my spine as I record the images—a shiver of fear.

And at the same time, surprisingly, one of excitement.

Even as my mind finds the scenery revolting and wrong in many aspects, my body appears to be reveling in it. My underwear are getting moist beneath my gown as heat pulses through my veins.

What is up with this place?

A maid in black offers me a drink and I take it, gulping down the contents of the shot glass in an effort to calm my nerves. I have no clue what it is, but its taste is surprisingly pleasant.

Spotlights turn on to shine on a stage at the front of the room. As the curtains are drawn, I see Damien Shore sitting in the middle like a king on a throne, naked women—no, girls and boys who look barely over sixteen—lined up on either side of him.

He claps his hands. "Let's begin the annual Valentine's auction, shall we?"

The crowd roars and the auction proceeds.

I stand there, too shocked to move.

How can Damien Shore, and all these other people, participate in such a barbaric event? The thought makes me sick to my stomach, and my fists clench. All of my principles shout for me to stop it, to help these helpless boys and girls, and I vow to do so. My article is already being written inside my head as my hidden camera records the show.

This will be your last Valentine's auction, you sick bastard.

The first girl gets sold to the highest bidder, who takes her away.

"Excuse me." I turn to Clark. "I think I need to go to the bathroom."

Without waiting for him to say anything, I leave his side, slipping into the crowd and emerging on the other side. Catching a glimpse of the girl and her buyer, I follow them down another corridor, where they disappear into a room. The man is so busy with his new purchase that he leaves the door open, and I peek in, letting my camera capture everything even as I close my eyes and try to shut out the sounds of their fornication.

I try... and fail.

The creaks of the bed springs, the slapping of skin against skin, the sucking, the groans, gasps, moans and cries of pleasure all seep into my ears and into my mind, conjuring images of another man—Clark— and myself on a bed. Sweat beads on my skin. My gown feels too warm, too tight, especially around my aching breasts. My underwear are drenched.

What is this sensation?

My shaking hand goes to the front of my gown, grabbing a fistful of satin over my wildly beating heart, which seems to be in the throes of a fever. A moment later, my purse slips and hits the floor.

The sound of the leather against the wood vibrates through me like the clanging of a gong, breaking me out of my trance.

And I'm not the only one.

The man on the bed stops and turns. "Who's there?"

Hastily picking up my purse, I leave the room, my head still spinning. Standing in the corridor, I wonder what to do next, but before I can come up with a solution, I hear footsteps approaching and see blurry shadows of burly men cast on the wall.

Shit.

Suddenly, a hand grabs my arm, pulling me. Again, my purse falls to the floor. My wrists are placed in handcuffs behind me as my body is pinned against the wall. I open my mouth to scream, only to gape as I recognize my assailant.

"Clark?"

In the next moment, his hand grasps my chin and his mouth descends on mine, robbing me of breath. With my lips parted, his tongue immediately slips in, and my knees buckle at the taste of him. Heat slides all the way to my toes.

"Hey!" one of the guards calls seconds later, approaching us.

I nearly whimper as Clark takes his mouth off mine. "Yes?"

The guard stares at us, frowning. "Get a room. Literally."

He unlocks a door and pushes it open, pointing to it.

"Thank you," Clark says, picking up my purse and ushering me into the bedroom. "You're very kind."

"Just get in," the guard says, shutting the door as soon as Clark is inside. "You have fifteen minutes," he calls from behind it.

My eyes grow wide as I sit on the edge of the king-sized four-poster bed.

Fifteen minutes? For what?

"Well, you heard the man," Clark says, tossing my purse on the bed and sitting beside me. "We have fifteen minutes to fuck."

"What?" I turn to him, eyes even wider.

He's got to be kidding.

"Isn't that why you came here with me, Lois? Isn't that why you were spying on that couple?"

"I wasn't..."

"Why, then?" He strokes my cheek. "Why are you here?"

"I..."

I try to think of an excuse but fail. The lips he has latched to the side of my neck and the finger circling my nipple through the satin empty my mind even as a gasp escapes my lips.

Clark's right. I did want this.

I do want this.

Now that I have my scoop, I might as well indulge in a little fun.

When he kisses me again, I kiss him back with all the passion I've built up since puberty, shivering in delight as my tongue mingles with his. He pushes me down on the bed and the soft mattress is like a cloud beneath me. My hair unravels past my shoulders as he rakes his fingers through it.

With each caress of our tongues, the combination of whiskey and tequila creates a far more intoxicating cocktail, muddling my brain and making every inch of my body burn.

His hand cups my breast and I moan into his mouth, my flesh stirring to life beneath his palm through the thin layer of satin. He unbuttons my collar, his hand slipping in to pinch one of my swollen nipples. I gasp, the pain and the pleasure mixing to create ripples of heat that travel through all my veins.

Suddenly he pulls away. Seeing my lipstick all around his mouth, I can't help but chuckle.

"What's funny?" he asks.

"Now you're wearing something else red," I tell him, planting another kiss on his cheek to prove my point.

He wipes it off with the back of his hand, frowning at the red tint.

"Oh, is that so?"

Without warning, his mouth finds my neck again, sucking on the patch of skin with so much force I whimper.

"What did you do?" I ask, frowning as I rub the skin after he's done.

He grins. "Now you have something else red, too."

This time he kisses my neck tenderly as he continues to rub my nipples. That wickedly wet tongue and his naughty fingers draw more gasps and moans from my lips and more of that warm, sticky liquid from between my legs.

When his hand creeps beneath my gown to stroke the stain on my underwear, I tremble, weak and dizzy from his touch.

Lifting his head, he holds my gaze as he pulls my underwear off. The cotton slides down my thighs to my ankles. Then Clark, too, slides down until the top of his head is all I can see.

He slips my underwear off my ankles and lifts my gown, then spreads my legs and disappears between them.

"Clark, what are you…?"

I stop talking as I feel his tongue dipping into the source of that warm, sticky spring. My thighs quiver and my back arches. My arms long to be free so that my fingers can hold on to something, anything, just so I won't be swept away.

"Clark, my hands…"

It's no use, though. He just keeps going, that tongue of his going places I never knew existed, doing things I never knew a tongue could do. And all I can do is throw my head back against the mattress and from side to side. My hands wring the sheets beneath me even as the metal cuffs dig into my skin, and my eyes squeeze shut as wave after wave of exquisite pleasure wash over me. My cries bounce off the walls.

"Oh God…"

Then his tongue pulls out, brushing against my swollen nub and setting off sparks throughout my body. My eyes fly open. My mouth opens in a silent scream.

A few more flicks of that tongue and I come undone, my body shaking and then shattering into pieces, the air sucked out of my lungs, tears blurring my eyes.

Closing them while I gasp for air, I feel like all time has stopped, like I'm drifting away aimlessly. Vaguely, I feel hands grip me, turning me around. Then a sudden, hard slap on my bare skin anchors me back to reality.

Opening my eyes, I find myself staring at the white sheets beneath a veil of my hair. My face is shoved against them and my knees are pressed to the carpet.

Another slap on my backside, and I wince. A third, and I whimper from the pain even as a fresh jolt of excitement surges up my spine.

"That's your punishment for behaving badly tonight," Clark hisses. "And this is your reward."

Gripping my hips, he enters me with one thrust, ripping a cry from my throat. Something stings, but only barely. My body is still numb from pleasure.

He moves, and my body jerks with his, the bed creaking beneath me. This time, it's not just my imagination. It's real. His cock is sheathed inside me, rubbing against the spots his tongue merely grazed, reaching into the depths of me.

"So this is what it feels like to be fucked," I whisper.

"What's that?" he asks.

"Faster," I tell him. "Harder."

The pleasure from my orgasm, which hasn't really died out, bursts into flames once more. My stiff nipples rub against the satin of the sheets, adding to the friction between my legs. My quivering thighs grow wetter. A strand of saliva trickles out from the corner of my mouth as my moans turn into new screams, eclipsed only by the slapping of skin against skin. My knees dig into the carpet.

Clark's grip tightens, almost bruising, as he speeds up even more. Then, with a sound between a grunt and a growl, he stops, pushing himself to the hilt as his quivering cock fills me with an explosion of warmth. The depth and force of that last thrust sends me into my second orgasm. It's a tremor compared to the massive quake that was the first, but it still leaves me breathless and trembling.

For a while, Clark lies still on top of me, panting. Then he gets off me and frees my wrists. I rub them as I slide off the bed to sit on the carpet.

"Twelve minutes," he says, glancing at his watch after he puts his pants on. "That's a record."

"Yes, it is," I agree.

I can't believe I lost my virginity in twelve minutes.

"But was that pleasurable enough for you?" he asks as he zips his pants.

I grin sheepishly as I rest my still reeling head on the edge of the bed. "It was super."

Now, this is how Valentine's Day is supposed to be.

That wasn't at all how it was supposed to be, I think as I pop a pain reliever into my mouth in the kitchen of my apartment. My head feels like it's splitting in half, being squeezed like an orange and pounding like a drum all at the same time.

What was that I drank, anyway?

What's even worse, though, is the sticky, sore feeling between my thighs—or rather, what it means.

How the hell could I have been so horny and so foolish as to give away my virginity to some stranger? Granted, he was hot, but was I really that desperate? What was I thinking?

I place a hand over my mouth, an idea dawning on me.

Was there something in that weirdly pleasant-tasting drink, maybe? Well, that would explain things. I just hope it doesn't have any harmful long-term effects. At any rate, it's over now. Last night is done and gone. At least I have my story.

As soon as the effects of the pain reliever have set in, making my headache bearable, I go back to my bedroom to check the now stained gown I wore to Damien Shore's party. Ignoring the stain, I check the collar. My eyes grow wide as I realize the camera isn't there.

What the...?

I sit on the bed, trying to remember when I last had it on.

I still had it when I was... spying on that guy who bought the girl from the auction, so I must have lost it afterwards, when...

I blush, remembering what happened next.

I stand up, shaking my head as I pace the room.

"No. No. This can't be happening. It can't be."

Still, it has happened. The camera is lost, probably having fallen off while I was having sex with that handsome stranger.

"Ugh." Groaning, I run my hands through my hair.

What have I done?

Suddenly, my phone rings. I grab it from the nightstand.

"Hello."

"Ingrid? Didn't you say you were going to Damien Shore's Valentine's party?" Samantha, my colleague from *The Dallas Times*, asks.

"I did," I tell her, sitting on my bed. "Why do you ask?"

"Let me guess. You found out something."

"I did."

"Something about Damien Shore liking whips and handcuffs and auctioning off underage girls?"

I straighten up, eyebrows furrowed. "How do you know that?"

Samantha sighs. "If that's your story, Ingrid, I suggest you write a different one, because that one's already been published on the website and will be in print by tomorrow."

"What?" I stand up. "But who wrote the story?"

"Actually, it's..."

"Conner Blake."

I say his name under my breath as I march towards his desk.

I've heard of him, alright, although I've never met him in person.

Even though he's less than thirty, he's one of the top reporters at *The Dallas Times*. Some say that's due to the fact that he's willing to do anything for a story, even sleep with a source—which isn't hard given his legendary looks.

At first, I thought he might just have stumbled onto the story the same way I did. What with all the masks, I couldn't tell if he was at that party. But then I took a closer look at the pictures and realized they were exactly the ones I took. In particular, the last one, with that buyer and the girl, couldn't have come from any other camera.

How on earth did he get those pictures? Well, he could have stolen my camera, but how...?

I stop a few feet away from his desk. There's a man seated behind it, a man with chestnut brown hair and thin lips, a slight cleft on his square chin, features apparent with or without a mask.

No way.

My purse falls from my fingers and my knees turn to mush so quickly that I have to lean on a nearby table to keep myself standing.

"You?" Conner stands up, the shock and recognition in his eyes mirroring the horror in mine.

Going around his desk, he walks towards me, eyes on the ID hanging from my neck. "Ingrid Halfield? You work here?"

I raise a finger. "Don't play dumb with me. You knew who I was."

"No." He shakes his head.

"Liar," I spit out.

"I only knew you were a reporter. I didn't know for which paper."

I point my finger at him. "You stole my story."

Conner shrugs. "You dropped your camera. I simply found it and used it."

"You used me."

"As you used me." He steps forward. "Admit it. You thought I was a handsome billionaire who could get you into the inner circle so you could get your scoop. And I did. Then you got in trouble and I saved you."

I pull my shoulders back. "Saved me?"

"Plus, you had the time of your life, so, really, I don't understand why you're complaining. You got the better end of the bargain."

I slap him. "How dare you!"

Conner raises an eyebrow as he rubs his reddened cheek. "So, we're into that now, are we?"

I feel an urge to slap him once more. Instead, I clench my fist at my side and square my shoulders. "You, Conner Blake, are the worst man I've ever met."

"Really? I thought you were quite smitten with me, Lois—I mean, Ingrid." He scratches his chin. "Didn't you say I was…"

"You're an asshole," I continue. "You're even sicker than Damien Shore is. I hope you rot in hell."

Picking up my purse, I stomp to the elevators, seething.

"By the way," he calls after me, "your gown was lovely. I'm sorry I ruined it."

I raise my middle finger at him. "You know what? If you think you're all that, why don't you shove your dick up your ass?"

I step into the elevator, banging my head on the wall after the door closes.

How could I have sex with that… that filthy scumbag? I don't even know what's worse—that he stole my virginity—and yes, he did steal it—or that he stole my story.

I let out a deep sigh.

Well, one thing's for sure—I'm leaving this paper. And then I'm going to forget about him and everything that happened last night. I'm going to pretend none of that ever happened and I'm going to get a better job and I'm going to get a nice boyfriend, have better sex with him and maybe marry him after a few years.

As the elevator doors slide open, I take a deep breath and step out, head and shoulders held high.

Today marks the beginning of the rest of my life, and nothing will stand in my way.

Chapter One
Conner

Six years later...

The redhead beside me groans as I toss her arm aside to get out of bed, but she continues sleeping, snuggling into the pillow.

I place the blanket back over her, watching her as I put my jeans and my shirt back on.

What was her name again? Leslie? Lisa?

A glance at the pen holder on the desk tells me it's the former.

Leslie. We met on the plane to Boulder, hit a bar straight from the airport and hooked up.

What else is new?

Walking to the kitchen, I open the fridge, empty except for a few cheese slices, half a loaf of fruit cake, a jar of pickles and some cookie dough. I grab one of the cheese slices, peeling off the plastic and munching on it as I sit on the stool by the window, watching the snow fall and paint the city a fresh layer of white.

There's definitely much more snow here than in Dallas.

Not that I prefer snow. I neither hate it nor like it. Kind of like shrimp. In fact, I'm not particular about climate. I can adapt to any kind. I'm cold-blooded that way.

I don't mind Dallas. A lot of restaurants serve great chili, which is good for mild hangovers. There are great bars, great women. Malls. Plenty of fresh produce. History. There are half a dozen pro sports teams and lots of politics and business going on, which also means there are plenty of stories if you know where to look, or just look hard enough.

That used to be enough, but not anymore.

I press my face close to the glass. A thirty-five-year-old man with weary eyes and a frown above an unshaved chin stares back at me.

In the past two years, I've started to wish I had something more to plan for, something to look forward to. When you're a journalist, working a job where you don't know what your next story will be, you want something to anchor yourself to, some measure of constancy or certainty.

You want a home, a family.

No, you need one.

My cheese slice is gone and the sky is starting to brighten up, so I head back to the bedroom to get my bag and my phone. Picking the latter up from the nightstand, I pause to look at Leslie.

Pretty. Witty. Successful in her own right.

Ah, but aren't they all?

All the women I've been with are the same, all boring and pretentious—save one ash-blonde beauty.

The only one I know willing to risk her life for a story. The only non-Asian woman I've seen wear a cheongsam and look ravishing in it. The only woman who let me cuff her and spank her and have amazing sex with her, all in the span of fifteen minutes.

No. Twelve.

Even now, the memory of that night still haunts me, sometimes giving me a hard-on in the shower. Why, just the thought of it makes my cock throb now, even though I can't remember how many times Leslie and I did it last night.

Yes, she was fascinating. Unfortunately, she was also the only one who's ever told me to shove my dick up my ass, which out of all the insults I've received from women is by far the worst.

Sighing, I bring my things to the living room, sweeping the magazines on the coffee table aside to make room for my laptop. While waiting for it to boot up, I pull the blanket off the armchair, wrapping it around my shoulders and rubbing my hands to ward off the chill.

I may not mind the cold, but that doesn't mean I don't get cold.

As soon as my screen's ready, I go straight to my latest story—allegations of corrupt alliances among farm owners—to continue editing it. I add a sentence here and there, check my notes to make sure I have the details right, listen to the interview again to make sure I didn't miss anything important. Then I change the starting sentence to make it catchier, then change it three times more.

When I'm done, I read the whole story two more times before formatting it and sending it to my editor with a quick note. I've barely hit send when my phone rings.

"Hello."

"Conner Blake?" a woman's unfamiliar voice asks.

"Speaking."

"This is Dana Hill, Ms. Cassandra Newton's secretary."

Oh, her. I don't know her, but I've heard of Cassandra Newton, Deputy Head of the News Division of newly listed SSJ Media, the company which, due to a dozen recent mergers and acquisitions, I now work for.

I stand up, the blanket falling off my shoulders. "Ms. Hill, what can I do for you?"

"Mr. Blake, are you in Boulder already?"

"As it so happens, I arrived last night. Why?"

"Something came up in Ms. Newton's schedule. She would like to see you this morning at ten-thirty instead of this afternoon."

I glance at the clock on the wall, which tells me it's only twenty minutes after six. That gives me plenty of time to shave, shower and have a heavy meal with at least two cups of coffee.

"Yeah. Sure. I'll be there."

~

At five past ten, I arrive by cab at the headquarters of SSJ Media, twin eleven-story towers in the heart of Boulder's business district. Each tower's lower half is clad in brick, like most of the historic homes in this city. The upper halves are covered with glass. It's likely a metaphor for building on the old to come up with something modern for all of society to look up to.

I like it.

Straightening my tie, I go up the brick steps of the first tower and walk past the glass doors. Even the lobby is a mix of brick and glass. A huge brick fireplace dominates one side, and pieces of glass sculpture, including a giant bottle with smaller bottles inside and a mother and child, decorate the other wall. In the middle of the lobby, the Christmas tree still stands surrounded by large, gift-wrapped boxes, its boughs heavy with tinsel and ornaments of all shapes, colors and sizes.

Well, it's still only the first week of January, after all.

I make my way to the reception desk at the other end of the room. The auburn-haired receptionist whose name tag reads Becky gives me my pass—and makes a pass at me. I play along, smiling, complimenting her earrings, then just before she gets any ideas, I head off to the elevators, taking them to the ninth floor.

Stepping off, I walk down the door-lined corridor until I find the one marked Conference Room 7B. There's a coat closet beside it, with two coats already hanging there—a pink fur-lined parka and a plaid jacket, size 46.

I frown. Wasn't this supposed to be a private meeting?

I glance at the door.

Then again, if we're meeting in a conference room instead of Cassandra's office, it makes sense that there are a few people involved.

As I shrug off my gray coat and place it on a hanger, I remember that first phone call from Cassandra Newton, telling me to come to Boulder for a job offer. That was all she said—a job offer. Given the company overhaul and my reputation for getting great stories, I can't say I'm surprised, but I have no idea what position or for which paper or how much higher the pay is. Hopefully significantly higher.

But basically I don't have a clue why I'm here in Boulder, and I'm eager to find out.

Shutting the coat closet, I enter the conference room, pausing as I see its other occupants—a mustached man in his forties who I recognize as another journalist, Ed Parker, and a raven-haired woman in her twenties, who I've never seen before but find absolutely stunning.

"Oh, shit," Ed scoffs, turning his chair towards me. "Why the hell are you here?"

Ah. Pleasant as always.

I shrug, taking the seat across from him, which is also beside the cover girl. "My guess is as good as yours, Ed."

A veteran, they all call him, since he's been a journalist for *The Arizona Daily* for nearly twenty years. Too old, I say. The wrinkles under his sleepless eyes and the thick lenses over them are proof of the toll the job is taking on him.

"What happened to your leg?" I ask, catching a glimpse of his cast from beneath the glass table.

"Hit-and-run," Ed answers. "Probably some teenager who was either drunk or texting or both."

"Did they catch him?"

He shakes his head.

I nod. "Sorry."

"Sorry about my leg, sorry the kid didn't get caught, or sorry he didn't finish me off?"

I narrow my eyes at him. "What?"

He leans forward. "Because by the end of this, you'll be the one who's sorry you dragged your pretty little ass all the way to Boulder for nothing."

"Hey," the woman beside me scolds. "Let's all play nice, okay?"

Ed shakes his head as he sits back. "Unlike pretty boy here, I don't play."

"That's the second time you called him pretty," she points out. "Maybe you have a crush on him."

Ed cocks his head, eyes furrowed in disgust. "Lady..."

"Easy, Ed." I raise a hand. "You don't want to get your blood pressure up and end up back in the hospital, do you? Besides, the lady was just joking."

He frowns.

"Good one, though," I whisper at my seatmate.

She smiles, offering me her hand. "The lady's name is Tiffany Jordan."

"Conner Blake." I shake her hand. "*Dallas Times*. Are you sure you're in the right room? Because you look like you should be getting ready for the runway or something."

From the corner of my eye, I see Ed roll his.

"Cute." Tiffany's pink-tinted lips curve into a grin as she lets my hand go, tucking hers under her chin. "But I don't do that anymore. Now, I just blog."

My eyebrows crease. "Wait. You were a runway model?"

"For two years," she answers. "I did a photo shoot for a magazine once, too."

"Ah." I move my chair closer to hers. "So, you like being in between the pages. How do you like being in between—?"

"Oh, for God's sake, Blake, cut it out," Ed interrupts.

I turn to him, shrugging. "What? I was just making friends."

"Yeah, right," he snorts. "I wasn't born yesterday."

"Nope, doesn't look like it," I mutter.

Ed glares.

"How about you?" Tiffany asks me. "Have you ever done modeling?"

"Me?" I point to my chest. "Nope."

She scratches her chin. "Hmm."

Just then, the door opens and a curvy, olive-skinned woman with wavy black hair enters in a long-sleeved green dress.

"Good morning, everyone," she greets us, standing at the front of the room where she leans on the table. "I'm Cassandra Newton, the one who called all of you here. I'm so sorry I had to reschedule the meeting on such short notice, but you know this industry. Things can be unpredictable."

"Don't I know it," Ed remarks, grinning at her.

Who's flirting now?

"You must be Edward Parker," Cassandra says, turning to him.

"Please call me Ed." He offers his hand. "I'd stand, but..."

"Oh, don't worry about it." She shakes his hand. "I'm sorry about your accident."

"Hey, I'm just glad I'm alive and here right now, Ms. Newton."

"You can call me Cassie," she tells him. "In fact, everyone here can call me Cassie. We're all comrades, after all, aren't we?"

She turns to Tiffany. "And you must be the famous blogger Tiffany Jordan. I'm a follower."

Tiffany stands up and shakes her hand. "Oh, I'm so honored."

"And you…"

I stand up, straightening the edges of my jacket before stretching my hand. "Conner Blake at your service."

Cassie smiles as she shakes my hand, her ebony eyes glistening. "I've heard a lot of things about you, Conner."

I simply return the smile.

She releases my hand. "And…"

Cassie stops, frowning. "Aren't there supposed to be four of you?"

I glance at the empty chairs.

She looks at her watch. "Oh, well. I guess we'll have to start without her."

Her?

"As you all know, a lot of print media have been brought together under the umbrella of SSJ Media," Cassie starts. "And I am Deputy Head of the News Division."

Ed lets out a whistle.

Cassie clasps her hands together. "I am pleased to announce that the powers that be have decided to launch our own news magazine."

My eyebrows go up. "A news magazine?"

"You know, the kind of magazine where they publish news stories instead of pictures of naked women," Ed tells me.

I throw him a pout.

"Like *Time*?" Tiffany asks.

"Exactly." Cassie taps her fingers on the table. "Now, you know what that means. New magazine. New staff. New editor-in-chief." She straightens up. "And one of you could be…"

Suddenly, the door opens and a woman in a knitted white sweater and black pants enters the room.

"Sorry I'm late," she mutters as she takes off her bonnet, revealing a head of ash-blonde hair. "I was…"

She stops, her blue eyes growing wider than her mouth as they recognize my own dark brown ones from across the table. Her face turns pale, as if she's seen a monster from her nightmares, which I probably am.

I sit up, grinning at her as I wave my hand. "Hello, Ingrid."

289

Chapter Two
Ingrid

Conner Blake. In the flesh. In Boulder. Right here in this very room.

I close my mouth, drawing a deep breath as I clutch the handle of my purse.

You have got to be kidding me.

"You know each other?" the woman in front of the room, who I'm guessing is Cassandra Newton, asks.

"No," I answer at the same time that Conner says yes.

The man with the glasses, who I recognize as Ed Parker, chuckles. "Oh, Blake, what did you do this time? Break this poor girl's heart?"

"No," I protest quickly, maybe too quickly. "Blake, you say? On second thought, I think I've heard of you."

"Come to think of it, didn't you use to work for *The Dallas Times*?" Cassandra asks.

"Yes," I answer, sitting down. "But it was a long time ago."

Six years ago, to be exact. Frankly, I never thought I'd see him again. I hoped I never would.

"Not that long," Conner contradicts. "I remember you as if it were yesterday."

I roll my eyes. Once a jerk, always a jerk.

"Well, take a seat, Ingrid," Cassandra tells me. "For those of you who don't know, Ingrid Halfield is from *The Colorado Chronicler*."

I pull out the chair closest to me, behind Ed.

"Tiffany," the woman across from me introduces herself, offering her hand.

I shake it, narrowing my eyes at her as I try to remember where I've seen her. Ah, yes. That famous fashion blog. They call her the woman who can never go wrong with fashion.

"I've read a few of your articles," I whisper. "They were helpful."

She smiles. "Thank you."

Cassandra speaks. "Now, as I was saying, SSJ Media is launching a news magazine. We'll be doing features that will appeal to a wide range of demographics, and we're looking for an editor-in-chief."

My heart skips. Editor-in-chief? Of a news magazine?

That means a higher-paying job, which I desperately need. And a desk job, which I need just as much, what with all my other responsibilities.

"As you may have already guessed, we'll be choosing from the four of you," Cassandra continues. "Yes, we could have chosen one of the other editors-in-chief, but we decided we want someone new. Plus, we chose you all for specific reasons—Conner, for your tenacity and hard work..."

Ed snorts before I can.

"Tiffany, for your creativity and understanding of what people want, especially young people. Ingrid, for the passion you have for your craft and your excellent writing skills..."

I nod, smiling.

"And Ed, for your experience, and well, because we know this accident makes it harder for you to be a reporter. Maybe it's about time you sit behind a desk."

"So it's out of pity?" Ed asks.

"Not at all." Cassandra shakes her head. "You are the most experienced person here, and you've done a lot for this company."

"And how will the winner be chosen?" Tiffany asks. "I mean, the editor-in-chief for this magazine."

"Good question." Cassandra walks to the window. "We decided that we'll start with blank slates and just give each of you the same test. Whoever does best at this test will get the job."

"And what will this test be?" Conner asks, swiveling his chair.

Cassandra turns to us. "You will all be tested at what you're best at, of course—writing. Each of you will have to write a story."

Ed chuckles. "That's way too easy."

"What story?" I ask.

"You'll have to impress us by writing a piece about the best love story you can find," Cassandra informs us. "A real love story, of course. No Romeo and Juliet or Edward and Bella here."

"A real love story?" Conner asks.

"It has to be new," Cassandra says. "It has to be genuine. It has to be powerful and of course, inspiring, moving."

"Unbelievable." Ed shakes his head. "You want me to write a cheesy article?"

"If you want the job, yes," Cassandra tells him, holding her chin high. "Any more problems? Tiffany?"

Tiffany shakes her head.

"Ingrid?"

"None," I tell her. "I think it's a good assignment, actually. I look forward to it."

"Great," Cassandra approves.

"Although, of course, Mr. Blake might have a problem," I add.

Conner turns to me with raised eyebrows.

"You see, I believe this kind of story requires heart, and I don't think Mr. Blake has one."

Ed feigns getting shot. "Ouch."

"You seem to know Mr. Blake better than you said," Cassandra says. "Well, I'm sure he'll manage. Won't you, Conner?"

Conner nods. "Yes, ma'am. I'll do my best."

To what? Sleep with women to get a lead? Sweet talk women into spilling their stories? Or steal someone else's story, maybe?

"Careful he doesn't steal your stories," I warn under my breath.

Conner's eyes grow wide.

"What was that, Ingrid?" Cassandra asks.

I put on a smile as I sit back. "Nothing."

"Well, that's it then." Cassandra sits down. "Deadline is two days before Valentine's Day. Come to my office, hand your stories to me in person and in the next twenty-four hours, you'll know who gets the job. In the meantime, Ed, Ingrid, Conner, you don't have to do your usual work. We want to be sure you can give this the best you've got. You'll still get paid, of course."

I blink in disbelief. "Really?"

"And Tiffany, just tell us how much you earn a month and we'll write you a check."

"Oh, no thanks." She shakes her head. "I need to keep my blog updated. Don't worry. I'll still give this my best shot."

"Fair enough," Cassandra says. "Any more questions?"

I shake my head. "None."

"Well, the clock is ticking. Your story's waiting. Go find it."

I pick up my purse, heading out the door first. Grabbing my black coat, I put it on while walking to the elevators. I want to be out of the building before Conner catches up to me.

No such luck.

"Hey." Conner runs after me. "It's good to see you again."

"You'll forgive me if the feeling isn't mutual," I tell him without looking at him, walking faster.

"You look great."

I snort. I'm well aware I've gained weight and lost a lot of sleep in the past six years.

"So, are you living here in Boulder now? Is this where you went after you left Dallas?"

I stop, taking a deep breath before turning to face him. "What do you want, Con—?"

The moment my eyes meet his, though, my breath gets stolen, my words fading.

How can he still be so damn good-looking after all these years?

"I'm just really glad to see you," he says, those chestnut brown eyes of his gleaming with warmth. "And I wanted to say I'm sorry about what happened before. I never did get the chance to say that."

At the mention of that, my temper simmers again and I cross my arms over my chest.

"Oh, really? You're sorry you used me?"

He frowns. "I thought you'd forgotten all about it."

"I've forgotten all about you, not all about it."

"Are you sure?" He steps forward, eyes gazing into mine, challenging. "Because that's not what I think."

I look away, stepping back with my fists clenched at my sides. "Why can't you just leave me alone?"

"I'm sorry, Ingrid." He reaches for my hand.

I pull it away. "Wow. You almost sound like you mean it."

"I do."

"And why apologize now, huh?" I push him back. "Because you want to sleep with me again? Because you want to use me again?"

"Because I don't want you to hate me."

I snort. "Yeah, right. I should have known Conner Blake can't stand to be hated."

He reaches for my hand again. "Ingrid…"

Again, I pull away, raising it. "Do us a favor, Conner, and just stop, okay? Just leave me alone. I…"

My phone rings, interrupting my train of thought. I fish it out of my purse, glancing at the screen before answering the call.

"Ms. Potter? Is Alexa okay?"

"I'm sorry, Ms. Halfield, but she's been taken to the hospital. She just wouldn't stop throwing up."

My heart stops. "Hospital?"

"Yes. She's at the Children's Hospital," Alexa's teacher tells me.

"Alright. I'm on my way there."

Ending the call, I toss my phone back into my purse and rush towards the elevator, sending up a prayer as my heart pounds in fear.

Please let Alexa be alright.

~

"Alexa is suffering from a case of acute food poisoning," Dr. Williams explains to me as soon as I reach her room at the hospital. "Dehydration was already setting in, so we decided to put her on IV fluids right away."

"Food poisoning?" I give the doctor a puzzled look. "From what?"

"We were hoping you could tell us," she says. "How long has she been having diarrhea? How long has she been vomiting? Can you think of anything she ate that might have caused this?"

"No." I shake my head even as I try to remember the past few days. "I can't think of anything she ate that was unusual. And she only threw up once last night. She said her stomach hurt this morning, but she said she was well enough to go to school."

"Maybe she ate something at school yesterday?" Dr. Williams suggests.

I shrug. "I make her lunch, but you know, sometimes she eats other kids' lunches, they swap…"

"I know." Dr. Williams places a hand on my shoulder. "Anyway, we already ran some tests so we're just waiting for results. In the meantime, we just need to keep her here so she can be observed and rehydrated."

"Yes, of course."

I stare at Alexa, who's currently asleep in her pink hospital gown, her hair turned to one side and her eyelids shut tight.

Poor girl. She must be exhausted from all that throwing up.

I run my fingers through her braided hair. Countless brown strands have already escaped from the rubber bands. I bring it to my lips, tears brimming in my eyes.

Alexa is all I have. She's my world, my everything. If anything worse than this happened to her, if I lost her, I don't know what I would do.

Dr. Williams squeezes my shoulder. "Don't worry, Mrs. Halfield. Your daughter will be just fine."

"Thank you," I tell her, patting her hand.

She leaves the room, but a moment later, someone else steps in. Turning my head, I see Conner standing in front of the door. His eyelids and eyebrows are pulled up, his mouth stretched.

I quickly wipe my eyes as I leave Alexa's side to face him. "What are you doing here?"

292

His gaze shifts from Alexa to me. "We have a daughter?"

Chapter Three
Conner

Staring at the girl lying on the hospital bed, taking note of how her hair is the same color as mine and calculating her age, I quickly put two and two together.

I have a daughter.

Ingrid and I have a child.

I know it. The explosion of warmth in my chest, taking over my heart and spreading throughout my body, and the coil in my gut tell me so.

I'm a father.

"Shh."

Ingrid holds a finger to her lips as she pushes me out of the room, glancing at the girl before closing the door behind her.

"What are you doing here?" she asks again.

"I overheard your phone call," I tell her. "It wasn't deliberate, just habit. I heard something about a hospital, and you looked so worried, so I thought you had a family emergency."

She folds her arms across her chest. "And you thought you'd take advantage of that."

"No. I thought you might need some help."

"What? You thought you'd be there for me to lean on? You'd be my hero so that I could feel like I owe you something and do you a favor, maybe find your story for you?"

I frown. "Do you really think I'm that low?"

"Yes," she answers without hesitation.

I sigh. "Fine. Think what you want of me, but answer my question. Is the girl in that room…" I point to the glass. "…our daughter?"

"She's *my* daughter," Ingrid corrects, placing a hand over her heart as she faces the glass. "I gave birth to her. I taught her to walk, to talk. I took care of her day and night. I raised her all on my own."

As she speaks, her voice softens, a gleam comes into her eyes and a tender smile plays on her lips. It's a side of her I've never seen, and once again, she has me blown me away.

I stand beside her. "And I admire you for that. I can only imagine all the hardships you've endured."

"No, you can't." She turns to me. "You can't imagine the pain of bringing a person into this world. You can't imagine the complete exhaustion of going through one sleepless night after another. You can't imagine the helplessness of hearing a baby cry and not knowing what to do. You can't imagine the scenarios that go through your mind when you're at work and your child is with a stranger. You can't imagine that tug on your heart or that feeling of self-loathing when your child needs something and you can't give it. You can't imagine the worry that eats you from the inside out when you send off your kid to school for the first time, not knowing if she'll make friends or if the teacher will be nice or if she'll come home unscathed and happy."

I nod slowly. "I understand."

Ingrid shakes her head. "No, you don't."

"Alright." I draw a deep breath. "I can't imagine and I can't understand, but you know what I can do? I can listen to you while you tell me everything about her. I can be here for you now, for both of you, and experience whatever hardships are yet to come together with you. I can take care of you, of both of you. You just have to let me."

She places her hands on her hips. "Just that easy, huh?"

"Yes." I place a hand on her shoulder, forcing her to look into my eyes. "I can't change the past or rewind it, but I can be here now and in the future."

"And what makes you think I want you in her future or in mine?"

"Because you know she needs me." I take my hand off. "Because I'm her father."

She snorts. "You're so sure of that, aren't you?"

I nod.

For a moment, Ingrid falls silent. Then she lets out a sigh as she leans against the wall.

"Alexa."

My eyebrows bunch up.

"Your daughter's name is Alexa," she explains.

I smile, my heart welling up as I repeat the name. "Alexa. It's a beautiful name."

She nods.

"Thank you, Ingrid."

She shrugs. "For what? I haven't said you could do anything yet."

She faces the window once more, hands in her pockets. "You can be in her life, but on two conditions."

"I'm listening."

"One, you don't get to make any major decisions about her life. I make the decisions."

"Okay."

"Two, you can't tell her you're her father."

"What?" I raise my hands in disbelief.

"Not at first," Ingrid clarifies. "I've told her that her father's dead."

I bite my lower lip. "You hated me that much, huh?"

"You have no idea." She turns to me. "I kept wondering why, of all the men in the world, did you have to be her father? Why you? I'd rather it be anyone else but you."

I wince.

I know it was wrong for me to take her camera and her story, but I never thought I'd regret it this much.

"Let me make this clear," she continues. "I may be letting you into my daughter's life but that doesn't mean I've forgiven you. I'm just doing this for Alexa, because I think it's what's best for her, but the moment I get the notion that it isn't, I can kick you out of her life as easily as I can flick an ant off a table. Do you understand?"

"I understand."

"Good." She exhales.

I rub my chin. "So, what do I tell her, then?"

"That you're an old friend?" Ingrid suggests.

I shrug. "Fine."

At this point, I'd do anything to get to know my daughter.

"Mrs. Halfield?" a plump nurse asks as she comes down the corridor.

Ingrid raises her hand. "Here, although it's Ms. Halfield."

"Oh, sorry." The nurse stops in front of her. "I need you to come with me and sign some papers."

"Of course."

"I can do it," I volunteer.

"Really?" Ingrid purses her lips. "Do you know Alexa's birthday?"

I start counting on my fingers. "November…"

"Do you know her blood type?"

I shake my head. "No."

"I'm sorry, Conner, but you know nothing about her." She tucks her hands into her pockets. "Just stay here and watch over her until I come back."

She walks off with the nurse, who glances at me with a suspicious look on her face.

"Just stay here and watch," I repeat, nodding. "Fine."

I go inside the hospital room, closing the door behind me. It almost looks like a child's bedroom, butterflies on the wall and stars on the ceiling, a box of wooden fruits on the table.

I sit on the only chair beside the bed, staring at Alexa, grinning at how she seems to be the spitting image of me.

My daughter.

I still can't believe I have a daughter. I never thought I'd have one.

Yes, I've been with many women, but I've always been careful. Well, except for that one night at Damien Shore's house when I was too excited to fuck the ravishing woman I was with and thought I didn't have time to put on a condom.

Yes, those were twelve minutes of heaven. Still, I never thought they would lead to an angel.

Slowly, I reach out to touch Alexa's hand, careful to avoid the needle attached to her.

I never thought I was cut out to be a father, because I'd barely had one of my own. Yet now, as I gaze down on my daughter, my chest so tight I can barely breathe, I wonder.

What if this was what I was really meant to be?

Suddenly, she stirs, her eyes fluttering open to reveal blue irises. Ah, that she got from her mother, that and her rounded chin. The rest she got from me—her hair, her nose, her cheeks, even her thin lips.

I've been attracted to many women before, yes, but this is the first time I've fallen in love with a girl at first sight.

She throws me a puzzled look. "Who are you?"

A lump forms in my throat as I feel an urge to tell her the truth, but remembering Ingrid's condition, I swallow.

"Conner. I'm a friend of your mother's."

"My mother doesn't have any guy friends," Alexa says.

"Really, now?"

That confirms my suspicion that Ingrid isn't dating anyone, which brings a satisfied smile to my face. Then again, I suppose with a child, she doesn't really have time for men.

"Maybe not here in Boulder," I tell Alexa. "But I was her friend in Dallas."

"Where's that?"

"You've never heard of Dallas?" I rub her hand. "It's in Texas. It's one of the largest cities in the United States."

"Texas? Are there cowboys there?"

I chuckle. "You bet there are."

"Are you a cowboy?"

"No, but I could dress like one if you like."

"Can you dance like one?" Alexa asks.

I scratch the back of my head. "I'm sorry, darling, but dancing isn't really…"

"Please?" Alexa begs, giving me puppy dog eyes.

And how can I refuse them?

"You're putting me on the spot here, Alexa." I get off the chair. "But fine, I'll do it as long as you promise me that you'll get better."

She grins, showing the gap between her front teeth. "I feel better already."

Smart girl. Charming. I'm falling more and more in love with her every second.

"Okay then."

Standing as far away from the bed as I can without hitting the wall, I turn around twice. Then, grabbing the buckle of my invisible belt, I cross my legs, kick them back and forth, and then swing them left and right in long strides.

"Yee-haw!" Alexa claps.

Just then, the door opens and Ingrid makes her entrance.

"Sweetheart, you're awake." She rushes to Alexa's side as I stop my performance. "And you're clapping. You're not supposed to be clapping."

"But Conner is so good at cowboy dancing," Alexa says.

"Still, you're not supposed to move this hand too much." Ingrid puts Alexa's left hand by her side. "You don't want the needle to come off, do you?"

"I don't want the needle at all."

"Oh, but sweetheart, you need it for now." Ingrid cups her cheeks. "You need it to be strong."

"You did promise me you'd get better," I pipe in.

"Okay." Alexa sighs.

"Good girl." Ingrid pinches her cheek lightly, then turns to me. "So, you've met."

"Yes. I've had the pleasure." I approach the bed. "Didn't I tell you I was her friend?"

"Mommy, why didn't you tell me you were friends with a cowboy?" Alexa asks.

Ingrid's jaw drops.

"Hey, I never said I was a cowboy, remember?" I tell Alexa. "In fact, I specifically said I wasn't."

Alexa's eyebrows furrow. "What's specificafally?"

"It means clearly," Ingrid answers before I can.

Alexa smiles. "Mommy's good with words. She's a writer."

I grin. "I know."

"Are you a writer, too?"

I rub the back of my head. "As a matter of fact, I am."

"Yes, he is," Ingrid confirms.

"Are you as good as Mommy?" Alexa asks.

I chuckle.

"No," Ingrid answers before I can again.

I frown but don't protest.

"Enough with the questions." Ingrid pats her head. "You should rest."

"But I just woke up," Alexa protests.

"You should rest some more," Ingrid tells her. "The doctor said if you stop throwing up so much and your stomach stops hurting and you look better, we can go home tomorrow."

"That's a lot of ands."

"Rest." Ingrid kisses her forehead. "The sooner you get better, the sooner we can get back to our apartment."

~

Setting Alexa's backpack down by the couch, I pause to admire Ingrid's apartment.

The same ivory wallpaper with blue flowers covers all the walls. The ceiling is cream; the floor of the living room is cloaked in wooden tiles, the kitchen in linoleum. A granite counter separates the two. Beyond it I can see a fridge, a stove and a sink beneath a cupboard. In the living room, the television hangs on the wall above a shelf filled to the brim with books. The top is littered with picture frames, mostly holding pictures of Alexa.

I pick one of them up, smiling at the sight of a baby Alexa trying to eat the ear of her teddy bear.

Behind me, Ingrid gathers the toys and books on the couch, shoving them in a corner so Alexa can lie down. After she does, Ingrid throws a quilt over her.

"There," she says, tucking the quilt under Alexa's chin. "Comfy?"

"I need my teddy bear," Alexa says.

"Right."

Ingrid disappears into one of the two doors I can see, the left one, and returns with a purple teddy bear.

"There you go." Ingrid hands the toy to Alexa, who welcomes it with open arms.

"Is purple your favorite color?" I ask Alexa.

She nods. "I like red, too, but Mommy doesn't."

"I see." I glance at Ingrid, who's glaring at Alexa.

"It's true," Alexa insists.

Ingrid turns to me. "Well, thanks for helping us get home. We're okay now."

In other words, I'm no longer needed.

"Alright." I nod, grabbing my suitcase. "I guess I'll go…"

Alexa sits up. "You're leaving?"

"Yeees," I drawl, the look of disappointment on her small face tugging at my heart.

"But I thought you were staying here."

"Honey." Ingrid places a hand on her shoulder. "Conner can't stay here."

"Why not? Where will he stay?"

Ingrid glances at me.

"I'm sure I can find a place where I can crash," I answer.

"Crash?" Alexa's thick eyebrows go up. "Why can't you crash here?"

"Well…"

"For one thing, our apartment is a mess," Ingrid tells Alexa.

"He doesn't mind," she answers. "Right, Conner?"

"Not at all," I answer.

Ingrid narrows her eyes at me. "And we don't have a spare bedroom, remember, sweetheart? We can't very well let a friend sleep on the couch."

"He can use my bedroom," Alexa says. "I don't really sleep in it."

Ingrid frowns.

"It's fine, really," I speak up. "Your mother has enough to worry about."

"But you can help her, right?" Alexa looks at me. "I thought you were friends."

"Well, yes, but…"

"Please?" Alexa begs, turning her puppy dog eyes towards me before giving them to her mother. "Please, Mommy? We've never had a guest before."

"What do you mean?" Ingrid asks. "Janine sleeps over sometimes."

"She's not a guest. She's a neighbor."

Ingrid sighs. "Sometimes I think you're too smart."

"You know, when you say that, it usually means you're going to say yes," Alexa says. "Are you going to say yes? Can Conner stay here? Please?"

Ingrid glances at me.

"If you want me to stay, I will," I tell her.

"Please, Mommy?" Alexa repeats.

Ingrid stands up. "Fine. Conner can stay, but only temporarily."

"What's tempirarily?"

"Temporarily," Ingrid corrects. "It means only for a little while."

"Yay!" Alexa cheers, throwing her fists in the air.

I smile, but I turn serious as Ingrid turns to me, hands on her hips.

"You understand what temporarily means, don't you?"

I put down my suitcase and give her a salute. "Yes, ma'am."

Chapter Four
Ingrid

I can't believe I let them talk me into this, I think as I sit on the couch and turn off the TV. Alexa is already tucked in my bed for the night.

I should have said no. I should have put my foot down and let Alexa know who's boss, just as I've told myself to do time and time again. Yet, like all the other times, I failed.

It's not that I'm spoiling Alexa. It's just that I can't refuse her whenever she asks me for something I can give which I think may not be entirely bad for her and which I know she deserves. And God knows she deserves a lot I haven't been able to give her.

Problem is, I have a feeling she knows it, which is why stuff like this keep happening.

I rest my head on the edge of the couch and stare at the ceiling, sighing.

Wait. No. This isn't Alexa's fault. It's Conner's for showing up here in Boulder, for following me to the hospital just because he can't shut off his nosiness, for demanding to be let into Alexa's life and for not giving her the right answers earlier, making her think it would be best if he stayed here.

Yes, it's all his fault.

Why does he have to show up now when I've already got this? Why does he decide to start acting like a father now?

I grab the pillow beside me, hugging it to my chest and tucking it under my chin. As I do, my gaze rests on the pile of toys and books in the corner and on a wayward Lego block under the coffee table before landing on one of Alexa's many pictures on the shelf.

Who am I kidding? I haven't got this. I never have and I often wonder if I ever will. And as for Conner just getting his father act together now, that's really my fault since he only found out now.

He took it rather well, actually.

I always thought the day he found out about Alexa, he'd either not care, get mad at me for getting pregnant even though he was the one who didn't use protection or deny it, deny her.

Yet from the moment he laid eyes on her, he knew he was her father. He felt it. I saw it in his eyes. And he wanted to be her father.

Remembering that teary look in his eyes, that smile on his face as he spoke to her in the hospital, I feel something clench my heart.

I wasn't ready for that. I suppose that's why I gave in so easily when he asked to be a part of Alexa's life. That and knowing Alexa deserves a father, needs a father. I did. I looked up to my father all throughout my childhood, and I know my life wouldn't have been the same without him.

It still isn't, I think as I glance at the lone picture on the shelf that has me as a child with my parents and my little sister.

Alexa needs her father, and now she finally has him. So, how could I kick him out the door?

I pick the Lego block from beneath the coffee table, toss it into the box against the wall and get off the couch. I turn off the lights in the living room before heading into the bedroom and then the adjoining bathroom.

Wiping my mouth on a hand towel after brushing my teeth, I remember that Conner doesn't have a towel.

Grabbing one from the top of the bedroom closet, I knock on the door to the other bedroom. When he doesn't answer, I push it open and find him lying on his chest on the bed, asleep.

I suppose he must be tired. He stayed awake most of the night watching over Alexa, refusing to leave until he was sure she was okay.

Placing the towel on a chair, I go to the bed and pull the blanket over Conner so he doesn't catch a chill. As I lean over him, I find myself staring at him, remembering the first time I saw him.

Not at the office, but at the party when he asked me if I wanted a drink.

He was dashing in his tux and his red-and-black mask back then. Just the memory of it makes my heart skip a beat.

He's still hot now. The past six years have done nothing to diminish those good looks. His lips still look kissable, his chin swoon-inducing, his broad shoulders grab-worthy, his backside still chunky.

In spite of myself, I grin. Then I slap a hand on my forehead to scold myself.

What am I thinking? I'm not a virgin anymore, so why am I acting like one? Again? Yes, technically, I've been celibate for the past six years, but I'm a mother now. I'm wiser now. After all that's happened, there's no way I'm having sex with Conner.

Still, staring at his face, I can't help but wonder how things would have been if only he hadn't stolen my story. Would we have dated? Would we be happy now?

He stirs, interrupting my thoughts, and before I can step back, his arm goes around me, pulling me into the bed and into his embrace.

Panicking, I hit his arms, then slap him across the cheek as soon as he's released me.

"Ingrid?" He rubs his cheek as he sits up.

"How dare you," I tell him in a whisper through gritted teeth, my fists clenched at my sides.

He glances around him, confused. "Whatever I did, I'm sorry. I didn't mean to. It was just habit."

"Habit again, huh? What a convenient excuse." I fold my arms over my chest. "Well, I guess some things really never change."

He scratches his head. "What were you doing in my room anyway?"

I grab the towel off the chair, tossing it at him.

"One, this isn't your room. It's Alexa's, in case you haven't seen the name on the wall. Two, this is my apartment, so I can do whatever I want. Three, you damn well better behave or I'll kick you out, regardless of Alexa's opinion." I hold a finger up. "Keep your hands off me."

"Okay." He raises his hands. "Hands off."

Still seething, I march out of the room, passing through the bathroom where I stop by the sink to wash my face in hopes of helping my temper simmer down.

Why, oh why, did I let those two talk me into letting Conner stay in my apartment?

Already, I smell trouble.

~

I smell bacon.

The whiff of salty, fatty, honey-cured goodness hits my nostrils as soon as I step out of my room, making my mouth water.

Stepping into the kitchen, my eyes grow wide as I see plates of bacon on the counter. Conner, wearing my apron, is standing in front of the stove.

He turns around, smiling at me. "Good morning. I hope you don't mind that I made breakfast."

I didn't even know he could make breakfast.

I rub the sleep off my eyes, still feeling that I'm dreaming.

"Please sit." He gestures to the stool. "Eggs are almost ready."

No, this isn't a dream.

I sit down, running my hands through my hair as I suddenly feel conscious about my appearance. I blow on my palm to smell my breath, then quickly put my hand away as Conner places a plate in front of me. Moments later, he places the plate of scrambled eggs on the counter and hands me a fork.

"Dig in."

I set my fork down on my saucer. "You didn't have to make breakfast, you know."

Conner shrugs. "I just thought it's the least I could do since I'm staying here and all. Plus, consider it an apology for whatever I did last night."

I blush, remembering it, but dismiss it with a wave of a hand. "Don't remind me."

"Right." He lifts a mug. "Coffee?"

"Please."

He pours coffee into the mug and places it in front of me.

I wrap my hands around it, savoring the warmth. "Thanks."

"You're welcome."

He pours himself a mug, then brings it to the counter and sits on the stool across from me.

"So, I was thinking…"

I stop stroking my mug and look at him.

"…that maybe we should work together on this assignment," he finishes.

I throw him a questioning look. "But we need a story each."

"Yes." He nods. "So we need two stories, and we can work on them together."

I still don't understand. "Why would we do that?"

"It'll be easier. You know, two heads are better than one." He drinks a sip of coffee. "Plus, with our combined knowledge and contacts, we'll be able to come up with two incredible stories which are more likely to get us the job."

I shake my head. "I still don't follow. You're saying that we should work together to get the job, but only of us can get the job."

"Better one of us than one of them," Conner answers. "At least, whether it's you or I who gets it, Alexa wins."

I tap the rim of my mug. I hate to admit it, but he does have a point.

"Also, this way, you won't have to worry about me stealing your story," he adds.

I raise my eyebrows. "Because I'm helping you write it?"

"Because we'll be helping each other," he corrects. "We'll be a team, not competitors. Or still competitors but still a team. You know what I mean."

I grab a strip of bacon off the plate, chewing on it. "Okay. But we'll only help each other with research. You write your story. I'll write mine."

He, too, gets a strip. "Fair enough. Though we can read each other's story when we're done just to…"

"I don't think so." I finish the strip of bacon and grab another.

"Okay." He wipes his fingers on a table napkin. "So, do you have any…?"

He stops, his gaze drawn to something behind me.

"Hey, kiddo," he greets.

Or someone.

"Good morning."

"Conner!" Alexa runs over to him, giving him a hug.

I frown. "Why don't I get that kind of greeting every morning?"

Alexa gives me a hug.

I kiss the top of her head. "Good morning, sweetheart. Are you hungry? You're up early."

"I'm excited." She rests her elbows on my lap.

"Because Conner's here?"

"Not just that," she answers. "Because you promised you'd get me new sneakers today. You didn't forget, did you?"

Actually, I did. I pause at the realization.

"I didn't forget," I lie.

"So we'll go buy new sneakers?" Alexa asks. "You know my old ones aren't good anymore. And I don't really like wearing those girly shoes to school."

I stroke her hair. "But sweetheart, you just…"

"Why not?" Conner interrupts me. "If she needs sneakers, I'd be happy to get her a pair."

"Really?" Alexa's eyes grow wide as saucers and she looks at me expectantly.

Conner nods as he touches my arm. Once again, I'm defeated.

"Okay," I give in with a sigh. "We'll all go to the mall to get you shoes."

Chapter Five
Conner

"There you go."

I pull on the shoelaces of the purple-and-pink sneakers Alexa picked, making sure they won't come undone.

"How do they feel?"

She kicks her feet, then jumps on the floor, turning around before giving me a thumbs-up.

"Perfect."

I smile, getting off my knees. "Glad you think so."

I gesture to the saleslady. "Excuse me. We'll take a pair of these."

"Yes, sir."

As the saleslady scurries off to get it, I sit on the bench beside Ingrid, stretching a shoulder.

"Who knew shopping for a kid could be so hard?"

She grins. "Oh, waiting for her to make up her mind is the easy part. Chasing her down and getting her to sit down and actually try something on is usually a lot harder."

I chuckle.

"Although it's easier now," Ingrid adds. "You should have seen us doing this when she was three."

I would have if I knew about her, I want to say. Then again, I'm not sure. Would I have been ready then?

Instead, I turn to her. "I should get you something, too."

Her blue eyes widen. "What?"

I nod. "Yeah, a present, you know, to let you know I appreciate everything you've done."

She waves her hands in front of her. "I didn't do them for you, so no need."

"I want to, though." I narrow my eyes at her. "Surely there must be something you want, something I can get you."

She shakes her head. "I…"

"Mommy needs a new dress," Alexa blurts out.

Ingrid and I both look at her.

"Alexa," Ingrid scolds. "I do not…"

"You've said so a lot of times," Alexa points out. "You keep saying I have more dresses than you and that your old ones don't look nice anymore."

"I do?" Ingrid asks.

Alexa nods.

Ingrid lifts her hands as she shrugs. "Wow. I didn't know you had such a good memory when it came to these things. Aren't you supposed to be remembering other things?"

Alexa sits in between us. "I have room to remember a lot."

Ingrid strokes Alexa's hair, shaking her head. "Oh, you sure are too smart for your own good."

"So, that means yes?" I ask her. "To the dress, I mean."

She shakes her head more quickly. "Really, you shouldn't."

"I want to." I get off the bench, offering Alexa my hand. "Shall we go get your mommy a new dress?"

~

"You really shouldn't have," Ingrid says. We're still discussing the matter as we stroll the mall about an hour after I got her the dress and minutes after we dropped Alexa off at an indoor playground.

"Please." I raise my hand. "I'm glad I did."

I really am. Seeing her in that black turtleneck dress that showed off her slender shoulders, clung to her breasts and tapered around her waist before flowing down, stopping just short of her knees, I felt smitten all over again. Granted, she still looked better—best—in that red cheongsam, but this dress was a runner-up, showing off her curves and taking my breath away.

How can the mother of a five year-old be so hot?

"Thank you." She slings the paper bag over her shoulder. "And thank you for Alexa's shoes. You didn't have to buy her an expensive pair. She'll outgrow them in no time."

"It's fine," I assure her. "I'll just buy her a new pair when she needs it."

Ingrid shakes her head. "You'll spoil her."

"I don't think so." I tuck my hand in my pocket. "I don't think she can be spoiled. She's a great girl. You've done a great job."

"Really?" She tucks a strand of hair behind her ear. "I often wonder if I'm doing good. Sometimes I feel like I have no clue at all what I'm doing."

"Really," I tell her. "She's amazing."

She's smart. She's sweet. She's confident. She's fun.

"Both of you are," I add, looking at her.

As Ingrid turns her head in surprise, our eyes meet and I find myself drawn to those sapphire pools, helplessly drowning in them.

She quickly looks away, though, wrapping her arms over her chest.

"You're only saying that because you haven't seen her throw a tantrum or me yell at her."

"What's the most trouble she's given you?" I ask. "Like the biggest mischief she's ever gotten into?"

"Hmm." Ingrid touches her chin. "That's a tough one, but I'd say it's that time when she got into my make-up kit and got my lipstick and mascara all over her face, and a pillow."

I laugh, imagining it.

"I didn't yell at her, though. I couldn't. She was too funny."

"Yeah." I nod. "I would have felt the same."

"Besides, when she looked at herself in the mirror, she cried because of how scary she looked," Ingrid adds.

"Really?" I chuckle.

She nods. "So I felt that was punishment enough."

I shrug. "I guess."

"Needless to say, she never went through my make-up kit again."

"Smart kid."

"Too smart."

"Nah." I stop walking. "She's just like her mother."

Ingrid stops, turning towards me, and just like before, her eyes create a spark in mine. Again, she looks away, blushing, walking faster as she rubs her arms.

I keep up with her. "Are you cold? I can lend you my coat."

"No, thanks." She stops rubbing her arms, reaching for her neck instead. "I just…"

She stops walking.

"What?" I ask her.

"My scarf." She places both hands around her neck. "My scarf is missing."

"It's not in the bag?"

She checks the paper bag and her purse, shaking her head. "I must have left it somewhere."

"At the restaurant, maybe?"

She touches her chin. "No. I don't think I had it there. The last time I remember I had it was…" She turns around, her gaze distant. "At the department store before I tried on the dress. I must have left it in the dressing room."

She walks off and I follow her, all the way back to the department store. She heads straight to the women's section and into the dressing room she used earlier.

I follow her there.

"Here it is." She takes the scarf off the peg. "I knew…"

I cut her off with a kiss, pushing her against the mirror as I become unable to restrain myself.

For a moment, she doesn't move. Her lips are frozen but soft beneath mine. Then she pushes me away, placing a hand over her mouth, her eyebrows pulled up in horror.

As she runs off, I frown, tempted to punch the mirror as I realize what I've done.

Damn.

"Ingrid!" I chase after her, making my way through the aisles of clothes, the salesladies and the shoppers.

She doesn't stop, rushing on.

"Ingrid, wait!"

"Conner?" A voice calls my attention and I turn my head to see Leslie in one of the aisles, walking towards me. "What happened to you? You just left."

"I had work to do," I tell her, glancing at Ingrid, who's slowed down and is glancing over her shoulder. "I have to go."

"Wait." Leslie clings to my arm. "How long are you staying in Boulder? Do you want to go to a bar again sometime? I know a few more good ones."

"Sorry," I mutter, freeing myself from her grip and running after Ingrid.

It's too late, though. She's running even faster now, disappearing in the crowd.

I stop running, resting my hands on my hips as I catch my breath.

Boy, am I in trouble now.

~

"Just to be clear, I'm not with that woman, okay?" I explain back at the apartment as I sit beside Ingrid on the couch. Alexa is taking a nap in the bedroom, exhausted after her shopping trip. "I'm not with any woman."

Ingrid raises a hand, her eyes on the TV screen. "I don't care, okay? It's none of my business."

"And I'm sorry about earlier. I shouldn't have sprung on you like that."

"Mm-hmm." She nods, still not looking at me. "That was totally a violation of the hands-off rule."

I lean over to her to whisper in her ear. "Well, technically, I kept my hands off…"

She silences me with a glare.

"Alright, alright." I raise my hands, then let them fall on my lap.

She shakes her head. "I don't want to talk about it."

"Okay."

"How about we just talk about work?" She picks up the remote control and turns the volume down. "Do you have any ideas for the assignment? Does anything, anyone come to mind? Any place to start?"

I can tell she's still annoyed, but at least she's talking to me.

I sit back. "Actually, someone does come to mind—this couple I know back in Dallas. They're in their sixties now, but they used to be in this orchestra traveling the world. The man was the conductor. The woman played the violin. They're still inseparable up to now."

"Romantic." Ingrid touches her cheek. "Nowadays, not too many relationships last, so that's sure to tug at some heartstrings and give some people hope. Also, I like how music plays a part in their story."

"I'm glad you like it. What about you?" I lean forward, elbows on my knees. "Any ideas?"

"I was thinking of a couple who fell in love against all odds, you know," she says. "Not exactly star-crossed, because that's outdated, but more like having a serious obstacle to overcome, like physical disabilities maybe."

"Like two blind people falling in love, or maybe a blind person falling in love with a deaf person?"

Ingrid's face lights up with excitement. "Exactly. That's the kind of thing that could be in a heartwarming reality show."

"Yeah. Good idea. You'll definitely nail the inspiring part."

"Thank you." She hugs the pillow on her lap. "Now I just need to find that couple."

Chapter Six
Ingrid

"So, you were blind when the two of you met?" I ask Maggie, the sixty-eight-year-old woman seated in front of me, my recorder on my lap.

She nods, a smile on her pale, thin lips as she appears to be recollecting the moment. Her milky eyes grow smaller as more lines appear around them, adding to the multitude already present on her timeworn face. Beside her, her husband, Dave, who is four years older than her, seems to be on the brink of dozing off, if he hasn't already. He's slumped on the chair with his head drooping and his belly out.

The three of us are seated at a corner of the lounge of their nursing home just outside Denver, where one of the nurses kindly agreed and arranged to have us meet. She's still in the room, all the way across, seemingly occupied with watching over the other elderly men and women who are chatting or playing Scrabble or bridge. I can feel her gaze on my back every now and then, though, like a hawk.

I adjust my scarf. "So, how did the two of you meet, then?"

"Oh, at the park. The wind blew my hat away and he got it for me and we just started talking," she says. "The next thing you know, we were a couple."

"How did you become a couple?"

Maggie shrugs. "Oh, he asked me if I wanted to go out with him and I said yes. Then on one of the dates, we kissed, and a few months later, we got married."

"I see." I tap the recorder on my lap.

Nothing unusual there.

"Was it hard because you were blind?" I ask.

"Not really. Actually, that was the first time in my life I didn't hate being blind, because he was so caring. If I wasn't blind, I'm not sure he would have acted the same way. Would you, Dave?"

She nudges her husband, who suddenly lifts his head. "Where's the fire?"

"There's no fire, Dave," Maggie tells him. "Dave here used to be a fireman."

"Oh. That's wonderful."

"He was wonderful." Maggie sighs, running her hands through her winter-white curls. "Now, I don't know."

I blink. Wasn't this supposed to be an endearing, perfect romance?

"Anyway, we got married and I had my eyes operated on and whatnot so I was able to see. Imagine my reaction when I first saw him."

"What was your reaction?"

She leans forward, holding a hand over her mouth as she whispers, "I thought he'd be hotter."

My eyes grow wide.

"But hey, he was fine. I didn't complain. We had our usual ups and downs, but we stuck together. Well, we almost didn't, especially when I found out he cheated on me with this nurse…"

"For God's sake, that was one time, woman," Dave says. "And it was centuries ago."

"You ain't a century yet," Maggie tells him. "Though you sure look it."

She turns back to me. "Anyway, one time, ten times—it doesn't matter how many, right? Once a man cheats on you, it just breaks your heart."

I pause, remembering the woman clinging to Conner at the mall and the tinge of jealousy I felt. I shouldn't be jealous, though. I have no right to be. Technically, Conner isn't cheating because we're not really together.

Why did I feel the claws of that green-eyed monster, then?

"But we got through that," Maggie continues. "I forgave him."

Dave rolls his eyes. "So she says."

Maggie ignores him. "And well, the rest is history. Here we are now, an old couple with our children living far away and with our roles reversed. Now he's the one who can't see and I'm the one who can. Funny, isn't it?"

I nod.

I have to admit it is amusing, and Maggie and Dave are both interesting people, Maggie especially. She reminds me of my own grandmother. Even so…

~

"The story just isn't good enough," I tell Conner at the cafe a few hours later, taking a sip of my coffee. "It's inspiring maybe, but powerful and unique? I don't think so."

"Unfortunately, I agree," Conner says, tapping his fingers on the table.

I lean forward. "I want something less real, you know, more magical."

"The stuff of fairytales. I understand."

I set down my cup in the middle of the table, and as I do, my fingers brush against his. The contact is fleeting but not unnoticed. I quickly pull my hands off the table, sitting back.

"What about you? How's your story going?"

"I haven't heard from the couple yet," he answers, folding his arms over the table. "They're still out of the country. Apparently they spend the holidays in Europe every year."

"Well, that's magical."

Conner shrugs. "I suppose some people can hold on to the magic."

As he speaks, his eyes, warm and brown like my coffee, find mine and hold them. And just like coffee, they give me a rush and a jolt of heat, waking something inside me.

I stand up. "I'll just go to the restroom."

"Okay. Don't take long."

Those last words make me pause just as I've left my chair. I draw a deep breath.

Jerk.

I head to the back of cafe where the restrooms are. Finding the door to the women's room closed, I stand outside, my eyes scouring the room to curb my impatience.

The quaint cafe has less than twenty tables, all round, coated in white linen and just big enough for two, maybe three. Stained glass pendant lights hang from the wooden ceiling and gilded mirrors of all shapes line the walls, which are still adorned with candy canes, red bows and holly leaves.

Aside from the table where Conner is sitting, only three other tables are occupied: one by a mother and daughter, making me think of Alexa; another by a man busy with something on his laptop; and the closest one to the bathroom by three college-age girls, giggling and chattering in between sips of coffee and glances at their expensive phones.

As I wait for my turn at the restroom, I end up eavesdropping—alright, so maybe it is a journalist's habit.

"Trust me, you don't want to go there." The girl in the red sweater rubs her arms as she shivers. "I still have goose bumps remembering the place."

"That's why I want to go there," says the girl beside her, who's wearing a green parka and earmuffs around her neck.

"Maybe your grandmother has something she wants your grandfather to do," says the girl with a pink bonnet and glasses. "That's why she's haunting the place."

A ghost story?

"Maybe she found out he cheated on her while she was still alive," the girl with earmuffs says.

"Nah." The girl in red shakes her head. "They loved each other so much. You should have seen them. They were all over each other even when they were already in their fifties."

Wait. It's a love story.

"Ew." The girl in the middle grimaces.

"Maybe that's why she's still there," the girl with glasses suggests. "Maybe she doesn't want to leave the house because she doesn't want to leave your grandfather."

"Maybe." The girl in red shrugs. "I just wish she wouldn't scare us all."

The girl with the earmuffs takes a sip of her coffee. "Maybe she's trying to scare your grandfather to death so he'll die and they'll be together."

A love story and a ghost story.

My curiosity piqued and my journalist senses tingling, I approach the table.

"Excuse me," I interrupt them. "I'm sorry, but I couldn't help but overhear you girls talking. Did you say something about your grandmother haunting your grandfather?"

~

"I have to say you really have a good nose for good stories," Conner says, walking alongside me as we make our way to our designated boarding area at the airport.

I shrug. "I just happened to be at the right place at the right time."

"Exactly. It's a gift."

I glance at him. "You didn't have to come with me all the way to Louisiana, you know."

"Why not? We said we'd work together, didn't we?" he answers. "Besides, the couple I'm interviewing aren't due back for a few more days, so I've nothing better to do."

"Maybe you could start looking for a back-up story," I suggest.

"Maybe," he says. "Also, I didn't want you to go to a haunted house all by yourself."

I pause. "I can take care of myself, thank you."

"I didn't say you couldn't. I just said I wanted to come along. You don't believe the house is really haunted, do you?"

"I hope it is, or this trip will be a waste."

I continue walking but stop again as a woman, busy talking to someone on her phone, bumps into me, the purse hanging from her elbow hitting my arm.

"Sorry," she mumbles, going on as if nothing happened while I stand there rubbing my arm.

And I would let her, except for the fact that something has slipped out of her purse—a red envelope that's now on the floor.

"Excuse me!" I call after the woman as I pick up the envelope.

She turns.

"You dropped this."

"Oh." She finally lowers her phone as she turns back towards me. "I don't know what I would have done if this got lost. Thank you. Thank you so much."

I hand her the envelope, only then noticing the familiar emblem on its wax seal, the initials D and S.

My eyes widen in surprise.

"That envelope was the same as the one for the invitations to Damien Shore's party years ago," I relay my observation to Conner. "And I'm pretty sure that emblem on its wax is his, too."

Conner nods, glancing at the woman. "You're probably right. I recognize that woman. She's the wife of someone important."

"But I thought Damien Shore's in jail. How can he throw a party if he's in…"

"He was released last year," Conner tells me. "Didn't you hear about it?"

"Um, no." I shake my head.

Shit. They let him out?

"Well, it wasn't too publicized," Conner says. "It's almost as if they were trying to keep it hushed."

"Or maybe I was just busy watching a marathon of *My Little Pony* with Alexa when that news was aired," I say. "But why did they let him go?"

"I'm sure you know why. He's rich, well-connected."

"But the charges…"

"He has a good lawyer, so he got away with only a few years in jail."

My hands drop to my side as my shoulders heave. "That… scumbag. And now he's throwing a party? Again?"

"Well, rumor has it he invited members of the jury to this one," Conner says in a low voice. "Also, he invited the press just to prove that nothing fishy will go on this time."

I sigh. "Well, at least he's decided to behave."

Conner chuckles. "Damien Shore behave? I doubt that."

He has a point.

"At the very least, no underage girls are going to get sold or hurt."

307

"Yeah, at least there's that." He moves closer to me. "You don't think we should go to the party, do you, for old time's sake? Just make a quick appearance?"

I stop, narrowing my eyes at him. "If that's a joke, it's not funny, Conner."

He raises his hands, backing off. "It was just a suggestion."

Yeah, right. He deliberately said that to make me remember the party, which I've been trying every day of my life since then not to.

"All passengers for Flight 103 bound for Lake Charles, Louisiana," a voice announces over the PA system. "Please proceed to Boarding Gate 4."

I glance at the speaker. "That's our flight."

Conner steps beside me. "Haunted house, here we come."

Chapter Seven
Conner

The house doesn't look at all haunted, I think as I stare at its non-creepy facade.

In fact, it looks like an ordinary, crumbling three-story house. No vines creeping up the walls. No shadows looming behind the windows. No screams or whispers from the inside. No hideous gargoyles or monstrous creatures sticking out. No full moon or ominous gray skies in the background.

Nothing.

I'm not even feeling a chill. The hairs on my arms are completely at ease.

"Are you sure we have the right address?" I ask Ingrid.

She glances at the paper in her hand and nods. "This is it."

She walks up the creaking stairs and crosses the porch, knocking on the front door. A few seconds later, an old man opens it. He's in his sixties, wearing a long-sleeved plaid shirt and round glasses.

"Mr. Murrow?" Ingrid asks.

"Yes." The old man scratches his bald head.

"I'm Ingrid Halfield from *The Colorado Chronicler*." Ingrid shows her ID. "We spoke on the phone."

"Ah, yes." Mr. Murrow pushes his glasses up. "I just didn't think you'd be here so soon, or that you'd look so young."

Ingrid smiles. "You're too kind, Mr. Murrow."

I frown. Is he flirting with her?

"Then again, these days everyone looks so young to me," he says. "Please come in."

He holds the door open and Ingrid goes in. I go in after her, shaking the old man's hand as I pass him. "Thank you for having us," I say.

"Don't mention it." He ushers me in. "An old man like me is always grateful for the company of the living."

I raise my eyebrows at the remark but let it go, looking around the living room.

Even the inside of the house doesn't look disturbing. The furniture is old but free of dust. Pictures—colored, not black and white—and colorful paintings of landscapes hang on the chartreuse walls. Behind the couch stands a shelf with books and vases. A wooden coffee table sitting on a fluffy brown rug is right in front of it, and there's a twenty-four-inch TV across the room.

Suddenly, I feel something wet against my hand. I turn my head to see a dog behind me, a Golden Retriever about four years old, a red collar around his neck and a friendly welcome in his eyes. Staring at me, it steps back, tail wagging.

"Hello, there." I kneel down to pet it.

"That's Shadow," Mr. Murrow introduces. "He's my only friend now. Problem is, I'm not his. Why, he'd even befriend a burglar if he could."

"Would you now?" I pet the dog behind the ears.

Ingrid sits on the couch and turns on her recorder. "Mr. Murrow, how long has it been since your wife passed?"

It's just like her not to waste any time.

Mr. Murrow sits on a chair. "Her name's Nancy, and it's been three years."

"What did Nancy die of?"

"Pneumonia."

"I'm sorry to hear it," Ingrid says. "But I also hear she hasn't really left you."

"Kelly told you that, did she?" Mr. Murrow scratches the back of his head. "That girl talks too much. She used to talk less when my wife was around, but now..."

"So it's true?" Ingrid asks.

I get off the floor and sit on the couch a few inches away from her so I can listen to the story.

Mr. Murrow nods, stroking his spade-shaped beard. "During the first few weeks after she died, the house was eerily quiet. Too quiet. And then maybe about three months later, on our forty-first wedding anniversary, I saw her right there in our bedroom. She was standing by the window, wearing her wedding dress."

He stands up and points to a picture hanging on the wall, their wedding portrait. "This dress."

A white dress with beads shaped into tiny, yellow flowers.

"And after that?" Ingrid asks.

"I'd see her regularly." Mr. Murrow gazes at the portrait. "Often there by our bedroom window, sometimes in the chair in the room where she used to spend the nights knitting while watching old soap operas or listening to Dolly Parton. Once or twice I even saw her sitting in the bathtub, always in that wedding dress. She's never showed up here, downstairs, though."

Ingrid nods. "I see."

He sits down, and Shadow lies down at his feet. "I was happy to see her, even though she never looked into my eyes—she was always looking away—and even though she never said a thing. Even when I didn't see her, I felt her presence and I was happy. I missed her very much, after all."

"Of course you did." Ingrid reaches across the table to place her hand over his.

"And she was always... nice?" I ask.

"To me," Mr. Murrow answers. "But when my children visited, or my friends or other relatives or the plumber or the man who wanted to buy the house, she'd throw a fit. They say she'd chase them or glare at them or shriek. They'd wake up in the middle of the night and she'd be floating above them. That's why they always sleep here in the living room now when they come over, though even then, they say they can hear her footsteps upstairs."

"Maybe she doesn't want them here," I suggest. "Then again, while it's understandable that she wouldn't want strangers here, it doesn't make sense that she wouldn't want her children or grandchildren."

"She wasn't exactly a doting mother or grandmother," Mr. Murrow says. "She was strict with them. Of course, contrary to what they think, she only did it because she loved them."

"Why only upstairs?" Ingrid asks.

"She died upstairs in our bedroom," Mr. Murrow explains, eyes on the floor. "I made the decision to bring her home from the hospital, knowing how weak she was. She asked me to."

Ingrid picks up the recorder and turns it off. "Do you think we can go upstairs?"

My eyes grow wide at the question.

After hearing everything Mr. Murrow just said, she wants to go upstairs?

Mr. Murrow shrugs. "If you want to, though like I said, she might give you a fright."

Ingrid stands up. "I'm hoping she will."

I grab her arm. "Are you sure about this?"

She nods, then leans over me to whisper in my ear. "I need to make sure there is a ghost story first. Then I'll ask for the love story."

"Fair enough."

"Are you coming with me?" she asks out loud.

"Of course." I get on my feet.

"Shall I accompany you?" Mr. Murrow asks, standing as well.

"Oh, please, you don't have to," Ingrid tells him. "We don't want to cause you trouble, though we'll call you if we can't find her."

"Oh, she'll find you," the old man says.

I frown. Great.

Ingrid gestures to me and I follow her up the stairs.

"Are you sure this is a good idea?" I ask her, my hand on the railing.

She stops, turning to me. "Are you scared, Conner Blake?"

"No."

Well, I am, but not of Nancy's ghost. I just don't want Ingrid to get hurt. But I don't tell her that.

"Let's get on with it then," she says, completely oblivious.

She continues up the stairs. Reaching the top, she stops, taking a deep breath.

"Are you scared, Ingrid Halfield?" I ask her.

"Shh." She holds a finger up. "I'm trying to listen."

Walking behind her down the corridor, I try to listen as well. All I can hear is the creaking of floorboards beneath our feet.

Where's Nancy?

We reach the end of the corridor after opening all the doors and checking all the rooms, including the one that looked like it must have been the Murrows' old bedroom.

Nothing.

Was Mr. Murrow lying? But what about all the others?

Ingrid sighs. "I guess she's not in the mood to appear today."

"Maybe she only appears at night," I tell her. "We can wait."

She says nothing.

"Hey." I place a hand on her shoulder. "Even if we don't see a ghost, you can still go with the story."

She turns to me. "Without proof of Nancy's haunting?"

"You get proof of a haunting and you'll have a bigger story than you bargained for," I point out. "Anyway, you have Mr. Murrow's word and you can interview the others."

"I guess," she says. "Still..."

Just then, we hear a thud upstairs. Then another. And another.

"Footsteps," Ingrid whispers excitedly. "She's all the way upstairs."

I glance up the stairs. "But I thought Mr. Murrow said..."

"He simply said upstairs," Ingrid says. She's already going up the second set of stairs to the third floor. I frown. Well, I knew she was stubborn. I don't know why I thought that was an endearing quality.

I follow her, listening to the sound of the footsteps and bracing myself to see Nancy. As soon as we get to the third floor, though, the sound vanishes and everything is silent.

"Maybe we scared her off," I remark.

"Shh," Ingrid hushes me again, pointing at the door at the end of the corridor, which is open. "Maybe she's in the attic."

Walking slowly but with shoulders straight, she heads for the open door and peeks inside.

I, too, take a peek, seeing nothing.

"Maybe she's hiding," Ingrid whispers, entering the room.

I step in beside her, looking around the attic. There's nothing but boxes everywhere, an old TV, an old chair and a pile of rugs, all covered in a thick layer of dust that can easily be seen in the afternoon sunlight drifting in through the lone window.

Some of it gets into my nose and I sneeze.

"Shh." Ingrid turns to me, a finger to her lips.

I open my mouth to apologize, but before I can, the door behind creaks and then falls shut. I turn around, grabbing the knob and turning it only to find that it won't budge.

I frown.

"What's wrong?" Ingrid asks.

"The knob's broken," I tell her, letting go of the knob and banging on the door. "Hey! Mr. Murrow! Shadow! Can you get us out of here, please?"

"You think someone locked us in?" Ingrid asks. "You think Nancy locked us in?"

"Nonsense," I tell her. "We didn't see Nancy, plus no one said anything about her touching or moving things around her. Frankly, I don't think ghosts can do that."

"But..."

"The breeze probably just closed the door." I gesture to the slightly open window. "You know, that same breeze that made me sneeze. And then it locked by itself. Sometimes doorknobs can do that, especially if they're old."

Ingrid doesn't look convinced. She rubs her arms. "But why was the door to the attic open in the first place? Shouldn't it be closed?"

Good point. Attic doors are usually kept closed.

I decide to think about that later, though. I bang on the door again.

"Mr. Murrow!" I pound my fists on the door.

"Maybe he can't hear us," Ingrid says.

"Maybe."

I smack my shoulder into the door, putting my weight behind it. It still won't budge.

"The knob may be old and faulty, but the door's still good as new," I say, knocking on it. "It's sturdy. And the hinges are outside, too."

Ingrid sighs. "So, we're stuck here, huh?"

"Just for a little while," I tell her. "I think Mr. Murrow will eventually get worried about us and he'll come check on us."

"And if Nancy's the one who checks on us?" she asks.

I pull my eyebrows together. "I thought you weren't scared."

"I never said I wasn't."

She takes the top rug off the pile near the window and sits on it, pulling her knees up and wrapping her arms around them. I notice for the first time that they're shaking.

She is scared.

I go to her.

"I won't let Nancy hurt you," I promise her.

She lifts her head to look at me. "I thought you said ghosts can't hurt people."

I shrug. "Well, you seem to think so."

She tucks her chin between her knees. "I sure hope Mr. Murrow finds us soon."

"Yeah." I sit beside her.

Not that I'm scared. I just don't want to be stuck in a dusty attic for long. Especially not so long that it gets dark.

I glance at Ingrid.

Then again, if it's with her…

"Distract me," she says, hugging her knees tighter.

"What?"

"Talk about something so I'll forget about the dire situation we're in," she says.

Okay.

"What do you want to talk about? Alexa?"

"No." She shakes her head. "Thinking about her will only make me more anxious. I mean, what if we never get out of here? What's going to happen to her?"

I reach for her hand. "We're going to get out of here. I promise."

She pulls her hand away.

I tap my fingers on my lap. "Why don't you ask me a question and I'll answer."

Ingrid gives me a puzzled look. "What?"

I fold my arms over my chest. "Make that three questions."

"Any question?"

"Yeah. It's time to put those journalistic skills to use."

She grins, then scratches her chin as she stares at the ceiling, thinking.

"Come on." I nudge her. "There must be a ton of things you want to ask me."

She turns her head to look at me. "Why did you decide to become a journalist?"

Ah. A serious question.

I sit back. "Well, I didn't really decide. It's not like it was my dream or anything. I just thought I'd try it and I realized I was good at it, and that it was fun and relatively easy."

"Easy?"

"I mean compared to working with numbers all day, or operating on someone. I'm not saying anyone can do it, though. It's hard, too. It takes a lot of hard work, resourcefulness and determination."

Ingrid nods. "Resourcefulness, huh? That brings me to my second question."

I hold my breath.

"How many women have you slept with to get a story?"

I take a deep breath, not sure I like this one. "A few."

"Give me a number," she demands.

I look at my fingers. "Five maybe. Six."

"Does that include me?"

"Is that your third question?"

She shrugs.

I take another deep breath. "No. Just to set the record straight, I did not intend to steal that story from you. I did not sleep with you just to get that story."

"Really?" She raises her eyebrows at me.

I nod. "Really. Believe it or not, you weren't the only one who smelled a story at Damien Shore's party. I was there because I was after the same story. I had no idea who you were. I just found out you were a journalist because I saw your camera, because I recognized that intense curiosity in your eyes. When you left me at that crazy party, I had a feeling you were going snooping. So I followed you. I was afraid you'd be in danger. And you were. I saved you the only way I knew how."

"By seducing me."

"I didn't mean to," I confess. "I got carried away. And then afterwards, I saw the camera and I just decided to run with it, literally."

"You stole my story."

"Okay, I did." I raise my hands. "But that wasn't my intention. The opportunity came up and I seized it."

"You stole my story," Ingrid repeats. "You knew I was a journalist. You saw I was taking pictures. You knew I was after the same story, and you stole it."

I look into her eyes, pursing my lips. "I'm sorry."

She looks away, silent for a moment. Then she bangs her head on the wall.

"I should never have gone up those stairs with you."

"Well, I did ask you if you were sure you wanted to," I remind her.

She pouts. "Are you saying this is all my fault?"

"I'm glad you said yes, though." I touch her shoulder as I look into her eyes. "Because that night was amazing."

She blushes.

I stroke her shoulder. "You in that gown with your eyes smiling from behind your mask... Now, that was magical."

She shakes her head slowly. "You tricked me. You seduced me. God knows you've had practice. You're just so good at putting women under your spell, aren't you?"

"On the contrary, it's you who has me under your spell."

Grasping her chin, I press my lips to hers.

She pulls away, eyes wide. "What are you doing?"

"Distracting you."

I kiss her again, more firmly this time. At first she doesn't move, her lips simply quivering beneath mine. Then, as I place my hand on her cheek and kiss her harder, she grips my arm and kisses me back.

Triumph swelling in my chest—along with something else—I move my hand behind her head, running it through her hair as I part her lips so that I can have a taste of her.

She shivers, letting out a soft moan.

Damn, I've missed this.

Pulling her close to me, I kiss her neck, savoring the taste of her, the feel of her skin, the smell of her...

Suddenly, I stop, smelling something else.

Smoke.

I look out the window. "Do you smell that?"

"Yeah." She nods. "Is that...?"

"Smoke," I say, though I can't see any.

It's not coming from outside the house, which means...

I stare at the door and see black wisps crawling in through the gap underneath.

"Shit."

313

I try to open the window, but it's jammed. Ingrid comes over to help me, but the window still won't budge.

Looking around, I grab the broken TV.

"Move away," I tell Ingrid.

After she does, I throw the appliance at the glass, which shatters into pieces.

Using the rug, I remove the sharp edges and then help Ingrid squeeze through to the roof. After that, I climb out myself.

"We have to climb down," I tell Ingrid. The smell of smoke is stronger now.

"What?"

"Hold my hand."

She stretches her arm out to me and I grab it, guiding her across the roof towards the tree. I get on the tree branch and climb down, jumping the last few feet. Then I look up at Ingrid.

"Jump," I tell her.

"Are you crazy?"

"Jump and I'll catch you," I tell her, stretching my arms. "I promise."

For a moment, she hesitates—then she leaps into my arms. I catch her but lose my balance and end up lying on the ground with her on top of me.

"Are you alright?" I ask her.

She nods, still too shocked to speak.

Moments later, the roof bursts into flames.

Grabbing Ingrid's hand, I run to the front of the house. Mr. Murrow and Shadow are there. Shadow starts barking at us.

"Oh, thank goodness you're safe," Mr. Murrow says, relief on his face.

"What happened?" I ask him.

"I don't know." He shrugs. "I was just watching TV and the next thing I knew, there was a fire. You don't think my Nancy started it, do you?"

I shake my head. Faulty wiring, maybe?

Or maybe…

I recall the footsteps Ingrid and I heard and then the door to the attic shutting, locking.

"Mr. Murrow, did you leave the attic door open?" I ask him.

"The attic?" He looks at me in surprise. "Why, I haven't been there in years. In fact, I think I might have lost the key."

I stare at the house, the smoke rising towards the sky.

I have a bad feeling about this.

Chapter Eight
Ingrid

"I feel so bad that Mr. Murrow's house got burned while we were there," I finally tell Conner when I return to the apartment after bringing Alexa to school.

I haven't really spoken to him since the fire. I ignored him throughout the flight back to Boulder last night, still in shock about what happened. Then when we arrived, I was so exhausted that I went straight to bed after picking Alexa up from Janine's. This morning, I was in a rush to bring Alexa to school, so we haven't had time to talk.

Until now.

Picking up a sock from the floor, I sit on the couch, sighing as I put my hand against my forehead.

"Hey." Conner stands behind me, squeezing my shoulder. "Don't go sounding like we started the fire now, because we didn't."

"I know, and I didn't say that, but…" I turn to him. "Do you really think that it was some old wire? That it was an accident? A coincidence?"

"You know what I think?" He sits on the other end of the couch. "I think that someone wanted to burn down the house before we got there and we were in the way—I mean, we could have easily stopped him, or at least we could have done it better than Mr. Murrow could—so we got locked in the attic and then the house got burned."

My eyes grow wide. "So, someone did try to burn us alive?"

"But they didn't," he says. "Mr. Murrow and Shadow were fine, too, so it's not much of a tragedy."

"Yeah. At least no one died," I agree, grateful for it. "But you don't think Nancy did it?"

"Absolutely not." Conner shakes his head. "Even if ghosts could start fires, why would she? It was her house."

"True." I stand up, picking another sock from the floor. "But now that it's burned down, she won't be able to haunt it anymore. Mr. Murrow won't see her anymore, and that kind of makes me sad."

"Who knows? She might follow him to his new home. And if she does, then that makes for an even better story, right?"

I snort, picking up a shirt. "I don't think Mr. Murrow will let us into his new home even if that happens. He didn't seem mad at us, but still…"

I feel his hand on my shoulder again. "We'll find a new story, okay?"

"Okay." I pick up a small pair of pants, the last item of clothing tossed on the living room floor. "I swear that little girl leaves a mess wherever she goes."

"And someday, she'll leave a mess of broken hearts."

I narrow my eyes at him. "Not funny."

"Okay."

The pile of laundry in my arms, I go into the bedroom and toss the clothes in the hamper. Then I sit on the edge of the bed, letting out another sigh.

I still can't believe Conner and I almost died yesterday, and I'm not sure what's worse—that or the fact that he kissed me in that dusty old attic.

And that I kissed him back.

Slapping my forehead, I lie on top of the bed, pouting as I stare at the ceiling.

How on earth did things lead to that? And why did I let it happen? How could I let it happen?

Still, I think as I run my fingers over my protruding lower lip, my cheeks growing warm at the memory, I have to admit it felt good.

I sit up, shaking my head.

What am I thinking? What am I doing?

I can't kiss Conner. I can't…

Ugh. Just think of work, Ingrid. Think of your story.

Taking a deep breath, I get out of the room. I find Conner in the kitchen, sitting at the counter drinking coffee.

I lean on the counter. "Do you think the others already have their stories?"

He lifts his cup to his lips. "You mean Ed and Tiffany?"

I nod.

"I don't know, but I've talked to a few friends," he says. "They'll tell me if they hear anything about what those two are up to, Ed especially."

"Oh."

I should have known.

As I go around the counter to grab my own cup of coffee, a phone rings—Conner's. Setting down his cup and getting off his stool, he goes into Alexa's bedroom. Through the open door, I hear him talking on the phone, but not clearly. Two minutes later, he comes out, laptop under his arm.

"That your story?" I ask him.

"Nope. But that was one of those friends I mentioned. They said Ed has an appointment at The Weeping Rose."

He sets his laptop on the coffee table, opening the lid.

I sit beside him, looking at his screen just as the search results come up. Conner clicks on the first one, which lists Weeping Rose as an exclusive club for art enthusiasts, a mansion located right at the foot of the Rockies.

"Do you think Ed is interviewing the owner of the club?" I ask. "Or maybe a client? It does seem like a fancy, romantic place."

"That it does," Conner agrees. "Do you want to find out?"

~

I thought I did.

Now that we're here at the place, though, now that the car has stopped in front of the massive, by no means welcoming cast iron gates, I'm starting to have second thoughts.

"Maybe we should turn back," I whisper to Conner, who's in the passenger seat.

"But we're already here," he says. "Why the cold feet?"

I shrug. "Maybe because I suddenly think it's not a good idea to spy on the others, after all? I mean, they might think we're trying to steal their stories."

"But we're not. We're just checking out the competition so we can stay ahead, and there's nothing wrong with that."

I shake my head. "I don't know."

"Relax." He squeezes my arm. "Everything will be fine."

The guard approaches the car and Conner spends a few minutes convincing the man to let us in, resorting to bribery when persuasion won't work. Moments later, the gates open and I drive in, parking in the slot from which I think we can most easily make our getaway if needed. After killing the engine, I glance at my watch.

"You said the appointment is at nine?"

"Yeah." Conner consults his own watch. "And we're right on time."

I take off my seatbelt. "Do you think Ed is already there?"

He grabs the door handle. "There's only one way to find out, honey."

I raise my eyebrows. "Honey?"

"Oh, did I forget to mention that we're posing as a couple? Because apparently, most of those who come here are."

"No," I tell him furiously, now wishing that I had turned back.

But it's too late. This time, we really are already here, with the gates already closed behind us.

I frown. "I wish you had told me."

"Sorry. It slipped my mind."

Yeah, right.

He circles around the car, offering me his arm as I get out.

"Do I have to?"

He grins. "Yes."

Clearly, he's enjoying this.

Rolling my eyes, I grab his arm. "You better not try anything funny."

"Oh, I don't have that much of a sense of humor."

"And we're not staying long," I add. "As soon as we find out who Ed is interviewing, we get out."

"Sure, honey."

He really is enjoying this.

We head to the mansion, a pair of butlers in coattails greeting us at the entrance. As soon as we step inside, a waiter in a similar tuxedo, but without the coattails, offers us hors d'oeuvres and champagne. I try an oyster, a stuffed olive and a tomato bruschetta. Conner samples the goat's cheese crostini and the stuffed jalapeno before grabbing two glasses of the sparkling, golden liquid—one for him and one for me.

Walking down the corridor, we see works of art lining the walls—ancient Egyptian drawings on papyrus, Renaissance pieces, Japanese paintings, modern sketches. They all seem to depict naked women, though, or men, making me slightly uncomfortable.

I shrug it off, taking a sip of champagne and telling myself that this is art and a fascination with the human body is common among artists. Besides, the works of art are probably arranged by theme. Maybe these were put here as conversation starters?

We reach the great room, which has a high, vaulted ceiling and a spiral staircase leading to the second floor. Chairs and tables from the Victorian Era are scattered throughout, making the room resemble a 19th century parlor. At the same time, there are life-sized Roman and Greek marble sculptures in between them, lending the atmosphere of a history museum. Like the men and women in the paintings, these, too, are naked.

I take a bigger sip of champagne, swallowing hard.

Okay. Maybe this is a continuation of the theme. Or maybe this is simply the classical section. God knows the Greeks and Romans liked their men and women naked.

Even so, that bad feeling in the pit of my stomach is rebelling.

"I wonder where everyone is," Conner voices out my other observation.

Indeed, the room is empty and quiet, although I can hear music coming from somewhere.

"Maybe they're all in another room," I say.

Conner approaches the doors hidden by a red velvet curtain at the end of the room, where the music seems to be coming from.

"They're here."

He opens the door and we step inside a larger room, my heart stopping the moment I realize what it is.

An exclusive club for art enthusiasts my ass. It's a BDSM club.

Unlike Damien Shore's 'club', this one doesn't have men and women tied to the walls and ceilings or dancing on poles, which is good, but there are men and women in skimpy leather clothes and collars crawling across the floor on all fours, led on leashes just like dogs, some gagged and others blindfolded. Some of them are sitting between their 'master's' legs, heads bobbing up and down, while others are on their laps, moaning as they are stroked. One 'couple' is on the stage, the man whipping a naked woman in a collar. behind him, there is a large emblem, one depicting a thorny rose in tears and a whip.

The Weeping Rose. Or is it actually the Whipping Rose?

At any rate, I've seen more than enough. Finishing my champagne in one gulp, I set it down on a table and grab Conner's arm.

"Let's go," I whisper. "I don't see Ed, and I doubt he'll be here."

Conner nods and we turn around, but suddenly someone calls our attention.

"Wait! I don't think I've ever seen you before."

Shit.

My face pale, I turn back around, facing a muscular, dark-skinned man with long hair wearing multiple earrings, a fishnet shirt and leather pants.

I feel even more blood drain from my face.

"Yes, we're new," Conner says with a grin. "We thought we'd just check out the place for now."

"Did you? But you've barely been here a minute."

My heart pounds. Has he been watching us this whole time?

"We'll come back some other time," Conner says.

"I think not." The man places his hands on his hips as two shirtless men with larger builds walk towards him.

Silence falls over the crowd and I grip Conner's arm tighter, trying to keep myself from shaking.

"Are you really enthusiasts of this art or have you just come here to snoop— or worse, to make fun of us? Are you reporters trying to take pictures for all the world to see so they can ridicule us, too?"

The crowd gasps.

"No." Conner waves his hand. "You're mistaken. Of course we're not reporters. We really are eager... enthusiasts."

"Prove it," the man challenges.

My heart clenches. Who does this man think he is? What is this? Some prank?

"If this is a prank, it isn't funny," I say, summoning every bit of my courage as I hold my head high. The man doesn't laugh.

"You heard my husband." I step forward, letting go of his arm. "We're leaving. We have a right to."

"And you heard me." The man steps forward as well, towering over me. "You're not."

The men behind him step beside him and I step back, glancing at Conner.

What are we going to do now?

"I think your wife needs a little discipline," the man in the fishnet shirt says. "Why don't you punish her on the stage right now and prove to us all that you're not intruders? Or should I punish you instead for your intrusion?"

His hand goes to his hip, where a whip hangs. One of the men beside him cracks his knuckles.

Punish us?

"I'll do it." Conner grabs my arm.

The man steps aside, gesturing to the stage.

Conner drags me to the front of the room.

No way.

"Conner," I whisper, trying to wriggle free.

"Sorry," he whispers back. "But if we don't do this, we're dead."

My heart beats faster. I know he's probably right, but surely there must be some other way. What is he planning on doing to me?

As soon as we reach the stage, someone offers Conner a collar with a leash, cuffs and a gag. He takes them and then, facing me, he kisses me hard before whispering in my ear.

"Trust me."

I give him a look of disbelief. Trust him? How can I trust him after all he's done, after what he's doing?

I know I have no choice, though, so I don't fight back. I let him place the leather collar around my neck and cuff my hands behind me. Next, he ties the gag over my mouth, silencing me.

Looking into Conner's narrow brown eyes, I see the spark of intensity in them, the unmistakable lust, and my heart flips, a lump forming in my throat.

He is enjoying this.

And something tells me he's not going to be the only one.

Chapter Nine
Conner

Staring at Ingrid standing there in the dress I bought her, her hands bound and her mouth gagged, my breath leaves my lungs and my heart hammers in my chest. My cock throbs, swelling against my briefs.

It's just like that night at Damien Shore's house.

Except this time, after all this time, I want her more.

"Here." The man in the fishnet shirt offers me a whip.

I glance at it, then at Ingrid, and seeing her eyes wide and her cheeks suddenly pale, I shake my head. "I'll do this my way."

Pulling her arm, I sit on a chair and bend her over my knee, her shoes falling off. I grab the hem of her dress, pulling it all the way to her waist to expose her black underwear. With one of my hands keeping her dress in place, I lift the other and let it fall, the crack of my palm against her skin through the thin lace barrier echoing throughout the room, breaking the silence.

Ingrid makes no sound, staying still on my lap, though I can feel her chest heaving against my thighs, her heart pounding.

I spank her again. And again. And again.

With each blow, I try to ignore her nipples rubbing against my thigh and how her body jerks across my lap. The image reminds me of what I did to her the last time I had her bent over. The memory makes my cock harder.

I want to fuck her. Now.

But not yet.

After that fourth blow, she moans, hands clenching in the cuffs.

Making sure not to hit her too hard, I let my open hand fall for the fifth time. She keeps moaning, her moans becoming louder with the succeeding blows. I finally understand why as I feel something wet beneath my fingertips.

I stop, pushing her off my lap as I get on my feet. Ingrid falls on her knees, too weak to stand, one of her cheeks stained with the trail of a tear.

"Why stop?" the man in the fishnet shirt asks.

"I'd like to perform the rest of the punishment in private," I tell him. "If you'll allow me."

The man scratches his chin as he toys with the notion. Then he turns to the man to his right.

"Take them to a room and stay by the door."

The man nods and walks off, glancing at me. Scooping Ingrid in my arms and picking up her shoes, I follow him inside a room with velvet-lined walls and a ceiling covered in mirrors. I set her down on the Victorian-style chaise in the middle, stroking her hair as I lean over her, gazing into her tear-filled, half-lidded cerulean eyes.

My heart clenches, guilt bursting in my chest.

I press my lips against those quivering lids and the corners, kissing her tears away in quiet apology.

Afterwards, I gaze into her eyes again. They're still moist, but this time there's a plea in them, a plea that tugs at my heart and at my cock.

Something tells me I'm not going to last even twelve minutes this time.

As soon as the man leaves us and the door falls shut, I remove her gag and without giving her a chance to speak or draw a breath, I let my lips crash down on hers and stick my tongue in her mouth, cupping her breast through her dress. She kisses me back, her tongue, tasting of champagne and something even more intoxicating, mingling with mine.

My fingers find her stiff nipple through the knitted fabric and her body trembles as she arches against me, moaning into my mouth.

I swallow up the sweet sound, letting it turn to heat as it ripples through my body. I move my hand lower, sliding it between her thighs and brushing against the stain in her panties.

She pulls away, eyes and mouth wide open, a loud gasp escaping from her wet, swollen lips.

I slip my hand beneath the black lace, finding her nub.

She shivers, squeezing her eyes shut as she throws her head back, gasping.

I stroke that bud of flesh, my fingers circling it and rubbing against it, coaxing it into full bloom. Then I place my mouth against her ear.

"Tell me you want me."

She nods.

"Tell me," I urge her impatiently, stroking her faster.

Her hips jerk. "I... want... you."

"Say please."

She trembles and moans, unable to speak.

"Say it."

"Please."

The word comes out as a gasp, but I hear it and I stop stroking her, sliding a finger inside her instead. Her slick, velvety skin clings to mine as she lets out a loud moan.

I put another finger in, stretching her.

She moans even louder. Then, with her gaze holding mine, she starts moving her hips.

I withdraw my fingers and she whimpers.

I take my belt off in record time and pull my zipper down even faster. My pants hanging on my hips, I let my cock spring free before climbing onto the chaise and kneeling between Ingrid's legs.

She cranes her head to take a peek at my cock, eyes wide.

I plant a hasty kiss on her lips before gripping her thighs and pushing in slowly, inch by inch.

"So tight," I murmur, more to myself than to her.

With her soft skin wrapped around me, her heat and her wetness swallowing me up, I can barely hold on, but I somehow manage, my cock throbbing inside her as soon as I've filled her to the hilt.

I pause just a moment to catch my breath and savor the sensation I've missed beyond words, then I gaze on her as I start jerking my hips.

Last time, I didn't have the chance to watch her while I pounded into her. Now, I do.

Seeing strands of her ash-blonde hair scattered across her forehead, her turquoise eyes glistening with tears and burning with lust, her lips parted as she forces air into her lungs only to have it escape in gasps, I almost come then and there.

I gather all my self-control as I bend her nearly in half and move in and out of her, the slurping sound and the slapping of skin against skin filling the room.

My cock grows numb from the friction. My knees dig into the velvet. Sweat breaks out on my back, the smell of it mingling with the scent of Ingrid's arousal and mine.

I reach between us, stroking that nub of hers once more as I continue moving in and out of her.

Suddenly she cries out, her body shaking as her eyes fall shut.

I manage a few more thrusts as her passage becomes tighter, then when I can't contain myself any longer, I empty myself deep inside her, grunting as my body grows taut.

The release leaves me completely satisfied and breathless.

Lifting a limp Ingrid, I lie down on the chaise, letting her rest on top of me. I stroke her hair as I chase after my breath, waiting for my heartbeat to slow down.

"Are you okay?" I ask her.

"Yeah," she whispers.

I plant a kiss on the top of her head, and drawing a deep breath, I slide out from under her to put my pants back on. Opening the door, I ask the man who's still outside for the key to her cuffs. After he gives it, I free her wrists.

She rubs them, sitting up.

I take off her collar, tossing it aside, then help her put her underwear and her shoes back on, kneeling in front of her as I do. After that, I pull her arm and hook it around my shoulder while I wrap mine around her waist, supporting her to her feet.

"Let's go home, shall we, honey?"

Chapter Ten
Ingrid

Staring at the bathroom mirror as I grip the edges of the sink, I see cobalt pools of dismay and regret gaze back at me, lips pursed tight.

Ingrid, what have you done?

Turning on the faucet, I roll up my sleeves and wash that sad look off my face with a handful of water—only to see the marks on my wrists.

I rub them, frowning.

I should have known the night would end the same way since it started the same way—with drinks and a walk through a corridor with strange paintings. Like before, I should have turned back when that voice in my head told me to. Like before, I should have kept my mouth shut and bolted. Like before, I should have resisted Conner, or at least fought harder instead of allowing myself to be seduced into surrender, to be swept away by that devilish mouth that has miles of experience on me and those wicked fingers.

Like before...

I turn off the faucet and step out of the bathroom, grabbing the overflowing laundry hamper in the bedroom. I'm supposed to bring it to the laundry room in the basement of the building so I can wash and dry the clothes like I do every Thursday. Instead, I stop just behind the front door, setting it down and backtracking to slump on the floor against the counter with my hands clasping my hair in frustration.

Why the hell did I make the same mistake last night that I made six years ago?

Alright, maybe I've told myself I would no longer think of that first night as a mistake, because someone as wonderful as Alexa came from it. But last night clearly was.

Why?

I thought I'd be wiser by now, stronger. Hell, I'm a mother now. I'm freaking thirty years old.

The first time I faltered, I blamed it on the alcohol and my virginity and maybe a suspicious substance. Last night, there was no such substance, I barely had any alcohol, and I definitely no longer had my virginity.

What's your excuse now, huh, Ingrid? And no, don't say it's because you haven't had sex for the past six years.

Letting my hair go, I pull my knees to my chest, letting out a breath to blow away the strands that have fallen across my face.

Alright. Maybe that was a factor. But that's not an excuse, not a good excuse by any measure nor a valid one, not for having sex with Conner again or for getting swept away by that whole BDSM thing again.

Frankly, I don't know which is worse.

What is with me and BDSM? Why do I somehow end up getting tangled up in it? And why do I end up enjoying it? Do I really like being spanked that much? Is it because I wasn't spanked as a child?

I bury my face in my arms.

Letting him spank and cuff me was humiliating enough. Getting turned on from the spanking and the cuffs—that's sick.

Am I sick?

Maybe I am. I feel sick. My stomach is a mess. My head is a mess. My heart is a mess. My body still feels sore. I don't even know how I managed to bring Alexa to school.

It's a good thing Conner isn't around. He'd be fawning over me, and I don't need that right now. The ride back home last night was unbearable enough.

I'm not ready to face him yet.

A knock on the door jolts me out of my thoughts. I lift my head and my feet slide across the floor as my arms fall to my sides and panic seizes me.

Don't tell me he's back already.

"Ingrid? You there?"

My shoulders sink in relief. It's just Janine, the brilliant, geeky home-based computer programmer who lives two floors above me. And I mean she lives there; she barely gets out, which is convenient because she's usually available to babysit Janine when I need her to, like last night. She also happens to be my best friend. We've bonded through our struggles—mine with being a single mom, hers with living in the real world. Not that she's anti-social. She just… doesn't like most people, or so she says.

"Come in," I tell her, knowing she has a key.

If she's here, it must be important. Besides, I can't deny I need a bit of company other than Conner's right now.

Keys rattle, and seconds later the knob turns and the door opens—knocking down the hamper and sending its contents spilling across the floor.

Janine hurriedly picks them up. "Oh, I'm so so—"

She stops as her eyes find me, eyebrows bunching up.

"What are you doing there?"

I shrug. "Talking to myself. Well, more like beating myself up."

"You sure look beaten."

Janine walks over to me, offering me her hand. I grab it, but since I barely have an ounce of energy to lift myself and my body is too heavy for her petite frame, my hand slips out of hers and I fall back to the floor.

"Ow." I rub my backside, which is still bruised.

"Are you okay?" Janine asks, offering both hands this time.

I take them, getting up slowly. I walk to the couch and sit down. She sits beside me, tucking chocolate-brown strands of hair behind her ears before pinning her hands between her thighs.

"Care to tell me what happened?"

I look at her, saying nothing. It's not that I don't want to tell her. It's just that I don't know where to start.

"Let me help." Janine moves closer to me. "Does it have something to do with the man who's been staying here?"

My eyes pop.

"I know you haven't told me about him," she goes on. "But I couldn't help but notice the men's clothes in Alexa's bedroom and the aftershave in the bathroom. Plus, Alexa keeps talking about him. Conner, am I right?"

I nod.

"So, new boyfriend? Not that I remember any old ones."

"No," I refute the suggestion immediately.

Janine lifts her hands as she leans back. "Okay. Not boyfriend. So…"

I sigh, facing her. "I'm sorry I haven't told you about him. I wasn't trying to hide him from you or anything."

She waves her hands. "No apologies required."

"The truth is, he's…" I take a deep breath.

Janine makes a rolling motion with her hand, urging me to continue.

"He's Alexa's father," I blurt out.

"What?" Janine stands up, her jaw dropping.

I nod. "Yup."

"But I thought you said…"

"He's dead. I know that's what I said, but it's not true. Conner is Alexa's father."

Janine sits down. "Okay. What else should I know about him?"

"That he's a journalist like me. That he works for *The Dallas Times*, the paper I used to work for before moving here. And that we met while I was working there."

"And why did you break up?"

"Well, technically, we weren't ever together. It was just… a one night stand."

"Wow," Janine gasps. "I seriously never saw that coming. No offense, but you don't strike me as a one-night-stand kind of girl."

"I'm not," I tell her. "It was unintentional, an assignment that went all wrong."

She nods slowly. "I see."

"After that, I moved out of Dallas. I didn't even know I was pregnant, and when I found out, I didn't even think about telling him. I stayed with my mom until I gave birth and… you know the rest of the story."

"Not the most recent events. Why is he here?" Janine glances around. "Why is he staying here?"

"He's here in Boulder because of a job offer, the same job offer that was made to me."

"What? So the two of you are after the same job?"

"Yeah."

"That still doesn't explain why he's staying here."

"He found out about Alexa," I explain. "He wanted to be in her life and he just looked so earnest about it that I couldn't refuse. I mean, he does have a right to get to know her and let her get to know him."

"Okay. So he's here to get to know her?"

"Also because he has no place to stay here in Boulder."

"Convenient." Janine stands up, leaning against the counter.

"We also decided to work together so that one of us would get the job. Whoever wins, Alexa wins."

"Ooh. You're a team already."

"I wouldn't call it that."

Are we?

"But Alexa doesn't know, does she?"

"Nope." I shake my head. "And please don't tell her. Conner and I will tell her when the time is right."

"Of course." She rests her elbows on the counter. "So, what is the problem with him exactly?"

"I hate him," I confess.

"No you don't," Janine disagrees. "If you hated him, you wouldn't have let him stay here with you."

"Alright. Maybe I don't anymore, but I still haven't forgiven him for what he did to me all those years ago. He stole my story."

And my virginity to boot.

Janine gasps. "He didn't."

"He did. It was the story about Damien Shore. A big one. It was what led to him being in jail."

"Wow. What can I say? He's a jerk."

"I know, and yet he's not all that bad. He's a good father, and…"

"Wait a minute." Janine returns to the couch. "You're in love with him."

I gape. "What?"

"That's why you were beating yourself up. Because you're in love with him but you're not supposed to be, or at least you don't want to be because of what he did to you."

I blink, unable to believe she put it all together just like that. Still, I have to admit it makes sense.

"You know, sometimes I forget you're a genius and then you say stuff like this and I remember."

She snorts. "I'm not a genius. You know what's going on. You just don't want to admit it."

I sit up, an idea sinking in.

"Wait. I'm in love with Conner?"

Janine nods. "You definitely are."

I get off the couch and walk around the coffee table. "No, that's not what's going on."

"You sort of just admitted it."

"No." I shake my head. "I'm not in love with him. I never have been and never will be."

"But you want to be. And yet you don't want to be."

I place my hands on my hips. "Now you're not making any sense."

"Have you slept with him?" Janine blurts out the question.

My eyebrows dart up. "Excuse me?"

"You heard me."

"Of course. That's how Alexa was born."

"That's not what I'm talking about." Janine places her knee on the couch, her arm on its back. "I mean since he got here."

I start pacing the living room. "If you're asking if we've had sex here in this apartment, the answer is no."

"But elsewhere?"

I sigh. This is what I get for having a perceptive best friend. Then again, I suppose that's why she's my best friend.

"Okay." I stop and look at her. "We did it. Last night."

"Any details?"

I think about telling her about the BDSM thing but decide against it. Even best friends are entitled to secrets from each other.

I shake my head. "That's all you'll get."

"Okay. I'll take it. And I'm guessing you regret it now, which I don't really understand. He's Alexa's father. You don't hate him. I'm guessing he's attractive…"

"Very." The word just comes out of my mouth.

"Okay. He's very attractive and you're both single. You have a kid together. What's the problem again?"

I shake my head some more. "This isn't going to work."

"Aren't you even going to give it a chance?"

"No. I don't need this. I don't want this."

"You're sure?"

I run my hands through my hair, pursing my lips.

"You don't look like you're sure," Janine says.

"Listen. The first time was never supposed to happen. Now, I know Alexa came out of that, and I'm forever grateful, but my life still got messed up. That's what Conner does—he messes my life up. I don't need that."

"But what if he loves you?" Janine asks, standing up.

I snort. "No way. This is a man who doesn't fall in love. He sleeps with women for stories, for Christ's sake."

"Like we said, he's a jerk. But that doesn't mean he can't fall in love."

Conner? In love? I can't even imagine it.

Yes, he smiles at me, and he gets this look in his eyes when he's looking at me, but that's not love. That's lust. Or maybe fascination. Whatever it is, it's not love.

Janine stands in front of me. "Do you maybe not want him to fall in love with you because that would mean you'd fall in love with him?"

I raise my hands. "You know what? I don't want to talk about it anymore. It was a good talk, but it's starting to get nonsensical now, and… Let's just stop, okay?"

For a moment, Janine just looks at me. Then she nods. "Okay. Fine."

I smile. "Thanks."

She grabs her bonnet, which is on the armchair. "I forgot this last time. I just came back for it."

"Okay."

She wrings it with her hands. "So, just for the record, what are you and Conner right now if you're not in love?"

"Colleagues," I say. "Professionals who are working together on a story."

"Right. And what story is it, exactly?"

"A love story," I answer without thinking.

"Right." Janine nods. "I rest my case."

I sigh. "Janine…"

She raises two fingers in the air. "You said you wanted to stop."

I cross my arms over my chest. "You just had to have the last word, didn't you?"

She gives me a sheepish grin as she holds the doorknob.

"I've got to go. See you when I see you."

"Not if I see you first," I respond as I usually do.

As soon as she's gone, I pick the laundry up, tossing it back in the hamper.

Well, that conversation was… confusing. I'm just going to pretend it didn't happen, just like I'm going to pretend last night never happened, which was what I intended to do the first time I had sex with Conner, except I couldn't because I had Alexa.

This time, I will.

And I swear if Conner brings it up, I'll punch him.

~

"I punched him," Conner relays as he eats a sandwich, having returned to the apartment shortly after lunch.

"You punched a man?" Alexa's eyes grow wide as she pauses in the act of eating her own sandwich.

I cover her ears. "But what did your friend say? Why did he… point us there?"

"He said he didn't know what it was and he seriously believed Ed was going to be there."

"And you believed him?"

"No." He takes another bite off his sandwich. "That's why I punched him."

I nod. "Serves him right."

Alexa glances at me. "Are you done? Because my ears are hurting."

"Sorry." I take my hands off her ears.

"Another friend of mine said he knows something about the lead Ed might be pursuing, though," Conner adds.

"No." I shake my head. "No more spying."

"We weren't…" He takes a deep breath. "Okay. Fine."

"I should focus on finding my own leads and pursuing them," I say.

"Oh, speaking of which, this other friend of mine might have something for you."

My eyes narrow. "What?"

Conner takes a business card out of his pocket and hands it to me.

"Unpetty," I read the word at the top of the card. "What is this?"

"Apparently it's a new business that opened in Colorado Springs just a few weeks ago," he tells me. "It's supposed to be this place where you can spend a day with your pets or arrange play dates with other pet owners. It's owned by a couple, both award-winning dog show handlers. They competed against each other a lot but somehow fell in love after one of the worst dog shows ever. Or so my friend told me."

"And this friend of yours isn't lying this time?" I ask.

I had to.

"She's more trustworthy."

"Oh, she's a she, huh?"

"Ingrid…"

I cut him off. "I have to say the story's got potential. At the very least, my curiosity is piqued."

"And Colorado Springs isn't far," Conner says. "We can give them a call now and maybe arrange an interview for tomorrow?"

I look at the business card in my hand once more, then tap it with my fingers. "Sounds like a plan."

Chapter Eleven
Conner

"We never planned to open this business," Eliza Richards says as she strokes the long-haired white cat curled on her lap. "Just as we never planned we'd fall in love. Then again, nobody really plans on falling in love, do they?"

She turns to her husband seated in the wicker chair beside her with an adoring smile, and he returns it while stroking the tabby cat on his own lap.

They're both in their late thirties, Eliza with a platinum blonde bob that has not a strand out of place beneath a crimson beret and Jack with darker curls and black earrings. Both are wearing matching calico silk scarves.

They're seated right across from us in the closed gazebo in the middle of the garden of their pet haven. Outside, snow is falling softly past the glass.

"I guess not," I answer as I sit back, elbows falling on the armrests of the chair.

Beside me, Ingrid says nothing, a somber expression on her face.

I frown. It's not like her to be so silent during an interview.

"Would you tell us how the two of you met?" I proceed.

"You'll never guess." Eliza holds her husband's hand. "It was at a pet shop. I was looking for a new collar and so was he. And we both went for the same thing."

"I saw it first," Jack teases.

"You did not," Eliza protests. "Anyway, it's like... serendipity, right? Except they happened to have two pieces, so we got one each. But while we were waiting for them to get the other from the stockroom, we started chatting and we were just so attracted to each other that we decided to go somewhere together afterwards, since we both happened to have some free time. We had dinner, went to a bar after, got a little drunk..."

"You were drunk, not me," Jack inserts.

"Okay, I was a little drunk," Eliza admits. "And then we kissed, we went back to his hotel room and..." She shrugs. "Well, you know what happens next."

"I do," Jack says.

Eliza looks at him, blushing.

"So, you had sex?" Ingrid asks in a serious tone.

"Mind-blowing sex," Eliza says with a smile.

"Now she admits it," Jack mutters.

"And then the next day, I see him at the dog show that I'm competing in. He never told me he was a handler, and neither did I, so imagine my shock when I found out we were in the same line of work."

"Yup, I can imagine," Ingrid remarks.

"Worse, we were competing with each other, like in the same division, like neck and neck." Eliza's eyes roll to the ceiling. "Oh, I hated him then. I wanted to kill him. I wished I'd never met him."

"Yeah." Jack nods. "You should have seen her. She was so mad. She almost strangled me."

"And that wasn't the only time. We kept seeing each other in these shows—dog shows, cat shows, even bunny shows..."

"Don't forget the duck show," Jack reminds her.

"I'd be there and he'd be there and we'd always be like competing for the top spot. Sometimes I'd end up first and sometimes he would and I'd hate him even more. I always thought he cheated whenever he won."

"Just to be clear, I never cheated," Jack says.

"I know, honey." Eliza squeezes his hand. "Then there was this one dog show where for some reason our dogs just wouldn't behave like we wanted them to. At one point they ran all over the place. Everything was a mess. We chased after them, of course. He ended up catching my dog. I ended up catching his, but by then, we were both, like, frazzled and haggard, and we had stuff on our clothes and on our hair, and then his dog, well, my dog that he had in his arms, just peed on his pants and I started laughing. But not the make-fun-of-him kind of laugh. It was just genuine laughter and he started laughing, too. I guess we both went crazy. Anyway, we just realized how stupid everything was and we kissed and we got back together."

"If you ask me, we were in love the whole time," Jack says. "We were just too proud to admit it."

"Oh," Eliza gushes. "I love you so much."

"I love you, too."

They lean over, about to kiss, but Ingrid clears her throat.

"So, you're saying you never really hated each other?" she asks.

"We did, but that also meant we loved each other," Eliza answers. "You know what some people say, that hate is just a twisted kind of love, that it isn't the opposite of love."

Ingrid's eyebrows crease. "Of course it is. How can it not be?"

Eliza taps her fingers on her knee. "Um…"

"We were stupid," Jack speaks. "We weren't fighting each other. We were fighting what we felt for each other, but we couldn't, not really. It was doomed to defeat from the start."

"The attraction was just too strong," Eliza adds. "That's why we just kept showing up at the same dog shows and ending up in the same situation over and over again."

"I just couldn't resist her." Jack squeezes Eliza's hand in turn. "So I just knew I was in love with her."

"But how could you be sure it was love and not lust?" Ingrid asks.

I glance at her in surprise.

"Oh, it always starts with a little lust," Eliza says. "We're stubborn. Our bodies decide for us before we can decide for ourselves, and we often try to overrule our bodies. That's why it gets complicated. Look at animals. They just follow their bodies, so it's simple."

"But that's not love," Ingrid tells her.

"No, but what I'm saying is that our bodies know these things. Everything starts with physical attraction and lust, but as humans, we feel the pressure to know better so we disregard all that. But if only we don't, if only we're a little less proud, then we can just go with the flow and eventually the attraction becomes something else, and…"

"I disagree," Ingrid cuts her off.

"What?" Eliza looks at her in shock.

I clear my throat. "Why don't you tell us about how you decided to start this business now?"

"Oh, that idea came naturally," Jack says. "We were just talking about it while we were walking our dogs, and we both thought it was a great idea and we just went for it, so here we are."

"We wanted a place for people to hang out with their pets," Eliza says. "And a place for pet lovers to hang out with each other and, you know, maybe fall in love."

"That's thoughtful," I say with a smile.

"That's bull," Ingrid blurts out. "Love and lust are two different things. If you…"

I place my hand over hers. "Ingrid."

She shuts up, her eyes meeting mine.

I squeeze her hand, shaking my head slightly in hopes of getting my message across.

That's enough, Ingrid.

She looks away but thankfully seems to calm down.

"Sorry about that," I tell the couple.

"It's okay," Jack says. "Not everyone shares the same opinions. That's why they're called opinions."

"Are the two of you a couple?" Eliza asks all of a sudden. "Because you two seem…"

Ingrid stands up. "Well, that's all for now. Thank you for your time."

She walks away, leaving me sitting there with my eyebrows raised.

Okay.

"Sorry, I apologize again. But, really, thank you for your time. Your story is so… fun."

"I think so, too," Eliza says, her smile back on.

I offer her my hand. "Thank you for sharing your story with us."

She shakes it. "You're so welcome."

"And I wish you all the luck with your business." I shake Jack's hand.

"Come over anytime," Jack says. "With a pet, though."

"Yeah. Maybe I'll get one someday."

I pat the cat on his lap before getting my things and following Ingrid. I catch up to her in the car, finding her leaning against it with her arms wrapped around her.

"Hey." I approach her. "Are you okay?"

She just looks at me.

"What happened back there?" I ask. "You know you're not supposed to…"

"I think I'll go for a drive." She opens the door to the driver's seat. "I need to clear my head. You can get a cab, can't you?"

"I…"

"Could you pick Alexa up from school for me?" she asks, not giving me a chance to speak.

I sigh. "Okay."

"Thanks."

She gets inside the car. Moments later, the engine starts and she drives off, leaving me behind.

I scratch my head.

What the hell just happened?

~

"What happened to Mommy?" Alexa asks me the same question when I pick her up.

"Oh, she just had to do some stuff for work," I say, slinging her tiny purple backpack over my shoulder.

"But I thought she didn't have work," Alexa says.

I place my hand on the top of her head. "Technically, she still does."

"Is she okay?" Alexa asks. "She looked upset yesterday. And this morning, too."

I frown.

Of course she noticed. How could she not?

"She's okay," I assure Alexa. "She just has a lot on her mind."

"I didn't do anything wrong, did I?"

I kneel in front of her, placing my hand on her shoulder. "Of course not. Whatever it is that's bothering your mom, I promise you it's not your fault."

"Then why didn't she fetch me?" Alexa asks, pouting. "She always fetches me even when she's so busy. Well, not always, but most of the time she does, and I kind of want her to."

I squeeze her shoulder. "Like I said, she just has a lot of stuff on her mind right now. You know, being a mom and working—it's not easy. But your mom is so good at it. She'll pull through. I know it."

Alexa says nothing.

I pinch her cheek. "Why? Am I not good enough for you?"

She looks at me.

"What about if I carry you on my shoulders, huh? Will that make you feel better?"

Slowly, her lips curve into a smile. "I always wanted someone to do that."

"Come here, then."

I help her get on my shoulders, then stand up. I wobble at first under her weight, drawing a squeal from her, but I steady myself, holding her hands.

"Are you alright up there?"

"Yup."

I don't see her face, but I can imagine how happy she looks, which makes my chest feel tight and warm.

To think such a little thing could make her so happy.

I start walking. "You know, your Mom and I went to this place with lots of animals earlier today."

"A zoo?" Alexa asks.

"No. It's called a pet haven. It's a place where people with pets can go and just have fun."

"I wanna go there."

"But you need to have a pet to go there."

"I wanna have a pet," she says. "I've always wanted one."

328

"Can you have pets at your apartment?"

"Yeah. Janine has a crab, and someone on our floor has hamsters."

"Really?"

"Mm-hmm."

"Well, if you could have a pet, what would you like?" I ask her.

"A mouse," she says. "Can I have one, please?"

I can imagine those puppy dog eyes on her.

"You'll have to ask your mom about that."

"But she's not here. Please, can we get one right now?"

"I don't know, sweetheart. Getting a pet isn't a decision you should make on the spur of a moment."

"But I've been wanting one forever," she argues.

"Having a pet isn't easy," I point out. "Even if it's just a small pet, it can be a huge responsibility."

"What's respinsobility?"

"If you don't even know that word, how can you have a pet?"

"I know it's not easy, but does that mean I can't try?" Alexa asks. "I'll do my best, I promise."

I sigh. She really is too smart. And too adorable.

"Please?" she begs, resting her head on top of mine.

"Fine," I give in, unable to resist. "I guess your mom won't mind."

Chapter Twelve
Ingrid

"What part of 'don't make major decisions about her life' did you not understand?"

Once again, I'm seething as I pace the living room. And this just after I went to a spa and the movie theater to relax.

"I didn't think it was a major decision," Conner argues, sitting in the middle of the couch.

"All I asked was for you to pick her up from school. That was all."

"And she begged me for a pet, so we stopped by the pet store."

I glance at the cage with two white mice on the coffee table.

"Just like that, huh?" I place my hands on my hips. "What? If she asked you for the moon, you'd give it to her?"

"If I could."

"You're the adult, Conner. You could have said no. You should have said no."

"It was just a present."

I stop walking and stand across him. "A present I decided long ago not to give her."

He crosses his arms over his chest. "Oh, is that what this is about? Because I made you look like the bad guy? Because you're afraid she'll like me more than she likes you? Is that it?"

I step forward, fists clenched at my sides. "How dare you."

He stands up. "Why don't you just admit it? You're afraid I might steal her from you."

"Well, you do have a record for stealing."

He chuckles, hands falling to his hips. "Finally, some honesty."

"What is that supposed to mean?"

"Isn't that why you ran away earlier? Because Mrs. Richards's words got to you? Because you couldn't bear to hear the truth or face the fact that other people can be true to themselves?"

I point a finger at him, shoulders heaving. "This isn't about me. It's about you breaking the rules, rules I made."

"What? Are you being like Damien Shore now, all obsessed with the rules?"

I plant my hand on my chest. "I have no choice. I need to make rules because I'm her mother."

"And I'm her…"

The door to the bedroom opens before he can finish, and Alexa comes out.

I take a deep breath. "Honey, I told you to stay in the room."

"You're scaring Lulu and Lily."

She kneels by the coffee table and scoops one of the mice out of the cage.

"Put the mouse back in the cage, sweetheart," I tell her.

She doesn't obey, holding the mouse against her heart instead.

"Alexa…"

"Why are you getting mad at him?" she asks. "I was the one who wanted the mice. Why don't you want them, anyway? I said I'd take care of them."

Great. Now I am the bad guy.

I point to the bedroom door. "Put the mouse back in the cage, sweetheart, and go back to the room."

"Why are you being so mean?"

"Alexa, this isn't…"

"Ow!" she yelps as the mouse tumbles to the rug.

I rush over to her to check her hand. "Sweetheart, are you okay?"

"I'm fine." She holds up her mitted hand. "I'm wearing a mitten so there's no cut. It just hurt a bit."

"See. This is why…"

I don't finish because the mouse scurries between my feet and I jump.

"Lulu!" Alexa shouts.

"Get that mouse!" I shout.

Conner goes after it, but it's scurrying too fast across the living room.

I chase after it as well. "Come here, you!"

I dive at the floor the same time Conner does, resulting in a head butt.

"Ouch!" I rub my head as I pick myself up.

"Sorry," Conner mumbles, rubbing his head as well.

"I got her!" Alexa says, following the mouse as it scurries into the bedroom.

My eyes grow wide. Not the bedroom!

I rush in there and find Alexa crawling under the bed. I prepare to crouch, too, but the mouse scurries out and races back to the living room. I chase after it, only to stumble across Conner, who's still sitting on the floor, and fall over his lap.

"Whoa!" Conner says. "You okay?"

"Don't you get any weird ideas." I push myself off his lap before he tries anything.

He puts his hands up. "Nope. No ideas."

I spot the mouse on the other side of the room and run after it. "Get up and help me catch that rat!"

"It's a mouse," Alexa corrects, rushing back into the living room.

And just in time. The mouse passes in front of her and she dives to the floor and snags it.

"I got it!"

I place my hand on my head, letting out a sigh of relief—which quickly vanishes as Alexa's elbow hits the stool while she's getting up. Its legs wobble alarmingly.

"Alexa, watch out!"

Conner rushes over to steady the stool, but it's too late. The paper bag that I've set down on it slides off the edge, and the jar inside, which I got from the spa, flies out. Its lid, which I must have neglected to close properly, flies as well, and the open jar lands on Conner's head with a plop. The green seaweed moisturizer oozes down his hair and face, some of it dripping onto his shirt.

I cover my mouth to gasp in horror, only to end up bursting into laughter seconds later.

I can't help it. With that green, foul-smelling slime on his head, he reminds me of some bizarre B movie menace, like a creature from the deep or a lake monster or something.

Alexa starts laughing along, and while for a moment Conner looks like he's about to get pissed, he, too, breaks into laughter.

Then Conner stops. "Oh, you think it's funny, do you?"

He grabs some of the goo and splatters it on Alexa.

"No!" she squeals, turning away.

Conner stands up, looking at me.

I put a finger up. "Oh no you don't."

He ignores my warning and rushes at me.

"No!" I scream as I run away.

Jumping over the couch, he catches me and starts rubbing the moisturizer on my cheeks as Alexa giggles in the background.

"Now you have something green on you, too," he says.

I ignore the allusion, wiping the substance off my cheek and staring at my fingers.

"Ew." I grimace. "That stinks."

"You're the one who bought it," Conner reminds me.

"Yeah. What was I thinking?"

I head to the bathroom, touching Alexa's shoulder on my way. "Let's go wash this stinky, slimy stuff off."

~

"Well, that's the last of it," I say as I wipe the last drop of green slime from the floor with a paper towel. I've been at the task since I finished taking a shower.

At least the stuff comes off easily and the smell doesn't linger once it's gone.

Throwing the paper towel into the wastebasket, I go to the couch and turn on the TV. As I'm flipping through the channels, Conner comes out of his room, drying his hair with a towel.

"So, did it come off?" I ask him.

He takes the towel off his head to show me his hair. "Did it?"

I nod. "I think you got most of it out."

"Good." He continues drying his hair. "That doesn't mean I like it any better."

"Just think of it as conditioner," I tell him. "Oh, you know what? You might have stumbled across a new product. Seaweed conditioners. Perfect for when you come out of the pool or for days when you just miss the sea so much that you want to smell like it."

"That's not funny." He sits beside me. "How's Alexa?"

"Better now. Inside the room, mesmerized by her mice."

He lets the towel fall to his shoulders. "I'm sorry I overstepped my bounds."

"Oh, now you admit it."

"Ingrid…"

"It's fine," I cut him off. "I didn't handle it well, either, but hey, everything got resolved by that jar of seaweed moisturizer."

I ruffle his hair.

"Hey," he complains.

"Alexa's happy," I say seriously. "Isn't that what matters?"

He nods. "She's got us wrapped around her finger, doesn't she?"

I chuckle, continuing to flip through the channels. When I get to the news channel, I stop, seeing Damien Shore's face on the screen.

"He's engaged?" I ask in surprise as I read the ticker beneath his face.

Conner shrugs. "Apparently."

"I thought he was married."

"Divorced," Conner corrects. "Twice."

"I've finally found love," Damien Shore says on the TV, turning to the brunette beside him, who looks at least a decade younger than him. "And I think it's all because I'm a changed man. Being in prison gave me time to reflect on my life, and…"

I shake my head, changing the channel. "Can you believe the man?"

Conner gives another shrug. "Maybe he has changed."

"Or maybe it's a publicity stunt," I say, stopping at the travel channel. "He seems too desperate to prove he's a changed man. Besides, you don't say you're a changed man. You just change."

"You know, you could interview him and find out." Conner sits back. "It is a love story."

"A fake love story." I set the remote control down on the coffee table. "I'm sure I can find something else, something better."

"What's wrong with the ex-dog handler couple?"

"I don't know." I shrug, eyes on the screen. "It's not powerful enough. My instincts tell me it's not the right story."

"And your instincts are always right. So just keep looking."

"Yeah. I have to. The deadline's approaching." I glance at the calendar on the wall. "You know, I didn't think it would be this hard. Maybe it's because the assignment is so vague. Like, it could be anything. Or maybe true love stories don't really exist. That's why there are books and movies. Maybe it's just a wild goose chase."

He turns to me. "If the assignment was easy, we'd all get the job."

"I know, but I didn't expect it to be this hard." I sigh. "Maybe my expectations are too high. Maybe I'm not looking at this the right way."

"Hey." Conner places a hand on my lap. "It's not your fault you haven't found a story yet, okay? You're a great journalist. The story's elusive. That's why you just need to look harder."

"It's not about looking hard enough. It's about knowing where to look."

"Well said." He pats my thigh. "Well, I'm sure you'll find your story soon."

I take his hand off me. "I hope so."

I glance at the calendar again. "I really hope so."

His phone rings and he picks it off the counter. I lower the volume, trying to listen in on his conversation, but he simply nods, puts the phone down, and returns to the couch.

"That was Cassie," he says.

My eyes grow wide. "Cassie?"

"Yes. She's probably going to call you in a minute, too. She wants to see us all tomorrow, just to check on our progress."

"Great." I stand up, pouting. "Just great."

Chapter Thirteen
Conner

"I expect nothing less than great things from you," Cassie tells me, pulling her oversized gray leather chair forward so she can lean over her sleek black desk. "Personally, I'm betting you."

I grin, sitting back. "Did you tell the others that, too?"

"The first, yes. The second, no. I do believe that of the four of you, you're the one who has what it takes to pull off this job."

"Thanks. You're too kind, but I'm afraid I don't agree. I believe we all have what it takes. That's why we're all being offered a chance at the job, right?"

She narrows her eyes at me curiously.

I know what she's thinking. The old me would have done anything to get this job, even if it meant sleeping with her. The old me wouldn't have cared about the others.

But that's the old me. The new me cares, at least about one other.

"Well, if you say so." She sits back.

"Are we done?"

Cassie nods. "You can send Ed in if he's already here."

I get off the chair, pick up my coat from the other chair, and head towards the door.

"Oh, one more thing," she calls after me.

I turn around.

"I found out something about you and Ingrid."

I tense. What exactly did she find out? That we have a child together?

"You two did work for *The Dallas Times* together at one point. Did you sleep with her?"

"No," I lie. "And frankly, I don't know how that's significant."

"I just wanted to make sure you don't mix business with pleasure—I mean, personal matters. You know, no conflicts of interest."

I nod. "I understand."

She clasps her hands over her stomach. "Also, I don't want you not to bring your A game just because you don't want to hurt her feelings or something like that."

"I'm focused, and I'm bringing my A game," I assure her.

"Good. Like I said, I expect something great from you."

I give another nod, about to turn around and leave, but the picture on the shelf behind Cassie catches my eye. It's a picture of her and an older man, one who I think I've seen somewhere before.

"What's wrong?" Cassie asks.

"Nothing," I tell her, dismissing my suspicion.

For all I know, it could be anyone important. As the Deputy Chief of the News Division of a large media company, I'm sure Cassie has her connections and no shortage of photo opportunities.

"Good day," I tell her.

Stepping outside, I find only Tiffany sitting in the hallway.

"Is Ed here yet?" I ask her.

"I don't think he's coming," Tiffany says, standing up. "Maybe his leg is hurting and he'll just call in his report."

"I see." I glance around. "Where's Ingrid?"

Tiffany shrugs. "Maybe she left already."

I'm not surprised. She looked upset earlier, after coming out of Cassie's office. There were actual tears brimming in her eyes.

"Why are you still here?" I ask her.

"I wanted to talk to you." She steps forward, lowering her voice. "I told Cassie I already had a story, but I lied. I don't. I was wondering if maybe you could help me."

I blink.

She touches my arm. "I know it's selfish of me, and maybe it's wrong, but you could just help me come up with some ideas, you know, point me in the right direction. After all, you are so good at this and I'm... I'm not even a journalist. I'm a blogger."

I eye her hand. "I'm sure you know a lot of people with great love stories to share."

"Actually, I don't know anyone." Tiffany shakes her head. "Most of the people I know have no luck with love. Just like me."

She traces circles on my arm.

"We're the same, you know. People throw themselves at us not because they love us but just because they want to feel good. So we throw them away after we've had our fun." She leans over to me, whispering my ear. "But if you throw yourself at me, I promise I won't throw you away. We'll have endless fun, and then I'll have something to write about—our own crazy love story."

I grab her hand. "Tiffany..."

I stop because I suddenly spot Ingrid coming out of the restroom at the end of the hall. Our eyes meet. Shit.

"Why don't you post something on your blog about finding a story?" I suggest before letting her hand go. "You should get plenty of ideas from your followers."

With that, I leave her, running towards Ingrid, who's already running away.

"Ingrid, wait!" I call after her.

She slows down but doesn't stop walking. "What?"

"I thought you'd already left."

"You mean you thought you and Tiffany were alone and it was a good time to whisper sweet nothings in each other's ears."

I shake my head. "Ingrid, it's not like that. I..."

"Save it. I don't care."

I frown but drop the subject, switching to the one I originally wanted to talk to her about. "Are you okay? You looked upset earlier after talking to Cassie. What did she say?"

"I'm fine," Ingrid answers. "Cassie didn't say anything. I'm just disappointed in myself. I should have a few great stories to choose from by now."

"Don't be so hard on yourself," I tell her. "Even Tiffany doesn't have a story yet."

She stops and turns to face me. "Oh, is that what you were talking about? Is she asking for your help?"

"Yes," I admit.

"Why don't you, then? She seemed like she was promising something nice in return."

She continues walking.

I roll my eyes but go after her. "Ingrid..."

"Ingrid?"

I turn my head at the voice at the same time Ingrid does. A man is approaching us with long strides, his beer belly bouncing. Smiling, he takes off his cap, revealing thinning golden hair. His eyes, blue like Ingrid's but a lighter shade, are fixed on her. Just her.

I frown.

I don't have a clue who this man is, but I already don't like him.

"Rick," Ingrid greets him, making my heart sink. "What are you doing here?"

"Work," he answers. "Which sure hasn't been the same since you stopped reporting to the office."

Is he flirting with her?

Ingrid shrugs. "Yeah. Well, you know, I'm busy."

"Don't I know all about it? Say, do you already have a story? Because if not, I have something that might interest you." He rubs the stubble on his chin. "Scratch that. I have something that will interest you." He gives her a nudge on the shoulder. "Between you and me, it could get you the job."

"You're kidding," Ingrid tells him.

"Do I look like I'm kidding?" Rick grins.

"What's it about?" she asks.

"Royalty. You know people dig love stories that involve royalty."

"You mean real royalty?" Ingrid's eyebrows furrow. "Here in America?"

"Vacationing and potentially staying for good," Rick says.

"Tell me more."

Rick waves a finger. "Nah-uh. If you want all the juicy details, you know what to do."

Ingrid frowns. "Really? You're going to bribe me into going on a date with you?"

"Is it working?" His grin makes me sick to my stomach.

For a moment, Ingrid falls silent, thinking—wait, she's thinking about his proposal?—then she crosses her arms over her chest and sighs.

"Fine. Just one dinner. And I get to pick where."

No way.

"Ingrid." I grab her arm. "Can we talk for a sec?"

"Um, who are you?" Rick asks.

"Sorry. Where are my manners?" I offer him my hand. "Conner Blake. I'm Alexa's..."

I pause as Ingrid glares at me.

"I'm Ingrid's friend."

"An old friend who's just visiting," Ingrid says to my dismay. "I'll call you and let you know what time and where."

Rick's grin widens. "You know I'll be waiting."

Ingrid walks away, and I follow her. "Ingrid, what are you doing?"

"I'm going to meet a colleague for dinner and he's going to help me with my story," she says. "That's all."

My eyebrows furrow. "You're seriously going on a date with that... that jerk?"

"Why not? You sleep with women for stories. Why can't I go out with a guy for one?"

"Because he can't be trusted. Have you seen the way he looks at you?"

Ingrid turns to face me. "Are you jealous?"

"No." I place my hands on my hips. "Well, yes."

"Well, you have no reason to be. You're not my boyfriend, and you're definitely not my husband. You have no say in the matter."

The words, though true, sting, and I wince.

"Are you doing this to get back at me because you think I was flirting with Tiffany?" I ask her.

Her eyes grow wide, then narrow dangerously. "How dare you suggest such a thing? What? You can do whatever you want and I can't?"

"So you are trying to..."

"I'm trying to get the best story I can so I can get this job," she cuts me off. "Which frankly, you haven't been helping me to do, even though you said you would."

Ouch.

"That's not fair, Ingrid. You know I've been passing leads to you."

"And they're no good," she says. "So I'm going to try this one."

I draw a deep breath. Once Ingrid makes up her mind, there sure is no way of talking her out of it. And while that can be an admirable quality, it can also be annoying, as it is now.

"I can't do anything to change your mind, can I?" I ask her.

Ingrid shakes her head. "My decision is made. But you can do something for me."

"What?"

"You can babysit Alexa while I'm out with Rick. But if you're not up to it, I can just ask—"

"Me babysit my own kid?" I interrupt her. "Of course I'll do it. You don't even have to ask."

She smiles. "Thanks."

End of discussion. She walks towards the doors and I stand there, frowning.

I have a very bad feeling about this.

Chapter Fourteen
Ingrid

I feel like throwing up, I think as I drink from my glass of water, my empty plate in front of me.

It's not just because I've eaten too much trying to limit my conversation with Rick, which somehow always strays to details about his life, which I find boring, or events in my life, which I don't want to discuss. No, it's mostly because my date is a lecher.

For the past hour and a half, I've been catching Rick staring at my breasts, peeling the top of my dress and maybe even my bra with his eyes. And when he's not trying that, he's dropping a not-so-subtle sexual innuendo or trying to reach across the table for my hand, if not my knee under the white tablecloth.

It makes my stomach churn.

The problem is, I knew what Rick was when I agreed to go out with him. I've seen that gaze before, at the office. Still, I agreed to this, so I have no choice but to endure it and wait until I finally get what I came for—the details of the story he promised.

But a person can only wait so long.

"Aren't you going to tell me about that story now?" I ask as I set down my empty glass, which a waiter promptly refills.

No alcohol for me. It might make the dinner more bearable, but it would probably give Rick the wrong idea.

"You said you'd give me the details after dinner," I remind him.

"But dinner isn't done yet," Rick says, wiping his mouth with the corner of the cloth napkin. "I haven't ordered dessert. I've heard they make the best chocolate cake here. Do you want some?"

I'm well aware of the fact, having chosen the bistro myself. I don't think I can eat another bite, though. "No."

"Don't you like sweet, sticky stuff?" Rick asks. "Or are you saving your appetite for something else?"

I glare at him. *You wish.*

"Suit yourself." He raises his hand. "Waiter!"

I let out a breath of exasperation as Rick smilingly orders his cake.

"You better not go back on your word," I tell him after the waiter has left.

"Don't worry, sweetheart. The story's all here." He takes out a small notebook from his pocket, showing it to me.

I try to swipe it from him, but he jerks it out of my reach, then tucks it back in his pocket as he waves a finger at me.

"Now, now, you have to be patient."

I roll my eyes, swearing that if he doesn't live up to his end of the bargain, I'll punch him in the face. If not in the balls.

The waiter arrives and sets Rick's chocolate cake slice in front of him. He digs into it with his fork, then shoves the fork at me.

"Open wide."

Unable to bear his company any longer, I get out of my chair. "Excuse me. I need to use the ladies' room."

Without waiting for him to say anything, I leave, grabbing my purse.

One of the reasons I chose this bistro was because of its restrooms; they're detached from the rest of the restaurant. Passing through the covered walkway that winds through the fragrant herb garden, I take sanctuary there now.

Leaning on the sink, I stare at it until I don't feel like throwing up in it. Then I lock myself in a cubicle, sitting on the toilet without really doing anything, just passing the time.

Hopefully, by the time I return, Rick will be finished with his cake and finished with his excuses.

As I stare at the cubicle door, my thoughts wander to another man—Conner. I wonder what he's doing with Alexa right now. Whatever it is, I wish I were there with them. I wish I'd listened to him and decided not to go on this date, which is feeling more and more stupid by the second.

Still, that look on his face when he admitted he was jealous was priceless. For once, I felt a power over him, and it felt good.

At the time, it made me want to go out with Rick all the more. Now, it just seems silly. Payback—and yes, this is payback—is a bitch that haunts both the one paying and the one making him pay.

It's too late for regret now, though.

After five minutes, I exit the cubicle and wash my hands out of habit before remembering that I haven't done anything to warrant it. Sighing, I dry them with a paper towel. Then I take a deep breath as I walk out of the bathroom.

I find Rick waiting for me in the small alcove outside the restrooms, which has a marble fountain between two wooden benches.

"What are you doing here?" I ask him, lowering the hand that I clapped to my chest in surprise.

"You were taking too long. I was beginning to think you'd abandoned me."

"Why would I do that when I don't have my story yet?"

He chuckles. "It's always work with you. Is that all that matters to you?"

"Don't forget, Rick. I only had dinner with you because you promised me a story."

"Now you're hurting my feelings." He places his hand over his heart. "Why would you do that, huh?"

He takes a step closer. I take a step back.

"Where's the story, Rick?" I ask him. "Give me your notebook."

He points to the back pocket of his pants. "Come and get it."

I exhale. "You told me you'd give me the story after dinner."

"And I am giving it to you." He taps the notebook.

Son of a bitch.

Fine. If he wants me to get it, I'll get it myself.

I approach him, reaching for the notebook, but as soon as I do, Rick grabs my wrist and wraps his other arm around my waist, pulling me close to him and pressing his lips to mine.

My stomach coiling, I try to wriggle free from his grasp, but he grips my wrist tighter. My purse falls to the floor as pain shoots up my arm. His other hand digs into my hip as well as he forces his tongue past my lips, effectively muffling my protests. Then he lets go to cup one of my breasts.

Panicking, I lift my knee and shove it right into his groin.

"Fuck!"

As he grabs his crotch in pain, I grab the notebook from his pocket, pick up my purse and run.

"Ingrid!" he calls after me. "Come back here, you bitch!"

I ignore him, running inside the bistro and making a beeline for the exit. Reaching the parking lot, I dash to the safety of my car, starting the engine as soon as I'm inside. I step on the gas and drive off without any hesitation or a backward glance. There's only one thing on my mind.

I need to get home.

~

As soon as I get back to my apartment, I rush to the bathroom, pausing only to glance at Alexa, who's fallen asleep on the couch with the TV still on.

I stand in front of the sink and open the faucet. Filling my palm with water, I bring it to my mouth, trying to get rid of every taste of Rick. As I do, I catch glimpses of my reflection in the mirror. My blue eyes are brimming with tears as I recall what Rick did. The scene is playing over and over again in my head in slow motion, every gruesome detail amplified.

I cringe.

How dare he force himself on me.

"Ingrid?"

Conner opens the bathroom's other door, standing in the doorway with just a towel wrapped around his waist. The toned muscles of his chest and his abdomen are laid bare to me for the first time.

He comes closer and cups my face in his hands.

"What did that bastard do to you?" he asks through gritted teeth. "I swear I'll—"

338

I place my hands behind his head and capture his lips, stealing both his breath and his words in one swoop.

When his lips remain still beneath mine, I pull away and drop my hands to his shoulders. He stares at me, his wide eyes searching mine.

I understand his confusion. I can't believe I just kissed him, either. Strangely, though, I don't regret it. If anything, I want to kiss him again, even if it's just so I can forget that filthy man devouring me.

I want him to kiss me.

"Kiss me," I tell him in a whisper.

For a moment, he still hesitates. Then he pulls me by the waist and his mouth falls onto mine.

Wrapping my arms around Conner's neck, I part my lips. His tongue quickly slips through the crack, and I suck on its tip before granting it full entry and letting him take control. My heart begins to pound, and my breathing grows ragged as we deprive each other of air.

His hands caress my back and shivers creep up my spine. Moaning into his mouth, I tug at his hair, my fingernails raking his scalp.

Tongues gliding and lips smacking, we stumble into the shower stall, Conner's hand gripping the back of my dress.

He unzips it, and I pull my arms through the sleeves. The dress wilts. He pushes it past my hips and it pools on the floor.

When his lips find mine again the force of the kiss slams me against the wall. The still-wet tiles are cold beneath my skin. I ignore it, and then forget about it entirely as the delicious friction from Conner's tongue sends heat coursing beneath my skin.

He grabs my wrists and pins them above me just before his mouth leaves mine. I gasp for air, only to have my breath stolen again as his tongue traces the lobe of my ear.

I shiver, but more heat ripples through my veins, gathering in my breasts and in between my legs. My breasts swell, tingling, and a puddle forms in my underwear as the heat leaks out between my legs.

Conner kisses my neck, which I bare to him, before moving lower and planting a kiss in the valley between my breasts. With one hand still holding my wrists in place, the other unhooks my bra. My breasts bounce free but my engorged nipples still ache.

He captures one in his mouth, sucking on the mound of flesh, and I let out a cry that bounces off the bathroom walls. His tongue circles the peak just before his curled lips tug on it.

My hips jerk. My knees buckle.

He does the same to the other mound, and by the time they're both wet, my panties are too.

He lets my wrists go, and his lips press against the curve of my belly before he drops on his knees. As he pulls my panties down, I grip his bare shoulders, leaning on them to maintain my balance. I almost lose it, though, when he clutches my hips and plants his mouth between my legs, his tongue delving inside.

My eyes fall shut, rolling back in my head as pleasure seizes me.

I'm at the mercy of that skillful tongue, which takes a break from exploring my core only to suck on the nub hidden in my curls. I cry out, trembling.

Getting off his knees, he cups my face and swallows my next cry. I taste myself on his tongue and another shiver goes through me.

My hands slide off his shoulders, gliding over muscle. I let my fingers trace them, following the trail that leads lower and lower, stopping when they rub against soft cotton.

With one hard pull, I get rid of the towel, letting it fall to the wet floor. I reach for his crotch and wrap my fingers around his hard cock.

This time, Conner is the one who shivers. A moan escapes from his lips to mine.

And once again, I feel my power over him.

Heady with it, I stroke him, feeling him throb against my palm. My thumb brushes across the leaking tip and he jerks.

"Ingrid." He speaks my name as a breathless warning.

When I don't heed it, stroking him faster in a flurry of mischief, he grabs my wrist to stop me.

Conner pulls me out of the shower stall and out of the bathroom, leading me to Alexa's bed. Throwing me on top of it, he kisses me again as he parts my thighs. The tongue dipping in my mouth reminds me of what's to come, and my heart flutters in anticipation.

The tip of his cock presses against me and I pull my mouth away from his, gaping, gasping. Every breath after that is a gasp, and my lungs are deprived of air as he enters me slowly.

This time, I cling to him because I can, fingers raking across his back.

When his hips start jerking, I grasp his firm buttocks, digging my nails into his skin. I gaze into his burning eyes and realize that my own are brimming with tears. I close them as I move my own hips in rhythm with his.

The bed creaks. The smell of sex and sweat fills the air.

Cries spilling out of my mouth, I throw my head back as I wrap my arms around his neck, feeling myself unravel little by little. When he moves even faster, I come undone, shouting his name to the ceiling.

"Conner, fu…!"

I tremble all over as my breath leaves me. My strength dwindles away.

But Conner still has his, and though I wouldn't have thought it possible, he picks up his pace another notch, managing a few wild thrusts before he buries himself deep inside me and lets go.

I hug him as his body jerks, and when the tremors finally stop I let my hands fall limply to my sides. I part my lips to catch my breath, my heart still in an uproar.

Conner moves off me and lies panting beside me. I reach for his hand with what strength I have left and give it a squeeze. He squeezes it back, turning his head towards me.

At the warmth in his eyes, my heart skips a beat.

"Thank you," I whisper.

"I'm still going to kill him."

I grin but shake my head. "He's not worth it."

"Yeah. You're probably right."

I smile.

Besides, I've already forgotten all about him.

Chapter Fifteen
Conner

I'd forgotten what home felt like, but now I remember it.

As I stand over the bed where Ingrid and Alexa are sleeping soundly, arms around each other, my heart dances to the beat of a soft melody playing inside my head. Before I know it, the corners of my lips curve up into a smile.

I move closer, seized with a desire to run my fingers through the ethereal mess of Ingrid's hair, to plant a kiss on the top of my daughter's head. I don't give in, though. I don't want to wake them. They both need their sleep, Ingrid especially after last night.

At the memory, my heart beats faster.

Ingrid might have been upset. She might simply have been looking for solace. Still, she came to me. She might not know it, but she bared more than her body to me.

She stirs, her head slanting to one side.

I step back and carefully make my way out of the room, glancing back at them one last time before closing the door.

On the kitchen counter, I scribble a note saying that I'm going back to Dallas to interview the couple for my story, something I didn't get the chance to tell Ingrid last night.

Smiling, I end the note with 'Yours, Conner'.

I put her mug over the note to hold it down and make sure she sees it, then grab my laptop and walk out of the apartment, humming.

I almost don't want to leave, but knowing they'll be here when I return spurs me on.

Glancing at the closed door behind me, I make a solemn promise.

I'll be back as soon as I can.

~

"Can you tell me more about that first meeting?" I ask Howard Boyle. I'm sitting across from him and his wife, Sylvia, in the music room of their elegant and, of course, immense Dallas home.

He strokes his pristine, winter-white chin curtain. "Well, it was a rehearsal for an upcoming concert for a small hall in Boston. I remember the piece well. It was Richard Wagner's 'Ride of the Valkyries'. She was a second violinist and she was taking the place of someone who'd gotten sick."

"Myrna," Sylvia supplies, her hands fidgeting with her pearl bracelet. "She got the flu."

"I already noticed her at first, with her messy red hair…"

"I was in a hurry," Sylvia says. "I was sound asleep when they called me and told me I had to fill in for Myrna. I had to rush to the hall. I barely had time to brush my teeth."

"Yeah, she looked like she had just gotten out of bed," Howard recalls, chuckling. "But then the rehearsal started. I began conducting, and when their section came, she held up that violin and she started playing and…"

"I messed up," Sylvia interrupts. "I got out of tune and he scolded me."

"He did?" I raise an eyebrow in surprise, not expecting that twist in the story.

"I did," Howard confirms. "And she started spouting excuses and I lost my temper a bit, so I asked her if she was serious about playing the violin or if she could, in fact, play it."

"I stood up and I started playing a Bartok concerto…" Sylvia stands up, reenacting the moment with an air instrument.

"It's a notoriously difficult piece," Howard informs me. "I've never been able to play it well myself, but she pulled it off and she blew everyone away, including me, of course. Needless to say, I didn't scold her after that."

"He didn't speak to me after that," Sylvia corrects, sitting down.

"Because I was already in love with her," Howard admits. "And I didn't know how to face her. You know, when you're in love with someone, you know you want to be with that person more than anything, but if you don't know whether that person feels the same, then you just feel so afraid. I was terrified."

"Unknown to him, I was already in love with him, too." Sylvia holds her husband's hand, giving him a tender smile. "The moment I saw him up there, I just knew he was the one."

I shift in my seat. "So, how did the two of you come to terms with your feelings? How did you each finally find out how the other felt?"

"I was playing the piano," Howard says. "After a rehearsal. I just felt like it. And she entered the room and played her violin. We played together and there was just this magic in the air."

"It was a concert just for two." Sylvia turns to her husband with a dreamy look in her eyes. "And when it was over, he stood up, I fell into his arms and we kissed."

He turns to her, their lips almost touching.

I look away, almost feeling like an intruder instead of an interviewer. "How long after that did you get married?"

"It was years later," Howard answers. "We decided we'd focus on our careers first. We traveled the world. She became my concert mistress. When we weren't rehearsing, we'd explore the cities or we'd simply lock ourselves up in a room and play our own music."

Sylvia blushes.

"It wasn't all champagne and roses, though," Howard adds. "We had our squabbles. We had our jealous fits."

Sylvia grins. "Oh, I remember."

"But by time we got off stage, everything was patched up," Howard says.

I rub my chin. "The music really was your connection, wasn't it?"

"It was," they answer in unison.

I make a note of it on my laptop.

"Now, could you please tell me about life after the orchestra?"

~

An orchestra of two, I type on my laptop in the middle of the hotel lobby.

Reviewing the screen, I put in a few more words, then I close the lid with a rush of satisfaction and sit back as I pick up my cup of coffee.

Bringing it to my lips, I look around.

The holly and the sparkling tinsel have come down now, replaced by pink hearts and colorful flowers.

In just over a week, it will be Valentine's Day, which means my story is nearly due, so it's a good thing I already have it done.

In just over a week, Tiffany, Ed, Ingrid and I will all find out who gets the job.

Speaking of Tiffany, I suddenly spot her crossing the lobby in a black-and-white dress, her electric pink heels clattering across the marble floor.

What on earth is she doing here?

Before I can look away, she turns her head and our eyes meet. Smiling, she walks over to me while I quickly gather my things to prepare for a hasty exit.

"Conner." She says my name with a smile that matches the gleam of her large earrings.

"Tiffany," I acknowledge without much enthusiasm.

Her hand goes to her hip. Her nails are the same shade as her shoes but with more glitter. "What are you doing here?"

"Work," I answer curtly.

"That's weird. Me too." She places her other hand on her cleavage. "You know, I'm so sorry for how I behaved last time. You did get the apologies I sent you, right? I hope you don't mind. I asked Cassie for your number."

I shake my head. "It's fine."

She lets out a deep breath. "I was desperate. I was going to do what you suggested, too, but I've had the most unbelievable stroke of luck."

"You found your story?"

"Yes, or rather, it found me."

She turns around, gesturing to the couple behind her—a brunette in her thirties dressed in red with a white shawl, arm in arm with a man in a crisp dark gray suit and a black scarf. Lifting his dark sunglasses to the top of his head of salt-and-pepper hair, he smiles.

A lump forms in my throat and my muscles tense as I recognize him.

Oh, fuck.

"Conner, this is Damien Shore and his fiancée, Margot," Tiffany introduces us. "Mr. Shore, this is Conner Blake, a colleague."

I stand up as Damien offers me his hand, swallowing before I shake it. "I'm pleased to meet you, Mr. Shore."

"No. I'm pleased to meet you," he says. "You don't know how long I've been waiting for this moment."

His grip tightens and my chest does as well.

"You know him?" Tiffany turns to Damien with raised eyebrows.

"You bet I do," he says, still not releasing my hand. "He was a guest at my party just before I went to prison."

The lump in my throat gets bigger.

"Tell me, Mr. Blake, did you enjoy that party? I do pride myself on throwing the best parties, you know, and satisfying all my guests."

"I did," I answer.

He lowers his voice. "That woman with you was something, wasn't she?"

My heart stops. He knows about Ingrid?

"Where is she now? I wonder."

I lower my gaze. "I…"

"Oh, Conner isn't with any woman at the moment," Tiffany says.

"Is that right?" Damien asks.

Why is he so interested?

He lets my hand go. "Well, not everyone thinks they need love." He strokes Margot's cheek. "It took me seven years in prison to realize otherwise. I'm grateful to you, really."

Tiffany's brows furrow. "Am I missing something here?"

"Oh, just that Mr. Blake here was the one who wrote that very interesting article that sent me to prison," Damien informs her. "Isn't that right, boys?"

He glances at the two heavily built men in black behind him and I swallow hard, suppressing a shiver.

"But I've already forgiven him." He pats my shoulder in a seemingly friendly gesture, though the force behind his hand lets me know it's anything but. "Like I said, I'm a changed man now."

I force a smile. Is he really? Has he forgiven me?

"Well, love can change a man," Tiffany says. "You know, Mr. Shore and Margot have a very touching love story. They…"

I stop listening, my attention diverted as Margot drops the purse she's been fidgeting with. She kneels down to pick it up, and so do I. As she stands up, her shawl slides off and I see bruises.

Marks from a whip.

Quickly, she pulls her shawl back in place.

"Thank you," she mutters, her eyes telling me something else.

Damien Shore is not a forgiving man.

I grab my laptop. "I'm sorry, Tiffany, but I have to go. Like I said, work."

"Of course." She turns to me. "I wouldn't want to keep you. It was nice bumping into you here, though."

"Yeah. It was nice," Damien seconds. "I look forward to reading more of your stories."

I simply nod before making my escape, holding my breath as I feel eyes pierce my back like daggers.

Only once I'm in a cab do I manage to breathe, but even then, fear still grips my gut just as hard as Damien Shore's hand gripped mine.

It was a threat. I know it. He's coming after me.

I take out my phone to type Ingrid a message. I know that I have to leave her alone so that at least she can be safe from Damien's reach. I end up staring at the screen, my hands shaking.

What do I tell her?

One of my hands clenches into a fist. How the hell did that bastard go free? Why does this have to happen now?

I don't want to leave Ingrid. Not now. Maybe not ever. But I have to, so with my gut wrenching, I type the letters, each one like a fragment breaking off my soul.

Suddenly, my phone vibrates.

Startled, I nearly drop it.

Muttering a curse, I hold it firmly and look at the screen. It tells me I have a message from Ingrid.

Discarding my message, I read hers.

Hope you're OK. Got my interview. It's at a ski resort in Aspen tomorrow. Wanna come along?

I sit back, drawing a deep breath.

I shouldn't. I know I shouldn't. Every moment she stays with me is another moment I'm risking her life, which I can't have.

Then again, if I'm leaving her, then I should tell her in person. She deserves that much.

I stare at my phone, fingers running over the screen.

I have to say goodbye. In Aspen.

With my heart sinking, I type a new message, this one just as painful.

I'll be back tonight. Looking forward to Aspen.

Chapter Sixteen
Ingrid

In all my years in Colorado, I've never been to Aspen, and now that I'm in a log cabin, staring out the window, I wonder why.

Under a thin blanket of snow, white hills and rows of pine trees stretch out before me, cream-capped mountains looming over them. I can catch a glimpse of some skiers, too, all wrapped up, and the smoke rising from the chimneys of the other cabins.

It's a whole other world, one that's enchanting, adventurous and serene all at once.

"I wish Alexa could see all this," I tell Conner. "I swear I'll bring her here someday."

Sitting in front of the fireplace with his gaze lost among the flames, Conner says nothing.

I call his name.

He turns to me. "What?"

I walk over to him, eyes narrowed suspiciously. "Are you okay?"

"Yeah." He nods, staring back at the fire. "Yeah, I'm fine."

But I know he's not. Ever since he returned from Dallas, he's been quieter, deep in thought and distant. Even when he was smiling at Alexa, I could see a glint of sorrow in his eyes, and twice I could swear he was avoiding me. He got off the couch just as soon as I got on it and left the bathroom as soon as I got there. He said he was done brushing his teeth, even though I could see he'd just started.

What happened in Dallas?

I'm about to ask but decide it's best to hold this conversation after my interview, which is starting in less than half an hour.

I place a hand on Conner's shoulder. "Shall we go get that story?"

~

"There's not much to tell, I'm afraid," Astrid says, her fingers fidgeting with the edge of her blue scarf.

She's seemed nervous since the interview started, even though it's just me, Conner, and her husband, Trevor, seated in front of the fire of their luxurious cabin.

"How did you meet?" I ask.

"Just online," she says, avoiding my gaze.

"We're both gamers," Trevor elaborates. "And we met in an online game. We started chatting, first about the game and then about other stuff, and we just got so interested in each other we decided to meet. I had no clue she was a princess."

"I'm not a princess," Astrid says. "I'm more of a duchess. It's my second half cousin who's a princess."

My eyebrows furrow. "I see."

"She's still a princess to me," Trevor says.

Astrid blushes.

And she looks like one, with hair like golden yarn from a fairy's loom, bluish green eyes under thick lashes and high cheekbones. The soft, caressing way she speaks and the finesse in her movements lends her an air of grace as well.

"Does your family know you're here?" I ask her.

She nods. "But they don't know I'm with Trevor yet."

"I thought this article you're writing might be a good way to tell them," Trevor says. "It's going to be available online, right?"

I nod. "But shouldn't you tell them in person first?"

"They won't like Trevor," Astrid says. "They don't even like me. I don't want to talk to them."

"But surely it's better if you do," I remark. "Right, Conner?"

He stares at his lap and doesn't answer.

"Conner." I tap his shoulder.

"Sorry," he mutters. "What did you say?"

I give him a hopeless frown.

"I'm sorry, but I thought this was an interview," Trevor says. "Not a counseling session or something."

"Sorry," I tell him, placing both hands back on my lap. "You're right. But are you sure you want to share your story with your family in this way? I mean, no offense, but you don't seem ready to tell them."

"Yeah, we are." Trevor holds Astrid's hand. "We're done with hiding. But we also don't want a confrontation or anything like that."

I touch my chin. "I see. Well, tell me more about your meeting, then. What was it like to see each other face to face for the first time?"

"I was blown away," Trevor admits. "She was much more beautiful than I imagined. I thought she wasn't real."

"I thought you weren't real," Astrid says, tucking a strand of hair behind her ear. "Because you look so much like your character in the game."

"When did you get married?" I ask, crossing my legs.

"Just last year," Trevor replies. "It was just an intimate ceremony in a tree house in Washington."

"A tree house?" I smile. "How romantic."

They both nod and smile but offer no further details.

I tap my fingers on my lap. "So, what are your hopes for the future?"

"Nothing set in stone," Astrid says. "We take each day as it comes."

Okay. No future planned.

"What makes you think your love will last?" I ask. "What do you do? Like, do you have a special routine or something the two of you do that strengthens your bond?"

"We just play together," Astrid says. "Video games, I mean."

"Or we dress up as our favorite video game characters by sprucing up ordinary clothes with items we see lying around the house," Trevor offers. "Just for each other. You know, to make each other laugh."

I smile as I imagine it. "Awesome."

"Sometimes, I dress up as a female character and she dresses up as a male. Just to keep it more interesting," Trevor blurts out.

Astrid falls silent.

"Oh." Trevor looks at her in concern. "I shouldn't have said that?"

"Please take that off the record," Astrid tells me.

I nod. "The cross-dressing part?"

"The whole dress-up thing," Astrid says to my dismay. "It's embarrassing."

"It's not," I tell her. "It's... fun." I glance at Conner, nudging his shoulder. "Right, Conner?"

"If she thinks it's best to leave it out, then maybe she's right," Conner answers, even more to my dismay.

What?

"Please leave it out," Astrid repeats.

My shoulders sink. "But..."

"If that's what she thinks, she must have a good reason for it," Conner says. "We shouldn't judge her. We should just respect her decision."

My jaw drops. Unbelievable. Did he just dis me in front of a source?

"Conner..."

"I think they've told us all they want us to know." Conner stands up. "Thank you for sharing your story."

He heads to the door.

I put on a smile for Astrid and Trevor and shake their hands. "Thank you so much for your story."

I gather my things and walk out of the cabin after Conner, who's already several feet ahead of me.

"Conner!" I shout after him. "Wait!"

To my relief, he stops.

"Conner, what's going on?" I ask him when I've caught up to him. "What happened back there?"

Averting his gaze, he doesn't answer.

"Look at me." I stand in front of him. "What happened in Dallas? What's the problem?"

He draws a deep breath. "I'm sorry, Ingrid, but we can't do this anymore."

"What?"

He walks away, leaving me with my hands on my hips, completely baffled.

We can't do this anymore? We can't do what anymore? And why?

Since he's already gone, I get no answers, of course, just more questions. I could chase after him, but I've already tried that.

If he doesn't want to talk to me, fine. If he doesn't want to stay around anymore, fine. I don't understand it one bit, but fine.

Tucking my hands in my pockets, I walk to town, thinking of stopping by a bar.

I need a drink.

~

I gulp down my second vodka and coke, wincing at the bitter taste as I set the empty glass down on the wooden counter with a soft thud. The liquid blazes down my throat and I loosen my scarf, feeling the heat.

Damn, that felt good.

Unfortunately, it hasn't made me feel good enough. I can still remember what Conner did.

Jerk.

I'm about to order a third glass, but a woman's voice interrupts.

"Sure you should be drinking?"

I turn my head to see Astrid sliding onto the stool next to mine.

"No," I tell her. "But I will anyway. What are you going to do about it?"

"Join you," she says, grinning.

Ah. The princess drinks.

"Two vodka and cokes, please," she tells the bartender.

"What are you doing here?" I ask her, resting my elbows on the counter.

"I thought I owed you an apology." She clasps her hands. "I'm sorry I didn't say much."

"It's okay."

"Frankly, it's not easy to talk about me and Trevor," she opens up. "It's not that I don't want to. It's just that it still feels unreal, and call me crazy, but that makes it magical for me. I feel like if I share the story then it'll somehow lose its magic. Does that make sense?"

I nod. "Sometimes speaking of something gives it power, and sometimes speaking of something makes it lose its power."

"Yeah. Something like that."

The bartender sets our drinks in front of us.

"Thanks," Astrid mutters.

"So, you don't really want your story published?" I ask her, turning my stool to face her.

She shakes her head. "But Trevor thinks it's not a bad idea."

"Maybe not, but if you don't feel like it should be published, then it shouldn't be. It's your story, after all. It's yours more than anyone's."

"Really?" Her blue eyes grow wide. "I thought you needed the story."

"It's fine." I shrug. "Maybe I'm only saying this because I'm drunk, but I don't mind letting go of a story just this once if it means someone else can hold on to happiness a little longer. Lord knows there's not enough in this world."

"Thank you." Astrid places her hand over mine.

"And I sure hope you can hold on to it." I squeeze her hand. "Don't let anyone, not even your royal family, tear you apart."

"Shh." She holds a finger to her lips.

I purse my lips. "Sorry. I forgot it was still a secret."

"I hope you can, too," Astrid says.

I tap my fingers on my glass. "What do you mean?"

"I saw you and… that guy with you fighting from our cabin. I'm sorry if I caused it."

I grab Astrid's hand. "You didn't cause it. I don't know what's wrong with him."

She shrugs. "Maybe Trevor will find out. I told him to see if he could talk to your boyfriend. You're not the only one who seems to need a friend."

"You did?" My eyebrows pull up. "Oh, and Conner's not my boyfriend."

"He's not?"

"We just... work together." I sip from my drink.

"Okay. I'm so sorry. It's just that you seemed..."

"It's fine," I tell her. "And don't worry about us. We'll be fine. I'll..."

I stop, placing my hands over my eyes as tears swell. What's wrong with me?

"Ingrid?" Astrid places her hand on my shoulder.

"I'll be okay," I assure her, wiping my tears and forcing the rest back. "I just don't know what's going on right now. I mean, I thought everything was going right and now... I just don't know. But I'll be okay. We girls always manage, right?"

"To us." Astrid raises her glass.

I raise mine, too. "To us."

I gulp down the contents of my third glass as she drains her first.

Afterwards, she frowns. "That's... strong. But good."

I chuckle. "Wait. Don't tell me this is your first time drinking?"

"No, but I've never tried this drink before."

I shake my head. "I am such a bad influence."

"No, you're not," Astrid tells me with a sweet smile. "You're a good friend."

My eyebrows go up. Friend?

Just then, I see someone familiar walking past the window on crutches.

Ed? What's Ed doing here?

"Is everything alright?" Astrid asks.

I nod. "Yeah. Everything's better than alright now that I've made a new friend."

Her eyes sparkle. "I don't really have a girlfriend, I mean a girl who's a friend, or a woman. You know what I mean."

"I do." I place my hand over hers. "So, girlfriend, tell me more about yourself."

~

"Can you believe Astrid knows twenty-two different languages?" I ask Conner, my arm over his as he hauls me out of the bar an hour later, having suddenly appeared with Trevor.

"Yes," he answers. "And I can believe she can't speak any of those right now. How could you get your source drunk?"

"She's not my source, not anymore," I tell him. "She's just my friend now."

"Okay."

"I think we'll be friends for life," I add. "After all, we both have Norwegian names."

"Well, it's good that you can still remember your name, seeing how much you drank."

I push him away, wobbling. "I am not drunk."

"Really?"

"And even if I am, what do you care?" I point a finger at him. "Didn't you toss me aside? Haven't you been avoiding me?"

"I..."

"I knew you'd always be a jerk," I cut him off, walking ahead.

I stumble and he offers to help me, but I shrug his arm off and continue.

He doesn't chase after me, lagging behind as we walk the rest of the way in silence broken only by the sound of our footsteps in the snow. Finally, after what feels like an eternity of stumbling, we reach our cabin.

Outside the door, I turn around, facing Conner. "You're still here."

"Of course I am. We need to talk, Ingrid."

"Oh, now we need to talk. And what if I don't want to, huh?"

"Ingrid…"

I shove him back with both hands. "Who do you think you are, always messing me up?"

"I…"

"Isn't it enough that you stole my story? You have to steal my heart, too?" The words gush out of my mouth without a pause for thought.

He falls silent, lips parted.

I clasp my hand over my mouth as I realize what I've just said, then quickly retreat inside the house.

For some reason, the door's open, which is good because I can't wait to get inside. But as soon as I do, I stop. My knees finally fail me and I drop to the floor at the sight before me.

Ed is lying on the floor, his neck bent in an impossible way, his eyes open and staring at the ceiling, lifeless.

I scream.

Chapter Seventeen
Conner

Ed is dead.

Pacing the floor in the living room of our new cabin, I still can't believe it. My gut coils and shivers break out across my back each time I think of it.

Worse, he was clearly murdered. No question of an accident, and whoever did it didn't even bother to make it look like suicide.

It was cold-blooded murder of a man who couldn't put up a fight.

Vile.

Why would anyone murder Ed Parker? Well, I can think of a few reasons. Maybe he set off someone at work. Ed isn't—wasn't—exactly a charming person, after all. Maybe one of his stories pissed off someone powerful. That's usually the way journalists go. Or maybe it's personal, though I don't know enough about his personal life to guess how.

And that's not all the mystery.

Why murder Ed in the cabin I'm sharing with Ingrid? Why not in his cabin? Or just dump his body outside and leave it to be covered in snow until summer? What, the murderer was cold-blooded enough to lie in wait and break Ed's neck but wouldn't stoop to concealing his body? Why did he want it to be discovered by Ingrid and me?

I sit on the edge of the couch, burying my face in my still shaking hands.

Come to think of it, it's a good thing I was with Trevor and Ingrid was with Astrid. Considering the competition we're in, we might have come under suspicion if we had no alibis. Even so, this is all such a mess.

Of course, Ingrid is shaken too, more so than I am since she found his body first. The last time I saw her, she was throwing up in the toilet.

Deciding to check on her, I head upstairs. I find her in the bedroom, sitting on the black sheepskin rug in front of the fire in her pajamas with her legs crossed. Her hands are clasped behind her neck, her eyes on the flames.

"Hey." I cross my legs beside her. "How are you doing?"

Ingrid turns to me with arched eyebrows, hands falling to her lap. "How do you think a person would do after seeing the corpse of someone she knows?"

"Worse," I answer simply, ignoring her barbed tone.

She turns back to the fire. "I saw him, you know, earlier. He was alive. I didn't see his face, but he seemed fine."

My eyebrows bunch up. "You did too?"

She looks at me. "What do you mean 'too'?"

"I saw him too, there in town," I inform her. "We spoke. As usual, he was trying to get me into an argument, but I didn't feel like it. And then Trevor found me and Ed just left. He was fine."

"What do you think he was doing here?" Ingrid asks me.

I shrug. "Your guess is as good as mine."

"And what was he doing in our cabin?"

I give another shrug.

Ingrid runs her fingers through her hair as she stands up. "I don't understand it. I don't understand anything. I don't even understand you. Why would you say that to me, huh? Why are you doing this to me?"

She shakes her head as she walks to the window, hands on her hips.

"You know, you're so unfair. You're no different from the guy who murdered Ed. I open myself to you a little and you barge right in and walk all over me, rip me apart and take everything from me. Why? What did I ever do to you?"

A lump forms in my throat as I stand up, my chest hurting from her words—both the ones she just said and those she said earlier.

She's right. She hasn't done anything to deserve all this. She didn't do anything to justify me stealing her story. I was a jerk. She didn't ask for a child. I was careless, even though I was the one who should have been careful. She didn't ask me back into her life. I barged in. I turned everything upside down. She told me to stay away because she knew I'd exploit her weakness. I couldn't.

Ingrid is right. I'm just as cold-blooded as Ed's murderer.

I hurt her. I took advantage of her. I tricked her. I tempted her. Worst of all, I stole her heart.

And now I'm thinking of leaving her?

What a fool I am. I can't leave her.

If there's anything Ed's death has taught me, it's that life is too short to mistakes, to walk away from the things that make you happy.

Besides, Ingrid and Alexa need me. And I need them.

Crossing the gap between us with long strides, I grab Ingrid's shoulders, turning her around. I pull her into my arms, my mouth holding hers captive.

She tries to shove me away, and when I don't let go, she beats my chest with her fists, her mouth squirming beneath mine.

I grab her wrists, pinning them above her head as I kiss her harder. Still, she struggles.

"If you want me to stop resisting you, you'll have to tie me up," she hisses, daggers in her eyes.

I stroke her cheek. "Is that a challenge?"

"What are you going to do? Run away?" she taunts. "What? You can tie me up when I'm not asking but not when I am?"

My jaw clenches. "If that's what you want, so be it."

I pull the sash off my robe, securing her wrists behind her.

"Better?"

She gives me a devilish grin. "Now fuck me like you mean it."

That's exactly what I intend to do. I press my mouth to hers as I cup her cheek. Her lips part and I suck on her tongue, tasting traces of vodka, coke and toothpaste before delving in.

As my tongue plays with hers, I let my hands have their fun, popping the buttons of her pajamas one by one. I cup both her breasts, one in each hand, thumbs pressing against her nipples.

She moans, trembling. The rosy peaks stiffen.

I lower my head to lick one as I slip my hand beneath two layers of garter. My fingers brush against the button in her curls and she cries out.

Moving my mouth to her other breast, I slip a finger inside her. The opening is already moist. Hot.

The heat goes all the way to my crotch. The front of my briefs grows tighter.

I slip another finger inside her, both fingers becoming coated in her sweet juices as they reach in deeply.

She gives a loud moan.

I swallow the next one as I pull out my fingers to tease her nub, now engorged and craving for attention. I strum it and she throws her head back. I bend it back even further, my tongue reaching as far as it can go.

When she pulls away to breathe, I lead her to the bed and bend her over its edge. Pulling her pants and underwear off, I toss them away and bend over to lick her from behind.

She thrashes on the bed, knees shaking.

"Conner," she gasps my name as she gets wetter.

A stain forms on my own briefs as my cock throbs.

I take it out, grip her hips, lift them slightly and enter her.

Her hands clench and unclench into fists behind her. Her cries are muffled by the sheets.

I pound into her, setting a hard pace from the start, and my robe falls off my shoulders. I reach for her breasts, letting them jiggle in my palms, and then I reach between her legs, stroking her as I jerk my hips.

Her hips move against mine. I can hear my heavy balls slapping against her skin. Then she stops and gives a particularly loud cry, her body trembling and squeezing me.

When she's done, she falls forward on the bed, but I'm unwilling to let her go. I grip one of her arms, my other hand clutching her hip as I manage a few more thrusts.

351

My jaw clenched, I release myself inside her, my muscles growing taut as I hold my breath. Only now do I release her, letting her fall on top of the bed as I stand above her, my chest heaving as my lungs pull in air.

When I've caught my breath, I free her wrists. She turns to face me, her eyes still teary, cheeks still flushed.

Discarding my robe, I lean over and kiss her still swollen lips. She kisses me back, her hand reaching for my crotch.

I jerk as her fingers brush against my cock, still erect and tingling from my recent ejaculation.

"Careful," I warn.

She moves her hand to stroke my balls instead, cupping them in her palm.

I plant a kiss just below her ear, sucking on the flesh. Suddenly, Ingrid pushes me away.

She kneels in front of me and, gripping my ass, starts licking the length of my cock.

I grab her shoulders, shuddering.

"Shit!"

"Am I being careful enough for you?" she asks, mischievous eyes glancing up at me.

Before I can answer, she wraps her lips around the tip of my cock, eyes still holding mine. Legs trembling, I purse my lips tight to hold back a moan.

She sucks on me and I let out a gasp. My hands go to her hair, becoming entangled with the soft tendrils. I pull at them, torn between pulling her close or pushing her away.

Her tongue glides across my sensitive skin. Her lips have me trapped, and the friction is building as she moves faster.

"Mmm…"

Grabbing her shoulders, I pull her off me and toss her onto the bed.

"Why did you have to do that, huh?" I ask her. "I intended to be gentle the second time."

"Maybe I don't want you to be gentle," Ingrid says, licking her lips as her fingertips dance across my wet cock, making me draw in a deep breath. "You and I, we're already a mess. Why hold back?"

She has a point. At any rate, I'm done holding back.

Ingrid cries out, throwing her head back as I sheath myself in her heat a second time, this time with one long thrust. She grips the sheets, her back arching.

Bending her nearly in half, the backs of her knees on my shoulders, I propel myself forward, moving in and out of that tight, exquisite passage. She clings to me, gasping and moaning, her body rocking with mine.

This time, we reach the peak of pleasure at the same time, her body quivering beneath mine as I spill out every last drop of me. Her cries mix with my grunts, both eventually fading to breathless gasps.

Pulling out, I lie down beside her, breathing heavily, my mind still spinning.

I can feel the buzz of sleep at the back of my head, but I push it away, keeping my eyes open as I pull Ingrid close. Still gasping for air, she rests her head on my shoulder. Her breasts are pinned against half my chest and one of her legs drapes over mine.

"What did you mean?" she asks in a whisper, lifting her head to look at me. "What did you mean when you said you didn't want to do this any longer?"

I gaze into her eyes as I run my fingers through her hair. "I meant we can't deny ourselves any longer." I stroke her cheek with my other hand. "Like you said, no more holding back."

Her eyebrows crease. "Why were you avoiding me, then?"

"I was struggling to say it, but now I can." I press my lips to her forehead. "I love you, Ingrid. I'm sorry for everything."

She shakes her head as she strokes my cheek. "I love you, Conner."

We kiss, slowly, savoring every second. My heart pounds. My chest floods with warmth.

Damn, I love her. And I'm never letting her go.

Ingrid pulls away, smiling. "You had to go to Dallas to realize it?"

"No." I kiss her hand. "I've loved you all along."

She nods and nuzzles against me, still with that sweet smile on.

I kiss the top of her head as I let my fingers entwine with hers.

Yes, I've been such a jerk, but that ends now. I'm going to take care of Ingrid and our daughter. And if Damien Shore threatens us, I'm going to do everything I can to protect my family.

No more running. No more messing around. No more games.

Pulling the blanket over us, I hug Ingrid tighter as I close my eyes, surrendering to the lull of sleep.

Chapter Eighteen
Ingrid

I wake up to a chill in the air.

I tug on the blanket, pulling it to my shoulders, only to realize I'm naked beneath it.

I open my eyes, staring at the pine ceiling. It still has a streak of gold from the glow of the lamp, but now that's not the only light in the room. Slivers of sunlight are drifting in through the window.

I turn my head, staring at Conner, who's still sleeping beside me. Remembering what he said last night, I smile.

He loves me.

I can't wipe the smile off my face as I get out of bed and put my pajamas back on.

I never thought we'd end up together. I thought for sure—and I sincerely hoped—that I was never going to see him again after I left Dallas. Yet here he is, the father of my child and my lover. And here I am, completely in love with him.

I guess I have been all along.

Eliza's right. Hate isn't the opposite of love. Although now that I think about it, maybe I never really hated him. I was just hurt. She was right, too, to say that it all starts with a little lust, which we humans strive to fight.

Well, the fight is over now. From now on, Conner and I will be together.

My smile vanishes when I think of Alexa pouting, getting mad at me because I didn't tell her Conner was her father. But it returns when I think of how happy she'll be to know it, to finally have a father.

We're going to be a family.

What started out as a night that got out of hand has has somehow ended up as a happy family.

Now, that's a love story.

I touch my chin. Well, that gives me an idea.

After slipping the last button of my pajama top in place, I head for the bathroom, but stop when I hear something vibrating.

A phone.

I check mine on the nightstand, but it's not the one making the sound. The vibration is coming from inside the nightstand.

Pulling the drawer out, I pick up Conner's phone. My eyebrows furrow at the unregistered number.

Curious, I swipe the screen to unlock it and open the message.

Conner, I need to talk to you as soon as possible. Can I call you?

Now I'm really curious.

I scroll down to the very bottom.

Conner, I'm sorry about earlier. Oh, and thanks for the tip.—Tiffany

Holding my breath, I read the rest, moving up. Then I stop at a more recent message.

It was so nice seeing you in Dallas. I knew you were naughty, but I didn't know you could be such a bad, bad boy!

My heart sinks and a lump rises in my throat. They met in Dallas?

The message is followed by another.

Hope you got back safely. I can't wait to see what other tricks you have up your sleeve. See you soon!

I sit on the edge of the bed. All of a sudden, my legs feel weak and my chest so tight I can barely breathe.

Conner was with Tiffany?

I shake my head. No, wait. Maybe I'm reading too much into this. Maybe they just bumped into each other and talked about work. But why would Tiffany be in Dallas and at the same time Conner was, and why did she say he was naughty?

My mind spinning, I check Conner's other messages. My eyebrows arch when I find the draft of a message he was going to send to me.

I read it.

I'm sorry, Ingrid, but I'm not coming back. I can't stay with you. I can't...

The message is unfinished, but the gist is clear.

When he was in Dallas, he was thinking of not coming back. He was thinking of leaving me after being with Tiffany.

That's why he said we can't do this anymore.

That's why he was avoiding me.

A tear rolls down my cheek. I let it.

I don't know what hurts more—the fact that Conner's a jerk or the fact that I'm a fool.

I've always been a fool when it came to love.

The phone in my hand vibrates again. It's a call from Tiffany.

"Who's that?" Conner asks, stirring behind me.

"Tiffany," I answer, getting off the bed and throwing the phone at him.

Rubbing his eyes, he gives me a puzzled look. "What's wrong?"

I cross my arms over my chest. "You met Tiffany in Dallas, didn't you?"

Conner glances at his phone. "You read my messages?"

"A small crime compared to stealing my story," I tell him. "Besides, I wanted to know if you really loved me. And guess what? You're just a jerk and a liar."

"You misunderstand." He sits up. "Yes, I bumped into Tiffany in Dallas..."

"Bumped into her?" I roll my eyes. "What a nice way of putting it."

"We just met. Nothing happened."

"You mean you did nothing naughty?" I ask him.

"Shit." He goes through his messages. "I don't even know what she texted. I didn't read her messages."

The phone vibrates again.

"Maybe you should answer that," I tell him. "It seems like she really misses you."

Conner frowns, dropping the phone and standing up. "It's not like that."

I step back. "And what about that message you were going to send me? The one which said you were never coming back."

He draws a deep breath.

"What? You just accidentally typed that? Were you practicing?"

"Fine. I wasn't going to come back. I was..."

"Because you like Tiffany better?"

"It has nothing to do with Tiffany."

"But you typed that message while you were with Tiffany, right?"

"It has nothing to do with Tiffany!" he repeats louder, shaking his head.

Rubbing my ears, I walk away.

"I'm sorry." He grabs my hand. "I didn't mean to shout. Seriously though, she..."

"I don't care, okay?" I shout in turn, wrenching my hand away. "You were thinking of not coming back."

"I..."

"You were thinking of just disappearing on Alexa and me." Another tear rolls down my cheek. "You were going to leave me just like that."

"But I came back," he says.

"Yes, but you were different. You were still contemplating leaving me, weren't you? That's why you were acting weird."

He sighs. "Fine. I admit it, but..."

I slap my forehead, my other hand on my chest as I struggle to breathe at his admission.

"Ingrid..."

He places his hand on my arm, but I jerk away. "Don't touch me! You're a liar. You don't love me. You can't love me. You've just been using me all this time."

"That's not true."

"Enough!" I shout at him. "I've had enough, Conner! Yes, you stole my heart, but that doesn't mean you can keep it. That doesn't mean you'll always have it. I'm taking it back."

I open the closet and shove my things inside my suitcase.

"Ingrid." He grabs my arm.

I shake his hand off. "Don't ever touch me again, and don't you even think about coming near Alexa again. Maybe I didn't hate you before, but now I do. And I'm not going to let you hurt me anymore."

"You're making a mistake, Ingrid."

"No. I'm making things right. Now, get out of my sight!" I point to the door.

"What?"

"Get out!"

He picks his robe off the floor, grabs his phone and goes to the door, glancing at me over his shoulder.

"Go to hell, Conner Blake."

I shut the door and lean against it with my shoulders still shaking. Then, as my tears break free, I slide down to the floor. My hands gripping my hair, I break into a sob, lamenting my crushed dreams of a happy family, my foolishness.

The worst part is that I still don't have my heart back, and a voice in my head is telling me I never will.

~

"Mommy, you're back!" Alexa rushes over to me as soon as I step inside Janine's apartment, a huge smile on her face.

I scoop her in my arms, whirling her around before hugging her tight. "Oh, sweetheart, I've missed you!"

"Mom, you're squishing me," she complains.

I let her go, stroking her hair. "Sorry. I got carried away."

"How was your trip?" Janine asks, coming out of the bedroom.

"Fine," I lie.

Janine comes closer. "Wait. Have you been crying? Your eyes look red."

"They're not," I protest, throwing her a reprimanding glance.

"Where's Conner?" Alexa asks. "Is he back at the apartment? Can we go there now? I have a lot of stuff to tell him about Luna and Lulu."

She glances at the mouse cage on the floor.

At the excitement in her eyes, my heart sinks and a lump forms in my throat. I swallow it, though, and summon my courage as I kneel before her.

"Alexa…"

"Where's Conner?" she repeats, some of the excitement in her eyes diminished.

She knows. Of course she does.

"Conner isn't here," I tell her.

"Where is he?"

"He's not coming back, sweetheart," I blurt out.

Janine gasps. The corners of Alexa's mouth droop along with her shoulders, and her small eyebrows bunch together.

"What do you mean?" she asks softly, on the brink of tears.

I stroke her hair. "Honey, Conner was never meant to stay. You know that, right? He was only staying with us for a little while."

"Temporarily," Alexa says. "So, he's gone now?"

I nod.

"Where did he go?"

"I don't know." I shrug. "But Mommy's here, and Mommy's not going anywhere."

Alexa steps back. "Did you two have a fight?"

"What?" I stand up slowly. "No, sweetheart."

"Are you lying?"

I scratch my forehead.

"You are lying. I can tell," Alexa says, her eyes narrow.

"Fine," I admit, having no other choice. "We had a small fight."

"So you made him leave?" Alexa asks.

I put my hands up. "I did not make him leave."

"He wasn't gonna leave. He told me so."

I roll my eyes.

Great. Just great.

"And he wouldn't leave without saying goodbye or telling me why," Alexa adds. "You made him leave, didn't you? Because he made you angry? Because he made you cry?"

I give her a look of disbelief. Am I seriously having to defend myself to my six-year-old daughter?

"I did not make him leave!"

"You're lying!" Alexa shouts back. "Bring him back!"

I sigh, shoulders heaving. "Alexa, I can't…"

"Until you bring him back, I'm not going back to the apartment with you!" Alexa turns her back to me, marching to the bedroom.

My hands roll into fists. "Alexa, come back here! Alexa! I'm your mother, for goodness' sake. You can't…"

She slams the door.

I let out a deep breath, rubbing my temples. Janine throws me a sympathetic look.

"I thought she wasn't going to rebel until she was fifteen," I tell her.

Janine shrugs. "What can I say? She's wise beyond her years. And sassy beyond her years."

I sit on the arm of the couch, hands gripping my hair. "What am I going to do?"

"Bring Conner back?" Janine suggests.

I narrow my eyes at her.

"Okay." She raises her hands. "So, that's not an option?"

"No," I confirm. "He's gone for good."

"Am I allowed to ask why?"

I say nothing.

"I'll take that as a no, but the fact that your eyes are red means that you didn't want him to leave."

"I did. I just…"

"See, you made him leave!" Alexa shouts from the bedroom.

I stand up, shoulders drooping. "Can we just not talk about this?"

"Okay," Janine says.

I glance at the closed bedroom door. "Can Alexa stay here with you for a while?"

"Are you seriously asking me that? Of course she can. Not that she'd have it any other way."

I look at Janine. "Sometimes I wonder if you're her best friend or mine."

"I'm your best friend and hers." Janine squeezes my shoulder. "Give it time. She'll be fine, and so will you. You're both strong women."

"She's a girl," I correct.

"You're both strong." Janine pats my shoulder. "And stubborn. You're very alike, actually. You really are mother and daughter."

"I used to think that bond was enough," I confess. "Now, I'm not so sure."

Hands on my shoulders, Janine turns me around. "Go get some rest. I'll bring Alexa to you the moment she asks."

I place my hand over hers. "Thank you."

I leave her apartment and walk slowly to mine, my feet and my heart heavy. As soon as I've closed the door behind me, I drop to the couch and sit staring at the wall.

It's so quiet. And so empty.

When did the apartment feel so empty?

I bury my face in my hands, the tears falling again. I was hoping Alexa would stop them. I was hoping she'd hug all my broken pieces together. But of course she thinks I made her father go away. And she doesn't even know Conner's her father.

Thank goodness for that. If she did, she might never speak to me again.

Yup. I'm the bad guy.

And now I wonder if I made a mistake, because it sure feels like it.

I grip my hair.

What was Conner trying to tell me? Why was he trying to leave me?

Just then, I hear footsteps outside the door.

Alexa?

Quickly, I get up and go to the counter, ripping off a paper towel so I can wipe my tears. I walk to the door, and as I'm reaching for the knob, it turns.

The door opens. A man in black stands in the doorway.

I cock my head to one side. "Who are...?"

The man presses a handkerchief to my mouth and nose. I stumble back, falling to the floor. A pair of shiny shoes is the last thing I see before everything turns dark.

Chapter Nineteen
Conner

It's too dark, I think with a gnawing suspicion as soon as I enter the house where Tiffany is staying. I had to break the back door to get in.

It's past sunset, and the sky is already turning from purple to black, but no lights are on. The fridge in the kitchen doesn't seem to be humming, either.

No power.

Seeing the phone hanging on the wall, I grab the receiver.

No dial tone.

Something is definitely wrong.

My heart hammering in my chest, I find a flashlight in the kitchen drawers. I pause, then grab a knife as well. One in each hand, I search the rest of the house.

In the living room, I find the TV cracked in the middle, pieces of a shattered vase in front of it. The books from the shelves lie scattered on the floor.

I swallow the lump in my throat.

There was a definitely a fight here. The question is: Who won?

I shine the flashlight around, and seeing red drops on the floor, I panic.

Blood.

There are more drops on the stairs, leading all the way up.

I hurry upstairs, keeping my senses sharp. I follow the trail, ending up in the bedroom, where I see a man lying face down on the floor, a puddle of blood around his knee and a bigger pool around his chest.

What the hell?

"I killed him," Tiffany's voice startles me.

Shining the light on her, I find her shaking in the corner of the bedroom. Her face is pale and her hands are stained with blood. A bloody knife is lying in front of her.

Carefully, I approach her. "What happened?"

"He tried to kill me," Tiffany says in a quivering voice that's barely above a whisper. "So I killed him."

Grabbing the bedsheet, I bend over to pick up the bloody knife from the carpet.

"How long have you been here?" I ask Tiffany.

She shrugs. "Hours."

I set the knife down on the table beside the one I got from the kitchen. Then I kneel down in front of Tiffany.

"Are you hurt?"

She points to her swollen ankle. My eyes grow wide as I shine the light on it.

"He grabbed it when I was trying to get away from him," Tiffany explains. "He twisted it, but I managed to stab him so he let me go."

It looks twisted, already red and swollen.

"Did you call 9-1-1?"

She shakes her head. "My phone's in the living room."

I take out my phone and call the emergency hotline to report the break-in. After the call, I stand up.

"I'll look for something cold to ice your ankle," I tell her.

I'm about to walk off when she grabs my leg. "No! Don't leave me!"

I nod, sitting beside her. "Come here."

I pull her into my arms, rubbing her back as she sobs.

"Shh. It's alright now."

I let Tiffany sob for a while, then offer her my handkerchief. She wipes her tears and blows her nose on the square piece of cloth until she finally calms down.

"Who is this man?" I ask her.

"I don't know."

"When you called me, you said you were in danger," I remind her. "You said someone was coming to get you. What made you say that?"

She blows her nose again. "It's because Margot warned me."

"Margot?"

"The fiancée of Damien Shore," Tiffany explains.

I tense at the name.

"After I interviewed them together, I asked if I could interview just Margot. I wanted to get to know her, because people know about him but not about her. Plus she's like the star of the story, the Cinderella. I wanted to see why Mr. Shore fell in love with her."

"And?"

"Mr. Shore was reluctant, but he agreed. He made all the arrangements. I interviewed Margot at a restaurant with her bodyguards at the table. At first it was just a regular interview, but we ended up talking about a lot of things, fashion mostly. She seemed to be knowledgeable. She knew about my blog. I guess we became friends."

"And Margot called you?"

"Yes. After I got back, she called me saying that someone was coming to kill me. She was whispering and she sounded scared. It was a short phone call, but the message got across."

I swallow the lump in my throat. "Who did she say was trying to kill you?"

"Her fiancé."

The flashlight falls from my shaking hand, clattering to the floor. I pick it up.

"She said Damien Shore was trying to kill you?" I clarify, although I already know the answer.

Tiffany nods.

I glance at the dead man. "Which means that man was sent by Damien Shore."

She gives another nod.

"Why didn't you run away and hide after Margot warned you?" I ask her.

"I wanted to, but where would I go?"

"To your apartment in Los Angeles," I suggest.

"What if the killer was already waiting there?"

Good point.

"And you didn't call the cops?"

"Would they have believed me?"

Another good point.

"I just stayed here and prepared for the worst," she adds.

I look at her. I thought she was just a pretty face. But she does have a brain behind that face.

"You prepared to fight?"

"I got a few lessons in self-defense back when I was still a model," she informs me. "A lot of men wanted to grope me, you see."

I nod. I can understand the impulse.

"And here I thought all you knew how to do was pick the right clothes."

She chuckles, then blows her nose again.

I turn to her. "Do you know why Damien Shore would want to kill you?"

Tiffany shrugs. "Maybe he changed his mind about having his story published. I mean, he and Margot don't seem happy. Or maybe he just didn't like my clothes?"

I pause, thinking.

"You used to be a runway model, right?"

She nods.

"And Damien Shore is a fashion magnate. Did your paths ever cross before?"

She falls silent.

"Tiffany?"

360

She draws a deep breath. "I went to his office once. I thought he had a job for me, but he just flirted with me and then told me he wanted me to come home with him. He offered me a lot of money for it, too, but I refused. When he grabbed me, I kicked him in the nuts and left."

My eyebrows furrow. "He tried to assault you?"

Tiffany nods.

"And you still interviewed him for your story?"

"I thought since he was getting married he wouldn't try anything funny. Also, he said he was a changed man. You heard him."

Alright. Maybe Tiffany's smarter than she looks, but she's still not that smart.

"And yet look what happened now," I remark, glancing at the body.

She cringes and squeezes her eyes shut.

A moment later, I hear sirens approaching. I stand up and look out the window to see the red and blue lights in the distance.

"Don't worry." I squeeze her shoulder. "You're safe now."

"But what about you and Ingrid?" she asks.

I kneel beside her. "What do you mean?"

"Margot said Damien Shore was after all of us."

I stand up, gaping. I figured he'd be after me, but why Ingrid?

"I'm sorry I forgot to tell you that at the start," Tiffany says.

I turn towards the door and walk out of the room.

"Conner!" she calls after me.

I ignore her, rushing down the stairs.

Damien Shore is after all of us. He's already tried to kill Tiffany. He's already succeeded in killing Ed. That leaves only me.

And Ingrid.

~

"Ingrid's gone," Janine confirms my fears as soon as I get to her apartment. "Alexa wanted to apologize to her so I brought her here, but when we got here, the door was unlocked and Ingrid was gone."

I clench my hand into a fist and punch the wall.

I'm too late. I never should have let her come back to Boulder alone.

"Conner!" Alexa shouts, rushing out of the bedroom.

Seeing her tearstained cheeks, I frown.

"Sweetheart." I pull her into my arms, hugging her tight.

For a moment there, I thought I'd never see her again.

She squeezes me in turn. "I knew you'd come back."

"Did you know?"

"You'll bring Mommy back, too, won't you? I made her go away, but you'll make her come back, right?"

I stroke her hair. "You didn't make her go away, sweetheart."

"Then why isn't she here?"

Good question.

Ed is dead and Tiffany almost got killed. Yet Ingrid's missing.

Why was she taken?

My phone rings and I take it out of my pocket.

"Is that Mommy?" Alexa asks.

"I don't think so," I say as I stand up, answering the call. "Hello."

"Conner Blake," the man on the other end says my name.

I grit my teeth. Damien Shore.

"Where's Ingrid?" I ask him. "What did you do to her?"

He laughs. "Nothing... yet."

My jaw clenches. "I swear, if you hurt her, I'll..."

361

"Oh, you should know by now that you can't touch me, Mr. Blake. Haven't you learned your lesson? Besides, you're in no position to make threats. I'm in a position to make demands. And I demand that you come to me tonight—or your precious girlfriend will die."

I swallow the lump in my throat. "Say the time and place and I'll be there."

"Be at the airport in half an hour."

The line goes dead.

Janine approaches me. "Was that...?"

I nod.

"Was that Mommy?" Alexa asks.

I place my hands on her shoulders. "Alexa, I promise you that your mother will come back to you safely."

She nods. "You'll bring her back with you, right?"

I don't answer that, but I plant a tender kiss on the top of her head. "I love you."

I turn to Janine. "I think the two of you should go back to your apartment. Lock the door."

Janine nods, gripping Alexa's shoulders. "I'll keep her safe."

"Thank you."

I walk to the door.

"Wait," Janine calls after me.

I turn around.

"Take care," she says.

I nod.

"And it was nice to finally meet you," she adds.

I give a weak smile. "Same here."

Alexa waves her hand at me and I wave back before I step out of the apartment, smiling at her even though my heart is breaking.

I don't know if I'll ever see her again, but if it means Ingrid will be safe, that's fine.

I swear I'll do everything I can to save her.

Chapter Twenty
Ingrid

When I force my heavy eyelids open, the first thing I see is a crack on the concrete wall across from me.

As my vision clears, I see other cracks, as well as windows without glass panes and a glimpse of the night sky beyond them. An electric lantern stands on a stool in a corner, shedding light on dusty floor tiles. A rat silently scurries across them.

Where am I? And what am I doing here?

The silhouette of a tall, broad-chested man with large arms shadowing one of the windows jolts my memory.

Right. One such man came to my apartment, and he...

I panic as the realization sinks in, but the moment I try to run I realize that my wrists are tied above my head by a half-inch-thick rope that hangs from a steel bar sticking out of the ceiling and is just long enough so the soles of my feet can touch the floor.

No way.

I tug at the rope but to no use. It's knotted firmly around my wrists, digging into my skin as I struggle while the other end clings to the bar, trapped between two notches.

I struggle anyway, ending up swaying to and fro.

A chuckle from behind me interrupts my attempts. I turn my head, and my heart stops as I see Damien Shore walking towards me with more of his goons.

"You?" I spit out, glaring at him as he passes by me even as fear creeps up my straight spine.

"I see you know me even though we haven't been formally introduced."

"Of course I do," I say through gritted teeth. "You're the child-molesting scumbag who wormed his way out of prison."

He gives another chuckle. "It seems my reputation precedes me, huh?"

His expression turns serious as he stops a few feet across from me and takes a puff of his cigarette.

"I know you, too. Ingrid Halfield, am I right?"

I don't answer.

"You used to work for *The Dallas Times*. Now, you work for that pathetic excuse for a paper, *The Colorado Chronicler*."

My jaw clenches. How dare he insult my hard work?

He takes another puff. "You know what else I know? That you have a daughter."

I freeze, my eyes popping out of their sockets.

No.

"She's still a little too young, but in time, she might make a good addition to my collection," he says.

Anger fills my chest and my hands clench into fists above me. I tug at the ropes harder and the hemp cuts into my skin.

"Don't you dare lay a filthy finger on my daughter," I growl.

"My, my, you really do enjoy pain, don't you?" Damien gives a mischievous grin, ignoring my threat. "Eric told me you did."

Eric?

"You know, the owner of The Weeping Rose."

My eyebrows shoot up. What?

"He's a good friend of mine. After all, our interests run along the same lines—whips, cuffs...He's even more strict with the rules, though. Why, he'd beat the life out of anyone who disobeyed them."

"You sent us there," I voice my suspicion out loud.

"Correct." Damien claps his hands. "As expected from a talented journalist."

I take no pleasure from the compliment, though I'm grateful for it, since it reminds me of the recorder chip I have hidden in my watch.

"Byline," I say to activate it.

"What did you say?" Damien throws me a puzzled look.

"Why did you send us to The Weeping Rose?" I ask him.

"Because I thought he'd kill you for me," he answers without pause, taking a final puff from his cigarette before tossing it to the floor and crushing it beneath his leather shoe. "I thought you would rather die than play his games, but boy, was I wrong."

He sits on a chair, crossing his legs.

"That wasn't the first time I tried to kill you, either. I tried to burn you alive, but that didn't work, either."

My jaw drops. "You burned down Mr. Murrow's house?"

"It was crumbling anyway. I did the old man a favor."

"Why, you fucking…"

"Of course, that was when I was still bent on trying to kill people and making it look like an accident." He hooks his arms around the back of the chair, letting them dangle. "Did you know I was also the one who arranged Ed's accident?"

A pang of sorrow stabs my chest.

Ed.

"But then I changed my mind. I thought, why go through all the trouble of making them look like accidents. It's more fun to just make it look like murder and blame it on someone else."

"You're crazy."

"I had a lot of time to think, you know, in prison. It really gives one plenty of opportunities to reflect. I have Conner Blake to thank for that."

Hearing Conner's name from his lips for the first time sends a mix of emotions through me—fear, anger, hatred… love.

"I thought 'What do some of the people I most want dead have in common?' and I realized they all liked to write, so I had my good friend, Paul Newton—"

"Paul Newton?"

"—arrange for the three of them to be in a competition where they'd all be going after the same job. After all, there's no more believable excuse for murder than money. Apart from passion, that is."

"You arranged that job offer?"

He leans forward in the chair. "What can I say? I like pulling strings."

Unbelievable. He went through all that trouble?

"But you said three. There are four of us," I point out.

"Now, that's the funny part." He stands up. "You were an extra. You were supposed to be there just to confuse everyone and lend the whole scheme a touch of authenticity. But then I realized something. You're not that innocent, are you?"

My eyebrows crease. What exactly did he find out?

"I found out that you're Conner Blake's girlfriend," he answers my unspoken question.

"I'm not his girlfriend," I argue.

He ignores me. "And more importantly from my point of view, that you were him that night he took the pictures that sent me to prison. Am I right?"

I say nothing.

"Even then, you already liked this sort of thing." He walks over to me, running his fingers along the rope above me. "Although I seem to remember you preferred cuffs. I prefer rope. It's more versatile. You can do so many things with it."

He grips my chin. "If you're a good girl, maybe I'll show you some of those things."

I wrench my chin away, fighting the sickening feeling in the pit of my stomach as I try to clear my mind.

What were we talking about again?

"You put us all together so you could pick us off one by one and blame the murders on someone else?" I ask.

"That was initially my plan, yes. One of you dies and another is the suspect. Then that person dies. You get the trend. It's like *The Hunger Games*, except there's no victor. Oh wait, there is—me."

"I understand why you want to kill me and Conner, but what about Tiffany and Ed? What did they ever do to you?"

"I'm glad you asked." He steps back, giving me an ounce of relief. "Tiffany hurt my pride once. Oh, and she kicked me, too."

"Serves you right," I mutter under my breath.

"She's feistier than she looks, that one, but not much smarter. And Ed? There was a story he wrote that he shouldn't have written. Nothing to do with this"—he gestures at the rope—"but it ruined a business deal for me, you know, cost me a lot of money."

"So you killed Ed?"

I try to fight the wave of disgust I feel at remembering the sight of Ed's corpse.

"I did," Damien admits shamelessly. "Did you like it? I believe you saw what I did to him."

"Why, you…"

"By that time, I had decided I'd blame the murders on Conner, since he's the one I hate the most. I sent Ed to that ski resort when you were there. I knew their paths would cross and they'd have an argument of some sort."

"But they didn't," I tell him. "Conner wasn't suspected of Ed's murder. You failed."

"Yes." He turns his back to me, clasping his hands behind him. "I didn't anticipate that, nor did I anticipate the fact that both of you would have other company."

"You failed," I repeat.

"It was frustrating, I admit. Then again, that's still one down. Bonus points for the fact that it gave you and Conner a scare."

My temper simmers anew. How dare he play with us like that?

"After all, it was so much fun seeing that scared look on Conner's face in Dallas."

My eyebrows arch. "You met in Dallas?"

"Didn't he tell you? Didn't Tiffany tell you? She was the one who introduced us. Now, that wasn't planned, but it sure was good, because I scared the shit out of him without really trying. Let me think." He touches his chin. "I think it was about the time I mentioned you that he started going pale. He was so scared at the thought of losing you. Frankly, that confirmed my intel that he had feelings for you."

Just then, something sinks in.

Dallas. He wanted to leave me after that, and I thought it was because of Tiffany, but I was wrong. It wasn't because of Tiffany. It was because of Damien Shore.

I stare at the man in front of me.

He threatened to hurt me, and Conner probably thought I was safer not being by his side. He couldn't have known that Damien Shore already intended to hurt me.

Conner was trying to protect me. He does love me.

That realization causes a burst of joy in my chest, which quickly diminishes when the next realization sinks in.

I got mad at Conner for no reason. I pushed him away.

Stupid.

No. It's not my fault. It's Damien's.

"Speaking of Tiffany, she was supposed to be dead by now, but by some miracle she survived."

I snort. "Another failure."

"It's Margot's fault, but she's already been dealt with."

"Margot?"

Damien chuckles. "Haven't you heard? I'm engaged. At least I was."

He places his hands on his hips as he continues. "Tiffany was supposed to die in Conner's arms as he desperately tried to save her. Then her blood would be all over him and he'd be pinned as the murderer, especially when information came out that they were lovers. He'd end up in prison, and my new friends there would have made him suffer."

My chest boils, but I try to hang on to my composure.

"It doesn't matter." Damien shrugs. "It'll be easy enough to kill her after I'm done with you and Conner. He's on his way here now, you know, thinking he can save you."

365

My anger fades. Conner's coming?

At first, that bit of information gives me relief, hope. But then I see the grin on Damien's face and the monsters with him and my heart sinks to my feet. A shiver goes up my spine.

No. Conner can't come here. He'll die.

The thought of losing him tears my chest apart.

"What's with that look? Now you look pale as a ghost. Do you care for Conner that much? No, wait. I know that look. You're in love with him, aren't you?"

I answer with a glare.

"I'll take that as a yes. And based on Conner's response earlier, I believe he feels the same." He rubs his hands together. "Boy, this is getting very interesting. I can't wait for him to arrive."

"Are you going to kill us both?"

"Of course." His answer makes my sweat run cold. "It's only a matter of who I kill first. After all, it's more painful to watch the person you love die. Something like that can break you. And if it doesn't, I surely will."

Damien walks towards me again, the grin on his face making the hairs on the back of my neck stand on end.

He reaches out to touch me but stops at the sound of approaching footsteps.

I glance behind me in their direction.

Conner?

He comes out of the shadows with one of Damien's men pointing a gun at his head, half his face swollen.

Blood drains from mine.

"Ah. Conner Blake." Damien turns to him. "How nice of you to join us." His brow furrows. "But what happened to his face?"

The man with the gun shrugs.

Damien frowns, hands on his hips. "I thought I said I'd be the one to make him suffer."

"Sorry, boss," the man mutters.

"Oh, never mind." Damien places his hand on his forehead. "I can make him suffer more."

"I'm here now," Conner tells him. "Let her go."

"That's funny." Damien rubs his chin. "I don't recall making that promise."

"Bastard!" Conner grits his teeth. "Let Ingrid go."

Damien waves a finger at him. "Didn't I tell you that you're in no position to make demands?"

"You said..."

"I said I'd let her live, not let her go. Big difference." Damien stands beside me. "I guess that answers my dilemma. Conner dies first. You'll watch him die. But not before I make him suffer, watching what I do to you."

Damien pulls a knife out of his pocket and I tense. He stands behind me, holding the blade to my throat. I close my eyes.

"Damien!" Conner shouts, his voice holding both a plea and a warning.

Damien chuckles, and the cold blade of the knife departs from my skin. I open my eyes just in time to see him rip the front of my shirt with it.

"Damien!"

Conner tries to run to me, but the man behind him blocks him, pressing the barrel of the gun to his forehead.

"Try anything funny and I'll blow your brains out."

"Go ahead, then," Conner tells him. "Kill me."

My insides coil. No.

"Stand down, Jim," Damien orders. "I do the killing around here."

He glances at another goon. "Tie him up."

The man obeys, heading to the pile of rope in the corner. As he picks it up, a red dot appears on his back and my eyes grow wide.

Isn't that…?

"Freeze!" a cop shouts.

I don't know how the cops got here, but I don't care. Relief floods through me. We're saved.

Chapter Twenty-One
Conner

"Don't move or we'll shoot!" another cop shouts.

From the corner of my eye, I try to count them. One, two, three...

"Well, well," Damien interrupts my count. "Look who we have here. Gatecrashers to my party? What, you want to watch the show, too?"

He rips Ingrid's shirt off, leaving her black bra in full view. She gasps.

Fear and anger rise to my throat. My fists clench, along with every muscle in my body.

I swear I'm going to kill him.

"We said don't move!" the cop repeats. "Or..."

"I know, I know. You'll shoot." Damien puts his hands up. "And so will we."

At his command, his men draw their guns, the man beside me pointing his gun away to direct it at the policemen.

I grab his wrist and bury my knee in his stomach. His gun clatters to the floor.

As the cops fire, a bullet sends him falling.

Picking up his gun, I run towards Damien amid the exchange of bullets, but he's already running off with a struggling Ingrid over his shoulder, having cut her rope with his knife.

I follow them up the stairs.

"Damien!"

He puts Ingrid down, holding her in front of him. She continues to struggle, but stops when Damien holds his knife to her throat.

"Put the gun down or she dies," he threatens.

I hesitate.

His knife draws blood and Ingrid gasps.

"Stop!" I tell him, putting my hands up in surrender.

"Put the gun down," Damien repeats.

I obey.

"Kick it over here," he orders.

I do it, but I kick it too hard on purpose, so that it slips past him.

Glancing at it, Damien grits his teeth. Then he grabs one of Ingrid's breasts.

"No!" I shout, despair gnawing at me. "Your fight is against me, Damien. Not her. She has nothing to do with this."

"Is that right?"

"Let her go. I'll do anything. Just let her go. Please."

For a moment, Damien falls silent. Then he laughs.

"Conner Blake begging? Well, this look is even better than your terrified look."

"Let her go," I repeat.

I don't care if I have to go on my knees. I'll do anything as long as Damien releases Ingrid.

"Well, it is you I want dead," Damien thinks out loud, eyes to the ceiling.

"Then take me instead," I tell him. "Kill me instead. Let Ingrid go."

I take a step closer, eyeing the gun behind him.

Downstairs, I can still hear guns firing. As long as that fight is going on, I have a chance to take Damien down.

Damien pauses to consider my offer.

"No!" Ingrid shouts, shaking her head as her eyes plead with me. "I'm not leaving here without you. I'm not living without you."

"Oh, how romantic," Damien says. "Maybe I'll just kill you both."

"No!" I shout, taking another step forward. "Let her go."

"You think he's the one who put you in prison?" Ingrid asks.

My brow furrows. What is she doing?

"What a fool you are," she tells him. "I'm the one who took those pictures."

"What?" Damien's eyes grow wide.

While he's distracted, I move closer.

"I'm the one who put you in prison, Damien Shore," Ingrid says. "You said so yourself. I was there that night. And not only that, I was the one with the camera. I would have published those photos myself if Conner hadn't stolen them."

Damien's jaw drops. Then he laughs.

As he does, his grip loosens and Ingrid bites his hand. The knife falls.

"You bitch!"

Damien kicks her, sending her stumbling forward before picking up his knife.

I rush him and grab his wrists. He butts his head against mine, sending me reeling back.

"You're too young to beat me, boy," Damien says, grinning.

From the corner of my eye, I see Ingrid crawling away.

Good. At least she's safe.

I raise my fists. "Aren't you a little too old for this?"

Damien snorts. "Who are you calling old?"

I make the first move, throwing a punch at his jaw. He avoids it, leaning sideways and making a swipe at me with his knife. It grazes my arm.

Shit.

Damien makes a clicking sound with his tongue. "You're going to die, Conner Blake. And then I'm going after the girl."

Without thinking, I lunge, aiming for his stomach this time. He blocks the jab and stabs the knife into my thigh.

I scream.

He kicks my leg, sending me falling to the ground. As I grip my thigh in pain, he stands above me, holding the knife with both hands. I kick his legs and he loses his footing and falls. The knife goes flying.

I climb on top of him and sit on him as I punch his face, my knuckles cracking his jaw. He reaches for my thigh and his fingers dig into the wound, drawing more blood and causing me incredible pain.

I let out another cry.

Taking advantage of my pain, he pushes me off, climbs on top of me, and wraps his hands around my neck. I swing my fists, punching him, but he doesn't let go.

My air supply decreases and my eyes dart around in panic. The gun inches away from me gives me a glimmer of hope.

"What are you going to do now, huh?" Damien asks, his grip tightening. "You may be younger than me, but I have more experience hurting people. You have no idea how many women I've strangled. I didn't always mean it then, but I certainly do this time."

I start choking. My chest hurts.

My vision blurs.

"Conner!" Ingrid's voice from across the room strengthens my will to fight.

Summoning all my strength, I lift my knee to hit Damien's groin. It draws a yelp, and his grip loosens.

I crawl away from him, snatching up the gun and pointing it at him.

"Don't move," I warn, finger on the trigger.

He chuckles. "Go ahead. Kill me. If you can, that is."

My finger quivers. My jaw clenches. Oh, I'd love to scatter his brains all over the floor right now.

"Go on," Damien urges.

I have no reason not to. He hurt Ingrid.

"Go on!"

I pull the trigger, shooting his thigh. He screams.

Now we're kind of even.

Moments later, I hear footsteps coming up the stairs. I point the gun, preparing to shoot at the bad guys, but it's the cops who appear.

"Drop the gun, son," one of them says.

I obey.

One of them goes to Damien, pins him to the ground and cuffs his wrists behind his back.

"Careful, will you?" he sneers. "I'm wounded here."

"How would you like to be cuffed now?" Ingrid asks, walking towards him with her hand on her lower back.

Damien growls.

"Oh, and this time, could you make sure he stays in prison?" Ingrid asks, handing a cop her watch. "I recorded all his confessions. He murdered Ed Parker. He tried to kill Tiffany Jordan, Conner Blake and me. Twice. Also, I don't know if his fiancée is still alive."

"What?" Damien's eyes pop out.

The cop takes her watch.

"Don't worry. He won't walk this time," he promises. "And we'll search his house right away."

"Thank you," Ingrid says.

She really is something.

Smiling, I try to get up but wince as I fail, gripping my thigh.

"Conner!" Ingrid rushes to me.

"The ambulance should be here any second," another cop informs us.

"Hear that?" I place my hand on Ingrid's cheek. "You don't have to worry about me. I'll be just fine."

Chapter Twenty-Two
Ingrid

"He's going to be alright," the doctor tells me as I stand outside Conner's hospital room in fresh clothes, my hair still wet from a hasty shower. "The cut on his thigh didn't hit any major arteries, so we just stitched him up. But he still lost quite a bit of blood, so he's on some IV fluids. We also did some X-rays and there are no broken bones. The cut on his arm was just a scratch, and the bruises on his face and his neck will go away in a few days."

The doctor smiles and pats my arm reassuringly.

"You'll get your good-looking boyfriend back in one piece."

I smile back. "Thank you so much."

She nods, leaving me.

I enter Conner's room and find him sitting up on his bed in his blue-and-white hospital gown, a tube attached to his arm.

"Hey," I greet him with a smile as I rest my hands on my back pockets.

"Hey." He smiles back, dimples showing.

I stop by his bed. "Nice shirt."

He glances at mine. "I like yours better."

I glance at it, too—a shirt with red and white stripes, the first shirt I pulled off the top of the pile in my closet. Not my favorite, but at least it's not tattered.

Conner touches my arm. "Are you alright?"

"You're the one in the hospital bed," I point out, lifting my head.

"Yeah, but he hurt you, too."

The sadness in his voice and in his eyes makes my heart melt.

I run my fingers over the Band-Aid on my neck. "I'm fine."

"That's not what I was referring to," Conner says. "Did he do anything to you before I got there?"

"Just words," I tell him. "He didn't really hurt me. I didn't let him."

Conner smiles.

"But he did threaten to hurt Alexa," I add.

The smile instantly vanishes from Conner's face. His jaw clenches.

"I should have killed that bastard."

"Shh." I place my hand over his. "He's the murderer, not you. Besides, death would have been too easy for him. He'll get what he's due now."

"Thanks to you. Again. Where do you get these tiny devices of yours?"

I sit on the stool. "Online. I had Janine modify the recorder, though, so that I could voice-activate it, which was really helpful."

"Wow." His brown eyes grow wide. "You're like Lois Lane and James Bond combined into one."

"And you were super," I tell him, touching his arm. "You brought the bad guy down."

He smiles.

"Speaking of Janine…"

We stop, having both spoken at the same time.

"You go first," I tell him.

Conner shrugs. "I was just going to say I met her. She was at your apartment with Alexa when I went to check on you."

"Yeah. She told me. She seems to like you."

"Really?" His eyebrows arch. "What did she say?"

I shake my head. "Not telling."

Well, she said Conner was hot and that I shouldn't let go of him.

"But I will tell you what we talked about earlier," I add. "Believe it or not, Janine was the one who sent the cops."

"I was wondering about that. They just appeared out of nowhere and right at the right time, too." Conner scratches his head. "How did Janine send them?"

"As you know, Janine is a genius. Apparently, she installed security cameras not only outside her apartment but outside mine. She just wasn't watching them live. After you left, she reviewed the footage and she found that the man had this tattoo…" My eyes narrow as I try to remember the details Janine gave me. "And she started running a search. She basically hacked into the city's security cameras to find the guy, and then she sent the cops to the location."

"Okay." Conner nods. "Remind me to be nice to Janine."

I grin. "Don't worry. She knows Alexa adores you. She also knows you're her father. I told her."

"Okay."

I let out a sigh. "I'm just glad all this is over. I still can't believe Damien Shore arranged that job offer, though."

"I thought I recognized the man in that photo with Cassie," Conner says. "He was at that party. He's friends with Damien Shore."

"Apparently he's Cassie's uncle," I inform him. "Cassie called me."

"What did she say?"

"That she's sorry about everything and she didn't know about it." My shoulders heave. "Frankly, I'm not sure I believe her."

"What about the job?" Conner asks. "Is there still one?"

I give another shrug. "All she said was that we still have to bring our stories to the office on the deadline."

"Which is just a few days away."

"I know, but I'm not worried."

He look surprised. "You're not?"

"I have a story," I tell him.

"You do?"

I nod. Somehow, while I was taking that hasty shower, an idea came to me.

"Besides, it's just you and me left, so whoever wins, it's fine, right?"

He nods. Then his eyebrows crease. "Wait. What do you mean it's just you and me left? Tiffany's still alive, right?"

"Yes. I spoke to her, too," I inform him. "She doesn't want this job anymore. She just wants her old life back."

"I don't blame her."

"She's starting a new blog, actually, with Margot, Damien's ex-pretend fiancée. They found her all tied up and beaten, but she'll be fine."

"Good for both of them."

"She also sends you a kiss," I add.

"What?"

I peck on his cheek.

Conner gives me a puzzled look. "Wait. You don't still think something happened between us, right? Because…"

I put my hand up. "No need to explain. Damien Shore did."

"He did?"

"He said he threatened you in Dallas, and I'm guessing that's why you wanted to leave me," I tell him.

"It was," he confirms. "I was trying to protect you."

"Except I already had a target on my back. Damien found out I was at that party with you."

"Yeah." Conner nods. "I think you said that. Still, things were made worse for you because he found out how much I cared about you. If the cops hadn't arrived…"

"But they did," I cut him off, holding a finger to his lips.

I've thought about it, too, and I think what could have happened will appear in my nightmares one of these days, but I'm not going to go there. I'm not going to let that cloud hang over me.

"Besides, it was my story all along that put him in prison. I'm the one he should have been after the whole time. If anything, I got you in trouble. I was the one who took those pictures."

"And I was the one who published them with an article that had my byline," Conner points out.

"Yeah. Big mistake, right? Your life would never have been in danger if you had never stolen my story."

"I'm sorry I stole your story," he says, holding my hand. "But I'm still glad it was me he went after, because I wouldn't have wanted anything bad to happen to you."

I purse my lips, placing my hand over his. "Also, Tiffany told me nothing happened between the two of you."

He grins. "You two sure had a long conversation."

"And I told her that you and I were together. It just... slipped out."

"You did?" Conner gives me a look of disbelief.

I nod. "I don't know, though, if we are together. I mean, I did sort of break up with you."

"You told me to go to hell," he reminds me.

"Yeah, I did. And we kind of did, didn't we? But now, we're back. We survived hell."

"We sure did," he agrees.

I squeeze his hand. "So, does it mean we're still together?"

"I don't think we were ever not together." He strokes my cheek. "I love you."

"I love you," I tell him, leaning over so I can press my lips to his.

"Wait," he says. "If you told Tiffany we were together, why did she still send me a kiss?"

I chuckle. "I was just teasing you. That kiss was from me. And this one."

I'm about to give him another kiss, but suddenly the door opens and Alexa bounces in.

"Mommy!" She throws herself at me.

"Hey, sweetheart." I stroke her hair.

"I'll be outside," Janine tells me from the doorway.

"Hi, Janine." Conner waves at her.

"Hi." She closes the door.

"Daddy!" Alexa stands on the tip of her toes to give Conner a hug.

My eyebrows furrow. "Wait. Daddy?"

She turns to me. "Conner is my daddy, isn't he? Janine told me."

I scratch my chin. "I see. No wonder she was in a hurry to get out."

"It's true, isn't it?" Alexa asks.

I glance at Conner who gives me a questioning look. I nod.

"It is," Conner answers the question, pinching Alexa's nose playfully. "You're my little girl."

"Yes!" She throws herself on Conner.

"Ouch!" Conner winces.

"Easy." I pull Alexa back. "Daddy is a little bit hurt."

"But only a little bit," Conner says. "I'm sure I'll get better faster if you dance for me."

"Of course."

Alexa starts dancing.

Watching her, I smile, my hand on my chest that seems about to explode with joy.

I thought she'd be mad at me for keeping her father a secret from her, but she's simply happy to have the father she needs and deserves. And I couldn't be happier for her.

"That means we're a family now, right?" Alexa turns to me.

I give her a hug. "Of course. Although you and I have always been a family."

Alexa's eyebrows crease. Then she shakes her head. "No. It's not the same."

"What do you mean?" I tickle her. "You sound like you didn't like me."

"I like you a lot," she tells me when she's done laughing. "But there are things only daddies can do."

"Like?"

"Like buy pets and carry me on his shoulders," Alexa answers.

Conner and I laugh.

"And make Mommy happy," she adds.

I touch her cheek. "Yeah, Daddy can make Mommy happy in a very special way."

Conner reaches for her hand. "I promise I'll always make Mommy happy."

I smile.

"One more thing," Alexa adds.

"What?" I ask her.

"Daddies let their kids eat pizza."

Conner laughs.

"Can we have pizza tonight?" Alexa asks. "Pretty please?"

I turn her around so she can face her father.

"Please?" Alexa begs him.

"Ask your mother," Conner says.

"Good answer," I tell him, grinning. Then I squeeze Alexa's shoulders. "Maybe not tonight, since Daddy still needs to stay here at the hospital, but tomorrow night we can have pizza—"

"Yay!" Alexa cheers before I can finish.

Above her, I gaze into Conner's eyes with a soft smile as I continue.

"To celebrate Daddy coming home... for good."

Chapter Twenty-Three
Conner

Home.

Sitting on the couch with a slice of pepperoni pizza in my hand, my daughter giggling beside me and a cage with two mice on the other side, I can't help but smile.

I've liked this apartment from the moment I got here, even though it's not exactly spic-and-span. It was always cozy. Warm.

Now, it's home.

"I think I'll go now," Janine announces from behind the counter. "Thanks for the pizza."

"You're welcome," I tell her.

"You're leaving already?" Ingrid comes out of the bedroom.

"Yeah. Time to go back to my apartment so I can slave away and leave your happy family to bask in your newfound joy."

"Oh, don't say that." Ingrid squeezes her shoulder. "You're family, too, and you're always welcome here."

Janine frowns. "Nah. I don't think so. Speaking of which…"

She hands Ingrid her key.

"Why?" Ingrid looks at her in surprise.

"You know, so I don't accidentally walk in when the two of you are…"

"Okay," Ingrid cuts her off as she takes the keys, blushing. "Alexa, say good night to Janine."

Alexa leaves the couch to give Janine a hug. "Good night."

"Good night." Janine kisses the top of her head before waving at me. "I'll see you around?"

"You will," I assure her.

After she leaves, I turn to Ingrid. "I like her."

Ingrid chuckles. "Why am I not surprised?"

"I thought she'd be weird since you said she coops herself up in her apartment most of the time. I was imagining someone with messy hair and thick glasses and… well, you get the picture."

"Janine's hair gets messy sometimes," Alexa pipes in.

"She's still a cool person, though," I say.

"Yeah." Alexa nods, sitting beside me again. "I agree."

"So do I." Ingrid points to the bedroom door. "I have to go finish that story."

"Okay."

She goes inside the bedroom, closing the door behind her.

She's been working on it all afternoon, and she hasn't given me any clues about what she's writing about. Still, that look on her face tells me she has something good.

"Don't you just love it when your Mommy is writing a good story?" I ask Alexa as I take another bite of my pizza. "She looks like she's on this journey, like she's in another world."

"Yeah. She doesn't hear a thing I say," Alexa says.

"I heard that!" Ingrid shouts from inside the bedroom.

Alexa and I laugh.

"Do you want to be a writer when you grow up?" I ask her, stroking her hair. "Or a journalist?"

"What's the difference?" she asks with furrowed eyebrows.

"Well, writers can write anything. Journalists only write things that happen in real life. You know, they report it. But both can make a difference in other people's lives."

"So journalists can't write about dragons?"

I bunch my eyebrows at her. "Dragons aren't real?"

She chuckles. "I think I want to be a doctor."

"An animal doctor or a people doctor?" I ask.

"I haven't figured it out, but I like the white coats."

"I'm sure you'll look good in one."

"And Janine says they make a lot of money."

I pinch her cheek. "Maybe Janine's right, but money isn't all that matters, okay?"

"I know. Mommy used to say that all the time." She lowers her voice to a whisper as she leans in my ear. "But she's still always sad when we don't have enough money, and I can always tell when we don't."

I squeeze her hand. "Don't worry, kiddo. I'm here now."

"Where were you?" Alexa asks me. "Mommy said you were dead. Did you come back to life?"

I chuckle, ruffling her hair. "I think I just did, sweetheart."

~

"Is our daughter adorable or what?" I tell Ingrid as I lie down on the bed—the bigger bed in the bigger bedroom. Alexa is now sleeping in the smaller one.

"What," Ingrid answers after gargling one last time at the bathroom sink. "She is not just adorable. She's amazing."

She wipes her mouth on a towel.

"Well, she's just like her mother," I say with a grin.

"Thank goodness for that." Ingrid closes the bathroom door and comes to the bed. "But you know what?"

"What?"

She lies down beside me. "You've been talking all about her. I think I'm getting a little jealous."

"Don't worry." I touch her cheek. "You'll always be my first love."

"Really now?"

"Really."

I turn on my side and grasp her chin, about to kiss her, but the position puts pressure on my wound and I wince.

"It still hurts?" Ingrid asks, glancing at my thigh.

"A bit."

"Maybe you shouldn't be moving too much."

My eyebrows crease. "What? You're not trying to get out of sex with me, are you?"

She chuckles, then turns serious as she touches my cheek. "Who said anything about not having sex?" She gets off the bed and walks over to the closet.

"All I said was that you shouldn't move too much, and to make sure of that..." She holds up a scarf.

My eyes grow wide as I realize what she's planning. "No way."

"Why not?" Ingrid climbs back on the bed with the scarf. "We are all for gender equality, are we not?"

"Of course, but..."

"Just this once." Ingrid rubs the tip of the scarf against my cheek.

I swallow the lump in my throat. "Alright, but only because I'm injured."

She grins. "Fine."

She holds her hand out. "Wrists, please."

I reluctantly offer them to her.

Still grinning, she ties the scarf around them, then pushes my arms above my head.

"How does that feel?"

"Okay," I answer in spite of my doubts.

She runs her fingers across my jaw. "Good. Now be a good boy and don't move."

Keeping her hand on my cheek, she lowers her mouth. Parting her lips, she dips her tongue inside mine and I close my eyes as the heat travels throughout my whole body, pooling in my groin.

As she crushes my mouth beneath hers, our tongues mingling, her hand slips under the hem of my shirt. It crawls across my tingling skin and over my quivering muscles, finally resting when it reaches one of my nipples and pinches the nub of flesh lightly.

My hands twitch and so does my cock. They're both becoming restless.

Ingrid pulls away and pulls her shift off so I'm staring at her teal bra. It seems too small for her; her breasts are almost bursting out. She keeps that on, along with her matching underwear, but tosses her pajamas aside.

She gives me just a moment to take in her beauty—her firm breasts, the soft curve of her belly, her thin waist and her smooth thighs—before she's on me again, kissing me. As she does, her fingers grab the hem of my shirt, pulling it up so that it bunches under my armpits.

Again, she tears her mouth away, and this time she takes her turn staring at my chest and my stomach, her sapphire eyes gleaming.

It's that same look that she has on when she's going after a story, a combination of curiosity, excitement and passion.

It makes my heart pound against my chest and my cock against my briefs. Suddenly, they both seem too tight to contain their frenzied prisoners.

Slowly, Ingrid traces the muscles of my chest.

"Have you always had this kind of body?" she asks.

"What? Is this an interview?"

She grins. "Why don't we make it one?"

Why didn't I just keep my mouth shut?

"So, what's the answer?" She plants a kiss right in the middle of my pectorals.

"Not always. I was a puny teenager, but in college I started running, getting…"

I gasp as she dips her tongue into my bellybutton, leaving me with a ticklish sensation.

"You were saying?" She lifts her head to meet my gaze.

"It's rude to interrupt the person you're interviewing, you know," I remind her.

"Sorry." She gives me a quick kiss as she traces circles on my rigid belly. "Please continue."

"I said I started getting fit in college."

"And what about this?" She cups my crotch. "When did you get this?"

I give another grasp as my cock throbs against her palm. "At birth, I think."

"Oh, I'm sorry. I wasn't clear. I meant this."

She slips her hand beneath my shorts and my briefs and wraps her fingers around my cock.

It hardens and I purse my lips to hold back a moan.

"You know, you should really answer when someone asks you a question," she tells me as she takes my stiff cock out and begins stroking it.

"And you know I'm going to get back at you for this," I promise her.

She responds by licking the tip of my cock, sending a jolt of pleasure through me that takes my breath away.

"Fuck."

Now I know what it feels like to have her touching me while I'm not touching her. Every brush of her fingertips and every swipe of that mischievous tongue makes me shudder.

"What did you say? Do you want to fuck me already?"

"Yes, please," I answer breathlessly.

Ingrid shakes her head. "I think not, but I'll give you a reward for being so polite."

She wraps her lips around me and sucks.

A moan escapes my lips, my body trembling.

It's a reward, alright, but it's also torture, pushing my self-control to its limits.

She cups my balls as she gives another suck and then licks the length of my cock.

I shudder.

"Ingrid," I gasp out her name.

"One last question," she says.

"Yes?"

"How does this feel?"

She takes the whole of my cock in her mouth and swallows.

My hips rise off the bed, the heat from my balls spreading through every inch of my body.

She pulls away, licking her lips. "Well?"

"I don't have words for it," I admit, shaking my head. "Are we done now? With the interview, I mean."

"Yes."

She takes off my pants and my briefs, planting a reverent kiss over the bandage around my thigh, then lifts herself up to claim my lips.

Breathless, she gets off the bed to take off her bra. Her firm breasts with their stiff, rosy peaks spring free. When she lowers her panties, my eyes grow wide at the stain inside them.

She returns to the bed, this time climbing on top of me. She gives me another kiss, longer, deeper, stealing my breath. Then she grabs my cock and slowly lowers herself onto me.

I hold my breath, my chest hurting.

She takes me all the way in to the hilt, sitting on top of me, and my breath leaves me in a sound between a gasp and a groan.

Ingrid, too, gasps, her shoulders heaving, trembling.

Putting her hands on my chest, she begins moving her hips up and down. Her breasts are suspended right in front of my face. I long to touch them, straining against the scarf, but since I can't, I lift my head to capture one in my mouth.

She moans, then leans back, beyond my reach. She throws her head back, her hair cascading behind her, dancing past her shoulders as she rolls her hips. Her eyes squeezed shut and her lashes fluttering, she moans, riding me.

She leans forward again, her hair a veil around her face. As she kisses me, her nipples rub against mine. Then she lifts herself up and moves faster. Grunting, I move my hips to meet hers. The sound of skin slapping against skin bounces off the walls.

Her eyes meet mine. "I thought I told you not to move."

"I can't help it," I tell her. "You're too sexy."

That said, I pull my wrists free, the scarf unraveling above me. Lifting her, I switch our positions and climb on top of her, gripping her thighs as I start pounding into her.

I kiss her to silence her protest, but even after I've pulled my mouth away, I hear none, only loud moans and soft cries as she wraps her arms and legs around me.

Pain shoots up my thigh but I ignore it, jerking my hips as I lose control.

It's amazing I've been able to hold back for this long.

With a long groan, I bury myself deep inside her, my feverish cock quivering with its release.

Clamping her hands on my ass, she trembles beneath me seconds later, her mouth open in a silent scream.

I lie down on the bed, completely out of breath. She snuggles next to me, gasping as well.

"How's your thigh?" she asks.

I jerk as she brushes against it. "I'm fine."

She slips a hand under me, squeezing my ass.

I turn my head towards her. "What was that for?"

"I've just been wanting to do it."

"Have you now?"

"No. Actually, this is what I've been wanting to do."

She pushes me onto my side and nips my ass.

"Ow," I complain at the pain from my wound and from the edge of her teeth.

Ingrid just gives me a mischievous grin.

"You know, you've been very naughty."

I sit up, tickling her. Her laughs and squeals fill the room.

"Stop!" she says, half laughing. "You'll wake Alexa."

I stop, realizing that it's true. Come to think of it, it's a miracle she's still asleep what with all the noise Ingrid and I have been making.

She pulls my shirt down and rests her head on my chest, right above my heart.

I glance at her, seeing her lips curved into a smile. "You're happy."

"Why shouldn't I be?" she asks, her eyes meeting mine. "You're here. Besides, I'm done with my story."

"I thought so."

"I'm not sure it's the right piece, but I love it."

I touch her cheek. "Then I'm sure everyone else will, too."

"What about you?" she asks me. "Are you done?"

"Almost."

"Don't slack off on my account, now," she warns, waving a finger at me.

"You know me. I'll give it my best," I promise her.

She smiles. "And may the best story win."

Chapter Twenty-Four
Ingrid

"Thank you for coming."

Cassie enters the conference room—Conference Room 2 this time—with two other people, an older, Asian-looking woman and a bald man in his fifties.

I straighten up in my seat, taking a deep breath.

"Once again, I apologize for all your troubles." Cassie sits down at the end of the table. "On behalf of my uncle, I am so sorry. He wanted to convey his apologies himself, but he has already resigned from the company."

I raise an eyebrow, glancing at Conner.

I'm not sure how much of that is fact and how much is the press release. At any rate, it doesn't matter.

"I also would like to inform you that the company has decided to compensate you for your troubles," Cassie continues. "As well as Ms. Tiffany Jordan, who has decided not to join us today."

"And Ed?" I ask.

"The company paid for all funeral expenses, and a trust fund has been arranged for his children."

I raise my eyebrows. "Ed had children?"

"Two," Cassie answers. "One in college and one seventeen. Both have been living with his wife and her second husband for over ten years now."

I nod.

Poor Ed.

"Of course, I would also like to thank you for stories," Cassie goes on. "They were both superb, no less than great and no less than we expected from each of you."

Her gaze goes from Conner to me, and I smile.

"Now, on to the important part. But first, allow me to introduce two other people at this company, Dan Smith and Gina Chang."

The people sitting beside Cassie smile.

"Pleasure to meet you." Conner stands, offering his hand. "I'm Conner Blake."

They shake his hand but say nothing. Cassie didn't even give their titles, which doesn't help me figure out why they're here. I'm guessing it has something to do with the job offer, if there is still one.

"Dan and Gina both helped me make the decision that I'll be announcing today." Cassie clasps her hands on the table. "First of all, the company has decided to push through with the news magazine, even though my uncle came up with it. We still think it's a good idea. As such, we still need an editor-in-chief. We…"

Suddenly, Conner raises his hand.

"Yes?" Cassie turns to him, along with all the other pairs of eyes in the room, mine most surprised of all.

What is he doing?

Conner stands up slowly, hands in his pockets. "I would just like to say that I think Ingrid should get the job."

My jaw drops. "What? But…"

"I think she's a better journalist than I am," Conner goes on. "Even though she is less experienced."

I shake my head, throwing him a look of disbelief.

"Ingrid, do you have anything to say?" Cassie asks me.

"Yes, if I may." I smooth the front of my white blouse as I stand up. "I think if it's a choice between me and Conner, then Conner should get it. Like he said, he's more experienced. He has more contacts. And he is very hard-working."

This time, Conner looks at me in disbelief, shoulders bunched up.

I ignore him, looking at Cassie. "Also, I have other reasons, selfish reasons maybe, but well… for one, I think I'd rather devote time to my daughter. She is growing up so fast. And two, if Conner doesn't get this job, he'll go back to Dallas, and I don't really want him to. Our daughter needs him."

Cassie's eyes pop out.

I glance at Conner. "And I need him."

I take my seat and for a moment, silence falls over the room.

Then Cassie exhales. "Well, I guess I know what the inspiration for your piece is. Are you saying you don't want the job, Ingrid?"

I nod.

"But..." Conner begins to protest, but Cassie holds up her hand.

"Well, like I said, the person who writes the best story becomes the editor-in-chief of our news magazine. And that person..."

She pauses, and I hold my breath. Across the table, I see Conner doing the same.

"Is Conner Blake," she finishes, turning to him.

Joy explodes in my chest.

"Your story was genuine and inspiring," Cassie tells him. "And it resonated with everyone. So, congratulations."

"Thank you," Conner mutters under his breath.

I turn to him with a wide smile, reaching across the table to squeeze his hand. "I'm so happy for you."

"Starting next week, you'll be working with Dan." Cassie gestures to the man beside her. "He will be the publisher of the magazine."

This time, he's the one who shakes Conner's hand. "I look forward to working with you."

"Me too," Conner tells him. "We'll work together to make this magazine a success."

Dan nods. "I have high hopes."

"As does everyone else in the company," Cassie adds.

"I'll try not to disappoint," Conner promises.

"We also decided that as the editor-in-chief, you will have the option to choose your own associate editor," Cassie informs him. "At least, for now."

The bit of information takes me by surprise. He does?

"After all, we want you to work alongside someone you can trust, someone you can get along with. These first few months will be bumpy."

Conner turns to me. "Then I'll choose..."

"Before you make your choice," Cassie interrupts, "I have something to say to Ingrid."

She turns to me as well. "Ingrid, your story wasn't exactly what we asked for, but it was a beautiful feature. You wrote straight from your heart, and you captured ours. That's why Gina thought she'd offer you a different job."

My eyebrows shoot up. What?

"Gina is a good friend of mine, and she is an editor for a publishing company that is soon to be a part of ours," Cassie explains. "Their company publishes popular magazines as well as non-fiction books. We thought you'd be a great fit."

I place my hand over my rapidly beating heart. "Really?"

Gina nods. "Our office is in Denver. You'll need to attend the meetings at the office twice a month, but otherwise you can work from home. That should give you plenty of time to take care of your daughter, yes?"

I nod. "It really is a wonderful offer."

"It is," Conner agrees.

I look at him.

"Well, Ingrid, it looks like you have a decision to make." Cassie stands up. "You'll let us know on Monday?"

I get out of my chair as well. "Thank you, Cassie. And Gina. And Dan."

They leave the room, leaving me with Conner.

"So..." Conner taps his fingers on the table. "You do have a decision to make. And a big one."

"I know."

He circles the table, standing over me and holding my hand. "Whatever your decision is, I promise I'll support you. I won't question it. I will respect it and be happy for you one hundred and one percent."

I smile. "Thank you. I'll think about it carefully."

"You do that. However, there's also something else I was hoping you could do."

"What?"

"I've actually made plans for Valentine's this year, so…"

"You did?" My eyes grow wide.

He kneels in front of me, and for a moment my heart stops. Is he going to give me a ring? Instead, he takes a card in a red envelope from his pocket—a Valentine's Day card.

"Will you be my Valentine? Or are you too busy thinking about the future?"

"Of course not." I pull him to his feet. "Yes, Conner, I will be your Valentine."

I give him a quick kiss. "So, where are you taking me?"

~

"I want you to close your eyes," Conner says. "And at the count of three, open them."

"Another surprise?" I ask, putting my hands over my eyes.

So far, the day has been full of surprises. He gave me flowers. We watched a movie. We watched the sunset from the top of a building. We had dinner at a fancy restaurant. And now, this.

"One…" I hear the door creaking and Conner gives me a gentle push. "Two. Three!"

I open my eyes, which then pop wide open just like my mouth as I look around the hotel room. Candles form a heart on the floor. Red rose petals are sprinkled on the bed, a heart-shaped box of chocolates lies on the pillow. On the table sits a bottle of wine with two glasses as well as a large bowl of strawberries and a smaller one filled with cream. On the window, more rose petals have been stuck to the glass, forming the words 'I LOVE YOU'.

I place my hand over my heart, which seems like it's either about to burst free with excitement or drown in so much joy.

"I love you too," I tell Conner, wrapping my hands around his neck and kissing him.

His hands on my waist, he pulls me closer, his tongue slipping into my mouth. I let it play with mine a bit before pulling away.

"Is something wrong?" He gives me a confused look.

I hold up a finger. "Just wait here."

I head to the bathroom, my purse still under my arm. Putting it down by the sink, I fish the small paper bag out from among its various contents.

I had a feeling something like this would happen, or at least I had hopes, which is why I bought a little something from Agent Provocateur.

Placing the bag on the other side of the sink, I begin to undress. First, I kick off my stilettos, savoring a sliver of relief at the fact that my feet are free. Next, I take off my pink sweater and my white dress, tossing both on top of my shoes. Finally, I remove my matching pink bra and panties and drop them on the rug.

Completely naked, I grab the paper bag and open it, pulling the red piece of lingerie out of the soft wrapping paper.

I slip on the red body suit made of sheer tulle and stand in front of the mirror to evaluate the effect. The fabric hugs my body, showing off every curve. My nipples poke out of the heart-shaped cut-outs on the cups, while the embroidered hearts along the sides and around the waist make my figure even more slender than it normally is. The back has a large heart cut-out in the middle and a single strap that runs along the center, all the way down the gap between my butt cheeks.

I draw a deep breath, knowing that it's a daring piece, almost next to nothing against my skin. It was expensive, too.

Still, tonight is special. It's worth it. I sure hope Conner likes it.

"Ingrid?" Conner knocks on the bathroom door, concern in his voice. "Are you okay in there?"

"Yup. I'm coming out," I answer, grabbing the robe off the peg behind the bathroom door.

Wrapping the white robe around me, I do two more things—let my hair flow free past my shoulders with a few shakes, and spray on a splash of Victoria's Secret Eau So Sexy. The floral and fruity scent fills the air.

Now, I'm ready.

I step out of the bathroom. Conner is waiting just outside.

"I was beginning to worry about you," he says.

Then his eyebrows arch as he notices what I'm wearing. "If you were going to take a shower, you should have said so. We…"

"I didn't." I hold a finger to his lips. "And instead of worrying, maybe you should have undressed, but since you didn't…"

I grab the front of his shirt and pop out the buttons one by one. As soon as the last button is undone, I push it off him and he shrugs it off the rest of the way. I reach for his pants, but before I can unbutton them, Conner grabs my wrists.

"I think that's enough."

"Okay."

"Now, will you show me what's beneath that robe?"

I push him so that he's sitting on the edge of the bed, then tug on the sash of my robe. I shrug it off slowly, and Conner's eyes grow wider with every inch of bare skin and sheer fabric revealed.

"Holy shit." The words escape his lips as he stands up. "You look… hot."

"Why, thank you for that very descriptive word." I put my hands on his shoulders.

"And you're wearing red. Again."

I grin. "Truth be told, it's always been my favorite color."

"It suits you."

Gripping my waist, Conner kisses me, picking up where we left off. Then, to my surprise, he picks me up in his arms, dropping me on top of the bed.

His tongue explores my mouth while his hands run through the tulle. Then he pulls away.

"I have something for you, too."

He pulls a pair of red handcuffs from his pocket.

I blink. "Wow. It's red, too."

"Mm-hmm." He opens them and places the key on the nightstand. "Let's see if they fit, shall we?"

I offer him my wrists and he cuffs them. I lift the cuffs to my face to take a closer look, finding all the metal parts covered in red fur.

"I like them."

"Good."

Conner pushes me down on the bed, my arms above me.

"Now, do you remember last time when I said I'd get back at you?"

"Um, yes?"

"This is payback," he promises with a mischievous grin.

A shudder of anticipation ascends my spine.

Conner grabs the bowl of cream and sets it down on the bed.

I raise my eyebrows. "You're going to get my new clothes dirty?"

"Don't worry." His fingers brush against my cheek. "I'll clean you up thoroughly."

My heart flutters. "That was what I was afraid of."

Getting some cream on his fingers and wiping them on his tongue, he kisses me again, sharing the sweet treat with me. Then he turns me around so that I'm lying on my belly.

Sweeping my hair aside, he paints a trail of cream down my spine, licking it off.

"You're going to get fat," I tease even as I shiver with excitement.

He doesn't answer, busy with his task. The end of the cream trail lies dangerously close to my other hole, and in spite of the fabric covering my skin, I gasp when he licks that spot.

I'm not sure if I'm relieved or disappointed when he doesn't go lower.

Getting more cream on his fingers, he adorns my butt cheeks, licking one and then biting the other.

"Ow!" I yelp.

"Now we're even," Conner says, reverently licking the patch of flesh which he nipped.

"You're not going to leave a mark there, are you?"

He turns me around. "No. I'll leave it here, like last time."

He kisses my neck and I throw my head back, baring more skin to him. He sucks on the flesh and I bite my lips at the sting. His wet tongue soothes it and I gasp.

"There you go," he says, smiling proudly at his work. "Now you're even more red."

"And you're not red enough," I tell him, lifting my leg so that my knee brushes against the tent in his pants.

He draws a deep breath. "Not yet."

Getting more cream, he covers my nipples, his fingers rubbing against the nubs and making them engorged. Heat swells in my breasts.

As he lowers his head, I hold my breath, bracing myself. I can never prepare myself enough for his tongue, though, and I let out a loud gasp as I feel its tip circling the stiff peak.

He rubs that peak as he moves on to the other and I give a moan, my back arching. The tingling heat from my breasts ripples down my belly and pools between my legs.

Shit.

I just bought this body suit and now it's getting stained.

Conner sucks on both of my breasts, drawing more moans from me. Then he moves lower.

"You're not going to put cream there, are you?" I ask, wondering if that's alright.

"Oh, I think there's enough cream there already," he answers.

He unhooks the bottom of the suit so that nothing stands in his way and parting my thighs, he settles between them. His tongue brushes against my clit and I let out a cry, trembling. His tongue slips inside me and I throw my head back, mouth open in a silent scream as I feel more 'cream' ooze out of me.

As his tongue turns me inside out, his fingers strum my engorged nub and I tremble even more. My back arching, I try to reach the wall, my nails grazing the plaster.

"Conner!" His name leaves me in a gasp as I struggle to breathe.

The pleasure from his tongue and his fingers is so great that the rest of my body has gone numb, my mind blank. It's sopping wet between my legs.

When I climax, the intensity of it knocks the breath from my lungs. My head rises off the pillow before crashing back down with the wave of pleasure that goes through me.

Still, Conner's tongue doesn't stop. Though he's withdrawn his fingers, his tongue continues to lick the sensitive skin and plunge in between, lapping up the 'cream'.

I squirm and move my hips, trying to get out from under him, but he holds me fast, hands pushing my thighs even farther apart.

As a result, a second orgasm comes on the heels of the first. I scream, feeling tiny explosions throughout my body.

Only after that does Conner stop, licking his lips as he sits beside me.

I turn towards him but don't speak, still trying to force air back into my lungs and recover my senses. He unties my wrists, kissing them before getting off the bed.

When my vision is no longer a blur, I lift my head to stare at him. He's standing at the edge of the bed, completely naked.

I pause to admire his long, thick cock. It's pointing straight at me, the tip swollen and glistening.

Going back to the bowl of cream, Conner brushes some on the tip of his cock.

"Your reward," he tells me.

Excitement buzzing in my veins once more, I kneel on the carpet in front of him, squeezing his butt and gripping tightly it as I lick the tip of his cock. His hands grip my shoulders in turn, his knees trembling.

I lick thoroughly long after the cream is all gone, tasting something even sweeter. Then I let the tip of my tongue dance along the length of him.

Conner gasps, grabbing my hair.

Looking up at him, holding his eyes, which are burning with lust, I open my mouth wide, letting his cock glide across my tongue, all the way down my throat. He pulls at my hair, grunting as I breathe through my nostrils, forcing my throat to relax so I don't gag. When I swallow around him, he lets out a curse as his body shakes.

"Fuck, Ingrid!"

I release him, pausing to take a gulp of air and hollow out my cheeks before sucking on him.

I move my head back and forth, his hand in my hair guiding my pace. His short curls tickle my nostrils. His balls slap against my saliva-coated chin.

Suddenly, Conner pulls me off him and sits on the edge of the bed.

"Come here, Ingrid." He crooks a finger at me.

I climb on Conner's lap and he slips a finger inside me to prepare me before pushing my hips down. I grab his shoulders, throwing my head back as he enters me.

When he's completely sheathed in my heat, he cups my cheek and kisses me fiercely. Then he grips my hips and lifts them, only to let them crash down again.

With his hands guiding me and my knees buried in the mattress, I move up and down, dancing on his lap. He captures one of my breasts in his mouth and I scream.

His thick cock rubs against my velvety channel, which is getting both wetter and hotter by the second. A tingling sensation travels throughout my body as shiver after shiver rack my spine.

When he releases inside me, hands holding my hips in an almost bruising grip, I explode anew, my nails raking across his back.

Afterwards, he lets me go and I collapse against him like a limp doll, completely breathless and exhausted.

"That was payback, alright," I tell him in a hoarse whisper as I rest my chin on his shoulder.

He plants a kiss on mine. "Happy Valentine's Day."

"Happy Valentine's Day," I greet him in turn. "And I have to say this has been the best Valentine's Day of my life."

"Mine, too," Conner confesses. "And by the way, your story was the best Valentine's Day piece I've ever read."

I smile.

The story I submitted to Cassie was published online today, and so far it's only received raves, but Conner's affirmation makes me even more proud of it.

I rest my cheek against Conner's neck. "What was your favorite part of the story?"

"I loved it all," he says. "Every word."

"Come on," I urge. "Tell me the ones you liked best."

"Fine. Let me see." He leans back. "I like the one where you said the best love stories are not the grand ones that people in Hollywood make movies about but the ordinary ones that creep up on ordinary people without them knowing it and linger long."

"I like that part, too."

"And that part where you mentioned that someone stole your heart, of course." He pushes me off his shoulder, hands on my waist and eyes on mine. "Because I think I know who did."

I grin. "Do you, know?"

He plants a kiss on my forehead. "Though I think it's a bit unfair. I don't think I stole your heart. I think you gave it to me."

I shrug. "Maybe. But saying you stole it makes it sound more romantic."

"Hmm."

He lifts me off him and I sit on the edge of the bed.

"I have one more gift to give you," he says.

He gets something else from his pockets, and when he returns, he genuflects in front of me, a satin box in his hand.

I cover my mouth as I gasp.

It can't be.

"Ingrid Halfield," Conner starts, opening the box to reveal the diamond ring inside. "You've already given me the greatest gift. And maybe I did steal your heart, but now I'm asking you to give me the rest of you for the rest of my life. Will you be my wife?"

I nod, too stunned to speak. My heart is pounding so hard I'm afraid it might fly off and take my whole body with it.

Conner takes the ring out of the box and slips it on my finger, then kisses the back of my hand. "I love you, Ingrid."

"I love you too, Conner."

I throw my arms around his neck, kissing the top of his head as a joyful tear trickles down my cheek.

This truly is the best Valentine's Day ever.

And to think it's just our second one.

Epilogue
Ingrid

Seven more years later...

Valentine's Day

"To ordinary love stories that never end," I say as I raise my glass of sparkling cranberry juice in the middle of the garden, my gaze on the debonair man beside me. He's holding the hand of our adorable four-year-old daughter, Celine, my stunning teenager, Alexa, beside him.

"To love," Conner and everyone else answer, raising their glasses of champagne in turn.

I take a sip of my drink, stopping when Celine wraps her arms around me.

"Careful," Conner tells her. "You know your baby brother is in there."

"Sorry," she mumbles.

I pat the top of her head. "It's okay. Now go play."

She runs off.

"Cool Valentine's Day party, Mom," Alexa says. "Although I still think we should have a live band."

"Maybe next year," I tell her.

Alexa sniffs my drink. "Can I have some of that?"

"Sure." I hand her my glass.

"Alexa!" Celine calls.

"Coming!" Alexa gulps down my drink and runs after her little sister.

Conner places his arm around me. "They get along so well."

I watch them playing with the heart-shaped balloons, a smile forming on my lips. "Why shouldn't they?"

"Now this is an amazing party!" Tiffany joins us. "You should do this every year."

I shrug. "Maybe. We've been wanting to throw a Valentine's Day party, actually, but the house just got finished and Conner is so busy..."

"Of course he is." Tiffany nudges his arm. "He's a Pulitzer Prize-winning journalist now."

Conner's eyebrows rise. "Why is it that you made that sound like I'm a prize stallion or something?"

I chuckle.

"Whatever," Tiffany dismisses his remark. "I'm so proud of you."

"Where's Margot?" I ask her.

"Oh, she's in the Maldives with her husband," Tiffany answers. "Lucky girl. I wish my husband would take me there. Oh, wait. I don't have a husband."

"But you do have your own fashion line now," I tell her. "Congratulations!"

"Thank you." She gives me a hug. "There's just so much to celebrate, isn't there?"

"Yes, there is." I glance at my stomach.

Tiffany does the same. "How far along are you?"

"Oh, not that far along yet. It's just almost the third month."

"Well, good luck." She smiles. "And let me know when the baby's out."

"I will," I promise her.

After she leaves, I head towards a bench. "I think I need to sit down."

"Do you need anything?" Conner asks.

"No. I'm fine. Go play with the kids or talk to some other guys." I shoo him away.

"Okay." He kisses my cheek before he leaves.

Just a few moments later, Janine and Astrid sit down beside me.

"I thought he was never going to leave your side," Janine says.

I narrow my eyes at her. "You mean like you were never going to leave your apartment?"

Astrid covers her mouth as she chuckles.

When Celine was born, I chose Astrid and Janine to be her godmothers. Now they're best friends, bonding over video games and other geeky stuff.

"So, how are things?" I ask Astrid, squeezing her hand.

"Everything's fine, actually," Astrid tells me. "My mother is really in love with the twins. Ever since they were born, she's just stayed around and refused to leave. Of course, that poses some problems, but at least she and I get along now. And she likes Trevor now, too."

"Of course," Janine says. "Grandchildren make all mothers-in-law fall in love with their sons-in-law."

"I loved your last book, by the way," Astrid tells me. "When is the next one coming out?"

"Next month, hopefully," I answer.

I've been writing non-fiction books for women for the past seven years, a vocation I've been enjoying immensely, especially since I get to spend a lot of time with my kids and my books have been selling so well.

Astrid squeezes my hand. "You're living the dream."

"I'm still not a princess, though," I tease her.

"I am not a princess," she argues.

"She is now," Janine says. "In that last video game I helped make, I named the princess after her."

Astrid's blue eyes widen. "You did not!"

"I did," Janine nods, taking a sip of her champagne. "Don't worry. No one will know it's you except the three of us."

Astrid raises her glass. "To secrets between lifelong friends."

"Sorry." I shrug. "I don't have a glass."

"Here. Take a sip of mine." Janine offers me her glass.

"No thanks." I shake my head. "Conner will freak out if he finds out I'm drinking."

"What?" Janine looks horrified. "Since when does he get to make the rules?"

"Um, since he became my husband," I say. "Which was six years ago."

"Trevor doesn't like me drinking when I'm pregnant, either," Astrid pipes in. "Actually, he doesn't like me drinking at all."

"That's because you can't hold your alcohol, Princess," Janine teases.

Astrid pouts.

I place a hand on Janine's shoulder. "Okay, that's enough. You're having too much fun."

"And you're not having fun at all." Janine stands up and pulls my arm. "Let's dance."

I throw her a puzzled look. "This from someone who doesn't like social gatherings?"

"I like this one," Janine says. "Come on."

I glance at my belly, hesitating.

"Dancing isn't against the pregnancy rules, is it?" Janine asks.

Oh, what the heck. I need to have some fun with my friends once in a while.

Smiling, I grab her arm, letting her pull me off the bench. I offer Astrid my other arm, and the three of us walk to the dance floor arm in arm.

"Let's party."

~

"You were partying earlier," Conner says, wrapping his arms around me from behind as I stand on the balcony under the starry night.

I touch his cheek. "Duh. It was a party, right?"

"I know one thing." He rests his head on my shoulder. "We throw better parties than Damien Shore."

I turn around to face him, leaning on the balustrade. "You just had to bring him up."

Conner shrugs. "Well, we met at his party."

"Like I can forget."

He tucks a strand of hair behind my cheek. "And now, several Valentine's Days later, we're still together. Who would have thought?"

"Every day is a Valentine's Day with you," I tell him.

He smiles and leans over to plant a tender kiss on my lips.

Even after all these years, Conner's kisses make my heart flutter like a butterfly.

After kissing my lips, he slides down to kiss the heart-shaped golden pendant he gave me on our first wedding anniversary. Since it's hanging between my breasts, the kiss makes me gasp. Then he moves even further down, kissing my belly reverently.

"I can't wait to meet you, Clark," he whispers.

I snort. "We don't even know if it's a boy yet. What if it's another girl?"

Conner stands up, hands on my waist. "It's okay. I'll just have another girl to win over."

"If you ask me, you're the one at the mercy of those girls." I glance inside the room, where Alexa and Celine are seated on the couch.

He nods. "You may be right."

I chuckle.

"But you'll always be my first girl." He rubs my arms.

"Really?" I arch my eyebrows.

"And my best." He strokes my cheek. "You're like this perfect red wine that once I had a taste of, I couldn't get enough, and nothing else could ever get me drunk."

I bunch up my eyebrows. "You're comparing me to wine?"

"I'm comparing you to a taste of heaven." He kisses my hand.

"Well, you are right." I wrap my hands behind his neck. "Ever since that first night, I've been your captive in more ways than one."

Conner pulls me close.

"I'll never let you go," he whispers against my forehead.

I smile as I press my cheek against his. "I never want you to."

It may have begun unexpectedly, and I don't know how it will end, but I know ours is the best love story of all.

All because we're in it.

~The End~

MARRIED TO THE ROYAL

Prologue
Steff

Outskirts of Aldnoah, Capital of Brelv

The percussion of the rain against the window masks the creaking of the dusty floorboards beneath my boots. I move one step at a time, steering clear of the cracked vase on the cobweb-coated stool and the boxes of mildew-infested clothes in the otherwise empty cabin.

At least, it was empty.

As I approach the corner, I hear voices, one of which I recognize as that of a woman I know well.

Natasia.

"This isn't my fault," she says shakily.

I catch a glimpse of auburn locks draped like curtains over an oval-shaped face. The strings of diamonds dangling from her ears through the gaps confirm my speculation. The muscles of her slender shoulders tense beneath her velvet cloak, fastened at the base of her throat with a brooch that is missing an onyx bead. Her hands tremble in their satin sheaths.

"I put the poison in his drink."

My eyes grow wide. Another speculation confirmed.

She grits her teeth between cherry-glossed lips. "Maybe I should just stab him."

Natasia's words and the hatred in them bring my heart to a halt as my chest constricts. My jaw drops. My breath hangs in the air.

"That would, of course, be your choice," the other voice replies.

I glance at him, unable to recognize his voice. Worse, his back is nearly against the wall, so I can only discern his black cloak, cotton instead of velvet and patched with flecks of dirt.

A commoner.

Why is a Princess of Brelv meeting with a commoner inside a filthy cabin, unaccompanied?

No. I already know the answer.

"Regardless, you owe me," the man says.

Natasia clicks her tongue disapprovingly and then tosses a leather pouch at his feet. The clink of coins rings out above the rain.

"Next time, the deed will be done," she promises as she turns around.

She walks towards the door and pulls the hood of her cloak over her head.

"I will not spend the rest of my life stuck in that hell."

I press my lips together and swallow the lump in my throat.

Hell?

All this time, I thought my brother's wife had nothing to be unhappy about. She has her own string of lavish chambers at the Palace, one of which houses a perfumed Turkish bath just for her. She has no shortage of maids, or jewelry, or gowns that are the envy of everyone else. My parents adore her. My sisters look up to her. Celia even used to imitate her every gesture. And Viktor...

I pause as I recall my conversation with my brother near the stables the other day.

Viktor's expression had suddenly turned serious. He seemed on the verge of confiding something in me, but Natasia interrupted us and he wasn't able to continue. When I brought it up again later on, he dismissed it with a shrug and said it was nothing. But the smile on his face was so wide it couldn't have been real.

Was he trying to tell me that his marriage to Natasia hasn't been working?

The front door of the cabin opens and closes. Moments later, the crack of a whip resonates through the air and the clatter of hooves fades into the distance.

Natasia's gone.

For a moment, I consider confronting the man she was speaking to, but I decide against it. This is no light matter. If I act now, my actions will have an effect on Viktor and possibly the entire royal family and even the country. I mustn't proceed without a plan.

I take a step back so that I can make my retreat, but in my hurry, my foot hits one of the legs of the stool. The vase on it wobbles, falls and shatters on the floor.

Fuck.

In the next instant, a strong arm wraps around my neck. At the same time, the tip of a knife enters my side. The sharp blade pierces layers of velvet, silk, reinforced leather and the skin between my ribs. Pain spreads throughout my chest and a strangled cry escapes my lips. My air passage narrows and a flurry of panic seizes me.

Then my adrenaline kicks in.

I grab the man's arm, go down on one knee and hurl him to the floor. I pull the knife from my side and throw it at him as he gets back on his feet. It strikes the back of his shoulder and he lets out a groan as he clutches at it. Drops of red trickle past his fingers and stain his cloak.

After arming myself with the largest remnant of the shattered vase, I take the chance to assess my opponent.

Disheveled brown hair. Ebony eyes. A scar atop the bridge of his nose.

Those dark eyes narrow and stare into mine intently. I glare back through platinum-blond wisps.

With a louder groan, he pulls the blade from his shoulder. I clench my jaw and tighten my grip on the porcelain shard in my hand, ready to attack. Then his gaze strays to the gleaming ring on my hand and his eyes grow wide beneath arched eyebrows.

Ah. He seems to have recognized me.

He turns on his heel and runs out the back door. I think of running after him, but my side throbs as I stand up. I peek under my cloak and frown at the sight of the crimson stain on my shirt.

Right. I'm injured as well.

Thanks to the inner layer of light armor I always wear, it's not a deep wound. Unluckily, it must have grazed an artery, and a fair amount of blood has gushed out. I can't afford to lose more. If I lose consciousness, the situation will slip out of my hands, and that's not something I can allow to happen right now.

I pull off my cravat and press it firmly against the cut in an effort to stop the bleeding. Then I sit down on the stool and take my phone out of my pocket. Six missed calls appear on the screen, all from the same person.

Danni.

Of course. She must be sick with worry looking for me after I gave her the slip. In fact, she must have tried to track my phone by now.

I tap the number to return the call before pressing the phone against my ear. After just a second, a loud, concerned voice answers.

"Your Highness?"

I frown. How many times have I asked her to call me Steff? Or Steffan at least?

"Stay put. I'm on my way to you now."

Just as I thought. In fact, I can already hear a motorcycle engine raging in the background.

I let out a sigh. "You're giving me orders as usual."

"I..."

"Don't worry, Danni," I cut her off as I glance at my roughly bandaged thigh, the blue silk already turned purple. "I'm not going anywhere, but do hurry. I'm afraid I have a small problem that needs immediate attention."

~

"A small problem?"

Danni crosses her arms over her chest as her dark brown eyes throw me a reprimanding scowl from behind her glasses. Her back rests against the chamber door, which she's just locked after sending the servants away. The tip of her boot beats against the carpet.

"Your Highness, you nearly got yourself killed."

I toss my cloak aside and take off my stained shirt and my pierced armor. I run my fingers over my wound, now stitched up, cleaned and bandaged properly thanks to Danni.

"Surely you don't think I'd die from a scratch like this."

"Your..."

"For the hundredth time, you don't need to address me so formally when it's just the two of us talking." I sit on the edge of the bed and remove one of my boots. "And you're my attendant, not my governess."

"And you are a Prince of Brelv." She genuflects in front of me and helps me with the straps of my other boot. "You mustn't be reckless."

"Ah. But where's the fun in that?"

I kick off the boot and begin to lie down on the bed.

"Steffan!"

My eyes grow wide at finally hearing my name on Danni's lips. I glance at her and find her head bowed down, her shoulders trembling. Her fist digs into the carpet.

I fold my arms behind my head and stare at the embroidered canopy. "I'm sorry I made you worry. But like I told you, I have my reasons."

"And you told me that once we got back here, you would tell me those reasons," she reminds me as she gets to her feet.

Her long shadow falls across my chest.

I draw a deep breath. "Someone has been trying to kill me."

Danni's lips part to let out a gasp. She lifts a hand to push her glasses up her nose.

"As I've said, you're a Prince of Brelv. There are inevitably a number of people who want you dead."

I know.

"What I mean is that lately, someone in the Palace has been trying to poison me."

"Poison?"

"I first noticed it a week ago after I spilled my glass of wine on the balcony."

"I remember that."

"In the morning, I noticed that the fingers of the maid who had cleaned up that mess looked burned. But she said she hadn't been near a fire. Later that day, I deliberately tipped my cup of tea into a potted plant. After a few hours, the plant wilted."

Danni slaps her forehead. "I should have noticed."

"You weren't the one being poisoned," I tell her.

"Then you should have told me. I could have hired a taster."

"And what? Have someone innocent die because of me?"

She grits her teeth.

"Besides, I wanted to find out who it was myself. One night, I..."

To my surprise, Danni slams her fist into the wall. The sound thunders throughout the room.

"Danni?" I sit up.

"Am I so untrustworthy that you didn't confide in me? Am I so incompetent that you won't rely on me? Am I useless after all?"

As her voice quakes, her shoulders tremble even more.

Is she crying?

I place a hand on my forehead. "I'm sorry, Danni. I didn't mean to make you feel useless. I just thought I'd try it my own way first."

No answer.

I rub my neck. "Well, I did call you, didn't I?"

For a moment, she remains still and silent. Then she lets out a deep breath. Her shoulders relax and she lifts her head.

"So what happened next?"

"One night, after you'd gone to bed, I told one of the maids that I wasn't feeling well and asked if she could prepare a tonic for me and serve it in the garden. She did and I pretended to drink it. I pretended to cough, too, and stagger back towards my room while clutching my stomach. On the way, I stopped to check behind some bushes and I saw an onyx bead on the ground."

"An onyx bead?"

"In the morning, I thanked the maid for the tonic," I continue. "It was only for an instant, but I thought Natasia looked annoyed."

"Princess Natasia?" Danni's eyebrows arch. "Are you saying...?"

"When I glimpsed her riding off on her horse after the downpour started, I followed her."

"And that's how you ended up at that cabin?"

"Yes," I answer. "She was talking to someone. A man with a scar above his nose."

I touch the spot on my own face to demonstrate.

"He was the one who attacked me after Natasia left, although he ran away when he saw my ring." I glance at the ring on my finger, a golden vine with purple sapphires to symbolize wolfsbane, the flower of the royal family. "I managed to wound him, too."

Danni nods and stands up. "I will look for him immediately."

"Wait." I grab her arm. "You don't need to. I heard Natasia confess."

"She confessed?" Danni turns to me with an expression of disbelief. "Then she must..."

"Nothing must be done." I look into Danni's eyes as I grip her arm more firmly. "No one must know."

Her eyebrows furrow. "But why? She..."

"Is my brother's wife, and everyone knows he loves her." I let go of her arm and let mine drop on my lap. "He will be crushed if he finds out."

"Of course he will be," Danni says. "You're his brother and she tried to kill you."

"She probably doesn't have anything against me personally," I reply. "She's probably just beginning to panic because she and Viktor still don't have any children. She knows that if they don't produce an heir, then I will be the one to inherit the throne."

"As the law commands."

"But my very presence must be a constant reminder of that. It must have been gnawing at her all this time. I should have realized that she's been suffering in silence."

"She tried to kill you," Danni reminds me.

"Because she's getting desperate," I say as I remember the pain in Natasia's words. "She's become so unhappy that she can't bear it any longer. It's starting to affect my brother, too."

"So you're going to let her kill you just to make Prince Viktor happy?" Danni holds her glasses in her outstretched hand. "Seriously, sometimes I wonder if the weight of your crown has impaired your thinking."

"I'm not going to let that happen, of course!" I walk towards the window and gaze down at the garden. "But I can't let things continue as they are."

"So what will you do, Prince Steffan?"

I touch my chin and turn to her with a grin. "I'll leave."

Danni's arm drops to her side. "What?"

"I'll get out of the Palace, of Brelv," I explain. "With me gone, Natasia will have a chance to be happy again. She might even be able to bear Viktor a child, which would surely make everyone happy."

"Are you going to ask the King and Queen to exile you?" Danni places her hands on her hips. "Because they won't do it. In spite of all the trouble you've caused them."

"I'll simply leave. I'll leave them a note saying I've gone on an adventure or something. As you said, I've caused them trouble before, so they won't be surprised. They'll think I'm just rebelling again."

"They will be angry, to say the least."

"I can live with that."

I clasp my hands behind me and turn back to the window, this time looking up at the gray sky.

Danni snorts. "You think you can just leave?"

"You'll help me, won't you, Danni?" I toss her a smile over my shoulder. "You are the only one I can rely on, after all."

Danni frowns and rubs her arms. "This is unfair."

"It's for the best," I say in a more serious tone. "Sometimes, sacrifices must be made in order to achieve the best outcome."

She sighs. "Why is it only now that you start acting like a prince?"

"Sorry." I walk over to her and place my hand on her rigid shoulder. "I've only ever made you worry, haven't I?"

She looks away. "It is my job to worry about you."

"So can I count on you?"

Her lower lip quivers, the rest of her body still. Then, slowly, she places her right fist above her heart and sinks to the floor on one knee. She lifts her left hand in the air before pressing two fingers to her lips as she bows her head.

It's a yes if there ever was one, a Brelvan's gesture of utter loyalty.

Truly, I could not ask for a better attendant.

I feel a thorn prick my chest as I pat the top of Danni's head gently, but I force a smile.

"Now, now, don't look so glum." I glance back past the window. "Who knows? This adventure might be the best for me, too."

Chapter 1
Jess

Los Angeles, California

I close my eyes against the bright lights and surrender to the music-to Kay's hypnotizing lead voice, to the clash of Riley's drums, to the poetry of Alice's keys, to the cries of Josh's guitar accompanying the rhythm of mine.

My fingers dance on the strings as if they have a life of their own. My shoe taps the wooden floor. My head bobs. The messy cascade of black and pink waves bounces off my cheeks, concealing the beads of sweat that travel down to the edge of my jaw and linger before dropping onto the back of my hand.

The tempo increases. Kay's notes ascend and Josh's guitar breaks into a screech. Then Kay falls silent and so do Alice and Josh. Only Riley's drumming and my plucking remain. After a few more beats, I, too, stop, and seconds later, the clang of Riley's cymbals ripples through the air.

And then silence.

Then faint applause.

I open my eyes to see the crowd at the bar, a sizable turnout even for a Saturday night, clapping their hands above their drinks-those of them who aren't too busy drinking or already too drunk to bother, that is.

No matter. I don't play for glory anyway.

As I catch my breath and wipe the sweat off my brow, I turn to the other members of the band. They're all sweaty and breathless just like me, tired, but I can tell they've all had just as much fun as me, too. That alone brings a smile to my lips.

"Thank you!" Kay shouts into the microphone after she recovers. "And have a good night, everyone!"

She goes down the stage and the rest of us follow. I lift my hand for the routine series of high fives that leaves my palm rosy. I pull the strap of my guitar over my head and put it to sleep in its case before following the band to the bar.

"Here you go."

Riley hands me an icy bottle of beer as soon as I occupy the stool between him and Josh. He lets his own clink against it.

"Cheers!"

"Cheers!" I tell him before taking a gulp.

The cold liquid feels good as it slides down my dry throat, and I let out a breath of satisfaction as I set the bottle down on the counter.

"Nothing like a cold beer after a performance," I say.

"Ditto," Josh seconds with a smile.

It's a dashing smile that shows off his dimples and gives a glimpse of perfectly white teeth with just a slight gap between the front two. Even after all this time, it still makes me weak at the knees.

I stare at those lips as they wrap around the mouth of his bottle, wishing they were pressed against mine.

Shit.

You'd think that after three years of hiding my feelings with him right next to me, my heart would have become immune to his charms and my mind would have stopped hoping that I'd be anything more than a friend.

For God's sake, he's taken, Jess. When are you going to get that stuck in your brain?

But I guess a girl never forgets her first real crush, or her first real kiss. I shared mine with Josh in my apartment after he brought me home from a party at Kay's house one night. We were both drunk, of course, and he apologized for it afterwards. I laughed it off even though I could feel tears welling up inside my chest. But my heart still goes crazy at the memory of it, which seems to be preserved in HD in my mind.

Besides, it's not like he's married, so I still have...

"Josh, didn't you mention that you've got something to say?" Kay's voice breaks into my thoughts.

"Um, yeah."

He puts his bottle down and touches his silver loop earring, as he usually does when he's nervous.

I take a sip of beer. I feel nervous, too.

"Well, I..." Josh rubs his neck and my heart skips a beat.

Even when he's nervous, he's still cute as hell.

He draws a deep breath. "Marianne is pregnant, so..."

"Oh my God!" Kay squeals as she gets off her stool. "You're having a baby?"

My hands freeze around my bottle of beer as my body suddenly grows numb. The bitter alcohol bubbles to my throat.

They are?

"I'm so happy for you." Kay wraps her arms around Josh. "Congratulations!"

"Yeah, man." Riley gives Josh another high five behind me, then a whistle. "You're the man, alright."

Alice, who doesn't talk much, gives Josh a thumbs-up as she takes a sip of her whiskey sour.

Now I'm the only one left to congratulate him.

I square my shoulders, put the shattered pieces of my heart together, and force a smile.

"Congratulations."

Josh smiles back. "Thanks."

This time, that smile nearly makes tears spill out of my eyes.

I quickly grab my bottle and swallow another gulp, and another.

"I don't really feel like celebrating, though," he says as his smile vanishes. "I still can't believe it's real."

No shit.

"But drinks are still on you," Kay says as she gets back on her stool. "Did you hear that, Benny?"

Josh pouts.

"You're ruthless." Riley pinches her cheek and then kisses it. "But I guess that's one of the things I love about you."

I roll my eyes.

Usually, I don't mind the lovebirds being all over each other, but for some reason, all of a sudden, it makes me sick. I take another swig of beer.

Josh sips from his bottle and sighs. "Anyway, what I wanted to say was that since Marianne and I are having a baby, I might have to quit the band."

"What?"

My jaw drops and the puddle of beer still in my mouth trickles down my chin. I quickly wipe it with the back of my hand.

"I need to get a real job," Josh explains. "A steady job."

"I guess that's understandable," Kay says.

"Can't be helped," Alice seconds.

Well, yes, I can understand that, but...

I look at Kay. "You're okay with it?"

She shrugs and tucks a strand of emerald hair behind her ear. "The truth is, Riley and I have been thinking of settling down, too."

My eyebrows arch. "What?"

"You know, we're not getting younger, and I want kids."

"I want you to have my kids," Riley pipes in as he wraps an arm around her.

"Don't get me wrong," Kay says. "I love the band. I love you guys. But maybe it's time to move on to the next stage and experience a different part of life. You know how basketball players eventually retire and then they take care of their families or run their own companies, or how beauty pageant queens have another career after they've given up their crowns? It's something like that."

My mouth gapes as I stare at my bottle. I don't say anything. I can't.

I can't believe I'm hearing this.

Yes, I understand what Kay is saying. Yes, I knew this day would come. But now?

"Hey." Riley squeezes my shoulder. "Don't worry. It won't happen right away. We still have to finish the gigs that have already been booked."

"I'm thinking we should save the best show for our final gig," Kay says. "How's that song you're working on coming along?"

"Um..." I tap my fingers against my bottle.

Are we really talking about this?

"I've barely started," I answer as I remember that notebook back at my apartment with all the torn and crossed-out pages.

"I was thinking we could use that for our final performance," Kay says. "What do you guys think?"

"Cool," Riley answers.

Alice gives another thumbs-up sign.

I shake my head. "I'm not sure I..."

"Hey." Josh places a hand on my shoulder. "I know you can do it."

And again, he flashes me that smile, and silly me feels a little better.

"I'll try," I end up promising him.

"Great!" Kay cheers.

She finishes the rest of her bottle in one go and sets it down with a thud. Then she grabs Riley's arm.

"Let's dance."

"Whoa." Riley nearly falls off his stool.

Next, Kay grabs Josh's arm. "You too."

"Me?" Josh gives her a look of disbelief.

But she's not looking, she's already dragging the two reluctant guys to the dance floor.

After a few steps, she stops.

"Jess, Alice, you should join us!" she shouts over the music.

Alice shakes her head.

I give her a sheepish grin and lift my nearly empty bottle. "I think I'll have another beer first."

"Okay."

She walks off with the boys in tow and gets lost in the crowd.

I let out a breath of relief, finish my bottle, and then order another. As I start on the second, Alice moves closer to me.

"Are you alright?" she asks.

I glance at her.

She might look like she doesn't give a fuck, what with her thick black eyeliner and her piercings and all, but I've been with her long enough to know that she's perceptive. In fact, she's the only one in the band who's noticed that I have a thing for Josh.

"I'm fine," I lie before taking another swig.

"Sure?"

I set my bottle down and wipe my lips. "Well, maybe I am upset. After all, I've just been told the band is breaking up. How can you not be upset about that?"

Alice shrugs.

Maybe she's just more mature than I am.

I enjoy another sip and sigh. "What am I supposed to do? I'll have to get another job."

"Don't you work at a cafe during the day?"

"That barely pays the rent," I answer. "And to make matters worse, I still haven't found a new roommate."

My old roommate, Sheila, left two months ago after she got engaged to some guy she met online.

Shit. Everyone around me is moving on in the romance department. And in life.

And me? I'll probably just stay a virgin forever, working two jobs and writing songs that no one really listens to.

"Want to move in with me?" Alice asks suddenly. "I've got a spare room."

My eyebrows go up.

Really?

"Nah," I answer before taking another sip. "Thanks for the offer, but I'm quite fond of my apartment."

"Okay. Anyway, my girlfriend probably wouldn't like me having a roommate."

Right.

"Good luck with finding one soon," she adds.

"Thanks."

I tip my bottle up and gulp down the rest. Then I catch the bartender's eye.

"I'll have one more, Benny."

"Sure."

After a few seconds, he places another icy bottle in front of me.

I grab it and quickly swallow a third.

"Wow," Alice remarks. "You're more upset than I thought."

"Or maybe I'm just thirsty," I say, stopping as I feel the alcohol settle in my stomach.

Alice says nothing.

Nah. Who the hell am I kidding?

~

"You have got to be kidding me," I mumble as I stand in front of the lone elevator in my apartment building.

I'm so drunk I'm starting to see double, but there's no mistaking that yellow 'Out of Order' sign on the door.

Was that there this afternoon? It doesn't matter. Right now, I have no choice but to take the stairs.

All the way to the seventh floor.

"Fuck."

I drag myself up the staircase one step at a time, stopping at every landing to catch my breath and keep myself from throwing up. At the third floor, I nearly do, but I take deep breaths and manage not to. By the time I get to the seventh floor, my vision is a blur and I have to lean against the wall of the corridor to keep myself from stumbling as I make my way to my apartment.

706... 706... 706...

I finally find the right door, but just then my tired legs give in. I fall to the floor and my purse falls out of my hands. Its contents spill out all over the place.

"Shit."

I start to pick them up. To my surprise, another pair of hands seems to be helping me.

My eyebrows furrow. Am I hallucinating?

The other pair of hands gathers all my things as mine stop moving. Eventually, everything ends up back inside the purse, which is then handed over to me.

"There you go. And here, let me help me you up as well."

The voice is a husky tenor. I look at the hand in front of me and then up at the face it belongs to. The dark lenses of gold-rimmed sunglasses throw my reflection back at me. Pale hair cascades out of the hood of a blue sweatshirt.

None of those can disguise the flawless complexion or the impeccable bone structure of the person in front of me, though.

A model? A nymph? A vampire, since she's pale as a moonbeam and wearing sunglasses in the middle of the night?

I must be dreaming.

And yet the hand that grips mine feels real. The palm is smoother than any I've ever touched, true, but it feels reassuringly warm. The long fingers entwine with my shorter ones, and somehow, I manage to get back on my feet.

"Who are you?" I ask.

"Steff."

Steff. Short for Stephanie, maybe?

"And you must be Jessica Campbell."

My eyebrows furrow. "How do you know?"

"I saw your ID when I was picking up your stuff. Also, your name was on your ad."

"Ad?"

Now I'm even more confused.

"I'm here for the room."

My eyes grow wide. Then I let out a gasp as reality sinks in.

"You're my new roommate?"

Steff shrugs. "If you'll allow it."

Allow it? I'd be jumping for joy if I didn't already feel like I was floating.

Unable to contain my excitement, I give her a hug.

"Of course. Welcome and thank you. Thank you so much!"

Filled with a fresh burst of energy, I quickly search for my keys, slowly select the right one, and somehow manage to slip it into the hole.

"Please come in."

I push the door open and step aside to let Steff in. I follow her inside and grab the papers from the counter.

"I've had this prepared for some time." I place the contract on the coffee table. "Now, if you can just sign and give me the initial deposit..."

She grabs my hand and places a thick wad of hundreds in it.

"Is that enough?"

I stare at the bills with wide eyes.

Even though I'm drunk, I can tell this money is real. It smells real. And it looks like more than enough. I trust my instincts more than my math skills right now, so I slip the cash into my pocket without bothering to count it.

"Now, just sign those papers and..."

I pause as my stomach churns.

Shit.

I rush to the bathroom and reach the toilet bowl just in time to throw up all that alcohol I shouldn't have drunk. My hair tumbles down and nearly gets drenched with vomit, but a hand pulls it up.

"Are you okay?" Steff asks behind me.

I nod and continue throwing up.

Now this is embarrassing. At the same time, though, I feel glad.

I finally have a roommate again, someone I can count on. And she completely understands the woes of someone with long hair-probably even better than I do; hers is gorgeous and she must spend hours on it.

"We'll talk about the rest in the morning, okay?" I answer afterwards as I flush the toilet. "I'm afraid I've had a rough night."

"No worries."

The hand lets go of my hair and I allow it to conceal my flushed cheeks as I wipe my mouth.

"Your room is right next to the kitchen. Good night."

"Good night."

After Steff leaves, I quickly brush my teeth then head to my bedroom and throw myself onto the bed. I don't even bother taking off my coat or my shoes. My head is still spinning. My heavy eyelids fall shut. Within moments, I drift off to sleep.

~

I wake up to the sound of the TV from the living room.

At first I think I'm dreaming, but the cobwebs of sleep soon melt away and my eyelids flutter open. I find myself staring at the clock on my bedside table. It tells me it's 11:43 AM.

That late already?

I lift my head off the pillow, which I've drooled on, and sit up. My body still feels heavy. My head aches and I frown as I rub it. Again, I hear the TV.

Did I leave it on last night? Or is there...?

I pause in fear at my other theory, but tell myself to calm down.

It can't be an intruder. An intruder wouldn't turn on the TV. I doubt it's a guest, either.

Then, as I place my hand on my forehead, the wheels of my alcohol-muddled mind start turning and my memories flash back. Some of them are hazy, but I do remember letting a woman inside my apartment. I even remember her kindly holding my hair as I threw up in the bathroom.

Right. I have a new roommate.

What was her name again? Stella? Sarah?

No. Stephanie.

A smile forms on my lips as I remember my luck, then vanishes as the voice in my head scolds me for being so careless.

You didn't even ask for an ID, stupid. What if she's a criminal? How could you have let her sleep in your apartment without interviewing her first?

I sigh.

True, I should have been more careful. And more decent.

Still, a roommate is a roommate, and I'm happy I have a new one.

I remember the money she gave me, too, and I run my hands over my coat to see if I still have it. The lump in one of the pockets confirms that I do. I shrug the coat off and take the money out, lay the bills out on the bed and count them.

It's real, alright, and it's more than three times the deposit I asked for.

That probably means she's not going to rob me or take advantage of me. Then again, it seems a little shady, too.

I grab the bills and get off my bed.

Oh, well. I just have to talk to her, right?

As I step out of my bedroom, the aroma of freshly baked pastry, cheese and tomatoes drifts into my nostrils. I follow the scent to the living room and see a head of platinum hair over the couch.

Her hair really is gorgeous.

She turns and I gaze into icy blue eyes that quickly take me captive.

"Good morning, Jessica." Thin lips moistened with olive oil, a thumb held captive between them, curve into a smile. "Care for some pizza?"

My throat goes dry.

Damn. That's sexy.

I blink.

Whoa. Did I just say sexy? But I'm not...

Then Steff stands up and I see the sculpted muscles through the loose front of a white robe.

No breasts. Just perfect ridges and dips of muscle that make my jaw drop and the bills slip out of my fingers.

No way.

In the blink of an eye, I grab the guitar hanging on the wall and point it at the man in my apartment.

"Don't you dare come any closer, you lying son of a bitch!"

Chapter 2
Steff

A lynx trying to defend her territory.

That is what Jessica reminds me of as her ebony eyes glare at me from beneath hooded eyelids and crinkled eyebrows. Her nostrils flare above thinned lips and I can almost hear her grinding her teeth behind them. Her chin pushes out.

Her knees are bent one in front of the other so that she can pounce at a moment's notice. Her fingers wrap firmly around the neck of her guitar, ready to swing it.

A guitar doesn't strike me as an ideal weapon, but I guess it's better than nothing. The real question is, why is it aimed at me?

I lift my hands. "Now, now, Jessica, let's not..."

"Stop calling me Jessica!"

She swings the guitar as she leaps forward. I jump back, narrowly avoiding it.

"But that's your name, isn't it?"

She answers with another swing. Again, I jump back. I'm running out of room.

"Liar!"

"What? I never lied to you."

I jump to the side as she takes another swing. The guitar hits the metal cylinder on the table by the window and the pens scatter to the floor.

"You told me you were my new roommate," she hisses.

"I thought I was. I even signed your contract and gave you money."

"You're a man!"

This time, the guitar hits the floor lamp in the corner. It wobbles and I straighten it to keep it from falling.

"I thought you knew," I tell her.

"How was I supposed to know when you didn't fucking tell me?"

"You didn't ask."

"Why, you..."

She growls low in her throat as she tries to hit me again. I pick up the lamp and use it as a shield. Mahogany clashes with metal as my back hits the wall.

"Calm down, Jessica!" I try to reason with her. "You'll damage your guitar."

"I'm gonna damage you, you sneaky jerk!"

Another clash.

I let out a deep breath.

Who'd have thought she could be so aggressive when she was acting all happy to see me last night?

As much as I've enjoyed seeing her so riled up and waving that guitar around so fiercely, this has gone on long enough. If she's not listening, I'll just have to make her.

The next time she swings, I drop the lamp and duck. Then, before she can recover, I pull her into my arms. One of them wraps around her waist. The other presses against her breasts as her back meets my chest.

She lets out a yelp.

Hmm. I thought her breasts were barely there, but they seem to be squishing nicely beneath my arm, soft and firm just as I like them. And her waist seems slender, too, and...

An elbow to my ribs, right on my just-healed wound, knocks away my breath and thought.

My arms loosen and Jessica escapes. The guitar is up in the air again.

I manage to roll out of the way before it smashes my head.

She prepares to hit me again, but suddenly, her eyes and her mouth gape.

I look down at my robe. Ah. It seems as if the sash has come undone-and I'm not wearing anything underneath.

She gives a girlish squeal as she drops the guitar. It lands on the coffee table with a crash.

"No!" Jessica cries out.

I stand up and approach her to try and comfort her, but she puts a hand up in front of my face.

"Go and put some clothes on, pervert! Why are you even wearing my robe anyway?"

I tie the sash and scratch the back of my head.

"Well, I lost my suitcase and..."

Jessica crosses her arms over her chest. "If you think I'm going to lend you some clothes, I'm not."

"Okay. I'll just wear this, then."

She scowls. She marches off to her bedroom and comes back with a shirt and a pair of pants which she throws at me.

"Put them on," she orders.

"Okay."

I slip my foot into a leg of the pants.

"Not here, dumbass!" She hurls a throw pillow at me. "Get changed and come back here."

I obey. I head to my bedroom to change into her clothes. The jeans are too tight for my liking, the shirt too loose, but they fit.

When I return to the living room, it's still a mess, but Jessica looks calmer. She's staring at her broken guitar. The contract I've signed lies beside it, along with the wad of bills I gave her last night.

I glance at the guitar as I approach her. "I'm sorry for..."

Again, she raises a hand. Then she points to the chair across her. I sit.

"Your name is Steffan?" she asks.

I nod. "Steffan... Olsen." I borrow the last name of my friend from Norway. Jessica can't know who I really am, after all. "But my friends call me Steff."

She sighs. "And you're from?"

"Norway," I lie.

I'm pretty sure she hasn't heard of Brelv, and I don't want her to be even more suspicious of me. Besides, I am trying to conceal my identity.

She stretches out her hand. "Passport?"

I rub my neck and give her a sheepish smile. "Sorry. It was in my suitcase."

Jessica frowns. "How am I supposed to know you're not an illegal immigrant or some fugitive?"

I sit back and shrug. "I guess you'll have to trust me."

Her frown deepens.

"Or you could kick me out."

She touches her knees. Her shoulders slump as she sighs.

"How did you find my ad?"

"I saw it online."

She looks at me. "You do know it says that the apartment belongs to a woman, right?"

I scratch my chin as I try to recall the ad.

"But you didn't say you were looking for a female roommate."

She snorts. "Anyone with common sense would know that."

She glares at me again.

"Unless you knew it and you've got some sick plan to..."

"No plans." I wave my hands in front of me before she can think of starting a ruckus again. "In my country, unmarried men and women share rooms all the time."

Jessica's eyes narrow.

"There's nothing wrong with it," I assure her.

Her gaze hovers over the contract. "So you have no problems with it?"

"None."

"Well, I do and I might," she says. "But I do need a roommate."

"I'll do my best not to cause you any trouble," I tell her.

"Too late for that." Jessica lets out another sigh. "Fine, I'll let you stay here in my apartment, but I have a few conditions."

I lean forward. "Okay."

"One, we'll tell everyone you're my cousin, okay?"

"Okay."

I suppose I shouldn't tell her that first-cousin marriage is fairly common in my country.

"Two. You will not lay a finger on me." She points hers at me. "Or try to peep while I'm changing, or... well, you get the idea."

She looks away with rosy cheeks.

I grip my chin and grin.

My, my. My roommate seems to be a virgin.

"Understand?" Jessica asks.

"Perfectly," I answer. "I'm not some mischievous little boy, you know."

"Whatever."

"I'm not going to do anything bad to you, Jessica," I promise her.

Stealing a kiss isn't bad, is it? Besides, she only said 'finger'.

"Three," she goes on. "Don't ever call me Jessica again."

My eyebrows crease. "But..."

"Jess," she says. "Call me Jess."

"Jess," I repeat.

She crosses her arms over her chest, sits back and lets out a deep breath.

"I guess that's settled then."

"Really? I'm glad to hear it."

After all that chaos, finally, we've reached an understanding.

"Yeah." She nods and glances at the table. "It's not going to mend my guitar, though."

"Well, you were the one..."

I stop as Jess glares again.

That must be her signature look.

"It's all my fault," I correct myself. "So why don't I buy you a new one?"

"Nope." Jess shakes her head.

"But you need one, don't you?"

"How...?"

She pauses and glances at the framed pictures on the wall.

Jimi Hendrix. John Deacon. An autograph from Carol Kaye. Pictures with Paul McCartney, Taylor Swift and John Mayer.

Then there's the massive collection of CDs on the shelf, along with the smaller collection of headphones. And the pile of music sheets.

Even without the guitar on the wall, anyone could see she's a musician.

Jess scratches her head. "Well, I guess I do."

"Then let me..."

"You paid me extra anyway. I can afford one," she cuts me off.

Right. I did.

I rub my hands together. "Then I guess all that's left to do is to buy one."

"Yeah." Jess nods.

She stands up and narrows her eyes at me.

"And while we're out shopping, you might as well get your own clothes."

~

"What do you think of this one?"

I pull a long-sleeved lavender shirt from the rack.

Jess slaps her forehead. "What? Don't tell me you don't know how to pick out your own clothes!"

Well, actually, I've always had someone pick my wardrobe for me.

"Just grab a few and pay for them," she says. "Men's clothes all look the same anyway. And hurry up. I want to get back before dark."

"Yes, ma'am."

Seriously, she's even bossier than Danni.

I get a few more shirts from the rack.

"What about you?" I ask her. "Don't you want to get anything?"

"I have enough clothes, thank you."

Funny. Until now, I didn't think a girl could have enough clothes. Natasia, my mother and my sisters certainly don't seem to think so.

I glance at the shirt I'm wearing and then at the one she's wearing. They look almost the same. "You mean you have enough oversized shirts."

Shirts that don't show off her curves, I might add.

My gaze goes to the red dress on the mannequin and I point to it with my chin.

"What about that dress?"

Jess glances at it. "Nope. I don't wear dresses."

Pity. She would look so much hotter if she did.

"Just get your clothes already and lay off mine," she snaps.

"Okay. Okay."

I grab another shirt on a hanger.

"What about this one?" The sales clerk, a woman with curly blonde hair and a name tag that says 'Vivian', approaches us with a black trench coat.

"Stylish," I remark.

"Yeah," Jess agrees. "But isn't that a woman's coat?"

Vivian looks at me and her eyes grow wide. Her cheeks grow red.

"Oh, I'm so sorry," she mumbles. "When you walked in, I thought..."

"It's okay." Jess waves her off. "You're not the only one who's made that mistake."

I give a sheepish grin.

After Vivian walks away, Jess turns to me with her hand on her chin.

"Amused, are you? Well, it's really inconvenient for other people."

I throw her a puzzled look. "But I haven't done..."

"How about we do something about this?" Jess takes a few strands of my hair and wraps them around her fingers.

I swallow. It's been a while since a woman has had the courage to do that to me.

She lets go of my hair. "And what's with the earrings?"

My hand goes to the earring dangling from my right ear. I've had the pair since I was sixteen.

"Well, in my country..." I begin to explain.

"Well, you're not in your country, are you?" she pouts.

I scratch my head. "I guess not."

I take off my earrings and hand them over to her. She tosses them inside her purse.

I bet she doesn't have a clue how much they cost.

"Better." Jess nods in approval. "But you still need a haircut."

I touch my hair.

I haven't had a haircut in years, and the last time I did, my mother was quite displeased. Then again, she's not around now.

Didn't I say this was supposed to be an adventure? I can't stay how I am or I'll never become a better person.

"Sure," I tell Jess with a smile. "Let's do it."

~

A few hours later, I walk away from a barber's chair with my hair so much shorter I can barely recognize myself. A man in a black shirt is already sweeping the locks I used to have from the floor.

I pay at the counter and head to the waiting area where Jess is.

At first, she doesn't notice I'm there but then she looks up and her onyx eyes grow wide. The magazine in her hands falls to her feet.

I give her a smile as I brush the short strands of hair out of my left eye.

"How do I look?"

Chapter 3
Jess

Scorching hot.

As Steff sits across me, eating a slice of pizza, I can barely take my eyes off him.

His pale blond hair has been neatly trimmed to his neck, but there are still strands long enough to tuck behind his right ear. Most of it, though, has been swept over the left side of his face. The strands seem to dance with his every move so that sometimes his eye is peeking through them and sometimes not. It adds an air of charm and mystery to his already fetching features. And when he brushes them away, like he's doing now, I can almost feel my heart stop.

He was good-looking before. Beautiful.

But now, he's so hot my panties are almost melting. Or maybe it's what's inside them that's almost melting.

I shift in my seat and close my legs as I take a sip from a can of soda just in case the wet spot is showing.

It's not just Steff's hair. It's also his clothes. In spite of everything, he picked them well. The midnight blue long-sleeved shirt he has on is hugging his chest and arms, making him look more manly than before. The pristine white jeans make his legs look even longer and leaner, and I can't even begin to describe how they looked like from behind when I was walking after him at the mall. I caught a few other women looking, too.

Am I really going to be living with this guy? Can my virgin heart handle it?

Steff finishes his pizza and slips his thumb and forefinger past his lips to clean the crumbs off them. Afterwards, he rubs his lips together, and then the tip of his tongue darts out to swipe the upper one.

I can feel my insides turning to goo.

"Are you alright, Jess?" His voice makes me jump and I nearly fall off my chair.

"Yes," I answer as I sit up and pull my shirt higher up my shoulders.

For the first time, I wonder why all of my shirts are so loose. Maybe I should have bought a new one like he suggested?

"Are you sure you don't want some?" He pushes the box of pizza towards me.

I shake my head. "No, thanks."

"It's quite good."

I know. At least, I thought so at first, but after months of going through the menu, the flavors have started to seem like nails on a chalkboard on my palate. Plus, my dad's pizzas are way better.

"You like pizza," I observe out loud.

Steff chuckles and some strands of his hair sway towards the right.

"It seems you've learned one of my weaknesses."

I'm suddenly curious to know about the others.

"That's why I thought your apartment would be perfect," he adds.

My eyebrows arch. "You chose my apartment because you knew I lived next door to a pizzeria?"

"You mentioned it in the ad," he points out.

I gaze up at the ceiling.

Right. I did. Whose suggestion was that again?

It doesn't matter. Actually, I was wondering why of all the ads for a roommate, he picked mine. Now I know.

I exhale. Thank God for Swizz Pizza.

Wait. Thank God? Wasn't I just thinking I was cursed this morning?

I take a bite of my chicken sandwich. "Anyway, you're not just going to eat pizza every day, are you?"

Steff scratches his chin.

No way. He's considering it.

"It's not healthy to eat just one kind of food," I tell him. "And don't tell me pizzas come in different flavors. Pizza is still pizza. You should have a varied, balanced diet."

Now I'm starting to sound like my mom.

"Wow." Steff tucks his hand under his chin. "You're really concerned about your roommates, aren't you?"

Concern?

"Don't get me wrong," I tell him with a pout as I try to keep myself from blushing. "I just don't want to take care of you if you get sick."

More importantly, I don't want him losing that perfect figure.

Steff chuckles. "Well, I guess you'll have to cook for me then. I don't know how."

My eyes grow wide.

"I'll pay you extra," he adds.

Unbelievable.

"What? Has someone else been cooking for you all this time?"

He shrugs. "Something like that."

Who? His mom? No. Somehow, I can't imagine it. A girlfriend, then? Girlfriends? A wife?

"You're not married, are you?" I ask in sudden alarm as I glance at his hand.

Well, there's a ring, but it doesn't look like a wedding ring.

He shakes his head. "This is a... family heirloom."

I nod. "Divorced?"

They have divorce in Norway, don't they?

"No," Steff answers.

I don't know why I'm so relieved.

"Just to be clear, I'm single," he goes on.

Heat bursts in my cheeks. My arms cross over my chest.

"I wasn't asking."

He smirks. My temper simmers.

"I only asked because I was wondering who's been doing your cooking for you," I say defensively. "I bet you've had endless women cooking for you."

"Yes," Steff answers.

Yes?

"And men, too."

What?

"We've had both male and female cooks."

I blink. Cooks?

Ah. I get it now.

"So you're from a rich family, huh?" I ask as I reach for my can of soda. That would explain the family heirloom. "What? Did you run away from home?"

"Something like that."

He's not even denying it.

I take a sip and sigh. "Oh well, we all have family issues. And I have money issues, so I guess I'll cook for you as long as you pay me extra."

"I can..."

I raise my hand to silence him. "But I'm not washing your clothes or doing anything else for you, you hear?"

I set my can down and slap the table.

"I'm your roommate, not your babysitter."

Steff gives me a thumbs-up sign. "Got it."

I finish my sandwich as he grabs another slice of pizza, then gulp down my soda and toss the empty can into the trash. I let out a yawn.

First I fought a man with a guitar, then I tagged along on a shopping spree. It's been a long day. Not to mention that my head still hurts a little from all that drinking last night.

"I'm going to bed," I tell Steff as I walk to my room. "I have work tomorrow, so I need to get up early."

~

407

I'm running late.

I thought I would be the moment I glanced at the clock on my bedside table, but now I know it for sure.

If I don't hurry, I'm not going to be at the cafe in time for my shift.

I stand in front of the bathroom mirror and brush my hair in a rush. As usual, the waves put up a fight against the bristles.

"Oh, come on." I grab my hair and try to disentangle the brush from its web. "Cooperate with me for once."

"Need help?" Steff asks me from behind.

His turquoise eyes meet mine through the mirror.

"No thanks." I step back as I yank the brush free. "I'm..."

I stop as I realize something is pressing against my lower back.

Something long.

And hard.

Heat explodes in my cheeks. The brush falls to the floor.

"What the hell?"

I turn around and push him away as my gaze descends to his crotch. I've caught a glimpse of it before when he was wearing my robe, but it wasn't up then.

And it is now.

Magnificently, fascinatingly...

"Fuck!"

I shove him out of the way as I squeeze my eyes shut in an effort to blot the sight from my mind before it becomes embedded in my memory.

"Could you please wear clothes while you're in my apartment?"

I run off without a backward glance. Then I grab my things from the living room, slip on my shoes and leave the apartment in even more of a hurry than before.

I already have a feeling this isn't going to be a great day.

~

"What's the matter?" Lisbeth asks me as we wipe the windows of the cafe. "You seem down today."

"I'm okay," I tell her. "I just had a bad morning."

A terrible morning, I correct myself. I don't even want to remember it.

"What did you do yesterday?" she asks as she squirts some water on the glass.

"Nothing," I answer.

I know Lisbeth is my friend, but the fewer people who know I'm living with a guy, the better.

"What about you?"

"I did the laundry," Lisbeth says. "I'd rather have been out on a date, though."

I glance at her. "Didn't you meet someone on Tinder?"

Lisbeth frowns. "He lied about his height. I want someone who's at least six feet tall."

I turn back to the window. "Maybe you shouldn't be so picky about who you date."

"And maybe you should start dating, period," she rebuts. "You don't want to stay a virgin forever, do you?"

"Shh." I hold a finger to my lips before glancing at the customers in the cafe.

Thankfully, there are only two, neither of them within earshot.

"Seriously, do you have something against men?" Lisbeth asks in a softer voice.

"Nothing," I tell her. "I've just been busy."

"With what?"

"Working here. Writing songs. Playing in a band."

And having a hopeless crush on the guitarist.

"Oh, come on. It only takes minutes to make an online dating profile."

"And you seriously think someone would be interested in me?" I ask her.

"Well, maybe if you change your hairstyle and put on some makeup," Lisbeth says. "And cherry chapstick does not count."

I grab a handful of my hair. "Well, I wish my hair was less stubborn."

"Wearing a dress wouldn't hurt either."

I shake my head. "No thanks."

Lisbeth sighs. "A better attitude would help, too."

"I'm fine, Lisbeth." I place a hand on her shoulder. "You don't need to worry about me.

She says nothing.

"Oh, by the way, I still owe you money from the other day, don't I?" I reach for the wallet in the back pocket of my pants. "How much...?"

I pause as my fingers don't come in contact with leather.

Lisbeth looks behind me. "What's wrong?"

"My wallet. It's not here."

I must have left it on the counter or on my bed.

Shit. If only I wasn't running late.

If only I hadn't been so flustered by...

"Jess!"

A familiar voice calls to me from the entrance and I turn my head. My eyes nearly pop out of their sockets.

"S-Steff?" I rush to him. "What are you doing here?"

"You forgot this."

He places my wallet on my palm.

I frown. "How did you even know I work here?"

"I saw the logo on your uniform."

I roll my eyes. Does this guy notice everything?

"Ahem." Lisbeth clears her throat. "For someone who claims to be uninterested in men, you seem to have quite the specimen here."

Great.

"Lisbeth..."

"Hi. I'm Lisbeth." She offers Steff her hand. "Sorry, I didn't catch your name."

"Steff," he answers as he gives Lisbeth's hand a shake.

"Nice name," Lisbeth remarks. "Can I get you anything? Coffee? A sandwich? A back rub? A kiss? A bl-"

"That's enough." I grab Lisbeth's shoulders and push her aside. Then I turn to Steff. "You should go."

"Is that any way to treat a customer?"

Tom, the manager of the cafe, approaches us.

I frown. Not him, too. Can this morning get any worse?

"He's not a customer," I clarify. "He's..."

"Yeah. Who is he?" Lisbeth puts her hands on her hips. "Because I'd sure like to know."

Shit. Lisbeth and Tom are both waiting for an explanation.

"He's my..."

"I'm her new roommate," Steff explains before I can. "I just dropped off her wallet because she left it at the apartment."

I glare at him.

"Your new roommate?" Lisbeth's jaw drops. She turns to me. "You're living with him?"

"Yeah," I agree since I'm left with no other choice. "But you don't have to be jealous or worried that I've become promiscuous or anything."

Tom doesn't seem to believe me.

Quick, Jess. Think of something.

I can't say Steff is my cousin. I've already told Lisbeth about my cousins, and I can't just add one now. What can I say?

Only one thing comes to mind.

409

I grab Steff's arm and give Lisbeth and Tom a wide smile. "After all, he's gay."

Chapter 4
Steff

Huh?

I glance at Jess from beneath raised eyebrows.

Where did that come from?

"No way!" Lisbeth gasps. "It can't be true."

She looks at me hopefully.

"But it is. Right, Steff?"

Jess squeezes my arm almost painfully before turning to me with her fake smile. It vanishes just long enough for her to glare at me in warning.

Fine. Fine. I get the hint.

I rub the back of my neck. "Jess is right. I'm afraid it's true."

Tom looks at me in surprise, then walks away with his eyebrows still crinkled. Lisbeth sticks out her lower lip as she stares at me. Her eyes look like they're about to well up.

"I'm... sorry?" I tell her.

"Now, now, don't cry." Jess pats Lisbeth's shoulder.

She turns to me. "You really should leave."

"Okay." I scratch my neck. "By the way, about what happened this morning..."

"Shush," Jess scolds with another glare.

I sigh as I watch her go back to the window she's cleaning.

I guess she doesn't want to talk about that.

Pity. She looked kind of cute when she was flustered, and I would have wanted to see that face again.

Well, she still looks cute now in her white blouse, her black capri pants and her frilled orange apron.

Especially the apron.

The thought of her wearing nothing but that apron makes my crotch throb.

Jess throws another glare in my direction. I take my cue and turn on my heel to walk out of the cafe. Once I reach the sidewalk, I hold my hand above my forehead to shield my eyes from the sun and look up at the sky. The vision of the white clusters amid the serene blue sea conjures memories of home.

Home.

I wonder how Mother and Father are doing. I wonder if Natasia and Viktor are happy now. I wonder if the twins are studying hard. I wonder if Danni is bored without me to watch over.

I hope they're all doing well without me.

I put my hand down and start walking.

I'm sure they're all fine and going on with their lives. I should do the same.

I glance at my watch.

It's still early. I guess I'll look around a bit before I go back to the apartment.

~

"Welcome back," I greet Jess from the living room couch as soon as she enters the apartment. "How was your day?"

"Good, in spite of everything."

She walks straight to the counter and sets a paper bag down on it.

"I brought you some food from the cafe since I'm too tired to cook," she says. "I've eaten as well."

I walk over to the counter and open the bag. The smell of roast chicken curls up to my nostrils.

I lick my lips. "Thanks."

"Don't thank me." Jess goes to the couch and takes off her shoes. "You're paying for food, remember?"

I walk over to her. "About this morning, I'm sorry I startled you..."

"I don't want to talk about it," she cuts me off again. "Just don't ever go walking around without clothes again."

"Sorry. Just an old habit."

411

Her eyebrows arch. "You walk around your house naked?"

"I sleep naked and I have my own bathroom," I explain with a grin.

"Okay. Well, you don't have your own bathroom now, so don't..." She blushes and looks away. "Just always have clothes on."

"Understood."

"Good." She stands up. "I'm going to bed."

She walks off but I place an arm on the wall to block her path.

She throws me a puzzled look. "Steff?"

I place my other arm on the other side of her head so that I'm hovering over her. She leans against the wall.

"You owe me," I tell her.

Her eyebrows furrow even more. "What?"

"You told your boss and Lisbeth I was gay," I remind her. "Which wasn't very nice of you, but I played along anyway."

Jess frowns. "Well, what was I supposed to say? I couldn't tell them you were my cousin because I've already told Lisbeth I have just four cousins. Besides, it's your fault for saying you were my roommate."

"They saw me hand you your wallet," I point out. "Should I have said I'm your boyfriend?"

She blushes. "Well, you shouldn't have come to the cafe."

"I only went there to bring you your wallet! You're welcome."

"I wouldn't have left it if you hadn't barged into the bathroom like that."

I grin. "I thought you didn't want to talk about that."

"I don't!" She looks away. "You're mean."

My eyebrows shoot up. "I'm the one who's mean? You told your..."

"I know, alright." Jess turns back to me. "Like I said, I didn't have a choice. Besides, I don't know you that well. Who knows? I might have been telling the truth."

My eyes narrow. Is that a challenge?

"For all I know, you..."

I cup her face and seal her lips with mine, silencing her. I feel her cheeks grow warm beneath my palms. Her lips quiver.

Ah. They're just as soft as I thought they would be. My cock swells in response. I can feel her lip balm rubbing off on mine. I can't help but want to taste it.

Suddenly, she puts her hands on my chest and pushes me away. Her gaze drops to her feet and her hair drapes over her face as her head bows down, but through the gaps, I can see the red tint on her cheeks.

I grin. "Now are you convinced I'm not gay?"

Jess says nothing. She just runs off into her room.

I lean against the wall and let out a deep breath.

What was with that reaction? I thought she'd glare at me and shout at me, hit me even. Instead, she ran away.

Why?

I stare at the ceiling.

Wait. Could it be that that was Jess's first kiss?

That thought sends a fresh thrill through me.

I grin and run a finger over my lips.

So I stole Jess's first kiss, huh?

Well, the kiss felt better than I thought it would. Even though neither of us used our tongues, I felt the heat all the way to my crotch. The bulge in my briefs is proof of it.

I might have been teasing her, but in the end, I was the one who got teased.

I scratch the back of my head and almost laugh at my own foolishness.

Well, I'll just have to tease her some more.

I rub my chin.

Now, what shall I do tomorrow morning?

"Good morning," I greet Jess as I set the plate of fried eggs on the table.

She stops on her way to the door. Her eyebrows furrow.

"What's this?"

"Breakfast." I pull out a chair. "You had a rough start to your day yesterday, so I thought today I'd try to help you start it the right way."

Jess's eyes narrow suspiciously. "But I thought you said you don't know how to cook."

"Well, I thought it wouldn't be bad to learn," I tell her. "Besides, it's just eggs."

I tap the back of the chair.

Finally, she sits down and stares at the plate.

"You made two fried eggs?"

"One with a hard yolk and one runny," I tell her with a grin. "I wanted just one egg that was both hard and runny, but I guess that's impossible."

Jess blushes.

Inwardly, I give a triumphant smile.

That's it.

"And I made coffee, too." I push the mug towards her.

She wraps her hands around it. "Smells good."

"You don't seem like you need it, though," I tell her. "You look like you slept well. Maybe you had a good dream?"

She frowns before lifting the mug to her lips.

Strike two.

Jess takes a sip of her coffee and puts the mug down. I move in to wipe the drop of warm liquid left on her lip with the pad of my thumb.

"You wouldn't want to go to work with..."

She pushes my hand away, wipes her mouth with the back of her own hand, and glares up at me.

Strike three.

"I don't want breakfast after all," she says as she stands up.

She grabs her things from the couch.

"What? No goodbye kiss?"

Jess clenches her jaw and says nothing. She opens the door but pauses at the doorway.

"Oh, by the way..."

"Yes?" I ask expectantly.

She throws me another glare over her shoulder. "Don't you dare show up at my workplace today."

"Don't worry," I tell her. "I'm going to stay in and do laundry. Want me to do yours, too? I should have room to throw in a few pairs of panties or-"

Jess slams the door shut.

I let out a sigh as I sit down. Well, that's a homerun.

Was it too much, though? Should I just have left her alone?

Then again, if I had, she would have run away from me anyway. She was already on her way out the door, in fact, probably still flustered from that kiss yesterday. And I'd rather she get mad at me than avoid me.

Besides, each time I see Jess's blushing cheeks and glaring eyes, I can't help but want to tease her even more.

This is turning out to be much more fun than I thought.

Chapter 5
Jess

He's toying with me.

As I tune my guitar behind the bar's back door just before the start of the evening's show, recent events flood back into my mind and I scowl.

First, Steff kisses me just to prove he's not gay like I told Lisbeth, which I only did because I couldn't think of any other excuse. Then he makes jokes at me at the breakfast table and then touches my lips, probably to remind me of the kiss last night.

The kiss.

At the memory of his lips on mine, I blush. Then I scowl even more.

How dare Steff kiss me? Didn't he promise he wouldn't lay a finger on me?

I don't even know what's worse, the fact that he kissed me, which was only the second time I've ever been kissed-or the fact that I actually liked it.

Even now, my heart hammers in my chest and with each beat and heat ripples through my body, a heat that not even the cool night breeze that blows through my hair can seem to extinguish.

I run a fingertip over my lower lip.

This is what his kiss feels like.

"Is everything okay?" Kay asks as she sits on the bench next to me.

"Yes," I answer quickly. I flash her a smile as I put my hand back on my guitar. "I'm just getting ready."

"Good." She smiles back. "Because last time, I think you drank a bit too much."

I scratch the back of my head. "I did, didn't I?"

"And just now, you seemed deep in thought. First you looked angry, and then all of a sudden, you looked happy."

I blink. She's been watching me all this time?

And I looked happy?

"I was starting to wonder if you were going crazy," Kay says.

"Me? Crazy?" I chuckle. "Well, I think I've been crazy for a while now."

She chuckles too.

"But I'm fine." I squeeze her hand. "Thanks."

"Good to hear you're fine," she says. "Because frankly, I'm worried."

"Why?"

"Josh still isn't here."

My eyebrows go up. "He isn't?"

Josh is usually one of the first people to show up.

I glance at my watch. Only sixteen minutes before the show is supposed to start.

"Have you tried calling him?" I ask.

Kay nods. "But he hasn't answered. He hasn't sent me any messages, either."

I touch my chin. That is a little worrying.

Maybe he's with his girlfriend and something happened to her?

I shake my head. No, I mustn't think that.

"I wonder what happened to him," Kay voices my thoughts out loud.

Just then, Alice comes out of the back door.

"Is Josh here?" Kay asks her before I can.

Alice shakes her head and glances over her shoulder. "But someone else is."

In the next instant, I see Steff emerge behind her wearing a dark gray cardigan over a white shirt and faded denims.

I gasp and get on my feet.

"Steff, what are you doing here?"

And why do I feel like this is deja vu?

"I came to watch you play," he answers as he walks down the steps.

I exhale. "Didn't I tell you not to come to my workplace?"

"I thought you only meant the cafe."

I roll my eyes.

Damn it. He's toying with me again.

"Who's this?" Kay asks as she stands up and steps forward.

Here we go again.

"This is Steff," I reluctantly introduce him to Kay. "He's... a friend of mine."

"Oh." Kay places her arm around me. "Well, that's a surprise. Jess doesn't have many friends."

"Then it's an honor for me to be one of the few," Steff answers.

I glance at him.

What? He's acting all mature and gentlemanly now?

Kay pulls me closer. "And I don't think you've mentioned him before."

"Oh, he and I just met recently at the cafe," I tell Kay. "He's not from around here."

Kay rubs her chin. "He does look foreign."

She whispers in my ear.

"Not to mention he looks hot."

My eyebrows arch. Is Kay allowed to say that when she has a serious boyfriend?

Speaking of serious boyfriend, Riley comes out of the back door.

"Whoa." He does a double take when he sees Steff. "Who's this?"

"A friend of Jess," Kay answers for me. "His name is Steff."

Steff extends his hand and Riley warily shakes it.

"I'm Riley."

"Nice to meet you, Riley," Steff says.

Riley walks over to me and lowers his voice. "Sure he's not your boyfriend?"

"No," I assure him.

He frowns, seemingly displeased by my answer. Then he stands beside Kay and puts an arm around her.

"Josh still isn't here," he says, loud enough for me to hear.

I throw him a look of disbelief. "He's not?"

I glance at my watch again.

Only eleven minutes left until the show starts. Where can Josh be?

Kay checks her phone. "Oh, he sent me a message."

I lean towards her to read it.

Sorry. Can't make it tonight. Marianne keeps throwing up and I can't leave her. Sorry.

I let out a groan. "What are we going to do?"

Kay puts her phone away and looks at me. "Well, at least we still have one guitarist."

"But all our songs are written for two," I whine.

"True," Riley agrees.

Steff raises his hand. "I can play."

"What?" Riley and I both say at the same time.

Steff puts his hand down. "I know how to play the guitar, so if you need another guitarist and you have another guitar, I can play."

My eyebrows shoot sky high.

Steff can play the guitar?

"You're joking," I tell him.

He turns to me. "What? I didn't tell you?"

He damn well knows he didn't. Then again, I should have known it from the way he looked at the guitars at the music store when we were shopping for a new one.

"I think Benny has an old guitar upstairs," Kay says. "I'll borrow it."

I look at her in disbelief. "You're taking his word for it?"

"Yup," she nods. But then she turns back to Steff before going inside. "If you're lying, I'll punch your pretty face."

From the corner of my eye, I catch Riley grinning.

"Okay," Steff agrees.

"But he doesn't know our songs," I argue with Kay.

"We'll just have to do covers tonight," Kay says. "Talk it over with him. Ask him what he knows."

She disappears through the door.

I sigh.

Riley pats my shoulder. "I'll leave the two of you."

He, too, disappears inside.

I throw Steff a warning glare. "This better not be a joke."

He shrugs. "Are you also going to punch me if it is?"

"I have enough reasons to punch you already," I tell him.

He chuckles.

I go up the steps with my guitar. "Come on. The list of songs we usually perform is in my purse."

"Okay."

I pause at the doorway to turn to him. "You better be as good as you think you are."

"Don't worry," Steff assures me with a confident grin that I want to wipe off his face. "I won't let you down."

~

And he didn't.

Steff played every note he was supposed to in every song with an unbelievable combination of poise and exuberance. Benny's guitar was like putty in his hands. He gave our music life and molded it into a dozen different masterpieces.

As much as I hate to admit it, he even plays better than me.

The crowd loved him. How could they not?

He was hot. He was cool.

Even I was enthralled by the way he played. I could not take my eyes off his face, which seemed to become more radiant beneath the spotlight as it glistened with sweat, or off his fingers as they commanded his instrument. Commanded? No. That's not the right word. He was in control, yes, but there was nothing forceful about the way he plucked at the strings. Instead, one could sense his passion flowing into the guitar and entwining with it. They were one.

I watch as the members of my band greet Steff jubilantly. Kay looks particularly ecstatic, Riley seems to have warmed up to him, and even Alice has a rare smile on her lips.

I stare at Steff, suddenly feeling as if I know him even less than before.

What kind of man do I have for a roommate, exactly?

"Whew." Kay wipes the sweat from her forehead as she walks over to me. "That was probably the most sizzling performance we've ever given."

"It was intense," I agree as I put my guitar away.

"Intense?" Kay chuckles. She leans over to me and whispers in my ear. "Don't tell Riley, but I swear I nearly had an orgasm at one point back there."

I look at her in surprise. "O-orgasm?"

She places a hand on my shoulder. "You do know what I'm talking about, don't you?"

A blush creeps under my already red cheeks. "Of course I do!"

What am I saying? I've only ever had two kisses in my life.

Kay grins like a little girl who's just played a prank on a boy.

I narrow my eyes at her. "Shouldn't you be more... well, behaved?"

She pats my shoulder. "Now, now, don't look at me like that. Didn't you feel the same way?"

I don't answer.

416

"How could you not?" She looks in Steff's direction. "The guy was practically making love to his guitar in front of everybody."

Huh?

"Just look at him." Kay crosses her arms over her chest. "Every woman in this bar wants to go to bed with him."

He is surrounded by a number of women now, all of whom seem to be gushing over him with wide smiles and googly eyes. And he seems to be enjoying their attention, flashing them smiles of his own.

Somehow, the sight makes my chest ache and my temper boil.

How can Steff be having fun with girls like this after he kissed me last night, after he teased me this morning, after he showed up supposedly to watch me play?

He is toying with me, after all.

"Are you sure he isn't your boyfriend?" Kay asks me. "Or that you don't want him to be? Because if you don't do something, one of those girls is going to sweep him away."

I snort. "Like I'd be interested in a guy like him."

So what if he's hot and plays the guitar well? He's mean. He's weird. He's a spoiled brat who couldn't even hold on to his own luggage.

Suddenly, I pause. My eyes widen.

That's right. I'm the only one who knows those things about him. Those girls don't.

"Wow. You really are something else." Kay pats my back. "I'm not sure if I want to punch you or salute you."

I let that go.

"Speaking of punching, I guess you're not going to do that to him since he played so well," I say.

"Of course not. I wouldn't want to put a dent in that pretty face."

Ah. So she was just bluffing.

"And like you said, he played very well." She puts a hand on my shoulder again. "Hey. Do you know how long he's staying? Maybe he could play for us again. Maybe he could even play for us until he leaves."

My eyebrows rise. "But what about Josh?"

"Let's face it. Josh has a lot on his plate right now," Kay answers. "Besides, there's no denying that Steff plays better."

My teeth clash. My hand rolls into a fist.

I know he plays better. But to replace Josh? That's insane. And completely unfair.

I brush Kay's hand off my shoulder. "Josh is an irreplaceable part of the band."

I walk off with my guitar.

"Jess?" Kay calls after me.

I ignore her as I start to make my way through the crowd.

"Jess," Riley calls after me, too. "Aren't you drinking tonight?"

"I'll pass," I tell him without glancing back.

I head towards the exit and walk down the street. The chilly wind kisses my cheeks and I put my hood on.

How could Kay have suggested that?

We've been playing with Josh for three years. We're not just a band. We're friends. We're a family. We can't just let him go.

I can't just let him go.

Yes, the band is about to break up. Yes, his girlfriend is going to have his baby. But as the other guitarist in the band, he's the one I'm closest to. He's my partner, and usually my inspiration.

He's irreplaceable.

"Hey, Jess, wait up!" Steff shouts from behind me.

I roll my eyes and keep walking.

He catches up to me and grabs my arm. "Wait."

"What do you want?" I whirl around. "Haven't you had enough fun already?"

It's all his fault. If he hadn't come to the bar, if he hadn't offered to play, things wouldn't have come to this.

Steff releases my arm. His eyebrows crease in concern.

"Are you... mad?"

I don't answer. I simply turn away from him and walk faster, even though my chest is threatening to burst.

"You are mad." I hear Steff's footsteps behind me. "Why? I thought you'd be glad..."

"Because you did me a favor?" I finish the sentence for him as I turn around once more. "Because you think you saved the band tonight?"

Steff falls silent.

"Well, you didn't." I hurl the words at him with a shake of my head. My fists tremble at my sides. "You're no hero. You're just a self-centered, insensitive, stupid jerk!"

With that, I turn on my heel and run off.

This time, I don't hear footsteps behind me.

Good. Steff should stay away from me right now, because I feel like punching his pretty face for real.

I clutch my chest as the wind blows through my hair. Tears threaten to trickle down my cheeks, and I run faster. I don't stop running until I've made it down three blocks to my apartment, and as soon as I get inside, I head straight to my bedroom and throw myself on my bed. I let the tears spill on my pillow.

How the hell did my life get so messed up? Everything was fine, and then all of a sudden Steff showed up and turned it all upside-down.

I sniff.

Why did Steff have to show up?

~

Why isn't Steff here?

I ask myself the question after reluctantly peeking into his bedroom to find his bed still made. No dirty clothes or boots lie on the floor.

My eyes grow wide.

Steff didn't come back?

No.

After crying myself to sleep last night, I felt better when I woke up. I felt calm enough to face him, to talk to him even.

But there was no sign of him in the living room or in the kitchen, and when I didn't see his boots by the door, I decided to check his room.

Now, my heart sinks as my eyelids lower.

Steff didn't come back.

Why? All because I got mad at him and said those mean things?

Now that I think about it, maybe I went a little too far. Maybe I shouldn't have said anything. Maybe I shouldn't have gotten mad at him at all. He did help the band out, after all, regardless of his intentions.

Still, I was only telling him how I felt. If he didn't want to hear it, he shouldn't have followed me.

Why did he follow me when he had all those girls drooling all over him?

I place a hand over my chest as I feel a stab of guilt.

This is my fault. My mother always used to say that I shouldn't get upset so easily, that I should learn to control my temper. I've failed. Again. And now, Steff might not be coming back.

I close the door to his room and let out a sigh.

Jess, what have you done?

Well, there's nothing I can do about it now. Steff will make his own decisions. And I have to go to work.

I grab my purse and head to the door but stop after a few steps.

Even if Steff is leaving, he'll come back for his things. The least I can do is say goodbye.

I turn back towards the counter and scribble a note.

Chapter 6
Steff

Steff,

I hope you're alright. What's left of your money is on your bed. You can keep the robe, too. You were great last night. I should have said that instead of the stuff I said. Hope you find a better roommate. (I will, too!) Take care.

Jess

I fold the note and put it inside my pocket. A smile forms on my lips.

So she was worried about me, huh? And she thought I did great last night.

I scratch the back of my head and let out a sigh.

That girl should really be more true to her feelings.

I take off my boots and go to my room.

The folded white robe that I wore on my first day here lies on top of the bed. A wad of bills sits on top of it just as Jess said in her note.

She really thought I'd leave, huh?

Not a chance.

I simply stayed away to give her some time to cool down, even though I wasn't even sure what upset her in the first place. I still don't know what it was and whether or not it was my fault. But I'm glad she seems to have calmed down.

I grab the bills and bring them to the counter, where I put a glass paperweight above them.

Nope. Not leaving.

I doubt I'd find a better roommate, after all.

I go around the counter into the kitchen and open the fridge. My gaze falls on the eggs and I remember the breakfast I cooked for her yesterday.

I touch my chin.

Hmm. Well, I did tease Jess yesterday, so maybe it's my fault she blew up like that. And I stole the limelight from her and her band, too. Maybe that's why she got upset and called me a self-centered, stupid, and-what else was it?-insensitive jerk.

I still remember the look on her face when she spat those words at me. The resentment in them took me by surprise then and they still make my chest ache now.

Maybe she wishes she could take them back now that she's calmed down, but I know for a fact that she meant them. Sometimes, the words one says in the heat of emotion are the ones that ring most true. They are the ones that come straight from the heart, after all, unhindered, unedited by the mind.

I must have hurt her, and so there's only one thing to do.

I close the door of the fridge, walk to the living room, and put my boots back on.

I have to make it up to Jess.

~

"You made dinner?"

Jess's raven eyes grow wide as they take in the feast I've spread out on the dining table-garlic butter prawns with peppers, Angus steak cooked medium rare, and some pan-roasted potatoes in rosemary and truffle oil.

It took me nearly all day to find the recipes I wanted, shop for the ingredients, and finally cook the meal, but I've managed to pull it off.

Erza, the head chef back at the Palace, would be proud.

I pull out a chair for Jess. "I hope you like it. I put a lot of work into it."

She sinks into the chair almost in a daze. Her gaze remains on the food.

"You really did all this?"

I grin. "I guess a person can do anything he puts his mind to."

419

"You mean you can do anything you put your mind to." Jess sighs. "Seriously, I'm beginning to think you're some kind of genius. Either that or you're an alien from another universe."

I chuckle as I begin to pour her a glass of wine. I stop, though, as she touches my bandaged fingers.

"Your hand."

I pull it away to rub the back of my head as I give her a sheepish grin.

"Well, shelling prawns is harder than I thought."

"Then you shouldn't have done it, silly," Jess reprimands me with a pout. "How will you be able to play the guitar now?"

"I have no plans to." I finish pouring. "Your guitarist will come back soon. And if not, the band has you."

I set the bottle down and take my seat.

"You're more talented than people give you credit for."

She might not be a performer-that's why the audience doesn't notice her-but I could tell how flawlessly and soulfully she played.

"Speak for yourself," Jess says as she picks up her glass. "You were the star last night. Kay and all those girls who were screaming at the bar last night are going to be disappointed when they hear you won't be performing again."

"Were you jealous?"

She coughs just after taking her first sip, then looks above her glass to glare at me.

Oops. I've teased her again.

I lift my hand. "Well, it can't be helped."

Jess sighs. "You didn't have to cook dinner, you know. It's enough that you came back."

Her cheeks turn a shade closer to the liquid in her glass.

I smile. "Where else would I find a roommate as fascinating as you?"

Her blush intensifies. Then her eyes narrow.

"You're making fun of me again, aren't you?"

I grab my knife and fork. "Plus you'll never find a roommate as hot as me."

Jess sets her glass down and gives another sigh. "You're still full of yourself, too. I guess some things never change."

I just grin.

She picks up her utensils and cuts into her steak.

"So where did you go last night?" she asks.

"I went to another bar," I answer. "I had a few drinks, then I stayed at a hotel."

Jess pokes her fork into the slice of steak.

"Don't worry," I tell her. "I wasn't with anyone."

Jess pauses. "I didn't ask."

She puts the steak inside her mouth.

"Good?" I ask her.

She finishes chewing. Then she wipes her lips with a table napkin and gives me a thumbs up sign.

I smile.

I've never cooked for anyone before. I must say it's satisfying.

"I'm glad you like it." I push the bowl of prawns towards her. "Please eat as much as you like."

~

"I think I ate too much." Jess rubs her belly as we sit on the couch after dinner. "Even after washing all those dishes, I still feel so full."

"Me too." I pat my own stomach. "I think I'll go to the gym tomorrow."

"You should," she tells me. "Women will stop throwing themselves at you if you gain weight."

I want to ask if that applies to her as well, but I don't.

Jess falls silent as she taps her pen on the notebook she has on her lap. Her eyebrows furrow.

"What are you doing?" I ask her curiously.

"Trying to write a song," she answers. "Kay wants to use it for our final show."

"Final?"

"Yeah." She stares at the ceiling. "The band is splitting up soon. Seems like everyone wants to grow up, move on and settle down."

"What about you?"

Jess shrugs. "I don't know yet."

I move closer to her and glance at her notebook.

"Doesn't seem like you've gotten very far yet."

She hugs the notebook to her chest. "Well, just so you know, writing a song isn't easy. In fact, most people can't do it."

"I know."

Jess closes her notebook and sighs. "Besides, I lack inspiration."

"Hmm." I scratch my chin. "Maybe I should take my clothes off."

She throws the pillow beside her at me.

"Don't even think about it." She crosses her arms over her chest. "Like that could be inspiring."

I just grin.

Suddenly, a phone rings. Jess gets off the couch and grabs hers off the counter.

"Hello," she greets her caller. "No. It's fine. I'm not busy. Why?"

Her voice trails off as she disappears into the bedroom.

I grab the remote and flip the channels in search of something interesting to watch. Jess returns before I find anything.

"Is everything alright?" I ask her as I put the remote back on the coffee table.

"Yeah." She sits down on the couch. "That was my sister checking on me. She does it from time to time."

I glance at one of the framed pictures on the shelf, one of Jess with a bride and groom, a man in uniform and an old couple.

I point to it. "Is that your sister?"

"Yup." Jess nods. "That was taken at her wedding. The other people in the picture are my brother and my parents."

"So you have an older brother and sister?"

"Yup. I'm the youngest." She turns to me. "What about you?"

"I've got an older brother and two younger sisters. They're twins."

"Really?" Her eyebrows arch. "They must be cute."

"They used to be."

She chuckles. "So you're the middle child, huh? I guess that's why you're the rebellious one."

I throw her a puzzled look. "Excuse me?"

"You know, they say the middle child ends up being the rebel because they're the easiest child to overlook."

I've never heard that.

"I don't think I'm-"

"Well, I don't believe it anyway," Jess cuts me off. "I mean, look at me. I'm the youngest child but I'm still the black sheep. That's why Laura worries about me a lot."

I feel more confused. "But you're doing fine on your own. You work at a nice cafe. You play the guitar well..."

"I didn't finish college like my parents wanted," she explains as she rests her head against the back of the couch. "They didn't want me to be in a band, either."

"Because?"

"They thought I'd end up becoming an alcoholic or doing drugs or getting a sleazy boyfriend."

"But you didn't," I point out.

"Besides, there's no future in playing in a band, and if there's one thing your parents want for you, it's a sure, bright future."

I nod. "Well, that I can agree with."

Jess turns to me. "What did your parents want you to be?"

"Obedient," I answer. "Responsible. Perfect."

Jess laughs. "Sounds like your parents and mine read the same manual."

I chuckle too. It's strange. Even though we're from very different backgrounds, we seem to be in the same boat.

Jess picks up her notebook. "Well, I really should be working on this song."

"I'll leave you alone." I stand up. "I've had a long day."

"I bet."

I walk to my room.

"Thanks for dinner," Jess calls after me.

I glance over my shoulder. "You're welcome."

"And good night."

"Good night."

As I hold the door knob, I hear a yawn behind me and I glance back at Jess again.

"Are you sure you don't want to go to bed yet? You look sleepy."

"I'm fine." She waves me off. "After all that food, I can last all night."

~

So she said.

Right now, though, I'm standing over a couch containing a soundly sleeping Jess. One of her hands rests on the open notebook that's on her belly. Her other hand is almost touching the floor near where the pen has fallen. Her soft snores add some rhythm to the humming of the air conditioner.

I sigh.

"You can last all night, huh?"

Gently, I pry the notebook from under Jess's hand and place it on the coffee table. Then I lift her in my arms.

She grunts but doesn't wake.

I carry her to her bedroom. She's lighter than I expected.

I set her down on the bed, and as I do, I notice that one of the buttons of her blouse has come off. Her black bra is peeking through the gap. I swallow.

I consider putting the button back in place but decide against it. Instead, I pull the blanket over her. She rolls to her side towards me.

I find myself staring at her face, at her thick lashes which I never noticed before, at her button nose and her full lips.

Yes, Jess is fascinating when she's all fired up, glowering and gritting her teeth, or when she's flustered and her cheeks are all red. But she's attractive like this, too, when she looks so peaceful and innocent.

Unable to resist, I brush back a pink strand of her hair. My finger grazes her warm cheek.

Just that is enough to send heat coursing through my veins. For a moment, I feel a strong urge to kiss her cheek, maybe even her lips. God knows I want to do more than kiss her.

But I keep myself in check and walk away from the bed.

After all, I'm pretty sure she's a virgin. If I give in to temptation, I'll just end up hurting her.

Strange. I've never had a woman that I wanted but couldn't have before. Nor have I ever had to worry about a woman's feelings, virgin or otherwise.

I place a hand on my heated forehead.

I guess Jess is one of a kind.

I walk out of her room, close the door behind me, and walk to my room. The bulge in my briefs throbs the whole way there.

She gets so mad at me when I tease her, but she teases me without even knowing it.

It's unfair.

I step inside my room and close the door.

It's going to be another long, hard night.

Chapter 7
Jess

It's morning?

I turn to the window and squint against the sunlight trying to sneak in through the blinds. I glance at my clock.

6:08.

Still early. Even so, I decide to get out of bed. As the blanket slips off me, I see the blouse I'm wearing and my eyebrows crease.

Why am I still wearing my work clothes? Didn't I change into my pajamas? And why is one button undone?

Then I remember that I was working on my song last night. I remember lying down on the couch, too, to rest when my mind was starting to feel tired.

Wait. Did I fall asleep on the couch? Then why am I on my bed?

Only one explanation comes to mind, and it sends me stomping out of my room.

"Steff!"

I find him in the living room, already dressed and putting on his shoes.

He looks up to greet me. "Good morning."

I cross my arms over my chest and tap my foot on the floor. "Did you carry me to my room last night?"

"Well, I wasn't about to just leave you asleep on the couch," he says. "Your back would hurt, or you could catch a cold."

I guess that's understandable. Still...

"And did you do anything else?" I ask him.

He touches his chin. "Anything else?"

"Yes. Anything else."

He nods. "Right."

I knew it.

"I put the blanket over you."

What?

I go over to him and grab the front of his sweater.

"I'm asking if you did something to me, dumbass."

"Oh. You mean if I kissed you or groped you or...?"

I grit my teeth and wait for his answer.

"Sorry to disappoint you, but no," Steff says. "I didn't do any of that. I just put you to bed."

I step back and glance at my blouse. "Then why...?"

"Oh, the button. That was already undone when I found you asleep on the couch."

I stare at the button. Come to think of it, it has come undone on its own before, although I usually don't notice it because I'm wearing my apron or a sweater.

"Sorry," Steff says.

I frown. What on earth is he apologizing for?

He stands up. "I would have done something, but I don't lay a hand on virgins."

My cheeks grow red. "Who said I was a virgin?"

Steff chuckles.

"So you're saying you're not?"

I say nothing.

Steff takes a step forward. "Fine. Prove it to me. Kiss me right now."

My jaw clenches.

"Why the hell should I-?"

"Kiss me."

His deep voice caresses my skin and echoes in my ears, which suddenly feel warm. His narrowed blue eyes gaze into mine.

I find myself drowning in them, completely under their spell.

Steff moves even closer to me, and my body stays still even as my heart begins to pound a million miles an hour. His face hovers just inches from mine. His chest lingers dangerously close to my breasts. They begin to ache. The smell of his cologne drifts into my nostrils and I can't breathe.

"Well?"

He lowers his face and the soft strands of his hair brush against my forehead. I see my reflection in his eyes.

I can't look away.

My cheeks are burning, and it's not just my cheeks. My chest is aflame. My belly feels hot and the skin between my legs is melting, leaking. It aches and feels good at the same time.

And I can't fight it.

I let my eyelids fall and move my face forward. The last time, the kiss happened too fast, but I still remember how soft Steff's lips were as they pressed against mine. I hold my breath and brace myself for that same exquisite sensation.

It doesn't come.

Instead, I feel a pair of strong hands on my shoulders, keeping me in place. I open my eyes and see the grin on Steff's lips.

Those lips that I had been about to kiss.

"Just kidding," he says. "I think one kiss between us is enough."

One kiss is enough? That means he doesn't intend to kiss me anymore?

Wait. He was just kidding?

My hands curl into fists. "Why, you..."

"See you later." Steff winks before walking out the door.

My nails dig into my palms. My foot goes flying into the magazine rack.

Damn that Steff.

First, he kisses me when I least expect it, when I don't want it. Then when I am expecting it, wanting it even, he just walks off.

I clutch my chest where my heart is now hammering with anger instead of passion.

What is it with men?

~

"Welcome to my problems," Lisbeth tells me as we enjoy a cup of coffee at the corner table during our break. "And don't even bother trying to find a solution. Men are all complicated jerks. There's no use trying to understand them, much less trying to make them act reasonably."

I tap the rim of my mug. "I just don't understand why men have to be so mean. What did we do to deserve this?"

"Nothing," Lisbeth answers before taking a sip from her mug. "Like I said, they're not reasonable beings. They get their strength from making us look weak. They get their fun preying on our bodies and playing with our emotions even though they haven't got any of their own."

I shake my head. I'm hearing what Lisbeth is saying, but it still doesn't make any sense.

She sets down her mug. "This is about Steff, isn't it?"

I look up from my coffee. "What?"

Lisbeth leans forward. "Come on. Surely you don't think I still believe he's gay."

I glance at the counter and see Tom a considerable distance away. Then I turn back to Lisbeth.

"You know?"

"At first, I admit I thought he might be," she answers as she lifts her mug. "But then I've been watching you lately and listening to all the things you've been saying and not saying about Steff, and there's just no way a woman would act like that about a gay guy."

"Like what?"

"You have a crush on him," Lisbeth blurts out.

I'm glad I haven't taken another sip of coffee. I would have spat it out.

"No way," I tell her. "That's impossible."

"Considering what I've seen, it's possible," Lisbeth argues. "A guy as hot as that can make even the most tepid of women weak at the knees."

My eyebrows furrow. "Are you saying I'm tepid?"

"I'm saying there's nothing wrong with liking the guy."

I touch my forehead and sigh. "Haven't you been listening? That guy is a jerk and a tease and so full of himself. There's no way I'd like someone like him."

"Maybe he's teasing you because he likes you," Lisbeth suggests.

I frown.

"Or maybe he's just teasing you because you're easy to tease," she adds.

I narrow my eyes at her. "What do you mean by that?"

"You get easily upset when someone taunts you, and you get easily embarrassed, too, which is probably due to the fact that you're a virgin."

I roll my eyes. That word again?

"I'm pretty sure he's just a jerk," I say. "Besides, he said he doesn't like virgins."

Lisbeth's eyes grow wide. "He said that?"

I shrug and lift my mug to my lips. "Not that I care. Why, is it important?"

"Hmm." Lisbeth leans her head on one arm. "A lot of men actually prefer virgins. But there are also plenty who don't like them. Maybe it's because sleeping with a virgin entails more responsibility, and you know how men are when it comes to responsibilities. Or maybe they just think the sex is better with an experienced woman."

Sex? I blush. How did we even get to talking about that?

I wave my hand. "You know what? Let's not talk about it anymore."

"Hey." Lisbeth reaches for my hand. "It doesn't matter. You've just got to be confident, alright?"

I take a sip of coffee. "Who cares if I'm not his type? He's definitely not my type, either. You know my type right?"

"I know. I know." Lisbeth drinks from her own mug. "Someone sickly sweet, like Josh."

I frown. "Josh would never tease me."

"Isn't that what he's been doing all these years?"

"No. I've just been hopelessly hoping all on my own. He hasn't done anything to lead me on."

Lisbeth sighs. "Boring."

"That's because he's a good guy," I point out. "He's loyal to his girlfriend."

"So you think if he didn't have a girlfriend, the two of you would be a couple by now?"

"Of course," I answer without hesitation.

"Well, that's confidence."

I say nothing. I finish the rest of my coffee in silence. My thoughts wander over to Josh.

I sure hope he shows up tonight.

~

"Josh, it's really great to have you back!" I end up giving Josh a hug instead of a high five after our show. "I knew it. The band really isn't the same without you."

"Of course not," Kay says. "It was different when Steff played." She sighs. "Are you sure he doesn't want to play with us anymore?"

"Kay," I scold her.

"Just kidding." She waves her hand. "I'm sure you want him all to yourself."

My eyes widen. "That's not-"

"I heard he was good," Josh interrupts.

"Yeah." I touch my neck. "But so are you. And I think you're a better fit for the band. We all play better with you."

"Thanks." He smiles and my heart flutters. "I think I play better with you, too. There's no one I'd rather play the guitar with."

My heart nearly stops.

He glances at Kay and the rest. "I'll surely miss the band."

My chest aches.

I'll miss you.

"Well, we just have to make the most of our final months," I say out loud. "And you have to be with us until the end."

"You're right," Josh agrees. "Sorry I wasn't here the other night."

I shake my head. "So, how's-?"

"Josh!"

I turn my head to see a woman with short, dark brown hair wearing a long sleeved yellow shirt and denim overalls walking towards us.

Even though I've never met her, I immediately guess who she is-and the fact that she goes straight to Josh to wrap an arm around his waist and kiss his cheek confirms it.

Marianne.

"You were great," she tells Josh. "I missed a lot of it, including the last part, because of all those trips to the bathroom, but hey, you were great."

"Are you okay?"

The concern on Josh's face as he looks at her makes my chest ache all the more.

"Yeah. I haven't thrown up once."

Finally, Marianne turns to me. "Hi there. I'm Marianne."

"Jess," I introduce myself.

She nods as she shakes my hand. "I see."

My eyebrows arch slightly. What's that supposed to mean?

"Hey, Josh," Riley calls. "Wanna go for a smoke?"

Josh looks at Marianne.

"Just one," she tells him.

He nods and they head for the back door, leaving me alone with Marianne.

"Drink?" I point to the bar.

She shakes her head and points to her tummy.

Oh, right. How could I forget?

"But I'll keep you company while you drink," she says.

Why do I have a feeling this isn't going to turn out well?

I ignore that feeling as I walk to the bar. I take my regular seat and signal Benny for a beer. Marianne sits beside me.

I decide to start the conversation.

"This is the first time you've watched us play?"

"Yup." She places her arms on the counter. "I've always wanted to, but I've just been busy."

"I'm glad you were able to make the time tonight."

Marianne shrugs. "I promised Josh I'd watch him play before the band broke up. He loves the band."

"And the band loves him," I say without thinking.

Benny puts my bottle of beer in front of me. I grab it and take a sip.

"You especially," Marianne says suddenly.

I lower the bottle so abruptly that some of the alcohol splatters on my shirt.

"I'm sorry?"

She props her head on an elbow and looks at me. "Josh talked about you a lot, you know."

He did?

"And from all those stories he told me, I got a sense that you had a crush on him. He wouldn't believe it, but I'm right, aren't I?"

I don't answer.

"I knew it the moment you started playing together."

My eyebrows shoot up and my jaw drops.

Shit.

"Poor girl." Marianne shakes her head. "You're in love with a man who'd never love you back."

My chest feels tight. I can't breathe.

"Even if he wasn't already taken, I'm sure he wouldn't fall in love with you," Marianne goes on. "Josh likes his women with spunk and sex appeal."

Every word stabs my heart like a dagger.

"Even though he's a guy, he likes being seduced, you see. And I'm sorry, but you don't look like you could seduce the last teenager on earth."

Something inside me cracks. I feel the blood drain from my face.

Marianne laughs. "To think I ever thought you were a threat."

She grabs my beer and places it between my hands. "Drink up. It won't mend your broken heart, but it should help you forget some of the pain of defeat. It's just as bitter."

She squeezes my shoulder and gets off her stool.

"Oh, and could you tell Josh I'll be waiting in the car? I don't think all this noise is good for the baby."

I say nothing. I'm out of words. Out of breath, thought, feeling.

Empty. Broken. Numb.

I can barely feel the bottle between my hands, but I'm seriously thinking about smashing it over the back of Marianne's head.

Instead, I lift it to my lips and gulp down its contents as fast as I can. Some of it trickles down my chin even as a tear makes its way past my cheek.

I'm hopeless, huh? I knew that already, but why did she have to say it? How could she be so mean? Are all pregnant women mean?

And isn't it enough that she already has Josh? Does she have to strip me of all my self-confidence, too?

No sex appeal, huh? No wonder Steff didn't bother to touch me when I was asleep. No wonder he didn't want to kiss me this morning even though I was practically begging him to.

I set the bottle down and wipe my mouth. I wait only a few seconds for the alcohol to reach my stomach before signaling Benny for another bottle.

Like Marianne said, there's only one thing I can do right now.

Drink.

~

I drank too much again.

I'm fumbling with my keys in front of the door to my apartment. I've tried three times and I still haven't been able to slip the right one into the hole.

Thankfully, before the fourth try, the door opens. Steff stands behind it.

"Jess?"

I stagger inside and Steff closes the door. I toss my purse at the couch and it lands between the pillows, but the force of the throw disrupts my balance and I stumble.

Steff catches me in his arms.

"Jess, what happened to you?"

I turn around and look straight up into his icy blue eyes.

Just as I thought, they're the prettiest eyes I've ever seen.

I clutch the front of his shirt as I gaze into them. Then I open my mouth to say the words I never thought I'd say.

"Kiss me, Steff."

Chapter 8
Steff

I blink as I gaze into quivering ebony eyes that send my heart thrumming in my ribcage.

Did I hear that right? Did Jess just ask me to kiss her?

For a moment, I think it's a joke. Maybe she's just trying to get back at me for what I did to her this morning. But as I search her eyes, I see no trace of anything other than a sincere, serious plea behind a glistening layer of tears that could break at any moment.

Her shoulders tremble as she holds the front of my shirt firmly captive in her fists. Her words echo in my ears.

Kiss me, Steff.

I swallow the lump in my throat even as another forms in my crotch.

What is with this request? And with this look, to boot?

I'm tempted to give in. Every buzzing vein in my body that suddenly feels spiking hot urges me to. Why not? Jess is asking for it.

Still, I pull her into my arms. I place my hand on the back of her head and press it against my chest. I want to kiss her. But not when she's like this. Not when she's drunk and clearly aching.

"Shh." I stroke her hair. "It's alright."

To my surprise, Jess starts sobbing against my shirt.

I grab her shoulders and push her gently away so I can look at her.

"Jess?"

She sniffs. Tears streak down her cheeks.

I press my palm against one.

Damn it. I'm no good with crying women.

"Jess, what happened?" I ask her.

Instead of giving me an answer, she sinks to the floor, her legs folding on either side of her. Then she buries her face in her hands and continues sobbing.

I kneel in front of her.

"Jess?"

"Why don't... you... want to kiss me?" she asks between sobs through her palms.

I scratch my head. "It's not that I don't want to kiss you. It's just..."

"It's because I'm boring, aren't I?" Her hands drop to her sides and she looks at me with those teary eyes. "It's because you don't see me as a woman, right?"

"What?"

Where on earth did Jess get that idea?

"Because I'm not like other women," she continues as she wipes her tears. "Because I'm not as sexy as they are, or as experienced."

I frown and put a hand on her shoulder. "Jess, that's not true. You're a woman, one of the most interesting women I've ever met."

"Then kiss me," she begs again. Her eyes gaze right into mine. "Make me feel like a woman."

At those words, my eyes grow wide. My heart stops and my breath catches.

I close my eyes and press my palm against my forehead beneath my hair. I draw a deep breath as I brush the strands up to the top of my head before letting them fall again.

I still don't want to kiss Jess when she's like this. But damn it, I don't want to see her like this either. Damn it all.

"You better not regret this," I whisper as I hold her gaze.

Then I let my mouth fall on hers.

As before, Jess's lips feel soft and warm beneath mine. The more I press against them, the more they quiver.

Unlike before, though, they push back against mine. My heart pounds. My cock throbs in my briefs.

She's really asking for it now.

My hand clasps the back of her head as I deepen the kiss. My fingers become lost in a forest of pink and black vines.

My tongue tastes the bitterness of alcohol on hers and I start to feel intoxicated.

Now we're both drunk.

I push my tongue in deeper. Jess lets out a moan that vibrates through my entire body.

My hand moves to her cheek. I can still feel the tears beneath my palm.

I let go of her lips so I can kiss and lick her tears away. The salty trails vanish beneath the tip of my tongue.

Jess's face suddenly slips from beneath me and her back hits the carpet.

My first thought is that she's passed out, but then she looks up at me with half-lidded eyes. Her cheeks burn a deep shade of red and her chest heaves as she chases after her breath.

"More?" she asks as she stretches her arms out to me.

The fresh plea sparks heat in my cock.

She has no idea what she's doing, but I can't hold myself back anymore.

I crouch over her and capture her mouth once more. Her hands go to the back of my neck. One of mine slips beneath her shirt and climbs up her ribs. My fingers reach the edge of black lace and press against the curve.

Jess lets out another moan, which I swallow. Her hands remain fastened on my neck until my thumb brushes against her nipple above the lace. Then they fall to her sides and she tears her mouth away from mine to let out a loud gasp. But no protest follows.

I continue rubbing her nipple as I plant a kiss next to her ear. The peak stiffens beneath the pad of my thumb and she trembles.

I brush her hair aside to kiss her neck next. She turns her head to the side, and for the first time, I notice the tattoo on her neck.

A black butterfly.

I wonder what it means.

I'll ask her later.

I trace the ink with the tip of my tongue and she shivers. Her arm drapes across her forehead and casts a shadow over her barely open eyes.

I move lower. My mouth descends on her other breast and plants a reverent kiss. Then I drag my lips down her shirt to the stretch of exposed skin. I plant another kiss on her belly and my chin comes in contact with the waistband of her jeans.

Suddenly, Jess laughs.

I look up at her in surprise.

"Your hair tickles," she says.

"Really?" I sweep the strands up my forehead. "But you seem to like it."

I kiss her belly some more, delighting in her laughter. My chin rubs against the denim and I look down. A sweet scent assaults my nostrils.

Unable to resist it, I pop the button of her jeans and pull down the shiny zipper. The scent grows stronger.

I pull down her pants and see a wet spot on her panties.

I press my nose against it to inhale even more of her scent. I can feel her curls poking against the cotton.

"Steff, what are you...?"

I start to lick the wet spot. The salty sweet puddle quickly coats my tongue.

Jess shivers and gasps. She moans.

Her hips rise off the carpet and I hold them fast.

Over and over, my tongue swipes against the front of her black panties. They get darker. The wet patch grows larger.

My fingers move towards the cotton. I feel the folds of skin beneath and part them with my thumbs. I press my tongue against the nub in between.

Jess lets out a cry. Then another, muffled by the back of her hand over her mouth. Her scent grows stronger and fills the air.

I continue until she's trembling, until her cries are spilling out one after another. Then the nub beneath my tongue retracts, the muscles of her belly contract and her back arches. A fresh wet spot forms under the one I've already made.

I stare at it as Jess pants and tries to catch her breath.

I should probably stop now, but I can't. I have my own wet spot in my briefs to worry about. Besides, Jess did ask me to make her feel like a woman, and this is the best way I know how.

I take off her pants, her soaked underwear and her shoes. I push my pants and my briefs down at the same time, all the way past my heavy balls. My painfully hard cock springs free.

I lift Jess's thighs so that her knees go up. The soles of her feet fall flat against the carpet. I part her legs and settle between them. My fingers wrap around the base of my cock.

"Here I come."

I push in and the tip of my cock is coated by her wetness. She gasps. It enters and she gasps even louder.

My hands go to the backs of her knees. I lift them as I keep pushing.

She's tight. Exquisitely tight. Her velvety skin clings to me like a glove. My teeth dig into my lower lip as I fight to maintain control.

Fuck.

I close my eyes and hold my breath until I'm completely inside her. When I open them, I find hers squeezed shut. Her hand remains over her mouth.

I push it away and her eyes open wide. I hold her hands at her sides as I gaze into the black pools.

I want to see her expression clearly. I want to hear her moans.

I want it all.

I hold her gaze as I begin to move. The friction is maddening and my cock swells inside her.

"Steff." My name escapes Jess's lips in a hoarse cry.

I capture them as I move my hips faster. My balls slap against her skin. The sheath clinging to my cock is wetter now, but still tight. I don't know how long I can last.

I let go of her hands and grip her thighs as I move even faster. Her arms remain at her sides. Her fingers curl against the carpet.

Heat swirls in my balls and leaks out of the tip of my cock. Beads of sweat break out on my forehead and back. My abdominal muscles tense.

"Coming."

That's all the warning I manage to give her before I bury myself deep inside her. Just as I do, she tightens around me and my cock quivers as she squeezes every last drop of my pent-up desire from me.

My eyes fall shut and I growl low in my throat as I lean over her. Then I open them along with my mouth as I force air into my lungs.

Jess is just as breathless as I am. Her eyes, though open, stare blankly past me at the ceiling. I can see the light in them fading.

I touch her cheek and plant a kiss on her forehead just as her eyes close. I pull out and put my clothes back on. By the time I'm done, she's already sound asleep.

I pinch her cheek and get no response.

Well, she did drink a lot. And she must be exhausted after her first time having sex.

Her first time.

As the haze of lust clears, the wheels of my mind start turning again and guilt threatens. But I shake my head.

She asked for this. She wanted it. I have no regrets.

Sometimes, alcohol gives us a chance to be true to ourselves.

I carry Jess to her bedroom and set her down on the bed. I brush the strands of hair out of her flushed face.

For a moment, I debate whether I should stay with her or go back to my own room. I decide on the former and crawl under the sheets beside her.

If she doesn't regret her decision, she'll be glad to see me here. If she does, she'll be furious anyway. My presence here won't make a difference.

I snuggle against the pillow and smile as I catch the scent of her shampoo.

I guess I'll find out which one it is in the morning.

~

"No way."

Jess is staring beneath the sheets with wide eyes.

I rub the sleep out of mine. "Good morning."

"We, we...?"

"Yes, we did it," I tell her to spare her the anguish as I sit up. "We kissed and had sex."

Her face pales.

"Just so you know, you asked for it."

She looks at me with crinkled eyebrows.

Shit. She doesn't remember?

She jumps out of bed, taking the blanket with her.

"Jess!" I call after her.

She runs out of the room. By the time I get out, too, she's already in the bathroom. As the door slams shut behind her, I hear a scream and a litany of curses. Then I hear the shower running.

I prepare coffee as I wait for her. When she finally appears in the kitchen in a brown robe, she looks calmer. Her cheeks are still red, though. Her uncombed hair drips on the cotton.

"Coffee?" I offer her a mug.

Jess sits down and stares at her lap. Her hands curl into fists on her knees.

"I'm sorry about last night," she says softly.

Ah. So she regrets it.

Her regret stings, but I suppose I should have expected it.

"It's okay," I assure her as best as I can.

Jess shakes her head. "Please forget about it."

My eyes grow wide. Then they narrow as my jaw clenches. My fingers tighten around the handle of my mug.

That stings even more.

How could she beg me to kiss her and make her feel like a woman and then beg me to forget about it all?

All the pain and anger vanish, though, as I look at her. Her head is still bowed down. Her shoulders tremble.

Jess isn't doing this to hurt me. She's just scared.

Of course she is. She was a virgin, after all.

I take a deep breath.

"No worries."

She lifts her chin and looks at me. Relief floods her face.

I lift my mug to my lips. "Are you going to tell me what happened?"

Jess looks away.

Okay. I guess not.

I take a sip and set my mug down. "Well, I don't mind it at all, but since I did help you out, you owe me."

Her jaw drops. "Huh?"

"You owe me," I repeat as I lean forward.

Jess crosses her arms as she sits back. "And what exactly do you want in return?"

I grin. "Well, I haven't been here long. Why don't you take me somewhere famous on your next day off? Somewhere fun."

She rubs her chin. "Somewhere famous and fun."

I tap my fingers on the table.
Then an idea comes to me.
"Why don't we go to...?"
"Disneyland?" Jess finishes the sentence.
I smile. "You read my mind."

Chapter 9
Jess

"So this is Disneyland, huh?" Steff asks as we stop in the middle of Main Street.

I draw a deep breath. "Yup."

I've been to Disneyland several times, but each time still feels like my first. The thrill never goes away.

As I see the fathers carrying children on their strong shoulders and the mothers chasing after older kids running around in their favorite costumes, memories of my childhood come back to me. As my gaze falls on the toys on display in the shop windows, I feel like a child again.

I close my eyes and hear laughter all around me, lively chatter, excited screams in the distance. I smell churros and corn dogs. I breathe the scent in, along with the exhilaration, the wonder in the air.

I open my eyes and smile.

Yup. It still feels like the first time.

I hear the click of a camera and turn my head. I catch Steff flashing away.

Come to think of it, this is my first time being here with a man.

Only Steff isn't just any man.

As usual, he looks like a runway model in his pale pink shirt. Frankly, I don't know how he can pull off that color so well.

The V neck runs just deep enough to give a glimpse of his pale chest. The sleeves bunch up inside his elbows. Half the hem is tucked into the waistband of his dark jeans, held up by a thick leather belt with a shiny buckle, while the other half hangs loose.

Seriously, what kind of man goes to Disneyland looking like he just stepped out of an issue of GQ? What kind of man goes to an amusement park wearing knee-high leather boots?

He's wearing a bowler hat, too, which casts a shadow over his features. And sunglasses. Well, that's not unusual. A lot of people have shades on. But his rectangular Gucci ones seem to suit him perfectly. It's almost bothering me how I can't decide whether he looks hotter with his sunglasses on or without them.

I exhale.

I had sex with this hunk?

I clasp a hand over my mouth, afraid I might have just said that out loud. Thankfully, as I glance around, it doesn't seem like I did. But I still blush.

How could I have had sex with Steff? And how can I not remember all of it?

I remember us kissing, and then I was on the floor, and then his mouth was on my...

I clasp my hand even tighter. Fire burns brighter in my cheeks as heat engulfs my body.

What on earth am I doing? Why am I thinking about that right now?

Suddenly, Steff grabs my hand and starts walking.

"Let's go," he says.

I stare at his hand firmly gripping mine and stop.

"Whoa." I pull my hand away. "Why are we holding hands?"

He turns to me. "Well, it would be bad if we got separated, right?"

I guess he does have a point.

"Besides..." Steff offers me his hand. "We know each other well enough now. We shouldn't have any problem doing this much, right?"

I frown. I know very well what he means by knowing each other well enough.

"Didn't you say you'd forget about it?" I ask him.

Steff scratches his head. "My bad."

I sigh. Well, it's not like I've forgotten about it, either. And I was drunk.

I take his hand. "Only because I don't want you to get lost or abducted."

Steff chuckles. Then he pulls my arm as he continues walking.

"Whoa! Slow down," I tell him.

But he doesn't listen.

He's just like those children, with the same smile on his face.

A smile forms on my lips, too.

I walk faster so that I'm beside him.

"So which ride do you want to try first?"

~

"Maybe we shouldn't have tried that one," I tell Steff as I glance over my shoulder to see how wet my shirt is.

We both ended up getting wet on Splash Mountain. Thankfully, most of the water went on my hair and just a little dripped down to dampen the back of my shirt.

As I look at Steff, though, I realize that he wasn't so lucky.

As he wipes his sunglasses, water drips from his hair to his face. He shakes his head like a wet dog and the blond strands whip back and forth.

I swallow.

Then I notice his soaked shirt. The thin fabric has turned translucent and I can see the outline of his muscles. And his nipples.

My jaw drops.

Hot.

Is this body really the one that was pressed against mine?

A gasp behind me jolts me back to reality.

I frown. Steff looks so sexy with his damp clothes on that he might as well be naked. And others are taking notice.

I take the sweater that's wrapped around my waist and drape it around his shoulders. Then I pull his arm.

"Where are we going?" Steff asks. "Aren't we going on another ride?"

"We'll get you a new shirt first," I answer as I drag him in the direction of the shops. "A dry one."

"But..."

"We can try the rest of the rides after."

~

Well, we didn't get to try all of the rides. Still, by sunset, I've lost track of how many we've been on.

I take off my shoes and rub my feet as we sit on a bench.

Too many, probably.

"Are you alright?" Steff asks me.

I nod and glance at him. "You?"

Steff pushes his sunglasses up to the top of his head and gazes up at the fiery sky. He turns to me with a wide smile.

"I don't think I've had this much fun in a while."

My heart skips a beat. I look away and put my shoe back on.

"Wow. You're even more childish than I thought."

"Huh?"

"Not in a bad way, though! I think the happiest people are those who haven't fully grown up. Then again, maybe I'm just saying that because I haven't grown up."

To my surprise, Steff pinches my cheek.

"Ouch!" I yelp.

"I hope you never do," he says with a grin.

I feel my cheeks turn the same color as the sky.

I tear my gaze away. "Only someone childish would say that."

Steff chuckles. "It's okay. I think the most interesting women are those who can act sweet and innocent like a little girl and fierce and sultry like a woman at the same time. Not everyone can manage that."

I pause. Did he just call me a woman? And interesting? And sultry?

Suddenly, I hear footsteps running towards us. I face forward and see a woman in her thirties stop in front of the bench. She places her hands on her knees as she catches her breath.

435

"Can we help you?" I ask her.

She looks at Steff. "You... Could you please help us?"

Steff points a finger at his chest. "Me?"

The woman nods. She takes out an ID from her pocket. It has the park's name on it.

"I'm on the staff here at the park. I'm in charge of the parade."

Right. There's a parade right before the park closes.

"The guy who was supposed to be Prince Charming just had an accident and we need someone to fill in for him," the woman goes on. "I've been running around the park for the past hour looking for someone who might fit the bill."

I narrow my eyes at her. "Don't you have an understudy or something?"

"Yes, but he's out sick." She scratches the back of her head. "Never rains but it pours, right? But we can't let that rain on the parade. The Cinderella float is a big part of it."

And I guess Cinderella wouldn't be Cinderella without her Prince Charming.

"So you want me to be the prince?" Steff asks.

"Please." The woman puts her hands together. "It'll be fun. And I'll give you gift shop coupons, too."

Steff looks down at his lap. "I'm not sure..."

Not sure? He doesn't usually shy from the spotlight, and he usually jumps at an opportunity to help out.

"Please?" the woman begs.

Steff sighs. "Fine. If it's okay with Jess."

He turns to me and so does the woman. She looks like she's about to cry.

Why me?

"Yeah, it's fine," I answer. "Go and be the star of that parade."

"Thank you!"

The woman gives me a hug. Then she drags Steff away.

"Follow me. Thankfully, you won't need much makeup because you already look the part. We'll just have to put on your robe and..."

Her voice trails off as they disappear from sight. I sigh and look up at the sky.

It's steadily getting darker.

I get up and stretch my legs.

Well, I guess I'll look for a good spot to watch the parade.

~

The parade is even more magical than I remember it, I think as I gaze up at the colorful, brightly lit floats from the sidewalk of Main Street.

There are more floats. They're grander. The characters look more lifelike than before.

And Steff is probably the most lifelike of them all.

Strange. He's just wearing a borrowed costume, yet it seems to suit him perfectly. Maybe they did some last-minute adjustments?

It's not just his costume, though. There's something about the way he's standing there, about the way he carries his shoulders and sticks out his chin, about the way he waves and nods at the crowd.

He really is like a prince.

As he smiles, I can hear the women scream. Some of them look like they're about to swoon. The flashes of dozens of cameras fire away.

I frown.

Can a guy like that really be at my side?

Wait. Does this mean I want him to be at my side?

I suddenly remember Lisbeth's accusation about me having a crush on Steff. Back then, I denied it. Now, I don't know.

Do I?

True, for the longest time, I had a crush on Josh. But after that talk with Marianne, I'm pretty sure that's over. So is Steff my new crush now?

I slap my forehead.

Well, I did have sex with him.

I blush as I remember.

Damn it, Jess. Stop remembering it already.

Okay. So what if I have a crush on Steff? Nothing will change, right?

Unless I want it to.

Do I want it to?

I'm so deep in thought that I barely notice the parade ending, or even the fireworks. Steff sits beside me just as the final ones light up the sky.

"What's wrong?" he asks. "Didn't you enjoy the parade?"

His thigh touches mine and my heart flutters.

I move away subtly. "I... I did."

He sweeps his hair aside. "What did you think of my performance?"

I look away and fight the blush threatening to coat my cheeks.

"It was... good. Being Prince Charming suits you."

"Really? I don't particularly like him, though. He's too... charming and not much else."

I narrow my eyes at him. "You just think you're more charming, don't you?"

Steff winks. "Of course."

I snort. "And I bet you loved having all those women go weak at the knees for you. It's a wonder Cinderella managed to keep standing."

"Well, I helped by keeping my arm around her waist," he says.

The pang of jealousy that hits me takes me by surprise.

"But hey, I was just a substitute."

A substitute, huh?

I glance at him. Is that what he is to me? A substitute for Josh? Yeah. Maybe that's it.

"Yeah. It's not like you're a real prince," I tell him.

For a moment, Steff falls silent. Then he chuckles.

"You're right. But if I were a real prince, I know who I'd ask to be my princess."

With eyes wide, I turn my head to find that Steff's face is just inches from mine.

I stand up. "You're teasing me again, aren't you? There's no way I'd pass for a princess. And I don't want to. Aren't princesses vain and snobbish and lazy?"

Steff stands beside me. "I think you can be any kind of princess you want to be."

I snort. "Just stop with the princess thing already."

"Okay."

Just then, the sky grows dark. The fireworks show is over.

"I guess that concludes our date," Steff says.

My eyes grow wide. "Date? Since when were we on a date?"

He turns to me with a grin. "Just kidding. But you did have fun, didn't you?"

I nod.

"So did I. Oh, and by the way, now we're even."

My eyebrows crease. "What?"

"We're even," Steff repeats. "I did you a favor. You treated me to Disneyland. We're even."

So he was just doing me a favor, was he? Why do I feel so annoyed?

He pats my shoulder. "Now we can put that incident behind us."

Incident?

I brush his hand off and cross my arms over my chest. "That goes without saying. In fact, it's already behind me."

Steff grins. "Good."

I grit my teeth.

There's no way I can have a crush on this guy.

Chapter 10
Steff

Why do I get the feeling Jess is mad at me?

She's been a little cold ever since we came back from Disneyland. At first, I thought she was simply tired from the excursion, so I left her alone. Then she started going to work earlier than usual so that we didn't see each other. I didn't even have a chance to make breakfast for her. She said that she had to work harder because she was saving up for something. And then, on the evenings when she didn't have a gig, she'd have her earphones on during dinner and afterwards she'd go straight to her room to work on her song. Sure, I'd hear her playing her guitar, so she wasn't lying about what she was doing in there-but she used to do it in the living room.

So what changed? Why is she avoiding me?

Is she really mad at me?

Right now, Jess is folding laundry on the couch, so I have a golden opportunity to find out.

I sit beside her and grab a shirt from the pile.

She turns to me with a puzzled look. "What are you doing?"

"Helping you," I answer. "You have more clothes than I do, don't you?"

"Yeah, right." She folds the sweater in front of her. "You have just as many clothes as I do."

Good. She's talking to me.

Then again, we have been having conversations, just not like the ones we used to have.

Like the ones we used to have.

What did we used to talk about?

"What do you want for dinner tomorrow night?" I ask her.

Crap. I sound like a boring husband.

Jess shrugs. "Whatever."

"You want steak again?"

Another shrug.

"Those pajamas look good on you," I tell her for a change of topic. "They're the ones you bought at Disneyland, right?"

Jess nods.

Suddenly, I remember something.

I stand up. "By the way, I had those pictures I took at Disneyland printed today. Want to see them?"

"It's fine." She grabs another piece of clothing from the pile.

I go and get them anyway, then sit back down on the couch and move closer to her.

"Look." I move close to her. "Some of them turned out really good. I especially like this picture of us with..."

To my shock, Jess slaps my hand away. The pictures scatter on the coffee table and the couch and the floor.

"I don't want to see them, okay?!?"

She gathers the clothes on the table. "I'll do this some other time. I'm tired. I'm going to bed."

I watch her as she disappears into her room. The door slams shut.

I sigh and slowly pick up the pictures.

So Jess is mad at me. The question is: Why?

~

"Is something wrong?" I ask Jess as I help her wash the dishes the next evening.

"No," she answers as she rinses a saucer. "I'm sorry about yesterday. I was just tired."

"You seem to be tired a lot lately. Is it that time of the month?"

That would explain her temper.

Jess doesn't answer. She just moves on to the next saucer.

"Or maybe you're coming down with something." I use the soap-soaked sponge on a glass. "Don't worry. If you do get sick, I'll take care of you."

"I'm fine."

There it is again. That 'I'm fine' that doesn't really mean 'I'm fine'.

Then I get an idea. If I want Jess to act like her usual self, maybe I should act like my usual self.

I whisper in her ear. "You know, I read that having sex improves your immune system."

I expect her to turn to me with a glare, but to my surprise, the saucer falls from her hand just as she's putting it on the rack.

Fuck.

Jess quickly bends down to pick up the pieces, but I grab her arm.

"Don't touch them with your bare hands," I tell her. "You might cut your fingers and then you won't be able to play."

She scowls at me and walks off.

Now I've done it.

I go after her. "Jess!"

She keeps walking.

"I'm sorry. I was just trying to cheer you up."

She glances over her shoulder. "So sex is a joke to you, is it?"

My eyebrows arch. What?

She faces forward. "I'm going to bed."

"Jess, wait!"

I manage to grab her arm before she reaches the door to her bedroom, but I pull too hard and she stumbles backwards. Her back slams against my chest, I fall backwards to the floor, and she lands right in front of me between my legs.

"Are you okay?" I ask her.

Jess doesn't answer, nor does she move. She just sits there between my legs.

Between my legs.

When she finally moves, she has a hard time getting up, so I decide to help her by putting my hands on her sides to give her a push. My fingertips end up grazing the curves of her breasts.

Jess lets out a squeal as she falls back down. Her arms cross over her chest.

"Sorry. I didn't mean to..."

I don't finish, because I realize her lower back is pressing against my crotch again. My gaze falls on the tattoo on her neck peeking out from her hair.

I still don't know what it means, but I'm as captivated by it now as I was the first time I saw it.

Without thinking, I press my lips against the ink.

Jess whirls around, hissing at me. Her hair whips against my face and her hand lands near my crotch, her knuckles brushing against the bulge I didn't even realize was there.

Fuck.

"Jess."

She stands up.

I grab her arm.

She pulls it away and turns to me with her hands on her hips.

"This is all a joke to you, isn't it?"

My eyebrows crease. "What? Jess, just calm down and..."

"You calm down!" She points at my erection. "You're unbelievable, doing that... showing that in front of me."

Huh?

"You're disgusting!"

Jess marches off to her bedroom. This time, I don't stop her.

I slap my forehead and sigh.

Damn it. I should have controlled myself better around her. I know better. I'm not some horny teenager or some beast in rut.

Still, did she have to react that way?

You're disgusting.

Is that really what Jess thinks of me? Why now all of a sudden? What did I do?

I pick myself up and sit on the couch. I lean forward on my elbows and clasp my hands beneath my chin. My eyebrows crease as I rummage through my thoughts.

What's done is done. Things are what they are.

For some reason, I've offended Jess and made her resent me. I don't know how or why, but that's how it is.

So what am I supposed to do?

~

"Jess."

I get off the couch as soon as she comes in through the door in her uniform.

"We need to talk."

Jess frowns. She turns her back to me as she takes off her shoes.

"What do you want?"

"I've been thinking that this isn't working, after all."

She turns around. Her eyebrows crease above narrowed eyes.

"What are you saying?"

I touch my neck. "I'm saying we shouldn't be living together. I'm a man. You're a woman, and an amazing one at that. I should have kept my self-control around you, but I couldn't, and now, I can't. Each time I see you, I want to touch you. I..."

"So you're moving out?" she interrupts me.

I sigh. "I've violated your conditions and there's no guarantee I won't violate them again. This is the only way to keep you safe from me."

Her gaze lowers. Her quivering lips purse as her shoulders tremble.

My eyebrows arch.

Wait. Is Jess mad? I thought she'd be relieved.

"You really are a stupid, insensitive jerk, aren't you?"

What?

Didn't she say I was disgusting? Doesn't she want me to leave?

Suddenly, her phone rings. She fishes it out of her purse and presses it against her ear.

"Hello."

I frown. Weren't we in the middle of an important conversation?

"What?" Her eyes grow wide. Then she nods. "Okay. I'll let you know if I hear from him."

She tosses the phone back into her purse.

"Who's that?" I ask her.

"Kay," Jess answers. "She said Marianne called her to say Josh didn't come home last night and now she can't contact him. She's sick with worry."

Josh? I try to remember who that is.

"Your guitarist, right?"

She touches her chin as her expression turns into one of worry. "I wonder where he could be."

Strange. Just a minute ago, she was angry. Now she's completely forgotten about it.

Well, I haven't.

I step forward. "Jess..."

Just then, the doorbell rings.

Now what?

"Just a sec," Jess shouts as she goes to the door.

She looks through the peephole and her jaw drops.

"Who is it?" I ask her again.

"It's Josh." She clasps a hand over her mouth. "My God, he's here."

440

"Well, then just let him..."

She clasps her hand over my mouth. "Shh. He doesn't know you're my roommate. He hasn't met you."

"Good thing you're here to introduce us, then."

Jess shoves me into my room. "Stay there and don't come out until I tell you to. And don't make a sound."

Okay.

I frown as she slams the bedroom door in my face. What on earth is going on?

Chapter 11
Jess

"Josh." I open the door for him. "This is a surprise."

"Jess."

He scratches the back of his head and forces a smile. I can tell from the rings under his eyes that he hasn't slept. His cheeks look a little pale as well.

"I'm sorry for dropping by. Are you busy?"

"No," I tell him. "I've just come home from work. Please come in."

Josh steps inside and I close the door behind him.

"Can I get you anything? Coffee? Food? I think there's still some leftover steak from the other night."

"I'm not hungry," Josh says.

"Okay." I gesture towards the couch. "What can I do for you, then?"

He doesn't answer. His forehead creases as he struggles for the words to say.

I sit on the couch and casually hide Steff's sweater behind a pillow. Then I pat the space next to me.

"You know, if there's something on your mind, I'll hear you out. You can say whatever you want and I'll just listen. I'm your friend, after all."

Yes, I might not be allowed to have a crush on Josh, but he's still my friend. The fact that he's here proves it.

Wait. He's here and not anywhere else. He's with me.

Doesn't that mean...?

My heart stops.

Truly, hope dies hard.

Josh sits on the couch beside me.

My heartbeat speeds up.

Josh scratches his head. "I don't quite know where to start."

I shrug. "Just say whatever you want to say first. Or the easiest thing to say."

"I'm not sure any of it is easy to say, but well, I guess the main thing is that..." He takes a deep breath. "I'm scared."

I blink. Scared?

"I'm not ready to be a father."

Of course he isn't.

"Well, I don't think anyone is," I tell him. "It's a huge responsibility, after all."

"You can say that again." Josh sighs. "I guess what I'm saying is, I don't want to be a father."

I look at him. "What?"

"I don't mind kids, but I don't particularly like them, either. And it's not just that. To be a father, you have to give up everything for your family. You have to set a good example for your kids. You have to do the right thing all the time."

"Well, maybe not that last part," I say. "Fathers are still human, you know."

"But you have to always try to do the right thing, right? Isn't that exhausting?"

I place my hand over his. "I think you're putting too much pressure on yourself. You don't have to change into a completely different person. You just have to find the strength, wisdom and love that you already have within you. And as for always trying to do the right thing, don't you do that anyway? I'm sure you that if you love your child and are always there for him or her, then everything else will fall into place."

Josh looks at me. "Wow. You make it sound so easy."

"It's not easy. Like I said, no one's ever ready to be a father. But at the same time, any man has the potential to be a great father."

He pulls his hand from under mine and clasps it with his other hand.

"But I still have to give up everything else, don't I?"

"Not everything."

"Yeah. Just all the fun stuff."

I sigh. Who knew Josh was childish, too? Just like me.

"Look, Josh," I tell him. "I think you're looking at all this too one-sidedly. Sure, you're giving up stuff, but look at what you're getting in return. You'll have a child who will look to you and fill your life with love and laughter."

"And who I'll have to yell at for the next eighteen years," he says sourly.

I pout. Was he always this negative?

"You'll have someone to teach how to play the guitar, someone to play the guitar with," I point out.

Josh's brown eyes grow wide. "I never thought about that."

"You're giving up some fun stuff, yes, but you're not giving up fun, Josh. You're getting a whole new world of fun, something that only you can enjoy."

He stays silent.

"The fact that you're scared right now means you don't just want to be a father," I add. "You want to be a good father. And you know what?"

I pat Josh on the back.

"I think you're going to make a great father."

He turns his head to look at me. Slowly, his lips curve into a smile.

"Wow. You're really good at this."

There it goes again. That smile that makes me melt from the inside out.

I sit back. "Maybe I should have become a guidance counselor or a motivational speaker. Or a therapist."

Josh chuckles.

I smile at him. "Now you sound better."

"Thanks to you. Now I won't have to run away."

I sit up. "What?"

"I was actually considering it because of all this pressure and this fear and confusion I'm feeling. But then I thought about the band and how I don't want to leave you guys hanging."

I let out a breath of relief. Saved by the band.

"Still, I needed someone to talk to." He puts his hand over mine. "I'm glad I came to you. Thank you."

The warmth from his hand flows up to my chest. My heart nearly melts.

I nod. "I'm just surprised you still remember where I live."

"How could I forget?"

My breath catches.

Right. The last time he was here, we kissed. Right in the middle of this living room.

I pull my hand away and tuck a strand of hair behind my ear. "Well, you were drunk, so..."

"So were you," Josh says. "But I wasn't drunk enough to forget how amazing that kiss was."

My eyebrows arch. He thought that kiss was amazing?

He rubs his neck. "Actually, I've been wanting to do it again."

I blink. What?

Didn't Marianne say Josh would never be attracted to me?

"Hey." His brown eyes bore into mine. "Do you think we can do it again? Just one more time."

Huh?

Suddenly, he leans towards me and touches my cheek. Then he closes his eyes. It's something I've dreamed of a hundred times, yet right now, for some reason, I can't bring myself to be overjoyed.

What is going on with me?

Suddenly, the door to Steff's bedroom opens. Josh opens his eyes just in time to see Steff pull him away from the couch. Then he pulls me away, too, and clasps me to his side. His arm goes around my shoulder.

"I think that's far enough," Steff tells Josh sternly.

I look up at him. The icy glare in his blue eyes takes my breath away.

I swallow.

I've never seen him like this before.

"Jess, who's this?" Josh asks me.

"Hey." Steff speaks before I can. "I'm the one talking to you."

Josh frowns. "Yeah, so who are you?"

"It's really none of your concern, is it? From what I've heard, you have enough worries, not least of which is growing a pair."

Josh's jaw clenches. "Why, you-"

"Josh," I interrupt. "Please just leave."

For a moment, he doesn't move. His clenched fists tremble at his side.

Then finally, he walks out. The door slams shut behind him.

I let out a sigh of relief as I touch my forehead.

Steff scoffs.

I free myself from his arm and stand in front of him with my hands on my hips.

"You didn't have to say that to Josh," I scold Steff. "He's in enough pain already."

"Apparently not enough to keep him from trying to kiss you," he replies.

I look away.

"Or was that what you wanted? For him to kiss you?" Steff asks. "He kissed you before, didn't he? Was he your first kiss?"

I cross my arms over my chest. "So?"

"And he did it while he had a girlfriend?"

"It wasn't entirely his fault," I defend Josh without thinking. "I wanted him to kiss me. I tempted him."

Steff grits his teeth. His hands fall on my shoulders.

"He's been using you, Jess. He's been playing with your feelings. Don't you see that?"

"So? Aren't you doing the same thing?" I meet his gaze squarely.

He growls low in his throat. "Don't you even lump me with that guy."

"He kissed me when we were both drunk. You had sex with me when I was drunk," I remind him.

"Because you asked."

"I asked him, too. And afterwards you acted as if nothing happened."

"So did he!" Steff places his hand on his forehead as he sighs in frustration.

"It's a lot easier to write off a kiss than taking someone's virginity!" I tell him. "If what happened between us really meant something to you, you wouldn't have been able to forget it so easily."

"Oh, is that what's been bothering you?"

Steff steps forward and grips my chin.

"You know, you gave some good advice earlier. Well, let me give you a piece-you really should start being true to your own feelings."

His mouth seals mine. His kiss robs me of breath.

Then he pulls away and looks into my eyes as he strokes my cheek.

"Do you want me, Jess?" Steff whispers softly.

I don't answer. I can't. I can barely breathe or think.

Even so, I can't look away.

"Do you want me to make you forget him?"

I pause.

Him?

Right.

Josh.

All this time, I've been wanting him, wanting him to smile at me, to kiss me, to hold me in his arms. And like a fool, I hoped he would. Like a fool, I clung to him.

No, not to him. To the image I painted of him, to what I hoped he would be.

That Josh that was here a while ago, that's the real Josh. That's the man I've been pining for.

And the thing is, I think a part of me has always known it.

I'm such a fool for loving someone I always knew would never love me back.

I don't want to be a fool anymore.

I look straight into the icy blue eyes in front of me.

"Yes," I tell Steff with tears brimming in mine. "Please."

His eyes widen slightly and then narrow as he places his hand on my other cheek. The warmth from his gaze and his palm seeps into my skin and somewhere deeper inside.

I close my eyes and brace for the feel of his lips on mine. My heart hammers in my chest.

Steff's lips do touch my skin, but not my lips. They press against one of my eyelids, then the other.

I open my eyes.

"Why must you always be in tears when you're asking me to kiss you?" he asks with a faint smile.

He kisses my cheek and whispers in my ear.

"Just so you know, this time I'm not doing it only because you asked."

The words make my eyes grow wide. My lips part slightly.

Steff captures them with his.

My eyes close. I can't breathe.

The kiss is so forceful it pushes me back. I cling to Steff's shoulders to keep myself from falling.

His arm goes around me, pulling me even closer to him as he slips his tongue in. When it comes in contact with mine, a shiver goes down my spine. Heat bursts in my chest.

As Steff's tongue stirs inside my mouth, the heat stirs inside my body. It moves lower and lower, melting my insides to goo as it goes. Some of it leaks out between my legs.

All this from just a kiss?

I feel weak. I feel like I'm on the brink of disappearing.

But I don't want to do it alone.

My hands move to his hair to caress the silky strands as I push his tongue back. My breasts tingle as they press against his chest. A moan vibrates in my throat.

Steff's hand slides down to my lower back. His leg slips between mine. His knee brushes my thigh, dangerously close to the hottest part of me. The puddle in my panties grows into a small pond.

Finally, he lets go of my mouth. I gasp for air but barely manage to catch my breath before it leaves me again as Steff's lips latch on to my neck.

I let out a moan as my arms fall to my sides. They have no strength left, nor do my legs, which are threatening to give way beneath me.

As I shift them, my thigh brushes against something hard. Steff grunts. My heart stops again.

He's hard. And like before, the knowledge of it sends my mind into a spin. A fresh explosion of heat erupts in my belly.

I know what I said before, but the truth is I've never found this reaction of his disgusting. A bit scary, yes, but not unpleasant. In fact, I feel excitement buzzing in my veins.

Steff wants me.

He wants me like a man wants a woman, like no one has ever wanted me before.

And it feels like nothing I've ever felt.

His tongue swipes my neck and I let out a moan. My knees buckle.

Suddenly, Steff stops.

I look at his face to see that he's just as breathless as I am. His lips are moist, his cheeks flushed. His eyes pierce through me.

"Let's continue in the bedroom," he says, pulling my arm. "We're doing it properly this time."

"Huh?"

He leads me to his bedroom and pushes me towards the bed. My knees hit the edge and I sit down.

Steff sits beside me.

"This time, I'll make sure you remember everything," he whispers in my ear.

His breath tickles my skin. His promise makes my heart race.

"Every kiss."

He kisses my neck again.

"Every touch."

His fingers brush against the curve of my breast.

Then Steff seals my mouth with his again. My eyes fall shut and my back hits the mattress.

His tongue dances inside my mouth as he works on the buttons of my blouse. Then his hand slips beneath my bra and his fingers trap a stiff nipple.

I moan into his mouth.

His fingers rub the nub and send heat swirling through my veins. He does the same to the other, and more moans spill past my lips into his. He pulls away and they escape into the air.

I cover my mouth.

Am I the one making those sounds?

"What's wrong?" Steff asks me.

I look away. "Nothing."

He takes my hand and traps my wrist beside my head. His other hand grips my chin and forces me to meet his gaze.

"Does it feel good? Should I stop?"

Slowly, I shake my head.

I may be a mess, but I don't want him to stop.

His eyebrows furrow. "So it doesn't feel good?"

I frown. "If it didn't, I would have kicked you a long time ago."

Steff grins. "I'm glad to hear it."

And he does look glad. Happy. His grin is from ear to ear.

Something like this makes him this happy?

My thoughts vanish as Steff presses a kiss to the valley between my breasts. His free hand skirts my belly and I suck in a breath.

"Your belly is really ticklish, isn't it?" he asks as he lifts his head.

I don't answer. He already knows it.

His fingers circle my bellybutton as his mouth envelops my breast through my bra. The muscles of my stomach tense. I squirm as laughter threatens to seize me.

"Steff," I say his name in both a plea and a warning.

Then I gasp as his hand cups me through my pants. At the same time, his nose moves my bra out of the way and his lips imprison my exposed nipple.

My eyes squeeze shut. My knees tremble.

Steff continues to rub me between my shaking legs. That part of me swells and melts and leaks.

Then he lets go of my hand and gets off the bed.

I open my eyes to see Steff above me, unbuttoning my pants and pulling on the zipper. Then he pulls them down my legs along with my soaked underwear. They catch on my ankles, but Steff kneels on the floor and yanks them off. He settles between my legs and I feel his burning gaze on the place where they meet.

I close them as I stare at the ceiling. Heat explodes in my cheeks.

Why is he staring? My curls are probably all tangled and I'm wet and sticky. There's nothing good for him to see.

But Steff pries my knees apart and pulls my hips closer to the edge of the bed.

I feel his warm breath on my skin.

I prop myself up on my elbows and lift my head.

"Steff, what are you do-?"

The rest of my sentence vanishes and I let out a cry as his fingers open me up and his tongue presses against my skin. My head falls to the bed as it slides up and down.

What on earth? He's licking me there?

"Steff, stop," I tell him as I squirm. "Isn't that dirty?"

"No," he answers without hesitation before taking another lick. "In fact, this is the purest, most honest part of you."

He presses a reverent kiss to my curls. Then the tip of his tongue rubs against the nub of flesh hidden beneath.

My back arches. My hands go to his head. My fingers grip strands of his hair.

"Shit."

The curse escapes my lips as Steff teases the nub. His finger slips inside me.

My eyes grow wide. What?

This feels weird. My whole body feels weird.

What's going on with me?

Steff switches so his thumb rubs against my nub as his tongue delves inside me.

My hips rise off the bed as I let out a cry.

He continues to tease that nub until it burns beneath the pad of his thumb. His tongue wriggles inside me and I melt even more.

"Steff!"

My body becomes suddenly numb, but only for a moment. In the next, it shatters. I feel my nub pushing against him. Something gushes out of me just as Steff's tongue leaves me. My back arches and my body trembles. My mouth and my eyes gape at the ceiling.

And then it's over. My back crashes against the bed and I close my eyes as I force air back into my lungs. My heart hammers in my chest as my muddled mind tries to make sense of what just happened.

What was that?

I lie there in a daze for some seconds, but I snap out of it as I feel Steff's hand on my thighs. My eyelids flutter open.

It's... not over?

But of course it isn't, I think as I lift my head and see Steff's bare cock between my legs. It curves up and out towards me, and I can see something glistening on the tip.

A lump forms in my throat as wonder seizes me. Then I swallow it as fear takes over.

That... thing is going inside me?

Well, it's not like this is the first time-but I can't really remember the first time.

Was it painful?

"Just relax, Jess," Steff says.

I frown. That's easy for him to say when he's not the one getting penetrated. He doesn't have anything to worry about.

Or so I think until I look up at his face and see the tension in his cheeks and in his jaw. His teeth dig into his lower lip.

He's not relaxed at all. In fact, Steff seems like he's... in pain?

He pushes in. I feel the tip of his cock enter me and I let out a gasp. I stare at the ceiling and hold my breath as he keeps pushing. His cock fills me inch by inch.

It stings. I feel like I'm being torn apart from the inside, and I want to cry.

But then Steff stops. He leans over me and traps my hands beneath his. His fingers entwine with mine. His hair grazes my forehead as his hooded eyes search my own.

They're still a pretty shade of blue, but there's nothing icy about them. They remind me of a blue flame. Scorching.

And just like that, all pain leaves me. I'm left with only the warmth of his body seeping into mine. My heart feels full.

"Jess," he whispers my name tenderly.

I smile. "I'm fine, Steff."

He kisses me and a tangle of desire, excitement and joy spreads through my veins.

I don't care if he hurts me anymore. Not even if he breaks me. I want him to feel good, too.

He lets go of my lips and starts moving his hips. The bed creaks.

His cock rubs against me, against parts of me that have never been rubbed before. It's hot and wet and pulsing.

I grip his hands and moan.

So this is what sex is like?

It's confusing. It's maddening. It's amazing.

I don't know how I've survived without it for so long.

Steff moves faster. The friction inside me intensifies and the heat builds.

I move my hips against him as I moan even louder. He grunts as his skin slaps against mine.

Then his movements become erratic, wild.

It's too much.

I feel myself shatter again as I throw my head back and cry out.

Steff continues to move inside me until finally he pushes in deeply, as if he's trying to carve himself into me, and then his cock quivers inside me and floods me with warmth.

Afterwards, he lets my hands go and places his above my head as he catches his breath. I see the stain of sweat on the front of his shirt.

For a while, he stays like this, hovering over me. His cock remains still inside me. I can feel it getting softer. I can also feel something sticky trickling down my butt.

Steff pulls out and tucks himself back into his clothes.

I sit up and clean myself with a wad of tissue from the box on the nightstand before putting my panties back on.

They're still sopping wet, but I don't care. Right now, I'm tired. And sore.

"Are you okay?" Steff brushes strands of my hair aside and touches my cheek.

"I'm fine," I assure him. "I'm not that fragile."

"No, you're not," he agrees.

I grab a pillow and hug it to me. "But you owe me, so you're cooking dinner."

Steff points a finger at his chest. "I owe you?"

I look away.

He sighs. "Well, I was going to cook you dinner one last time before I left."

I glance at him. "You're not still leaving, are you?"

"Of course not," Steff answers. "Where else would I find a roommate who likes to be kissed so much?"

I frown and blush at the same time.

He chuckles. Then I feel his hand on the top of my head. His fingers ruffle my hair.

"Don't you worry about a thing. Just rest."

Why is he treating me like a child? Still, I can't deny that his hand feels nice. Or that his pillow smells nice.

My eyelids drop.

Everything feels so nice I could almost fall asleep.

Chapter 12
Steff

I smile as I stare at Jess's sleeping face beside me.

It's already nearly seven and she's still sound asleep. She fell asleep so quickly yesterday that I didn't even have time to make her dinner.

I guess she must be tired.

Well, she did have a long day yesterday. And today is her day off, so I guess I'll let her sleep in.

I toss the blanket aside, get out of bed and head to the bathroom in my briefs.

Now that Jess and I have had sex-twice-she shouldn't mind me walking around like this.

On my way back from the bathroom, I hear the doorbell ring.

My forehead creases.

Who could that be so early in the morning?

Someone from the cafe who wants Jess to come to work? Someone from the band?

Josh?

My eyes widen at that possibility. A frown forms on my lips as I reach for the door knob.

That asshole. Doesn't he know when to give up? Hasn't he already caused Jess enough trouble?

I open the door.

"You-"

I pause with wider eyes as I see who's outside Jess's apartment.

It's a man, alright, but it isn't Josh. This man has black hair and eyes just like Jess. A thin beard coats his chin. He's older than Josh, too. And taller. Nearly as tall as me. And he has a heavier physique. The gray shirt he's wearing shows off muscles that can only come from frequent trips to the gym. Or military training, I think as I glimpse the silver chain around his neck and make out the dog tags behind the cotton. A frown forms on his face as he assesses me with a displeased gaze.

I place a hand on my hip. "I'm sorry, but who are-?"

To my surprise, he kicks the door open. I jump back. He throws a fist at me and I duck.

Is he a burglar?

I don't know, but I can tell by the way he's throwing those punches that he knows how to fight.

Fortunately, so do I.

From the corner of my eye, I see the phone charger on the coffee table. I grab it and coil the wire around my fist as I jump onto the couch. He glances behind him and sees the guitar on the wall.

The blood drains from my face. Not again.

I jump down. "No. Not Jess's guitar!"

I try to wrestle the instrument from him, but I can't employ my full strength without damaging it.

Fuck.

At this rate, he's either going to break the guitar or break my skull with it.

"Who the hell are you?" I ask him through gritted teeth.

"Me?" His eyes grow wide. "Who the hell are you?"

"Stop it!" Jess's sudden scream interrupts our little getting-to-know-you talk.

I let go of the guitar, but the moment I do, the man swings it at me. I barely evade it.

"I said stop it, Keith!" Jess grabs the guitar.

My eyebrows arch. Keith?

Finally, the man goes still. Then he lets out a deep breath as he surrenders the guitar to her. She hangs it back on the wall.

He crosses his arms and leans back, fingers tapping his biceps.

"Who's this?" he asks.

Jess turns to me. When she sees what I'm wearing, she slaps her forehead. Then she looks down at her panties and open shirt and her cheeks turn red.

I grab the sweater from the couch and wrap it around my waist. She hastily buttons her shirt, which unfortunately isn't long enough to completely cover her underwear.

"Who's this?" the man asks again.

Jess sighs. "Keith, this is Steff. Steff, meet my brother."

Brother?

Now that she's said it, I can see the resemblance even more. So he's Jess's older brother, huh?

I smile and extend my hand. "Nice to-"

"Who is he?" Keith interrupts. His arms remain on his chest. "Why is he here in your apartment?"

Jess scratches the top of her head. "Well, actually, he's staying here."

"Staying here?" Keith turns to her with narrowed eyes.

"He's... um, my..."

I wait for Jess to come up with an explanation. What will she say now? She can't say I'm her cousin, and given what he caught us wearing, he's not going to believe her if she says I'm just her roommate. Unless maybe I'm her gay roommate? Is she going to pull that again?

"He's my boyfriend," Jess blurts out.

My jaw drops. I wasn't expecting that.

"What?" Keith's arms fall to his sides.

Jess stands beside me and grabs my arm. "Steff is my boyfriend, so he sleeps here sometimes."

I glance at her.

What's with that sheepish grin? We're both consenting adults, after all.

"More importantly, when did you get back?" Jess asks as she grabs a pillow to hold in front of her panties. "Why didn't you call me?"

"I was planning on surprising you," Keith says. He doesn't look so angry anymore.

Jess shrugs. "Well, consider me surprised."

Keith says nothing.

"Now, why don't I just go get dressed and then we can talk?"

Without waiting for an answer, Jess hurries off to her room.

I frown.

Is she just going to leave me here? Has she forgotten that I'm not fully clothed, either?

Keith hasn't.

"Go put some clothes on," he orders.

I nod and head to my own room.

When I come back out with a pair of pants, Jess and Keith are in the kitchen. Keith is sitting on a chair and Jess, now wearing a shirt and jeans, is preparing a pot of coffee.

"So how long until your next assignment?" Jess asks her brother.

"What? Are you sending me away already?"

"Of course not." Jess turns to him. "I just want to know how long I'll be seeing you before you disappear again."

"You mean how long you'll have to endure having me around watching you like a hawk?"

Jess sighs. "Do you have any idea how hard it is to have a nosy older brother?"

"I'm not nosy," he argues. Then he turns to me. "So how long have you and my sister been going out?"

"Nosy," Jess tells him before I can say anything. "And just a couple of months."

She glances at me.

"Just a couple of months," I repeat as I sit across from Keith.

"You don't look American." Keith leans forward. "What country are you from? Are you an immigrant or a tourist? What do you do for a living?"

"Nosy." Jess pushes Keith back. "I will not have you interrogating someone in my apartment."

Keith sighs. "I'm just concerned, Jess. After all, he is your first boyfriend."

Jess blushes.

Ah. That confirms one of my suspicions.

"So what?" Jess crosses her arms over her chest and sticks her chin out. "I'm not a child, you know. I'm a twenty-seven-year-old woman."

"Who still acts like she's eleven," Keith teases.

Jess scowls at him.

450

"See. You still lose your temper so easily."

"Because you still tease me like a mean little boy," Jess points out.

I grin in amusement.

"Does she still wear Minnie Mouse pajamas?" Keith asks me.

"Yes," I nod. "When she's not running around half naked, that is."

Jess glares at me. Keith laughs.

"You know, the two of you are supposed to be grown gentlemen, and yet here you are bullying a girl," Jess says. "Who's being immature now?"

"Oh, come on." Keith pats her shoulder. "I was just teasing you."

She frowns.

Just then, a phone rings. I look around for Jess's phone, but it turns out to be Keith's.

"Hello." He answers the call as he gets off his seat.

As he walks off, Jess leans on my shoulder.

"You see what I've had to put up with all my life," she says.

I say nothing.

After a few seconds, Keith returns.

"Sorry," he says. "But I have to go."

"But the coffee is almost done," Jess whines.

"Don't worry." He pats Jess's head. "We'll see each other soon."

Jess pouts. "Like that's what I'm worried about."

Keith scratches his beard. "Actually, I have an idea. You see, there's a party being thrown for me and my buddies tonight. Family is invited, too. You and Steff should come. Be a good chance for us to get to know each other better."

He places his hand on my shoulder.

"You mean a good chance to interrogate him some more," Jess says.

"We'll be able to catch up, too," he tells Jess. "And I can show off my beautiful little sister."

"Yeah, right."

"I'll bring somebody, too, so it will be like a double date."

Jess raises her hand. "No thank you."

"I'm guessing Mom and Dad don't know you have a boyfriend yet, do they?" Keith asks her.

Jess's face grows pale.

"Not even Laura?"

Jess glares at him. "Are you threatening me?"

"Come to the party and I'll zip my mouth for now." Keith makes a zipping motion with his fingers.

Jess sighs. "You really are such a pain in the ass."

Keith grins. "I'll take that as a yes."

He turns to me. "You have a suit, don't you?"

"Um, no. The airline lost my luggage."

He glances at his watch. "Then you have about eleven hours to buy one. I'll pick you guys up at six."

"Okay."

Keith smiles. "See you guys then."

He walks to the door and lets himself out.

As soon as he's gone, Jess sinks into a chair.

"What are we gonna do?"

"I don't think we have any choice," I tell her. "Well, you don't have any choice."

She frowns. "You have an older brother, too, right?"

I nod.

"Is he this difficult?"

I touch my chin. Come to think of it, he's always been concerned about me, but I feel like I've always watched out for him more than he's done for me.

"We get along well," I answer.

Jess pouts.

I touch her arm. "I think you're lucky to have a brother who cares about you a lot."

"Well, I don't feel lucky."

She gets up and goes to the counter.

She says that, but I think she cares just as much about him.

"So after breakfast, we'll go buy clothes?" I ask as I glance at her. "Like your brother said, I need a suit. What about you? Do you have a dress?"

She turns to me. "Do I look like I own a dress?"

I shake my head. "I guess we'll just have to get you one."

~

I knew Jess would look amazing in a dress, but I wasn't expecting this.

As she stands in front of the bathroom mirror with her salon-straightened, black-dyed hair cascading past her shoulders, I can't help but stare.

The dress that she chose is black, of course, and it's simple, with a plain, round collar and no sleeves or embellishments. It looks classy, though, with the skirt draped beautifully over her legs and the hem dropping just below her knees. And it fits her well. The fabric glides over her breasts and hugs her waist. The sheer lace back exposes the soft curve of her spine.

Sexy.

As I stare at her, my own expensive suit starts to feel uncomfortably tight in the crotch. I wonder how it would feel to rip that dress off her.

I tell myself I won't, though.

Tonight, I'm going to treat her like a lady. No. A princess.

I push myself off the wall I've been leaning on and glance at my watch.

"Ready to go?" I ask her. "Your brother will be here any minute."

Jess turns to me with a ruby smile that makes my heart stop.

"I'm ready."

Chapter 13
Jess

I said I was ready, but now that I'm here in the hotel ballroom, I don't know.

All the women around me seem to be better dressed than I am in spite of all the effort I put into my appearance for this evening. Their ears and necks glitter with diamonds. Their gowns rustle and flow around their curves. Their cheeks, eyes and lips make them look almost unreal, whereas all I put on were lipstick, some powder and mascara.

It's not just the women, though.

The ballroom looks so grand. The tables are covered in immaculate white linen. The silverware gleams under the light of the chandeliers. Soft music streams from speakers that blend in with the tapestries.

I sigh.

Just as I thought, I don't really belong here.

"You'll be just fine," Steff assures me.

I turn to him.

Unlike me, he doesn't look the least bit nervous, even though I can tell a few heads have already turned in his direction. He looks impeccable in his suit, too, so much so that I don't even feel like I belong at his side.

What am I doing at this party?

"It's amazing, isn't it?" Keith asks me. "All this just for us."

I frown at him. "Well, you're enjoying yourself, aren't you?"

"As should you." He winks at me.

Why do I get the feeling I'm being teased again?

"Come on." He gestures for Steff and me to follow him. "Let's go find our seats. I think the program will be starting soon."

~

After the short program, which consists mostly of speeches from various people, dinner is served.

The food is good, at least, and I enjoy it, though I have trouble figuring out the cutlery. Steff seems to pull it off effortlessly.

He must be used to events like this. Well, he is from a rich family, a fact I often forget.

After dinner, the guests start circulating from one table to another to chat. Some couples get up to dance, and Keith invites his date, Annie, to join them on the dance floor. To my surprise, Steff offers me his hand as well.

"Shall we dance?"

I turn to him with arched eyebrows.

"Do I look like I can dance?"

"Surely, someone who loves music and plays guitar can at least move to the beat."

I let out a deep breath.

"Besides..." He gets out of his chair and pulls my arm. "I'll be the one leading."

My mouth gapes as he drags me to the middle of the ballroom.

What the hell is he doing? Doesn't he know I'm uncomfortable enough already?

When we reach the dance floor, Steff puts my hand on his shoulder. Then he places his hand on my waist and pulls me close. He clasps my other hand.

I glare at him. "You and my brother really like putting me through hell, don't you? Maybe that's why you're getting along so well."

Indeed, they talked a lot during dinner since they were seated next to each other. They even shared a good laugh.

Steff smiles. "I have no idea what you're talking about."

I pout and stay silent as we sway to the music.

His thumb moves slowly across my hip until I feel it graze the garter of my panties.

"What are you doing?" I ask him in a low voice.

"Just making sure you're wearing something under that lovely dress," Steff answers.

I blush and glare at him. "Of course I am. Why wouldn't I be?"

He chuckles. "There. You're more relaxed now, aren't you?"

He whirls me around.

"Just be your usual self," he adds. "You're a remarkable woman and you look stunning in that dress."

When Steff pulls me close again, he whispers in my ear.

"So stunning, in fact, that it's the one piece of clothing I'd rather not take off you."

My breath catches. My cheeks turn even warmer.

Still, I glare. "As if I'd ever let you do such a thing."

"Now, now. That's not the way to talk to your boyfriend, is it?"

I frown. I'm still kicking myself for introducing him as my boyfriend. But what could I do? My brother dropped by at the worst moment, catching us both with barely any clothes on.

I hear some murmurs from the tables behind me.

"So handsome!"

"Is he a soldier, too?"

"No, I think he must be a model."

"Is he really with her?"

My frown deepens.

"You really like being the center of attention, don't you?" I ask Steff.

His eyebrows arch. "Huh?"

I sigh. Then I stop moving.

"I think I need to go to the ladies' room," I tell him as I take my hand off his shoulder and free my hand from his. "Excuse me."

I walk off. I hear the gossip intensify, but I pay it no heed.

I walk past the doors, down the corridor and round the corner to the restroom I had spotted earlier. Inside, I lean on the sink and stare at the mirror.

Steff really is hot, isn't he? He's cool, too. He's amazing. There's nothing he can't seem to do.

And I can't believe I've had sex with him twice already.

I slap my forehead.

Really, Jess, what are you doing? You're just setting yourself up for a heartbreak, you know. A man like that deserves more than you, and he'll get it, too.

I sigh.

And to think I introduced him as my boyfriend.

It almost feels like I've committed some kind of crime.

And yet, Steff doesn't seem to mind. Then again, he's always played along with my lies and schemes. He's nice that way.

Nice? I blush as I remember his words earlier. How can I say he's nice when he's being so mean to me?

I draw a deep breath.

Calm down, Jess. You're just on edge because you're not used to this kind of environment. After this, everything will go back to normal and you and Steff will be fine.

I narrow my eyes at my reflection.

Right. This is all just pretend. There's no reason for me to take this seriously or to think that something has changed between Steff and me. There's no reason for me to be jealous.

I walk out of the bathroom. I stop as I see Keith waiting for me around the corner.

"You were taking so long I was beginning to worry," he says.

"What are you doing here?" I ask him. "You left Annie alone?"

"So? You left your boyfriend alone, too, didn't you? You should hurry back before someone steals him from you."

My hands rise to my hips. "What?"

Keith chuckles. "Just kidding. He may smile kindly at other women, but he doesn't look like a man who can be stolen."

My arms cross my chest. "You seem to know him surprisingly well for somebody you just met today. What, are the two of you best buddies now?"

"Of course not," Keith answers. "But I have to say I do like him."

I raise an eyebrow. "You do?"

"He's smart, witty, gutsy. And he looks reliable."

"All this from your conversation at dinner? You didn't do a background check, did you?"

"He's not from here, so that will take a while," Keith answers.

I sigh.

"Plus I can tell from the way we fought this morning that he knows how to fight," Keith adds in a more serious tone. "That means he'll be able to protect you when I'm not around."

I glance at him. His eyes stare beyond the glance into the distance.

He really does like Steff.

So he's even won my brother over, huh?

"Hey." I punch his shoulder playfully. "You're not going to steal my boyfriend from me, are you?"

Keith's eyes widen. "What the...?"

I start laughing. "Got you."

He laughs as well. Then he puts his hand on my head.

"So my little sister knows how to tease me back now, does she?"

"Stop that!" I tell him as I step away. "You have no idea how long I had to sit still to get my stubborn hair to end up this way."

Keith laughs so hard he grips his belly. He's still chuckling when his phone rings. As he gets it from his pocket, I decide to check my own. I fish it out of my purse and discover that I have three missed calls, all from Laura. There's a message from her, too.

Dad collapsed. We're bringing him to the hospital now.

The phone nearly slips out of my fingers, which have suddenly turned cold. What could have happened to Dad?

"Jess." Keith turns to me. "That was Laura."

From the look on his face, I already know what he's going to say. I swallow.

"We have to go back home, don't we?"

~

By the time Keith and I arrive in our hometown, Prairie du Chien, Wisconsin, it's already morning. We go straight to the hospital and a nurse leads us to Dad's room.

I find my mother sitting by my father's bed.

"Mom!" I throw myself into her arms.

"Jess!" She hugs me tight and then pulls away to look at me. "Look at you! You've finally learned how to put more effort into how you look."

I frown. In all my haste and worry, I barely had time to change, much less remove my makeup. My face looks the same as it did at the party, and although my hair has already started rebelling, most of it still cascades down my shoulders in a straight line.

Seriously, that's the first thing my mother says to me?

"Mom..."

"How's Dad?" Keith approaches the bed.

"Keith!" Mom hugs him in turn.

I place my hand over my father's and take a close look at his face. It seems a little paler and more wrinkled than when I last saw him. Otherwise, he seems fine.

"We thought your Dad had a stroke," Mom explains. "Thankfully, it wasn't that bad, but we still have to make sure he doesn't strain his heart. He's not as young as he used to be, after all."

"I'm not that old, either," Dad says suddenly as he opens his eyes.

My mother sighs. "What? Were you pretending to be asleep? Did you want your daughter to cry?"

"Of course not." He touches my cheek. "I'd never want to see her cry."

"Oh, Dad." I place my hand over his. "I'm so glad you're alright."

"I'm perfectly fine," Dad tells me. "Especially now that you're here."

"There you go spoiling her again," Mom complains. "Are you sure you didn't collapse on purpose just so she'd come running home?"

Dad chuckles.

I squeeze his hand. "I should have come home more often. I'm sorry."

Dad shakes his head. "I'm sure you're busy, but your Mom and I do worry that you're not taking care of yourself."

"Speak for yourself," my mother tells him. "And what do you mean busy? What, do you have a real job now?"

"Maggie," my father scolds her before turning to me with a smile. "Don't mind your mother. She's just like that because she hasn't had breakfast yet."

Mom snorts.

"But, well, are you taking care of yourself?" Dad asks.

I exhale and put his hand down by his side. "Dad, you're the one in a hospital bed. You shouldn't be worrying about me."

"That's right," Keith says. "Besides, you shouldn't worry about Jess anymore. She's all grown up now. Why, she even managed to get a boyfriend."

Mom gasps. Dad and I gape. I turn to Keith with a deathly glare, which he tries to fend off with a sheepish grin.

"Keith..."

Chapter 14
Steff

"So Keith ratted you out to your family, huh?" I ask Jess during the drive from the airport to her house.

She lifts one hand off the wheel to rub her temples. "And after all the trouble I went through, too, at that silly party."

"You mean the one where you ditched me?"

She puts her hand back on the wheel and frowns. "I didn't ditch you. I had to leave because of my family emergency and I decided to let you stay behind and enjoy the party. After all, you did seem to be enjoying yourself."

"You ditched me," I repeat.

Jess sighs. "Fine. Sorry."

"Apology accepted. So, why did Keith tell your family after he said he wouldn't?"

Another sigh. "He said he wanted my dad to have one less thing to worry about, given his health. And really, I would have been okay with it if only it was true. I mean, what if he finds out it isn't? Then he'll be more upset, right?"

I place my hand over hers. "Don't worry. I'll keep your secret."

Jess glances at me. "Thanks. I'm sorry for dragging you into this."

I scratch my chin. "Well, that's unusual. You seem to be in an apologetic mood. You didn't eat something weird, did you?"

She glares at me.

I chuckle. "That's more like the Jess I know."

I look out the window.

"Really, though, it's fine."

At least now I can find out more about Jess. Also, I've been in LA all this time and I think a change of scenery is in order. How can I call it an adventure if all I do is stay in one place?

"So this is Wisconsin, right? And your hometown is called Prairie du Chien?"

"Yes."

"Want to tell me more about it?"

"More importantly, we should talk about what we're going to tell my family," Jess says. "That's why I insisted on picking you up at the airport."

I sit back. "And here I thought it was because you missed me."

Jess ignores the remark as she lowers the volume of the music.

"So when my family asks how we met, what do we say?" she asks me.

I shrug. "What do you have in mind?"

"That we met online," she says. "And that we've been corresponding online for two years now."

"Two years?" My eyebrows crease. "That's long."

Jess says nothing.

"And meeting online is fine," I add. "But it's a little boring, if you ask me. I think we should go with us meeting at a concert."

"Not bad," Jess approves. "It doesn't have to be a big name band. We'll just say there were a few local bands playing."

I nod. "A friend of mine who played in one of the bands invited me, and you came, because, well, that's your scene."

"I came with a friend but I lost her," she continues. "We bumped into each other and we started talking about the guitar. Then we ended up leaving and having coffee, talking some more. We hung out for the next few days before you had to leave. We continued corresponding online."

"And while we were apart, we fell in love," I supply. "And so I decided to come back and now, here we are."

I notice Jess stick out her lower lip at the word 'love', but she says nothing.

"So to summarize, we met at a concert, we've been corresponding for two years, and I came back last month. How does that sound?"

Jess nods. "Sounds good."

"Anything else we have to talk about?"

She shrugs. "I think that's about it."

"Then we're all good." I give her a grin. "See, we're a great team. We've got nothing to worry about."

Jess exhales. "I sure hope so."

"Now, tell me more about your hometown and your family."

~

"This is my older sister, Laura." Jess introduces the woman with the child on her hip as soon as we arrive at her house. "And this is her daughter, Lucia, and her son, Raffy, should be somewhere in the house."

"You can't miss him," Laura says as she shakes my hand. "He always has his gaming console."

"And this is my mother, Maggie," Jess continues.

I take the hand of the woman with the eyeglasses and the salt and pepper hair and plant a kiss on the back of it.

"It's a pleasure to meet you."

"My, my." She touches her cheek. "You didn't say your boyfriend was such a hunk."

"Mom," Jess reprimands. "Dad can hear you."

Jess stands beside the bearded man who is sitting on a wicker chair.

"This is my dad, Don Campbell," Jess says. "Dad, this is Steff, Steffan Olsen, my boyfriend."

I smile at him as I shake his hand. "I'm glad to see you're doing well."

"And that's it." Jess shrugs.

"What about me?" Keith complains.

Jess ignores him and crosses her arms over her chest.

"So how did you two meet?" Maggie asks.

Jess tells her the story we've settled on.

Maggie smiles. "How romantic. You came back just for Jess!"

"Of course," I say. "How could I not?"

I reach for Jess's hand. "She has truly captured my heart."

Maggie applauds and Laura whistles. Jess narrows her eyes at me.

"I'm happy to hear it," Don says. "I know Jess can be a handful, but-"

"Dad," Jess interrupts him with a frown.

"What did you see in her?" Laura asks.

Jess turns to her. "Not you too!"

"I mean, what do you like best about her?" Laura asks me.

I touch my chin. "Well, I like everything about her, but what I like best?"

That's a tough one. But then I remember how we first met, or at least, our first meeting when she was sober and knew I was a guy.

"I guess her spirit."

Laura laughs out loud. "That's Jess, alright."

Jess glances at her. "Laura."

"Tell me..." Maggie places a hand on my shoulder. "How do you handle her tantrums?"

"Mom," Jess whines.

"Yeah. Have you guys fought?" Laura asks.

"Sometimes," I answer just as Jess answers, "Never."

Shit.

"What I mean is sometimes we argue," I explain. "But we've never had a real fight."

Laura touches her cheek. "Aww."

"And who got whose Skype ID first?" Keith asks.

"He got mine," Jess answers as I say, "I got hers."

I almost sigh with relief that we agreed on that detail. It's funny how we read each other's minds.

458

Jess turns to Keith. "By the way, you don't get to ask any more questions."

"Hey!" Keith protests.

"Actually, none of you get to ask any more questions," Jess announces. "He's here, isn't he?"

"Well, I surely am glad to meet you," Don tells me. "And I'm sure you're tired, so please head inside. Our home is your home."

~

Jess's home, huh?

As I stand in the living room while Jess talks to her mother about dinner in the kitchen, I pause to look around.

Floor pillows of various shapes in colorful knitted cases surround a low, round wooden table in front of the fireplace. Five pairs of tiny mittens hang from the mantel; two are noticeably newer than the other three, and my guess is that Maggie made them all for her three children and two grandchildren.

To the left of the fireplace, French windows extend from floor to ceiling, giving a glimpse of the garden outside-and access thereto, if one wished. Across from it, a couch with a floral pattern sits in front of a forty-plus-inch TV. A glass coffee table stands between them.

I spot a boy, about six years old, on the couch, busy pressing the buttons of his gadget.

I approach him with a smile.

"You must be Raffy," I say.

He just glances up at me then continues playing.

I look behind me and see the dining room with its table for eight and the cabinet that houses all the china. Beside that is the door through which Jess disappeared.

"Why don't you go ahead upstairs?" Laura suggests as she enters the house. "I'll show you where you'll be staying."

I nod. "Thank you."

I follow her up the stairs and down a hall with doors on either side. She stops in front of the second door to the right.

"Here we go." She grabs the knob and pushes the door open. "This is Jess's old room, which is where you'll be staying. I'm afraid the kids and I stay in the guest room since my old room was turned into Mom's craft room. You don't mind, do you? After all, you're Jess's boyfriend."

I grin. "I don't mind."

But I wonder if she does. Does she know?

Laura pats my shoulder. "I'll leave you to it."

She leaves and I enter the room. I put down my things and close the door behind me.

It's a small room, even smaller than the bedroom I have in Jess's apartment. The twin-sized bed stands against the wall, made up with pink and green sheets. A desk occupies the corner near the window, and opposite that is the closet. There's a bookshelf across from the bed, but instead of books, it's filled with CDs. A ukulele sits on top of it.

I pick the instrument up and give it a strum. The notes fill the air.

So Jess loved playing even when she was little? How little? Was this her first instrument?

I set down the ukulele and go to her desk. There are no pictures on it, but I do see a jewelry box filled with odds and ends-charms from a broken bracelet, a quarter, rubber bands, a baby tooth, tickets to Disneyland, a ribbon from school that says '2nd Place'.

I smile as I close the box. The contents may not mean anything to me, but they're remnants of a childhood, Jess's childhood, and as I look out the window, I remember mine.

Lessons. Endless lessons. Training. Parties. Fittings. Times when I played pranks on Danni, times when I ran away from my governess to play in the snow, times when I snuck sweets into my brother's bedroom, times when I hurt myself climbing things I wasn't supposed to.

The door opens, breaking into my thoughts. I turn to smile at Jess.

"What are you doing?" she asks me.

"Reminiscing," I tell her honestly. "Being here has somehow reminded me of my childhood."

"No, I mean what are you doing here in my room?"

"Laura said I'm staying here," I explain.

She sits on the edge of her bed and sighs.

Just as I thought, she does mind.

"At least our story will be more believable this way, won't it?" I say to console her.

She looks at me. "Fine. But we're not sleeping in the same bed. My old sleeping bag should still be in the attic."

She heads back to the door, but stops to glance over her shoulder.

"Oh. And since we're sharing my room, maybe you can tell me some stories about your childhood later."

Chapter 15
Jess

"So how are things at the cafe?" I ask Lisbeth with a yawn.

I stayed up late last night listening to Steff tell stories of his childhood and sharing some of my own. I would have preferred to sleep in, but I promised Lisbeth I'd call her on Skype, which is why I'm in the living room right now with my laptop in front of me. She, on the other hand, is on her first coffee break of the day.

"Good." She glances behind her. "Not that busy."

"I can see that."

She leans closer to the screen. "But you seem to have been busy last night. Isn't that why you're sleepy?"

My eyebrows shoot up. My sleepiness suddenly vanishes.

"What are you talking about?"

"You're there with Steff, aren't you?" Lisbeth asks with a mischievous grin. "Tell me, did you share a room last night?"

"Well, yes, but-"

"And did he keep you up?"

"Yes, but-"

"I knew it!" Lisbeth cheers.

I sigh. "Lisbeth, that's not-"

"Hey, keep it down," I hear Tom's voice in the background.

"Sorry," Lisbeth apologizes.

I wave a reprimanding finger at Lisbeth.

That's what she gets for teasing me.

Suddenly, Tom's face appears on the screen.

"Jess?"

I sit up straight. "Hi, Tom. I'm sorry I couldn't come to work today. I'm here in Wisconsin."

"Yeah. Lisbeth told me about your father," Tom says. "How is he?"

"He's out of the woods now," I tell him.

"That's good."

"But I won't be back until Monday. My family hasn't seen me in a while, so..."

"That's fine," Tom says. "You've always come to work until now anyway, even during holidays. You deserve a break."

I smile. "Thanks, Tom."

"You're too soft, Tom," Lisbeth teases him.

"You think so?" Tom turns to her. "Isn't it time you got back to work?"

Lisbeth pouts.

Tom chuckles. "Just kidding."

He peers into the screen again. "Just take the time to..."

He pauses and gives me a puzzled look.

"Is that your gay roommate?"

I glance behind me to see Steff at the bottom of the stairs. What's worse, though, is that he's not the only one around. My mom has just come in from the garden. Her gardening shears slip from her fingers and clatter to the floor.

She gasps. "G-gay roommate?"

I slap my forehead and look at the screen. "I'll get back to you later."

I terminate the call and lift my hands as I face my mother. "Mom, I can explain."

~

"Explain," Laura demands as soon as she, Mom, Keith and Steff are gathered in the living room.

461

We decided to leave Dad out in consideration of his health.

I rub my temples. "It's a misunderstanding, okay? I didn't want to tell my boss that I had a boyfriend, so I said Steff was my roommate and that he's gay."

"So he's not gay?" Mom asks.

"Why didn't you want to tell your boss?" Laura asks. "He seems like a good guy."

"He is, so I didn't want him to worry about me." I glance at Keith. "You know, like an older brother would."

Keith crosses his arms over his chest. "I'm not convinced. Is Steff really your boyfriend? How can I be sure he's who you say he is when he's not even who he says he is?"

My eyebrows crease. "Excuse me?"

"The intel I received says no Steffan Olsen from Norway entered the country within the last few months," Keith reveals.

Gasps fill the living room.

"Well, that's because I'm not actually a Norwegian citizen," Steff explains as he steps forward. "I was born in a small Baltic country called Brelv, but I grew up in Norway. I usually say I'm from there because very few Americans have heard of Brelv."

"And where did you study?" Keith asks. "Where do you work?"

"I studied all over Europe. I work in Brelv now."

Keith touches his chin and falls silent.

"And you're not gay?" Mom asks him.

"No," Steff answers.

"You caught us, remember?" I remind Keith with a scowl. "Or have you forgotten that when you dropped by my apartment, Steff and I barely had any clothes on?"

Laura gasps.

"But I didn't actually see you doing anything," Keith supplies.

God, I want to punch him right now.

Steff grabs my hand. "Should I kiss your sister in front of you to prove I'm not gay and that I'm in love with her?"

"Ooh." Mom grins.

I narrow my eyes at Steff.

"A kiss wouldn't prove much, though," Laura says.

"What do you want me to do?" Steff asks.

"Prove to us that you and Jess are really in a serious relationship," Laura answers. She glances at me. "Just show us some proof."

I snort. "Why do I have to prove anything to you guys? If you don't believe me..."

"Well, you didn't even know where he's really from," Mom points out. "We just want to make sure he's actually your boyfriend."

Keith nods.

I slap my forehead. This is such a pain. "What, are you guys immigration officers now?!?"

"Even just a few romantic messages will do," Laura says.

I frown. "Sorry, but they were all on my old laptop."

"How convenient," Keith says.

I glare at him. All this is his fault. I wouldn't be in this situation right now if he'd kept his mouth shut.

"So you have no proof?" Laura asks.

I glance at Steff, who looks deep in thought.

I try to think as well.

Think, Jess. Think. How can you convince them that you and Steff are in a serious relationship?

Should I just come clean and tell them the truth? Keith doesn't believe I had sex with Steff anyway. But if I do that, Dad will get more worried than ever about me.

I don't want him to worry. I don't want any of them to worry about me anymore.

I've caused them enough trouble.

What to do?

Then my gaze falls on Steff's hand and something comes to mind.

I sigh. "You know, I wasn't ready to tell you guys yet, but I guess you're forcing my hand."

Steff looks at me with arched eyebrows.

I grab his hand and hold it behind mine.

"Ready to tell us what?" Mom asks.

"Well, you're right," I tell them. "Steff isn't my boyfriend."

I slip the ring off his finger and put it on mine.

"I thought so," Keith says.

"He's my fiance," I announce as I show the ring on my finger. The gold band and purple gems glint under the light.

Unfortunately, it's too big for my ring finger, so I had to put it on my thumb, but at least I'm wearing it.

Laura gives me a puzzled look. "That doesn't look like an engagement ring."

"It is in his country," I answer, since Steff still looks as surprised as my Mom.

"And it's on the wrong finger," Laura adds. "Is that part of the custom, too?"

"He got the size wrong," I say. "But hey, it's the thought that counts, right?"

I hug Steff's arm.

"Um, wasn't he wearing that before?" Keith asks.

He just has to make things difficult, doesn't he?

"Of course he was," I say with as much confidence as I can muster. "He proposed the moment he arrived at the airport. I told him I'd think about it, and he's been wearing it ever since so he'd always have it ready in case I said yes."

"Then you're not engaged," Laura points out. "Because you didn't say yes."

"I was going to at that fancy party, but then we found out about Dad and I had to leave. I finally said yes just last night."

Mom clasps her hand over her mouth as she gets on her feet. "You're engaged?"

"Yes," I tell her as I run my hands through my hair. "Though I still can't believe it myself."

I give Steff's arm a squeeze.

"It's true," he confirms with a grin. "I did ask her to marry me, and thank goodness she finally said yes."

For a moment, everyone in the room falls silent. I hold my breath.

Do they believe me? Do they still think Steff and I aren't in a serious relationship? Do they think this, too, is a lie?

Then Mom runs to me and squeezes me tight. Laura joins the hug.

"I'm so happy for you!" Laura says.

"Wait," Keith says. "We don't believe Jess has a boyfriend but we believe she's engaged?"

"Oh, shut up," Mom tells him. "You're just jealous because you're not engaged."

I smile and resist the urge to stick my tongue out at him.

Thank you, Mom.

"But he was, wasn't he?" Laura says. "It just got broken off."

"Hey," Keith complains. "This is not about me. It's about Jess."

"She might lie about having a boyfriend, but not about being engaged," Laura says. "Especially not with the man concerned in the room. Do you think a guy would go along with that?"

She gives Steff a hug. "So when's the wedding? And where do you guys plan on getting married?"

"No date yet," Steff says coolly. "And we don't have a venue, either."

"I just said yes, after all," I remind my sister.

"Well, make sure you let me help with the planning," Laura says.

"Okay," I promise her.

Keith gets off the couch and looks into my eyes. "You really are engaged?"

Steff squares his shoulders. "If you're questioning the engagement, we can have a duel. That is how it's done in my country."

Keith's eyes grow wide. "A duel? Sounds interesting."

"There will be no such thing," Mom says.

She grabs my hand and Steff's.

"Come. We must tell your father."

~

"I'm sorry about all that," I tell Steff later on when we're finally alone in my room.

I let out a sigh as I let my arm fall across my forehead. Today has probably been the craziest day of my life.

I thought they'd leave me alone after hearing that Steff and I were engaged, but no.

After Steff and I talked to my dad, who was so overjoyed that I started to feel even more guilty about lying, my mom and Laura wouldn't stop talking about weddings. My mom brought her friends over and threw an impromptu bridal shower for me. Laura brought over her wedding dress and made me try it on. And then Keith dragged Steff off for their 'duel' at the boxing gym, which ended up a draw.

"I should have thought of something else."

"But you couldn't, could you?" Steff folds his arms behind his head on the sleeping bag and stares at the ceiling. "It's fine. I was surprised. That's all."

"So was I."

I hold up my hand and stare at the ring on my thumb.

"You said this ring was a family heirloom, right?"

Steff grunts in assent.

That must be why the design looks so unique. All of my mother's friends said so.

I run my other thumb over the purple gems. "What are these? Amethysts?"

"Sapphires."

I glance at him with wide eyes. "Sapphires? I thought sapphires were-"

"Blue?" Steff finishes my sentence. "There are purple ones, but they're very rare."

I swallow as I glance at the ring again.

No wonder he's never taken it off. It must be worth a fortune. I'd better take good care of it.

"I'm sorry I have to borrow this," I tell him. "I promise I'll take good care of it and give it back when-"

"You're being apologetic again," Steff cuts me off.

I pout as I hug my pillow. "Well, that's because I'm feeling guilty."

"In that case, do you want me to help you ease your guilt?"

I lean over the bed to throw him a puzzled look. "Huh?"

Steff reaches up to touch my cheek. My heart skips a beat.

"You're feeling guilty because you feel like you're using me."

Well, he's not wrong.

"You think it's unfair, and you don't like owing me."

That's not wrong, either.

"So why don't we make it even?" His thumb touches the corner of my lips. "If you don't want to owe me, you know a way to pay me, don't you?"

I look into his eyes as mine grow wide. Is he suggesting...?

"Of course, you don't have to," Steff tells me as his hand falls away. "I just brought it up because you seem to be in pain and you're reflecting that on me. That's why you keep apologizing. But feel free to deal with it in your own way."

He turns on his side away from the bed.

"Good night."

For a moment, I just stare at Steff as I try to digest what he just said.

Me? In pain? Well, I am feeling guilty. I don't like using other people, not even Steff.

He's right. It is unfair to him. Well, it's unfair to everyone, but to him most of all.

Didn't my sister say no man would go along with such a big lie?

And it's true, I don't like being in his debt.

So there's only one thing to do.

I have to pay Steff. I have to give him something in return.

Thankfully, I know just what he wants.

I get off the bed and put my arms around him. My nose digs into the pale strands of hair that gleam under the lamplight. His scent drifts into my nostrils.

And just like that, my worries vanish.

I close my eyes and press my lips against his neck. I feel Steff's body stiffen.

I'm inexperienced at this, I know. I'm still a virgin in many ways.

But right now, his scent is putting me in a daze. The taste of his skin is making me dizzy. The heat of his body is lighting a fire in mine, and as the flames spread through my veins, my body begins to move as if it has a life of its own.

My hand slips under the blanket and reaches around him to touch the bulge in his crotch. I part my lips and his name escapes me in a whisper.

"Steff..."

Chapter 16
Steff

Jess's hot breath tickles my skin. The sound of my name on her lips vibrates through my body all the way down to my crotch. My cock quivers against her palm.

I glance behind me. "Are you sure you want to do this?"

"You suggested it," she answers as her palm rubs against my erection through its cotton prison.

I suck in a breath.

Yes, I did suggest it, but I didn't actually think Jess would take my suggestion.

Maybe I've underestimated her?

I grin. "Go ahead, then. After all, we're practically married, aren't we?"

Let's see what she can do, how far she can go.

Jess plants another kiss on my neck. Then she withdraws her hand to unzip the sleeping bag. The thick flap that serves as the blanket falls aside.

When her hand returns, it pushes the waistband of my pants and the garter of my briefs past my hips. My cock springs free and pulses in the cool air.

Jess leans over me and wraps her fingers around the rod of flesh.

I feel the cold metal of her ring-my ring-against my heated skin and gasp.

The heat disperses throughout my body.

She starts stroking me. I stare blankly at the stack of CDs in front of me as my heart hammers in my chest.

Her strokes lack experience and finesse, and yet, I tremble. The friction sends sparks through my veins.

It's not just Jess's hands that are sending me into a fever.

Her ebony eyes scorch me as they watch intently over my shoulder. Her hair tickles my cheeks and the scent of her shampoo drifts into my nostrils.

I can feel the curve of her breast pressed against my arm. I can feel her slender body spooned against mine. Even through the layers of fabric between us, I can feel her heat seeping into me.

"You're concentrating," I tell her.

"Well, I want you to feel good."

The answer takes me by surprise. Excitement erupts in my chest and tightens around my heart, causing it to skip a beat. My cock swells.

"Ha!" Jess exclaims in wonder. "It got thicker."

"It's got a mind of its own," I answer breathlessly.

Jess's hand suddenly starts moving faster. The pad of her thumb brushes over the moist tip of my cock. The ring rubs the skin just beneath that.

I suck in a deep breath and grip the edges of the pillow beneath my head.

Strange. I've been with several women-more experienced, skilled women-but none of them has ever reduced me to this state, especially not with just fingers.

Then Jess's fingers go still.

She sits up and moves on top of me. I lie on my back and she kneels between my legs.

"Getting bolder, are we?" I tease her as I lift myself on my elbows.

Jess doesn't answer, just stares at my cock for a few seconds. Then she lowers her head and her tongue brushes against the tip.

A shiver climbs up my spine. My jaw tightens.

"It tastes odd, but not bad," she says with creased eyebrows.

The tip of her tongue travels down the curved shaft.

I bite down on my lower lip to hold back a moan. It ends up resounding in my throat. My arms tremble and my elbows wobble.

Still, I keep watching her.

I can't tell what's more exciting-the sight of Jess savoring me like I'm an exquisite treat or the feel of her tongue on my sensitive skin.

Finally, she wraps her lips around my cock.

My hands curl into fists. I can feel my sanity slipping away as I get sucked little by little into that mouth.

Jess fails to take all of me inside her mouth, but what she manages is almost too much.

I quickly grab her shoulders and push her away. Then I push her down on the couch and lean over her. I stare right into those quivering black eyes.

"I think I'll take it from here."

I pull off her pajama pants and her panties and toss them aside. I claim her mouth as I slip a finger inside her.

She's wet. Even though she was the one giving me such pleasure, she must have been feeling it, too.

Jess wraps her arms around my back. I withdraw my finger and guide my cock slowly inside her. She moans into my mouth.

I break the kiss and grip her thighs as I start moving. Her hands clutch my shoulders. I feel her nails through my cotton shirt.

I grunt as I move faster. She moans and squeezes her eyes shut. Her body squeezes me as well. The sheath around my cock grows tighter and robs me of air I'm already short of.

Fuck. I'm not going to last long.

I pause to reach between us and play with her nub. I bend over to suck one of her breasts through the cotton of her pajama top.

Jess trembles. Her moans turn into cries. Her nails dig into my shoulder.

"Steff!"

As she comes undone, I put my hands behind her knees and move again. I go in faster, deeper, even as she trembles and tightens around me.

My hips rock. Heat swirls in my balls as they slap against her skin.

"Co... ming."

A series of grunts escapes my throat as I give a few more rapid thrusts. Then I bury myself deep inside her and fill her up before collapsing on top of her.

Jess's arms fall to her sides. Her heart beats wildly against mine as our heavy breathing fills the room.

"So," Jess speaks first. "We're even now?"

I nod. "I'd say we're more than even."

I pull myself up on my elbows and look at her.

Her cheeks, still rosy, glow under the yellow light of the lamp. Her eyes glimmer like a moonless sky dotted with stars.

"Then consider it an advance," Jess says with a grin. "After all, we're going to have to keep this act up until Sunday."

I smile. "Let's give them a good show."

~

"That was quite a show," Laura says at the family barbecue the next day. She's eating the grilled mushroom off the top of her vegetable kebab. "Not sure how I felt about it, though."

I look away from the grill to give her a puzzled look. "I'm sorry?"

"Oh, come on. You think you guys can fool me?"

I glance at Jess, who's standing beside me frozen in the act of biting a zucchini slice from her own kebab. Panic flickers in her eyes and flutters in my chest.

Have we been discovered?

"You guys might look innocent and all, but I know that shaking above me last night was no earthquake," Laura goes on to explain.

She gives me a wink. A blush creeps across my cheeks as I understand what she's saying.

I scratch the back of my head. "Oh, that."

"You felt it, too, didn't you, Keith?" Laura asks him.

Keith groans beside me as he flips a burger patty on the grill.

"Don't remind me."

467

Laura places a hand on her jaw and gives me a playful grin. "I guess the two of you really are engaged. Passionately engaged."

I ruefully return a sheepish grin of my own.

Well, at least we seem to have them convinced.

Unexpectedly, Jess, too, has a grin on her lips as she chews on her zucchini slice within the hollows of her burning cheeks.

I thought she'd be embarrassed, but she seems to be... amused?

"You're just jealous," she tells her sister.

Laura's jaw drops. Then she grins.

"My, my, Keith, did you just hear what our little sister said?" she asks Keith. "Sounds like someone's all grown up already."

Keith doesn't answer. He flips another burger patty. I flip the one in front of me.

"She said we're just jealous," Laura repeats.

"I heard," Keith says. "But I think she was just talking to you."

"Really?" Laura gives him a nudge. "When was the last time you had any?"

"None of your business. And please spare me yours." He glances at Jess. "Both of yours."

"Laura started it," Jess points out.

Laura places an arm around Jess and me.

"So tell me, who's the wilder one, hmm?" Laura asks in a low voice. "Also, want me to give you some tips?"

Jess shrugs off Laura's arm. "No thanks. And stop acting like you're single. You have two children, for God's sake."

"So?" Laura shrugs. "That just means I know a lot of stuff about-"

"We're leaving," Jess interrupts her as she grabs my arm.

She pulls me away from the grill and towards the swing under the shade of an oak tree.

"Sorry," she says as she sits down. "I just couldn't stand it anymore."

There she goes, apologizing again.

I sit down beside her. "It's fine."

She sits back. "My family's really crazy, huh?"

"Maybe."

I look across the yard at Keith, who's still at the grill; Laura, who's now tending to her daughter; and Maggie and Don, who are eating their skewered vegetables on the front porch.

"You said you're the rebel and that they're disappointed in you, but I think they all care a great deal about you. You're lucky to have them."

I can't remember the last time my entire family had fun like this. We attend a lot of parties together, yes, but that's because we have to. I wouldn't really call them fun. I used to have picnics with my sisters when they were younger, but not recently.

Jess's hand falls to my lap. "Tell me more about your family. What's your father like?"

"Strict," I say the first word that comes to my mind. "Old-fashioned. Wise. Ruthless."

Jess wrinkles her eyebrows. "Okay. And your mother?"

"She supports him in everything, and she can be just as brave and just as frightening. But she's also kind and thoughtful."

"She sounds like a good mother," Jess says. "I bet she's beautiful, too."

"Well, they say I look more like her," I tell her. "The same hair. The same eyes."

Jess nods. "She must really be beautiful."

"My brother looks more like my father, but other than that, I don't think they have anything else in common. My sisters have mixed features."

"They're twins, right?"

I nod.

"They must adore you."

I say nothing. They must really be pissed that I left without saying goodbye to them.

"Don't you miss them?" Jess asks suddenly.

I turn to her in surprise. I smile.

"Yes," I admit. "But it was best for me to leave."

I really hope it turned out to be for the best.

"Sometimes, you have to make what seem like the wrong choices to-"

I stop as I hear the sound of glass shattering. Then Maggie screams.

I stand up and turn towards the front porch. Don is hanging limp in her arms.

Jess drops her kebab and rushes off.

"Daddy!"

Chapter 17
Jess

The squeak of rubber soles on the freshly mopped floor sets the beat for the hospital corridor. The smell of bleach reminds me of the days Mom took her woes out on the bathroom tiles. The chatter of the nurses around the corner provides the vocals. Every now and then, a chime sounds from above like a note from a keyboard. Then a different voice, a mechanical-sounding one, spills out of the speakers to give a fresh layer of dynamics to the piece. Every now and then, a wail cuts through like the screech of a guitar. The anxious tapping of my foot provides the percussion.

Beside me on the bench, Steff sits quietly, apparently relaxed. He sips his coffee as his other hand holds mine. My mother, sister and brother are all quiet, too, though they are by no means relaxed.

Mom looks pale. Her shaking hands clasp a string of prayer beads that someone gave to her. Laura is holding the napping Lucia tight. Keith is chewing on a piece of gum while his knee goes up and down to rock the bench.

We are all anxiously waiting for news about Dad's condition, hoping for the best and trying not to think of the worst even as it repeatedly knocks on our minds.

Finally, a man in a white coat appears in front of us. I'm the first to stand up and speak.

"Is my father alright?"

He pulls his glasses into place from the side. "You're Donald Campbell's daughter?"

"Yes."

"We're his family," Keith says.

"I'm Dr. Steve Partridge," he introduces himself as he offers his hand to Keith. "I'm afraid the patient has suffered a transient ischemic attack. In other words, it's a mild stroke."

A stroke?

I sink into the bench as my knees shake. Steff squeezes my hand.

"He's out of the woods now," Dr. Partridge goes on. "He is conscious, but he's still weak. Given his age, he will likely not be able to move around like he used to."

Laura gasps.

"He may have a hard time speaking as well."

I clasp a hand over my gaping mouth. My dad will be unable to run or to talk to me like he used to?

"Also, the chances of him having another stroke are high. And I'm afraid the second one is undoubtedly going to be worse."

He means the second one could be fatal.

"When?" Keith asks. "When is he likely to suffer another?"

"There's no telling." Dr. Partridge shakes his head. "Some patients have another within a week, some within a month, but for some it's not for five or ten years."

My eyes grow wide. A week? A month?

"I want to see him," Mom speaks up.

She's holding her shoulders up, but I can see them trembling.

Dr. Partridge nods. "You should be able to see him in a bit. I'll have the nurse inform you when you can. However, remember that he can't talk properly. Also, he needs a lot of rest, and I recommend not saying anything to make him worry or get upset or excited. We're monitoring his heart activity closely, and we'd like to keep it stable."

"Of course." Mom nods.

"Then if you'll excuse me..." Dr. Partridge walks off.

As soon as he's gone, Laura grabs Keith's arm and starts crying into his sleeve. Mom sinks back into a chair. Her eyes stare blankly at the wall across from her.

I touch her arm. "Mom?"

"I'm fine," she tells me in a shaky voice. "We have to be strong for your father. If he sees us worried, he'll worry, too."

I know. And I admire Mom for doing her best to be strong. She's always been strong. Still, I don't know if I can do it.

I stand up. "I'll just head to the restroom."

I walk down the corridor slowly. My feet feel heavy.

Somehow I manage to drag myself to the lobby and past the doors to the small garden facing the parking lot.

I sit down on the stool.

I know I said I was going to the restroom, but the truth is I just wanted to be alone and maybe get some fresh air. My chest feels wound up so tight I can barely breathe.

As I gaze up at the cloudy sky, I think of Dad.

I remember how he used to carry me on his shoulders when we went to watch parades. I remember how he taught me to ride a bike and bandaged my knee when I fell. I remember how we'd cook in the kitchen together when Mom wasn't around. I remember when he bought me my first guitar, how he applauded for me at my first recital, how he defended me against Mom after I said I wanted to be in a band more than anything.

Dad.

He was always on my side.

The doors behind me slide open and a man and a little girl come out. The little girl has her arm in a sling but has a smile on her face. It must be because her father is smiling, too.

Tears spill out of my eyes.

Dad has always been there for me, and I thought that was the way things would always be. But I was wrong. Dad isn't as young or as healthy as he used to be, and now there's a chance I may lose him soon.

My fingers tighten around the edge of the stool as my shoulders tremble.

This is so unfair. I'm not ready to lose my dad.

I lift my eyes to the sky once more. Tears blur my vision and one of them rolls down my neck.

I know I haven't been the best daughter, but please, please don't take him away.

I sit there until my tears stop falling, until my shoulders stop trembling. Then I go to the restroom and wash my face. The water feels cool against my skin.

When I return to the bench, only Steff is still sitting there. He holds a crumpled coffee cup in his hand.

"There you are," he says when our eyes meet.

"Where did they go?" I ask him.

"To your father's room. Do you want to go?"

I nod. I'm ready to see him now. I feel a little stronger now after crying. At the very least, I'm not on the brink of tears.

To my surprise, Steff wraps his arms around me.

"It's okay," he whispers. "I'm here."

I nod. I know. And I'm glad he's here. His mere presence gives me an added ounce of strength, that extra ounce that keeps me standing.

He holds my hand and leads me down the corridor.

I follow him quietly, slowly.

Finally, he stops in front of a door and steps aside. I draw a deep breath and knock before opening the door.

Keith and Laura turn their heads towards me. Sitting by the bed, Mom keeps talking to Dad.

"How many times have I told you that you should take better care of yourself?" she scolds him. "But you never listen, do you?"

He smiles at her weakly.

Mom sighs.

Dad's eyes meet mine.

"Jess," he says my name.

It sounds more like 'Jesh', and just that tiny detail tugs at my heart. Still, I force a smile as I step forward.

"How are you feeling, Dad?"

He gives me a shaky thumbs-up sign, but I can tell he's weaker now. It seems as if he's aged years in just a few hours.

I swallow. "I'm glad. And I know you'll be fine. You probably just got too happy that Keith and I are home."

"Or that you got engaged," Laura says.

My eyes grow wide. "But-"

"Lau...ra," my father interrupts.

"Sorry," Laura mumbles.

Dad glances past me at Steff. Then he turns to Mom.

"Could leave us... alone?"

I look at my dad with wide eyes.

Mom nods. "I should go home and get some of your stuff. Dr. Partridge said you'll be here for around four days."

"I need to change Lucia's diaper and get back to Raffy," Laura says. "But I'll come back later, Dad."

"I'll be just outside," Keith says.

He squeezes my shoulder and puts his hand on Steff's to usher him out of the room. But Dad struggles to lift his hand. His eyes let out a plea.

"Sht..."

I glance at Steff. "I think he wants you to stay, Steff."

Steff nods and turns around. Keith walks out the door and closes it.

I occupy the stool that Mom vacated.

"I'm here, Dad. Is there something you wanted to tell me?"

He reaches for my hand.

I take his.

"Have I told you... you're my favorite child?"

I chuckle. "Too many times."

"And that you're... talented and... beautiful... and smart?"

My lower lip quivers. "I think so."

"And that I'm p... proud of you?"

My chest aches. A lump forms in my throat.

I feel Steff's hand on my shoulder.

"Yes," I force the word out of my mouth.

"Good." Dad lets out a sigh of relief. "Seems... I've said all... wanted to say."

I squeeze his hand. "Don't talk like that, Dad. You'll be fine."

To my horror, he shakes his head.

"My body... Don't know how long... go on."

"You should stop talking, Dad," I tell him as my chest threatens to burst. "You're tiring yourself out."

"I just wish..." He glances at Steff before gazing back at me. "Could have walked you..."

He stops there, but I understand what he's saying. My throat cracks as I try to hold back tears.

Dad closes his eyes. I plant a kiss on his forehead and run out of the room before the tears fall.

Steff follows me.

"Jess."

I run down the corridor.

"Jess, are you alright?" I hear Keith ask behind me, but I ignore him as well.

I keep going until I get back outside. Tears spill down my cheeks as I stare up at the sky.

"Jess." Steff stands beside me and holds my shaking hand.

"I can't believe it," I tell him. "One moment he was fine, and then..."

I shake my head as the words fail me.

Steff pulls me into his arms. I cry against his chest.

"I don't... like seeing him... like this," I tell him between sobs.

"I know." He rubs my back. "And it's okay for you not to. It's okay for you to cry."

"He's... the one person... who's always been on my side," I sputter.

"Then be grateful. You're lucky you had a father like that."

"And yet... all I've done is... make him worry."

Steff's fingers run through my hair. "That's not true. You've made him happy and proud. He said it himself."

I shake my head. "It's not enough. I want to do something for him. I want to show him how much I appreciate all he's done for me."

But how? What can I do for my father?

Then his words come back to me.

I just wish I could have walked you down the aisle.

I pull away from Steff and wipe my eyes.

I sniff. "Steff?"

"Yes?"

I stare into his blue eyes. "Do you think we can get married?"

Chapter 18
Steff

I comb my hair back in front of the bathroom mirror and apply a small mound of gel from the bottle Keith lent me to keep the strands in place. I wash my hands to get rid of the sticky substance before straightening my tie. From the glass, a pair of placid blue pools stare back at me.

Well, they look calm enough, but beneath the surface, I can barely quell the unease that's entwined with every nerve in my body.

I draw a deep breath.

Am I really getting married?

Ever since I can remember, I've known it would happen. My governesses kept talking about it. I kept hearing the maids wondering which woman from which noble family I'd end up marrying. Last I heard, all bets were on Yrena, the daughter of the Duke of Olvant, who also happens to be the sister of Osvald, my brother's attendant and best friend.

Well, Yrena isn't bad. She's beautiful and she's kind. She's not as pompous or spiteful as a lot of the other women in court. By all accounts, she's the right choice-but she's not my choice. And I've told myself I would never get tied to a woman not of my own choosing. I've told my parents on a few occasions, too.

True, Viktor was able to stomach it, and he even fell hard for Natasia. But I'm not like him. I can't do that.

When I get married, it will be to my own chosen bride on my own terms.

Or so I thought.

I grip the edges of the sink and let out a sigh.

My family and Danni would certainly freak out if they found out what I'm about to do. Why, the whole country would.

Then again, this ceremony is just a sham. Lisbeth helped us find someone to play the role of a parson, and I helped to pay him off. There are no papers to be signed. Even if there were, they wouldn't be valid since I'm not using my real name and I don't have the necessary supporting documents from my embassy.

It's all just for show, really, all for Jess's dad.

Still...

I glance at the empty finger on my hand.

This is all not real, huh?

Well, real or not, I've told Jess that I'll go along with her plan, and I intend to do just that.

How can I not, after hearing her father's wish from his own pale lips and after seeing all her tears?

A knock on the door breaks into my thoughts.

"Steff?" It's Keith. "You're still there, aren't you?"

I turn around and open the door.

"Did you think I jumped out the window?"

He glances at the window and scratches his head. "Well, I won't say you couldn't have done it."

I fold my arms over my chest. "As flattered as I am by your assessment of my physical abilities, I am not running away from your sister."

"Are you sure?" Keith's expression and tone turn serious. "I know you just got engaged recently. I also know why Jess is doing this."

He sighs.

"Seriously, that girl and her crazy ideas, which is what this is, so I wouldn't blame you if you tried to run away."

"I didn't and I won't," I assure him. "I'm here for Jess."

Keith strokes his freshly shaved chin. "Well, you did come all the way here."

He puts his arm around me.

"Come on. We better go downstairs. I'm your best man, so it's my job to make sure you're there before the bride is."

I raise my eyebrows at him. "You are?"

"Well, your brother couldn't make it from Brelv, so who else would it be?" He pauses. "But I guess you're Jess's best man now."

I narrow my eyes. "You're not going to cry, are you, Keith?"

"Me? Cry?" He laughs out loud. "Like I would do such a thing."

He pats my shoulder and walks on ahead. Then he stops again.

"You will take care of Jess, won't you?"

My eyebrows arch. Just as I thought, Keith really cares about Jess. Well, he is Jess's big brother, after all.

"You have my word." I squeeze his shoulder as I pass him by. "Let's go."

~

The front yard has been turned into a wedding venue for the ceremony. A short white carpet covered in flower petals leads from the porch steps to an arch of flowers, and baskets of fresh flowers line the sides of the walkway.

There are already people gathered-neighbors, Don and Maggie's friends, Laura's friends. Even though Jess wanted the wedding to be a relatively secret family affair, Maggie and Laura still managed to gather a small crowd.

That small crowd falls silent as I make my way to the arch. Wide, unfamiliar eyes stare at me. Then whispers erupt into the air.

I sigh.

Keith pats my shoulder. "I guess they can't believe Jess managed to hook a guy like you."

Finally, a familiar face appears in front of me.

"Steff," Lisbeth greets me. "Nice suit."

It's not as nice as the purple pinstripe one on the dark-skinned, thirty-something man she's with, but I accept the compliment graciously. "Thanks. And thanks again for all your help."

"No worries. By the way, this is Raymond." Lisbeth gestures to her companion. "He's the one officiating today."

I shake his hand. "I'm counting on you."

I glance around. "So you're her only friend who came, huh? No one from the band?"

She leans over to me and whispers in my ear. "She said that she wanted as few people as possible to know about it."

Well, it is a sham, after all.

Keith steps up and shakes her hand. "So you're Lisbeth, huh? Thanks for watching out for Jess."

"Oh, we watch out for each other," Lisbeth says with a smile. "And I've heard so much about you."

"Really?"

I leave the two of them alone to chat and step under the arch. Raymond stands beside me.

I stare at the front porch and let out a deep breath. After a few moments, the front door opens and organ music drifts out from inside.

I inhale.

This is it. The ceremony is finally starting.

Laura comes out first in a peach dress with two kids in tow. Then Maggie in a floral dress. Finally, Jess emerges holding Don's arm, supporting him as he takes one step after another with the help of his cane.

I suppose she's walking him down the aisle instead of him walking her, but it doesn't matter. Don looks better than he has in the past few days. And he looks happy.

And Jess...

I hold my breath as I stare at her in that sleek, white dress. The boat neck emphasizes her elegant collar bones but doesn't reveal too much skin. Her knee peeks through the slit of the skirt that flows around her. The hem rustles above the carpet.

Her hair is swept up and long crystals dangle from her ears, the only piece of jewelry she has on apart from my ring. Colorful flowers bloom within some of the strands.

To think that this is just the second time I'm seeing her in a dress.

Just as I thought, it suits her better than a shirt and pants.

Jess smiles as she walks. Her rosy cheeks glow.

She's mostly looking at her dad, but when our gazes finally meet, my heart stops. A lump forms in my throat.

Who would have thought she would make such a ravishing bride?

I step forward to shake Don's hand as they approach. After Maggie leads him away, I offer Jess my arm. She hands Laura her bouquet of lilies before taking it and allowing me to lead her under the arch.

The music stops and Raymond clears his throat.

"Dearly beloved, we are gathered here today..."

~

"Congratulations," Laura greets Jess and me after the ceremony. "I wish you both all the best."

"Thank you," I tell her.

She looks at Jess. "In the end, we didn't get to do much planning, but it was okay. Right?"

"It was beautiful," Jess assures her. "And I appreciate all your help, especially this dress you lent me."

She gives a whirl and her skirt billows.

"Hey, don't ruin it," Laura says. "I still want it back."

"So that's why it looked familiar." Keith touches his chin. "Although I must say it looked better on Laura."

Jess pouts. "You never get tired of teasing me, do you?"

He places his hand on her shoulder. "Well, married or not, you're still my little sister."

She glares at her. "Who are you calling little?"

He looks at her chest. "Well, certain parts of you still are..."

She hits him with her bouquet.

"Hey!" Lisbeth shouts from a few feet away. "If you're just going to destroy that, give it to me."

Jess tosses it. Lisbeth catches the bouquet and hugs it with a wide smile.

"Anyway..." Keith clears his throat. "I wanted to give you guys this."

He hands Jess an envelope.

Jess stares at it. "What is it?"

"Open it," Keith urges.

I look over Jess's shoulder as she opens it and two plane tickets appear.

"Tickets?" Jess's eyebrows crease.

"I figured every married couple needs a honeymoon," Keith explains. "No matter how rushed their wedding is."

Jess looks at him with wide eyes.

I narrow my eyes at him. "A honeymoon?"

"In Florida," Keith answers. "My friend happens to have a villa in New Smyrna Beach, which is just near Orlando, and he said I could borrow it. Well, technically I reminded him that he owes me big time and then he said I could borrow it, but..."

Jess wraps her arms around him. "Thank you!"

She pulls away and gives me a hug of my own.

"I can't believe we're going to Florida!"

Florida, huh?

My gaze falls on the tickets in her hand.

It seems the real adventure has just begun.

Chapter 19
Jess

"Woohoo!"

I let loose the scream at the top of my lungs as I gaze at the ocean stretching endlessly before me. The turquoise surface glimmers under the glaring sunlight. The white-tipped waves rise and fall like the heartbeat of the ocean. One of them crashes around my bare feet and buries them in sand. The cool water clings lovingly to my ankles before ebbing away.

I close my eyes and breathe in the salty air. The breeze kisses my cheeks and blows my floppy straw hat off my head, but I manage to catch it just before it drifts away. I hold it firmly as I stare at the cloudless sky through the amber lenses of my sunglasses.

"Jess!" Steff shouts behind me.

I turn around and find him standing on the porch of Keith's friend's house in his sunglasses and shorts. The corners of his barely buttoned Hawaiian shirt flap in the wind.

"Isn't it too hot to be out on the beach?" he asks.

I hold my arm under the sun and wince.

He's right. It's just past noon, so the sun is directly overhead. And even though I have my hat and sunglasses on, it's not enough. I didn't apply any sunscreen.

I run back to the house, picking up the shoes I've discarded along the way. After a few steps, the soft sand begins to scorch my feet, making me feel like I'm walking on burning coals. I run faster. As soon as I get to the porch, I sit down on the steps and breathe a sigh of relief.

"What were you thinking?" Steff asks me as he hands me a small towel to dry my feet.

"That I haven't been to the beach in a while," I answer.

"I thought there were beaches in LA," he says. "I'm pretty sure I saw some in a brochure."

"Yeah, but they're crowded."

And I'm not confident enough to be around strangers in my swimsuit. This beach, on the other hand, is private. For now, it belongs just to Steff and me.

Thank you, Keith, for always coming through for me.

"Are there beaches in... where you're from?" I ask Steff.

"Yes. But the water is cold most of the year. It's only during the height of summer that people can swim, so the public beaches are crowded during that time. I do know a private, secluded cove, though."

I get up. "Oh. You mean the one reserved for the rich kids?"

"Sort of."

I frown. He doesn't even deny it. Well, at least he's honest.

I stretch my arms and peer into the glass. "So, how's the house?"

"Good," Steff answers. "There's a guitar upstairs."

"A guitar?"

I try to rush inside, but Steff's arm blocks my path.

"What?" I scowl. "My feet are clean now."

"That's not it," he says.

In the next moment, he takes me in his arms and carries me into the house. He sets me down in the living room.

"Isn't the groom supposed to carry the bride over the threshold?" Steff asks me.

I blink. A blush coats my cheeks as I remember how he looked in his suit yesterday as he stood under the arch of flowers.

He was dazzling, like the light at the end of a tunnel.

I turn away from him and cross my arms over my chest. "Make no mistake. We're not really married."

"I know."

Still, there was a moment back there, that moment when he slipped the golden band onto my finger, that everything almost felt real. My heart skips a beat at the memory.

I lift my hand to look at the simple golden band and then at the other, more elaborate ring that I'm wearing.

477

I take it off and hand it to Steff.

"I should give this back to you. After all, we're not engaged anymore."

He steps back and raises his hands in the air.

"Keep it. It's bad luck to give it back."

"Oh." I stare at the ring on my palm. "But..."

"So soon," Steff adds. "Wear it for now. After all, it's not like we're parting ways already."

I nod and slip it back on. "Okay."

He sits on a chair. "What do you plan on doing for the rest of the day?"

I touch my chin. "Well, it's too late to go to Orlando. And we're too tired from our flight to go sightseeing anyway. I say we go out and buy some food. After that, we'll come back, stay here and do something we haven't been able to do in a while."

Steff's eyebrows crease. "And what's that?"

I slump into a chair. "Relax."

~

Now, this is relaxing.

I stare up at the moonlit sky as I float on the surface of the pool. The calm, warm water all around me creates a thin sheet over my skin and my swimsuit and forms a barrier over my ears that muffles the sound of everything else.

I close my eyes and surrender to it, willing it to melt all my exhaustion, all my tension and troubles away.

The past weeks have been stressful, what with having to handle my new roommate and then dealing with Dad's stroke and then having to pretend to get married.

Now, finally, I can rest and relax.

I let out a sound between a sigh and a moan.

I could do this all night.

Or so I think until I feel a drop of water on my cheek, then another on my forehead.

Is it raining?

I open my eyes just as more water splashes over me. I straighten up and wipe my face with my hand. As my toes touch the cold floor, I turn around and see Steff standing at the edge of the pool in...

Nothing. He's completely naked.

My eyebrows furrow. "What the hell are you do-?"

I don't finish, because he jumps into the pool. I turn away in time to let the water splash on my hair.

"What are you doing? I thought you were asleep."

"I was, but I woke up and thought I'd check on you." Steff walks towards me. "You looked so serious, so I thought I'd help you relax a little."

"I was relaxing," I tell him with a glare.

He answers by giving me another splash.

I frown. "Oh, is that what you want, huh?"

I splash some water at him, too. It lands right on his face and I laugh.

Steff frowns. Then slowly, his lips curve into a grin.

"Oh, it is on."

He splashes at me as I turn my back on him and give him another splash. I swim away and he follows me.

"You're not getting away from me that easily."

He gives me another splash and I let out a squeal of laughter.

"That's... enough!"

I hold my hands in front of my face as my back hits the edge of the pool.

He throws another splash in my direction. I turn my head and squeeze my eyes shut. Most of the water lands on my palms and cheeks.

When I open my eyes, Steff is standing beside me running his dripping fingers through his hair.

At first, I let out a sigh of relief that he's finally stopped splashing me. But then my gaze drops. I catch a glimpse of his body beneath the water and my cheeks burn.

Right. I almost forgot he's not wearing anything.

I place my hand on his shoulder and push him away. "Don't get too close to me, will you?"

His eyebrows arch. Then he grins mischievously as he moves even closer.

"Why not? It's not like you haven't seen me naked before."

I move away and he follows me.

"Besides, we're a married couple on our honeymoon."

"No, we're not," I remind him with a scowl. "Don't tell me you've forgotten that it was just an act."

Steff stands in front of me. "And don't tell me you've forgotten our agreement."

My eyes grow wide.

No. I haven't forgotten.

I remember that conversation we had about our marriage very clearly. He asked me what I had to offer him in exchange for his agreeing to that fake ceremony, and I told him that I'd pay him the same way I'd been paying him.

With my body.

Steff grabs my waist and leans forward until his face is just an inch from mine. I grab his shoulders and push him away.

"Here? Outside? In the open?" I ask him. "Are you crazy? People could see us."

His blue eyes narrow. "So you're saying you knew there was a chance people could see you and you still wore that alluring swimsuit?"

Alluring?

I glance down at what I'm wearing. It's just an old two-piece black swimsuit I've had for ages. The top is a simple crisscross bandeau and the bottom has a high waist and high leg cuts.

What could be so alluring about that?

I shake my head. "You're not making any sense, Steff."

"Maybe," he agrees with me to my surprise.

His hands, which are still on my waist, go up my sides. He leans over to whisper in my ear.

"The more time I spend with you, the more I seem to lose my mind."

His tongue flicks against my earlobe. I let out a gasp.

"Don't worry," Steff whispers. "I think we're alone here, which means you can make as much noise as you want."

I frown. "Who said I'm noi-?"

His kiss cuts me off. His tongue slips between my lips and I get a taste of wine, toothpaste and chlorine.

And him. As usual, Steff tastes great.

And feels good.

His tongue glides over mine and my mind begins to spin. He plunders my mouth and my defenses melt away. Heat erupts in my chest. It flows through my veins and my body comes alive.

My hands move to Steff's neck and my fingers caress the skin there as I kiss him back.

His hands move up even higher until his thumbs reach my bikini top. He hooks them beneath the fabric and pushes it up.

My breasts spill out. I let out a moan as my nipples stiffen in the water.

His thumbs press against the engorged peaks as his tongue wrestles mine and forces it into submission. He takes the nubs between his fingers to twist them lightly and I tremble.

My fingers tug at his hair. I press my hips against his as my body pleads for more.

A chuckle escapes Steff's lips. "And here I thought you weren't in the mood."

"And whose fault is that?" I ask breathlessly.

Ever since we had sex, my body hasn't felt the same. It burns. It yearns.

It feels like I'm Pandora's Box and now all the desires and all the naughtiness I never knew were inside me have been unleashed.

Steff grins.

I narrow my eyes. "I swear if you keep making fun of me, I'll drown you in this pool."

"Well, we can't have that, can we?"

Steff starts nibbling on my neck. I gasp.

"You know you're better when you have your mouth shut," I say as I close my eyes.

"And you're better when you let your body give me the answers I need."

He captures my lips again. His hands grip my waist and then slide to my butt as he grinds against me. I moan.

Then his fingers creep to the front and slip inside my panties. His knuckles brush against my nub.

I step back with a jolt. A gasp escapes my gaping mouth.

Steff kisses my neck again as he starts teasing that nub.

My knees wobble and I lean against the edge of the pool.

One of his knees slides between mine. His fingers move lower, and one of them slips inside me.

I grab his shoulders.

Even though we're immersed in the water, I can feel myself getting wetter, coating his finger. He slips in another and I let out a cry. My skin burns and I wonder if the water might boil.

Once again, Steff seals my mouth with his. His fingers move in and out.

Feeling weak but not wanting to surrender, I reach for his crotch. My fingers wrap around his hard cock.

He grunts but continues to stroke me. I moan and start stroking him.

For a while, our tongues mingle as our hands work in tandem. It's as if we're moving-dancing-to one rhythm. My hips move on their own as I melt from the inside out. His cock quivers against my fingers and makes them sticky.

Then Steff stops. He turns me around and pulls down my bikini bottom. Then he grips my hips and enters me from behind with one thrust.

I let out a cry as my fingers grip the edge of the pool. My toes curl. The soles of my feet rise off the floor.

This position... it's strange.

Steff seems to be going in deeper. He seems to be more in control.

I'm losing my mind.

I squeeze my eyes shut. My nails scrape the stone.

Steff moves faster. I hear his balls slapping against my skin and the water splashing faintly around us. I feel my breasts swaying beneath me. They tingle as they seem to grow heavier.

When Steff cups them in his hands as he thrusts into me, another cry spills past my lips. His fingers lightly pinch my nipples and I'm swept away.

My body trembles as wave after wave of pleasure washes over me.

Still, Steff moves behind me, pounding into me. His fingers dig into my hips.

Just when I feel I'm about to break, he grabs my leg and lifts it.

His cock plunges deeper and hits a spot inside me that sends fresh ripples of heat throughout my body.

"God!"

The word escapes me as I feel another huge wave of pleasure sweep me away. This time, as I tremble, Steff trembles as well.

He lets my leg down and manages a few more thrusts before pushing in deeper. Heat explodes inside me. His ragged breathing sounds in my ears.

As soon as Steff pulls out, I feel my legs grow weak and I grip the edge of the pool to keep myself from drowning. I fold my arms and use them as a pillow beneath my head as I catch my breath. My eyes refuse to stay open.

I feel Steff's arms around me. He's carrying me again like I weigh nothing. He lifts me out of the pool.

The breeze caresses my wet skin and I shiver. But the sound of Steff's heartbeat fills me with warmth. It echoes in my ears along with the roar of the waves in the distance.

And once again, I'm floating.

Chapter 20
Steff

I sink into the couch and run my hands through my hair in frustration.

What have I done?

Last night, I lost my self-control with Jess.

As soon as I stepped outside, I saw her floating on the surface of the pool in those skimpy pieces of clothing that barely covered her body, and my blood simmered. I saw her skin gleaming under the moonlight, her hair scattered around her head. I saw her in such a state of surrender that it inevitably awakened my desire to take. And when she let out that moan, I couldn't just keep away.

So I took her. Right then and there. I gave her body pleasure with my own.

But I should have been more gentle.

By the time I realized it, it was too late. Jess was already on the verge of passing out, and all I could do was carry her into the house, dry her off and tuck her to bed.

I went to my own bed afterward, but I could barely sleep. The voice in my head, the voice of guilt, kept haunting me, scolding me.

I sit back against the couch and let out a sigh.

What have I done?

The sound of footsteps coming down the stairs makes me sit up. Moments later, Jess appears in a striped robe.

She yawns. "Good morning."

"Good morning," I greet her softly. "Did you sleep well?"

"I think so, although I remember feeling cold during the night."

Jess wraps her arms around her.

I stand up and walk over to her. "I'm sorry."

Her eyebrows arch.

I bow my head. "I shouldn't have been so rough."

For a moment, Jess says nothing. Then she sighs. "It's fine."

I look up. "But..."

"I owed you, didn't I?" She meets my gaze. "Now the debt is paid."

I slap my forehead.

So Jess let me have my way with her just so she could pay her debt? I wasn't even serious when we made that agreement.

"I still should have been gentler," I tell her through gritted teeth. "I should have controlled myself."

"Well, it wasn't so bad," Jess says softly.

She rubs her arms as she gazes into the distance. A blush coats her cheeks.

My eyes grow wide.

"What I mean is that it's good to know that even you can lose control," she tells me as she meets my gaze. "What's wrong with that? I lose control of my temper all the time. It just means you're human."

I frown. "Even so..."

Jess pinches my cheek. "Enough with that already. As you can see, I'm fine."

My eyebrows crease as I rub my cheek. "Are you sure?"

Jess rubs her lower back.

"Well, I'm a little sore down there, and my back aches. Maybe I pulled a muscle. And my stomach seems a little upset this morning..."

"I'm sorry," I apologize again with my head bowed.

Jess lets out a chuckle. I lift my head.

"I was just kidding," she says. "Geez. You're acting strange."

I just stare at her.

"If you're feeling that guilty, just be more gentle next time."

Next time?

Heat stirs in my crotch at the thought.

I shake my head. No. I have to calm down. If I don't, I'll mess up again next time.

"Anyway, let that be the end of it."

Jess walks to the kitchen.

"Are you sure you're fine?" I call after her. "You don't want to stay at home?"

"No way," she tells me over her shoulder. "We've got amusement parks to visit, remember?"

~

She really does love amusement parks, I think as I glance at Jess towards the end of the Rock N' Roller Coaster.

Today, our fourth and last day in Florida, we decided to visit Disney's Hollywood Studios. Yesterday, we spent the whole day at Universal Island of Adventure, and the day before that, we were at Legoland.

I can tell she's been having lots of fun, which has made the experience fun for me as well. She's had nothing but a smile on her face, and she seems to be full of boundless energy as she drags me from one ride to another.

Then again, even when we were in Disneyland, she was already having fun. In some ways, she really is like a little girl. Amusement parks must bring out the child in her, full of wonder and excitement. It makes me want to be like a child as well.

"Why are you smiling?" Jess asks.

My eyebrows go up. I didn't even realize I was smiling.

"I'm just glad to see you having fun again," I tell her.

"Well, to be honest, there were times when I thought of my dad," she says. "Because he's the one I used to go to amusement parks with. But I just kept thinking that I want to remember him just as he was during those times and that I should be happy that we had such wonderful times together."

"That's the spirit," I cheer her on.

The ride stops and we get off. I hold her hand as we walk towards the exit.

"So, do we go around one more time, or-?"

"Your Highness!" The shout comes from the queue on the other side, the one that leads to the entrance of the ride.

I freeze.

Fuck. Did someone just recognize me?

Well, Orlando is a popular tourist destination, after all, so some Brelvans must visit. And of course they'd recognize me.

Why didn't I think of that?

"Steff?" Jess looks at me.

I take her hand and run.

"Your High..."

The voice fades as we leave the ride. Still, I keep running until we're far from it, almost at the park entrance. Only then do I stop and let Jess's hand go. I sit on a bench as I catch my breath.

She sits beside me, panting. "What... on earth... was that?"

I shrug.

"Wait. That woman... called you 'Your Highness', didn't she?"

My eyebrows shoot up.

Jess heard?

"Maybe she was at Disneyland, too, and she recognized you?"

I look at her.

Right. I was a prince there.

I smile. "Yeah. I thought that was it, and I didn't want her to make a fuss over it, so I ran."

"Still, did you have to run this far?"

"Sorry."

Jess sighs. "It's your fault you like being in the spotlight so much."

"Hey," I complain. "I wasn't the one who asked to be in the spotlight that time."

"I know. I guess you just looked too much like a prince. If we had gone to Magic Kingdom, they might have asked you to play the part again."

I fall silent.

Is that why she didn't want to go to Magic Kingdom?

"Anyway, I'm tired now." Jess stands up. "So how about we get dinner and head back? I want to spend our last night in Florida on the beach."

~

I hug my knees to my chest as I stare at the invisible horizon. The sand feels cool beneath my feet. The salty wind blows through my hair.

I listen to Jess playing the guitar against the background of the rolling waves. When she's done, I applaud.

"You really are a talented guitarist," I praise her.

Jess smiles. "I'm not as flashy as you, though."

"You're right," I agree with her. "And that's why your music can reach the hearts of your listeners even more than mine can. The people who watched me play with your band were in awe of me, but those who hear you play end up getting moved."

She falls silent.

Even under the moonlight, I can see the rosy hue on her cheeks.

I grab a handful of sand. "Have you figured out what you're going to do after your band breaks up? Are you going to join another band? Or start your own, maybe?"

She shrugs as she sets the guitar down beside her.

"I don't know yet. All I know is that I can't give up music."

"And you shouldn't," I tell her.

Suddenly, the sand spills from my fingers as an idea comes to me.

What if I help her get signed with a record label? Surely someone I know must know someone. And if connections don't work, maybe I can pay someone to give Jess a chance? But she wouldn't like that, would she?

"I don't want to think about it, though," Jess interrupts my thoughts. "I don't want to worry about a thing right now when I'm having so much fun."

I nod. "I'm sorry I brought it up."

Jess glances at me. "Now who's being overly apologetic?"

I grin.

"I've really had so much fun here in Florida." She leans back on her arms and crosses her ankles. "And it's all thanks to you."

"Me?"

"If not for our wedding, we wouldn't be having this honeymoon," Jess answers.

"Won't Keith be pissed off when he finds out we're not really married?"

Jess frowns. "Probably, but if you ask me, it's only fair. He hasn't given me a present since my seventh birthday, you know, so he owes me."

"Okay..."

"Besides, if he finds out, he'll be more pissed off that we lied to him," Jess adds. "And he'll probably be most pissed off at you."

I frown. I hope it doesn't come to that.

"What about you?" Jess asks.

She lies down on the blanket with her arms behind her head.

"Did you have fun?"

I nod as I mimic her. "Tons. And not just here in Florida. Even in Prairie du Chien. Well, not fun, exactly, but in spite of everything that happened, I'm glad I was there."

"Really?"

"I feel like I know you better now."

"It's unfair," Jess complains. "You know me better, but I still feel like I don't know you well."

She turns her head towards me.

"Tell me..."

"What?"

"Tell me something about you that I don't know already."

I pause. My heart screeches to a stop in my chest.

This is my chance to tell Jess who I really am. If I do, I won't have to run for fear of discovery the next time someone recognizes me.

And a part of me wants to. A part of me doesn't want to hide secrets from her any longer.

But the voice of reason prevails in my head.

If I tell her who I am, she'll be upset with me for not telling her in the first place. And then she'll start treating me differently. She'll distance herself from me. She'll probably even kick me out of the apartment.

No. I can't tell her. I don't want to.

I don't want to leave her side.

"Well?" Jess props her head on her elbow as she turns on her side.

"I... like to ride horses," I finally tell her.

"Hmm." Jess's eyebrows furrow. "But all rich people like to ride horses, right? Tell me something only you can do, or something that's only happened to you."

"Well..." I scratch my head. "A girl once threw a whole chocolate cake at my face."

It was when Danni and I were kids and I told her I wished I didn't have her for my attendant. She got in trouble for it, but I defended her because I realized I'd been wrong.

Jess laughs. "Hmm. There's an idea."

I frown. "Don't you dare try it."

"Just kidding," she says. "I wouldn't waste a chocolate cake on you."

She lies back down.

"Speaking of chocolate cake, I haven't had one in a while. I wanted our wedding cake to be chocolate, but of course Mom had her way. She said she didn't want it to be messy. Anyway, do you want me to bring one home from the cafe when we get back to LA?"

"Sure," I answer. "If Tom will take you back after all this time."

"He will." Jess sighs. "I guess we have to go back to being grown-ups and facing reality, huh?"

"Yup." I sit up. "But hey, think of the bright side. At least you'll get to play with your band again. They must miss you."

Chapter 21
Jess

"We've missed you," Kay says as she puts an arm around me after our show, my first show since I've returned to LA. "You really are the heart of the band."

"I thought I was," Riley complains.

"No. You're the beat of the band," Kay tells him. "But you do have my heart."

She gives him a quick kiss.

"It's good to have you back," Alice tells me.

"Yeah, we should drink to it," Riley says.

He sits on his stool at the bar.

"One round of drinks for everyone, please, Benny."

I sit down and smile. "It looks like nothing has changed around here at all."

"You will play with us from now on, won't you?" Josh asks me as he occupies the stool on my other side. "After all, you told me to keep playing with you guys until the end. It's unfair if you don't do the same."

I look at him.

Strange. In the past, it would have made me so happy just to hear that he wanted to keep playing with me, but not anymore. He doesn't make my heart skip beats anymore.

Does this mean I'm over Josh now?

"I will," I promise him just the same. "If not for what happened to my dad, I wouldn't have missed any of the shows."

"Are you sure it's not because of that jerk?" Josh asks.

My eyes narrow. "Excuse me?"

"You know, that jerk at your apartment," he explains.

"Oh, right," Riley says. "Josh said that Steff is staying at your apartment. Is that right?"

"Yeah," I say. For some reason, I don't feel so flustered about that anymore. "But only because he has nowhere else to stay."

"Wow," Kay says. "You're lucky."

"Yeah," I agree. "He's a good guy, after all, once you get to know him. He's only a jerk to guys who act like one."

Josh's eyebrows arch.

I reach for my bottle of beer and take a sip.

"By the way, how's that song going?" Kay asks me. "You're still working on it, I hope."

I nod. "That's the problem. I'm still working on it. But hey, who knows? Maybe inspiration will strike soon."

From the corner of my eye, I see Josh frown.

"Hmm." Kay leans on her elbow. "I smell a budding romance."

I almost choke on my beer.

I put the bottle down. "What are you talking about?"

Kay walks over to me and places a hand on my shoulder.

"You know, a single man and a single woman staying together can't stay away from each other for too long, especially not if the man is as hot as that and the woman is... well, let's just say she's not too aware of things."

I narrow my eyes at her.

"What things?"

Kay shrugs. "What she can do."

I take another sip. "I have no idea what you're talking about."

"Exactly."

I turn to her. "You're making fun of me, aren't you?"

Kay sighs. "Never mind. How about you just tell me all the details, hmm? What is Steff like when it's just the two of you? Does he like his coffee with sugar? Does he sleep naked? Does he look even hotter when he's asleep?"

Hotter when he's asleep, huh?

I stare at Steff's face, which is illuminated by the TV screen as he snores softly on the couch.

It seems he left the TV on and fell asleep right here in the living room.

I sigh and slap my forehead. How can he be so careless? Does he think I can carry him to his room? Then my eyebrows arch as my hand falls.

Wait. Was he waiting up for me?

I glance at the empty glass of water on the coffee table beside the saucer of crumbs.

Steff has his arms crossed over his chest. His hands are tucked under his armpits.

Usually, people who are sleeping like that didn't intend to fall asleep. And if his arms haven't fallen to his sides, it means he fell asleep only a short while ago.

Steff was waiting up for me?

The thought makes my heart race, but I shake it off as I shake my head.

No way. Why would he?

Then Kay's words come back to me.

A budding romance? Is that what this is?

Well, I've never really stopped having a crush on Steff. And he no longer teases me as much as he used to. And we've both had fun times together, and shared some bad times.

My gaze goes back to Steff's face.

What are we, exactly?

I decide not to think about it right now. I'm too tired. Instead, I turn off the TV.

For a moment, I consider waking Steff up so I can send him to his room. In the end, though, I leave him alone. I simply put a blanket over him so he doesn't feel cold.

As I do, I find myself staring even more closely at his face.

His eyelids twitch ever so slightly beneath his hair and so do his thick lashes. His lower lip extends out just a little.

I guess he is hot even when he's asleep. I don't know if he's hotter when he's awake, though.

I step away from him and pick up the dirty dishes to put them in the sink. I yawn and stretch my arms as I go to my bedroom.

I should get some sleep, too.

~

I wake up to the sound of a rap on the door.

With a yawn, I drag myself out of bed. I get to the front door at the same time that Steff does. I open it and find the FedEx guy standing just outside.

I greet him with a smile. "Good morning! What a surprise!"

Inwardly, I wonder what he's doing here so early.

Then I glance down and see the parcels at his feet. Some of them are wrapped in ivory and silver wrapping paper with white ribbons. One of them even has a huge tag that has 'Best Wishes' and my name and Steff's on it.

My jaw drops.

No.

I told Laura that Steff and I didn't want any presents, so we left them back at home. What are they doing here?

"These were sent Priority Overnight," the guy explains with a stroke of his mustache. "Wedding presents, it looks like. Congratulations, you guys!"

He walks off. Steff and I look at each other bemusedly and then start carrying everything inside.

When we're done, Steff pats my shoulder. "I'm going to take a shower. I feel dusty and sweaty after carrying so much stuff."

I nod. "I'll take a shower after you."

Steff walks off. I go to the kitchen to get a glass of water. I take it to the living room and sit down on the couch. I reach for the remote, about to turn the TV on, when I spot the pile of wedding presents.

I might as well open them.

I go over to the pile and grab the largest box. I tear open the wrapping paper like a child on Christmas morning. Inside, I find a mixer.

Not bad.

I open the smallest one next. This one's so soft that I guess it must be a tablecloth. As soon as I've torn the paper, though, I realize that it isn't.

It is made of lace, dainty golden lace, but it's too small to be tablecloth.

I lift it up. It looks like a one-piece swimsuit with a scalloped neckline that plunges all the way down to... the waist? There's a ribbon around the waist as well, and delicate frills around the hips to conceal the high leg cuts. There are snap fasteners at the lowest part, too. Well, that will be convenient for trips to the restroom.

On a whim, I decide to try it on in my room. I step into the leg cuts and pull it up. It fits snugly around my waist. I lift the front up and clasp the elastic strap behind my neck. I turn my back to the mirror and realize that there's practically nothing there.

I frown. It's too revealing for my tastes.

Then I turn around and find out just how revealing it is.

My eyes grow wide.

Wait. This isn't a swimsuit. It's a piece of lingerie.

Which means it's for...

Just then, the door opens.

"Jess, it's your turn to..."

Steff stops. The comb in his hand clatters to the floor.

"What are you wearing?"

Chapter 22
Steff

The flimsy lace, like a thin layer of gold leaves all sewn together, hangs from Jess's neck over her breasts, leaving her shoulders and arms bare. Her curves peek out from the plunging neckline. Her dark nipples poke through the sheer fabric, which also hugs the soft curve of her belly. I can even make out the curls between her legs.

"Is that... a piece of lingerie?"

Jess covers her chest with her arms. "What does it look like to you?"

"What does it look like?"

Well, it looks beautiful and very... sexy.

My cock throbs in my briefs in approval.

"Never mind," Jess says as she turns her back to me. "If you know what it is, stop staring already."

But I can't.

I can see her spine and the smooth skin of her back through the gaps in her hair. I can see that line between her butt cheeks. Those firm mounds of flesh are threatening to spill out of the bodysuit just like they did with her bikini bottom.

My cock stiffens.

Jess glances over her shoulder. "Just so you know, I didn't buy it. It was in one of those boxes sent from home."

Oh? I walk towards her.

"Also, I didn't know it was lingerie when I tried it on," she says with a pout.

I chuckle. "What did you think it was?"

"A swimsuit."

"A swimsuit?"

"And just because I'm wearing it doesn't mean that I..."

I stop in front of her just to see the furious blush on her cheeks.

"It doesn't mean anything," she continues as she looks away. "It's just an undergarment, right? Like a bra and panties."

"Trust me, Jess," I tell her as I admire what she's wearing up close. "This wasn't meant to be under anything."

I've seen women in their undergarments back at home. None of them were ever this... arousing.

"Unless maybe a man's body," I say.

I reach out to touch the lace, but Jess turns and walks off.

I grab her arm. "Where are you going?"

"To take it off and take a shower," she answers.

"Or would you like me to take it off in the shower?" I offer.

Jess stops. Her lips part, tremble and then close.

"It is our wedding gift, after all," I tell her. "That means we're both meant to enjoy it."

"How can a man enjoy...?"

The rest of her sentence vanishes as her gaze drops to the tent in my robe. She swallows.

I narrow my eyes at her and whisper her name.

"Jess."

I know we're not really married. I know we're just two people living together.

But damn, I want her. And if the stiff peaks beneath the lace are any indication, Jess wants me too.

But if she really wants me, she has to reach out like she did the first time.

She scratches her cheek. "Well, I guess I do still owe you..."

I frown. That excuse again.

After all this time, she still won't admit her feelings. Even after all the times we've had sex, she still acts like a virgin.

Well, it's not like I dislike that.

If Jess needs an excuse, then fine. I'll give it to her. And I'll take what's mine.

I pull her close to me and lift her in my arms.

Jess screams. "What are you doing?"

"Carrying you to the bathroom," I tell her.

I carry Jess out of the room. Once we're in the bathroom, I set her down on her feet inside the tub. Then I shrug off my robe and step in with her.

I cup Jess's face in my hands and kiss her on the mouth. She grips my waist and parts her lips. I push my tongue in and allow it to mingle with hers. She lets out a moan.

My hands slide down to her back. I pull her closer. My fingers trace her spine beneath her hair.

Jess's hands move behind me as well. They clench around my backside. I grunt.

I move my hands to the front and follow the curves of her breasts from the sides. I squeeze those mounds of flesh and then run my thumb over the peaks through the lace.

Another moan sounds low in Jess's throat. It goes straight to my cock and a stain forms in my briefs. And this was a fresh pair of underwear, too.

Jess's palm presses against the damp cotton. My cock quivers and pushes against her hand.

She starts stroking me.

I twist her nipples lightly.

She pushes my briefs down and grabs my aching cock.

I slip my hands beneath the lace and cup her firm breasts.

She plays with my cock and I grunt.

I play with her nipples and she moans.

Suddenly, Jess pulls her mouth away, gasping for air.

"I thought we were taking a shower," she says.

She reaches behind me to turn the knob. Cold water rains down on my skin. I turn around to adjust it to the right temperature. By the time I turn back, Jess is on her knees.

"Jess?"

She wraps her fingers around the base of my cock and her lips around the tip.

I place a hand against the wall.

As the water trickles down my skin, she takes me in her mouth inch by inch. Her tongue presses against me. Heat spreads through my body.

My cock hits the back of her throat and she gags.

I look down at her and place my hand on the top of her head. "Jess, it's fine. You don't have to..."

Then she tries again. This time, my cock slides down her throat.

My hands curl into fists. The one against the wall scrapes the tiles. The other pulls at black strands. Fuck.

When she swallows, I throw my head back. The drops of water land on my face and I close my eyes. When did she learn to do this? Isn't this just her second attempt?

Suddenly, she lets go, coughing violently.

I kneel on the floor and place my hand on her cheek. As I look at her face, I see tears in her eyes. I wipe them away.

"You've done enough," I tell her. "Now it's my turn."

I sit at the end of the tub across from the shower. Then I pull her against me.

I grasp her chin and turn her head so I can capture her lips. I taste myself on my tongue and my heart races.

I play with her nipples through the lace. Now that it's wet, it clings to her like a second skin.

She moans into my mouth. I slip my hand between her legs.

I feel the buttons and I undo them. They come off with a snap.

"Well, that's convenient," I remark.

"I thought so at first," Jess says. "But now..."

Her words turn into a cry as my fingers find her nub. I tease it as I slip a finger inside her.

Jess lets out a loud gasp. Her head falls back against my shoulder. Her body trembles.

I nip her ear as I let my fingers do their work. I remember my promise and make a deliberate effort to be gentle. That, however, seems to make her shudder and gasp all the more.

I abandon her swollen nub in favor of an engorged nipple. I slip another finger inside and stroke her. Her hips begin to rock. Her head falls forward.

Through the gap between her hair, I see her tattoo.

I kiss it.

"You know, I've always wondered what your tattoo meant. It's a black butterfly, right?"

"Moth," Jess answers softly. "Butterflies... have their wings up, not spread out."

Now that I think of it, that's true, and this one does have its wings spread out.

My eyebrows crease. "Why a moth?"

Jess glares at me impatiently. "Do you want to chat, or do you want to keep going?"

I chuckle. "You know the answer."

I suck on her shoulder as I continue stroking her. Her moans fill the tub even as water splatters on the porcelain.

Then Jess turns around.

"That's enough," she says as she moves to the other end. "If you're going to do it, just do it."

My eyebrows furrow.

What ever happened to asking nicely?

"Not yet," I tell her as I crawl towards her.

The water splashes off my back.

"I want to make sure you're ready."

I crouch between her legs and start licking. My chin touches the bottom of the tub.

Jess grabs my hair. At first, she seems to be pushing away. Then she pulls as gasps escape her.

More of her sweet nectar spills out on my tongue. The scent of it saturates my nostrils.

I dig in.

I keep at it until she seems to be on the verge of going over the edge. Then I lift my head and stand up. I take off my briefs and toss them out of the tub. I offer Jess my hand.

I pull Jess to her feet and keep lifting. The tip of my cock catches on the folds of her skin and I slip it inside.

She wraps her arms and legs around me as she gasps. I wrap my arm around her and take a breast inside my mouth. Then I press her against the wall and begin to move.

Jess's hands wrap around my neck. I hear her skin rub against the tiles.

I lift her off the wall so as not to hurt her, supporting her weight with my own body. I grunt as I move my hips. The lace rubs against my chest.

I move as fast as I can. The muscles of my abdomen tense. The ones behind my legs begin to burn.

Jess grips me tighter and trembles.

"Steff!"

She cries out my name and it bounces off the walls as she squeezes me.

Damn.

I manage one more thrust into the impossibly tight passage before I feel my cock spurt inside her.

I slowly let her down and sit at the bottom of the tub. Jess sits beside me and leans against my shoulder.

We stay still and silent as the shower keeps running. The sound of the water masks that of our heavy breathing.

"Are you okay?" I ask Jess when I've caught my breath.

She looks up at me. "Shouldn't I be the one asking you that?"

"I'm fine."

I kiss the top of her head. Then I run my fingers across the soaked lace.

"You've ruined it," Jess accuses me. "You said you'd take it off, but you didn't."

"Well, the point of lingerie is to have sex while wearing it," I tell her.

She turns to me with narrowed eyes. "You seem to know a lot about lingerie, don't you?"

"I..."

"And you seem to have a thing about skimpy clothes," Jess adds.

I grin. Guilty.

"And about wet surroundings."

"Now, that's not..."

Jess stands up and pulls me to my feet. She pushes me out of the tub.

"Out!" She points to the door. "I'm going to have a shower now."

She draws the shower curtain.

I sigh.

So much for putting Jess in a better mood.

I grab my towel to dry myself off, then pick up my robe and briefs from the floor. I walk out of the bathroom and close the door behind me.

As I see all the boxes in the living room, I frown.

I guess tomorrow is going to be another busy day.

~

Is it morning already? I wonder as I hear a guitar playing in the living room.

I glance at the glowing numbers of the clock on my bedside table and realize it's not. It's not even midnight, in fact. And yet the guitar continues to play.

Jess is still awake?

I get out of bed and go outside the room.

I find Jess on the couch with her guitar. Her notebook is spread out on the coffee table in front of her.

I rub my eyes. "Aren't you supposed to be sleeping?"

Jess stops abruptly. Then she turns to me.

"I couldn't sleep, so I thought I'd work on that song. Kay seems to be getting impatient about it."

I walk over to her and peer over her shoulder. The pages of the notebook seem to have more lines now.

"Looks like you're finally getting somewhere," I say.

"Well, I have to. Our final performance is only a week away."

I squint at the lines and start reading one out loud.

"The times we-"

Jess closes the notebook and hugs it to her chest.

"Will you please not look at my song? It's my masterpiece, you know. Until I'm ready to share it, it's a secret, precious part of me."

"Okay. Okay." I step back. "But I'm glad it's coming together."

"Well, you're partly responsible for it."

My eyebrows arch. "Oh?"

"Not that I'm saying you inspired me or anything," Jess adds. "Just that... Well, a lot of stuff has happened since you came along, and..."

She stands up.

"Never mind. I'm going to bed."

Jess disappears into her bedroom with her notebook, her guitar and her red cheeks.

I grin.

She might have been a little bolder earlier, but she's still got a long way to go with being honest with her feelings.

Even so, to think that she'd write a song about me or for me!

I don't think anyone's done that before.

Chapter 23
Jess

"You're writing Steff a song?" Lisbeth asks me as we wipe the washed mugs on the kitchen table.

"I'm not writing him a song," I argue. "I'm just... Well, everything just started to come together in my head as I thought of him, and so now I'm just trying to capture stuff that we shared and..."

"You are writing Steff a song," Lisbeth affirms. "And if that's not proof you're in love with him, I don't know what is."

I sigh as I reach for another mug.

First, Kay keeps going on about Steff and me being romantically involved, and now Lisbeth insists I'm in love with him.

"Am I missing something-I mean I am still a novice when it comes to all this men and relationship stuff-or are other people just quicker to find out when you're... well, in love?"

"It's not about experience." Lisbeth puts another mug on the tray. "And I don't think finding out is your problem."

My eyebrows crease. "Then what is my problem?"

"You know how you feel. You're just... not being honest," Lisbeth answers.

I point to my chin. "I know how I feel?"

Lisbeth lets out a loud sigh. "Well, you certainly know that you don't feel nothing, don't you? Otherwise, why did you introduce him as your boyfriend and then your fiance and then ask him to marry you?"

"I only did it because he happened to be there."

"And do you only have sex with him because he happens to be there?" Lisbeth asks.

I blush.

"Are you saying you'd do it with any other man who happened to be there?"

"Of course not," I tell her without hesitation.

"Then you do feel something for him."

I reach for another mug. "Well, I used to just be annoyed at him, but now I feel at ease around him. And I was glad he was there when my dad had a stroke. And I had a lot of fun with him in Florida."

I look at Lisbeth.

"But that's not love, is it?"

She exhales. "Why? What were you expecting? Did you think you'd get swept off your feet right away and just fall head over heels? Then you're even more naive than I thought. Love isn't just one feeling. It's joy. It's pain. It's peace. It's excitement. And it doesn't always have to be intense. Sometimes it's subtle but it lingers."

"Hmm." I touch my chin. "For someone who's not married, you seem to be an expert on love."

"Don't mock me." Lisbeth suddenly wraps her arm around me.

"Hey!"

I almost drop the mug in my hand but manage to transfer it to my other one.

I breathe out a sigh of relief.

"Just because you're in love right now with a perfect hunk doesn't give you the right to be cheeky," Lisbeth says.

"I didn't..."

She pinches my cheek. "Just you wait. I'll get a boyfriend soon."

"Ouch!" I rub my cheek as I get away from her. Then I frown. "I wasn't trying to challenge you or anything, okay? I was just trying to lighten up the conversation because it was so serious."

"Love is serious." Lisbeth lifts a finger. "This is a serious conversation we're having between two serious women who..."

"I hate to interrupt such a serious conversation," Tom cuts in. "But someone's looking for Jess."

"Tom." Lisbeth gives him a smile as she faces him. "Don't worry. Even though we were having a serious conversation, we were working just as seriously."

"Who's looking for me?" I ask Tom.

"He said his name is Josh," Tom answers.

My eyebrows arch.

Josh? What's he doing here?

"Go ahead and take a five-minute break," Tom tells me.

"Thanks." I turn to Lisbeth and put the mug down. "I guess I'll be back in five minutes. Leave me some mugs to wipe... or not."

Lisbeth just frowns.

I go out to the dining area and see Josh at a table near the window. He turns his head and our eyes meet.

"Hey!" I wave as I walk over to him.

He waves back.

I pull out a chair and sit down. "To what do I owe this surprise?"

"I just wanted to talk to you," Josh says.

"About?"

"Well, I wanted to thank you again for all the things you said before. They've really helped. Marianne told me to thank you as well."

I shake my head. "I just did what a friend should."

"And are we still friends?" He scratches his head. "Because lately, I feel like you hate me and... well, things just aren't the same between us."

He places his hands down on the table.

"To tell you the truth, it bothers me."

My eyebrows go up.

Now this is a surprise.

Come to think of it, though, I guess there has been some distance between us lately. Of course, there would be, considering how close we used to be and everything that's happened.

"I just want us all to enjoy playing together and enjoy each other's company for the remaining performances, you know," Josh adds. "I mean, there are only a few left."

I nod. "I understand. And don't worry. Even though things may have changed between us, that doesn't mean I hate you. I'm sorry if you've been feeling that way."

Have I really been that harsh?

Josh touches his neck and looks away. "Well, you do have a reason to after what I did to you."

Ah. So he knows he did something wrong, after all.

"If you're sorry then that's fine," I tell him. "We can forget about it now, okay?"

"So we're still friends?" Josh asks hopefully as he meets my gaze. "But if it's not okay with your boyfriend, I'd under-"

"We're still friends," I interrupt him as I offer him my hand.

He smiles as he shakes it.

It's still a nice smile, but it doesn't shake the foundations of my being anymore.

"And more importantly, we're band mates," I add. "So let's make our final memories as a band amazing, okay?"

Josh nods.

I glance at the clock on the wall and stand up.

I still have two minutes to go, but I think we've already said all we wanted to say. The air is clear now and I even feel like I can breathe a little easier.

"I have to go back to work," I tell Josh. "See you tonight?"

He stands up. "See you."

I give him a final wave before heading back to the kitchen. Lisbeth is standing there, waiting for me with her arms crossed over her chest.

I glance at the mugs behind her. "You really did leave me some mugs to wipe."

"So?" She taps her arm. "What did he say?"

"Nothing," I answer. "He just wanted to clear the air. Frankly, I'm glad he did."

Lisbeth's eyes narrow. "What exactly does that mean?"

"It means we're going to carry on as friends, at least until the band breaks up," I explain. "Which is fine by me."

"And is it fine with Steff?" Lisbeth asks. "Or haven't you told him about your crush on Josh?"

"I don't have a crush on Josh anymore," I state plainly. "So there's no reason for Steff not to be fine with it."

"Oh?"

"Why wouldn't he be? We're not in a relationship, remember?"

"But you are sort of exclusively sleeping with each other, aren't you?" Lisbeth points out. "And you're in love. Frankly, I don't know why the two of you aren't in a romantic relationship."

I shrug as I pick up a mug. "Because he's not in love with me?"

"Jess, he married you."

"So he could have sex with me."

"And how many times have you had sex already, huh?"

I look at her. "I thought sex and love were different things."

"Yes, but..." Lisbeth scratches her head. "Forget it. If you can't figure it out, you don't deserve him."

My eyebrows arch.

Huh? What was I supposed to be trying to figure out again?

"Just hurry, though," Lisbeth adds. "Or someone might snatch him away. You know guys like him sell out as soon as they hit the shelf."

"Huh?"

"Speaking of shelf, weren't you thinking of buying a chocolate cake today? You better tell Tom not to bring it out or someone else might."

"Oh, right." I put the mug down and hurry off.

Romance is complicated. But chocolate cake? Simple. And divine.

And I did promise Steff I'd finally bring one home.

~

"It's as good as you said it would be," Steff remarks after eating a forkful off his slice of chocolate cake.

"Told you." I eat another forkful off my own. "Is it as good as the one that got thrown at you?"

"Frankly, I didn't get to taste much of that."

I chuckle. "Of course you didn't."

He touches his chin. "Maybe I should try making one."

I shake my head. "Don't even go there. Baking is tricky. And baking cakes? Very tricky. Even professionals have trouble with them."

"If you say so."

"I say so."

I grab my glass of water and take a sip.

"By the way, Lisbeth says hello."

Steff wipes his mouth with a paper towel. "Tell her hello, too. Or maybe I should drop by and say it myself?"

"No," I protest immediately. "Bad idea."

Who knows what Lisbeth might say to him if he dropped by?

"Okay," Steff accedes.

I pick up my fork. "Also, Josh dropped by. He said sorry."

I watch Steff's eyes for a flicker of jealousy but see none.

Surprise? Yes. Jealousy? No.

See. He isn't in love with me.

"Finally."

Steff leans on one arm and smiles. Then his expression turns serious.

"For his girlfriend and his child's sake, I hope he can become a better man."

I nod.

Just then, the phone in the apartment starts to ring.

Who could it be?

Steff goes over to the counter and picks up the receiver.

"Hello?"

His eyebrows arch slightly, then crease.

He puts the receiver down.

"Who was that?" I ask him.

"No one," Steff answers as he walks back to the table. "Just some static."

"A prank call?"

He shrugs.

I glance at the phone again.

Who could it have been?

Chapter 24
Steff

"You shouldn't have called the apartment," I scold Danni as I sit across from her at the elegant restaurant of the Four Seasons. "What if someone else answered?"

"By 'someone else', you mean Jessica Campbell?" Danni asks as she picks up her cup of tea.

I frown. As usual, she's well-informed.

I pick up my own cup and take a sip. "It is her apartment. Or didn't you get that little piece of information?"

"Why are you staying in someone else's apartment? And a woman's, no less?"

"Why not? You and I have adjoining quarters at the Palace. It's practically the same thing."

"It's not," Danni says firmly as she sets down her cup. "I know your place and I know mine. But she doesn't know who you are, does she, Steffan Olsen?"

I put my cup down. "Should I have told her? Should I have told everyone who I was?"

Danni sighs. "You haven't changed, Your..."

"Steff," I correct her promptly.

She meets my gaze through the lenses of her eyeglasses. "You're still as troublesome as ever."

"What? Did you think I'd become a saint? Someone worthy of your worship?"

"I was hoping you'd grow up a little more," Danni answers. "I see that hasn't happened."

I sit back in the cushioned chair.

"Why are you here? Surely you didn't go through the trouble of tracking my phone, installing surveillance cameras outside Jess's apartment and calling me here just to scold me." I narrow my eyes at her. "Or did you miss it that much?"

Danni pushes her glasses up her nose. "I'm here to tell you that you can come home."

My eyes grow wide.

"Princess Natasia is with child."

For a moment, I go still. Then I lean on one arm.

"Is she? I haven't read it in the news."

"It's good that Your... you still read news from Brelv. But this is something that hasn't made it to the headlines yet, because it hasn't been announced yet. In fact, I'm not even sure Prince Viktor knows."

My eyebrows arch. "My brother doesn't know?"

"I only know because I caught the Princess by surprise while she was holding her pregnancy test," Danni tells me as she picks up her cup of tea again. "She made me swear not to tell anyone."

"I see." I tap my fingers on the arm of the chair. "So you didn't tell my brother but you're telling me?"

"My loyalty is to you," she reminds me.

"But why hasn't she told Viktor?" I wonder out loud. "He'd surely be thrilled."

"Maybe she's just waiting for a perfect opportunity to surprise him," Danni answers. "He is busy, after all, what with the Midsummer Festival coming soon. Maybe she's planning to tell him at the Festival, for that matter."

"You mean those pretend festivities," I say.

It's supposed to be a week for the Brelvan nobles to come together with each other and mingle with the common folk, but all the nobles ever do is squabble at court and try every means they can think of to curry favor with my father and brother.

"Anyway," Danni goes on after clearing her throat. "I believe you theorized before you left that she was threatening your life because she felt threatened herself, because she did not have an heir. Now that that is no longer true, it makes sense for you to come back. If you return at once, the King may even be lenient with you."

I pause to think. Then I shake my head. "I won't."

"What?"

Danni's cup hits the saucer with a soft clatter.

"I'm sorry, Danni, but I'm not going back," I tell her. "Not yet. Yes, Natasia may be pregnant, but who's to say she'll be satisfied with that? Besides, my return may upset her, and she can't be upset in her condition. I have to wait until the new Prince or Princess is born."

Danni leans forward. "But that won't be for nine months."

I clasp my hands on the table and exhale. "It can't be helped. I started this plan. I have to see it through."

"But..."

She puts her hand on the table and stands up, but stops as her gaze falls on my hand.

Shit.

I quickly pull my hand back under the table, but it's too late.

She's noticed.

Danni sits down. "Where is your ring?"

"Someone is keeping it safe for me," I answer.

"Jessica?"

I snort. "She doesn't like being called that."

"She's the real reason you don't want to come back, isn't she?" Danni asks. "Is she also the reason you cut your hair?"

I say nothing.

"She's bewitched you, hasn't she? She lured you to her bed and filled your head with fantasies so that you'd give her your ring. How could you?"

I lift my hand. "Calm down, Danni."

"This is unacceptable." She shakes her head. "She is not even Brelvan. And she..."

"Danni," I interrupt her. "I'm warning you. If you speak ill of her..."

"Does this mean you don't plan on coming back at all?" Danni asks with a worried look. "Are you renouncing your claim to the throne?"

"No."

"Are you marrying her?"

I don't answer.

We are married. Well, sort of. Danni would freak if she found that out.

Danni walks over to me and grabs my hand. "We're going back."

"No." I pull my hand away.

"Your High-"

"I said no!" I raise my voice.

A hush falls over the room as heads turn in my direction.

I take a deep breath and lower my voice. "Danni, I'm not going back with you."

"Because you've fallen in love with her?"

My eyebrows go up as her words take me by surprise. Then I close my eyes and grin.

Ah, Danni, you know me so well.

"It will not do," she says. "I will tell the King."

I open my eyes and meet her gaze. "No, you won't."

"You are a-"

"I know very well who I am," I tell her as I stand up. "But you, perhaps, have forgotten it. I will not go back, and you will not speak of it further. That is an order."

With that, I march out of the restaurant.

~

Later, at the apartment, I regret my actions. Maybe I shouldn't have left Danni like that. She only followed me here because she was concerned about me. She's known me since we were children and she's been loyal to me since she pledged herself to me. She's done everything I've asked her to do and a lot that I didn't need to ask. Yes, she's difficult sometimes and we've argued, but never like this. I shouldn't have treated her like that.

Oh, Steff, what have you done?

"Steff?" Jess calls my name.

I turn to her. "Sorry. I was thinking of something."

"Clearly. Want to tell me what it is?"

"Nothing important. Just what I'm doing tomorrow," I answer. "Did you want something?"

"I was just asking if you wanted the last cake slice," she answers.

I shake my head. "You can have it. I know how much you like it."

Jess gives me a wide smile and runs off. She reminds me of a kid who's just been given permission to play for five more minutes.

I sigh.

If only Danni could meet Jess, she'd see what I can see in her. She'd understand me.

She'd understand why I can't leave Jess.

But they can't meet. Not until I've told Jess my secret, which I still haven't found the right opportunity to do.

Still, that's my decision. This whole trip was my decision, so I can't blame Danni for it. She's only fulfilling her duty. I can't fault her for that.

Besides, Danni is the closest friend I've got.

I glance out the window.

Tomorrow, if Danni's still around, I'll make sure to patch things up with her.

~

A few minutes after Jess leaves, I head out of the apartment as well. I walk down the street towards the corner to hail a cab but stop as I get the feeling that someone's following me.

I let out a deep breath.

"I know you're there," I say softly.

I hear footsteps behind me, then a familiar voice.

"I'm leaving this evening."

I nod and turn around to look at Danni. "Then why don't I show you around a bit before you leave? That way, you'll have some nice memories of this place."

She steps beside me and we continue walking side by side.

"I know this great pizzeria, too, where we can have lunch," I add.

Danni sighs. "If you like pizza so much, why didn't you go to Italy instead? It's a little closer to home."

"Maybe too close," I say. "Besides, the weather here is great. And it's always lively here."

"Too lively."

I glance at her and grin.

"Hey, while I show you around, maybe you can tell me everything I've missed at home."

"I would be glad to. Where do you want me to start?"

We stop at the corner and wait for the light to turn green.

"How are Celia and Charisse?" I ask.

"They weren't happy to learn you'd gone. Princess Celia wanted to come after you. If Princess Charisse hadn't talked her out of it, she might have."

I nod. "I can imagine that."

"And Princess Charisse's studies are going well. Already, there is talk that she will make one of the finest doctors in Brelv."

I smile proudly. "As I expected."

"And Princess Celia is designing most of the gowns for the Midsummer Festival."

"Really?" I throw Danni a puzzled look. "I thought Father didn't approve of her designs."

"Well, she promised to tone things down a little."

I touch my chin. "I see. Though it's not like her to back down."

"Maybe she's outgrown you."

I chuckle.

"Well, they sound like they're doing fine without me. Anyway, I should get them some presents for you to bring home. They would love that."

Chapter 25
Jess

"Ah. It must be wonderful to be in love," Lisbeth says dreamily from across the table during our break.

I glance up from my notebook.

My eyebrows crinkle. "I have no idea what you're talking about."

"Look at you, you're writing a song," she says. "Also, you've been smiling a lot lately and putting on lipstick instead of chapstick."

I quickly cover my mouth. "What has that got to do with it?"

Lisbeth chuckles.

"It only means that you've gone past the agonizing stage and now everything is roses and butterflies."

I narrow my eyes at her. "You're still not making sense. You didn't spike your coffee, did you?"

She rolls her eyes. "Fine. I'll tell you outright since your head's up in the clouds. Or up somewhere. You and Steff are finally in a relationship, aren't you? You've finally figured it out, right?"

"You got that from just my lipstick?"

"Oh, come on." Lisbeth leans forward. "You can tell me all the details, like how he introduced you to his sister and how you plan on moving to Norway."

"Me move to Norway?"

Now I feel even more confused.

"And what's this about Steff's sister?"

"Now, now, don't play dumb, Jess." Lisbeth waves a finger at me. "I know for a fact that Steff was with a foreign-looking woman yesterday."

My eyebrows arch. "A woman?"

"And that they went to that new building, the one that houses a few European consulates."

"They did?"

"My silly roommate thought they were some kind of celebrity couple and took a picture of them," Lisbeth explains. "She showed it to me last night."

My eyes grow wide. "Do you have a copy?"

"Hmm." Lisbeth takes out her phone. "She didn't send me a copy, but I think she uploaded it to the computer at home. I should be able to access that drive from my phone."

I rub my cheek. "You know, you're such a goofball sometimes that I tend to forget you're a techie."

"Shut up. I just go out of my way not to look like a geek because guys don't like girls with brains."

After a few moments, she hands me her phone.

"There you go. That's Steff, isn't it?"

I stare at the picture on the screen.

It is Steff. There's no mistaking that hair, that sense of style, or that physique. And he is with a woman, one who shares his pale complexion and has some similar facial features. She has darker hair, though. I can see the building behind them as well, with a row of European flags. I recognize it from the news.

Why did Steff go there with this woman? Who is she?

"Well?" Lisbeth puts her hand on my shoulder.

I grip the phone in my hands. "That is Steff, but I don't know who that woman is. She looks foreign, too, but I don't think she's his sister."

"What?"

"If I remember correctly, Steff said he had two younger sisters. Twins. This woman looks just as old as he is, if not older."

"Crap." Lisbeth grabs the phone and looks closely at the screen. "You're right. She does look a little older."

"Steff doesn't have an older sister," I tell Lisbeth.

"So this woman is...?"

Lisbeth gasps and covers her mouth.

"I'm so sorry, Jess."

She's thinking the same thing I'm thinking-that Steff was seeing another woman.

I feel a sharp prick in my chest.

"But hey, maybe they're just friends," Lisbeth says as she leans over me. "Maybe she's a visiting friend."

"Then why didn't he introduce her to me? Why didn't he even tell me about her?"

"Maybe he was going to. You went straight to the bar yesterday, remember? You came home late and this morning you were rushing to work and he didn't have time to tell you."

I touch my chin.

It's probable.

But then I remember how Steff's been acting strange lately, lost in thought and easily getting startled. I remember the phone call and my eyes grow wide.

Could that woman have called our apartment and asked him to meet her?

If so, Steff had a chance to tell me, but he didn't.

"Or maybe she's an ex. Maybe he was seeing her back in Norway and he's decided to cut ties with her."

I say nothing.

Maybe. But they definitely looked like they were getting along well in the picture. Also, why would he go to his country's consulate with an ex?

"He might not even know her. I mean, they might just happen to be from the same country. She might have lost her luggage and her papers and he accompanied her to the consulate to get new ones. You know how Steff is. He can't resist helping someone in need."

That's another possibility. Still, I can't shake off this unpleasant feeling that's crept into my chest and taken root in my heart.

Something is off.

And I intend to find out what.

I grab my notebook and stand up. "Sorry, Lisbeth, but I'm telling Tom that I'm going home early today."

~

I intended to talk to Steff as soon as I got back, but he's not here at the apartment.

My trembling hands roll into fists.

Did he meet that woman again? Where did they go this time?

I shake my head and take a deep breath.

No. I should calm down.

What am I even acting jealous for anyway? It's not like Steff and I have a romantic relationship.

And yet my chest aches so much I feel it's about to break and my heart is going to spill out.

I clutch the front of my shirt.

I guess I am in love with Steff, after all.

And to think that in spite of all my denial, I thought that there was a chance he'd feel the same way.

I hoped.

I run my hands through my hair in frustration.

Oh, Jess. I thought you'd become wiser, but you're still a silly naive fool.

I glance at the door to Steff's bedroom.

No. I won't make the same mistake as before. If Steff really isn't in love with me, if he'd rather be with someone else, I'll let him go. I won't hang around and hope.

But I have to know.

I go inside his bedroom and start looking through his things.

I don't really know what I'm looking for, but I have a feeling I'll know it when I see it.

Steff doesn't have much. Mostly clothes. Some of the drawers in his room are empty. One of them, though, has a phone in the back.

I grab it.

Steff has a phone? Why has he never used it, then?

I turn it on, but I can't seem to get past the security, so I turn it back off and put it back in the drawer. I keep looking.

I go through the pile of laundry in the corner. I grab the pair of pants Steff used yesterday and check the pockets. My eyes grow wide as I see receipts. Receipts for perfume, for scarves, for chocolates. And I haven't seen any of them-which means they're with someone else.

I clamp a hand over my mouth. The tears that have been pricking my eyes trickle down my cheeks.

I think of stopping my search, but then my gaze falls on an envelope under the bed.

I wipe my tears, grab it and look inside.

Travel documents from the consulate. And a ticket. An airline ticket.

The envelope drops from my hand.

So he was thinking of leaving me? He was thinking of going back home with that woman?

I hastily put the envelope back under the bed but leave everything else a mess. I head over to my room with more tears coating my cheeks, but just as I grab the knob, the door to the apartment opens.

I grow still.

"Jess?" I hear the surprise in Steff's voice. "You're home early."

I say nothing. The lump in my throat quivers.

Why? Even though I'm in so much pain, why does the sound of his voice still make me happy?

I said I'd let him go, didn't I? Then why am I hesitating? Why am I dreading it?

Why are my hands shaking in fear?

"Jess, is something wrong?" Steff asks as he approaches me.

I turn my face away, but he must have seen my tear-stained cheeks.

He grabs my hand. "Jess..."

"Don't touch me!" I pull my hand away. "Don't... Just go away."

"What?"

"I said you should just leave." I turn to face him. "After all, that's what you're planning on doing, aren't you? You were planning on going back home with your girlfriend?"

His eyebrows crease. "Jess, what are you talking about?"

"Lisbeth's roommate saw you together, so don't deny it!" I shout. "And I saw the stuff in your room, too, so I know you were with her."

Steff lets out a deep breath. "Jess..."

"Just go!" I point to the door. "There's no reason for you to stay here, after all. I'm not your girlfriend. I'm nothing to you."

"That's not-"

"Maybe just a sex friend, someone you used. Well, I used you too, so we're even, right?"

I wrap my arms around my chest.

"Let me get this straight," Steff says. "You want me to leave?"

I nod even as my mind screams the opposite.

No. Don't go. Don't leave me.

"And all because I was with another woman?"

Ah. He's not even denying it anymore.

"If you understand it, then..."

Suddenly, he grabs my face. His palms press against my wet cheeks.

I look at him and see a smile on his lips.

Why?

I glare at him. "What are you smiling for?"

"Because now I know how you feel about me."

"Huh?"

"Here I thought I'd never get your true feelings out of you, but it seems I just did." Steff strokes my cheek. "You want me to stay with you, don't you, Jess?"

I feel puzzled. Didn't I just tell him to leave?

"Good," he tells me as his blue eyes pierce mine. "Because I feel the same way."

What?

Suddenly, Steff presses his mouth to mine. The warmth spreads throughout my body and melts away my pain, my fears.

My hands stop shaking. My eyelids fall.

Steff... feels the same way I do?

He pulls away and kisses the corners of my eyes.

"Seriously, why must you always be crying?" he asks. "I don't think I've ever seen a woman cry over me as much as you."

My lips curve into a grin. "Then you should make up for it, shouldn't you?"

Steff strokes my cheek. "As you wish."

His mouth descends on mine again, and this time the kiss forces me to take a step back. I hit the door. It swings open and Steff pushes me against it as his hands drop to my shoulders. I hear the door hit the wall. I feel the wood behind me.

I wrap my hands around the back of his neck and kiss him back as fiercely as I can. Our tongues mingle and excitement flutters in my chest.

Earlier, my heart was shattering. Now, it's threatening to spill out of my chest for a different reason.

Heat swirls through my veins. And joy.

Strange. This isn't the first kiss I've shared with Steff, but I've never been as happy as I am now. Or more alive.

I push my tongue against his and moan.

I can't get enough of this feeling. I can't get enough of him.

I want more.

I reach down to cup his crotch. The heat from his cock seeps into my palm through the layers of fabric. I press against it and it quivers.

I tremble in delight.

Steff's hands cradle the curves of my breasts. His fingers find my pert nipples. Then his mouth travels to my neck as he strokes me between my legs.

I gasp. My fingers freeze around his cock.

It escapes my clutches as Steff lower his head to take one of my breasts in his mouth. His fingers free the button of my pants and pull down the zipper. Then they slip beneath my underwear in search of my sensitive nub.

When they find it, I let out a cry. My hands grip his shoulders.

Steff lifts my shirt and my bra up to lick my nipple. His other hand continues to play with the bud of flesh peeking out of the folds of my skin.

Both buds swell. My skin grows even hotter.

Then Steff slips two fingers inside me.

I shiver. Gasps escape my lips as I throw my head back against the door.

Again, Steff captures my lips. Then he looks into my eyes.

His glimmer with desire, and with something else I've never quite seen so clearly before, something that makes my racing heart stop.

Is this... love?

"Sorry," Steff says. "But I don't think I can hold back today."

I smile as I shake my head. My fingers brush away the strands of his hair.

"Then don't."

I put my hands around his waist as I give him a full kiss on the lips. Then I grab the hem of his shirt and pull it over him before pushing him towards the bed.

Steff narrows an eye at me. "Someone's eager."

I push him onto the bed and go down on my knees so my face is level with his erection.

"Look who's talking."

I pull his jeans and his briefs down and his stiff cock springs free. I wrap my fingers around it and give it a lick. The taste of soap rubs off on my tongue.

"Where were you?" I ask him before gathering the moisture on the mushroom head of his cock with the tip of my tongue.

"The gym," he breathes out.

I hold my hair back with one hand and wrap my lips around his cock. I take it slowly inside my mouth, letting it glide across my tongue and hollowing out my cheeks to make space.

Steff grunts.

I look up and see his hooded eyes and his flushed cheeks. I can see the lines running along the taut muscles of his chest and abdomen.

Come to think of it, in the past, I wasn't really paying attention to his upper body. Now that I am, the sight of it sends a fresh burst of excitement through my veins. I notice the faded scar on his left side for the first time, too, somewhere between his ribs.

I let his cock go and lift my head to kiss it. Steff shivers in response.

Then I continue. I don't really remember how I did what I did last time, but I try to fit his cock slowly inside my mouth all the way to the back of my throat. Just as it's about to push down my throat, though, Steff grips my shoulders.

"If you do that, I won't be able to last," he threatens.

I stare at him.

Half of me wants him to lose control and explode in my mouth, but the half that wants to be connected with him prevails.

Now that the bond between us feels stronger, I want to feel one with him.

I pull away.

Steff removes my shirt and pulls me towards the bed. Then he pulls off the rest of my clothes and climbs on top of me.

He kisses my mouth, my neck and my breasts. Then he settles between my legs and grips my thighs.

For the first time, I lift my head to watch Steff as he enters me. I hold my breath as he slides the tip in and then let out a loud gasp as he fills me all the way to the brim with one thrust.

"Are you alright?" Steff asks hoarsely.

I nod and put my arms around his back. My legs entwine around his waist. I push lightly against him.

"Give me all you've got."

Steff frowns and I feel puzzled.

Did I say something wrong?

Then he starts moving. Fast.

The bed creaks. The cries from my gaping mouth fill the room.

I cling to Steff as he pounds into me.

I feel on the verge of breaking, but I don't care.

My body is his to claim. My heart is his to own.

My vision blurs with fresh tears, but I strive to keep my eyes open so I can stare at his face. His eyebrows are furrowed, his nostrils flared. I can see the lines of tension on his chin.

Then Steff moves even faster, without a rhythm now, and my eyes squeeze shut as a cry escapes my throat. My hips rise as my head falls back against the mattress. My nails dig into his skin.

He manages one more thrust, even deeper than before, and then he explodes inside me. Grunts vibrate low in his throat.

When he collapses on top of me, I wrap my arms around him and plant a kiss on his shoulder.

"I love you, Steff," I whisper.

Steff lifts himself up to look into my eyes. His are the warmest I've ever seen. His lips curve into a smile and my chest tightens all over again, but it's the words I hear next that make my heart stop, melt and explode all at the same time.

"And I love you, Jess."

Chapter 26
Steff

I do love her, I think as I run my hands through Jess's hair.

Just by looking at her sleeping face, warmth and peace wash over me. At the memory of what happened last night, pride and joy burst in my chest.

I've never felt like this before. I've fancied women, yes. I've been attracted to them. I've wanted to have them.

But this is nothing like that. I don't just want to have her. I want her to give herself wholly to me and I want to give myself to her. I want to protect her. I want to be strong for her. I want to make her stronger.

I don't even know why. She's not as stunning as the women back home vying for my affections. She's rough around the edges. She's a crybaby. She has a short temper. She's a child.

But I love her just the same.

I take her hand and press a reverent kiss on my ring, which she hasn't taken off her thumb since Florida. With the gesture, I make a vow.

Jess, I will treasure you no matter what.

"Good morning." Her voice breaks into my thoughts.

I smile. "I'm sorry. Did I wake you?"

Jess shakes her head.

I brush the hair off her cheeks and stroke it. "Good morning."

She presses a kiss against my palm.

The tiny gesture reminds me of how bold she was last night, and I grin.

"You've changed," I tell her.

"Maybe," Jess says. "After all, they say love changes everything."

I shrug. "Maybe."

I slide my hand down to her jaw and to her neck. I lift her hair.

"You know, you haven't told me about your tattoo," I remind her. "Why a moth?"

"Because I'm plain and not easily noticed," Jess answers.

I frown.

"That's not true. You're only plain because you choose to be plain. If you wanted to stand out, you could."

"But that's too much trouble," she says. "Besides, when you're in the shadows, you're not afraid of them."

My eyebrows crease. "Is that the poetic songwriter in you speaking?"

"Don't make fun of me." Jess punches my arm playfully.

"I wasn't."

She glances over her shoulder. "Also, it's a moth because I like the night better than the day. Simple."

I nod. "I see."

She sits up. "And what about you? Do you have a tattoo?"

I turn around so she can see the howling wolf on my lower back.

"A wolf?" Jess takes a close look. "That's cool."

"My parents didn't think so. They threatened to have me skinned."

"What?" She runs her fingers over it. "Why did you get it?"

"I was being rebellious, as usual," I answer.

And because I wanted the pain from the needle to help me forget the pain from losing to Osvald in a tournament.

Jess moves in front of me. "And what about your scar? How did you get that?"

I glance down at my chest.

"A knife. I was careless."

The wound is already completely healed, thanks to Danni's treatment and the verise, that rare herb endemic only to Brelv that accelerates wound healing, which she applied on it afterwards.

Jess hugs a pillow and rests her chin on it. "So are you going to tell me who that woman was?"

That woman?

Ah, I remember.

"Her name is Danni. She's just a friend, although she practically grew up with me."

"Is she from a rich family, too?"

"Yes. She just wanted to see if I was alright."

"Did she try to convince you to come home?"

"Yeah, she did. But I told her I wasn't leaving you."

Jess blushes and buries her face further into the pillow.

I reach for her hand. "I'm sorry I didn't tell you about her."

Jess looks at me. "What about the presents?"

"They were for my sisters."

"Ah."

"And the trip to the consulate? What did you do there?"

"She went to talk to someone," I answer.

"And the ticket?"

I exhale. "You really went through my things, didn't you?"

She just looks at me.

"It's my return ticket," I explain. "I've had it all this time. But I'm not using it anytime soon, and not without you."

Jess looks away. Then she straightens up and scratches her head. "I'm sorry I accused you of... a lot of things."

I shake my head. "You were just jealous."

She frowns. "Don't remind me. It's an awful feeling."

I squeeze her hand. "I will do my best not to make you feel it again."

"So Danni's gone now?" Jess asks.

I nod. "She left last night."

"And is there anything else you want to tell me? Any other secrets I might need to know so we don't misunderstand each other anymore?"

I pause.

There is, of course, still one more secret. The big one.

I've been thinking about it all night. I've decided I should tell Jess in spite of my fears. I should choose trust over fear. That's what love means. Besides, only when she knows who I really am and loves me for it can this love we share be real.

But not right now.

"Actually, there is something I want to tell you," I say to her.

Jess's eyebrows arch. "What?"

"I'll tell you after your final show with your band," I promise her. "After I hear your song."

Jess frowns. "That's not fair."

"It's only a few days."

"Why not now? Why...?"

Jess trails off and clasps her hand over her mouth.

"Jess?"

She runs out of the room. I follow her to the bathroom and find her throwing up over the toilet. I gather her hair in my hand and pull it back.

The belching sounds go on for a few more minutes before Jess finally flushes the toilet and gets up. She heads to the sink and washes her face and mouth.

"Sorry you had to see that... again."

I shake my head. "It makes me feel nostalgic."

Jess chuckles. "Yeah, you did that when we first met, too."

I nod.

"Back when I thought you were a girl," she adds.

I grin. I remember it well.

"You didn't drink last night, though," I tell her with narrowed eyes. "Are you okay?"

"Yeah. I'm just..."

She wobbles and I put my arm around her to keep her from falling.

"I don't think you're okay."

"I'm just... dizzy," Jess tells me. "Maybe it's because of everything that went on yesterday."

"Well, it's a good thing it's your day off." I help her out of the bathroom. "You can rest today."

"But I need to finish the song," Jess protests. "Like you said, there's only a few days..."

She covers her mouth again.

"Bathroom?" I ask.

Jess shakes her head. "I'm just a little nauseous. That's all."

"You really should rest today. You haven't been taking care of yourself lately."

"But..."

"I'll take care of you," I promise her.

Jess's lips curve into a grin. "In that case, I'll take you up on your offer."

~

She seems to be feeling better, I think as I set the mug of coffee down on the coffee table that evening.

Jess's cheeks have more color now, and she hasn't thrown up all day. She slept all afternoon, but now she seems refreshed and she's back to writing her song.

"How are you feeling?" I ask her as I sit beside her.

"Good." She puts the guitar down. "Like I said, maybe it's just stress from everything that happened yesterday."

I nod.

I glance at her closed notebook. "How's the song going?"

"Almost done." Jess picks up the mug. "It just needs some final tweaks."

"That's good to hear."

She lifts a finger. "Don't you forget that you have something to tell me afterwards."

"I won't," I promise her.

Jess sighs. "You're keeping me in suspense, you know, so this secret better be worth it."

I shrug. "I guess you'll find out."

She frowns.

I get off the couch. "At any rate, I'm glad you're feeling fine. Maybe you just needed some pampering."

"I'm not a baby," she says with a glare.

"You sure cry like one sometimes."

Her frown deepens.

I pinch her cheek lightly. "Just kidding."

"And here I thought you'd be nicer to me."

"Because I'm your boyfriend now?"

Jess blushes.

I guess she's still not used to that word.

"By the way, I just remembered something," Jess says. "Didn't you say something about sex strengthening the immune system? Apparently, you're wrong, because I felt unwell today."

"I thought you said it was because you were tired," I tell her. "Though we could definitely have sex more often if you want."

Her blush intensifies.

I lean over to whisper in her ear. "And that's not a joke."

I start to walk off, but Jess grabs my arm.

"One more thing."

I turn around. "What?"

"You have a phone, don't you?"

So she saw that, too. Then there's no point denying it.

"Yeah."

"How come you've never used it?" Jess asks me.

I shrug. "Because I didn't want to pay roaming charges?"

Jess doesn't look convinced.

"Because I didn't want to get calls from home," I confess.

That seems to do it.

She lets my hand go. "You should use it, though, or get a new one. That way, you can call me if you need to go off somewhere, and I can call you if I need anything."

"Sure."

I was already considering that anyway.

"Also, so you can call to tell me you love me whenever you want," I add.

Jess scowls.

"Just kidding." I grin.

Then again, that doesn't sound so bad.

"This is bad," I tell Lisbeth as I sit down and rub my temples. "I'm having a headache again."

She throws me a puzzled look. "Again?"

"I've been having headaches these past few days," I tell her. "They go on and off. Also, sometimes, I feel dizzy."

"Have you been eating well?" Lisbeth asks.

"The usual amount," I answer. "I don't think I've eaten anything weird, though I do feel nauseous sometimes."

"Have you been sleeping well?"

"Well, I've been staying up late to finish the song." I put my hands down and sit back. "I finally finished it last night and I think it sounds great. You better come and hear it tonight."

"I already said I'd be there, okay? Tomorrow is my day off, after all."

"I just hope my head feels better tonight," I say. "It usually goes away, but if it doesn't, I guess I'll finally take an aspirin."

Lisbeth leans over me. "Or maybe a kiss from your boyfriend will do the trick.

I frown.

I wasn't going to tell her about it, actually, but Steff dropped by yesterday and I was forced to spill the beans. Lisbeth ended up jumping up and down so much that I had to hold her and then lie to Tom that it was because Steff had a friend to introduce to her. After all, I couldn't very well tell Tom that Steff was my boyfriend when... well, he already knew that.

Lisbeth sighs. "I wish he really did have a friend he could introduce me to, though."

I shrug. "Maybe he does."

"You think?"

Just then, the chime behind Lisbeth rings.

I stand up. "I'll get it."

"Sure?"

I grab the plate of eggs on toast, but as I lift it, the aromas of the egg yolk and the garlic from the bread assault my nostrils. A wave of nausea washes over me and my stomach churns. My head spins and the plate falls from my hand.

"Whoa!" Lisbeth catches it just in time.

"Sorry." I lean against the wall.

"Are you okay?" she asks.

The smells from the plate drift up to my nose again and I pinch it.

"Just take that away from me."

She goes off to deliver the dish. I head to the bathroom and close the door behind me. Only then do I let go of my nose. I grip the edges of the sink and close my eyes as I force deep breaths into my lungs.

Breathe, Jess. Breathe.

The scent of lavender from the freshener swirls around me and my stomach calms down. The nausea passes.

I open my eyes.

Thank goodness.

"Jess, are you alright?" Lisbeth asks outside the door.

I open it and she comes in.

She cups my cheeks. "What happened to you?"

"I'm fine," I tell her. "Thank you for rescuing the plate."

"You seemed to be allergic to it."

I shake my head. "It's not allergies. It's... The smell was just..."

Just remembering it makes me queasy.

Lisbeth gasps.

I throw her a puzzled look. "What?"

"Jess, when was the last time you had your period?"

"Last month, I think."

Or was it the month before?

"I'm not very regular. Sometimes it comes on the first week, sometimes on the third week. Sometimes, when I'm sick or stressed, it gets delayed for days, and I have been stressed and sick lately. Why?"

"And you're not on pills, right?"

My eyebrows crinkle. "No."

"And Steff's never used a condom."

My eyes narrow. "Not that I know of."

I've never seen him use one. In fact, I've never seen one out of its box.

Lisbeth grabs my shoulders. "You know what I'm getting at, right?"

"Huh?"

"Jess, you might be pregnant."

~

I stare at the blue-and-white pregnancy test I've just taken out of the box.

It feels light in my hands, and it looks relatively simple. No lights. No batteries. No buttons.

Can this device really tell me if I'm pregnant?

Pregnant.

When Lisbeth first mentioned that word, I thought it was impossible. There's no way I can be pregnant. It's never even remotely crossed my mind.

But then Lisbeth enumerated the facts to support her theory.

I'm a woman past puberty, but not too far past.

I have a boyfriend who I've been having unprotected sex with for a while now.

I haven't had my period.

I've thrown up for no reason.

I have headaches.

I feel tired all the time.

I feel dizzy and nauseous.

I hate the smell of eggs and garlic. And maybe even cilantro. And sausages.

I even remember that my breasts were a bit more tender and sensitive the last time Steff and I had sex. At the time I thought it was just because I was excited to be with a man who felt the same way for me as I did for him.

Yup. The signs were there, which was why I had no choice but to give in to Lisbeth's suggestion and buy a pregnancy test.

Now, here I am, back in the bathroom and about to try out her crazy suggestion.

But is it really crazy?

What if I am pregnant?

Am I ready to be a mother?

Suddenly, my conversation with Josh floods back.

What did I say to him again? That no one was ever ready but that everyone could do it?

Weird. It was my own advice, but I can't even bring myself to believe it right now. I sounded so confident back then, but now I'm so scared that my hands and knees are shaking.

I square my shoulders and draw a deep breath.

Before I start reacting or overreacting, I have to know the results.

I follow the instructions on the piece of paper that comes with the test, and then I lean against the wall as I wait for something to appear in the tiny white space.

Two lines means I'm pregnant.

Just one means I'm not.

I hold my breath. My heart pounds in my chest.

At first, only one blue line appears, but then I see another parallel one becoming visible.

Shit.

"Jess?"

The sound of Lisbeth's voice from the other side of the door makes me jump so hard I nearly drop the test.

"Jess, what is it?"

I stare at the two pale blue lines on the test as my back slides down the wall.

"Come on. Don't keep me in suspense. One knock for negative and two knocks for positive."

I draw a deep breath. Then I knock once.

And one more time.

Outside, Lisbeth screams. I hear cheers and applause.

And just like that, excitement overtakes the fear in my chest.

I'm pregnant.

With Steff's baby.

I jump to my feet and step outside. Lisbeth, Tom and a few of our regular customers are waiting for me.

"I'm pregnant!"

"Told you so." Lisbeth gives me a tight hug.

Then she steps back.

"Oops. I shouldn't squeeze you so tight. I might hurt the baby."

I glance down and tentatively touch my belly.

A baby.

"Congratulations, Jess," Tom says.

"Thanks," I tell him.

I glance at everyone else. They all seem to be as exhilarated as I am.

"Thank you all."

"Well, aren't you going to call Steff?" Lisbeth asks.

Good question.

I head to the staff room and give Steff a call.

He answers after two rings.

"Jess?"

"I love you," I tell him.

He chuckles. "Wow. You're really doing it."

I smile. "You'll be at the bar later, right?"

"Yup. I'll meet you there. Why? Do you need me to bring anything from the apartment?"

"No," I answer. "I just wanted to be sure you'll be there."

"Of course I will. I can't wait to hear my song."

I sigh. I've told him so many times it's not his song, but right now, I'm not in a mood to argue.

Anyway, it's partly true.

"I just wanted to be sure," I repeat. "Because, well, remember when you said you have a secret to tell me?"

"Don't worry. I haven't forgotten, although I was hoping we'd discuss that when we get back to the apartment. You know, in private."

"Okay. But I have something I need to tell you, too."

"Really? What is it?"

"It's a secret," I tell him.

"Oh. Now I see what's going on here."

"See you later. I love you." I make a kissing sound into the phone.

He does the same. "Love you too."

I hang up first, but I hold the phone against my wildly beating heart.

Now, I have three reasons to look forward to tonight-our final show, Steff's secret and my announcement.

I feel so excited I'm almost wetting my pants.

511

I take a deep breath and smile.

Tonight is going to be a night I'll never forget.

Chapter 28
Steff

I didn't forget anything, did I?

I glance around the apartment one more time to make sure, then draw a deep breath as I place my hand on the door knob.

I don't know what Jess is going to tell me-though she definitely sounded excited earlier-but depending on how she reacts to what I tell her, this might be my last day at this apartment.

I pause.

In truth, I'm starting to feel scared.

What if Jess can't accept the truth? What if she resents me for not telling her right away? What if she never wants to see me again?

Then again, I've prepared myself for that.

Whatever happens, I'm going to face it. And I'm not just going to let Jess go.

With my mind made up, I turn the knob and pull the door open. My eyes grow wide as they rest on Danni, who's standing at the doorway, about to ring the bell.

My eyebrows crease. "Danni?"

I peek out the door to check if anyone else is there. Then I turn back to Danni.

"What are you doing here? I thought you were back in Brelv."

"I was," she admits. "But then something happened."

She peers inside the apartment.

"Is Jess there?"

"No. She's waiting for me at the..."

"Good."

Danni grabs my arm and pulls me inside the apartment.

"Your Highness, we need to talk."

~

"Viktor... fell from his horse?"

I feel the blood drain from my face at the news. My breath leaves my body. A lump forms in my throat. No.

"His Royal Highness went out riding on his own," Danni goes on. "When the stable boys found him, he was lying unconscious on the ground."

"Stable boys? Riding on his own?" I get to my feet as my temper rises. "Where was Osvald?"

"He was attending to some other matter, I believe."

"But..."

"Please, Your Highness, calm down." Danni takes off her glasses and wipes them with the hem of her shirt. "This is a serious matter that needs serious thought, and if you let your emotions get ahead of you, you will not be able to think clearly."

I exhale.

She's right, of course.

I sit down.

Calm down, Steff. Think.

Well, I do send Danni off to do things for me from time to time, often things I don't want anyone else knowing about. It's not that unusual.

It is unusual, though, for the Crown Prince to be completely alone.

"Why wasn't anyone else with him?" I ask.

Danni puts her glasses back on.

"According to the groom at the stables, he was in a rush. It seemed like he wanted to be on his own."

I frown. My hands roll into fists on my lap.

I should have been there.

"How is he now?"

"His condition is still critical. It seems he hit his head. He broke a leg as well."

My fists tighten. My nails dig into my palms.

I force a deep breath into my lungs.

"How's Natasia?"

"She's locked herself up."

That's understandable. Hopefully she won't lose the baby.

"My brother will be fine," I say more to myself than to Danni. "He fell from his horse once before, remember? And he turned out just fine."

That was actually my fault. I was the one who asked him to ride with me, and then I raced him. I went too fast and left him behind. He fell trying to catch up.

"You were children then," Danni points out.

"I know. Even so, I'm sure he has the best doctors tending to him."

"Yes. Princess Charisse is helping as well."

"Then he will surely be fine," I say.

Please be fine, Viktor.

"Do you not want to go and make sure of it yourself?" Danni asks me. "Do you still not want to return?"

I don't answer.

"Even if His Royal Highness recovers..."

"He will recover," I say with conviction.

"It will not be in time for the Festival," Danni continues. "And the kingdom will worry if they don't see a Prince."

Unfortunately, Danni has a point.

"Besides, do you not wish to be by your brother's side at this time? Do you still think that your presence will simply result in chaos?"

I clasp my hands beneath my chin.

"Your Highness..."

"Steff."

"Princess Natasia is already upset, and I'm sure His Royal Highness will feel better when he wakes up and sees you there. He needs you right now."

"I know."

I know it all too well.

I place my hands on the top of my head.

I know my country and my brother need me, but I can't just leave Jess behind.

I glance at the clock on the wall.

Wait. Maybe I don't have to. Maybe after her band plays, I can bring her with me to Brelv. I can just tell her who I am there, and maybe...

"There is one more thing you need to know," Danni interrupts my thoughts.

I look at her. "What is it?"

"Prince Viktor's accident... was not an accident. Not this time."

My eyes grow wide.

"What do you mean, Danni?"

"The horse was given something. There was a needle found under the saddle."

My eyebrows go up. "Are you saying...?"

"I'm saying that an attempt was made on Prince Viktor's life," Danni states plainly as she pushes her glasses up her nose.

My jaw drops. Then I close my mouth and swallow.

"Who knows?"

"The King. The Queen. The Wolfsbane."

"And what about the others? What have they been told?"

"Simply that it was an accident."

I nod.

Again, my fists clench.

First, someone made an attempt on my life. And now, my brother's.

Still, there's no proof the two are related. Natasia was the one who wanted me out of the way. There's no reason for her to want Viktor out of the way, especially not now that they're expecting a child.

Or is there?

"I know what you're thinking," Danni says. "You're wondering if the same one who tried to poison you poisoned your brother's horse and caused this accident."

I shake my head. "It can't be."

"Can't it?"

I look into Danni's eyes.

"At any rate, whoever tried to kill His Royal Highness is still out there."

"And yet you want me to return?"

"Yes," Danni answers without a shred of reluctance. "Because I believe that you can help sort all this out. You can end this madness and help bring the man who tried to kill Prince Viktor to justice."

I snort. "I never knew you thought so highly of me, Danni."

"I'm serious," she says firmly. "You must return. Brelv needs you."

I let out a deep breath.

As much as I want to argue some more, I know I've lost. Danni speaks the truth, after all.

I found out who was plotting to take my life. Maybe I can resolve this plot as well. At the very least, I can help find out who's behind this attempt on my brother's life. And I owe Viktor that much.

Besides, what if this attempt on Viktor's life is just part of a grander plot? What if the King and Queen and my sisters are also in danger?

I must go back.

And the hardest thing of all is that I know I cannot take Jess with me.

Not now.

If I brought her to Brelv, she might get caught up in this mess. What if someone tried to kill her, too? I can't do my duty and protect her at the same time. And I will not risk her safety.

Jess must stay.

And I must go.

Danni stands up. "If you've made up your mind, a car is waiting downstairs. A plane is waiting at the airport, too."

I look at her. "You mean we're leaving right now?"

I glance at the clock.

In less than an hour, Jess's band will start their final show. I bet she's already worried about me, wondering why I'm not there.

I take my new phone out of my pocket.

Three missed calls. Six messages. All from Jess.

Should I call her and say goodbye? But if I do, I'll mess up her last show with the band.

"There's no time to waste, Steffan," Danni tells me. "We must go back."

With a heavy sigh, I turn off the phone and put it back in my pocket.

Jess won't like it. She'll cry for sure. She'll go mad wondering where I've gone.

Unless...

"I need to leave Jess a note," I tell Danni.

She hands me a pen and paper.

I scribble a note on the coffee table, then hand it back to Danni along with the pen.

"Put it there on the counter. I'll just get something."

Danni nods.

I grab the picture of Jess and me in Disneyland from the drawer of my bedside table and put it in my pocket. I grab my wedding band as well. This way, I'll be able to keep her in my thoughts and keep a part of her with me.

As for a part of me being with her, my ring should be more than enough.

It will have to be.

I walk out of the room and find Danni already waiting by the open door. I glance at the counter and see the folded note under the phone.

I tuck my hands into my pocket and draw a deep breath.

"Let's go home, Danni."

Chapter 29
Jess

I hurry home faster than I ever have before.

The sound of my ragged breathing fills the elevator. My heart ticks like a clock in my heavy chest. A glance at the mirror reflects the beads of sweat on my forehead.

And all to answer one question-Where is Steff?

He said he'd be at the bar early, so when he wasn't there an hour before the show, I started to worry. When he didn't answer my calls or my messages, I grew anxious. And when I realized he'd turned off his phone, I nearly rushed home then and there.

The only thing that kept me at the bar was my band mates and the knowledge that I was playing with them for the last time. But even that was not enough to make me play my best.

Far from it. I was distracted. I made mistakes. And after four songs, Kay told me to just leave and come back in time for the final song.

I tap my fingers on the handrail. My other hand tightens around my keys.

I sure hope I can get back in time.

More than that, though, I hope Steff is okay.

Yes, I'm angry that he didn't come to the bar. But I'm more worried.

What if something bad has happened to him?

Finally, the elevator stops. As soon as the doors slide open, I rush out. My rushed footsteps thunder through the empty corridor.

When I get to my apartment, I quickly open the door.

The first thing that greets me is darkness. The second is silence.

I turn on the lamp by the door. My heart hammers in my chest.

"Steff?"

No sign of him.

I check the bedrooms then the bathroom.

Nothing.

Where can Steff be?

I glance at the phone on the counter.

Should I call the police?

Then I see the note. I unfold it with shaking hands and hold my breath as I read.

Jess,

Thank you for everything, but we can't be together after all. I've gone home. I'm not sure if I'm coming back, so don't wait for me. In fact, it's better if you don't think of me. Some things just aren't meant to be.

Steffan

A teardrop falls on the piece of paper and blots the ink. Then another. And another. One falls on my ring, too.

Steff's ring.

I drop the note and take off the ring. I clench it in my fist as I walk to the window.

I open it and the breeze blows the tears off my cheeks. The sound of the traffic spills into the apartment.

I draw a deep breath and lift my hand to hurl the ring out. But my hand stops in midair. My arm refuses to move. My chest hurts.

Why?

Even with that note that deprives me of all hope, even with all this pain, I still can't let Steff go?

I hold the ring against my aching chest as I sink towards the floor. My head droops. My tears spill over my hand and land between my knees.

A gust of wind from the open window knocks a vase down and the smashing of the glass into a hundred smaller pieces echoes the shattering of my heart. As the water flows out to form a puddle on the carpet, I cry my heart out.

Like a moth, I snuggle against the shadows and hope to disappear until morning.

"Jess, wake up!"

The familiar voice echoes inside my head like ripples on a pond.

I force my heavy eyelids open and squint against the sunlight.

It's morning?

"Jess!"

A soft palm caresses my tear-stained cheek.

Steff?

No.

As I open my eyes, the ones I see in front of me are not the blue ones I've been wanting to see.

Just brown eyes filled with worry.

Lisbeth's.

As my mind clears, I sit up.

"Lisbeth, what are you doing...?"

I pause as I realize I'm on the floor. And then my memories return.

Right. I came home to an empty apartment, and I must have cried myself to sleep in this corner.

Lisbeth sweeps away the hair from my face.

"What happened to you?"

She looks around.

"Where's Steff?"

I shake my head. "He's gone."

"Gone?" Lisbeth's eyebrows furrow. "What do you mean he's gone?"

I see the note under a chair a few feet away and I point to it. Lisbeth picks it up. She clamps a hand over her mouth as she gasps.

"No way." She throws the note on the counter. "That note does not make sense."

"I know."

"'We can't be together after all'? 'Some things aren't meant to be'? Bullshit." She kicks the garbage bin. "Who in his right mind would write crap like that?"

I sniff and rub my swollen nose. "Steff believed in fate. He once told me it brought us together."

"That's right. Fate brings people together. It does not tear them apart. See, if Steff said that, there's no way he'd say what was on that piece of shit-paper."

Well, that makes sense. Still...

"But Steff's not here anymore. He's gone home."

"And what are you going to do about it? Cry yourself to death?"

Lisbeth offers me her hand.

"Come on. Get up. You've been on the cold floor long enough."

I grab her arm and get up on my feet. My legs ache as blood starts to flow through them again.

"Ouch."

Lisbeth sighs. "See what happens when you fall asleep sitting down? What were you thinking?"

She places her arm around my waist and I limp to the couch. I sit down and rub my legs.

"Let me get you something to eat," Lisbeth says as she heads off to the kitchen. "It's not good for a pregnant woman to starve."

I glance over my shoulder. "I'll help."

"No." Lisbeth holds a warning finger up. "You stay right there. I haven't swept the broken glass yet, and you might step on it."

Broken glass?

I turn my head and see the fragments of glass on the floor.

Right. The vase broke because I left the window open.

"How did you get in here?" I ask Lisbeth.

She picks up the keys from the counter. "You left your keys outside the door. Really, you are too careless."

I rest my head against the back of the couch. It feels good to have something soft behind me for a change.

"I guess last night, I just didn't care," I say. "Steff was gone and nothing else seemed to matter."

Lisbeth stands in front of me with her hands on her hips and a scowl on her face.

"Well, don't you dare think like that again, you hear me? If you do, I'll slap you right across your cheek."

I touch my cheek and wince at the thought.

Lisbeth sits beside me and pulls me into her arms.

"I know it hurts like hell right now, but I'm here. You're not alone."

I pat her arm and manage a weak smile. "Thanks, Lis."

She pulls away. "We are going to solve this together."

My eyebrows arch. "Solve this? I don't understand."

"What?" She narrows her eyes at me. "Don't tell me you've given up hope."

I glance at the ring on my thumb. Sometime before I fell asleep, I must have slipped it back on. I run my other thumb over it.

"What exactly do you want me to do?"

"Go after Steff, of course."

I look at her with wide eyes. "What? Are you crazy?"

"No." Lisbeth points at my chest. "You're crazy if you just let that man go."

"He left me, Lisbeth," I point out. "Regardless of all that destiny crap, Steff left me. And he's not coming back. He told me not to wait for him."

"But he didn't tell you not to come after him."

I sigh. "Why would I do that?"

Lisbeth holds my hands. "So that you can convince him to come back."

I shake my head. "But he doesn't love me anymore."

"Did the fucking note say that?"

"No, but..."

"Sweetheart, you're still new to love, so let me tell you this. Love is not something that can just be discarded or forgotten. Yes, Steff left. But what's the reason, really? I doubt it's because he doesn't love you."

I shrug.

"So you have no idea why he left?"

I shake my head. "But he said he had something important to tell me yesterday."

"Then you should find out what it is, shouldn't you? That alone is enough reason for you to go after him. Ask him what he was going to say. Demand an explanation, and then, whatever that may be, tell him you love him, that you want to be with him."

"And if he tells me he doesn't want to be with me?" I ask fearfully.

Lisbeth squeezes my hand. "Then at least you know for sure and you know why. And that way, you'll be able to say goodbye and move on."

Again, my gaze falls on Steff's ring. It's a family heirloom and yet he didn't ask for it back, so maybe that's a sign that there's still hope, that I should go after him. And if it turns out to be a mistake, then I'll just return the ring and say goodbye, I guess.

Goodbye.

Just the thought of that word makes my heart ache all over again.

"But before that, tell him about the baby," Lisbeth says.

"What baby?"

I turn my head to see Keith standing a few feet away. He looks at the broken vase on the floor.

"What happened here?"

"Why are you here?" I ask him.

"I thought I'd drop by to see you, and the door was open." Keith glances at the door. "You really shouldn't leave it like that."

"Oops," Lisbeth says. "My bad."

I frown. "You were getting mad at me for leaving the door unlocked but you left it open?"

"You left the door unlocked?" Keith asks.

He glances around.

"Where's Steff?"

I slap my forehead. "Here we go again."

"He's gone," Lisbeth explains as she gets off the couch. "He went home and so Jess here is upset, but she's okay now. She's going after him."

Keith takes the spot Lisbeth vacated on the couch. "What do you mean he went home? Without you?"

I sigh. "Lisbeth here thinks something must have happened and since he didn't say what, I should go and ask him myself."

"And what's this about a baby?" Keith asks.

I draw a deep breath. "I'm pregnant."

His eyes grow wide. "You're...?"

I nod.

"And yet he left you without an explanation?" Keith stands up. "I'm going with you so that I can punch him."

"I'll do it myself," I say.

"So you're going, then?" Lisbeth looks up from the pile of glass shards she's sweeping.

I give another nod. "But I won't tell him about the baby. I don't want him to come back with me just out of some sense of obligation."

"But he does have an obligation," Keith points out.

"I don't need a man who doesn't love me to be the father of my child," I tell him.

"And what about what your child needs, hmm?" Keith puts his hands on his hips. "Are you just going to ignore that?"

I glance down at my belly. "I'm all my child needs."

"Really?" Keith shakes his head. "You really believe that?"

"I'm with your brother on this one," Lisbeth says. "Steff deserves to know about his child. And his child deserves a father."

"And what about me?" I stand up. "Don't I deserve a chance to be happy, to be loved and not just be pitied?

I shake my head.

"I'm going after Steff, but I'm not telling him about the baby, and that's final."

"Fine." Lisbeth nods. "That's your decision."

"It is," I tell her.

Lisbeth throws the glass shards into the trash bin.

Keith turns to me. "So you're going to Norway?"

"It's not Norway, remember?" I answer. "I believe it's Brelv."

"Brelv? Oh, right. But what about travel documents?" Keith asks. "You're talking about going to a different country here, one you've never been to before. Do you even know where Steff lives? How will you find him."

I shrug. "I guess I'll have to go to the Brelvan consulate. Maybe they can help me."

"I'll go with you," Keith offers.

I nod.

"But first, breakfast," Lisbeth cuts in. "A pregnant woman needs her strength, especially when she's going after the man she loves."

I gaze out the window.

Going after the man I love, huh?

It sounds like something from a movie, although in movies, it's usually the man who goes after the woman he loves.

But I guess I have no choice.

Like Lisbeth said, I have to get myself some closure, or at least some answers.

I can't let things end this way.

Chapter 30
Steff

The morning sunlight filters through the high branches above me and paints my white silk shirt with flecks of gold. The breeze from the lake sweeps through my hair and caresses my cheeks. I close my eyes to savor it, and the smell of flowers at the height of their bloom drifts into my nostrils. Birdsong reaches my ears from the canopy of the trees.

I let out a deep breath.

I've missed mornings like this. I've missed the Palace gardens. I've missed Brelv.

And yet, Brelv is not what it used to be.

This morning in the gardens may seem peaceful, but my brother still lies unconscious in his chamber in the Palace, and the person responsible for it still roams free, lurking in the shadows.

And I am not what I used to be.

I may smile on the outside, but my heart aches because the woman I love is so far away.

I open my eyes and gaze beyond the lake. The image of Jess's face appears in my mind.

I wonder how her last gig with her band went. I wonder how her song sounded. I wonder if she got my note. Is she lonely right now, or is she trying to be strong, patiently waiting for me? Is she smiling, believing I'll return?

Damn. I miss her.

I never got to hear what she was going to tell me, either. I wonder what it could be.

"Your Highness," a man's voice calls my attention.

I turn my head to see a member of the Wolfsbane, the royal army, standing in front of me in his black armor adorned with the flower of the royal family.

I stand up. "What is it?"

"The King and Queen wish to see you."

Of course they would. frankly, I've been waiting for them to summon me.

"Please lead the way."

I follow the soldier into the Palace and towards the Hallowed Hall. The ever-present pair of guards at the massive gem-encrusted doors open them and I step inside. As I walk down the hall, I notice that the chairs on either side of me-usually filled with nobles and members of the Royal Council-are unoccupied.

As I thought, this is a private audience.

I stop just in front of the waterfall. I hold my fist over my heart and bow my head as I go down on one knee.

The water vanishes into a cloud of mist. In the pool it leaves behind, I see the reflection of the King and Queen of Brelv.

Father and Mother.

"So, Prince Steffan, you have the gall to appear before us once more," the King says. "And after that ridiculous note you left about going on an adventure."

"My apologies, Majesties." I bow my head lower. "It was not my intention to cause you worry."

"And what was your intention?"

"To learn of things I could not learn of here in Brelv. To have experiences as a man and not as a Prince, so that I might become a better man and so a better Prince of Brelv."

My father pauses. "And have you become a better man?"

"I hope so," I answer. "Though I have much yet to learn, and much better to become."

Another pause.

"Rise."

I stand up.

My father appraises me from head to toe. My mother's eyes smile behind her fan.

"In light of recent events, of which I am sure you have been made aware, and of the upcoming Midsummer Festival, you will not receive any punishment," the King declares. "Consider this a mercy."

I beat my fist against my heart. "I am most honored."

"And speaking of the Midsummer Festival, since Prince Viktor is unable to attend, you will take his place."

I try not to frown. I'm not being punished, huh? Somehow this feels worse than any punishment.

"Of course," I give the only answer that will suffice.

"And you will act in every manner befitting a Prince."

"Naturally."

"That is all. You are dismissed."

"Welcome home, Prince," my mother adds. "Even if it is under the strain of bitter circumstances."

"We will not speak of such circumstances here or elsewhere," my father says.

"Of course," I reply. "And in spite of them, I am glad to be home, Majesties."

They say no more, and after a few moments the waterfall returns. The side door opens and I walk out of it and down another hall.

"Prince Steffan," Osvald greets me as I round the corner. "So it's true you've returned."

"Osvald." I pat his shoulder. "It is good to see you again."

"I'm afraid I cannot present myself to you in good conscience, though. It is my fault Prince Viktor lies in bed."

I shake my head. "Of course not. And he would not approve of you thinking so."

I start walking. Osvald steps in beside me.

"Besides," I tell him. "There is no use lamenting the past. We must simply do what we can to ensure it does not repeat itself."

"I understand."

I glance around to make sure no one is listening. "Is there anything you can tell me about what happened? Anything at all."

Osvald also glances around. Then he moves closer to me.

"There are rumors of a man being spotted at the royal stables on the day Prince Viktor went for his fateful ride," he whispers as he runs his thumb over the dent in his chin. "A man with some kind of scar on his face."

My eyes grow wide.

"I've tried searching for him, of course, and I've heard that he's been spotted at the taverns near the docks, but I can't seem to get my clutches on him. If you ask me, he seems to be under the protection of a noble."

A noble? Natasia?

"By the way, Prince Steffan, I would ask that you leave Princess Natasia alone for now."

Huh?

"She is in a dire mood, which is only understandable given what's befallen Prince Viktor."

Oh. Of course that's what he meant.

"I understand."

"She has fallen ill as well and has been confined to her bed."

"Ill?"

I touch my chin.

That's strange. Does no one else in the Palace know that she is with child yet?

"Well, I certainly hope both she and my brother have a full recovery," I say. "And soon."

Osvald nods. "Oh, and by the way, my sister Yrena wonders if you would like to take her to the Midsummer Ball."

Of course she does.

Truthfully, I'm reluctant since I feel like I'll be cheating on Jess, but I suppose while I'm in Brelv, I can't escape from my duties.

Besides, I'm not actually cheating on her. I'm just allowing a woman to accompany me to royal functions. Yes, in the past, that might have led to a different kind of company, but not this time.

Not anymore.

"It would be my pleasure to be in the company of Lady Yrena at the Ball," I tell Osvald.

"And it would be the honor of our family," Osvald replies. "I will surely tell her the news next time I see her. She will no doubt be thrilled. I believe she's already had Princess Celia make her a wonderful gown."

"I think half the women of the court have," I say. "Which is probably why I haven't yet seen my sister."

Osvald chuckles. "Well, I'm sure you will see the Princesses at the parade in a few days."

The annual parade signifies the beginning of the Midsummer Festival, and all members of the royal family are required to attend. It's one of my least favorite activities of the year.

I sigh. "I suppose so."

Osvald bows. "Well, if you would kindly excuse me, I must return to Prince Viktor's side."

"Of course. I will visit him again soon."

"Oh, and by the way," he adds. "You seem to have had a new ring made. Did you lose the original one in your travels?"

I lift my gloved hand.

I was hoping no one would notice that I'm wearing my wedding band and not my Brelvan ring beneath my glove, but I guess Osvald is Viktor's attendant for good reason.

Nothing escapes him.

"I'm afraid so." I rub my hand.

"Pity." Osvald sighs. "It was a magnificent ring. Well, at least you did not lose your finger. Some savages will stoop to that in order to steal jewelry."

"Indeed."

He gives another bow before walking off.

I stare at the back of my hand.

Lost my ring, huh? I guess that's one way of putting it.

I glance out the tall window at the blue sky and think about the person I lost it to.

I wonder what Jess is doing right now.

Chapter 31
Jess

What am I doing here?

I look around me at the crowd gathered on the sidewalks of Aldnoah. They're mostly men, women and children with long, straight, blonde hair, and they all seem to be wearing their best clothes. I, on the other hand, am just wearing jeans and a gray sweater, my mess of wavy black strands trapped under a red bonnet.

I can't help but feel like I'm not supposed to be here.

And yet, I came to Brelv because Lisbeth insisted that it was the right thing to do.

And I'm here on the sidewalk right now because the kind woman at the consulate told me to be.

One look at my ring, Steff's ring, made her eyes grow wide as saucers, and apparently it was also enough to get me a visa. She wouldn't tell me where Steff lived, though. She just told me to be here on this day at this time. She said I would surely see Steff.

But how can I when there are so many people?

I consider leaving.

I don't really like crowds, and I'm worried I might get squished.

Or my baby might. I place a hand over my belly.

We've both had it tough lately. I threw up so many times on the plane that the stewardess had to reassign me to a seat closer to the restroom so I wouldn't bother the other passengers. Ever since I arrived in Brelv, though, I've been feeling fine. Maybe it's the clean, cool air. Maybe it's the smell of freshly baked bread that seems to fill the city. Maybe it's just how kind and warm and beautiful the people are, or how much slower life seems to be here. But I haven't had a single headache or felt nauseous once. I haven't had a worry about my health.

Until now.

The last thing I want is to get trampled, or to faint on the sidewalk in a country where I don't even know if I know anyone.

I'm about to turn around and leave, but then I hear music drifting out from the speakers at the crossroads. Trumpets blare in the distance. Horses' hooves clatter against the cobblestones.

I let out a deep breath.

Oh well. Since I'm already here, I might as well see the parade.

It starts and I see the horses all dressed up and adorned with jewels. A string of carriages in various colors and designs follows, with men, women and children waving from inside. Then there's a group of dancing women and children throwing flowers, followed by soldiers, first in purple and then in black.

Finally, I see a huge float that looks like a cake with several tiers, sparkling under the sunlight.

The crowd begins to cheer. Necks crane. Handkerchiefs wave. Excited children are hoisted up on their parents' shoulders.

So this is the main attraction, hmm?

The float itself, made of flowers and fabrics and crystals and even fruits, looks grander than any I've seen. But I don't think it's the float the people are cheering for.

On the lowermost tier, two women stand in nearly identical gowns, one midnight blue and the other magenta. They look almost the same, too, except one has her pale hair in a braid and the other has it twisted in a chignon.

Twins?

The crowns on their heads gleam under the sunlight.

Twin princesses?

Then my eyes move further up and I see a man dressed in black and gold. A purple sash hangs from one of his shoulders to his waist. His light blond hair falls over his eyes and...

I stop.

My heart stops as the float passes right in front of me and I get a better look at that face.

It's Steff.

There's no mistaking it.

I pat the shoulder of the man next to me.

"Who is that?" I point to the float just as it passes by.

"Who?"

"The man on the float," I answer. "The one in black and gold."

"Oh, you mean Prince Steffan?"

My breath catches.

Prince?

"Prince Steffan Alezzander Aldnoah," the man informs me proudly. "The second son of King Darien and Queen Celene and Second Prince of Brelv."

"Second?"

"The Crown Prince had an accident, I'm afraid." He beats his hand over his chest. "May the great gods restore his health."

My gaze drops.

Steff is a prince? A real prince?

No wonder he always seemed to have this air of grace and charm about him. No wonder he was so... noble. No wonder he knew so much. No wonder he was used to being in the spotlight.

And no wonder he could pull off the role of a prince so well. He was born for it. Literally.

Suddenly, I remember that time in Orlando when someone called him 'Your Highness'. That's why he ran-because someone recognized him and he didn't want his secret to be discovered.

But why? Why didn't he tell me who he really was?

Well, he did tell me he was from a wealthy family, which wasn't a lie.

Just a gross understatement.

Why didn't Steff tell me the truth?

Wait. Was that what he was planning on telling me the night he ran away instead?

"Is it your first time here in Brelv?" the man beside me asks.

I nod.

"No wonder you look shocked," he says. "Never seen royalty before?"

Well, I have but...

"Or are you in love with the Prince?"

My eyes grow wide.

"That's it, isn't it? Every woman who sees him falls in love with him. Prince Steffan, that is. He is more charming than Prince Viktor, after all-no offense meant-and the fact that he's got a rebellious streak seems to make the girls go wild."

I can see that. Even now, I can hear screams in the distance where the float is passing by.

"Well, it's not just the women who admire him. Us men, too. He's brave, and he often mingles with us common folk. He's the people's prince, if you ask me."

The people's prince. And yet he's been living with me in LA all this time.

Why?

"Did he just return from a trip?" I ask.

The man turns to me with look of surprise.

"I'm only asking because I heard he was away," I lie.

"It's not the first time," the man answers. "But he's always around when the kingdom needs him."

So this man doesn't know where Steff has been and why. But now, I know why he left me.

"Excuse me," I say as I turn to leave.

"If you wait a little longer, there will be some free food and drinks," the man says.

"I'm fine," I tell him. "Thank you."

"Oh, and if you have time, visit the caves of Anturion and the meadows of Larein. They are the most beautiful parts of Brelv."

"Thank you," I say again.

I give him a faint smile and make my way out of the crowd.

It's not easy. There really are a lot of people. It's almost as if all of Brelv is here right now.

I end up getting led here and there, pushed this way and that, and when I finally manage to get myself untangled from the crowd, I don't know where I am.

I frown.

Oh, shit.

I decide to keep walking until I find a place where I can sit and think. Unfortunately, all the stores seem to be closed.

Eventually, I come to a quiet, secluded alley away from the crowd. I'm so tired I sit on a low stool beside a pile of broken furniture.

I rest my head against the cold wall and look up at the narrow strip of blue sky.

What am I really doing here?

Well, I came to find out why Steff left, and now I know.

He's a prince. His kingdom needs him.

Now I know why he said we couldn't be together.

My chest hurts and I place my hand over it. Tears sting my eyes.

Lisbeth said that I shouldn't come home without telling Steff I love him, but there's no way that can happen now.

So what if I love Steff? So what if he loves me? He's a prince, and everyone knows that princes can't marry nobodies.

Nor do they live with nobodies. But Steff did.

That voice in my head-or is it from my heart?-gives me a flicker of hope, but I extinguish it quickly with a shake of my head.

There's no way this is going to work.

No way.

If I stay, I'll only cause him trouble and end up hurting myself.

I touch my belly.

Sorry, sweetheart. But it'll just have to be the two of us.

"That damn prince," a voice says from the other side of the pile. "He should never have come back."

My eyebrows go up.

Are they talking about Steff?

"You should have killed him when you had the chance," another voice says.

This one belongs to a man, too, but it's deeper and sounds more refined.

"I panicked, okay? I'm not used to killing royalty."

"Just fucking them?"

I hear a laugh.

What are they talking about?

"Anyway, it doesn't matter," the deeper voice says. "It doesn't matter that he's back. We'll get rid of him once and for all. He won't escape this time."

Fear clutches my chest. I clamp my hand over my mouth to suppress a gasp.

They're planning on getting rid of... Steff?

Their laughter crisps the air before their footsteps fade into the distance.

In the silence, I sit still with my trembling hands and my racing heart.

I can't just leave now.

I might have been willing to let him go, but I don't want him dead. And if I don't say anything, he might end up that way.

How could I be a good mother knowing I'd let my child's father die?

Slowly, I stand up. I take a deep breath and square my shoulders.

I have to warn Steff that his life is in danger.

~

"Please," I tell the black-clad soldier, who doesn't even seem to be blinking. "I have to speak with Prince Steffan. It's an urgent matter."

527

The soldier stays still as a statue.

"Please. His life is in danger!"

Still nothing.

I put a hand over my forehead.

Oh, what was I thinking? That they would believe I knew the prince and open these huge golden gates for me? I'm not even Brelvan.

Still, I can't just give up now.

I pace back and forth.

How can I convince them to let me speak to Steffan?

Then I remember the ring. I haven't been wearing it, because the woman at the consulate told me not to, but I have it in my pocket. I take it out now and show it to the guard.

His eyes grow wide.

Finally, a reaction.

"Please," I beg him. "I just need a few moments with him. If you could just tell him I'm here. Please, he has to know..."

"Who's this?" a voice from beyond the gates interrupts me.

I turn my head and see a tall man in his late thirties with pale shoulder-length hair and a slight cleft in his chin. His white-and-gold attire suggest he's not a guard nor a servant.

Who is he, then? A noble, I suppose.

He approaches the gates, and when he sees the ring in my hand, his eyes grow wide as well.

"That ring."

It does seem to get that reaction.

"I didn't steal it, I promise," I tell him. "And I'll give it back. I just need to see Ste... Prince Steffan."

For a moment, the man says nothing. Then he nods.

"Of course. Please forgive the delay."

He opens the gate and offers me his hand. I take it as I put the ring back in my pocket. His lips curve into a grin.

"Please come with me."

Chapter 32
Steff

"Come on, Vik. You're not just going to lie there and make me do all the work, are you?"

I speak to my brother as I sit on the chair beside his bed. As before, though, I get no response.

Not a word. Not a smile. Not a nod. Not a bat of an eyelash.

I glance at all the screens around him and all the tubes attached to his body.

I run my hands through my hair.

Why isn't he awake yet? Didn't they say he was out of the woods?

I remember the last time he was like this. That was when he fell from his horse, too, years ago. He had tubes attached to him, too, and bandages, but fewer. And he woke up just the day after.

I was right by his side, trying to hold back tears of relief. Viktor noticed it and patted my head and promised me he would never scare me like that again.

Yet here I am, scared once more about what will become of my brother.

"It's unfair," I whisper under my breath. "You're being unfair, Viktor."

Just then, a hand falls on my shoulder.

I turn around and find myself gazing into blue eyes just like mine.

"Charisse."

"Don't rush him," she says. "His body is repairing itself."

"I know." I place my hand over hers. "I just don't like seeing him like this, I guess." I look at her. "We haven't been able to talk much."

"Well, you've been busy with princely duties. It can't be helped," Charisse says.

I sigh. "Why did this have to happen to Viktor at a time like this?"

"Oh, come on." She pats my back, none too gently. "You don't get to act like a prince very often."

I narrow my eyes at her. "What's that supposed to mean?"

"Besides, didn't you hear the crowd cheering, the women screaming your name?" Charisse adds. "They were so happy to see you back."

"And what about you?" I ask her. "Are you happy to see me back?"

"Are you happy to be back?"

I fall silent.

My sister pinches my cheek.

"Ouch." I rub my cheek as I glance at her. "What was that for?"

"For leaving without saying a word," Charisse answers. "For getting me a doll. How old do you think I am?"

"It was supposed to be a souvenir, not a toy," I tell her.

"And most of all, for coming back with something missing."

I glance at my hand. "My ring?"

She punches my shoulder playfully. "Not that, silly."

"Oh."

Of course she'd notice that I'm not my usual self. Nothing escapes her, either.

"Celia's thrilled to have you back, though," Charisse says. "At least, she would be if she wasn't buried under a ton of dresses. I told her she couldn't do it, but as always, she never listens to me."

"I thought you stopped her when she tried to come after me."

"Well, usually, she doesn't listen to me," Charisse corrects herself.

I get off the chair and pat her head. "You've grown up to be such a fine woman, you know. You and Celia. I'm proud of you both."

Charisse smiles.

I glance at the bed. "I'm sure Viktor is proud of you, too."

"Hey, Steff." Charisse tugs at my shirt.

I turn to her. "What?"

"Do you really think you know Viktor?"

My eyebrows arch. "What kind of a question is that?"

Instead of answering, she walks away.

"Charisse?"

She crooks a finger at me.

I follow her out of Viktor's chambers and towards the fountain down the hall. When she sits on the bench, I sit beside her.

"What do you mean?" I ask her.

"You always thought Viktor was perfect, didn't you?"

"Compared to me, yeah."

She sighs. "Maybe that's why he tried to hide it."

"Hide what?"

Charisse draws a deep breath.

"When Viktor had his 'accident', I was one of the first in his room. One of the doctors asked me to look in his medicine cabinet for some verise to treat his less serious wounds. I found it, but I also found something else. It looked like verise at first, but I knew it wasn't. When I did some research later on, I found out it was a different herb, not as rare as verise but not too common, either."

"What kind of herb?" I ask.

"It's something that's supposed to help with... impotence."

My eyes grow wide. "Are you saying...?"

"I investigated some more," Charisse goes on. "And I talked to the doctor who treated him when he fell from his horse the first time. He told me it was possible that he... well, due to that..."

I place my hand on my forehead. So it's my fault.

"He should have told me."

Was that what he had been trying to say that time we were near the stables? Before Natasia interrupted us?

Natasia.

"Wait," I tell Charisse. "But Natasia is..."

"What?"

Charisse doesn't know. But I do. Danni said Natasia's pregnant, but if Viktor can't have a child, that means...

I stand up.

"Steff?"

"I'm sorry," I tell my sister. "But I have to go. I have some questions that need immediate answers."

~

"You're saying you followed this man with the scar and he disappeared into Lord Kester's house here in Aldnoah?" I ask Danni after hearing her report.

"Yes," she confirms.

I touch my chin.

I can't believe it. The Duke of Olvant has always been one of the royal family's closest friends and strongest allies. Why would he harbor a mercenary in his home? Or is that man under his employ? Is he the one behind all this?

"What are you thinking?" Danni asks me. "What have you found out?"

I tell her what Charisse told me and also what I've learned from questioning a few of Natasia's maids.

"You believe the child Princess Natasia is carrying is not your brother's?"

I nod. "That's why she wasn't eager to make her pregnancy known. No one is supposed to know until after Viktor is gone. Then everyone will believe she's carrying his child, and she will retain her position. In fact, she may become Queen Regent."

"But Prince Viktor found out she was pregnant, didn't he? And so she tried to get rid of him."

"That's what I thought at first, but then I realized that she's not the only one who benefits from this. Also, the more I think of it, the more I believe Natasia isn't capable of pulling all this off on her own. Maybe she wasn't even capable of conceiving such a plot. It should have occurred to me before."

"So someone put her up to it?"

I nod. "And who better to do it than her lover, the father of her child? A Queen Regent is not forbidden to remarry. With Viktor out of the way, she'd be able to marry that man, and they would both hold power over the kingdom."

Danni pushes her glasses up. "And now you think the Duke of Olvant is her lover?"

I give another nod.

"Well, he has been seeking a new wife lately," Danni adds. "And I suppose a man can never have enough power."

I sigh. "I just didn't think Lord Kester was that kind of man. He has my father's trust."

"Which is why he has the confidence to do this," Danni says. "What will you do, then? Do you want me to go to his house and get proof of his crimes? Do you want me to make Natasia confess?"

I shake my head. "I will go to Lord Kester's mansion myself. And if I find proof, I will bring him back here to the Palace in chains."

Chapter 33
Jess

I tug at the ropes around my wrists, but to no avail. The hemp digs into my skin with each tug, and it's obvious that it will soon scrape it away.

I can't have that. I can't have myself losing blood.

I can't just sit still in this dark cellar and do nothing, though. If only I can free my wrists, I'm sure I can get to that small window near the ceiling and crawl out. I'm sure I can escape.

I have to.

I have to warn Steff of the grave danger he's in. The fact that I'm being held prisoner right now is proof of how serious it is.

I don't remember exactly what happened. All I know is that I was following that guy and then I smelled something funny and then I fainted. When I woke up, I was here in this dank cellar that stinks of dead rats. At least, I hope they're all dead. The smell is enough to make me queasy, but I'm doing my best not to think of it.

I have to be strong. For Steff's sake and my baby's sake, I can't fall apart right now.

I have to escape.

But how?

Keith gave me a personal safety pen before I left, and I have it hidden beneath my sweater. It has an LED flashlight on one end, a button that activates an ear-piercing alarm in the middle, and a laser pointer on the other end-but no cutting edge.

I look around the room. Nothing but a shelf full of cobwebs, some crates, some empty bottles and...

Empty bottles.

If I break one of those, then I can use the sharp edge of a fragment to...

My idea trails away as the door opens.

The man with the cleft chin appears, a flashlight in his gloved hand. The bright light shines on my face and I look away.

"Ah. I see you're awake," he says.

He puts the flashlight down on the table near the door and leans against it.

"I'm sorry I couldn't provide you with better accommodations. I know you must think you deserve a chamber in the Palace, but I'm afraid things aren't going smoothly there right now. And they're about to get worse."

He grins.

"I do believe the real Midsummer Festivities are about to begin."

I glare at him. "Who are you?"

"The question is: Who are you?" He steps forward. "I thought Steffan might have given his ring away. Imagine my surprise when I saw it in your hand."

My eyebrows crease.

What is up with this ring? Why is it such a big deal?

"I never thought you'd show up at the Palace, of course, but it's good that you did. Your presence works in nicely with my plans."

"What are you planning?" I ask him through gritted teeth.

He laughs.

My eyes grow wide.

That laugh...

"You're the one I heard plotting to kill Steff in that alley, aren't you?"

He frowns. "My, my. I was sure we were alone. I guess I'll have to kill you, after all, after I kill your precious prince."

Anger erupts in my chest.

"You won't get away with it," I tell him. "No. You won't succeed. Steff won't let you."

His eyebrows arch. "You think Steffan can defeat me?"

He comes even closer to me.

"Let me tell you something, since you don't seem to know anything." He leans forward. "I'm the only one who's ever defeated Prince Steffan."

My eyes widen in horror.

No.

"And I can do it again."

"No!" I shout. "You won't succeed! You won't be able to lay a hand on him!"

"Are you sure?" He touches my chin. "Can you really say that when I have you here, the woman with his ring?"

My eyes grow even wider.

No way. He's using me as hostage. And if Steff finds out he has me, then...

"Now you understand?" The man in front of me gives a wicked grin.

Calm down, Jess.

"You're the one who doesn't understand," I tell him. "Steff and I have nothing going on. I came here to return the ring."

"Really? Well, that's unexpected and unheard of. Poor Steff."

"I mean nothing to him."

I say the words firmly. So why don't I believe them? And why doesn't this man seem to believe me?

He just grins. "I guess we'll find out, shall we?"

He grabs the flashlight and leaves the room.

I let out a deep sigh, but it's not one of relief. My heart is racing even faster now in the darkness.

I can't let this man use me as a hostage. If I do, then I'll be the one putting Steff's life in danger.

As soon as I no longer hear his footsteps, I lift the chair behind me and head to the corner. I lean to the side to get the bottle from the floor. I nearly fall but manage not to. I grip the bottle between my fingers.

Now I just need to break it.

I can't make a sound, though, so I decide to put the bottle down on an old rug. Using my feet, I wrap the bottle in the rug and step on it. Then I slowly lay the chair down on its side and reach for one of the shards.

Some of the smaller ones dig into my arm and I wince at the pain, but I keep going.

Finally my fingers close around a shard large enough to cut the rope. I start trying to, biting my lips to hold down a cry each time I cut skin instead of hemp.

After a few minutes, the rope gets loose. I give it a tug and it breaks.

I get up and stare at my hands.

Blood. Lots of blood.

I tear off my sleeves to wrap my hands and stop the bleeding. Then I step onto one of the crates and crawl out the window.

It's a tough squeeze, and for a moment I fear I'm stuck. Still, I manage to wriggle through. I rub my belly after.

I'm sorry, baby. I hope you're okay.

I glance around quickly, and when I don't see anyone, I start running through the gardens. My eyes search for a door, a way out.

How do I get out of here?

Suddenly, someone grabs me. A hand wraps around my waist and another clamps over my mouth.

I can't breathe. My limbs start shaking.

Have I been caught?

"It's alright, Jess," a familiar voice whispers in my ear.

As the hand on my mouth falls away, I turn around.

My jaw drops as my gaze meets Steff's.

"Steff!" I throw my arms around him.

I'm so happy to see him I can't put it into words.

Then I pull away. "What are you doing here?"

"Shouldn't I be asking you that?" he asks.

"I came after you," I explain. "I..."

He holds a finger over my lips.

"We can talk later. For now, let's get you out of here."

I nod. "Good idea."

We can't have that horrible man catching up to us, after all.

Steff grabs my arm and leads me through the shadows further down the garden. We reach a hedge maze and I follow him through it, running as fast as I can. My heart hammers in my chest and my breath leaves me in gasps.

Still, I run.

Suddenly, though, as we reach the middle of the maze, someone grabs me again. As my hand is wrenched from Steff's, a knife presses against my throat. I feel the cold blade against my skin as I swallow.

"No!" Steff shouts. "Don't hurt her."

The man behind me laughs.

"Ah. You mean something to him after all," he says in my ear.

He steps forward and Steff's eyes grow wide.

"Good evening, Your Highness."

Chapter 34
Steff

"Osvald?"

I stare at the man standing in front of me with wide eyes.

"You're working with Lord Kester?"

I never suspected he'd be working with his father. After all, I know for a fact that they hate each other. Yrena told me so on several occasions. But I suppose blood is blood. And even though Osvald may be Lord Kester's bastard son, they still share the same blood.

Osvald laughs. "You really think I'd work for that filthy old man?"

My eyebrows arch.

Ah. They're not working together, which means...

"It was never Lord Kester, was it? It was always you."

After all, he was the one who told me about the man with the scar and where to find him. Being close to Viktor, he must have known about Viktor's condition and seen an opportunity. Also, now that I think about it, he and Natasia did spend a lot of time with each other.

Besides, Natasia would never take an old man for a lover, not even a duke. But someone like Osvald...

"Steff, watch out!" Jess screams.

I turn around, but it's too late. A knife stabs my shoulder and pain spreads throughout my chest. I grip it as my knees hit the ground.

"Steff!"

"Quiet!" Osvald warns her.

I glance at my shoulder and see the blood streaming out. I look up and see the man with the scar above his nose standing above me.

"You..."

"That's payback," he says with a grin.

"I believe you've met my brother, Edmur," Osvald says.

"Brother?"

"Well, half-brother. We share the same whore of a mother."

"I should have killed you before," Edmur says. "I wasn't ready. Now, you bet I am."

My hand clenches into a fist.

"Now, now, don't fight back," Osvald warns me. "If you do, your precious woman is going to get hurt."

I glare at him. My nostrils flare.

"Don't you dare hurt her," I tell him.

"It's up to you. Stay still and let Edmur kill you and she might live."

Might.

"Fight back and she dies for sure."

I look into Jess's eyes. They flicker with fear beneath the moonlight.

No. I can't risk putting her life in danger.

But I can't die here, either. If I die, I'll lose her just the same, and I can't have that.

Think, Steff. Think very carefully.

"You'll have me killed?" I ask him in an effort to stall him as I wait for an opportunity to strike back.

"It's your fault for coming back," Osvald says.

"And you think your father will finally accept you afterwards? You think he'll let you get away with this?"

"In the morning, your corpse will be found in this garden and your blood will be on my father's hands."

"And why would anyone believe he killed me?"

"Because you hurt his daughter."

Shit.

"Yrena will..."

"Do whatever I ask her to do," Osvald finishes. "And so I'll finally have vengeance on my father. You out of the way. Vengeance. Two birds with one stone."

535

"And Viktor? And the King and Queen? And my sisters? Are you getting rid of the entire royal family?"

"Not the entire family," Osvald says. "Maybe I'll spare your sisters. Maybe I'll give one of them to my brother. Or both."

Edmur laughs.

My gut coils.

"And of course Princess Natasia will live. She will be the new Queen, and our child will be the next ruler of Brelv."

"What of my parents?" I ask him with my jaw clenched.

"They're old. They won't be hard to dispose of."

My chest tightens.

"And Viktor?"

"He could be dead right now," Osvald answers. "If Natasia does her job."

I hiss through my teeth.

"How could you do this, Osvald? You grew up with my brother. He treated you like a brother, too. He..."

A boot hits my stomach. I wrap my arms around it as I curl on the ground. It hurts to breathe.

It hits me from the side next, and I lie down on my back. A punch lands in my jaw and I taste blood.

"Ste-!" Jess gives a muffled cry.

I force my eyelids open and stare up at the moon. I force air into my lungs and try to ignore the pain.

"Finish him off," Osvald orders.

Edmur stands above me with his knife in his hands. He looks into my eyes and he laughs.

I crane my neck to glance at Jess. I see the tears in her eyes.

I suppose this is goodbye.

I start to mouth the words 'I love you' but stop as I hear an extremely loud electronic shrieking noise.

It seems to be coming from Jess's hand.

Osvald looks too-and suddenly a bright flash of red light leaps from her hand and hits him in the eye. He lurches backwards, the knife clatters to the ground, and Jess picks it up.

Finally, an opportunity to strike.

I ram my knee into Edmur's crotch. As the knife drops from his hand, I catch it by the hilt, turn it around and press the blade into his chest. I kick him off me as he dies.

As I get on my feet, I see Osvald trying to wrestle the other knife away from Jess. He punches her across the face and the knife falls. Jess crashes to the ground as well.

"No!"

I run over to her as Osvald runs away with his knife. I cup her face in my hands.

"Jess."

"I'm fine," she tells me weakly. "I'll be okay. Go after him."

I hesitate.

"You have to go after him," Jess repeats.

I press a kiss to her forehead and stand up. I pull the knife from Edmur's corpse.

"And Steff," Jess calls after me. "Don't die."

I nod.

I start after Osvald through the maze, walking slowly and listening for the slightest movements, for the sound of footsteps, for the rustle of leaves.

Something rustles behind me and I turn just in time to parry a blow from Osvald's knife with my own. The weapons fly into the air over the hedge.

He hurls his fist at me and I duck. I swing at his stomach, but he twists his body to the side. Then he lands a quick punch on my wounded shoulder.

I cry out as I grip it. Fresh blood seeps through my fingers.

"You think you can defeat me?" Osvald challenges. "I defeated you before, remember?"

"Yes, I remember," I tell him. "But I'm not the man I used to be."

When he tries to punch me again, I grab his wrist and pull his arm so that he ends up behind me. He wraps his arm around my neck and begins choking me. I can barely breathe, but I summon all my strength to hurl him to the ground.

He groans.

I climb on top of him to wrap my hands around his neck, but his knuckles fly towards my chin. He kicks me off and I land on a hedge. The twigs prick my back.

I grip my shoulder and gasp for air.

As Osvald runs towards me, a memory floods back to my mind.

At the last moment, I turn my body out of the way. Osvald crashes into the hedge. Then I lift my leg and swing towards his head. The tip of my boot hits the back of his neck just as he turns his head.

He falls to the ground.

Panting, I sink to my knees. I check Osvald's body for a pulse and find a weak one.

Good. He's unconscious but alive, just as I want him to be.

To think that I'd defeat Osvald with a move Keith taught me.

"Steffan!"

Danni suddenly appears in front of me.

"Is Viktor safe?" I ask her.

She nods. "The Princess is confessing her crimes to the King and Queen right now."

I nod. "Good. Take Osvald away."

She kneels down and ties his wrists. I lean against a hedge and grip my still bleeding shoulder.

"You're hurt," Danni says.

"I'm fine," I tell her, even though I feel on the verge of passing out myself.

"We need to get you to a doctor."

Maybe, but there's one more thing I have to do.

I force the strength back into my legs and run back to Jess.

Chapter 35
Jess

I open my eyes to find myself staring into the depths of turquoise pools that seem to go on forever, like a cloudless sky above a grassy meadow.

At first, I think I'm dreaming. But then I feel the warmth of a palm against my cheek and I smile. This hand, this warmth is real.

"How are you feeling, Jess?" Steff asks me.

His voice sounds like a perfect melody to my ears.

"Okay," I answer.

"Are you in pain anywhere?"

I shake my head and place my hand over his. "Shouldn't I be asking you that?"

I glance at his shoulder and see the bump of the bandages beneath his shirt. The sight brings back memories I would rather never remember again.

I kiss his hand. "Are you alright?"

Steff nods.

"What happened to... Osvald?"

I can barely bring myself to say the name of that monster.

"He will be punished appropriately," Steff assures me. "Though the Royal Council has agreed to wait until my brother wakes to decide exactly how. The Princess will be stripped of her crown and exiled."

"Exiled? But what about the baby?" I ask. "Didn't he say he and the Princess have a child?"

"The Duke of Olvant has promised he will look after the child," Steff explains. "He is probably more shocked by Osvald's action than anyone."

I rub his hand. "Well, at least the plot didn't succeed. The royal family is safe. Your family is safe."

Steff kisses the back of my hand.

"You're right. My family is safe." He kisses my belly. "You and my baby are safe."

My eyes grow wide.

He knows?

"I know," Steff tells me. "The doctors told me."

Oh.

"Why didn't you tell me?"

"I was going to tell you after the show, remember?" I remind him. "But you disappeared."

"I had to come home because of what happened to my brother," Steff explains. "Because of what was going on. I couldn't take you because I wasn't sure you'd be safe here. And I was right."

I frown. "You didn't tell me."

"But I left a note."

"You mean that note that said we're not meant to be together?"

His eyebrows crease. "What?"

I take the note that I've been carrying in my pocket and hand it to him. As I do, I notice the ring on my finger.

"Your ring," I say as I lift my hand.

"I put it back," Steff tells me. "It belongs on your finger."

"Everyone seemed to be making a fuss over it and I didn't even know why," I tell him. "What does it mean?"

He draws a deep breath. "Every Brelvan male has a ring, and he only gives it to the woman he's chosen to spend the rest of his life with, the woman he's pledged to protect."

I touch the ring. So that's what it means.

"And this ring happens to be distinctly mine. It was given to me at my coronation when I was sixteen. The whole kingdom saw it, so everyone knows it's my ring."

I gasp. "So every Brelvan who saw it thought I belonged to... the Second Prince?"

Steff nods.

Unbelievable.

And to think I practically yanked it off his finger.

I look at him. "Why didn't you tell me you were a prince?"

"I was going to after the show."

I nod. "Right."

"How was that show, anyway?"

"A disaster. I heard the band didn't perform that song I wrote. Also, they're all mad at me now."

"I'll talk to them."

I shake my head. "We've got more important problems, don't you think?"

Steff says nothing. He unfolds the note I've handed him and reads it.

His eyes grow wide.

"This is not my writing," he says. "This is..."

He crumples the note.

"It doesn't matter. What's written there is not true, and we're together now."

"But we can't be together, can we?" I ask him. "Isn't that why you didn't tell me you were a prince even though you had countless chances to do so?"

Steff lets out a deep breath.

"I didn't tell you because I was scared that you wouldn't accept me, that you would run away."

I blink.

That was what he was afraid of?

"But I was wrong." He clasps my hand between his. "Jess, I should have trusted you. I should have trusted in us."

Steff looks into my eyes.

"I should have told you the truth."

"You were afraid I wouldn't love you anymore if I found out you were a prince?" I ask him.

He nods.

I scratch my cheek and look away. "Well, I guess I am kind of scared knowing I'm in love with a prince. And I guess I'm tempted to run away."

Steff squeezes my hand. "But I'm still Steff, your Steff."

"Are you sure?" I look at him. "Steff, you belong to your kingdom. And I don't belong here."

"You belong by my side. You and our child."

"But..."

"I love you," Steff interrupts. "When I thought I was going to lose you, it hurt me so much I almost wanted to die."

I say nothing.

"Don't you... love me, Jess?" Steff asks me.

My lips quiver.

I remember what Lisbeth told me-to not come back home without telling Steff I love him. And yet I find myself hesitating.

After all, even if I say it, it won't change a thing. Even if I say it, it won't be enough.

"Don't you remember, Steff?" I tell him in a shaky voice. "I'm not fit to be a princess."

His blue eyes grow wide.

"I'm sure your parents will..."

Steff stands up. I swallow as I see the serious expression on his face.

"If my parents approve, you'll be my princess?" he asks me.

I turn away from his burning gaze. "I guess."

"Then I'll go talk to them. And I won't come back until they approve."

He turns on his heel and walks out the door.

Chapter 36
Steff

As soon as I get out of Jess's room, I see Danni waiting for me.

I frown. "You changed the note, didn't you?"

Her eyebrows arch.

"You think she's not fit to be a princess, do you? You were hoping she'd forget about me?"

"I didn't know she was pregnant," Danni says. "I just..."

I raise my hand to silence her.

"I know your intentions were good, but you were wrong this time, Danni. Anyone who thinks Jess doesn't belong with me is wrong. Even if that's what the whole kingdom thinks, they're wrong. I'll prove them all wrong."

I walk off.

"Where are you going?" Danni shouts after me.

I square my shoulders and lift my chin. "I'm starting with the King and Queen."

~

"You wish us to sanction your... relationship with this American woman?" my father asks.

The Royal Council and the rows of nobles on either side of me turn into a sea of murmurs.

I draw a deep breath. "Yes, Majesties."

"Preposterous!" The King's fist thuds on the arm of his throne. "Have you forgotten who you are, Steffan Alezzander Aldnoah?"

"With all due respect, I am well aware of who I am," I answer with my head held high.

Then I turn to the crowd.

"I am also well aware of my past actions, but allow me to tell you that in these past few weeks that I was not here and these past few days that I have been here, I've become even more aware of what is required of me as a prince, and of the kind of prince that I want to be."

The crowd grows silent.

I turn back to the thrones.

"I want to be a good prince, but I've realized that in order to do that, I must first become a good man. And a good man is someone who does not judge based on appearances. A good man is someone who is not afraid to do what is good even when no one is looking, to do what is right even when it earns the displeasure of others. He does not become what other people tell him to be but finds himself and believes in himself. Most of all, a good man is a man who, when he loves, gives his all and expects nothing in return, and does so until his death."

My father says nothing.

I wish to be a good man, so allow me to be," I continue. "And then I promise I will become a good prince, a prince who does not oppress but liberates because he himself feels free."

Still nothing.

I draw another deep breath.

"Grant me this and I will never ask for anything more ever again."

My father sits back. "You want this woman that much?"

"Her name is Jessica Campbell. Jess," I say. "And I've never wanted a woman more in my life. She knows she is weak, but that is why she tries to be strong. She fiercely protects those she loves. She fights for what is right. She never loses hope. If those are not qualities fit for a princess, I don't know what are."

Again, I hear whispers from the crowd.

"Silence!" my father shouts.

And silence falls.

"And does this woman... does Jess feel the same way for you? How can you be sure she will not turn her back on you and Brelv?"

"I swear I will not."

I turn my head and see Jess entering the Hallowed Hall.

My eyes grow wide.

What is she doing here? How did she...?

Then I glimpse Danni at the doors and the unconscious guard at her feet, and I understand.

Our eyes meet. She bows and beats her hand against her chest. I nod in gratitude.

As always, I can count on you, my faithful attendant.

"What is she doing here?" Lord Galden asks as he stands up. "Only nobles are allowed in this Hallowed Hall."

"This matter concerns her as well," Lord Kester says. "Let her speak."

The Duke glances at my father, who says nothing, then at me. I give another nod of gratitude.

"Your Majesties." Jess stops and curtsies. "I may not know much about Brelv, but in the few days I've been here, I've seen it is much like your son-warm and kind and full of passion and life. So I have no doubt I will love it."

She glances at me and I smile.

"So what if I was not born to be a princess? I choose to be one. And I will choose to be one each day for the rest of my life, just as I've chosen to love your son, your Prince..." She turns to the nobles. "And will keep doing so for as long as I live."

My heart bursts with pride and joy. I run to her and hold her hand.

"I never expected you'd come here," I whisper to her.

"I've decided I'm not running away anymore," Jess answers. "Oh, and Danni helped me."

"I know."

I kiss Jess's hand, then clutch it firmly as I meet my father's gaze.

"Your Majesties, we ask that you give us your blessing."

"And I ask that you give me leave to renounce my claim to the throne."

I turn to the side door with my eyes wide and see Viktor in a wheelchair being pushed in by a servant.

The crowd murmurs once more.

I stare at my brother. When did he wake up?

"My brother is a better man and a better prince than I am," Viktor says. "If not for him, I'd be dead. We could all be."

He looks at me and I smile.

I'm truly honored to have such great people supporting me.

"I'm sure that they and their children can lead Brelv into the future," Viktor goes on.

The crowd quiets. For a moment, the King says nothing. Then as he opens his mouth, my mother speaks.

"I see no reason not to grant your request, Prince Steffan, Miss Campbell."

My father looks at her and sighs.

"And after all the recent events here at the Palace, I do believe that a celebration is in order. Perhaps a royal wedding in lieu of the Midsummer Ball?"

My eyebrows arch.

"When is that?" Jess asks me.

"In three days."

"Three days?"

The King stands up. "So be it. In three days hence, Prince Steffan will marry his chosen woman and she will be crowned Princess of Brelv. Their child will be recognized as an heir to this throne."

I kiss Jess's hand once more. My heart races in my chest.

My father looks at me. "I only ask that you remember the words you have uttered this day and be a good man and a good Prince."

I bow. "As you wish, Father."

~

"Did you see that look on Father's face earlier?" Viktor asks me as I wheel him through the gardens.

"When you said you were going to step aside, or when Mother stepped in?"

Viktor chuckles. "Anyway, I think that's the most fun I've had in that room in ages."

He reaches for my hand.

"And I'm truly happy for you. You've always fought for the things you wanted, so I always knew you'd marry only a woman of your choosing. I only hoped she'd be a good one, and I can see that she is. You are lucky."

I nod. "Thank you, brother. You have always been my greatest ally."

"As I will always be."

"I'm sorry I was not here recently, and that..."

Viktor raises a hand.

"Please, let us not talk of mistakes and failures and sad things. You are getting married. In three days."

He gazes into the distance.

"Brelv will have a Princess once more."

Chapter 37
Jess

"Princess Jess."

I say the words for what feels like the hundredth time as I stare at my reflection in the mirror.

No matter how many times I've said them, though, they still don't feel real, just as the reflection in front of me does not seem like me.

The woman in the mirror has the same black hair as me, but the strands have been twisted into a hundred small, intricate braids, all woven into one larger braid. The gown she has on looks like a dream. The lace coats her arms but leaves her shoulders bare, bordering the sweetheart neckline and seamlessly flowing over the satin. Diamonds adorn her neck and ears. Pink blooms in her lips and on her powdered cheeks.

Is that really me?

Am I really getting married? Am I really going to become a princess?

Everything seems unreal.

Unbelievable.

I run my fingers over my necklace as the nerves set in.

What if I can't do this? I said I'd choose to be a princess, but what if that turns out to be a bad choice? What if I can't be a princess after all? What if I fail Steff and all of Brelv?

My thoughts are interrupted by a knock on the door.

"Come in," I say, thinking it's another servant.

Instead, my eyes meet blue ones through the mirror.

I turn around. "Steff."

He stares at me with wide eyes, his lips parted in awe.

"What are you doing here?" I ask him. "Should you be here?"

"You're... stunning," he says.

I exhale. "You're not too bad yourself."

In fact, he looks dashing in white and gold, a purple sash hanging from his shoulder just as it did in the parade.

My heart feels like it's about to leap out just looking at him.

"You've even outdone Prince Charming," I add.

"As you've outdone Cinderella," he says with a dazzling smile. "Anyway, I just came to make sure you're alright. I know this is all a bit much."

"It is," I agree. "And I admit I'm nervous."

And yet, seeing him has made all my fears go away, leaving only the excitement.

"But I'll be fine," I assure him as I reach for his gloved hands.

He nods.

Just then, the door opens.

"Brother!" Princess Celia scolds Steff. "Get out! You're not supposed to be here."

"Alright, alright."

Steff raises his hands and leaves.

Celia sighs. "What on earth was he thinking? He just ruined his own wedding. He's supposed to be stunned when he sees you walk down the aisle. Enchanted even. Head over heels in love."

"I think he still will be," I say.

Celia smiles. "Well, are you ready for your wedding, Princess Jess?"

I take a deep breath and smile back.

"Yes. I think I finally am."

~

"Congratulations... again," Lisbeth greets me with a hug after the ceremony.

Then she steps back. "Wait. Was I supposed to do that? Sorry, I've never had a princess for a friend before."

"Shut up," I chastise her. "You can treat me just like you used to. You're my friend, after all."

"Jess told me you're the one who convinced her to come here to Brelv," Steff says.

Lisbeth nods. "Yup."

"Thank you."

Lisbeth shakes her head. "I just had this feeling that you were meant for each other."

I smile at her.

"And I wanted her to make sure the two of you made up so I could meet your friends," she adds. "By the way, you have some gorgeous friends."

"I do believe I do," Steff says.

"I'll go introduce myself to them." Lisbeth walks off.

I grab Steff's arm. "She's having fun."

He turns to me. "Are you?"

I nod.

Well, everything still feels unreal to me, but yes, I am happy.

"Thank you for bringing Lisbeth here, and my family."

I can see Laura talking to Princess Celia and Keith talking to Danni. My mother and father both have proud smiles on their faces.

"Oh, they're not all I brought," Steff says.

I throw him a puzzled look.

He takes off my crown. "I'll hold this for you."

"What?"

"We don't want it falling off, after all."

"Why would it fall off?"

Then a man speaks at the microphone.

"Your Highnesses, lords, ladies and gentlemen, let us now hear a song composed by our very own new Princess."

I gasp. The curtains go up and I see everyone from the band-Kay, Riley, Josh and Alice. I see my guitar as well.

"This is it," Steff tells me. "Your final show. Make it the best."

I kiss him on the cheek. "Thank you."

"Go!"

I pick up my skirts and run towards the stage as fast as I can.

544

Chapter 38
Steff

"Slow down, Jess."

I grip Jess's shoulders as her head moves back and forth over my quivering cock.

"If you keep doing that, I'll-"

She suddenly takes me in her throat and swallows around me.

A shudder goes through my entire body. A gasp escapes my lips. My nails dig into her shoulders.

"Jess," I warn hoarsely as I try to push her way.

She grips my buttocks firmly, though. Her eyes remain closed as tears glisten in their corners. A trail of saliva trickles down her chin.

She swallows around me again and I feel the swirl of heat in my balls.

Fuck.

My cock spills inside her mouth. Gasps leave my trembling body.

Jess finally pulls away. She wipes her mouth with the back of her hand.

I lean over her. "Are you alright?"

She gives me a smile.

I narrow my eyes at her. "What was that?"

"A wedding present," Jess answers. "Did you like it?"

Like it? It was so damn good it drove me crazy.

Even so, I'm still hard.

"In that case, let me give you yours," I tell her.

I carry her towards the massive bed and set her down on it. Then I run my hands through her hair as I kiss her lips.

My fingers get caught in the braids.

"It seems your hair still has a mind of its own," I remark.

"Good," Jess says. "Even though I'm a princess now, I'm still a fighter."

"That's what will make you such a good princess."

I kiss her breasts.

"And a good mother."

I plant a reverent kiss on her belly.

Jess lifts her head to look at me and smiles.

"I think you'll be a good father, too."

I settle between Jess's legs and grip her thighs.

"But for now, I think I'll be a little naughty."

I spread her legs and push my cock between them. Jess gasps.

"Tell me if I'm hurting you," I tell her.

She shakes her head. "I'm fine."

I hold my breath as I push in slowly. Once I'm completely inside her, I stop and let it out. I close my eyes and savor the feel of that velvety skin clinging to me.

No, this is not the first time, but each time is still as good as the first.

"Are you going to move, Your Highness?" Jess asks.

I grin. "Right away, Your Highness."

And I start moving my hips. Slowly.

I reach down to tease her nub as well.

Jess lets out a loud gasp. Her hands grip the edges of the pillow behind her head.

I move both my hips and my hand faster. She trembles.

Then her back arches off the bed as she lets out a cry.

Afterwards, I stop to stare at her breathless, satisfied expression. It takes my own breath away.

"Did you like your present?" I ask her.

Jess nods.

"Good. Here's one I think both of us will enjoy."

I continue moving, faster this time. I keep my eyes on Jess's face for a while before closing my eyes to savor each thrust.

Good. Damn good.

And to think I'll have this for many years to come.

I'll never get tired of it.

I press a kiss to Jess's lips and move even faster. Jess starts moaning and gasping once more. My own breathing becomes ragged.

I can feel the heat swirling in my balls again. The muscles of my stomach coil.

My hips move erratically. My jaw clenches.

Jess trembles again. She cries out as she tightens around me.

I spill myself deep inside her this time, emptying myself of every drop with a series of grunts.

Then I pull out and lie down beside her. I pull her into my arms.

For a moment, she stays still as she catches her breath. Then she looks up at me and smiles.

I kiss the top of her head.

"What are you thinking?"

"That I can't believe I've been having sex with a prince all this time," she says.

I chuckle and touch the tip of her nose.

"And that's all you're going to have sex with for the rest of your life."

Jess grins. "That doesn't sound so bad."

She snuggles against me.

"Looking back now, everything feels so weird. You weren't supposed to be my roommate, but you were. We weren't supposed to be a couple, but we became one. We even had a fake wedding ceremony before we had a real one."

I stroke her cheek.

"And I never intended to fall in love with you, but I did."

Jess looks up and meets my gaze. "And I fell in love with you before I knew it, maybe the first time I swung that guitar at you."

I chuckle. "I remember it well."

I press my lips to hers tenderly, fleetingly. Then I plant a kiss on her forehead.

"I love you, Princess Jess."

"Stop calling me that," she says. "Everyone else calls me that. Not you, too. I'll always be your Jess."

"My Jess," I repeat. "I like that."

I take her hand. "And I'll always be your Prince."

Jess smiles.

"Then all that's left to do is live happily ever after."

~*The End*~

ACCIDENTALLY INTO YOU

Chapter One
Lilly

I should've called in sick.

That's the first thought that ran through my head when I glanced up and caught the eyes of my boss. Henry Burke rarely came to The Verve. In fact, I could count the number of times I'd seen him here on one hand, and I'd worked at this nightclub for two years.

The man was obscenely rich, having made his first million as a real estate mogul back before I was even born. Now, he owned a variety of businesses, including this place.

Why did he have to show up tonight, of all times? As a new manager of the club, there was a ton of pressures on me to prove myself and tonight was not my best showing. The local band I had booked for the night showed up late and had yet to start playing, leaving the dance floor full of people milling around with drinks in their hands, waiting. Not exactly the party atmosphere that the owner of a night club would want to see on a Saturday night.

On top of that, one of my bartenders had called in sick, so the two guys I did have manning the bar area were struggling to keep up. I was doing my best to help out, but I had just lost my grip on a highball glass, sending it tumbling to the ground where it shattered into a million pieces and splashed a Vodka Mojito all over my pants. That's when the prickling awareness of being watched made me snap my eyes to the door.

There he was, my boss, with his eyes locked on me. Great timing. Just great.

"Damn it," I muttered, looking at the mess at my feet and the dozens of impatient customers crowding the bar area.

Yep, definitely should've just stayed home.

Taking a deep breath, I tried to compartmentalize. First things first, clean the mess. I grabbed a broom and flagged down my best waitress.

"What's up, boss lady?" Tina asked with a grin, leaning on the bar and watching as I swept up the shards of broken glass.

"I've told you to call me Lilly," I said. I nodded my head toward Mr. Burke hovering near the entrance. "See the older man over there by the door?"

"You mean the guy in the expensive suit with the two barely legal and barely dressed girls hanging off his arms?" Tina asked, wrinkling her nose in disgust.

"That's the one. It's Henry Burke."

"The same Henry Burke that signs my paycheck?"

"Yep," I said, dumping the broken glass into a small trash can under the bar.

"Wow, talk about VIP. What's he doing here?"

"No idea. And his timing isn't the best. So, I need you to take care of him. Seat him upstairs, of course. Wait on him and his...companions. Do your best to make sure he's happy."

"What are you gonna do?"

"I have to get the music going, even if I have to learn to play guitar myself," I said, eyeing the stage where the band had just finished assembling their drum set.

"That's something I'd like to see." Tina shot me a grin before hurrying away to take care of our unexpected guest.

***

It was nearly 20 minutes later that the band finally picked up their instruments and started their set. Rock music filled the large space and I could feel the bass reverberating in my chest. The crowd reacted immediately. It was a sight to see as the dancefloor flooded with dancers; their bodies writhing to the beat under the dancing neon lights that twirled above them.

The band was good but I already knew that. I had watched them perform at a bar last month. It was why I booked them but I knew they wouldn't be back here. Starting the show nearly an hour late was unacceptable. Besides, there were plenty of bands to choose from around here.

With the proper night club atmosphere in place and things running as smoothly as they ever do, I made my way to the stairs leading to the second floor. The steps were always flanked by a pair of bouncers since they led to our VIP seating. All seats on the upper level were semi-private booths along a metal railing that overlooked the dancefloor. The seating areas were separated by partial walls, giving a level of seclusion that wasn't available below.

Henry Burke was seated in the booth at the far end, furthest from the stage area with arguably the best view in the place. He could see everything from here - the bar, the dance floor, the stage. As I approached, I couldn't help but think of a king on his throne. He was seated comfortably, lounging with a scotch in his hand, but his calculating gaze never stopped roaming the place, seeming to take in everything. There was something about the man, the way he held himself, that projected the power he held here. This was a man that took charge.

Refusing to show that I was intimidated by him, I squared my shoulders and straightened my back, making sure to look him in the eye as I stopped at his table. His eyes snapped to me before slowly traveling over my body, taking in the hint of cleavage and traveling down the curve of my hip. I wasn't dressed provocatively, but his heated gaze made me wish I was wearing a parka. I felt my skin crawl. I shifted my weight uncomfortably but refused to wilt under his stare.

"Mr. Burke, it's a pleasure to see you again," I said, forcing a smile onto my face. Finally, his eyes returned to my face. Thank God.

"You as well, Miss Monroe," he said, his voice smooth as velvet. I was mildly surprised that he even knew my name. He wasn't involved in the day-to-day running of the club at all. The general manager of the club was a man named Trent who had been in charge since long before I started working here. I had only met Mr. Burke once before and that was almost a year ago when I was still a waitress.

"I trust that Tina has been taking good care of you?" I asked, trying to sound as professional as possible. I knew that my young age made people question my position as manager, despite my degree. I didn't want this man to think they had a point, so I chose my words carefully. I really just wanted to ask him why he was here.

"Oh, yes. She's been quite accommodating." he replied, sipping his scotch. My eyes traveled over to the women he had brought along. They looked younger than me, which raised some questions about the alcohol in their hands. Were they even 21?

My greater concern was their behavior. They were huddled together in the booth, chattering together nonsensically. There was a manic euphoria about them that I had never seen from simply drinking. I suspected they were high on something. I really hoped that they didn't take it here, whatever it was. I suspected cocaine because of the peculiar way one of the girls kept sniffling.

"I'm expecting some company this evening. A man named Clint will be here within the hour. Let the bouncers know to grant him access immediately," Mr. Burke spoke with a dismissive tone that irked me.

"Of course. Please let us know if you need anything else," I replied before pivoting on my heel and heading back to work. There was an uneasy feeling in the pit of my stomach. What was this man up to?

As I stepped off the bottom stair, one of the bouncers working the door waved me over. Weaving my way through the crowd, I saw that there was a man standing there with an arrogant smirk on his face. The uneasy feeling in my stomach got worse as I approached. I was never a fan of judging a book by its cover, but this guy looked like trouble.

He was wearing a black leather jacket, despite the warm weather, and combat boots. His head was shaved and there was a teardrop tattoo under his left eye. As he looked my way, I was struck by the cold look in his eyes. He seemed tense, the way he held himself showing that he was prepared for a fight at any moment. I had a feeling that this was the man Mr. Burke was waiting for.

"Who're you?" he asked as I reached him. The bouncer beside him crossed his arms over his chest, aggression pouring from him in waves as he clearly didn't like the way this stranger spoke to me.

"Are you Clint?" I asked, deciding not to answer his question.

"Yeah," he jerked his head in a rough nod. "Burke here?"

"Yes," I replied shortly, turning to the bouncer that was still standing there with a frown. "Jack, can you take our friend here upstairs to Mr. Burke's table?"

I stayed by the door and watched as the men made their way to the second floor. I didn't know what was going on, but I was suddenly eager for the night to be over.

The night air was humid as I pushed open the back door, stepping out into the poorly-lit alley. The dumpster was near the corner of the building and I made my way toward it, carrying an overstuffed trash bag with me. It was just after midnight and things had been calm for the last few hours.

Well, maybe not calm, but normal. No more unexpected guests and I hadn't seen Mr. Burke or his company. I hoped that they had left without me noticing while I was busy helping out behind the bar.

My mind was wandering aimlessly while I walked. I glanced up at the sky and saw that thick gray clouds were hiding the stars from view - not that they were especially easy to see with all these city lights anyway.

A man's voice reached my ears and I froze. Fear filled me, but not because there was a stranger nearby in the darkness. My anxiety came from the pleading quality in his words. I had never heard such a desperate, terrified tone of voice before.

"Please, don't do this," the man begged. I told myself to turn around and go right back inside. There was something dangerous happening around the side of the building and I needed to get away from it. I would call the police to come check it out, once I was safe.

Except I couldn't do that. I couldn't leave some man behind without at least seeing what was happening. He sounded so scared. I crept forward slowly, pressed against the brick wall of the building, the trash bag still clutched tightly in my hand. I knew I was being an idiot, but I couldn't seem to stop myself.

"I can get the money to you, I swear. Just give me a week and you'll have it all. Plus interest," the man spoke again. This time his voice cracked as if he were fighting tears. My heart raced as I edged around the dumpster just enough to peek at the three men gathered only 30 feet away.

"You've had plenty of time. Besides, we both know it's not really about the money. God knows I don't need it. It's about respect. You stole product from me. Do you really think that I'd let you get away with that?"

My legs began to shake as I recognized the man speaking as Henry Burke. He had his back to me, but his voice was unmistakable, as was the leather jacket on the man standing next to him. Clint was holding his arm out in front of him and I realized with a sickening jolt that he was pointing a gun at the third man, the terrified one.

"Henry, I'm sor-"

"It's too late for that," Mr. Burke's voice interrupted. He turned to Clint, "Do it."

Without hesitation, Clint pulled the trigger. There was a popping sound, not nearly as loud as I would have expected, and the pleading man was knocked backward off his feet as he was hit square in the chest. He landed in a crumpled heap and didn't move.

I let out a gasp, shock loosening my grip on the trash bag in my hand. It slipped out of my hand as I stood frozen, helpless to stop it. The trash landed on the ground with the sound of beer bottles clashing together, deafening in the narrow alleyway.

Time seemed to ground to a halt as Mr. Burke and Clint whipped around, their eyes taking me in. I saw my own shock reflected in Mr. Burke's face. For a long, pulse-stopping moment, we stood staring at each other.

Then Clint took a small step toward me and the tension broke. Mr. Burke's eyes flashed with determination and I knew, with gut-wrenching certainty, that I was about to join the pleading man in the afterlife.

My body reacted before I made a conscious decision to move. I shot up the alley toward the door to the club with a frantic urgency that gave me a speed I'd never possessed before. My breathing was ragged as my panicked mind kept replaying the scene I had just witnessed.

I just saw a man die.

He's dead.

Dead!

Hysteria was threatening to take over and I had no idea how to stop it. A scream was trying to claw its way up my throat, but I was panting too hard for it to explode out of me yet.

I was closing in on the metal door of the club when another popping noise sounded behind me and a section of the brick wall beside my head seemed to explode. Debris lashed against my bare arms as I shielded my face impulsively. I stumbled, my heart lurching as my panicked mind struggled to understand what was happening.

"Stop her, damn it!"

Mr. Burke's voice cleared up my confusion. They were shooting at me. They were trying to kill me.

That thought should have made me panic more, but all I could focus on was the need to get away, to flee danger and death. Pitching forward, my hand grasped the door handle as I heard footsteps racing after me. Yanking the door open, I threw myself inside and pulled it closed behind me.

Cursing myself for leaving my keys in my purse behind the bar, I knew that I couldn't stop running now. I couldn't lock the door without them and Clint was hot on my trail. The sound of the band's music was getting louder as I tore up the hallway toward the storeroom. In my mind, I latched onto the sound. I just had to reach the bar area. Then I could lose him at the dancefloor. Hopefully.

I was passing through the storeroom when I heard a bang behind me that I assumed was the back door bouncing off the outer brick wall. Throwing myself against one of the freestanding shelving units, I pushed with all my might until it came crashing to the floor. I didn't stop to watch, but the sound of shattering glassware gave me hope of slowing Clint down even further.

I slammed the storeroom door behind me and hurried past the bathrooms. Finally, I was back in the bar area. Elbowing my way through the crowded dance floor, I couldn't believe how surreal this seemed. Was I really only here ten minutes ago?

I felt like my entire life had changed and it was strange that all these people had no idea what was happening. The bodies around me twirled and gyrated to the music while I tried to slow my rapidly beating heart and get out on the other side.

I didn't dare look behind me and see if Clint had spotted me in this crowd. I was barely holding onto my sanity as it was. Pushing my way to the far side of the room, I broke free of the mass of people. I instinctively made my way to the front door; the need to escape propelling me, keeping me from thinking things through.

People around me were staring wide-eyed and I knew the terror I felt was reflected on my face. I heard someone tentatively calling out my name as I passed the bar, but I didn't stop to acknowledge it. Instead, I shoved my shoulder against the door and stumbled out into the night once again.

This was nothing like the isolated darkness of the alley had been. The front of the night club was brightly lit, with a huge sign hanging above and spilling red light upon the people gathered on the sidewalk. There was a line of people waiting to get in and there were two bouncers staring at me with surprise.

Movement from the corner of my eye drew my attention to Mr. Burke as he came barreling around the side of the club, clearly meaning to cut me off while Clint closed in from behind. It looked unnatural, seeing him run in his nice suit, his hair disheveled. I never imagined I'd see the man as anything less than put together.

"I need to borrow your car," I said to the bouncer, Jack, my own urgent voice sounding unfamiliar to my ears.

"What? Why?"

"Just give me the keys, please!" I could hear the same pleading tone in my voice that I had heard the dead man use. It made me feel sick to share that connection with him.

"Are you okay?" he pulled his keys from his pocket as he spoke, his face lined with worry. I snatched them from his hands and whipped away toward his car parked a block down the street. A painful stitch formed in my chest, but I couldn't slow down now. They were too close.

I skidded to a halt next to the black Jeep, fumbling with the key fob to get the doors unlocked. I half-expected to feel hands grabbing me from behind any second, or worse, the barrel of gun pressing against my back. Finally, I got my shaking fingers to cooperate long enough to press the unlock button.

I had just turned the key in the ignition when I looked up and saw both men were closing in on me. Without thinking about where I would go, I moved the shifter into drive and stomped on the gas pedal. There was a loud screech as the tires spun against the pavement before getting traction and propelling me forward. I shot out into the street, cutting the wheel sharply to avoid hitting any cars parked nearby. As I sped away, I refused to look back.

I couldn't say how long I sped along the road, my body trembling from the shock and adrenaline flooding my system. All I knew was that I had to keep going because the thought of stopping made me want to scream.

Then, a large brick building came into view. It was the police station. I honestly didn't know if I had driven here purposely, or if it was just a lucky coincidence. My thoughts were too scattered to be sure either way.

I parked the Jeep and took a steadying breath. Clinging to the idea of safety that a police station could provide, I climbed out of the vehicle and started inside. As I reached the glass door, it opened outward, nearly hitting me. A tired-looking man with brown hair was walking out, looking down at his cellphone.

"Sorry," he mumbled, glancing at me before looking at his phone again. I started to walk past him when he looked back up at me, doing a double-take. I couldn't imagine what I must have looked like after my crazy night, but something about my appearance caught his attention because he stopped in his tracks and tucked his phone into his pocket.

"Are you okay?" he asked softly, placing his hand on my shoulder gently.

"Um, no. I don't think…I don't think I am," I croaked.

"I'm Detective Samson. You want to tell me what happened?" he asked, turning to lead me inside the building with a light grip on my upper arm.

"He's dead. I don't why. I mean, I saw it happen, but I don't know why." I knew I wasn't making much sense, but my sluggish brain wasn't working properly.

"Okay, let's just take it slowly," the detective said as we stopped at an elevator. He pushed the up button.

"It was my boss," I told him, needing him to understand. "Henry Burke. You have to get him. And Clint. You have to stop them!"

The detective froze, his grip tightening on my arm as he stared at me. A muscle in his jaw twitched before he turned and started back toward the door, dragging me along with him.

"What are you doing?" I exclaimed, trying to pull away.

"We have to get you out of here, now," he said, his head was swiveling around as we walked. He sounded almost scared.

"Why?"

"There are too many cops here that work for Burke. You'll never make it out of here alive if you tell your story."

My heart plummeted, and I felt light-headed. Would this nightmare never end?

"What can I do?" I asked as he ushered me into his car.

"I know a place you can go. Somewhere safe," he said, climbing into the driver's seat. I wanted to believe him but I couldn't help wondering if I'd ever truly be safe again.

Chapter Two
Grant

I couldn't sleep.

This was nothing new, I had a history of letting anxiety and tension keep me awake. This time it was because of my old obsession: Henry Burke.

Burke was a snake, a billionaire with ties to the criminal world that I had never been able to substantially prove. My vendetta against the man had begun when I was fifteen years old, far too young to really do anything about it. Now, thirteen years later, I had worked my way up in the world and was his social equal.

Yet, even with my massive resources, I hadn't been able to find evidence of his crimes. He was careful, and I had to admit, despite my loathing of the man, he was too damn smart.

I let out a heavy sigh and got out of bed. It was nearly 1:30 in the morning but sleep still eluded me. Leigh's birthday had me worked up. It was in three days and he would have been 32. Every year, it tortured me that my brother was still missing, and I might never have the closure I needed.

Wearing only a pair of plaid pajama pants, I headed downstairs to the kitchen; the hardwood floor cool against my bare feet. I flicked on the light, flinching against the sudden harsh glare before heading straight to the pantry. Grabbing a box of Chocolate Lucky Charms, my guilty pleasure, I poured a heaping bowl full.

I settled onto a cushioned stool at the kitchen island and dug into the chocolatey goodness. Propping my phone up against the salt shaker, I pulled up my news app and jolted as I saw Burke's face. It was a video. Pushing aside my cereal, I picked up the phone and pressed play.

"We're here with billionaire Henry Burke, real estate mogul and owner of popular nightclub The Verve, where there was a shooting earlier this evening." The reporter was standing with Burke in front of the club, talking into the microphone with an air of seriousness that was a little too perfect, like the guy had practiced his mock-concern in front of the mirror a thousand times. "Now, Mr. Burke, can you tell us what happened."

"It's truly a tragedy," Burke began, his face properly contrite. "I often visit my various businesses to make sure things are running smoothly. Tonight, here at The Verve, I stepped outside for a smoke and saw my new manager having an altercation with someone. The next thing I knew, she had shot the poor man and fled."

"Oh my, that must have been quite a shock for you."

"Yes, indeed. I tried to stop her, but she's a few decades younger than I am," he shot the reporter a self-deprecating grin.

"Well, I think it's fair to say that you're a hero for your efforts," the reporter responded. I rolled my eyes. Why didn't he just drop to knees and kiss the guy's ass for the camera?

"Thank you, Tom. I just hope the police can find Miss Monroe before she hurts anyone else."

"And here's a picture of the young woman in question." The screen changed to a picture of a strikingly beautiful young woman with auburn hair and a bright smile. It looked like a selfie and I'd wager money that it was pulled from one of the girl's social media pages. "This is Lilly Monroe. She's twenty-three years old with red hair and was last seen driving a black Jeep Wrangler. If you see her, please call the number at the bottom of your screen. Do not attempt to-"

My doorbell ringing drowned out the reporters next words. I hit the pause button and glanced at the digital clock on my stove.

1:48 a.m.

What the hell?

I briefly contemplated running upstairs and grabbing my gun from its safe, but that seemed like an overreaction. Yeah, it was late, but I had a security system with a pin pad right next to the door. I was also fully capable of defending myself if needed.

The doorbell rang again as I was walking to the front door, followed by the thundering sound of a fist slamming against the door.

"Open up, Grant. It's Jim."

I picked up my pace, keying in the alarm code before I pulled the door open to reveal my oldest friend standing at the threshold next to...

Holy shit.

It was that Monroe woman, the one I had just seen on my phone. What was Jim, a cop, doing with her?

"Are you going to let us in?" Jim asked. His hand was placed on the woman's lower back and she looked jittery, her hands shaking and her eyes darting around, looking around wildly for something. Danger, maybe?

I hesitated. This woman was wanted for murder. Even if she didn't do it, which I was inclined to believe since Burke was the witness, I wasn't sure that letting her come in was a good idea. It could only mean trouble for me.

"Come on," Jim snapped impatiently. I stepped aside without further thinking. If there was one person I trusted, it was Jim Samson. He must have brought the girl here for a reason.

Jim led her into the house, guiding her to the living room where she sat heavily on the couch, as if her legs couldn't hold her weight anymore. Jim stayed standing but didn't leave her side.

"What's going on here?" I asked, crossing my arms over my chest.

"There was a shooting tonight at The Verve," Jim said, rubbing his hand across his forehead as if he had a headache coming on.

"I know. It's all over the news."

"What?" the girl asked, her voice soft.

"Yeah, I was watching it when you guys showed up."

I pulled my phone out of my pocket and handed it to Jim. He started the video over at the beginning. After a few seconds, the girl was standing at his side, her eyes wide as she watched. When her picture was displayed on the screen, she let out a strangled sound and looked positively sick. Jim stopped the video and guided her back to her seat, his forehead creased in concern.

"It's okay. It'll be okay," he told her. I wanted to contradict him because I was sure that things were absolutely not going to be okay, but I bit my tongue when he shot me a warning look. He knew me too well.

"How can you say that? He framed me. Everyone thinks I'm a murderer. That I killed that poor man." She sounded hysterical, but I couldn't blame her. It looked like Burke had ruined another person's life. "Oh my God, I'm going to be sick." She shot to her feet, staggering as her face paled.

"This way," I said, jogging ahead to lead her to the half-bath by the kitchen. I hoped she'd make it. I really didn't want to clean up a mess.

I slammed the door open and turned on the light just as she shoved past me and fell to her knees in front of the toilet. The sound of her retching filled the small space. I almost left her to it, but I couldn't bring myself to do that. She looked so small and pitiful wrapped around my toilet. Instead, I knelt beside her and gathered her long hair in my hands, pulling it back from her face while she heaved.

It lasted for several moments until the sounds were replaced by her whimpering and she pulled away from the toilet. I snagged the hand towel from its holder and handed it to her silently. She took it without looking me in the eye. I was sure she must be embarrassed. I should probably give her some privacy.

"We'll be out in the living room. Take your time," I said, pushing myself to my feet and closing the bathroom door behind me.

"She okay?" Jim asked as I returned to the living room.

"Well, she's done vomiting," I said with a frown. "But I don't think she's okay at all. What the fuck is this? Why did you bring her here?"

"Hell, I don't know," Jim sighed and perched himself on the arm of the couch. "I couldn't think of anywhere else that she'd be safe."

"You want her to stay here?" I asked disbelievingly. He had to be kidding.

"She saw the murder. It was Burke. Or at least, he ordered it. She's a witness."

"It doesn't matter what she witnessed. She's the suspect now. That makes her word useless."

"But it does put her in serious danger. She needs a place to lay low, to stay safe until we can figure out a way to clear her name."

"That's not my problem," I retorted.

"Don't be an ass. You of all people know that Burke will kill her. You'll never forgive yourself if you turn her away." Jim's rationalizing was irksome.

"I have been trying to bring this guy down for years and he doesn't even know it. That's my only advantage over him. He doesn't realize I'm an enemy. Bringing the girl into this…it's too much risk."

"The girl has a name, you know," a voice said from behind me. I turned to see her standing in the living room doorway. She looked much better, her red eyes the only evidence of her traumatic bathroom episode.

"I'm sorry, Miss Monroe," I sighed. "I'm just trying to wrap my head around all this."

"You're trying to wrap your head around this?" Her eyes narrowed in anger. "What about me? Two hours ago, my life was normal, almost boring. I was doing my job and looking forward to having a day off tomorrow. The biggest problem I had was being short-staffed at the bar," she laughed humorlessly. "Now, my life is over. I can't go home. I have nothing but the clothes on my back. Nothing. Showing my face in public will get me arrested. I did nothing wrong here. Simply wrong place, wrong time, and now my life will never be the same. I'm so sorry if you're feeling a little overwhelmed, but the least you can do is refer to me by name when you talk about me as if I'm not even here!"

As she ended her rant, her chest heaving and her lips forming a tight line, I felt a tightening in my lower stomach and a twitch in my pants. Was I getting turned on?

I must be losing my mind.

But her words weren't lost on me. 'Wrong place, wrong time.' She was a victim here. I might have been an asshole, but I couldn't turn her away, no matter how much I didn't need the trouble in my life.

"Okay, Miss Monroe-"

"Lilly. Call me Lilly," she interrupted.

"Lilly, then. You can stay here for a while until we figure out something else," I said, causing her eyebrows to pop in surprise.

"You sure?" Jim asked.

"Yeah. Enemy of my enemy and all that. If Burke wants her, I'd say it's my duty to stand in his way."

"What a hero," Lilly said, rolling her eyes.

"I'm not going for sainthood here," I shrugged. "But I am on your side. Burke is a real piece of shit."

"It's settled then," Jim said, clapping his hands together.

Lilly had opened her mouth to speak but closed it with a sour look on her face. That was too bad. I almost wanted to hear what kind of fiery retort she had for me. I liked this argumentative attitude much more than the frightened bunny state she was in when she arrived. I didn't want to pity this woman that was turning my life upside down.

"I guess it is," she grumbled.

"You're welcome," I said wryly.

"Why don't you go lay down? You look dead on your feet," Jim said to Lilly, playing peacekeeper. That was fine and dandy, but how were we going to get along without him here?

"Yeah, I guess that's a good idea," she conceded. "Thanks for helping me."

I frowned. He gets a 'thank you.'

"Of course. We'll get you out of this mess," Jim said, heading for the door. "Grant, I'll be in touch."

When Jim was gone, the atmosphere in the room became tense immediately. Lilly shifted uncomfortably on her feet. "Follow me," I said shortly, leading her up the stairs to the guest room.

She followed along silently, and I was glad. I was feeling overwhelmed, having this woman I didn't even know in my personal space so suddenly. It didn't help that she came with some serious baggage.

"Here ya go," I grunted, stopping outside the guest room. "Bathroom's on the right."

I started to walk away before she'd responded. I was getting a headache and it did nothing to improve my foul mood. I had only walked a few feet when her voice rang out from behind me.

"Do you have something I can wear? These are the only clothes I have." I turned back, and she gestured at her outfit. She was wearing black, high-waisted dress pants with a white blouse tucked into them. Not exactly sleepwear.

"Uh, yeah. Hang on," I said, continuing to my room.

I didn't have any women's clothes and she was tiny compared to me. So, I grabbed a random t-shirt and a pair of basketball shorts with a drawstring. That would have to work.

When I returned to her, she was standing just inside the guest room, with the door open. I lingered in the doorway for a moment and watched as she walked around the space. She looked so lost and small, with her shoulders hunched and her arms wrapped around herself, as if she was trying to protect herself in some small way. I felt that stab of pity once again. Damn it.

I needed to get some space from this woman and get my head on right. I cleared my throat to catch her attention.

"Here. This'll have to do for now," I said, setting the outfit on the dresser by the door. "See ya in the morning."

I closed the door behind me and walked back to my own room, trying not to think about the vulnerability I just saw in Lilly's eyes. Her shields were down now, and the stark fear she was clearly trying to suppress was shining through. This was such a shit situation. The woman's life was in danger and, whether I liked it or not, I was her new protector.

Chapter Three
Lilly

What an asshole.

I stared at the door for a long moment after he closed it, leaving me alone in this unfamiliar place. I stifled the feeling of dismay that threatened to overwhelm me. My emotions were too raw; I felt like I was barely holding myself together and the deafening quiet of this large, impersonal guest bedroom made me feel more alone than I ever had in my life.

I paced the room, fueled by nervous energy. Based on the size of this room, of the whole house, this guy must be loaded. The room had the same dark hardwood flooring that ran throughout the home, which contrasted appealingly with the cream-colored walls. Everything, from the furniture to the huge area rug, looked expensive. A king-sized bed sat in the middle of the wall opposite the door and I was sure that it would be the most comfortable mattress I'd ever laid on. Too bad I wasn't tired at all.

The thought of sleep was laughable at this point. I already couldn't get the horrifying memories of the evening out of my head. The last thing I needed was nightmares.

Picking up the clothes Grant had left me, I opened the bedroom door and peeked out into the hallway. I felt oddly disappointed when I saw that it was deserted. It wasn't that I expected him to be lingering outside my door, or even wanted him to be. He hadn't exactly been welcoming to me.

But it was oddly soothing to be around someone else right now. Even if he was a jerk. A hot jerk.

Whoa, where did that thought come from?

I shook my head at myself as I entered the bathroom. Okay, maybe I noticed that his body was amazing. How could I not? He was shirtless, after all. Even with my own drama to contend with, my eyes couldn't help taking in the obvious strength of his body, with well-defined arms and hard ridges of muscle that made up his sculpted chest. The low-slung pajama pants he wore did nothing to hide the sexy v-shaped muscles of his lower abdomen.

The ink along his right arm, forming a half-sleeve tattoo in an intricate tribal pattern, was mesmerizing. It highlighted and defined the thick cords of muscle along his shoulder and bicep, making him even more alluring.

Feeling hot and bothered by my own thoughts, I stripped out of my clothes, leaving them in a careless heap on the floor. I turned the shower on, cranking it the far left, then adjusting to the hottest setting I could stand. I hoped that the noise of the water running didn't keep Grant awake. I was in no mood for any more hostility from him tonight.

That thought was like being doused with cold water, despite the warm shower. It didn't matter how attractive the man might have been physically, his attitude was a libido killer.

Killer.

Just thinking that one word made my chest tighten and my breathing turn shallow. I bent over and placed my hands on my knees as my vision went blurry with tears. The hot water pounded against my back as I finally let myself cry. My body was wracked with sobs that I tried desperately to keep quiet.

I couldn't say how long I stayed like that, bent over with tears streaking my cheeks. But when they finally ceased, I felt lighter, like I was able to breathe more freely. Nothing about my situation had changed, but the burden seemed slightly less formidable on the other side of my crying session.

I hurried through the rest of my shower, scrubbing my body with the Axe body wash that was in there. I didn't care if I smelled like a man.

By the time I stepped out of the shower, the mirror was coated with a thick layer of condensation, but I felt better. Much better than I would've thought possible, as if I had been cleaned inside and out. The fear was still there, and I was flirting with despair if I thought too hard about the state of my life, but at least I was safe for now.

I opened all the drawers and peeked in the medicine cabinet, hoping to find some toothpaste and a toothbrush, preferably new. No luck with either. There was a tiny, travel-size bottle of mouthwash in the vanity, so I opened it up and gave my mouth a thorough rinsing, twice. It wasn't as good as brushing my teeth, especially after retching earlier, but I supposed it was my only option for tonight.

Unfolding the clothes that Grant had brought me, I slipped the t-shirt over my head. It was way too big, flowing around me loosely and settling around my thighs. I thought about skipping the shorts, since the shirt was so long, but I didn't have any clean underwear. The shorts would have to cover my lower half. They were also large, but pulling the drawstring tight kept them up around my hips. I looked down at my body and felt so small in these clothes, but it would have to do.

Once I was back in the bedroom, I settled into the bed, leaving the bedside lamp on. It felt childish, but I couldn't stand the thought of total darkness. I was already dealing with spine-tingling anxiety that would make sleeping hard enough.

I was right about the comfort of the bed, but it didn't keep away dark thoughts. No matter how hard I tried to clear my mind, the image of that man crumpling to the ground haunted me. I didn't even know his name, but I knew I would never forget seeing him die.

It was hours before sleep finally took me, and even then, it was fitful. My dreams were filled with terror and death until my mind seemed unable to take any more. Finally, I reached a deep slumber and mercifully remembered nothing else until morning.

***

I slept late the next morning. Jolting awake suddenly at nearly 11 am, There was a moment, as soon as I opened my eyes, that I was overcome with confusion. Waking up in a completely unfamiliar place was startling, but it was seconds later, when the memory of my circumstances came crashing in, that I sat bolt upright in bed with a gasp.

There was something about waking up to this realization that made it more real. There was no pretending it was all a bad dream now.

Taking a moment to steel myself, I forcefully pushed aside my negative thoughts. I wasn't going to fall to pieces over this situation. I had allowed myself a good cry last night, but now it was time to put on my big girl panties and make the best of this.

Still, I hesitated before climbing out of bed. A small part of me wanted to hide out in the bedroom to avoid Grant, at least for a little while.

It was my rumbling stomach that made the decision for me. I hadn't eaten in nearly eighteen hours, and I'd expelled that meal into Grant's toilet. I needed food, now.

Making my way downstairs, I took the time to notice everything that I had missed the night before. I was right in thinking that this was a nice house. I'd say it qualified as a mansion. Looking both ways down the hallway, there were at least eight rooms on the second floor alone. The ceilings were high, with crown molding throughout, and not a single stair creaked or squeaked as I made my way down.

Passing through the living room I'd been in last night, I took note of the black leather furniture and stone fireplace. Onward to the kitchen, which was huge, and I was immediately drawn to the smell of coffee. There was half a pot on the warmer by the stove and I didn't hesitate to search the Cherrywood cabinets until I found a mug. A few heaping spoonfuls from the sugar bowl later, I was clutching a perfect cup of joe as I continued my self-guided tour of the house.

The kitchen opened into a great room. This room was clearly the heart of the home. There was a huge flat screen TV mounted on the far wall and pool table off to the side. A big gray sectional took up most of the space in the room, along with an overstuffed recliner. There were small details that showed Grant spent time here – a pair of slippers that had been carelessly kicked off by the couch, a half-finished bottle of water along the edge of the pool table, a book on the end table by the chair with a pair of reading glasses laying on top.

A pair of French double doors led out into the backyard and I could see a huge inground pool. That was something I'd have to try out soon. But right now, I was drawn to a door behind the pool table. I could hear the unmistakable sounds of a treadmill being used on the other side and, before I could stop to overthink it, I pushed the door open. Grant was there, running all out on the inclined treadmill, wearing only a pair of basketball shorts similar to the ones on my own body. Sweat glistened on his bronze skin and I felt my insides clench with need.

His cobalt blue eyes met my own and he pushed a button on the treadmill, causing it to slow down before coming to a stop. His chest heaved as he panted, and I found myself staring at the movement, wondering what his skin would feel like pressed against my bare breasts.

Damn, I really needed to get myself under control.

Grant grabbed a towel off the side of the treadmill and wiped his face. He looked around the room, his forehead furrowed. Taking an educated guess, I reached behind myself and grabbed his water bottle.

"Looking for this?" I asked, holding it up.

"Yeah, thanks," he said, stepping closer to take it from my hand. I could feel the raw heat radiating from his body as he drew near.

The second he had ahold of the bottle, I took a step back. I couldn't get too close to this man while he was barely dressed like this. It was causing the most ridiculous thoughts. Thoughts I couldn't handle right now.

"How'd you sleep?" he asked, taking a swig of the bottle, downing half of it in one huge gulp.

"Uh, fine," I said, surprised by the question. I guess we're playing nice today.

"I'd say so. It's damn near noon," he said with a smirk. I frowned. Okay, maybe nice was wishful thinking.

"Well, I had a rough night."

Something primal flashed in his eyes then, but it was gone before I had a chance to analyze what it was.

"You missed breakfast, but feel free to help yourself to anything in the kitchen." He eyed the mug in my hand and I felt my face flush. "I'm guessing you won't have a problem with that."

"Are you really giving me shit over a cup of coffee?" I asked, unwilling to overlook his passive-aggressive attitude.

"No," he sighed. "At least, I don't mean to."

He wrapped his towel around the back of his neck and started forward, squeezing past me into the great room. I held my breath as he came within inches of touching me.

"I'm just not used to having someone in my space," he continued with a frown. "I'm a loner, haven't lived with anyone in years. Damn near a decade."

"I know this isn't ideal for either of us. But I'm not trying to encroach on your territory," I dropped my eyes to the pool table, not wanting to look into his piercing gaze. I felt vulnerable, depending on this man's hospitality and protection. "I just want to make the best of this."

"Fuck," he said before draining the rest of his water bottle. He walked into the kitchen and tossed it carelessly into the trash. I watched as he stalked back over to me, looking pensive. "Okay, you're right. We need to make the best of this."

"I am?" This guy kept surprising me.

"Yeah, don't get used to it," he said with a small smile. I rolled my eyes.

"What do you suggest then?"

"Let's start over." He held out his hand to me, humor dancing in his eyes. "I'm Grant Donovan, a grumpy bastard that can't help himself sometimes."

I let out a startled giggle before grasping his hand in my own. It was warm and slightly rough, indicating he was no stranger to working with his hands.

"Well, Grant, I'm Lilly Monroe. I'm having a streak of bad luck you wouldn't believe, and I'll be your roommate for the foreseeable future."

"Alrighty then. Grab something to eat while I take a shower," he said, releasing my hand and starting to walk away.

"Tell me, Grant, are you always this bossy?" I asked, trying to emulate our fun banter to cover up my real annoyance with him.

"Yep," he called over his shoulder as he passed through the kitchen. He stopped in the doorway and turned around. "Oh, I washed your clothes. They're back in your bathroom so you can get dressed after you eat. We're going shopping."

"Shopping?" He wanted me to go out in public? Was he crazy?

558

"Yep," he called out again before I heard his footsteps on the stairs.

I groaned in frustration. This fresh start thing was a cute idea, but we were never going to get along if he kept ordering me around. Deciding the argument could wait until after lunch, I headed to the kitchen to scrounge up a meal.

Chapter Four
Grant

"Come on, let's go in," I urged Lilly as she hesitated to open the car door. It had been a pain in the ass to get her here at all and now that we were finally at the boutique she refused to open her car door.

I ground my teeth in irritation. We had already argued about the idea of shopping at home. She was afraid to leave the house, but I insisted. She needed clothes. I'd talked her into it by agreeing to take her to one small women's boutique in a wealthy neighborhood, so it wasn't likely to be crowded. She had still insisted on stopping at a convenience store on the way and buying big round sunglasses and a floppy hat. She looked ridiculous, pairing that with her business casual clothing, but I didn't want to go another round with her over it. Besides, it was kind of funny.

I was just glad that she was back in her own clothes. I hadn't been prepared this morning, when she walked into my gym, for my body's reaction. What was it about seeing women in our clothing that got men so worked up?

It didn't help that Lilly had long, toned legs that looked like they'd fit perfectly wrapped around my waist. I also knew that she was wearing nothing underneath, since I had found her underwear in the bathroom with her other clothes this morning. There was a tightening in my pants now at just the thought of her bare body rubbing against my clothing. Those shorts were so loose on her, too. It would've been easy to gain access to the core of her. God, I wanted access to that.

Forcefully derailing that train of thought, I brought my attention back to the present. Lilly seemed jumpy, head swiveling around to track the people on the street, trying to detect any danger. But there was none to be found.

"Look at me," I commanded, and she turned her head to face me. I could see my own reflection within the frames of her sunglasses, which kept her captivating gray eyes hidden from view. "You're going to be fine. I'll be with you the whole time."

"You think you can keep me safe? What if the police show up to arrest me?"

"That's unlikely. Any other customers in this store are going to be too wrapped up in their own little lives to pay us any attention at all. We shouldn't see a bunch of people here anyway, but I'll keep an eye on our surroundings. We'll leave if someone is paying you undue attention. I just need you to trust me," I said earnestly. I may not have been happy about our living situation, but I would protect her if she needed it. I wasn't a monster, after all.

I watched the lines of her body become more rigid and her jaw clench. I could literally see determination taking over her body and wasn't surprised when she suddenly nodded curtly to me and grasped the car door handle. "Okay. I'll trust you," she said before pushing the door open and stepping out into the sunshine.

There was a foreign feeling swelling within my chest at her words. She was putting her faith in me and it filled me with pride.

I had to admire her ability to push aside her fears and her resolve to follow through. As I walked behind her, that wasn't the only thing I admired. The black pants she wore outlined her firm ass in an eye-catching way.

Pure lust shot through me once again and I clenched my fists. I had known this woman less than twenty-four hours, yet she was proving to be both a thorn in my side and an alluring temptress. I needed to keep some distance between us.

Practicing some self-control might be a good idea, too.

The boutique was a squat building with large glass windows in front, where they had mannequins wearing dresses. It was connected to other businesses on each side, sharing one wall with a doggy treat bakery and the other with a home décor store. The whole street was laid out in an old-fashioned but charming way, with exposed brick giving the buildings and shops a historical feeling.

There were many eclectic shops in this area, along with art galleries, bars, and restaurants. It was all upscale, though, catering to the wealthiest people in the Chicago area with prices the average person would never be able to pay. So, we saw few people on the street as we headed toward our destination.

A bell above the door dinged as we entered the little shop. There were only two other customers in the place, both women chattering animatedly together as they loaded their arms up with blouses and dresses.

The woman behind the counter greeted us warmly but didn't attempt to approach. Good. I wasn't a fan of pushy salespeople and Lilly was nervous enough already.

Lilly faltered just inside the door, looking around at the racks of clothing scattered throughout and nibbling on her bottom lip. Striding forward to the nearest rack, I beckoned her to follow. She had nothing but the clothes she was wearing at the moment, so I would be buying her a whole wardrobe today.

But I wasn't a huge fan of shopping. I wanted to get this over with.

I was pawing through the dresses carelessly, the silky material soft against my rough palms, when I realized that I had no idea what I was doing. I didn't know her size or what she'd like to wear. I guessed that meant I would be standing around bored, probably holding whatever she wanted to buy.

Shopping was the worst.

I felt myself grow agitated with Lilly for a brief moment. I was stuck doing this because she had been thrust upon me. It was only the first day and I was already being inconvenienced.

"Oh my God, look at this price!" Lilly exclaimed, holding out a yellow wrap-around dress with a low-neckline that I was sure would make her breasts look amazing. We were definitely buying that. I glanced at the price tag.

"Don't worry about that," I said.

"Grant, I can't afford this place," she hissed, glancing toward the sales clerk to make sure she wasn't being overheard. "This one dress is almost as much as my rent. That's crazy."

"You can't pay for this stuff."

"That's what I'm saying!" she said, exasperated.

"No, I mean the police will be tracking your credit and debit cards. You can't use them."

"Oh," she said, her cheeks turning an adorable shade of red. "Of course, I should've thought of that."

"So, don't worry about the price."

"Why would you want to pay so much for clothes for me? That doesn't make sense."

"Money isn't a problem for me. I'm a billionaire," I said. It felt awkward saying those words out loud. Most of the people I spent time with already knew about my money.

"What?" Lilly's eyes bulged as she looked at me.

"Yeah. I would've thought it was obvious from the house and all."

"Well, yeah, I guess. I mean, the house is nice, but a billionaire? I can't even comprehend that type of money."

She looked at me thoughtfully and I was worried that she was seeing me differently now that she knew about the money. Not that I cared what she thought.

Not at all.

"So, don't worry about the price. I could buy everything in this store if I wanted to. It's no big deal."

"I'm not looking for a handout though. Just a safe place to stay."

"You need more than one outfit," I told her, reasonably, "and we're already here. Let's just get this done."

"Fine, but I want the receipt. I'll pay you back." She looked at the price tag on another dress and grimaced. "I might have to make payments for the rest of my life, though."

"Don't worry about that. Seriously," I caught hold of her arm and squeezed gently. "I won't take a dime."

Lilly froze for a moment, her gaze drawn down to where my hand touched her. There was a tingling sensation spreading through my body from the contact. The air between us seemed charged and I quickly broke the connection, taking a small step back so I was out of her personal space.

"So, uh, yeah," I cleared my throat, "let's just get this over with already. Don't even check the price tags."

"Whatever," she mumbled, but I saw that she didn't look at them anymore.

She skimmed through the racks of clothing quickly, pulling out dresses, blouses, even jeans. When her hands were full, I took the load from her and followed her around the store like a lost puppy. It was going fine, perhaps a bit boring, but fine, until we reached the back of the store. This was the lingerie section.

I tried to remain indifferent, to ignore the way my blood heated as she picked up a red lace bra and panty set, but it proved to be impossible. I tried to cling to my convictions, that this woman was a burden that I didn't want around, but my body was a traitor.

"I think I'll take these clothes to the register, have her hold onto them up there," I said, my voice uneven. She was looking at a silky nightie that looked like it would be see-through. This woman was killing me.

"Okay, I'll meet you over there," she called carelessly over her shoulder, but I could've sworn I saw the hint of a smile on her face. Did she know what she was doing to me?

***

"Really? You eat at McDonald's?" Lilly asked as I turned into the parking lot and joined a long drive-thru line. We had just left the boutique and I was starving.

"Sure. Why wouldn't I?" I asked, turning to look at her.

"I don't know. I guess I just never thought of someone so rich eating fast food like the rest of us."

"I'm still a human," I said with an eye roll.

"I know. I guess it's silly, I just think of people with so much money going to fine dining restaurants for steak and lobster."

"Steak is good, but sometimes a man just wants a decent burger." My stomach chose that moment to growl, as if demonstrating my point. Lilly laughed lightly.

"Were you born into it?" she asked thoughtfully.

"Into what?"

"Your wealth. Are you a trust fund baby?"

"Not at all. I grew up on the south side of the city, the younger of two boys raised by a single mom. She worked as a nurse at South Shore Hospital for years," I smiled, thinking of my mom. "We definitely weren't rich, but I didn't have it too bad. Learned to appreciate a good old Mickey D's burger for a dollar."

"Wow. Does your mom still live in Chicago?"

"No," I said curtly, my defenses coming up. Family was a sore subject with me.

"Well, she must be proud of your success. What about your brother? Does he live nearby?"

I tightened my grip on the steering wheel until my knuckles turned white. Why did she have to bring him up?

"Success is putting it lightly," I said, clinging to any subject that wasn't my family. I tried to sound casual, but my voice was strained. "I started D-Tech. You heard of it?"

"I don't think so," Lilly said.

"It's an internet and technology firm. Between D-Tech and our subsidiary companies, we do it all, from e-commerce to AI to social networks. I'm one of the youngest self-made billionaires out there. So yeah, I'm not just a success, I'm the American dream," I smirked.

I knew I was coming across as an arrogant jerk, but I had to push her buttons to get her to stop asking these questions. It was bad enough that I had this intense attraction to her, the last thing I needed was to open up about all my personal problems and see the pity in her eyes. I couldn't stand any more of that.

"Okay, then. Good for you, I guess," Lilly replied. She propped her elbow up on the passenger door and stared out the window, facing away from me.

She was completely shut down and I felt a lump in my throat, knowing that I was responsible. Why did I have to be such a dick?

I told myself it was better this way, keeping distance between us. I needed to focus on my vengeance against Burke anyway. Lilly Monroe was a distraction that I did not need.

Chapter Five
Lilly

It had been five days since Grant took me shopping and I had since settled into a routine here at Chez Donovan. Grant woke up early every day and worked out, usually leaving for work around the time that I crawled out of bed and stumbled down the stairs. I was used to working nights at the club and horrible dreams plagued my nighttime hours, so I tended to sleep in a bit.

After that, I'd have the whole day to myself in this gorgeous mansion. There were five bedrooms - and one master suite that Grant kept locked when he wasn't home-, four bathrooms, a home office, a living room, a great room, a big kitchen, a formal dining room that looked like it'd never been used and an outdoor living area complete with a heated pool, firepit and grill.

It was a lovely home.

I was already bored.

There was only so much TV I could watch, or so many books I could read. Grant had a cleaning lady come twice a week, so there was nothing to clean. I had been here less than a week and I felt like the walls were closing in on me.

I knew a part of the problem was loneliness. I had no family that I was close to, so there was nothing to miss there, and I had devoted much of my time over the last few years to work and school, so I didn't have many friends. But I was still used to interacting with people regularly; coworkers, customers, the barista at my favorite coffee shop.

I wondered if Andre had noticed that I hadn't been in to pick up my normal coffee order in a while. Though he may not have been surprised if he watched the news.

Now, the only person I interacted with was Grant, and that was hardly better than being alone. I had thought that we were making progress on Sunday when we talked about a new start and went shopping. Then, he shut down and had been avoiding me as much as possible ever since.

I didn't want to care if he was around, but the man was my only company at this point. He was my connection to the outside world.

Sometimes he wasn't bad company either.

Lately, he had been coming home from the office, eating dinner with me, then disappearing upstairs for the night. Dinner conversation was stilted at best. I would try to engage him but his grunts and one-word responses made it impossible. At least I had figured out one topic to avoid: his brother. Nothing made Grant shut down, or even lash out, as quickly as bringing him up.

I was getting frustrated and stir-crazy.

Part of the frustration was sexual. Damn that man and his hard body. I had caught a glimpse of his workout routine this morning when he left the door to the gym cracked. He was lying flat on a workout bench, using a bar with several large weights at each end. His breathing was steady as he pushed the bar out from his body and brought it back toward his chest with a controlled steadiness. The thick cords of muscles in his arms bulged and I had the absurd impulse to go straddle his hips. I wanted to feel all that strength beneath me, preferably while we were both naked. I wanted to taste him. All of him.

It was crazy. I had no experience with that. Between my troubled teenage years and working to better myself in school and work for the last four years, I hadn't found time to date someone seriously. A few groping sessions in the back of movie theaters or in a car were as far as I'd ever gotten with a man.

Yet, my mind had no trouble conjuring up images and cravings that made my core throb with need. It was almost cruel, to be so close to this man, this Adonis, and to not even be seen. Who was I kidding, anyway? The man was an unbelievably sexy billionaire. He could have any woman he wanted. There was no way he'd look twice at the virgin that had disrupted his life so much.

The only thing that occupied my time was cooking. I had taken it upon myself to prepare dinner every night. It wasn't something that Grant had asked me to do; in fact, he seemed shocked the first time I did it. I also thought I'd seen a warm expression flash across his face. Then it was gone.

I didn't know if that brief softening of his features was real, but I kept cooking every night anyway. I told myself it was just to have something to do, but it's hard to lie to yourself. I was chasing that warmth, hoping to break through the hardened exterior that Grant kept around himself and see what was underneath, to find the kindness that I had convinced myself was there. So far, that hadn't happened, and it just served to make my mood worse.

What was I doing here? How long could I keep this up?

I was attracted to a man that didn't want me around, the police wanted to arrest me for murder, and my boss – well, ex-boss – probably wanted me dead. Here I was playing house, with no plan for my future, no way out of this mess.

How did my whole life unravel so quickly? I hadn't realized it was so fragile in the first place, that one bad night could change everything. A feeling of hopelessness washed over me. I felt like I was waiting for something to happen. How long could I sit around and wait? Did I even have any other option?

These thoughts swirled through my mind as I sat at the massive kitchen island, eating dinner alone. I had made chicken alfredo, one of my favorites and the only thing my mom had taught me to cook before she died. Grant was late. Every night he had been coming home at six o'clock. The food was fresh and delicious then.

It was now almost two hours later, and I had given up on waiting for him. I nuked my own food in the microwave and left his sitting, a ball of anger forming in my stomach and growing bigger the longer I sat there looking at it.

Finally, as I finished eating my own food, I heard the garage door opening. He was strolling into the house a minute later, his face buried in his phone and seemingly oblivious to my agitation.

He strolled to the refrigerator without acknowledging me at all, grabbing a beer before he finally looked up from the screen in his hand. My temper must have been reflected in my face, because he stood rooted to the spot, staring at me.

"Hey, what's up?" he asked, fueling my anger more. That was the most he'd spoken to me in days.

"'What's up?' Where have you been?" I asked, my hands on my hips.

"What?"

"I asked where you were. Why you left me waiting here for you for two hours."

"I was at work," he snapped, his face looking confused.

"Why were you there so late? I expected you at six. I had dinner ready and everything."

"I never asked you to make me dinner."

"This isn't about dinner."

"Then what's your problem? You're being irrational."

Was I? I couldn't bring myself to care.

"My problem is you. And Mr. Burke. And the whole damn police force. My problem is that the only person I see day-in and day-out doesn't even care enough to tell me that he won't be here," I felt so weak, admitting that his indifference bothered me.

"My life doesn't revolve around you, Lilly. I'm not here for your entertainment. I'm just providing a safe house."

"I'm not asking for entertainment. Can't we just be friendly to one another?"

"We're not friends. While I'm at it, we're not lovers, so I don't owe you any explanation of my whereabouts. You're my responsibility. That's all."

With those hurtful words, he pivoted on his heel and marched out of the kitchen. I heard him stomping up the stairs until he slammed his bedroom door like a teenager throwing a tantrum. I wanted to follow him and continue the fight, as unhealthy and pointless as that may have been. At least I wouldn't be alone.

Instead, I tossed his untouched plate into the sink and wandered into the great room. I already regretted picking a fight with Grant. I was lashing out because of my own unhappiness and insecurities.

He was right, it wasn't his job to entertain me, and it wasn't his fault that I was in this situation. That blame lay solely with Mr. Burke.

I paced the length of the great room, making a few laps before the sight of the pool caught my eye. I had tons of nervous energy, maybe a quick dip in the pool could help with that.

I didn't have a swimsuit, but my bra and panties were black and fit well. I would probably be fine in that. Stepping through the French doors, I pulled my short navy-blue dress over my head, tossing it onto a patio chair before kicking my sandals off.

It was invigorating, being outside in my underwear. They were no more revealing than a string bikini, even less so perhaps, but a tingle ran along my spine and I felt risqué. I looked around, even though Grant had an eight-foot-tall fence and no one could see me.

Walking to the edge of the pool, I looked down into the clear water. There were blue lights built into the sides of the pool, lighting it from beneath. Taking a deep breath, I dove headfirst into the warm water. Starting to swim to the far edge of the pool, I slid through the water with ease.

This pool was amazing, large and rectangular, it was four feet at the shallow end and gradually got deeper and deeper until it reached twelve feet. He even had a high rise diving board on that end. This was the type of pool you'd find in a high-class gym or maybe a well-funded high school. I usually swam at a public pool, not being anywhere near financially secure enough to buy a home with one, but the community pool I went to was nothing compared to this. It was probably half the size and usually full of teenagers horseplaying. So, this was a hell of a luxurious swim. If I was lucky, I'd tire myself out doing this and actually get some peaceful sleep tonight.

Chapter Six
Grant

This wasn't working. Avoiding Lilly was futile at this point. She was everywhere in this house; if not physically, then there were signs of her lingering, memories of her presence and how it affected me. The only exception was this room, my master suite. It was the one room I actually wanted her in. If she would just step through that door, I may never have let her out again. I desperately wanted her in my bed, beneath me.

But the more we interacted, the further that fantasy drifted away from me. I couldn't seem to stop myself from lashing out, pushing her away. As far as the argument we just had, I should've seen it coming.

I had been avoiding her as much as possible all week and it didn't occur to me that she had no one else to talk to, no other companion to share things with. I had been a selfish ass and then acted defensively when she called me out on it.

It was amazing how she would call me on my bullshit anytime. No one else in my life did that. Maybe it was the money making them nervous, but nearly everyone I interacted with kissed my ass all the time.

Not Lilly.

Not my fiery temptress.

She wasn't intimidated by me at all. Damn, that was so hot. Every time she squared up to me, ready for an argument, I wanted to throw her down on the closest surface and ravage her sweet body. I wanted to hear her scream my name in pleasure, not anger.

Fuck, this was hopeless. It was starting to feel inevitable. But I had unfinished business to deal with. Burke was still a free man and I had made it my mission to take him down. I couldn't let myself get so distracted by this gray-eyed beauty with a sharp tongue.

Speaking of distractions, a shadow passed over the ceiling above my bed, where I lay staring at the ceiling and fighting off an erection at the thought of Lilly. The light in my room came from the pool below in the backyard. I had glass double doors in my master suite that lead to a balcony overlooking my outdoor living space. So, what was that shadow?

Standing, I walked to the doors and peered down. There she was, the woman that was driving me crazy. Lilly's body was silhouetted against the bright lights in the pool, so I could just make out the outline of her slender form as it slid through the water. She had a grace that I never could've imagined, flowing smoothly as if she were a part of the water itself.

My immediate compulsion was to go down there.

Nope. Not going to happen. Couldn't happen. It was a bad idea.

I kept up this stream of internal dialogue all the way down the stairs, through the kitchen and great room, and was thinking it as I came to a stop at the pool's edge. A lot of good it did. Apparently, my mind didn't have control of my body, which was drawn to Lilly as if she had a gravitational pull I couldn't break free of.

Did I even really want to?

As Lilly caught sight of me, she swam over to the steps and climbed out. As I got a good look at her dripping body, my mouth went dry. My dick gave a painful jerk in my pants as my eyes trailed down her back and took in the sight of her little ass hanging out the bottom of her underwear.

Then she turned around. Her auburn hair looked darker while it was wet, trailing over her shoulders and laying against the tops of her breasts. Lucky hair.

The swells were barely contained by her wet bra and I could just barely see the outline of her hardened nipples through the fabric. Raw want overcame me, and my entire body became aware of hers, making my skin feel overly sensitive.

Her smooth pale skin contrasted sharply with the dark material of her underwear, and the sight caused maddening arousal. The fight to control myself was almost painful as she walked near, her cheeks turning pink as she approached. She crossed her arms over her chest and I wanted to growl as I lost sight of her large breasts.

"Hey, I hope it's okay that I used the pool…"

I just nodded. I didn't trust myself to speak.

"I forgot a towel. Let me grab one and then we can talk, okay?" She sounded timid, almost afraid. That brought me out of my aroused state in a flash.

"Yeah," I said, my voice deeper than usual. I cleared my throat. "I'll wait for you here."

I took a seat on one of the patio chairs as she made her way inside, carefully adjusting myself so that my throbbing erection was less noticeable. She was back out in minutes, a thick towel wrapped around her chest, covering her body. What a crime.

She moved a chair in front of me and sat down, crossing her long legs. I noticed that her toenails were painted a bright red color. Cute.

"Listen, I think I owe you an apology. I know I jumped down your throat earlier," she began.

"Aw, hell. Lilly. It's not like I didn't have it coming. We both know that things have been tense around here lately. It's toxic for us both."

"I think I'm just feeling lonely. That's not your problem, but you're the only person I have to communicate with right now. I don't even have a cell phone," she sounded so defeated, not at all like the fiery temptress I was used to. I hated that she was trying so hard to get on my good side and taking all the blame, because it showed that I had been treating her like shit.

"No, I told you already, I'm a grumpy bastard. But I'll work on it."

"I guess you don't play well with others, huh?"

"Is it that obvious?" I asked, with a little grin.

"I think I'm the opposite actually. I thrive around people. That's why I worked at the nightclub. I just got my business degree a few months ago, but I had options. I chose to stay there, where I had already worked for years, because I like the people. I know and trust my employees. The customers can get rowdy sometimes, but there's a certain energy to them, to the whole place. It makes me feel connected."

"Do you have anyone in your life that will be missing you right now? Family, friends, boyfriend?" I could hear my blood rush through my veins as I asked that last one. A primal possessive urge was threatening to overtake me. I was starting to wonder if my mind even had control of my body.

"No. No close friends or boyfriend, I've had other priorities for the past few years. No close family, either. My parents died in a car accident when I was fifteen. I lived with my aunt until I was an adult, then she gave me the boot when I turned eighteen. She didn't really want to take me in in the first place, I think. She was the only option though, so she felt that there wasn't a choice."

"She sounds like a bitch."

"Maybe," Lilly said, her mouth quirking up for a second, but her eyes seemed far away. "But I was a handful back then."

"You?" I couldn't imagine it.

"Yep. I took my parents deaths hard, fell in with a bad crowd when I switched to a new school in the district where my aunt lived. We mostly just got drunk and partied. One of my friends was an amazing artist but didn't have a good outlet for it. So, she'd graffiti buildings, bridges, even stopped trains. Whatever was around. Once we all broke into an empty house that was for sale and had a party. Absolutely trashed the place. The cops came and rounded up as many of us as they could. I was one of them."

"Yikes."

"I know. It feels like a different lifetime. I got community service out of that ordeal. Also had to live with my aunt's crushing disappointment, but things changed after high school. I got my life on track and now I'm basically in witness protection at a billionaire's mansion and wanted for murder," she said sardonically.

I chuckled. "Good to see you can joke about it."

"Sometimes you gotta laugh to keep from crying" She looked at me thoughtfully for a moment. "Listen," she began. I cringed internally, sure that she was going to ask me about my family since I had asked about hers. I may have opened that door, but I still didn't want to talk about it. "We have to find some common ground here, make living together more bearable."

"Well, neither of us is a fan of Henry Burke, so there's that commonality," I said lightly.

"What's the deal with that? What did he do to you?"

"Honestly, I don't want to get into that tonight. Let's just say he made an enemy of me a long time ago and I've wanted to see him behind bars ever since." If I were honest, I'd like to see him in a casket, but I had to get some information out of him first.

"You know, I never cared for him. He always looked at me like I was a piece of meat. No, it was more than that. He looked at me like I was a piece of his property, something he owned because he signed my paychecks."

"The man thinks he's king of the world, that he can do or have anything he wants. He's a complete narcissist."

"I can see that," she said, nodding. She looked at me thoughtfully. "What I want to know is, how do you know Jim? You being such a loner, I have to wonder about the one guy I know you're friends with."

"Jim is one of those people you've known so long that it's hard to even recall a time he wasn't around. Like, I don't have a story about how we met because he's just always been a part of my life. I know our moms were friendly and we were in the same class all throughout Elementary school. He's just... he's always been a friend. I remember when we were younger, his mom used to keep his hair in this horrible bowl cut," I chuckled thinking about it, the unexpected sound of my own laughter in the quiet night startling me.

There was silence between us for a few long moments, but it wasn't uncomfortable. I looked out over the calm pool water, letting my mind wander.

"You know, his name was Mark." Lilly's soft voice broke the quiet unexpectedly. I had the feeling she was simply speaking her thoughts out loud. "The man that Mr. Burke killed. I looked it up the other day." She was staring up at the stars while speaking.

"Why did you look that up?"

"I don't know. I guess that I owed it to him or something. I watched the man die. I saw his last moments. I should at least try to know who he was," her voice sounded haunted.

"So, who was he?"

"Mark Lewis. According to the paper, he had an ex-wife and an arrest record. I guess he had a history of drug dealing."

"That's probably his connection to Burke," I said, then realized that wasn't very sensitive. "You must be pretty upset about it."

"I keep reliving it in my dreams. Hearing him beg for his life, the pop of the gun, I think it must have had a silencer because it wasn't very loud, then he just fell. He was gone so quickly. Everything he ever was, just gone in an instant," her voice cracked.

Without thinking about it, I reached out and grasped her hand. It was so small compared to my own and her skin was extraordinarily soft. I ran my thumb over the back of her hand, offering my comfort without words.

Her gaze returned to my face, staring at me as if she could see right into my soul. I felt my heart flutter. This was more than just lust, I was drawn to her because of who she was, because of the strength I could so clearly see. It terrified me.

Then she leaned in close, brushing her lips against my own. The kiss was gentle but powerful enough to terrify me. Every nerve ending in my body flared to life, making my skin feel more sensitive than usual. My muscles tensed and I longed to take control of the kiss, to take it to the next level, but I didn't want to ruin the sweetness of the moment.

When Lilly pulled away, I stared at her, speechless for the first time in my life. I wasn't expecting this, not after the fight we had just a few short hours ago. It felt like there was a shift in the chemistry between us now, a nonverbal acknowledgment of the attraction we shared. But we hadn't quite crossed that line yet.

"I'm, uh, I think I'll go to bed now," Lilly said, rising to her feet. "Good night, Grant."

With that she was gone, practically fleeing into the house. I wondered if she regretted the kiss, but I didn't think that was it. She seemed almost embarrassed. I had seen a hint of something in her stare...was it innocence?

The thought excited me, but I knew that was dangerous thinking. One kiss didn't make us lovers. But that didn't stop my imagination from filling my dreams with the image of her writhing beneath me, moaning in pleasure. I woke up needing a shower and hoping that some dreams do come true.

Chapter Seven
Lilly

What was I thinking?

I kissed him. I got caught up in the moment, in the comfort he provided and the intimate setting, with the moonlight and my body so exposed under the towel I was wearing. I knew that it was silly; the impetuous action of a girl clinging to any kindness she could get after going through a traumatic event. That was all it was.

So, why did my heart skip a beat when I thought of him?

It wasn't just sexual anymore. The kiss was amazing, making my body come to life in ways that it never had before, but I also felt drawn to Grant on a deeper level. There was a connection between us, an invisible tether that kept urging me to get closer, to get to know the man underneath the snarky comments and the distance that he forcefully kept between us. I knew, I could sense, that there was more to him. There was pain hidden within him and, I suspected, loneliness. I had seen glimpses of it over the last week, while he was doing his best to evade me. It just made me want to know him even more.

I had briefly considered hiding out in my room this morning, mortified about initiating the kiss. He had responded, his surprisingly soft lips molding to my own with ease, but I felt like I had crossed a line. How awkward would things be now? Or, even worse, would he simply go back to avoiding me as much as possible?

It was a Saturday, so I knew he didn't have to go to work. Guess I'll find out right away then.

As I left my bedroom – when did I start thinking of it as mine, instead of a guest room? – I heard the doorbell ring. In the time I had been here, only one person had come to the house, the housekeeper, Anna. She was a serious woman in her 50s, with blonde hair that she kept pulled back in a tight bun at the nape of her neck. I kept myself locked up in my room when she was around, trying to avoid being recognized, despite Grant's assurances that I needn't worry. Anna was unlikely to realize I was one of Chicago PD's most wanted since he had introduced me to her as his girlfriend visiting from out of town. If she thought it was odd that I was staying in a guest room, she kept it to herself.

Today was not one of Anna's normal cleaning days, and she had a key, so it surely wasn't her at the door. I lingered on the landing, just out of sight, as I heard Grant approach the door.

"Don't worry, it's Jim," he called out to me before opening the door. I had no idea how he knew I was there, but I was glad to hear his reassurance. I let out the breath I had been holding, hating that I felt so jumpy and worried all the time.

I stepped off the bottom stair as Jim stepped over the threshold. He and Grant clasped hands and patted each other's backs in the way that men greeted one another when they were old friends, like they wanted to hug, but were too manly for it. I wanted to snigger but restrained myself.

I followed them into the living room, noting that the air between the three of us was much more relaxed than it had been the last time we were here. Grant was less aggressive, seeming stoic and reserved as he settled into a straight-backed chair by the fire.

I took a moment to let my eyes roam over him as I stood near the doorway, unsure if I was welcome to join them. Grant was wearing a tight black t-shirt that showed off the hard lines of his body and allowed his tattoo to peek out from under the sleeve. The worn jeans hugged his hips and thick thighs, and I appreciated the view.

He had been wearing suits all week to the office, and while the man filled out a suit nicely, I preferred him like this. He was so relaxed in his casual clothes, seeming much more approachable, or maybe I felt that way because I was thinking of the way our mouths felt pressed together.

I pried my eyes away from Grant to greet Jim and found that he was already watching me with a knowing look in his eye. Oh, shit. My ogling must have been obvious.

"Hey, Lilly. How you doing?" The amusement was clear in his voice.

"I'm, uh-" I cleared my throat, feeling flustered. "I'm fine."

Was it really that obvious that I was attracted to Grant? He never indicated that he knew the effect he had on me, but if Jim had picked up on it so easily...

God, there's that feeling of mortification again.

"Why don't you take a seat?" Jim suggested, indicating the chair beside Grant. I purposefully sat on the couch instead.

"Any news on Burke?" Grant asked.

"Kind of. We got the autopsy report on our victim," Jim said, all traces of humor gone. I felt my blood freeze in my veins. Grant glanced at me.

"Do you want to go in the other room?" he asked, an uncharacteristic softness in his voice. I suddenly wished that I had taken the seat beside him. Why did I feel like I had to prove something to Jim anyway?

"I'd better stay," I said. I needed to know what was going on or I'd drive myself crazy.

"I need you to take a look at this picture, anyway," Jim said, pulling one out of a folder in his hand. As he handed it over, I immediately recognized the woman staring up at me. "Do you know her?"

"She was at the club that night, with Mr. Burke. She and another girl."

"Well, she has come forward as a witness. She says she was there with a friend, no mention of Burke, and saw you being intimate with the victim earlier in the evening."

"What?"

"Don't you see? They're painting the picture of a lover's quarrel. According to Mindy here," he took the picture back from me, "she saw the two of you with your tongues down each other's throats early in the evening. Then, just hours later, someone else saw the two of you argue and you shoot him. It's thought to be a crime of passion at this point."

"But that didn't happen, none of that happened! I didn't even know the man's name until it was reported in the news," I exclaimed. Grant's face was frozen, showing no expression, but I saw that he was tightly gripping the arms of his chair.

"I know. My point is that Burke is covering his tracks. You're the scapegoat," Jim said solemnly.

"Could this get any worse?" I asked desperately.

"Well, the good news is that he doesn't know where you are. He only knows Grant as a fellow billionaire entrepreneur that he rubs elbows with at fancy charity events and all that. He'd never suspect that Grant would hide you from him."

I was burning with renewed curiosity about Grant's connection to Mr. Burke – or Burke as Jim and Grant called him – but now didn't seem like the right time to ask him about it.

"What about the autopsy?" Grant asked, his voice cold.

"Not much there," he opened his folder again, his eyes scanning a piece of paper. "Victim's name was Mark Lewis. He had a single gunshot wound to the chest, perforating the heart and lung. Ruled a homicide, of course. The only surprise was the cocaine in his system. Lewis had a history of dealing, with a couple of prior arrests, but we didn't have him pegged as a user. Guess that changed."

"That makes sense," I said, my mind conjuring a memory from that night."

"It does?" Jim looked mildly surprised.

"Well, maybe. Before they...killed him," I swallowed thickly. "Burke said something about stolen product and that it was disrespectful. The man, Mark, said he'd pay him back. I bet the product was the drugs!" I felt like a regular sleuth.

"Could be," Jim said, thoughtfully.

"I knew that fucker was in the drug business. I'm telling you, he smuggles it in somehow," Grant told Jim.

"You're probably right, but we can't prove it yet. Hell, look at this situation," he nodded toward me. "The man murdered someone in public, outside a busy night club, and it's looking like he might get away with it. He knows how to cover his tracks."

"He won't get away with it. We just have to figure out a way to get to him," Grant replied, but he was looking at me.

I wanted to believe him but I couldn't see how we would ever be able to clear my name. It wasn't just my word against Burke's anymore. Now he had at least one witness against me, probably more if he needed them. My mind was a million miles away as Jim and Grant talked more. I vaguely heard them make plans for Jim to come over for dinner that evening, bringing his daughter who he had joint custody of since he got divorced last year, but not much else tracked. I was busy trying not to sink into despair.

It was beginning to look like I'd never be a free woman again.

***

By the time Jim left the house, I was feeling disheartened. I had fallen into the routine here, but it couldn't last forever. I had a life outside of this drama. Yeah, it centered mostly around work – which I clearly could never go back to even if I found a way to clear my name – but it was still mine.

I didn't belong here.

"I'm gonna throw some steaks on the grill for lunch. If you want to, uh, come outside or whatever…I mean, I don't mind…" Grant rubbed the back of his neck uncomfortably.

Adorable.

I suppressed a giggle, amazed at how much lighter he could make me feel with just a few stammered words.

"That'd be great. I could use some fresh air anyway."

Grant started gathering supplies in the kitchen, waving me away when I offered to help. So, I grabbed a couple of beers and walked outside onto the concrete patio. Being out here brought forth memories of the night before and the kiss I was trying not to think about. Best to act like it never happened, I decided, taking a seat.

The day was overcast, with gray clouds blocking out the blue sky. It made the summer day cool, with a light breeze that made goosebumps rise on my exposed arms. The tank top I wore didn't account for the weather.

I had just stood to my feet, prepared to go inside for a jacket, when Grant walked through the patio doors. His hands were full of plates, food, and cooking tongs. He also had two pullover hoodies draped over one arm. My heart seemed to swell as he carefully sat everything down on the patio table before handing me one of the sweatshirts.

I couldn't resist giving him a huge grin as I took the hoodie from his hand. He faltered for a moment, staring at me with a heated expression before he slowly blinked and turned away. I slipped the hoodie over my head and noticed that it smelled like Grant's body wash. He must have worn this recently.

The corners of my mouth stayed upturned as I settled back into my seat, watching Grant fire up the grill and season the steaks. He also had a couple of ears of corn in the husks. I watched as he carefully arranged everything on the grill before closing the lid.

"Do you grill out a lot?" I asked, twisting the top off my bottle of beer and taking a sip.

"All the time. I built this house, you know," he said. He wasn't bragging and being obnoxious like he had in the past. He was just talking to me and I found myself craving more, wanting to know everything. "I picked this land because I could envision this outdoor space. I put up these concrete walls around the backyard for security, but I own three acres. So, I have no close neighbors and complete privacy."

The idea of having complete privacy with Grant immediately made my mind conjure images of the two of us naked, maybe in the pool. Or against the wall, with him using those muscles of his to support my weight. Or even entwined on this very chair.

Stop, I commanded myself.

"When I was growing up, we lived in an apartment building with the world's thinnest walls. You couldn't flush the toilet without your neighbors hearing it. It drove me nuts, the way that we were all on top of each other like that. I always swore I'd live in the middle of the woods someday. Not a neighbor for miles around," he continued.

I looked around at the trees that were visible just beyond the perimeter of the backyard. I remembered the night that I was brought here; his long driveway wound from a busy road into a thick canopy of trees before his massive home came into view.

"I'd say you're pretty close to that," I said with a smile.

"Not quite, but I'm happy with this place. We didn't have a yard of our own at the apartment, obviously. Much less a patio or pool. This right here," he spread his arms out wide, beer still in his hand, "is my favorite part of my home."

"Me too, that I know of. I've never seen the master suite, so I can't be sure," I said. I hadn't meant for that to sound so suggestive. It had slipped out before I even considered the way it would sound.

As those words left my mouth, the air between felt charged with an energy that almost scared me. There was an intensity on Grant's face that made my legs tremble. I knew in that moment, without a doubt, that the attraction wasn't just one-sided. He wanted me too.

Before either of us could decide if we were going to act on those feelings, the jarring sound of a phone ringing cut through the quiet. Grant broke eye contact, fishing his phone out of his pocket and putting it up to his ear as he lifted the grill lid and flipped our steaks. I didn't know if I was relieved or disappointed at the interruption. I finished off my drink and Grant's was almost gone, so I went inside to grab two more while he talked.

"Fine. Make the arrangements. I'll leave first thing in the morning," Grant said into the phone as I walked back outside. He did not sound happy.

"You okay?" I asked as he ended the call abruptly.

"No, I have to fly to Oklahoma for business," he said, frowning.

"At the weekend?"

"Yeah, tomorrow morning. There's some serious accounting problem at one of my subsidiary companies. Our CFO thinks that the guy managing the company for us is fudging the numbers, recording more revenue than the company is actually earning."

"Wow. That's serious," I said. Grant could have a real mess on his hands.

"Yeah. If he's committing fraud, it can come back on D-Tech and spell big trouble for us. I have to go tomorrow so I have a chance to look things over on site while he's not there. If I find evidence of fraud, I can deal with it first thing Monday."

"So, you'll be gone for days?" I couldn't disguise the unhappiness in my voice.

"Probably. Unless I get lucky and it's all a big mistake. I could find nothing and be back tomorrow night." He didn't sound very confident.

"I hope so," I said. Then, realizing I sounded needy, I added, "for the sake of D-Tech."

In truth, I hated to see him go. We were finally starting to act like friends and I was afraid that he would revert to his aloof ways if he left now.

**

"Can you open a bottle of wine?" Grant asked as he laid out four marinated chicken breasts on a tray.

"Sure. Is red okay?"

"White is better with this meal. When it's dark meat, red is best."

"It's the best, period. I hate white wine," I said, scrunching up my nose in distaste.

"Are you crazy? What do you drink with fish?"

"I don't know. Water?"

Grant rolled his eyes and turned back to his meal preparations, but I could have sworn I heard him mumble the words "crazy woman" under his breath.

"Whatever, butthead," I said, using the corkscrew to open a bottle of red. He just laughed. I froze for a moment, startled at my body's reaction to the sound. I felt like there were tingles spreading all over my body.

What was this man doing to me?

I walked into the dining room and set the table. It was the first time I had even seen this room used, and I was sure that everything in here would've been covered in dust if Grant didn't have a maid come by twice a week. Jim was bringing his daughter to dinner. According to Grant, she was a five-year-old firecracker.

I gave her water to drink while pouring the wine into the other three glasses. I heard the patio doors open and close. Grant must have stepped outside to start grilling the meat. I headed back to the kitchen and tossed a salad together, marveling at how comfortable I felt here. This place wasn't what I would've expected for a billionaire's home.

I would've thought he'd have thirty rooms and separate wings of the house. Multiple floors and live-in servants. Maybe I watched too much TV as I was picturing Daddy Warbucks' house.

Grant's home was so much cozier. It felt lived in. The rooms had purpose, even if they weren't actually used often, like the dining room. It was so big that it felt cold, no matter the temperature. It was more personal.

I liked the house and I was starting to like Grant - a little too much.

The doorbell rang, derailing that train of thought, and I was grateful. I hurried to answer it just as Grant came back inside with four cooked chicken breasts that smelled heavenly.

A quick check of the peephole showed Jim, so I pulled the door open with a smile. He was wearing a pair of jeans and a polo shirt. Next to him, clasping his hand tightly, was a little girl with big brown curls and blue eyes. She looked up at me and my heart melted. Her eyelashes were miles long and when she smiled I saw that a front tooth was missing. She was wearing a red dress and white sandals.

"Welcome Jim," I said, then bent my knees until I was down at her level. "And what's your name, little lady?"

"Macy," she mumbled shyly.

"Welcome Macy, my name's Lilly."

I held my hand out to her and she shook it firmly. "Nice to meet you," she said, a slight lisp to her words because of the missing tooth.

So cute.

"Well, come on in, guys," I said, moving aside so they could pass. I closed the door behind them and followed Jim to the dining room.

"Something smells delicious," Jim said as he helped Macy into her chair.

"It's chicken," Grant said, walking into the room. "Ah, Miss Macy. Lovely to see you again," he said, adopting a posh accent and bowing low to her as she were a queen. Macy giggled, delighted.

I couldn't believe what I was seeing as Grant interacted with her playfully, shaking her hand and dramatically acting like she had crushed his fingers with her strong grip. It was a side of Grant that I never would have guessed existed. Grant pulled her out of the chair Jim had helped her into and demanded she help him in the kitchen, leading her as if he was the leader of a marching band.

"He's great with her, isn't he," Jim asked, as if reading my mind.

"Uh, yeah. It's shocking actually."

"I know he can be gruff, but that's the guy I knew when I was younger. The guy I grew up with."

"Then why is he-"

I cut myself off as Grant and Macy walked back into the room.

Grant was carrying the big bowl of salad while Macy had two pairs of tongs in her hands.

"Thank you, m'lady," Grant said, as she handed them over to him and he placed one pair in the bowl and the other with the meat.

"I have a couple of baked potatoes in the oven, staying warm," I said. "I'll grab those, and we can eat."

I made quick work of the potatoes, placing them on a plate and grabbing some butter and sour cream too. My hands were full as I walked back into the dining room, but I almost dropped everything in my hands when I heard Macy ask, "Uncle Grant, is Lilly your girlfriend?"

There was a beat where we all just stood there looking at each other. Then Jim answered.

"Lilly is a friend of ours."

I continued to the table and sat down everything, cursing myself for reacting so strongly to an innocent question posed by a child. Why was I so jumpy?

"But don't you think she's pretty?" Macy asked Grant.

I felt my face grow hot and I set about straightening silverware that didn't need it and unfolding napkins just to refold them again. Whatever I could find to keep myself busy.

"Yes, I do," Grant said, his voice tight. The fun accent was gone. Sensing the shift in the atmosphere of the room, Jim swooped in and picked Macy up under her arms, planting her back in her seat.

"Are you hungry, little monkey?" he asked, tickling her sides. She screamed and giggled, restoring the fun air. Thank God.

We all settled in to eat, Jim cutting up Macy's food and warning her sternly about the hot potato. I felt guilty for not letting hers cool a bit.

Jim and Grant made conversation easily, while I listened, contributing occasionally. Towards the end of the meal, I noticed with a jolt that this felt like Grant and I were entertaining as a couple.

Just like that, I could see that happening. I could envision a future where we had Jim and Macy over, maybe along with a woman he was dating at some point, welcoming them into our home. We would all eat a meal that Grant and I had prepared together. Then everyone would leave, and we would decide to leave the cleanup until morning because we just couldn't wait to get into the bedroom...

The fantasy was frightening in how real and attainable it seemed. My God, I had only kissed the guy once. Was I crazy?

"-he took a swing at me," I tuned back into the conversation as Jim was in the middle of a story. "I avoided it easily, but the gall this guy had, it was nuts. And he was a real deadbeat dad too, never-"

"Mommy says you're a deadbeat dad. What's that mean?"

Macy's words brought everything to a grinding halt. Jim froze for a second, then seemed to almost inflate in anger. His face was turning red and he was gripping his fork so tightly that I was afraid he'd bent it.

"What?" Jim asked, his voice so smooth that it caused goosebumps to rise on my arms. It was like being in the calm before the storm. Macy looked confused, clearly having picked up on the tension but not understanding where it came from.

"Hey, Macy, do you like to paint fingernails?" I asked, cutting across anything else Jim might say before he could think through the consequences of his words.

"I don't know. I've never done that before."

"Well, do you want to try? Because I have a pretty pink color that I have been wanting to put on for ages," I said, wiggling my unpainted nails in the air. "I bet you'd be great at it."

"Can I?" she asked Jim excitedly, her eyes lighting up and the gap in her teeth making an appearance as she smiled.

I shot Jim a significant look while Grant placed a hand on his arm and whispered lowly to him.

"Sure, princess. Go ahead," Jim said with a smile, but it seemed forced.

Taking Lilly by the hand, I led her to the guest bedroom I had been staying in. As soon as I closed the door, I heard indistinct shouting from downstairs. I was sure that Jim was raging against his ex-wife down there and, though we couldn't make any words, I didn't want Macy to pick up on anything amiss.

"Tell me, Macy, have you seen the movie Frozen?"

I knew I had struck gold when her face transformed into a look of glee.

"It's my absolute favorite movie ever!" she said in that dramatic way that kids do. "Do you like it?"

"Actually, I've never seen it, but I have heard some of the songs. Would you like to sing them with me while you paint my nails?"

"Yes, yes, yes!"

So, I handed over the nail polish and watched as Macy painted just as much finger as nail while we sang "Let It Go" over and over until she had taught me all the words. Then we moved onto my toenails.

In the time that we were upstairs together, I let Macy make a mess of my fingernails and toenails while we worked our way through quite the collection of Disney classic tunes. Then I painted her fingernails as she told me endless stories about her kindergarten classmates. By that time, the shouting had long since stopped, so I wasn't worried about what she might hear. I just listened to her.

It was the best time I had had in weeks. Macy was a bundle of energy and life. She experienced everything so fully, completely submerging herself into every experience. It was awe inspiring.

That was how Jim and Grant found us. Sitting side by side on the floor with our backs propped up against the bed as she talked, and we blew on our nails to dry them faster.

"Time to go home, princess," Jim said as he stepped into the room and helped her to her feet. He mouthed a "thank you" to me when her back was turned, and I just smiled.

I trailed along behind as Grant walked them to the front door. We both said goodbye and Macy told me she loved painting nails. When we closed the door behind them, my mind flashed to my fantasy from earlier.

At this point, we would go up to the bedroom and make love.

"You were amazing with her," Grant said, an emotion I'd never seen from him before shining in his eyes.

"She's a great kid," I said, trying not to sound too breathless as my mind stayed locked on the fantasy.

"I better go to bed. I have to leave early in the morning," Grant said. It was like being doused with cold water. Not only were we definitely not a couple and not going to bed together, he was leaving in the morning and I'd be trapped in this house alone for days.

"Okay. Well, goodnight," I said.

Then Grant stepped forward and, before I even knew what he had planned, he brushed his lips against my own. It was just a gentle touching of the lips before he pulled back, but it made my blood boil. His soft lips sent electricity dancing across the surface of my skin, making me crave so much more.

"Goodnight, Lilly," he said, looking into my eyes. I gulped as he turned and walked up the stairs. That man was going to be the death of me.

Chapter Eight
Grant

It was a long three days in Oklahoma. We had acquired JumpStart Media, a small startup that developed third-party gaming apps last year and it had done well in that time, or so we thought. It turned out that the guy we put in charge, a man named Steve that had seemed well-qualified, was misleading us. The company was struggling, and we didn't know.

Steve was arrested, and I spent the next two days dealing with the shitstorm that followed. I had to deal with angry shareholders that wanted answers, then decide the future of Jumpstart Media. Revenue was in the toilet because the poor performance hadn't been addressed before now. At this point, the company was a liability and it made more sense to shut it down.

But I was reluctant to do that. Some hard-working people would lose their jobs if I walked away from it now. Besides, I had bought the company because it had potential. D-Tech was doing great, but I liked the idea of getting into the gaming app business.

My success in business came from following my instincts, so I decided to find a new GM for the company and keep a close eye on things for a while. It wasn't an easy task and was made even more difficult by the resistance of D-Tech's Board of Directors.

Now, it was Wednesday morning and I was finally back in Chicago. My mind was focused solely on the comforts of home as I drove away from the airport: my own bed…a home-cooked meal…Lilly…

If I were honest with myself, I was looking forward to seeing her the most. How did I grow so attached to this woman?

There was just something about her, a sweetness that was reflected in the way that she tried to get to know me, even when I made it difficult for her, and the pain she carried from the killing she had witnessed. I was amazed to learn that her nightmares and dark thoughts centered almost entirely on that moment, when she had seen the man die. She was in serious danger – hell, she had been pursued by a man shooting at her – but the greatest horror of this situation for her wasn't about that or the fact that her life and reputation were decimated. It was the death of a stranger.

I could so easily see her heart, as she wore it on her sleeve, and it drew me to her, despite my best efforts to create distance between us. I could also see how much she wanted me and it set my blood on fire.

There was a break in the trees on my left as my driveway came into view. I turned and made my way up the twisty drive until the big white house finally came into view. I felt my heart surge up into my throat as I took the car into the driveway, a silver Aston Martin that looked a little too familiar. But it couldn't be…

I sped up, causing gravel to fly into the grass along the sides of the driveway, but I didn't care. I had to get to the house, now. I didn't understand how it was possible, but that was Burke's car. Had he come for Lilly?

Cursing myself for leaving her alone, I jumped out of the car as it skidded to a stop in front of the garage. Taking the porch steps two at a time, I didn't hesitate to let myself into the house, noting that the door was unlocked.

The foyer was empty, and I wanted to call out to Lilly, to locate her immediately, but a small part of my mind held onto rationality and demanded I proceed with caution. I strode to the living room, adrenaline coursing through my body and preparing for a fight if needed. He better not have hurt her.

The living room was empty, and dread pooled in the pit of my stomach as I continued into the kitchen. This room was empty too, but there was an open bottle of wine on the counter, a Prieur Montrachet. I knew that Lilly didn't like white wine, so she was unlikely to have opened it. Hot rage filled me at the thought of Burke in my home, helping himself to my wine and possibly hurting my girl.

My girl? Where did that come from?

Now wasn't the time. I pushed the thought aside for later and rounded the kitchen island, coming to a stop in the great room. There he was, sitting on the end of the couch with a wine glass in his hand and his feet up on the ottoman. He had certainly made himself at home.

Lilly was nowhere to be seen and I hoped that meant she was hiding, perhaps upstairs. I focused my attention on the man in front of me. Burke was eyeing me with a calculated gaze and I could see the smugness clearly in his expression. He was trying to rattle me. The question was: why?

"What are you doing here?" I asked, my voice was cold enough to freeze water.

"Welcome home, Mr. Donovan," he said, as if he were a welcome guest. I scowled.

"How did you get in my house?"

"The door was unlocked, and the security system wasn't set. I must say, that is quite irresponsible. You've been out of town for, what, three days?"

If he thought that his knowledge of my whereabouts would impress or unnerve me, he was mistaken. It was a business trip, no big secret. I was far more concerned about his knowledge of Lilly's whereabouts. I felt like a tightly coiled spring of tension.

"You're right, that was irresponsible of me. Any riff-raff could just let themselves right in," I said, crossing my arms, to hide my shaking hands, and leaning against the doorframe. "Now, I'll ask one more time, what are you doing here?"

"I should think you would know," Burke said, rising to his feet. I straightened up, planting my feet. Burke had a few decades on me and was more thin than muscular, so there would be no match in a fight, if it came to that. If he had a weapon, that would complicate things. "You seem to know so much about me, after all."

Okay, that surprised me. It must have shown in my face, because he chuckled.

"What? You thought I wouldn't find out that you've been snooping around about me, investigating my business?" He dropped the calm and in control act, his face contorting in anger. "I'm Henry Burke, you little worm. You can't pull one over on me."

Okay, I needed to think fast.

No mention of Lilly, so that's not why he's here. No mention of my brother, either. So, he probably doesn't know my history. Is he just here because he found out that I've been keeping track of him? Could that really be all?

"I don't know what you're talking about," I said smoothly. I certainly wasn't going to confirm anything.

"Please," he sneered, rolling his eyes. "Let's not play games. I know you've been tracking my special business deals. At first, I couldn't figure out why some kid I barely know was sticking his nose where it doesn't belong, but then I realized, you think you can muscle me out!"

I had no idea what he was talking about, so I stayed silent. It didn't seem to matter, he was on a roll now.

"I'll have you know, I've been in this business a long time and I can handle a little competition. You won't be able to get rid of me. I'm not afraid to do what needs to be done." The threat in his voice was unmistakable. "Can you say the same? You have no idea what it's taken to become a top supplier."

I schooled my expression, because I still didn't know what the man was talking about, but I didn't want him to know that. How was I a business competition? I worked exclusively in the tech industry. While Burke had a variety of businesses under his belt these days, nothing overlapped with D-Tech's interests. So, what did he mean...

Realization slammed into me and everything suddenly made sense. He thought I was trying to infringe on his criminal dealings. What had he said? He was a top supplier? So, it must be drugs, as I thought, and he suspected that I was a smuggler too.

This presented an interesting opportunity. Maybe I could get some information out of him if I played along. Besides, it was better that he thought I was as shady as him, instead of the truth.

"Top supplier, huh? Maybe for now, but you might want to make way for some new blood," I smirked. My loathing for this man made playing along more difficult, but I hoped it would pay off in the end.

"That cocky attitude of yours is going to get you in trouble one day."

"Is that a threat?" I asked.

"It's a warning. There's a darker side to this world than you know, Mr. Donavan. But you'll find out if you don't back off."

With that, he drained his wine glass and sat it on the coffee table before striding toward me. I braced myself, but he stopped five feet away. His superior grin had returned.

"It sounds like I could learn from you," I said, almost cringing. I was trying not to let this opportunity slip through my fingers.

"I don't think so, kid," he replied patronizingly. "You should stick to robots and internet games. That's the only advice I have for you. I'll show myself out." He slipped past me before I could respond.

Moments later, I heard the front door open and close. Walking to the living room, I peeked out through the curtains to see Burke's expensive car turning around. An immature part of me wished I'd taken the time to key the sides. It'd serve him right for coming to my home, invading my space.

I punched in the security code, arming the system, and peeked back out just in time to see the car disappear around a curve in the driveway. There was a loosening of my taut muscles that was almost painful. It was jarring to have my personal space invaded by the man I considered my greatest enemy. Now that the shock had worn off, I was livid.

But first things first, "Lilly?" I called out her name, hoping she was hidden and safe.

There wasn't an immediate response. I headed toward the stairs, calling our louder, "Lilly, he's gone. We're alone."

I was greeted with more silence. Panic started to creep up on me. "Lilly!"

"I'm here," a timid voice said from behind me. I whipped around to see Lilly standing there, her face pale.

I hurried forward and wrapped her in my arms. She felt so small when I wrapped my body around her like this. Too small, too vulnerable.

She was shaking like a leaf, but she clung to me like a life preserver, her grip on my back almost painful. Her breathing was uneven, but there were no tears, as I had expected. Instead, she exuded a desperate need for comfort, like she needed me to hold her together and I was happy to do it.

Honestly, I needed it too. I needed to hold her and feel that she was solid, she was okay. The fear I had felt when I got home was a lingering echo that made me realize that I was right before. She was my girl.

Chapter Nine
Lilly

I was close to a panic attack by the time Grant came home. I had been walking downstairs this morning when I heard the purr of a car engine. Assuming it was him, I strolled toward the front door, not even caring that I was acting like a dog rushing to greet its master. Punching in the security code, I unlocked the door and placed my hand on the doorknob to pull it open when the sound of a man's voice stopped me. It's wasn't Grant.

Rushing to the window by the door, I glanced out, barely moving the curtains. Terror shot through me as I recognized the man walking toward the porch, talking into a cell phone pressed against his ear, as none other than Henry Burke. My throat constricted as I stumbled backward, away from the window. Now he was so close that I could hear his sure steps on the wooden porch.

My eyes darted to the deadbolt that I had just unlocked. Stupid, stupid, stupid.

If I locked the door now, he'd hear it and know someone was here. Shit, I had to hide. Cold sweat broke out on my forehead as I hurried through the house, past the living room and kitchen. In the great room, I hesitated. I only had two options from here: outside or Grant's gym.

Outside felt too exposed, too open. So, I instinctively ran into the gym, closing the door softly behind myself as I heard Burke entering the house. I could hear him talking on the phone, but he was still at the opposite end of the house, so I couldn't make out his words.

I leaned against the wall, but my legs felt weak. I slowly slid down until I was huddled on the floor, my legs bent and my head resting on my knees. Not daring to turn on the lights, I sat there in the dark, the only illumination provided by the thin strip of light coming from under the door.

I couldn't say how long I was there. It could've been minutes, but it felt like days.

Hell, it felt like years.

My ears were straining to hear what Burke was doing, but only picking up the thumping of my own heart, which felt like it was going to break free of the confines of my chest, it was working so hard. Whether it was the darkness or adrenaline and fear heightening my senses, I felt hyper-aware of the world around me in an almost painful way. I knew the second that Burke stepped into the great room. His footsteps were light, almost silent, but I could feel his presence. So close.

Why did I run in here? There was no lock on this door, nothing to stop him from opening it and finding me here, defenseless. Every moment that I spent waiting for him to discover me made my chest feel tight. I felt like I couldn't catch my breath.

It was the sound of the front door opening that caused me to snap my head up. Hope filled me as I heard Grant speak. In my mind, I pictured Grant's powerful body. Instead of the lust I was used to, I was filled with pride. He was so strong, and he was my protector. Reluctant or not, he had agreed to keep me safe.

The conversation between the two men was short but intense. I could hear the threats that Burke leveled at Grant, but he didn't seem fazed by it. I marveled at his ability to stay calm.

I heard footsteps leading away and let out a sigh of relief, but I didn't dare move until I heard Grant calling out for me. Even then, it took a moment to make my body respond.

Grant enveloped me in his arms when he caught sight of me and I surrendered myself to the strength he provided. His warmth surrounded me and I inhaled deeply, taking in the lingering scent of his body wash.

I had so much to ask him; questions about his history with Burke. But, in this moment, I couldn't seem to get the words out. So, I buried my face further into his chest and reveled in the fact that he was as content to stay this way as I was.

***

"I can't believe you're eating that," Grant said with his nose crinkled in disgust.

"What? It's the best pizza there is!"

"Are you crazy? Black olives and sausage? That's gross."

"At least it's not boring. Plain cheese is so lame," I told him, mimicking a valley high girl's voice.

"You're lame," he grumbled, taking a huge bite of pizza while I sniggered at his response.

We were sitting at the kitchen island, eating pizza that Grant had delivered for dinner. It had been a low-key day for us, spent watching TV and talking about anything but Henry Burke. Neither of us seemed to want to bring him up. For my part, my emotional state was too fragile after his surprise visit to the house and I had spent most of the day purposefully not thinking about it. But it was time to take the bull by the horns.

"Listen," I started, "we have to talk about Burke."

Grant sobered up immediately, setting his uneaten pizza crust back into the open box beside him. "I had no idea he'd show up here like that."

"I know that," I reassured him. "But I have to know, why do you hate him? He seems to barely know you."

"He doesn't know me, really. To his mind, we met almost three years ago, right after D-Tech took off and I started to count myself among the wealthy. I was invited to a fundraising gala for the NICU at Northwestern Memorial. It was an upscale, black tie party. I was introduced to Burke there, and that's when he thinks we first met."

"But it isn't?"

"No, we met thirteen years ago, when I was fifteen years old," Grant said, his eyes glazed as if he wasn't seeing me or the kitchen around us anymore. He was envisioning the past. "My last name was different then, it was Foster, and the meeting was nothing, just a brief introduction to my brother's boss at the time. It was insignificant, and I'm sure he doesn't even remember it."

I nodded, because it seemed like I should respond in some way, but I didn't know what to say.

"Two weeks later, my brother went missing. Leigh was only nineteen and working for Burke as a driver was his first job."

"A driver?"

"Yeah, he drove Burke to and from work, social events, whatever he needed. And the man paid well, of course."

"You think that Burke had something to do with your brother's disappearance?" I asked, though I was sure that I already knew the answer.

"I know he did," Grant responded, his eyes blazing with intensity. "Right before Leigh went missing, just days before, he told me that his new boss wasn't a good man, that he wanted to quit, but didn't think he could. He was scared. I was only fifteen at the time, just a stupid kid, so I didn't press for details, just told him to 'man up' and quit if he wanted to." Grant made air quotes with his fingers and looked disgusted with himself.

"Do you think he's…" I couldn't bring myself to say the word dead. It was too horrible.

"Yes," Grant said, his shoulders slumping as he stared down at the granite top of the island.

"But, why? Why would Burke kill him?"

"I think," Grant met my eyes and I saw emotion swirling within the depths of his blue orbs, "that he must've seen something he shouldn't have. A crime of some kind, maybe a murder."

I understood the significance in Grant's words. This was why he had taken me in, despite his clear reluctance to do so. He saw a connection between my situation and Leigh's disappearance. That was why Jim brought me here.

"I found out years later that another man went missing around that same time. The exact day isn't known because he had no close family in his life. By the time anyone realized he was missing and reported it, Leigh had been gone for three days. But I think they went missing at the same time."

"Who was he?"

"Victor Costa, a low-level criminal much like Mark Lewis. He had a history of violent crime, nothing related to drugs, but I did a lot of digging and found out that he worked as hired muscle for crime bosses. He had also deposited a huge sum of money into his checking account every week for a month before he disappeared."

"Wow. How did you find this stuff?"

"Money talks. Honestly, there are very few doors closed to me. Unfortunately, Burke is rich too. So, he has the means to cover his tracks better than Costa did."

"Burke really doesn't recognize you? Aren't you worried that he'll remember your name?"

"I changed my last name years ago. If he dug deep enough, he might be able to find that paperwork and make the connection. But I'm hoping that doesn't happen."

"This is all so crazy. Isn't Burke rich because of his legitimate business? I don't understand why he would get involved in all this shady shit. It seems like too much risk to me."

"Maybe he gets off on the risk," Grant shrugged. "I don't know, but I have to prove that he's doing all this illicit shit. I have to," his voice was almost pleading, and I could see, for the first time, just how fixated he was on this. I thought that Burke's framing of me was personal, but it was nothing compared to Grant's battle with him.

"You will," I reassured him. "You'll get the bastard. For Leigh," I reached out and placed my hand on top of his, squeezing gently.

"For Leigh," he repeated. "And… for my mom."

"Your mom?"

He nodded.

"She died six years ago, while I was in my senior year of college. Breast cancer. It was horrible, losing her like that, but the worst part was that she never knew what happened to Leigh. She never got answers and it tormented her until her dying breath," Grant shuddered. "It messed me up for a long time, losing her like that. Her mind was foggy from the drugs and she kept asking for Leigh, kept begging me to tell her where he was."

Grant's voice was soft, and I could clearly see the pain on his face. He had never looked so vulnerable to me and I found that I wanted to protect him, as silly as that sounded. I wanted to protect him from his own demons, if only I knew how.

"I'm so sorry," I said.

In truth, "sorry" didn't even begin to cover what I felt. I was devastated for him but I didn't know how to put it into words. So, I continued to hold his hand, trying to tell him all the unsaid things I felt with my eyes and my touch. I wasn't sure if he understood that, but he did turn his hand and entwine our fingers. We sat like that for a long time, our pizza all but forgotten.

***

Grant put a movie on the TV in the great room after dinner. After giving me a hard time because I hadn't seen many of his favorite comedies, which he proudly proclaimed to be classics, he demanded I sit with him and watch "Ghostbusters".

I liked the movie, but I couldn't stop sneaking glances at Grant. Maybe it was because he was watching one of his favorite movies, or maybe it was because he had opened up and shared his painful family history with me – whatever the reason, he seemed so much more comfortable than I had ever seen him before. He laughed openly at the movie, even quoting a few lines occasionally, and excitedly told me to pay attention to a good part, even if I was already focused on the screen.

He was nestled onto the end of the couch, with his feet up on the ottoman and a bowl of popcorn in his lap. I had to sit right next to him to eat from the bowl, and our fingers kept brushing as we reached in at the same time, causing a tingling sensation to spread through my body. It felt like a date, which was a dangerous thought.

"You want a pop?" he asked me as the movie credits rolled and he started to climb to his feet.

"No, thanks," I said, scooting over to give him room.

As I watched him walk into the kitchen and pull a can of Coke from the refrigerator, my gaze lingering far too long, I knew that I should keep distance between us. This heat in my body, spreading from my throbbing core, was only going to get worse if I stayed snuggled up to him like this. We were getting too cozy.

I didn't think I could keep my hands to myself for much longer.

"What do you say to a game of pool?" he asked, as he walked back into the room. He took a sip of his drink and my eyes zeroed in on the movement of his throat as he swallowed. How did he make everything seems sexy?

"I've never played before," I told him, my mouth suddenly dry. Maybe I should've taken a pop after all.

"I'll teach you, then," he said, walking to the pool sticks that were mounted on the wall and pulling two down.

"Don't you need to sleep?" I asked. It was nearing midnight.

"Nope. I'm taking the rest of the week off."

"Is that a good idea with all the Jumpstart issues you have to oversee?" I didn't know why I was arguing. Having him here for the next few days sounded great.

"I can do that from home. Do you not want my company?" he asked with a playful smile. I grinned and rolled my eyes at him while he started rubbing chalk on the tips of the pool sticks.

"Well, if you're going to be here, I expect some entertainment. This place gets boring."

"That's okay, we have plenty of movies that I still have to introduce you to. Have you seen 'Young Frankenstein'?"

"Nope."

"Have you been living under a rock?" he asked, clutching his chest dramatically.

"Just give me the stick and show me what to do with it," I said, holding my hand out. Grant's smile turned flirtatious and I realized what I had said. My eyes widened. "Pool stick. Give me the pool stick."

"Sure thing," he said, his voice deeper than usual. He handed it over and started racking up the pool balls. "I'll break," he said.

I didn't know what that meant, so I just nodded. Placing the white ball on the opposite end of the table from the other balls, Grant bent low, lining his stick up carefully. The long lines of his body were coiled gracefully around the end of the table. Then, he hit the white ball and it shot to the other end, colliding with the balls there and scattering them. Two balls went into the pockets.

"Okay, I'm stripes. That means you have to try to get the solid colored balls in the pockets. Don't knock the black one in, that's the eight-ball and it's got to be the last one you go for. If you knock it into a pocket before the rest of your solids are in, you'll lose. Got it?"

"Yep," I nodded. Sounded simple enough.

"You can only directly hit the white ball. Use it to knock the others around. But if it goes into the pocket, your turn is over and I get two shots. Otherwise, your turn continues until you don't get any balls in, then it's the other player's shot. Now, watch how I do it."

He bent low over the table again, at a more awkward angle this time because of where the white ball was. He hit it with the stick, clearly aiming for the striped orange ball, but it went wide.

"Damn," he muttered, straightening up.

"My turn?" I asked eagerly.

"Yeah. First, you need to pick a ball to try to get it the pocket. What do you think?"

"The blue one," I said, pointing to the ball that was closest to the corner pocket.

"Okay, bend on over so you can see how the balls line up."

I did so, trying to find the best angle to put the pool stick. How had he held his? It seemed to glide through his hands easily, but I was too busy looking at his poised figure to notice how he did it. Grant saw me fumbling and came up behind me.

I felt my body stiffen as he molded his against me, looking at the balls from my position to help me line up the shot. "You'll want to shift to the left just a bit," he said, his mouth at my ear.

His breath fanned over my neck, sending a pleasant chill down my spine. Placing his big hands on my hips, he adjusted my stance a bit. I was further to the left now, but I was also pressed more firmly against him. I bit my lip.

"And your hands should be like this," he said, reaching out to correct the way my hands were holding the stick. This aligned his groin with my ass and I felt the unmistakable bulge in his pants press against me. I gasped.

To hell with pool. I couldn't take this sexual tension anymore. Deciding one of us had to act on it, I boldly arched my back and rubbed my backside against his erection, turning to look at his face as I did so.

Grant's eyes widened before he let out a low groan, dropping his hands to the edge of the pool table as if he needed to hold himself up. He looked at me with a question in his eyes and leaned forward, once again connecting our lips.

This kiss wasn't gentle and sweet as the last one had been. This was all fire and passion. I turned all the way around until our chests were pressed together. I was bent at a difficult angle over the edge of the table, but I didn't care. Grant licked his way into my mouth and I gripped his shoulders tightly as his tongue ran over my own.

Reaching down and gripping the back of my thighs, he lifted me until my legs were wrapped around his waist. Our lips were still molded together as he started walking, taking me to the sectional and sitting me roughly so that I was straddling him.

I pulled lightly on his hair and broke the kiss, only to trail my lips across his cheek and down his neck, where I nipped at the skin lightly. My dress was pooled around my thighs, meaning that I could feel the rough material of his jeans against the thin fabric of my panties and it was driving me crazy. I needed more. I ground myself against him, earning another low groan that made me feel so powerful.

"Shit, Lilly. I want you so fucking bad," he said, almost panting.

"Then do it, Grant. Please," I pulled back to look into his face. I needed him to see how serious I was. "Take me."

I was more than ready for him.

Chapter Ten
Grant

Hearing her beg nearly led to my undoing. I was holding on by a thread already. Lilly's voice was husky with need and it made every nerve ending in my body light up.

Shifting our positions, I laid her out on the couch and covered her body with my own, careful to keep the bulk of my weight off her even as she spread her legs so that I could settle into the space between them. Her long hair was spread out around her head as she looked up at me through her eyelashes. I couldn't help thinking that she looked angelic like this. Far too good for a man like me.

But I wasn't going to let that stop me.

"I want to see you, all of you," I told her. Hell, I wasn't sure I could survive another minute without her bare before my eyes.

She was quick to oblige, reaching down to the hem of her dress and arching her back as she pulled it over her head in one swift motion. She let it flutter to the floor beneath her and looked up at me once again, this time with a hint of shyness.

"God, look at you," I murmured as my eyes took in the white lace bra and panties she was wearing. The swells of her breasts were barely contained, and I could see the dark outline of her nipple through the thin fabric. Holy hell.

She had a long, flat stomach and hips that flared out just enough to form a delicious curve along her side. I wanted to touch, and taste, every part of her.

Planting soft kisses along her collarbone, I brought one hand up and traced my finger along the cup of her bra, making her shudder. Spurred on by that reaction, I traced the same line with my tongue. That's when I realized, there was a clasp on the front of her bra. Fuck, yes.

I flicked the clasp with my fingers and the bra popped open, exposing her perfectly formed breasts. I latched onto one of her nipples, sucking on it lightly until it hardened. I blew lightly across it, making Lilly's back arch, before giving the same treatment to her other bud. Her skin was so unbelievably soft, like nothing I'd ever felt before.

Sweeping my hand down her side, along that sexy curve, I ran my fingers along the edge of her small white panties. Her loud moan told me that she approved, so I slipped my hand down further and cupped her sex.

Lilly jacked up at the touch, nearly flying off the couch, but my face was still pressed against her chest, worshipping her breasts, and it helped to steady her. I felt my erection straining against my pants as I rubbed her shaved pussy and found that it was dripping wet. She was killing me.

I had to taste it.

Reluctantly pulling away from her breast, I pulled her panties down her long legs, sliding my hands back up until they reached her inner thigh, spreading her wide. She fidgeted, and I looked at her face to see that she looked nervous.

"What's wrong, sweetheart?" I asked. I was so hungry for her, the only thing that could stop me now would be her request. I prayed that she didn't ask that of me.

"I've never... I mean, I'm a..." Her cheeks flushed, and she looked away, embarrassed.

"You're a virgin?" I asked. My body roared at the thought of being her first. I had never been so consumed by a woman, or so far from sanity.

"Yeah," she mumbled, still not looking at me. I cupped her chin in my hand and turned her face back to mine. I waited until she looked at me again before speaking.

"Do you want to stop?"

"No!" she exclaimed, her eyes widening. "I'm just inexperienced and thought you should know. Just in case I'm not very...good."

I wanted to laugh at how cute she was, but I thought that might make her feel mocked, so I stifled it.

"Lilly, my fiery little temptress, you have nothing to worry about," I said, reaching down to her core once again, dipping a finger inside slowly.

"Grant!" she cried out, squirming beneath me.

"See, your body knows what it wants," I said, removing my finger that was covered with her juices and holding it up. "You don't need experience, just follow your instincts. That's what I plan to do." Holding her eyes, I brought the finger to my mouth, licking it clean. Lilly's mouth parted, and her eyes dilated.

Her sweetness exploded in my mouth and I had to have more. Repositioning myself, I knelt before her. Her legs were spread wide, opening her weeping core to me. She was so exposed, all smooth skin and feminine curves, and I couldn't believe that I was lucky enough to be the first man to see her like this.

The only man.

That thought was crazy, but a feeling of possessiveness had taken over my body and drove me forward until my face was buried between her legs. Lilly gave a guttural cry as I licked up the center of her, lapping up the wetness there.

Her thigh muscles clenched around me and I snaked my hands beneath her, cupping her ass and lifting it slightly, angling her hips so my mouth had better access to her. I felt like an animal as I ravaged her with my tongue, dipping into her opening before moving up to swirl around her clit. She whimpered and panted, making incoherent noises that urged me on.

Then she started rubbing herself against my face, her hips thrusting frantically, and I knew she was close to orgasming. My own hard-on was almost painful now, as the need to penetrate her became too much. But I kept going with my mouth, squeezing her ass as I drove my tongue deeper inside.

Lilly finally snapped. Gripping my hair tightly, she held my head in place while her whole body went rigid and my name tumbled from her lips. I kept my tongue buried inside her and felt her contracting even as she got wetter.

A warm snugness filled my chest when I pulled away and looked down to find her with a dazed smile stretched across her face. But we weren't done. Her sex was dripping, so ready for me.

I pulled my shirt over my head and started to unbutton my jeans. She was watching me closely, her gaze so intense it felt like a caress against my skin. When I shoved my jeans and boxers down my hips, freeing my aching cock, her eyes widened.

"It's so big...will it fit?" she asked timidly.

Talk about making a guy feel fucking amazing.

"We'll go slow. It might hurt a little at first, though. Are you sure you want to do this? We can stop any time you want." I suddenly had a tiny sliver of doubt. Should I do this? Taking her innocence seemed wrong, I wasn't worthy of such a thing.

"No, I don't want to stop. Please, Grant, I need more. My body needs you."

Well, so much for my doubt. I didn't think I could deny her anything right now, with her gorgeous body laid out beneath me and her taste still on my lips. I reached into the back pocket of my jeans and pulled out my wallet. Leigh had once told me to always keep a condom in there and I'd never been so grateful.

Positioning myself between her legs once again, I lined myself up with her entrance. The heat from her sex made my whole body quiver. I was no virgin myself, far from it, but with Lilly everything felt new, more intense. It had never been like this before and, as I slowly entered her, I knew she was ruining me for anyone else ever again.

She was so tight and hot. I clenched my teeth and fought the impulse to thrust wildly, pounding her into the couch with all my strength. I couldn't do that, so I used all my willpower to go slow until I was fully inside, every inch encased in her body. Then, I froze.

Lilly's eyes were shut tight and her breathing was shallow. I leaned down and kissed her eyelids before lowering my mouth to her ear. "It's okay, sweetheart. Just relax. I promise it'll feel better if you do," I whispered.

When I pulled back, her eyes were open and the look she gave me took my breath away. It was the sincerest expression of trust I'd ever seen on a person's face. The open vulnerability she was showing tore me up. Fuck, I didn't deserve that. Her faith should have been placed in a better man than me.

But then that damn possessive monster within me reared its ugly head. She was mine.

I pressed my mouth against hers once more, trying to put so many unsaid things into the kiss. Then, she wrapped her legs around my hips and let out a low moan, her body relaxing around me.

"Yes," I moaned into the kiss, beginning to thrust in and out of her in earnest. I found my rhythm quickly, losing myself in the sensation of her warmth around my cock. God, it was so good. I didn't know how much more I could stand.

Lilly's hands were flying all over my body, tracing every dip and curve of my abdomen, my back, my thighs. Her light touch was driving me mad, making me feel like a sex God as she purred in pleasure.

I wasn't going to last much longer.

"Fuck, Lilly," I growled, picking up speed. I could feel her moving with me, chasing her second orgasm as she whined and moaned.

"Do it, baby. Come with me. Do it, now!" I yelled, as I came hard, my hips pumping wildly as I felt her reach her release at the same time, screaming my name as she clutched my arms with surprising strength. Her walls pulsed around my twitching cock and the pleasure was primal, more powerful than anything I had ever felt before.

This was the best sex I'd ever had.

***

The sunrise streaming in through the patio doors awoke me five hours later. We were still in the great room, the chaise longue on the end of the sectional allowing plenty of room for Lilly to curl up against my chest after we had exhausted ourselves. My morning hard-on twitched at the memory and the feeling of her body still pressed against me.

I looked down into her sleeping face. Her pale skin seemed to glow where the sunlight touched it, making her seem even more surreal. She was an enigma, this woman that was dropped into my lap, sweet and strong at the same time.

This was probably a bad idea, if I looked at it objectively. Sex with a woman that was here temporarily, that was on the run from my worst enemy, was playing with fire. Too bad that I enjoyed it too much to give a damn about the consequences.

Slowly shifting my body and pulling my arm out from under Lilly's head, I slid off the couch, careful not to jostle her more than necessary. Making my way to the kitchen, I grabbed my cellphone and pulled the phone number of a security firm that I had used before on occasion. Lilly would not be left alone in this house again, not even while I was at work.

Fury, which had been simmering just beneath the surface since Burke had left the day before, engulfed me as I remembered the fear in Lilly's eyes. That bastard wasn't getting near her again. I walked upstairs to talk on the phone without disturbing Lilly's sleep.

The phone picked up on the third ring, "Hello?" the voice on the other end of the line sounded alert despite the time of day.

"Tyler? This is Grant Donovan. I've got a job for you."

"Mr. Donovan, good to hear from you." Tyler was all business and I could hear the sound of papers being shuffled in the background. "What can I do for you?"

"I need a bodyguard, here at my house during the week while I'm at work."

"With the house unoccupied?"

"No, there's a woman staying with me, I need to know that she's safe when I'm not here."

"There's a threat?" Tyler asked, his tone of voice unwavering. That was why I liked the guy. He was tight, always on the ball and took his job very seriously. Just the credentials the owner of a security firm needed.

"Yes, a well-connected one. I need this off the books, no record of her being her at all."

"Sounds serious."

"It is. I need discretion on this one."

"You sure you don't want someone there around the clock?"

"No, if there's trouble while I'm here, I can handle it," I said confidently. Let the son of a bitch show up again, there'd be no opportunity for strained conversation or veiled threats this time. I couldn't guarantee that I wouldn't lose control and end the man once and for all.

"If you're sure. When do you want the guard there?"

"I'm taking a few days off. Have him start Monday."

"Got it. I'll assign Dwight. He's ex-Army."

"Good."

I ended the call, resisting the temptation to tell Tyler that Lilly was off-limits. That was crazy, and not just because Tyler was a professional and would never allow his employees to screw around with clients. One amazing round of sex didn't make Lilly mine.

I ignored the pain in the center of my chest at that thought. Stripping out of my boxers, I stepped into the bathroom nude. I caught a glimpse of myself in the mirror and smiled when I saw scratch marks along my biceps, where Lilly had been gripping me when she orgasmed. I hadn't even felt them at the time.

Those memories caused an immediate response in my body. My cock stood at attention, ready for another round. Damn, I couldn't get enough of her.

I stepped into the shower stall, cranking the water on and hissing when it came out cold. I had been hoping that the shock of cold water would help cool my blood, but no luck. I couldn't get the image of Lilly's sweet body out of my head.

As the water turned warm and I ran a washrag over my body, I remembered the feel of her hands on me. What the hell? I was acting like a sex-starved teenage boy, not like I had just had the best sex of my life hours ago.

Lilly was too intoxicating, if I wasn't careful, I'd get addicted.

Chapter Eleven
Lilly

I was disappointed to wake up alone. It was early, based on the positioning of the sun through the patio doors. Yet Grant was no longer beside me.

I sat up and stretched, my body deliciously sore. I looked down at the Guns N' Roses t-shirt I was wearing and smiled. It was Grant's, the one he had been wearing yesterday. After our carnal activities, he had strolled through the house naked, disposing of the condom in the bathroom and bringing back a hand towel for me to clean up with. I felt self-conscious as I wiped myself in front of him but he didn't seem to mind. Instead, he was pulling on his boxers and looked utterly spent.

I had searched around until I finally found my discarded panties on the floor. After slipping them on, I reached out for my dress, but Grant stopped me.

"Here," he said, holding out his t-shirt to me. "Sleep in this."

So, I had pulled it on, feeling sexy as hell when he ran his eyes up and down my body, biting his lower lip. We had settled onto the couch then, my back pressed against his front as we both slipped off to sleep.

As I stood from the couch, I tried not to read too much into the sex. As much as I wanted it to mean something, I wasn't too sure that Grant felt the same way. I wondered where he was. He told me that he wasn't working today, but maybe he changed his mind?

Walking through the kitchen, I stopped just long enough to start the coffee maker. As the fresh smell of coffee filled the kitchen and the drip-drip-drip started, I headed up to the second floor. I supposed that I should have a shower and put on my own clothes, even though I loved the feeling of wearing Grant's. It made me feel like we were a real couple.

Yikes. So much for not getting ahead of myself.

Speaking of showers, was that water running that I could hear? I walked by my room and down the hall to Grant's suite. Stopping outside the door, I pressed my ear against it.

Yep, he was showering.

I couldn't believe it, but my insides clenched with need. Despite the earth-shattering orgasms I'd had the night before, I wanted him again. The image of his naked body, wet and slick as the showerhead rained down upon him filled my mind and I was turning the doorknob to his room before I'd even thoroughly thought it through.

Stepping into his private space, I looked around. The whole house was decorated in a masculine way, showcasing that it was a bachelor pad, but it was most pronounced here. The room had the same hardwood flooring that ran throughout the house, but there was a big gray area rug that took up most of the room here. It was thick and oh, so soft against my bare feet. The walls were also gray, though a darker shade.

My eyes were drawn to the bed, which was big - a king size for sure, and unmade. I could see black satin sheets and a white duvet. Would I get to sleep here now?

I shook the thought away and I walked over to the patio doors. Unlike the ones downstairs, these had black curtains that blocked out the light when they weren't tied back. Pushing these aside, I saw that there was a balcony out there overlooking the backyard. There was a small metal table and two cushioned chairs next to the railing. I could just imagine Grant sitting out there with his laptop, working on some business, or eating a meal in his beloved outdoor space.

Turning away from the window, I saw a stone fireplace on the opposite wall. Next to that was a white dresser with a TV mounted on the wall behind it. All-in-all the room felt warm and comfortable. There were two doors next to the bed. I assumed one was a closet, while I could hear the shower running behind the other door. I hesitated outside this door.

Was I confident enough to do this?

I stood there, toying with the hem of my shirt – well, Grant's shirt. My mind flashed to Grant hovering above me, fire in his eyes as he stripped my clothing from my body. He seemed to appreciate the view...

Fuck it. I ripped the shirt off and shimmied my panties down my legs. Standing in Grant's bedroom exhilarated me. I was just going to stroll into the bathroom and join him. What was the worst that could happen?

Opening the bathroom door, I was shocked to see that his shower stall was made of clear glass. No sneaking up on him now. What really blew me away was the sight that met my eyes.

I could see every inch of his magnificent body, from his damp hair to the suds on his chest to the erection that twitched as I looked at it. Turning as he ran a washcloth over his tight abs, Grant froze as he caught sight of me. I watched his eyes narrow, taking his own assessment of my appearance.

Then, with a heated look, he continued to trail the washcloth down his stomach, moving painfully slow. When he reached his swollen member, he held my eyes while he gripped himself, leisurely sliding his hand up and down while I stared, transfixed. His other hand rested on his lower stomach.

There was something primal about watching him pleasure himself, knowing that he was thinking of me as his gaze lingered on my breasts, my hips, my dripping pussy. I walked forward, as if in a trance, letting myself into the shower stall with him. The heat of the water was nothing compared to the warmth spreading through my body.

No words were spoken as we stood there, assessing each other's nude bodies. I had never felt so desirable as when his eyes were on me. I could get addicted to this feeling.

Feeling bold, I took a step closer to him before dropping to my knees. Pulling his hand away, I wrapped my own smaller fingers around his thick member. It was hard, but smooth. As I got a good look, I was amazed at the length of him. How had this fit inside me? It seemed impossible. Yet, I craved to feel him within me again, to have this thick head push into the folds of my body until I couldn't stand the pleasure of it all.

I ran my thumb over the head, looking up into his face and seeing that he was staring at me intensely. Now wasn't the time to back down.

"I want to taste you, Grant. Can I? I want to see how much of your big cock will fit in my mouth." I spoke softly, trying to be seductive. I had never spoken like this before, but I wanted to turn him on. It must have worked, or perhaps my language was getting him hot, because his hips jerked, and he braced himself against the wall with a drawn out, "Fuuuuuck."

I took that as permission. Tightening my grip around his base, I ran my tongue up the underside of his cock, swirling it when I reached the head. Careful of my teeth, I took him into my mouth, lowering myself until I felt him hitting the back of my throat.

Moving my hand in sync with my mouth, I pulled back until my lips were at his tip, then I took him all the way in once again. I settled into this rhythm, experimenting with sweeping my tongue along the underside and hollowing my cheeks as I sucked.

I read the responses of his body, hearing his heavy breathing over the light pattering of the water hitting the tile and feeling his thigh muscles tense where I was pressed up against them. I learned what he liked as I worked him with my mouth, feeling powerful as I commanded these reactions from him.

It was when I picked up the pace that he let out a snarl and buried his hands in my wet hair. He didn't push my head down, just held on as I brought him closer and closer to the edge. A tremor ran through his body as I took him even deeper, relaxing my throat to bring him this pleasure.

"Oh, God. I'm gonna…I'm gonna come," he said. I flipped my eyes up to his face and let out a moan around his cock. "Lilly!" He shouted my name as his face twisted into a raw expression of absolute pleasure.

Then I felt the hot jets streaming into the back of my throat, his cock pulsing as it unloaded. I swallowed it all, looking up at him and watching his orgasm play out. The muscles of his abdomen seemed to be spasming as he tossed his head back and made a noise that I could only describe as a howl. Looking at him like this, losing himself in the gratification that I was providing, I didn't think I'd ever seen anything so beautiful.

Maybe that wasn't a very masculine way to describe him but it was fitting. He was so alluring like this, with the tough front he put up softened. I felt my heart lurch.

Shit, I was really falling for him.

I pulled back, making sure to keep my lips wrapped around him until the head popped out of my mouth. I smiled at him as I stood. Grant leaned against the wall, looking like he needed the support as he looked at me with awe on his face.

"You are amazing. I can't even tell you how good that was. I don't have the words," he said, weakly, trying to catch his breath.

I felt like my face might crack, I was grinning so wide.

***

The next few days were a blur of sex, classic comedies, and sleeping wrapped up in Grant's arms. He even got around to actually teaching me how to play pool. I sucked at it, but he enjoyed poking fun at me when I failed so miserably at getting a single ball into a pocket. I didn't take it too hard.

We had the awkward birth control conversation. I had an arm implant that kept me from getting pregnant. I had been a virgin, but my doctor had pushed for it just in case. Now I was glad she did. Grant assured me that he didn't have any STDs, so we made the decision to ditch the condoms. I didn't notice much of a difference, but I could tell that Grant preferred it this way. It was also thrilling to me to know that we were skin to skin, even if it felt the same.

I felt like we were living in a bubble, a secure sanctuary where we were sheltered from anything that would come between us. It didn't matter that he was filthy rich, while I didn't even have a job at this point - not that I even wanted to think about that, anyway. All the drama with Burke and the murder investigation, none of it could touch us here in the bubble.

But I knew it wasn't real. We were stealing a few days and I couldn't get enough of him but it wasn't meant to last like this. Real life was approaching fast. Grant was going back to work, and a bodyguard was staying here with me during the day. Talk about getting slapped in the face with a harsh dose of reality.

I was sitting on the balcony attached to his bedroom, drinking a cup of coffee as he got ready for the day. It was almost eight in the morning, but I found that my sleeping schedule had adjusted to a more traditional one in the last week or so. I guessed that made it official, no more night club life for me.

A surprising feeling of bitterness swept over me. I felt like I didn't have anything anymore. My job and home were ripped away. Hell, I couldn't even leave the house at this point. A house which wasn't mine. Then there was Grant. The man rocked my world, but he wasn't mine. He had carefully avoided any conversation about that, and I wasn't so dense that I didn't understand what that meant. Everything felt so fleeting at this point.

I heard the door behind me open and turned to see Grant standing there. He was wearing a navy suit with a white shirt and blue tie, looking every bit a businessman.

"Dwight should be here any minute. You want to come down with me and meet him before I leave?"

"Sure," I said, clutching my coffee cup in my hand as I stood. It was the same mug I had used when I first arrived at the house, which seemed so long ago. Had it really only been two weeks? I felt like I had changed so much in that time.

I followed Grant down the stairs, trying to shake myself out of this melancholy attitude. The doorbell rang as I stepped off the bottom stair. Grant moved toward the door, looking through the peephole before his shoulders relaxed and he punched in the security code.

When the door swung open, I was surprised to see such a young man walk in. He looked close to my own age, with close-cropped blonde hair and classically handsome features. He was shorter than Grant, but built like a boxer, stocky with a broad chest. He was wearing all black, from his boots up to his sunglasses, which he took off as he entered the house. There was also a gun strapped to his side, which was also black. I was picking up on a theme here.

"Hello, Mr. Donovan," he said, holding out his hand to shake with Grant. I was surprised to see Grant's frown as he looked at Dwight and the firm grip he had when he finally took the man's hand, his bicep bulged so much that it was visible even through his suit.

"This is Lilly," Grant said, walking over and putting his arm around my waist.

"Nice to meet you, Lilly," Dwight said, shooting me a charming smile. I took his hand briefly as Grant's body stiffened beside me. Was he jealous? The thought was so ridiculous that I wanted to laugh.

"Well, Dwight, I have to head out to work. If you could stay in your car out front and keep an eye on the place-"

"Outside? Grant, it's summer. He'll bake alive out there. Why doesn't he just sit in here?" I asked. I saw a muscle tick in his jaw before he looked at me with a smile.

"I just thought you might like your privacy," he said with a rigid smile.

"I'd prefer company, honestly."

"It's okay, Lilly. I can sit outside. No problem," Dwight interrupted, shrugging his shoulders.

"Grant, you're being silly," I said. He frowned, a crease forming between his eyebrows.

"Fine," he said after a moment. "Just keep an eye out for any visitors," he told Dwight with a hint of aggression in his voice. Dwight looked confused but nodded.

"I have to go," Grant said, turning to face me full-on. He looked quite unhappy.

"Let me walk you out," I said, striding ahead without waiting for an answer. Grant followed behind and I waited until we were alone on the front porch to stop and round on him. "What the hell was that?"

"What?" he asked, his look of wide-eyed innocence a little too exaggerated to be believed.

"Why are you acting so jealous?"

"I'm not," he insisted.

"Then what was that? Why were you aggressive to my new bodyguard? Why don't you want us in the house together?"

"Because I don't trust him."

"Based on what? Didn't you just meet?"

"I didn't like the way he looked at you," he said, his eyes looking anywhere but at me. "I didn't know he'd be so young. So... I don't know. I just don't like the idea of you around someone like that all day long."

I considered Grant for a moment. When he said "someone like that" I assumed he meant an attractive man. So, this was jealousy. I wasn't sure how to feel about that. On the one hand, it was nice that he was so worried about losing me and the possessiveness was sexy as hell, to be honest.

But, it was also uncalled for. Dwight wasn't my type at all. Besides, I was loyal to Grant, whether we were an official couple or not. I supposed he didn't know that.

"You know that I want you, right?" I asked. His eyes flared with a now familiar heat. "No, not like that. Well, okay, yeah, like that. Always like that. But that's not what I meant. I know things are complicated, but I want to be with you. Only with you."

Grant stood still for a moment longer, staring at me. I was beginning to think I'd misread this situation, making a fool out of myself. But then he reached out and grabbed my shoulders, pulling me to him and taking my mouth in a hot, toe-tingling kiss. He held me against him as he dominated my mouth, penetrating me with his tongue. I felt marked, branded by the passion he was pouring into this kiss and I realized that words weren't always necessary. He was showing me that he wanted me too.

And possibly showing Dwight too, if the man was looking out through the window.

"Good to hear that, Temptress," he said as he broke the kiss but kept me close to him. "Because you're mine."

***

Dwight was a nice guy; not quite the reserved, emotionless robot that I expected from a bodyguard. Things were a little awkward at first, being thrust into this situation where I was alone with a stranger, but my natural charm eventually broke the ice.

Okay, so my "charm" consisted of turning on reruns of Parks and Recreation to avoid small talk. It turned out to be one of his favorite shows too. I got lucky for once.

It didn't take long for the two of us to fall into easy conversation, mostly about the show we were watching. Though, I did discover that the two of us had grown up just a few blocks away from each other in downtown Chicago. He was a little younger than me, though, so I couldn't recall seeing him at school.

A package was delivered to the house in the early afternoon. Dwight didn't seem surprised by it, but I had no idea it was coming. It was addressed to Grant, but Dwight insisted I open it, saying it was really for me. Inside was a cellphone.

I was thrilled that he would think to buy me such a thing and quickly started setting it up, sending him a thank you text as soon as I could. He responded immediately: You deserve it, Temptress.

God, I loved that nickname. It made me feel like the most desirable woman in the world. Also, it demonstrated how personal our relationship had become.

The day passed quickly after that and we were in the great room watching tv when we heard the front door open earlier than usual. I assumed Grant must have come home early, but Dwight was off the couch in a flash, striding toward the front of the house with his hand resting on the butt of his gun.

My stomach flip-flopped and I wondered if I should hide. Was it Burke? Fear flooded me and I started to get up from the recliner and make a beeline for the gym once again, but the sound of Grant's voice eased my fears. He came walking into the room with Dwight trailing behind, looking relaxed.

"What the hell?" I asked Dwight, "You scared the hell out of me!"

"He was protecting you," Grant said, his face showing his approval. "I told him I'd be home around five, but I took off an hour early."

"Wow, three days off and you leave early on your first day back. They're lucky to have you running the joint," I joked, throwing him a wink to be sure that he took it light-heartedly.

"Hey, they're fine if I leave a little early sometimes. That's what happens when you build a successful business. They don't need you as much." Ah, there was that old Grant Donovan arrogance. It didn't bother me like it used to, though. It seemed less obnoxious, somehow.

"I'll take off then. See you guys tomorrow," Dwight said, leaving the house a moment later.

"So, I've been thinking, you seem a little... cooped up lately. This situation getting to you?" he asked and I felt my jaw drop. I had just been thinking along those lines this morning. His ability to notice that touched me more than anything else between us had. He saw me.

"Yeah, it's been a little rough," I said, not wanting to complain about being trapped in the beautiful home that he had opened up to me. He had really done so much, the home, the bodyguard, the sex - not that I thought of that as a fringe benefit. I just didn't want him to think I was ungrateful for everything.

"Let's do something about that," he said, clapping his hands together. "What is something you've always wanted to do, but never been able to?"

"What?"

"You heard me. Name it and I'll make it happen. Something you could never afford or have time for or something like that. Let's cross something off your bucket list."

"I shouldn't go anywhere."

"No, not just anywhere, a carefully selected location. I took you to the boutique and things were fine. We just need to take your circumstances into consideration. If it would make you more comfortable, I have a private jet. We could put a hell of a lot of miles between us and Burke if we had to."

"You're serious about this?" I asked, already having something in mind.

"As a heart attack."

"Well, something that I've always wanted to do..." I twisted my hands together, nervous for some reason, "...is get a tattoo."

"Really?" Grant's eyebrows popped in surprise.

"Yeah, I've always wanted to get one to commemorate my parents."

Grant's face broke out into a smile. "That's perfect," he grabbed my hand and started to pull me along behind him. "I know just the place to go."

Before I knew it, we were in his car, speeding down the road. The sun was still brightly shining and I rolled down my window, sticking my hand out to enjoy the feeling of the wind rushing across my skin. I had been outside a lot over the last few weeks, taking advantage of the privacy at Grant's house, but this felt different. The sun felt warmer, the air smelled sweeter. This was the freedom I had been missing. I already felt a weight lifting from my shoulders and we hadn't even gone anywhere yet.

I didn't even care where we were going, to be honest. I just needed something beyond those four walls and I trusted Grant to take me somewhere safe.

It was almost half an hour later that we pulled up in front of a small brick building with a glass front. The sign hanging on the front proclaimed it Billy Jean's Tattoo Parlour. I followed Grant inside, looking around at the art hanging on the walls in the tiled shop. It was amazing, the creativity and artistic vision on display. There were three large cushioned chairs in the space, one of which was occupied by a large man getting a skull tattooed on his calf.

"Grant!" A woman had just walked out from back-room and called out happily at the sight of Grant. She was a tiny woman that looked to be in her mid-forties with tattoos visible along her arms, legs and neck. She had a nose piercing and short blonde hair that was spiked up.

"Billy Jean, great to see you," Grant said, stepping forward to pull her into a quick hug. "This is my friend, Lilly," he said, placing his hand on my lower back, sending shivers up my spine.

"Nice to meet you," she said, taking my hand in a quick and firm shake. "What can I do for you guys?"

"I want you to give Lilly anything she wants."

"Nice! Well, Lilly, what did you have in mind?" she asked, linking her arm with my own and guiding me to one of the empty chairs.

"I've always pictured a pair of birds in flight on my back, up around my shoulder blades. It's in memory of my parents. I've always liked to think of them flying free on the other side."

"Fantastic, any idea what kind of birds?"

"No," I admitted.

"Not a problem," she said, pulling out an Ipad and pushing a few buttons before handing it to me. "See if there are any here that you like."

I looked through the photos before me, picture after picture of hand-drawn birds filled the screen. So many to choose from. As I perused the options, Grant and Billie Jean talked. I gathered from their conversation that she had done his half sleeve, so I knew that she did excellent work.

I found a type of bird that I liked and showed it to Billie Jean.

"Excellent. That's a Swallow," she said, pulling out a notepad and starting to sketch two of them in flight together. "They represent love."

"Then it's perfect," I said with a smile. I looked at Grant and saw softness in his eyes. I thought of his mom and brother. We were such different people, but we shared this; the pain of being alone in the world, with no one to call family.

Once I was happy with the hand-drawn image, Billie Jean pulled a curtain around the chair, the kind you would find in a hospital, and I took my shirt off. Grant bit his lip as I unhooked my bra as well, presenting my bare back to Billie Jean. The chair tilted back and I laid on my stomach, feeling so exposed, but so excited.

I couldn't believe that I was doing this and Grant made it happen. As Billie Jean started her work and I grimaced in pain, he leaned forward and grasped my hand, holding on firmly and providing the support I needed.

Billie Jean didn't miss this action. I saw her smirk as she turned to her instruments. She looked almost amused.

"So, Lilly, did Grant tell you how we know each other?" she asked while she worked.

"No." I wanted to say that he wasn't exactly an open book, but that seemed unnecessarily catty when he was paying for my tattoo.

"I was his neighbor in the apartment building that he grew up in. It was my first apartment ever and when I moved in this little hellion must have been...What? Ten? Eleven?" she asked Grant.

"Something like that," he replied, watching her work on my back.

"Yeah, well, this guy and his older brother thought it would be hilarious to haze the new neighbor. So they bought a huge fake spider and attached a hook to my ceiling outside my apartment door. They used fishing wire to tie one end of a long string to my doorknob and the other end to the spider, with the middle of the string threaded through the hook. Long story short, when I opened my door the next morning, it looked like a giant spider was jumping into the air inches in front of me."

I chuckled lightly, trying not to move my back. Grant laughed out loud at the memory.

"You should've heard her scream bloody murder," he said.

"And you still associate with this guy?" I asked her, giving him a grin.

"Well, the kid grows on you. Like a fungus," she added snarkily, making Grant stick out his tongue like a child. "I'm sure you know how he is."

"Yeah, I do." As the needle traveled over my spine and I tightened my grip on his hand, Grant squeezed back.

"I know it hurts, but it's looking awesome," he reassured me.

Billie Jean was right, he had grown on me. In fact, I was beginning to realize exactly the kind of man that Grant was. A protector. A supporter.

A man I was beginning to love.

Chapter Twelve
Grant

I didn't know what the hell I was doing. Things were escalating with Lilly. Emotions were getting involved, and that was a dangerous game to play. Our living situation was meant to be temporary. What would happen when we cleared her name and she went back to her life? Would we be able to maintain this?

Did I want to?

I wasn't sure that would be fair to her. I'd been in a bad place after Leigh went missing. It was even worse when my mother died. The hatred and anger engulfed me. At this point, I'd spent nearly half my life clinging to that darkness and I felt like it had poisoned me. Tainted my soul. Was I really enough of a bastard to expose Lilly to that, especially when it was still unfinished business?

I wasn't sure. Here, at work, I could tell myself not to get too attached, but at home, when she looked at me with her gray eyes and bright smile, it wasn't so easy.

Damn it, I didn't know what to do anymore.

I looked at the time in the corner of my computer screen. It was a little early, but I wasn't getting any work done, anyway. Lilly was such a distraction.

I decided to go home. Turning my computer off, I grabbed my suit jacket from the back of my chair and shrugged it on while walking out of the office. I approached my secretary, an older woman with graying hair and an uncanny ability to see right through me.

"I'm heading home for the day, Bonnie," I said, making her look up from her computer screen.

"You got a hot date, boss?" she asked with a knowing smile.

"No, just finished for the day," I shrugged.

"Yeah, I've noticed that you've been wrapping up your work earlier and earlier lately. You used to be the last one here every night, but now… Heck, I don't think you've even stayed until five since you took those few days off. Matter of fact, that was weird too. I've worked here almost three years and you've never taken time off."

"Then I suppose it was long overdue."

"Maybe," she said, chewing on the end of her pen cap as she looked at me thoughtfully. "But I reckon you've got yourself a woman."

"You do, huh?" I asked, trying not to let my surprise show.

"Yep, and if I may say so, I think that's something else that's long overdue," she added with a wink. I rolled my eyes and chuckled before heading to the elevator. Maybe Bonnie had a point.

I heard Lilly's laughter when I walked through the front door of my home nearly 20 minutes later. Following the sound, I found her sitting cross-legged on one of the kitchen stools, with Dwight across from her at the island. They each held playing cards in their hands and the layout on the island in front of them looked like they were playing Texas Hold'em, using pennies, dimes and nickels as chips. Lilly looked up as I entered the room and beamed.

"Welcome home," she said and that sounded too fucking good. Who knew it would be so nice having someone to come home to? I swooped in and planted a kiss on her lips, lingering for just a second longer than I normally would.

I couldn't help the jealousy I felt seeing her so comfortable with Dwight. It wasn't just that the guy was closer to her own age and good looking. It was the knowledge in the back of my mind, that I was too messed up for this, for her. I couldn't shake the thought that being around Dwight would make her realize that. A part of me thought that she had only chosen me because I was her only option at this point.

"Poker?" I asked, gesturing to the cards on the island.

"Yep. I'm educating Dwight here. He's never played before."

"Yet, you show me no mercy," Dwight said. "She's already won-" he counted the small stacks of coins in front of him "-$3.40. I'll be in the poor house before I know it."

Lilly smiled at him and shook her head. "I warned you in advance. My house, my rules. And we play for keeps around here."

My chest felt tight as she referred to this as her house. Why did that feel so right?

It shouldn't, I told myself. It was too fast, and she was just laying low here for a while. I couldn't let myself feel so happy that she might like it here, that she might care about me. I couldn't want her to stay.

A prickling feeling of unease ran up my spine. I was starting to need her and that was bad news. This thing between us was too fragile and playing house was never a part of the plan. If things kept going like this, I would be destroyed when she wised up and left my ass.

Lilly and Dwight kept talking, but I lost track of the conversation. I was shocked at my own feelings. I had slept around plenty over the years, but this was the first time that I felt like someone was touching my heart, claiming me. I couldn't be this stuck on her. I just couldn't.

"Are you okay?" Lilly asked me, those three words tearing me up because they were so sincere. She was too damn good.

"Yeah. I'm, uh, I have a headache is all. I think I'll go lay down."

Lilly put her cards down and stood, the game apparently forgotten. Walking over, she put her hand on my arm. I could feel the warmth of her touch even through my suit jacket.

"Can I do anything for you?"

"No. I'd better just relax. It's probably just work stress," I said, stepping away and breaking our contact. I hated the concern that was on her face, hated that I was lying to her because I suddenly needed space and didn't know how to explain it without hurting her.

"I'd better head out too," Dwight said, nodding to me as he stood. "I'll see you tomorrow," he added to Lilly before walking out of the kitchen.

I followed behind him, turning to the stairs as he let himself out the front door. I heard Lilly activating the security system as soon as the door closed behind Dwight. She stayed below on the first floor, but I could sense her eyes following me as I climbed the stairs, making me feel ashamed of the disappearing act I was pulling on her.

But I kept walking.

***

It was hours later that I heard the knock on my door. I wasn't surprised that she came. We had been sleeping in my bed every night for a week.

In the last few hours whiled away in my bedroom, I had come to a conclusion about this relationship. The sex was out of this world, and I didn't want to stop. Hell, I didn't know if I could stop. Just knowing that she was standing on the other side of the door made my blood roar and my body demand release.

But I couldn't let this be more than sex. I had other shit to do. Burke was living it up out there while my brother was gone and my girl was stuck-

No. Not my girl.

Lilly was stuck here, hiding and missing out on her life.

I needed to get back on track, keep in mind what was important. No more staking a claim on her in front of the bodyguard or evening trips to tattoo parlors, which felt far too much like a date. This was just sex to relieve stress, to break the sexual tension. I could do that.

"Come in," I called out, staying seated on the bed with a book in my lap and my reading glasses perched on my nose.

"How are you feeling?" she asked as she came in, closing the door behind her. She was wearing low cut, hip-hugging jeans and a fitted t-shirt. A small sliver of skin was exposed along her midriff and I stared at the pale skin as she walked toward me.

"I'm better," I told her, looking up into her face as she stopped beside me. I could see her nipples through the thin material of her shirt, the buds pebbled and straining. She wasn't wearing a bra. I felt my cock throb as that realization hit me and I licked my lips. I moved my book to the nightstand and grasped her hand, pulling her down onto the bed across my lap. She giggled lightly, and I was transfixed by the movement of her unencumbered breasts.

"You seem to be much better," she said, looking at my bare chest. "But maybe I should give you a thorough examination, just in case."

"Well, if you insist," I said, slipping my reading glasses off and adding them to the nightstand as Lilly repositioned herself so she was kneeling beside me.

597

"Let's take a look, shall we?" she asked before grabbing the blankets that I had pulled up to my waist and ripping them off me. The sexual aggression was incredibly hot.

Lilly began trailing her hand along my chest, tracing the lines of my body with a light touch that made my head spin. "We'd better dive right into the physical exam," she said in a seductive voice.

"Whatever you say, doctor," I replied, leaning my head back against the pillow and relishing the sensations pulsing through my body. It was hard to believe that she had been a virgin just last week; she was so good at this.

She ran her hand all the way down to the waist of my boxers but refused to go lower. It was torture to have her fingers so close, but not feel them wrap around me. I let out a frustrated groan.

"Oh, no. Are you in pain? Well, I'd better do something about that," she said before straddling me. She rubbed her jean clad mound against my erection, increasing my frustration. Based on her smile, she knew it too.

"You're killing me," I said, but it was so damn good. The anticipation was like a drug, making my need for her climb higher and higher. She chuckled.

"I think it's time to check your reflexes," she said, diving forward to flick her tongue over my nipple. I thrust my hips up into her as electricity shot through my body.

"Very good," she said, her grin teasing. Straightening until she was upright over me, Lilly stripped out of her shirt, confirming that she was braless. The heavy swells made her waist look even smaller and I ran my hand along her sides, loving her hourglass figure.

As amazing as this role-playing was, I couldn't take much more. I needed to bury myself inside of her. Flipping our positions, I wasted no time in stripping her out of the rest of her clothes.

I could see that she was already wet, so ready for me. Refusing to delay any longer, I gripped her hip in one hand as I used the other to guide the head of my cock against her entrance. There was no gentle building of intensity this time, no playing around. I took her with a rough jerk of my hips, sheathing myself inside of her up to the hilt.

Lilly sucked in a deep breath but didn't shy away. Instead, she met my roughness with her own, bringing her hips up to meet mine as I pounded her into the mattress. The sweet friction around my member was bliss, the tight heat of her drawing me in.

But I wanted more.

I pulled myself out of her, drawing an arduous protest from her lips, then flipped her over, onto her stomach. My eyes locked on the tattoo on her shoulder blade, beautiful and delicate, and I reached out to run my hand along it, causing Lilly to arch her back. I used that as an opportunity to enter her again.

I let out a hiss as her sex gripped me. I had never been this deep before and I already felt an orgasm building. I gritted my teeth and used all my concentration to keep it from exploding out of me, the effort almost painful, but in the best way.

My hands gripped Lilly's hips as I rode her from behind, making her cry out in pleasure. I resumed my frantic rhythm, making the entire bed rock beneath us as I dominated her body, loving the sounds she was making, the way her sweet pussy clenched around me. It was too much, I couldn't hold back much longer.

"Come for me, my Temptress," I said hoarsely. "I need to feel your juice around my cock."

"Grant!" she let out a rasping scream as her entire body convulsed, the pulses driving me over the edge with her. I growled as I filled her with my seed, tightening my hold on her hips to steady myself. It was so intense that I saw spots before my eyes.

My orgasm seemed to last for several long minutes. Not that time mattered when I felt this gratified. Nothing mattered but the point where our bodies joined together, the source of so much heat and overwhelming sensation.

Lilly collapsed beneath me, as if her arms couldn't hold her up anymore, but her hips stayed in the air, holding that connection for just a few more seconds before I started to pull out. This I did slowly, the loss of contact almost painful as my spent cock was exposed to the cool air of the room.

I fell on my back beside her and realized that I was panting. I felt like I'd just run 10 miles on the treadmill, but that had never been quite this satisfying. In fact, nothing ever had.

I gathered Lilly in my arms, too exhausted to bother with clean-up or conversation. My last thought before sleep claimed me was that I shouldn't hold her like this if I wanted to keep emotion out of the relationship, but I just couldn't bring myself to pull away.

***

I turned the shower off and heard the incessant ringing of my phone. "Shit," I mumbled. I was soaking wet. Snagging a towel off the towel rack, I used it to wipe my hands as I streaked through the bathroom and into the bedroom, dripping water all over the floor along the way. Just as I reached out my semi-dry hand to pick up the phone, the voicemail picked it up.

I sighed and unlocked it, checking the call log. It was Bonnie and she had already called twice. My thumb moved to push the voicemail button when the shrill ringtone started again. It was her.

"Hey, Bonnie, what's wrong?" I asked. There was nothing positive that would require three phone calls in a row, especially not when I was due at the office in about an hour anyway.

"Someone broke into your office," she said without preamble.

"What? Did they take anything?" I asked, putting her on speakerphone so I could dry myself off quickly.

"Nothing obvious, but it's hard to tell. They ransacked the place."

"Just my office?" I asked, a sneaking suspicion forming in my mind. I heard footsteps behind me and turned to see Lilly walking into the room, her signature cup o' joe one hand. She looked at me curiously.

"It looks that way. The door looks like it was kicked in. I noticed it right away when I came in this morning," Bonnie said.

"Security didn't see anything or hear it?" I started pulling on my clothes quickly, not paying much attention to how I looked. What did it matter, anyway? The priority was getting to the office and seeing the damage.

"No, they saw no one enter all night and your office is on the top floor, while they're in the lobby. They didn't hear a thing."

"Fuck," I said under my breath. "I'll be there soon. Don't let anyone else into that office until I get there."

"Do you want me to call the police?" Bonnie asked.

"Not yet. I want to take a look first. I'll call them when I get there." I finished buttoning my dress shirt and ended the call. When I turned around Lilly was still standing there, looking concerned. "I've got to head in early. Will you be okay until Dwight gets here?"

I suppressed the unease I felt leaving her alone. It was for less than an hour. She'd be fine.

"Of course," she said.

I nodded and walked toward the door, planting a chaste kiss on her lips as I passed. I was out the door and on my way to work in record time. When I walked into the building, Bonnie was waiting for me by the elevators, looking nervous.

"It's bad, boss," she said, pushing the up button. The doors opened right away, and we stepped inside.

"See about the security cameras for the elevator," I told her, but I didn't have much hope. If the guy had avoided the security guards, he probably didn't take the elevator. Unfortunately, I didn't have cameras set up throughout the whole building. With around-the-clock security in the lobby, I didn't think it was necessary. So, the only cameras were here in the elevator, because that was standard.

As the elevator dinged and the doors opened on the top floor, I could immediately see that the person who did this wanted to make a point. That made it even more likely that Burke had a hand in it. It wasn't just my office, it was Bonnie's work area too.

My office was the only one on the top floor, one of the fringe benefits of being the founder of the company. So, when the doors opened, Bonnie's desk was the first thing in sight. Everything she usually kept on her desk - her computer, paperwork, pictures of her kids - had been swept off onto the floor. I clenched my jaw and walked toward my office door.

It was just as she'd said. The doorjamb was broken from the force of a kick that had dented the door itself as well. I pushed the remains of the door open to find complete chaos within. Books were knocked off the shelf behind my desk, my chair was overturned, papers were scattered everywhere, and every drawer in my desk was open.

The items on top of my desk had also been swept onto the floor, but I had taken my laptop home with me, so it escaped damage. Overall, it didn't look like they had taken anything, but I wouldn't be sure until I went through it all. Most of the paperwork should be of no use to anyone outside of the company unless industrial espionage was at play. I doubted that, though. That would surely be subtler, and this mess was designed to send a message.

There was only one possibility, the man that had already invaded my home did this to tell me that he knew I was still investigating him. Fucking Burke.

A sickening fury filled me as I made my way across the room, kicking debris out of my way as I went. This was to show me that he could get to me, to threaten me without words. How did he know that I was still tracking his movements? I had tried to be careful after his visit to the house.

I called Jim and started picking through the mess while I waited for him to arrive. Sorting through the paperwork was going to be the biggest hassle. Bonnie tried to help, but I sent her on a coffee run. I was going to need a pick-me-up. Besides, she could have probably used a breather. I'd never seen her so rattled.

I understood it, though. Someone had invaded our space, gone through her things. I felt violated myself.

I hung my jacket up and rolled my sleeves up to the elbows. I had kept a glass paperweight on my desk, which was now shattered on the floor. Jim found me ten minutes later on my knees, picking up the shards carefully and tossing them into the trash.

"Don't you rich guys usually pay someone to clean up messes for you?" he asked, looking around at the wrecked office.

"That is my preference, but I need to go through everything, make sure nothing was taken," I replied.

"Damn," Jim said, letting out a whistle, "they sure did a number on this place. You have any idea who it was?"

"Aren't you the cop?"

"Yeah and as such I'll ask the questions," he said, striding over to the desk and moving some pens from the seat of my chair before sitting down himself and propping his feet up on the desk. He pulled a notepad from his back pocket and popped the cap from one of the pens. "So...tell me, who do you think it was?"

"This isn't funny," I said, rolling my eyes as I climbed to my feet.

"Believe me, I know that," he said, suddenly serious. "But if anyone has an idea of who would do this, it's you."

"I think it was Burke."

"Why? You're the one that has a problem with him. He has no reason to break into your office."

"About that..."

"What?" he frowned, lowering his feet to the floor and leaning forward.

"He's onto me."

"He knows who you are?"

"Not yet. But he knows I've been keeping an eye on him. He showed up at the house last week and threatened me."

"Did he see Lilly?"

"No, she hid until he was gone."

Jim's face clearly showed his relief. He was protective of her.

"How could he know that you've been checking up on him?"

"I don't know. I get my information from a man that works for Burke, but he didn't return my call last week."

"What man?"

"Mitch Conway. Works as an IT guy at Burke's real estate firm. He keeps his ear to the ground and lets me know about anything he catches wind of, shipments, 'business meetings' at odd times of day, unsavory visitors. That sort of thing."

"I had no idea you had that kind of arrangement," Jim said, frowning and shooting me a calculating look. "I thought you hired a PI."

"Well, that didn't yield results."

"So, you think this Mitch guy might've turned on you?"

"Maybe. I pay him three times his yearly salary every month, but I guess that anyone can get too greedy. Maybe he switched sides for more money."

"Grant," Jim began, his tone cautious. "Don't you think that this is getting a little out of hand? You have a spy in his company now? How far will you go to bring him down?"

"I'll do whatever it takes," I said coldly.

"To be honest, I hope that isn't true. Burke's a killer and you're so desperate to get to him that you're getting reckless. I'm worried what it'll cost you."

For some reason, that statement had me pulling out my cell phone to call Lilly. Excusing myself from Jim, I stepped out into the hall and saw that Bonnie had already cleaned up the mess out here. As the phone rang, I told myself that I was just checking because I was responsible for her safety, but that didn't quite explain the relief that flooded my body at the sound of her carefree voice.

I kept the conversation short, just confirming that Dwight had arrived and everything was quiet there before hanging up. I had work to do here, starting with cleaning this mess up while Jim processed the scene. Then, I had to figure out what my next move would be with Burke. The dynamic between us was changing, he was no longer my secret obsession. He may not have known my reasons, but the man was aware of my crusade against him. We were now enemies.

Chapter Thirteen
Lilly

Something was wrong. I could sense it. The way that Grant looked at me was changing, the affection that had been growing in his eyes was now barely a glimmer when he looked at me.

There was some invisible obstacle growing between us, a wall that I was desperately trying to scale, but he wouldn't let me. The tighter I tried to cling to him, the further he seemed to back away.

He spent more time at the office, no longer showing up early after work. More often than not, he was late, coming home long after I had eaten dinner. I didn't fight with him about it, afraid that it would drive him further away from me.

Which may have been the objective.

When he was present, his mind seemed to be a million miles away. There were no more engaging conversations or deep confessions shared between us. Sometimes, it was like I wasn't even there, which hurt the most.

The only exception was in the bedroom, or rather, wherever we got physical. He lavished my body with the warmth that he was forcibly withholding otherwise. His touch was reverent and his passion raw. I couldn't keep my eyes off him when we were intimate because I still saw him there, the Grant that I had been getting to know over the last few weeks; my protector and the man that had shown he cared through his actions. I had always suspected that I was the only one that got to see him like that and that the tough front he had shown me initially was his way of handling most of the world. But the real Grant came out for me.

I held onto the belief that that version of him would return. If I could still connect with him on the physical level, then I wasn't losing him, right?

So, I had been initiating sex as often as possible, stealing the love he showed my body to nourish my soul as he retreated from me emotionally. I knew it probably wasn't healthy, but I was holding onto him in any way that I could.

I stared at him as he sat at the kitchen island, his laptop perched in his lap and his eyes focused on the screen. He ignored the plate of food sitting beside him while I quietly enjoyed my pasta. It was a Sunday, but he had spent most of the day staring at that screen, working with a concentration that made me wonder if he even realized I was here at all.

There was so much distance between us, despite the island being three feet wide. I felt like an entire desert separated me from him and there was no way across. He couldn't be reached.

"Do you want me to reheat your dinner? It's probably cold by now." I said, trying to break this thick ice.

"No, I'm not that hungry." He said, not even looking at me.

I let out a heavy sigh that was ignored, before walking over to the sink. I started washing the dishes that I had used to make dinner. Irritation swept through me. I had made a meal for us and instead of eating it, he let it sit untouched and was now leaving the clean-up to me.

What the hell was his problem?

I had tried being understanding, giving him time, but there was only so much I could take. I deserved respect, damn it. I started slamming things around in my anger, loading my plate into the dishwasher before slamming it shut, not even caring if I broke the thing. It wasn't like Mr. Billionaire couldn't afford a replacement.

Filling up the sink with hot, sudsy water, I started cleaning the pans with rough, jerky movements. I wasn't going to take this change in attitude lying down. Whatever his problem was, he was just going to have to talk to me about it. If he thought that he was just going to ice me out, he had another thing com-

I let out a gasp as a sharp pain shot through my right hand. Ripping it out of the water, I realized that there had been a knife in the sink that I forgot about and I had just grabbed it. The water turned crimson as blood poured from a cut on the fleshy part of my palm, beneath my thumb.

"Shit," I mumbled, turning to grab a towel, but Grant was already there. Before I even registered his movement, he had sprung from his seat, grabbed a dishtowel, and was wrapping it tightly around my hand with concern written all over his face.

"Use this to keep the pressure on it. Come on, I have a first aid kit upstairs," he said, leading me to the master suite.

I follow along obediently, shocked at this rapid change in demeanor. My hand was throbbing painfully. Grant wrapped his big hands around my hips and lifted me effortlessly onto the vanity counter as he rummaged in the drawers. Finally, he pulled out a small plastic box and set it on the counter before washing his hands.

"Okay, let's take a look," he said, holding his hand out. I placed my hand in his outstretched one and he carefully unwrapped the towel. It was still bleeding a little, but not badly. Unfortunately, there was too much blood around it to clearly see how bad the wound was. Grant turned on the faucet to cold water and stuck my hand under it.

There was a slight sting as the water ran over the cut, but I just bit my lip and watched as the blood washed away all the red. The incision was long, maybe two inches, but not deep.

"Well, I don't think you'll need stitches, which is good," Grant said, pulling a small tube and a big band-aid from the kit. He turned off the water and no more blood pooled on my skin; it looked like it had stopped. He grabbed a new towel from the cabinet by the shower stall and used it to gently pat my hand dry.

The way he handled me, the soft touches, the worried look, made my heart warm. Why was he hiding this part of himself from me lately?

"This is antibiotic ointment," he said, opening the tube and squeezing out a greasy, goopy line of ointment along the cut and pressing the band-aid over the top of it.

"Thanks," I said, looking into his eyes.

"You have to be more careful," he admonished, but I could see beneath the reproach to the anxiety. He cared.

Perhaps that thought showed in my face, because he suddenly stepped back, the emotions on his face disappearing the way the sun could be blocked out by shutters. "Because I can't always be around to take care of you," he added, his voice clipped. After a moment's hesitation, during which I said nothing, he turned and stalked out of the bathroom without glancing back.

I sat there for a moment, replaying that scene in my head. His words didn't match his actions. Just as our love-making demonstrated his affection despite his recent detachment, his quick reaction and tender attention to my wound painted a picture that words couldn't.

So, why was he trying to ice me out?

***

"Can you teach me some self-defense?" I asked Dwight on Monday afternoon.

I had been thinking about how helpless I felt when Burke showed up at the house. Even though I hadn't been left alone since then, I wanted to have some idea of how to defend myself. I hoped it would be empowering.

"Of course, but you won't need it. That's why I'm here," Dwight assured me.

"Still...just a few basics?"

"Okay," he said after a moment's hesitation. I wasn't sure what made him reluctant, but I wasn't going to ask.

"Great, I'll go change and we can use Grant's gym. The flooring in there is black rubber, so it won't hurt when I knock you on your ass," I said with a grin.

The sound of Dwight's laughter followed me up the stairs, where I changed into yoga pants and a sports bra. I almost walked back to Dwight like that but decided at the last minute to slip a tank top over my head. There was no attraction between the two of us, but Grant wouldn't like it if I was so unclothed around another guy.

At least, I didn't think he'd like it. It was hard to tell these days.

I tied my hair back as I walked down the stairs and met Dwight in the gym. He was standing in the middle of the room, looking around at the exercise equipment. It was no wonder that Grant's body was so delectable. He had a little bit of everything in here and started almost every day on one machine or another.

I bounced around on the balls of my feet, energy flowing through me as I lightly stretched. Dwight watched me without moving, looking amused at my excitement.

"Where do we start?" I asked him.

"Well, the best defense is really avoidance. Run if you can, scream to get attention, whatever it takes."

I wanted to roll my eyes. Avoidance was great unless you had a knack for trouble, like me. I saw a murder while taking out the trash, for fuck's sake. And I already knew a thing or two about running.

"If it comes to actual defense, you need to know how to block attacks."

"Great. Show me that."

Almost an hour later, I was starting to think that self-defense training wasn't my best idea. I was breathing hard, my body was covered in sweat, and my arms were feeling bruised. Dwight had shown me how to blocks hits using my forearms and we had been practicing it over and over and over again.

"Can we move on to something else?" I asked, gulping down half a bottle of water in one go.

"Okay, I'm gonna choke you."

"What?" I spluttered.

"Fake choking and you'll try to get out of it," he clarified.

"Oh. Right." Duh.

"Okay, you will be up against the wall," I moved into position. "If I were attacking you with a frontal choke like this," his hands wrapped around my neck, making me feel uncomfortably vulnerable despite trusting Dwight, "you would bring your hands together like you were praying, up between my arms, and forcefully thrust your arms out, breaking my hold."

I tried it as he spoke, and he moved his arms off my neck easily to demonstrate. "That was easy," I said.

"Yeah too easy. Let's try again."

This time Dwight locked his arms as he wrapped his hands around my neck. He still didn't apply pressure to my throat, but his arms were rigid, and the move didn't budge him. "Keep trying, it'll be difficult if your attacker is this strong," he said.

I tried again and again, grunting with the effort as it had no effect. I couldn't see it working.

Suddenly Dwight's hands were no longer around my neck. In fact, he went flying backward, making me gasp. He landed on his back and Grant positioned himself in front of me, in a defensive stance. I could see the back of his neck was red and his fists were clenched at his sides.

"What the fuck are you doing to her?" he snarled as Dwight climbed to his feet. My heart stuttered, and I didn't know if it was because I was afraid that he would attack Dwight or because Grant's protective reaction was such a turn-on.

"No, no, no," I said, coming around to stand beside him. "I asked him to teach me self-defense. He wasn't hurting me. See," I gestured to my unblemished neck as Grant's eyes, looking darker than usual, snapped to me.

"Self-defense?" Grant asked, deflating slightly.

"Yeah, just self-defense."

"Why didn't you ask me if you wanted to learn that?"

Yeah, because you've been so approachable lately, I thought bitterly.

"I'm gonna head out," Dwight said, looking uncomfortable.

"See you tomorrow," I called out as he practically fled the room.

"You should've asked me to teach you. I don't want his hands on you," Grant said, possessiveness clear in his voice.

"How was I supposed to know that? You haven't exactly been an open book lately."

The air was thick with tension. It was the first time either of us had spoken about the rift that had been forming between us. Now that it was out in the open, it felt like a physical presence in the room, unavoidable and intrusive.

"Stay here," he said, walking out of the room.

He was back ten minutes later dressed in a pair of basketball shorts. I kept my eyes glued to his face, refusing to admire his body.

"What are you doing?"

"You want to learn self-defense. I'm going to teach you."

"I don't know..."

"You'd rather learn from Dwight?" he asked, his tone dark.

Not really.

"I'm just tired."

"How long were you in here with him?"

"Almost an hour."

"And you're tired?" he smirked. "Come on, I know you have better stamina than that."

Heat spread through my core, but I ignored it.

"We were working on blocking hits the whole time. It was exhausting."

"Blocking?" Grant shook his head. "That is exhausting. In fact, an attacker that knows what he's doing is relying on that. You wear yourself out fending him off until you're too tired to fight back anymore."

"Oh."

"You need to know how to incapacitate an attacker long enough to get away."

I nodded. That made so much sense. Grant stepped closer to me.

"The weakest parts of the body are the eyes, nose, ears, throat and knee. Hit one of these and run. Period. No getting cocky and trying to take things further. Even if you hurt him, it won't take a determined man long to recover enough to catch you. You need to take advantage of any head start you get."

"Just poke him in the eye and run?"

"Kind of. Actually, unless he's already very close to you, I say go for the knee. You don't want to have to move in closer to get access to his face. You have more reach with a kick. Besides, your legs are stronger than your arms, so you're more likely to do some damage that way. Go for the side of the knee. That way you can probably knock him off his feet."

"Got it," I said, regretting the hour that I had wasted with Dwight. This was what I wanted to learn; this made me feel like I might have a fighting chance if it came down to that.

We spent another hour in the gym together, practicing various moves. He would pretend to attack me, and I would carry out the maneuver he recommended. At the end of the session, he promised to buy padded gear so that we could continue training together.

This, more than anything else, gave me a feeling of hope for us. He had been engaged during my lesson in a way that I had been missing the last few days. The idea of doing this more in the future, of having any impending plans at all, made me think that things might go back to normal between us.

Chapter Fourteen
Grant

"Bad news," Jim said, as soon as I answered the phone. I sighed.

"Lay it on me," I replied.

"Mitch Connelly is missing."

"You're sure?" When I had stopped hearing back from Mitch, I assumed that he'd decided not to spy on Burke for me anymore. He'd always been nervous about it, but the money I gave him was too good for him to pass up.

"His dad filed a report two days ago." Shit. That was the day that my office had been broken into. My chest felt tight as I realized that I had probably gotten this man killed. Now he was another missing person, just like Leigh. Would his family ever find out what happened to him? "I know what you're thinking, but don't. We don't know that Burke did something to him. It could be unrelated. People go missing all the time," Jim was trying a little too hard to be convincing.

"You really believe that?"

There was a short pause.

"Okay, no. I'm sure that Burke had something to do with it. The timings are a little too coincidental for my liking. But I don't want you to blame yourself."

"I deserve the blame."

"No. Burke is responsible. He's the bad guy here," Jim argued.

"And I put Mitch right into his path. Listen, thanks for the heads up but you're not going to convince me that I'm blameless here."

"I didn't really think I would," he conceded, sounding grave. "But there's something else you should know."

"More good news?"

"Is it ever? One of the beat cops has been asking me about you. He's trying to be casual about it, but he sucks at lying. I'm thinking he might be one of Burke's guys, trying to get some dirt on you. Everyone knows you're a friend of mine."

"Are you in danger?" I asked, fear creeping up my spine.

"I don't think so, but I thought you should know about it."

"Watch your back. I wouldn't put anything past Burke."

"Yeah, you too."

As I hung up the call I wanted to hit something, scream, act out my frustrations in some way. But when I looked up, Lilly was standing there.

"Hey, are you okay?"

My first instinct was to tell her the truth, to take the comfort I knew she would provide, but I didn't deserve that. I had likely gotten a man killed. Besides, it wouldn't help with the whole distancing myself thing.

"Yeah, I'm fine," I said. She didn't look entirely convinced but I knew she wouldn't press it.

"Well, I made dinner for us and set it up on the patio," she said happily. I knew she was trying to please me, to make me happy, but I wished she wouldn't. I didn't know how to convince her that I simply wasn't worth it.

Instead, I followed her outside and ate dinner. I told myself that I had to stop putting this off and make a decision about her. But after dinner, I let her pull me into the kitchen and bend her over the island instead. Tomorrow then, I'd make a decision tomorrow.

***

I had to end it. This thing with Lilly was throwing me off my game too much. I hadn't held onto this grudge against Burke for so long just to let myself get distracted by a woman now. It was too late for that. I had invested too much of myself into this vendetta.

I had come to this conclusion when I received a call from one of my contacts about a shipment that arrived from Argentina this morning. It was supposedly an import of art for a gallery that Burke owned.

What upset me was that I missed it. I was supposed to be keeping an eye on Burke's business dealings so that I could intercept things like this, find the proof I needed of his misdeeds. Now the shipment had already been sitting at the dock for nearly two hours and it wasn't nearby.

Oh, no. That would be too easy.

This shipment came by boat to a pier in Charleston, South Carolina. I was having my private jet prepped, but it would still be hours before I got there. Would Burke move it before I arrived? I was sure that he must be using this art to smuggle in his drugs.

This had to be it.

If it wasn't, I was back at square one and didn't even want to think about that. I pulled out a duffle bag and started throwing things into it haphazardly. Lilly was in the shower and I was listening for it to shut off. I wanted to be ready to go before I talked to her because I knew it wouldn't go well and I didn't want to hang around afterward.

This was hard enough, but I had to do it. I knew from the beginning that she was a distraction. Her smooth skin, her warm smile and her damn caring nature was too appealing to a monster like me. She'd be better off in the long run and I could fulfill the promise I made to myself years ago. I was going to get revenge on Burke by ruining his life and nothing would stop me.

I pulled out my phone as I walked down the stairs, calling Tyler to tell him I was ready. He was coming with me to South Carolina - you knew you were a VIP customer when the owner of the security firm himself escorts you somewhere potentially dangerous.

Dwight would be staying here with Lilly. She would still need protection until I managed to get Burke behind bars.

I ended the call and realized that the shower was off. She was coming. I was standing in the bedroom when she emerged from the bathroom a few minutes later, her pale skin glowing after the hot shower. The sundress she had put on flowed loosely around her body but left those long legs exposed. Her hair was wet and she carried a towel with her, drying the dark locks as she walked along, humming to herself.

For just a second, I let myself admire her, the beauty she exuded without even trying. It was just a part of who she was. She was a light that had illuminated my darkness, chasing away some of the pain I was used to living with.

But it couldn't last. My demons would swallow her whole if I walk away now. I'd never get my closure if Burke slipped through my fingers and the anger and the obsession would take over my life again. It would take over her life if I let it.

With those thoughts in mind, steeling my resolve, I folded my arms across my chest. When she looked up and saw me standing there, her face started to transform into a smile. A warm, loving smile that fucking killed me; but she must have seen something in my expression that told her something was wrong.

"Grant? What's going on?" she asked, freezing on the other side of the room.

"We need to talk," I said. I wanted to roll my eyes at my own word choice, talk about a cliché.

"Okay…"

"I can't do this anymore," I swallowed thickly. "Us. I can't keep this up."

"What do you mean," she asked, her brow furrowing.

"I didn't mean for this to happen, this… whatever it is we have going on. I need to be chasing Burke, getting him back for what he did to my family, but I can't focus properly with you around. You're a distraction that I don't need."

"I never asked you to stop going after him. Hell, I want you to get him. Then I won't be a murder suspect anymore. I won't have to fear him."

"It's not about you asking me not to. It's about succumbing to the comfort of being with you. It's about coming home early from work to see you. It's about being wrapped up in a relationship when all I wanted was a good fuck."

Lilly didn't move a muscle, but she looked like I'd gutted her. I fucking hated myself right then, but I didn't take the words back. I needed to drive her away from me, make her hate me, because I knew that I couldn't resist her otherwise. I wasn't as strong as her.

"You said I was yours," she said softly, there was a pleading tone to her voice that I couldn't stand to hear. It was so different from the fight she usually had, the fierce retorts she threw at me no matter what I said.

Now she sounded broken. I did that. I broke her because I was a piece of shit, but there was no stopping now. I couldn't allow this attachment any longer.

"You were my fuck buddy. And that was great, really. But it's over now." I turned away and strode to the door, I couldn't keep looking at her. "I'm going out of town for a day or two. Dwight will be here while I'm gone."

I left the room without waiting for a response. The doorbell rang as I bounded down the stairs and I hurried to answer it. Dwight stood on the porch while Tyler waited by my car. I pushed past Dwight without a greeting; my anger was rising and I wasn't in a place to speak to anyone.

I was angry at Burke for all of his shady shit, angry at Dwight because he was probably going to be a shoulder for Lilly to cry on, angry at her for making me care about her so much. But mostly I was angry at myself. I loathed myself for hurting Lilly in any way.

At least there was one good thing to come from all of this, my self-loathing was tinged with the satisfaction of knowing that I had just destroyed myself. It turned out that Burke wasn't my worst enemy after all. I held that title myself.

Chapter Fifteen
Lilly

What the hell just happened?

I stood frozen in the middle of Grant's bedroom, which I had foolishly been thinking of as ours, since I stopped sleeping in the guest room after we had sex for the first time. God, what a sap I was.

He had called me a Fuck buddy. No more cute nicknames like Temptress for me, I guessed. It felt like he had canceled out all the sweet words he'd whispered in my ear during sex, all the warmth he had filled me with. Those were an illusion.

I was a Fuck buddy.

The truth was clear. He didn't care about me. I was used for sex.

I couldn't stay here.

My body seemed to unfreeze as that thought occurred to me. I bolted to the closet, where a searing pain entered my chest at the sight of my few clothes hanging beside his, a reminder of the future I had so desperately wanted.

Ripping my clothing from the hangers, I threw it all onto his bed. I returned to the closet and foraged around for a bag of some kind, coming up with a set of suitcases that I knew he used for business trips. I brought the smallest one of them into the bedroom, unceremoniously stuffing my clothes into it.

A small voice in the back of my mind told me that I was being irrational. That I wouldn't be safe if I left this house.

I suppressed it. Like hell was I going to be waiting here for him when he got home, sleeping in the guest bedroom again and acting like everything was fine.

Part of my decision-making process was fear. I felt sick at the thought of his eyes looking at me with cold indifference, as they had when I first arrived at the house. I was afraid that I'd show him just how heartbroken I was if that happened.

He didn't get to know that.

I grabbed my toiletries from the bathroom and threw them in on top of the clothes, not caring that the shower bottles were still wet. That was a problem for later.

Looking around the room, I tried not to remember the times that Grant and I had been together here, the taste of his skin, the sound of his voice moaning my name. There was nothing left here for me but pain.

I closed the suitcase, not even half-full with the pitiful amount of possessions I had, and took it off the bed. I strode out of the room and down the stairs to find Dwight standing in the living room, looking at his phone.

Making my way past him, I went to the kitchen. When we'd ordered pizza a few weeks ago, I had seen Grant pull cash out of an old coffee tin that he kept in the cabinet above the refrigerator. I didn't feel good about it, but I grabbed a handful of twenties and stuffed them into a side pocket of the suitcase. Promising myself that I would send Grant a check in the future, when I found a way to clear my name, I returned the tin to the cabinet as Dwight entered the kitchen.

"Morning," he said, eyeing me curiously.

"Hi, Dwight. Thanks for coming, but I won't be needing your services today."

"What?"

"You can go home," I said, walking to the great room and scanning it for anything that might be mine. I tried my hardest not to look at the couch where I'd lost my virginity. Walking to the coffee table, I picked up a book that Grant had ordered for me when I told him that my favorite romance author had released a new one that I wanted.

A foolish, hopeful part of myself still wanted to believe that he must care about me. Why else would he order this book? Why else would he take me to get a tattoo that I wanted? Why would he tell me about his brother and mom?

If he cared, it must not be enough. Or maybe it was the problem. Caring about me wasn't a part of his plans.

Shoving the book into the suitcase, I let out a shaky sigh. That was it. That was every trace of me in the house. Now, it was like I was never here at all.

My eyes glanced out through the patio doors. Our first kiss had been right out there, initiated by me. Everything that had happened since then, included this suffocating feeling in the center of my chest, had stemmed from that moment.

I felt curiously ashamed as I stood there, reliving that moment. I had felt a connection to Grant after that kiss. Despite telling myself that I shouldn't get attached, that was exactly what I had done. Standing here, reliving that very first kiss, I knew that I was falling for him from the very beginning.

I turned and was surprised to see Dwight standing in the kitchen, watching me. He was wearing a look of understanding that made me want to scream. I had been so happy here. I hadn't expected it, but I guessed that love did that to a person.

"Why are you still here?" I asked tiredly. I was stalling out, for some reason. After my whirlwind packing and determination to leave, I wasn't sure why I didn't just do it.

Then, I looked beyond Dwight and into to the kitchen, my eyes falling on the island. I remembered Grant telling me about his painful past that still haunted him. His tortured heart was on display that night and I fell in love with him then. I didn't realize it at the time, but it was so clear now.

My entire path to heartache was laid out for me to retrace as long as I stayed.

"Where are you going?" Dwight asked, his face inscrutable.

"I don't know yet. Away from here. I probably need to leave Chicago. That'd be safest," I said, talking more to myself than to him. I was looking at the pool table, which inevitably led to thoughts of my first time having sex.

"Does Grant know?"

"That I'm leaving?"

"Yeah."

"It doesn't matter. I'm a burden on him. I have been since the beginning."

"It doesn't look that way to me," Dwight said.

"Well, you're wrong," I snapped.

I walked past him to the front door, pulling my phone out as I went. Pulling up the app, I ordered an Uber to pick me up down the road. I didn't want anyone to associate me with Grant if I was recognized as the woman the police were looking for. No need to bring him down with me.

I thought about leaving the phone behind, but I really needed one. I would send it back to Grant later.

"Lilly, don't leave," Dwight called out as I opened the front door.

"Don't worry, I'll be fine. I don't need your protection anymore."

"But I don't work for you. I work for Grant and he told me to keep an eye on you here at the house."

"Well, that creates a problem because I won't be at the house," I said, turning away and walking down the porch steps.

I started walking down the driveway, dragging the suitcase along behind me, its wheels unable to get good traction on the rocks. With each step I took, I felt a heart-wrenching sorrow come over me. I could barely breathe with this pain.

A burning sensation started in my throat and my vision blurred. I didn't want to cry, not here. I wanted to wait until I was alone, probably in a hotel room, if I could find one that accepted cash. My tears didn't care what I wanted though. They came unbidden, making me feel pathetic.

How had my life derailed so much? A part of me wished I'd never met Grant. Although, if I were making wishes, I would wish that I never went to work at all that night. Then I wouldn't have had any of these problems.

I wouldn't have had any of the pleasure either, but that would have probably been for the best. Too bad that wishes didn't come true.

I was just clear of the garage when I heard a noise behind me, a shifting of gravel that sounded far different than the sounds being made by suitcases or footsteps. Sniffling, I came to a stop. I started to turn around when a blinding pain shot through my head. My legs crumpled beneath me but I had succumbed to darkness before I even hit the ground.

Chapter Sixteen
Grant

"This is it. Container C-14," I said, putting the car in park and stepping out while Tyler did the same on my other side. We were at the docks in Charleston, South Carolina and facing a wall of massive shipping containers stacked on top of each other and arranged in rows.

The one I was looking for - Burke's container - was right in front of us, luckily on the ground so it was accessible. I popped the trunk of my car and grabbed a pair of bolt cutters that I had bought at a hardware store after leaving the airport.

A feeling of giddy anticipation ran through me. This was it. I was finally going to find evidence that Burke was smuggling in drugs.

"Shouldn't you get the cops here before you break in? I mean, it looks suspicious that you would be in there first."

"The FDA can verify the origins of the drugs. I read the shipping manifest for this container. Most of this art is from Argentina. If the drugs came from there, they'll be able to tie it directly to Burke. Once we find them, I'll make an anonymous call and the investigators don't need to ever know we were here."

I expected Tyler to object to that, but he just nodded.

"Why didn't you just call in the tip anyway, instead of flying here yourself? Then, if the drugs are here, they could find them. If not, no harm done."

"I don't want to spook him. The only chance I have of catching Burke is if he gets comfortable and makes a mistake, like leaving this container unattended. Besides, he's well-connected and smart. I can't assume that he wouldn't be able to trace the call to me. Then, there's a lot of harm done."

With that, I walked forward and used the bolt cutters to cut through the lock on the outside of the container. I was overcome with a heavy sense of purpose as I pulled the metal door open, a loud creaking noise disturbing the still air.

Inside, I could see various shapes, shadows in this dark space. I pulled out my phone and turned the flashlight on as Tyler did the same beside me. There were crates stacked all over the interior of the container.

Tyler ran out to the car and grabbed a crowbar out of the trunk, prying open the boxes as I sifted through their contents. The first one was full of tribal masks and packing peanuts. Nothing there.

Refusing to get discouraged, I moved on to the next one. It was full of metal pieces and seemed to assemble into some kind of art. Then, a third one had paintings. A fourth one yielded more paintings, as well as a fifth. What the hell?

Frustration mounting, I looked through another box to find clay bowls that looked ancient. These were also just packed in peanuts. I was already feeling the crushing disappointment setting in.

Tyler was double-checking the crates I had already looked at, confirming my conclusions that there was nothing illegal there. I started moving more frantically, determined to find something, anything. As I feared, all fifteen crates were packed with legitimate art.

"Son of a bitch!" I clenched my teeth until I thought my teeth might crack. Kicking the side of one of the crates, I heard the contents rattle. The sudden urge to destroy something was almost overwhelming, but I forced myself to walk back to the car instead.

How could there be nothing? I was so sure that I had him this time. An import from South America? Come on, it had to be how he was bringing them in.

Striking out against the dash in anger, I let out a string of curses. I had been trying to pin something on Burke for years. So much time lost to this obsession, and now I was back at square one. I had nothing.

Lilly's face flashed through my mind.

Yeah, because that was really helpful right now, adding guilt to my frustration. Tyler came out of the shipping container five minutes later. "I put the lids back on the crates as well as I could. If you're lucky, Burke will just assume that they were packed poorly to begin with," Tyler said.

"Thanks, man."

None of this was a part of Tyler's job description as a bodyguard, so I was grateful, but I also wasn't in a good place mentally. I felt like I was falling down a black hole, my own incompetence pulling me into a place of hopelessness.

"Let's just go back to the hotel. You can get your head on straight there," he said, his voice almost cautious.

I must have look wrecked, but who could blame me. I sure knew how to fuck up my life, dedicating my whole existence to getting revenge on a man that bested me constantly; and now I had nothing outside of my work and this sick fixation on him. I had snuffed out the light in my life.

***

A stiff drink sounded so good, but I wanted to check in with Dwight before I drowned my sorrows in a bottle of scotch.

After driving to a hotel in northern Charleston, I collapsed onto the bed in a heap. I allowed myself a few minutes to wallow in the reality of such a shitty day. I had been so certain about this shipping container, I felt like the rug had been pulled out from beneath me now.

I wasn't even sure why I had hung all my hopes on it in the first place, but I suspected that it was because I wanted to be done with this. Over the years, I had grown so intent on avenging my brother that it felt wrong to do anything for myself until I reached that goal.

Sitting here, alone on the top floor of a fancy hotel, things seemed clearer to me. I had fallen for Lilly. I loved her.

But I didn't deserve her. Falling in love was a privilege that I hadn't earned yet. I couldn't even fulfill my promise to take down my brother's killer and the pursuit of the man had made me a broody nightmare of a person. I knew it.

Lilly had broken through my layers of cynicism and anger to show me the man beneath, the man I wanted to be. But I couldn't, not yet. I had thought… if this had been my shot to catch Burke, maybe I could finally put the pain behind me. Maybe I could be the man she thought I was.

That shipping crate being drug-free was a devastating situation, not just because Burke was still free, but because it meant that I had so much more to do before I could move on with my life. Abandoning the cause wasn't an option.

I picked up my phone. It was hard to believe that less than four hours had passed since I'd left the house, it felt like a lifetime since I'd looked into Lilly's big gray eyes. I pulled up my contacts information, my finger hovering over her name for a moment before I scrolled up to Dwight's number.

I couldn't talk to her now, not after I'd stomped her heart into the floor and didn't even have good news to give her on the Burke situation. We could have a face-to-face when I returned. Maybe I would try to explain my real feelings to her. She understood me better than anyone, she might get where I was coming from.

I listened to the phone ring five times before the voicemail picked up. Frowning, I disconnected the call and tried again. Still no answer.

Sitting up in the bed, I pulled up Lilly's number again, pushing the call button this time. The dread I felt made any awkward conversation a secondary concern. When her voicemail picked up too, I left the room to head to Tyler's next door.

"What's wrong?" he asked as soon as he opened the door.

"I can't reach Dwight or my - or Lilly. Can you try him?"

"Sure," Tyler said, pulling out his phone. I tried Lilly again. No answer and Tyler shook his head at me before leaving a voicemail for Dwight.

"Pack up, we're leaving as soon as possible."

Going back to my own room, I picked up my unopened duffle bag and called my pilot. I had planned to stay overnight and return in the morning, but there was no way that was happening now. I had a horrible feeling in the pit of my stomach.

I was checking us out of our rooms when Tyler came up to me with a grave expression. I braced myself for bad news.

"I sent one of my guys over to your house to check things out. It was deserted. No Dwight. No Lilly. No car." My head spun as he spoke. "They found a cellphone in the driveway with a cracked screen and a little blood on the gravel."

Tyler pulled out his own phone and showed me a picture.

"It's Lilly's," I croaked.

Tyler was talking but I couldn't seem to hear it past the roaring sound in my ears. All I could hear were the last words I spoke to her. My harsh attempts to drive her away from me like a fucking moron were replaying in my mind, drowning out everything else. Would those be the last words I ever spoke to her? Would she just disappear, like Leigh?

No. No, that couldn't happen because I wouldn't survive it. It was hard losing Leigh, it was devastating losing my mom, but this...

There was no life if Lilly was gone. I couldn't even picture it. The only thing I knew for sure was that I would kill him. Forget ruining his reputation and putting him behind bars. If he hurt Lilly I would kill the bastard with my bare hands.

Chapter Seventeen
Lilly

The first thing I became aware of, before I'd even opened my eyes, was a throbbing pain in the back of my head. This was no typical headache. The pain radiated throughout my skull and made me whimper. That was when I snapped my eyes open, suddenly aware that I was in a strange place.

I flinched as the fluorescent lighting stung my sensitive eyes and made my head ache more. Where the hell was I?

Secondary to the pain in my head, I realized that my body was stiff and the exposed skin on the left side of my body felt chafed because it was pressed against rough concrete. I wondered how long I had been on this floor.

The room around me was bare, with no furniture or fixtures of any kind. Just that bright light, four walls, and a door. It was small, the size of a bathroom, or perhaps a storeroom. Why was I here? Everything was murky, I couldn't think straight.

I started to maneuver my body into a sitting position but had to stop when I got lightheaded from the pain in my head. If I wasn't careful, I might have passed out again. Fueled by mounting fear, I took several deep breaths and moved slowly until I was sitting up against the wall opposite the door.

I was confused, my sluggish brain unable to comprehend what was going on. How had I gotten here? I tried to remember.

My mind conjured up the memory of Grant's rejection. Yeah, because that was so helpful right now. Knowing I couldn't dwell on it, I pushed that whole incident aside. What happened next?

Right, packing and fleeing. Then…

Nothing. I couldn't remember anything after leaving the house. Panic threatened to overtake me, but I crushed it, using all the willpower I had. It was bad enough that my mind was moving so slowly, like I was swimming through tar, I didn't need a panic attack on top of that.

I was positive that I didn't meet the Uber that I ordered, so something must have happened on the way. I suddenly noticed a dark stain on the floor where I had been laying.

Tentatively prodding around my head, I let out a hiss of pain as my fingers brushed against a wound on the back of my skull. My hair felt wet and sticky around the spot and when I pulled my hand away, I saw blood.

Well, that explained the pain. Someone must have hit me from behind, knocking me out. Not just anyone, it must have been Burke or someone working for him.

I heard the distinct sound of footsteps echoing on the other side of the door. Before I could even decide what to do, a key was inserted into the lock and the door swung open. I saw Dwight standing there.

Relief flooded me.

"Dwight! How did you find me?"

He didn't answer, just walked into the room. I held my hand out to him.

"Help me up. We need to get out of here," I said. Uneasiness trickled down my spine when he didn't grab my hand. He just stepped to the side of the room and turned to face the door. His expression was blank.

"Dwight?"

At that moment, more footsteps sounded, and I didn't have a chance to brace myself before Henry Burke himself strode into the room like he owned the place. Hell, he probably did.

The man looked the same as always, perfectly pressed suit and shiny loafers adorning his thin body. He looked calm, with a slight uptick in the corners of his mouth giving him the expression of a man that was mildly amused by this situation. I immediately wanted to slap that look off his face.

"I see sleeping beauty is finally awake. Tell me, Miss Monroe, how are you liking your accommodations?" Burke said lightly.

I glared at him, refusing to speak.

"I know it's a far cry from a billionaire's mansion…" My eyes widened in surprise and he chuckled. "Oh yes, I know you've been staying with Grant Donovan."

I looked at Dwight. "You're working for him, now?" I asked. That had to be how Burke knew where I was.

"Yes," Dwight finally spoke, barely moving his mouth and not looking at me.

"Why? Why would you do that? I thought you were a good guy. God, I thought you were my friend." I was disgusted. "Are you the one that hit me?"

"I had to do something. Burke was already on his way to get you. You couldn't be allowed to leave."

"So, you bashed me over the head? You could have killed me!"

"I tried to convince you to stay. You're the one that had to be so stubborn."

"You're a real piece of work. How could you betray me like this, you dick?"

"Now, now, don't be so hard on the ole boy. Everyone has their price, Miss Monroe. Lucky for me, I can always afford to pay it."

I hated that they were standing over me like this. I felt too vulnerable, more so than I already was. Using the wall to brace myself, I slowly climbed to my feet. The pain in my head roared, making my stomach flop and I thought I might vomit for a moment.

If that happened I would aim for Burke's annoyingly perfect loafers.

But the feeling passed, and I was able to at least look them in the eyes. "Why am I here?"

"Because you're useful to me for now. You'll bring Donovan."

"You want Grant?" I asked, then cringed. My feelings for him were clear from the way I said his name.

"Oh yes, I do. Donovan's snooping around is a complication that I don't need. So, you're here because he'll come for you."

"And then what?"

"Then I eliminate the problem," Burke said with a cold smile. A chill ran down my spine. He was going to kill Grant. I couldn't let that happen.

"And what about me?"

"Well, you're part of the problem."

I had to do something. I couldn't just stand here and talk about my own death with the man planning to kill me. It was surreal.

My vision strayed to Dwight. He was standing just a few feet away, his body turned toward Burke and his arms crossed over his chest. I locked my eyes on the gun he carried at his hip.

"He won't come for me," I said, trying to keep Burke talking. I subtly pushed myself away from the wall, pleased when I was able to stand without my head spinning. The pain was becoming more of a dull ache.

"Silly little girl. No man would leave the woman he loves in the hands of his enemy."

"Loves?" I asked, distracted momentarily.

"Don't be silly. Dwight's told me everything."

The feeling of betrayal that coursed through my veins gave me the fuel I needed to dive toward Dwight, grabbing his gun and ripping it out of the holster. I backed away from the two men, holding the gun out with shaking hands. My back pressed against the wall.

"Now, get out of my way. I'm leaving!" I exclaimed. I had never even held a gun before.

Both men stood staring at me for a moment, then Burke started laughing.

"I said move!"

"You have to love it when a plan comes together," Burke said to Dwight, ignoring me completely. I was confused.

I was the one with the gun. Why weren't they listening to me?

Dwight took a step toward me. I trained the barrel of the gun on him. "Stay back," I said, my voice unsteady. I told myself to pull the trigger as he kept advancing toward me. I had to do it.

Despite the voice in my head shouting Shoot, I couldn't bring myself to do it. I just stood there, frantic, until Dwight reached out and plucked the gun from my hands easily. I noticed that he was wearing leather gloves on his hands.

"Show her," Burke instructed, and Dwight pointed the gun toward the floor, pulling the trigger twice. I expected a deafening bang in this small space, but nothing happened. Just two small clicking sounds

"It's empty," Burke said, taking in my puzzled expression. "No bullets."

I felt like an idiot as I watched. If I had paid attention, I would have realized that this wasn't even Dwight's normal gun. Everything he wore was black, even his gun. I remembered noticing it the first time we met. I had always assumed it was part of his bodyguard job, like a uniform. The gun currently in Dwight's hand was silver. It was crushing, the realization that my bid for freedom was pointless.

"Why?" I asked feebly.

"Now, your fingerprints are on the gun," Burke explained almost eagerly. He looked proud of himself. Dwight placed the gun back into his holster before pulling off his gloves. My fingerprints...

They must be framing me again. I was so stupid.

"When your boyfriend gets here, this is the gun that'll take him out. Can't you see how perfect it is? You're once again a jilted lover, murdering your boyfriend in cold blood."

"Mark Lewis was never my boyfriend."

"Of course not," Burke rolled his eyes. "But the truth hardly matters. You won't be around to defend yourself anyway."

"Isn't it going to look suspicious if I'm dead too?"

"Not when you killed Donovan right in front of his bodyguard," Burke said, gesturing to Dwight. "He had no choice but to take you out."

I stared hard at Dwight, hating him even more than Burke. I had played cards with him, watched TV, trusted him with my life. The bastard betrayed me and now he would kill me.

This was hopeless. Burke had thought of everything.

"You're wasting your time with this. Grant won't come for me," I repeated, praying that I was right.

I wanted to be rescued, of course, but I was terrified that I would have to watch Grant die in front of me if he came. The idea was abhorrent. Better to be left here.

"We'll see about that," Burke replied. "Dwight's going to give him a call now. Don't worry," he said as he and Dwight walked out the door. "I'll give the young lovers a chance to say goodbye first. I'm not entirely heartless."

He slammed the door behind him and I heard the lock engage before they walked away, their footsteps fading rapidly. All I could think about was Grant. The last time we spoke was horrible, would that be our last interaction?

I should've told him I loved him. Now he'd never know.

Chapter Eighteen
Grant

The plane ride was excruciating. Despite the fact that the aircraft was hurtling through the air at hundreds of miles an hour, I felt idle. A car may move much slower, but at least it gave me a sense of doing something, moving toward a goal.

I spent the whole two-hour flight pacing up and down the length of the plane while Tyler made phone calls, trying to track down Dwight using his cell phone GPS. He had no luck.

Horrible scenarios ran through my head. I had called Jim and asked that he try to track down Burke's current location, but he had to work within the confines of his position on the force. There was red tape to contend with, so it would take time.

Time. It was something that Lilly may not have.

The most horrid thing about this situation was that, no matter how hard I tried, I couldn't think of a reason that Burke wouldn't kill her immediately. That made it hard to breathe.

When the plane landed, I dropped off Tyler at his office. He needed to track down his man, as we didn't know if Dwight was in trouble too. He promised to update me as soon as he heard anything, though. Tyler barely had time to grab his overnight bag from his trunk before I was peeling away from the curb, heading home.

It seemed the most logical place to start. There was a hollow feeling in the center of my chest, as if my heart had been ripped right out, when the house came into view. It didn't feel like home anymore, just knowing that Lilly wasn't there. I wasn't sure when I had started to think of her that way, possibly when we started sleeping together, but this house that I called mine for years was now just a cold, empty building.

I parked outside the garage. No point pulling in when I would be leaving soon anyway. As I stepped onto the gravel, the dark splatter on the ground caught my eye. This must have been the blood Tyler's men found. I swallowed a knot in my throat and stepped over it, heading to the house.

The memory of the last time I saw Lilly haunted me as I entered the bedroom. I headed to the closet, to the small fireproof safe I kept in there. I froze in the doorway.

All the clothes I had bought Lilly, which had been hanging on the right side of the closet, were gone. The closet looked just as it had before she ever came into my life, the way it had been since the house was built.

But now, it looked so wrong.

Why would Burke take her clothes?

The answer was obvious. He wouldn't. She must have been leaving the house, leaving me. I should've expected that. I pushed her away after all. Of course she wasn't going to stick around for my bullshit. That would explain why she was in the driveway, too.

I could see it all play out as if I had been here. She grabbed her things, put them in a bag of some kind, and walked right out the front door.

But where was she going?

Following a hunch, I pulled out my phone and called Tyler. He answered on the first ring.

"Any update?" he asked tensely.

"Her stuff is gone. You have her phone there?"

"Yeah, hang on." I could hear shuffling on the other end of the line. I hurried to my safe while I waited, unlocking it with my fingerprint and pulling out my handgun. I tucked it into the back of my pants and grabbed a small box of ammo before shutting the safe.

"Okay, I've got it," Tyler's voice came back on the line.

"And it still works?"

"Yeah. Screens cracked, but I can work around that."

"Check for an Uber app."

"I'll be damned," Tyler said after a short pause. "It's here. Looks like she ordered one this morning but didn't show up to meet the guy."

Another piece to the puzzle. But it didn't actually get me any closer to her. I ended the call and left the house. I wasn't even sure where to go, but I knew she wasn't just going to show back up at home. I had to find her.

***

It was almost an hour later that I got the phone call. I had gone to Burke's home, simply because I didn't have any other starting point. It was deserted, not a soul in sight.

Burke lived next to Interstate 90, so I jumped on it. What was I even doing? I had chosen to head south because I knew that there were bad neighborhoods on that side of the city and I associated them with Burke's criminal activities. I had no plan and was starting to feel like I was spiraling out of control. At the very least I was grasping at straws, but what choice did I have?

My phone rang and my heart leapt, hoping it was Jim or Tyler with an update. I damn near crashed the car when I glanced at the screen and saw Dwight's name there. Pulling off the side of the Interstate, I turned on my hazard lights and answered the call.

"Dwight? Where are you?" I didn't have the patience for salutations.

"Lilly and I were taken by some thugs. They're keeping us in a warehouse."

"Where?" I asked, even as doubt crept into my mind. He rattled off an address that I punched into my car's GPS. I was only ten minutes from there.

"Is Lilly okay? Let me talk to her," I demanded as I pulled back onto the road. I was so close to her.

"She's unconscious, but I think she'll be fine. Listen, they gave me my phone to call you. They want you to come here, alone. If they see anyone else, they say they'll kill us both."

I was skeptical about his version of events. Maybe I was paranoid, but I had a feeling that I wasn't talking to a victim at all. In the end, it didn't matter. If Burke wanted me, he'd get me. Anything to find my girl.

"Don't worry about that. I'll be there soon," I said, then disconnected the call.

I checked the GPS, five minutes away. Phone still in hand, I called Jim.

"Hello?"

"I think I know where she is. I got a call from Dwight, claiming they were both kidnapped. But my instincts tell me that he's in on it. I think he's in league with Burke. Damn it, why didn't I see that before now?"

Scanning my memory, I couldn't pinpoint any warning signs whatsoever, but that didn't assuage my guilt. If he was in on it, it was my fault. I had hired the man to watch over her. I had trusted him to keep her safe.

"Don't focus on regrets right now. We need to get her back first. Then you can beat yourself up over it."

"You're right," I said. I reeled off the address Dwight had provided as I took an exit, leaving the Interstate behind.

"Okay, give me a little time to mobilize-"

"No, I'm only a couple minutes away. I'm going in."

"You are not. This isn't an action movie; real life doesn't work that way. Cops have to wait for backup."

"I'm not a cop."

Jim let out a string of curses.

"Dwight said I had to come alone or they'd kill her," I told him. Nothing he said would change my mind.

"Grant, they'll just kill you both."

"Then I'll die with her, if that's what it takes. But I can't just stay outside with a bunch of cops while she's alone in there." I pulled up to the warehouse. It wasn't a huge space, but it was old and clearly unused. The structure was metal with signs of rust and boarded up windows.

"I don't like this," Jim said, his voice resigned.

"Me neither. I'll see you soon," I said, then hung up the phone.

Checking that my gun was loaded, I stepped from the car and once again tucked it in at my back. I strode to the big metal door and was unsurprised to find it unlocked.

The interior of the warehouse was a largely open space with steel rafters and a concrete floor. There were three doors along the side of the room, presumably office spaces. Burke was standing in the middle of the room, with his arms folded in front of himself and an expression of mild interest on his face.

"Hello, Mr. Donovan," he said pleasantly as the door closed behind me. I was reminded sharply of the day he broke into my home and I hoped that Lilly was hidden somewhere nearby just as she had been on that day.

"Where is she?"

"Who?" he asked, raising one eyebrow. I fought the desire to attack him.

"Where's Lilly."

"Ah, the lovely Miss Monroe, yes. She's around here somewhere, but I was hoping we could have a conversation first."

I just stared at him. He held all the cards here and he knew it. I had no choice but to talk to him if that was what he wanted.

"Something doesn't add up to me, about why you are so interested in my business dealings. When I discovered that Mitch was supplying information to you, I was most displeased. But even he didn't know why you wanted to know what I was up to."

"So, you killed him." It wasn't a question.

"He was insignificant. A man like that disappears and no one really cares," My blood boiled, thinking of Leigh. This is what he must have thought of my brother. "You, however, are more problematic. A young billionaire goes missing or turns up dead and people will ask questions."

"What's your point?"

"Why are you so interested in me? At first, I thought it was because you were looking to get into the same business, but that's not it, is it? There's something more… personal about your obsession."

"You know, this has been my problem," I said coolly. "You may be a son of a bitch, but you are intuitive. It's made it difficult to get ahead of you."

Hatred coursed through me as I stared at Burke. It looked like I never would get the best of him. I sighed.

"I want to know what happened to Leigh Harris," I said, looking him straight in the eye. "I want to know what you did to him."

Burke looked startled for a fraction of a second, it was just a flicker in his eyes. Then, his gaze was assessing. I could almost see his mind putting the pieces together, possibly recalling the time we met, when I was a wisp of a man.

"My, my, my," Burke said, his smile turning predatory. "You must be Leigh's baby bro'. Been holding a grudge all this time?"

"What did you do to him?" I asked again. I had come so far, I had to get my answers.

"Leigh was such a good kid, a real straight arrow. Hiring him was a bad idea. He saw a few things that he shouldn't have, drug use and prostitutes mostly, but seemed content to look the other way until I had to put an end to a muscle-head named Victor. Poor Leigh was so upset when he saw Victor's body, I knew he couldn't be trusted to keep his mouth shut this time. I made him drive me to my lake house, so I could dispose of Victor's body, and I killed him too. Both bodies are at the bottom of Lake Michigan."

The way that Burke spoke, with a carefree confidence, as if he was discussing nothing more pressing than the weather, had two effects on me. It made me sure that he intended to kill me, as he would never have spoken so candidly about his crimes otherwise. It also filled me with sorrow.

I was mildly surprised by this. Rage, I expected. Satisfaction at finding the truth, perhaps. But this bone-deep sorrow for my brother, who was only nineteen years old, left me reeling. I couldn't help comparing his circumstance to Lilly's. She came so close to being killed after seeing the real Henry Burke, the murdering psycho. I never would have even met her then. Some of the grief I felt was for her too, because I was afraid that neither of us was getting out of here alive.

"Is that why I'm here? To join my brother at the bottom of a lake?"

"No. Remember what I said? People like you aren't so easy to get rid of." The sound of a door opening drew my attention to the left. "Ah, here she is," Burke exclaimed, gesturing to Lilly who was being pulled into the room by Dwight. That two-faced asshole.

Lilly was a sight for sore eyes. She was still wearing the yellow dress she had on this morning the last time I saw her. It was hard to believe that had only been about ten hours ago. It felt like years had passed.

Lilly's face dropped when she saw me. She looked positively devastated. That couldn't be a good sign.

"Grant, get out of here! Go! Before they-"

"That's enough Miss Monroe," Burke said sharply. I looked back at him to see that he was pulling on a pair of white gloves.

"Let her go. You wanted me and I'm here. She won't tell anyone what she saw at the club. Besides, who would believe her?"

Now that I saw Lilly alive, I had a frantic need to get her away from here. I would do anything, say anything, if I thought it might convince him to leave her alone.

"This has gone beyond the club," Burke said, pulling a gun out of his pocket. I wished Lilly were closer, so I could block her body, but Dwight had brought her closer to Burke than me. At least Burke seemed keen to keep the weapon trained on me for now.

"Tell me, Dwight," I said, knowing that stalling was my only option at this point. Jim was on his way. We just had to last long enough for the cavalry to arrive. "What's Burke paying you? He's worth billions, you know, so whatever it is, he can afford more. I can afford more. You get Lilly out of here and I'll pay anything you want. Name it."

Dwight looked at me flatly. "Wish I could believe that, but there's no way you'll forgive and forget this little incident. You think I haven't seen how protective you are of her?"

I clenched my jaw. While he was right, I had been trying to stir up discord between the men. My time was running out, I could feel it.

"How do you expect to get away with this?" I asked, desperate for a delay.

"The only prints on this gun belong to your girlfriend there," Burke replied, gesturing toward Lilly with the gun, making my heart skip a beat. "There'll be no missing person's report for you. It's a homicide."

Shit. He had planned this too well. The bastard might actually get away with it by framing Lilly once again.

"Any last words, Mr. Donovan?" Burke asked, as he raised the gun and turned off the safety. My fingers twitched with the desire to go for my own weapon, but there was no way I'd get my hand on it before Burke fired. He was watching me too closely.

So, I took that opportunity to look straight into Lilly's eyes. The captivating gray orbs that had stolen my heart and changed me. She made me a better man. Maybe that was what I had been running from all along, but now I embraced it. The warmth she implanted in the center of my chest compelled me to confess my feelings to her, despite the shitty circumstances and the presence of these two men I loathed. If these were indeed my last words, I wanted to make them count.

"Lilly, I love you with all that I am. You chase away my demons and make me whole. You are my light."

I saw her eyes mist with tears as she heard my dying declaration. I'd done a lot of things wrong with my life, but she wasn't one of them. Taking her into my home had turned out to be the best thing that ever happened to me and now she knew it.

"How precious." Burke's smooth voice broke the moment. The room filled with tension until the air itself felt thick. All I could see was the gun when I turned back to him. It was aimed at my head and as I watched, he moved his finger to the trigger.

I braced myself for the shot, but it didn't come. Instead, we all swiveled around as Lilly let out a scream.

Chapter Nineteen
Lilly

I couldn't stand by and watch the man I loved die without even trying to stop it. Dwight had a tight, bruising grip on my arm, so I ran through my one day of self-defense training in my head.

Grant had emphasized planting my feet. What else?

Right, the sensitive areas. Eyes, ears, nose, throat, and knees. But did he tell me how to get out of a tight grip like this? My mind raced, but I couldn't come up with anything.

Then, I saw Burke's finger move to the trigger and all rational thinking went out the window. Letting out a scream of fear and anger, I let my instincts take over. Bending my legs, I launched myself at Dwight, my hands twisted into claws as I went for his face.

My thin body collided with his firm one. I had clearly taken him by surprise, as he released my arm, but he didn't even stumble backward from the impact. His stocky build not only kept him upright but allowed him to easily fling me off him and onto the floor, knocking the wind out of me. Looking up, I felt a deep satisfaction at the sight of three long scratches down the side of his face. He glared down at me with a rage-filled expression and started to step toward me, surely to inflict pain, when several things happened at once.

It happened so fast, I could barely comprehend it all and my own adrenaline was the only thing that allowed my mind to keep up. Burke had turned in our direction when I attacked Dwight, distracted for just a second. But it was enough.

Grant had a gun tucked into the small of his back and used Burke's brief lapse of attention to pull it out and point it at Burke. When he realized this, Burke lifted his own weapon once again and both men pulled their triggers.

The sound was deafening and only seemed to echo in the large space. Time froze as my eyes darted back and forth between the two men, anxiously looking for signs of injury. Dwight was forgotten as I held my breath.

Then, Burke let out a weak grunt before clutching his stomach and falling to the floor. His gun skidded away, coming near me. I scrambled to get to it, seeing Dwight step forward in my peripheral vision.

"Not another step, asshole," Grant's voice rang out and Dwight stopped moving, his own gun still holstered on his hip.

I snatched Burke's gun off the floor and moved to Dwight. I reached to take his from where it was strapped to his body, but he moved his hips as I reached out, his hand moving out as if he was going to grab me.

"Give me an excuse," Grant said. I glanced over my shoulder and saw that he was moving toward us. "Any excuse and I'll pull this trigger, I promise you. Don't touch her. Hell, don't even look at her." Dwight lifted his hands into the air and I disarmed him.

Burke groaned from his place on the ground. I spared him a glance but decided I didn't care what happened to him. I had his weapon and Grant was watching both men intently, so they were no longer a threat.

All I wanted to do was throw my arms around Grant and kiss him. I wanted a tender moment together where I could declare my feelings for him without these men listening in, but it looked like that would have to wait.

Instead, I moved to his side, trying to be satisfied with simply being close to him. He didn't dare even look at me, His focus on Dwight and Burke was so absolute.

"I heard two shots. You aren't hurt are you?" I asked, my eyes running over his entire body, looking for any sign of blood.

"No, sweetheart. I'm perfectly fine. Bastard is a terrible shot."

I looked at Burke curled up on the ground. He was panting now. A small, hateful part of me was glad to see him suffering, but I knew we needed to get him an ambulance.

"Do you have your phone?" I asked Grant. "We should call the police."

No sooner had those words left my mouth than the door of the warehouse burst open and uniformed officers flooded the place, guns drawn. I froze, Burke's gun still in my hands as they surrounded all four of us.

"Drop your weapons!" One of the many faces around us shouted.

Everything was a flurry of movement after that, it all happened so quickly. The first wave of police had been wearing jackets that said SWAT on the back, then the FBI came in, along with Chicago PD to help maintain a perimeter. It was chaos. An ambulance arrived for Burke, and I finally found myself in Grant's arms.

Too bad it didn't last long.

"Lilly Monroe, you're under arrest for the murder of Mark Lewis..." a voice recited as I was pulled away from Grant and cuffs were slapped on my wrists. It happened so fast, I found myself being led away as Grant struggled to get past the officers that held him back. I could hear him arguing and cursing, but it did no good. They were arresting me.

"No, you can't do this. I didn't kill anyone. It was Henry Burke and a man named Clint. Please, Burke kidnapped me! Just ask Grant." I tried to reason with the man as he pulled me toward the door of the warehouse.

"You can give us a statement at the station," he replied.

"Whoa, what do you think you're doing?" Jim's voice spoke from behind me and I wanted to cry at the relief of hearing it. Surely, he wouldn't let them take me in.

"You aren't in charge here, Sampson," the cop that had read me my rights said. "The feds are calling the shots."

"She's injured," Jim argued, gesturing to the back of my head. "You can't take her in like that, she needs medical treatment."

"Fine," the arresting officer said, after a moment of hesitation. "You escort her to the hospital and stay with her at all times. She's considered a flight risk. Bring her to the station when you're done."

The cuffs were removed from my wrists and Jim led me through the warehouse and out into the fresh air. The sun was just going down and I marveled that so much had happened in a single day. To my right, I saw Dwight sitting in the back a police cruiser, his hands cuffed behind his back and a sour look on his face.

"This is a mess," Jim said. "You're still wanted for murder. It'll surely get all sorted out now, once we take statements from you and Grant. And the security guard," he nodded in Dwight's direction. "Maybe we can cut him a deal or something. But for now, there's only so much I can do."

I didn't know what to say, so I just nodded and got into his car. I had foolishly hoped that things were fine now, that the truth would come out and I would be able to go home a free woman. I hadn't even gotten a moment alone with Grant yet.

It turned out that I had a mild concussion and needed three stitches on the back of my head. The doctor gave me pain medicine and told me to avoid too much activity or stress.

Yeah, right. How could I do that when I was going to jail after this?

That thought made me realize that Jim had left the room. He had stayed with me during the long wait to be seen and the exam, but now I was in the hospital room alone.

I sat on the stiff hospital bed, trying to stay calm. I wondered how serious Burke's injury was. Would he live? He took a slug to the gut, so it was hard to know if any organs had been hit. As much as I hated the man, I hoped he lived. I didn't want Grant to become a murderer. Despite what he thought, he was a good man.

The hospital door opened, and I looked toward it, expecting a nurse or perhaps Jim to enter. I was delighted to see Grant walk in. He closed the door behind himself, shutting us in together. Finally, alone.

"I love you too," I blurted out. I slapped my hand over my mouth, mortified. I had been dying to tell him that I felt the same since he made his confession to me, but I had hoped to be smoother about it. All his elegant and heartfelt words were a worthy testament to such feelings, and I just shouted it at him with no tact at all.

Grant laughed and walked over, placing a searing kiss against my lips that was far too short. "I know you do, Temptress." He craned his neck to the side and looked at the back of my head, "Does it hurt?"

"Not nearly as bad as it did." It was true. In the hours since I woke up, the pain had dulled to the level of an average headache; unpleasant, but livable. "I'll be okay."

"Listen, about what I said this morning-"

"Forget it," I interrupted him. We were so far beyond our breakup that it wasn't even worth discussing. I'd almost watched him die. It made a few harsh words irrelevant. "I know you love me. Let's leave it at that."

Grant smiled, looking relieved. Another chaste kiss and he was pulling away as the door opened again. Jim walked in, putting away his phone and looking somber.

"I'm glad you're here. Listen, you're not going to like it, but I have to take Lilly in," he said to Grant. He stiffened beside me.

"You can't do that until she's released from here, right?"

"They're writing up the paperwork for that now. But it should just be temporary. We'll get her story and all our ducks in a row."

"No, the doctors won't release her."

"It's just a mild concussion. They have no reason to hold her here."

The door opened yet again, and a nurse came bustling in. "The doctor has decided to keep you overnight for observation, dear. Just to be safe. There are gowns in this cabinet," she pointed to a tall cabinet by the bathroom, "if you want to change. I'll be back in a few hours with more pain medicine."

As she left, I turned to Grant with wide eyes. He had a smug look on his face that I knew very well. "What did you do?" I asked him.

"I don't know what you're talking about," he said. "But did you hear that this hospital will be opening a new wing within the next year?"

"Yeah?" asked Jim with a knowing smile.

"Yep. Apparently, some anonymous donor gave them a ton of money today."

"Must be a nice guy," Jim said. "I wonder if he got anything out of it."

"I think he did," Grant said, reaching out and grabbing my hand.

"I'm going to go check Burke's status. They were doing surgery on him, last I heard. I'll be right back," Jim said, walking back out of the room. I had the feeling that he was giving us privacy and I appreciated it.

"The hospital agreed to keep me overnight because you gave them money?"

"What can I say? The Dean of Medicine is a smart man. He could see how much good that money would do for his hospital and that it was worth putting a little pressure on your doctor."

"How much money are we talking about here?"

"A hundred million," Grant said, shrugging as if it were no big deal.

"What? You paid a hundred million dollars just to keep me out of jail overnight?"

"Let me make something clear," he said, sitting on the bed and pulling me into his lap. "I'm your protector and I'll do whatever it takes to take care of you. If that means bribing - I mean donating - a bunch of money to a good cause, that's what I'm going to do." He looked me in the eyes and I saw the depth of my own emotions reflected back at me. "If it means confronting my enemy or taking a bullet, then I'll do that too. You're worth it."

I didn't know what to say, having no words that could match the sincere expression of love. So, I kissed him.

***

The FBI showed up first thing in the morning to talk to me. Jim had already taken my official statement the night before, but they wanted to hear it again. I told them everything, beginning with the night I saw Burke and Clint murder a man, confessing that I had been in hiding at Grant's house - though I left out the steamy details of my stay - and ending with my abduction.

I was clear and honest, but I knew that they were probably going to take me to jail the second that my doctor signed the release forms. They had no reason to take my word as truth and Burke had done a hell of a thorough job framing me for Mark Lewis' murder.

Grant stayed by my side the whole time, refusing to leave the room for my statement. He held my hand while I spoke, our fingers intertwined. He was my rock, providing the support that I needed as I relieved the trauma of being held captive.

The FBI left without me though. It wasn't until almost an hour later, just after my doctor came in with a list of things to avoid, sex among them, unfortunately, and delivered my discharge papers that Jim came into the room grinning broadly.

"Great news. So, the FBI spent all night interrogating the bodyguard."

"Dwight," Grant provided as Jim flipped through his notebook looking for the name.

"That's it. Anyway, Dwight cut a deal. He's only looking at two years for abducting Lilly," Grant spluttered angrily. Jim talked over him, "but he flipped on Burke. I guess he told Dwight about the murder at the nightclub. It cleared your name."

I sat, stunned. It was hard to grasp, this turn of good fortune. I had spent all morning mentally preparing myself to be carted away, photographed, fingerprinted, and placed in a cage. Could this be true? Was it really over?

Jim's face told me it was.

A smile formed on my face and I laughed, the emotion exploding from me in a sudden loud outburst. Then, before I was even aware of what was happening, I was crying. The tears spilling down my cheeks as Grant wrapped his strong arms around me, whispering soothing words in my ear.

I was embarrassed by my tears, but I couldn't seem to stop them. Just like the laughter, they burst forth in a great release of pent up tension. As they poured down my cheeks, I felt like the tears were taking all my stress and worry with them, hollowing out all those negative feelings and leaving behind plenty of room for the good stuff, for love.

Which was good because snuggled into Grant's embrace, I had a feeling I was going to receive an endless supply of that from now on.

Chapter Twenty
Grant

Lilly officially moved into my home the day she left the hospital. No temporary arrangement this time. I was jumping into this relationship with both feet. I wanted to have her here, to wake up to her face every morning and worship her body at night.

I didn't have a single reservation about loving her, not anymore. I guessed almost dying did that to a person. I almost missed out on this because of my own stupidity and I wouldn't be making that mistake again.

It was almost a week later that I realized I wasn't completely okay.

I had thought, all these years, that I would be able to move past my trauma when I got revenge on Burke. Which I had done. He wasn't behind bars yet, still recovering from his gunshot wound and abdominal surgery, but charges were being filed. It started with the murder of Mark Lewis and the abduction of Lilly. Then, the DEA started snooping around after Dwight's plea bargain confession mentioned drug smuggling.

Jim called me two days after the incident at the warehouse to tell me that they had finally found the evidence I had been fixated on for so long. A shipment from Colombia had come in by plane and there were several kilos of cocaine hidden among fruit supposedly meant for a restaurant Burke owned.

That added several federal charges to an ever-growing list and the police hadn't even located Leigh's body yet. They were dredging Lake Michigan, but it would take time.

I had fulfilled my vendetta, there was no doubt about it. I even got to injure the man, which was a fringe benefit for sure. Yet, I didn't feel fixed.

My darkness was chased away by Lilly's light. But, in the night, while she slept peacefully, I would find that I couldn't rest beside my fiery Temptress. I would leave the bed and wander the dark house. I felt anxious and lost.

I had defined my existence around Burke. It was unhealthy and I knew it, but I had made my anger toward him a priority in my life. I thought that closure would help button that all up, allowing me to cast aside the resentful feelings and just move on with my life, but now I found that I didn't know how to do that.

I tried to hide these things from Lilly, fearing that she would think I was unhappy to be with her. It was the opposite, actually. The only time I felt like my life was on the right track was in her arms.

"Guess what?" she said excitedly as she found me out on the patio, trying to make myself relax.

"You got the job?"

"Yes!" she exclaimed, her bright smile dazzling me.

She had been trying to go back to work since her doctor removed her stitches and gave her a clean bill of health three days ago. I told her she didn't have to work, money wasn't an issue, but she wanted to do it and I couldn't deny her anything.

I suspected that she would hate being unemployed now that she was no longer forced into hiding. In fact, she was taking every opportunity she could to leave the house, even if it was just to run mundane errands. The happiness she got just from being out in public was infectious.

"You're looking at the new Event Coordinator at the Northview Convention Center," she said with a flourish.

"Congratulations, sweetheart."

"The pay isn't great, but I'll be booking shows and musicians, marketing, all that. It's perfect for me."

"I'm proud of you," I said, pulling her down for a quick kiss.

"Thanks." She sat down in a chair next to me, fidgeting with her hands. She bit her lip and looked out over the pool.

"What's on your mind?" I asked. She looked nervous.

"Grant, I'm worried about you. I want you to talk to someone."

"What?" I sat up, leaning forward with my elbows rested on my knees. "Where's this coming from?"

"You think I haven't noticed what's going on with you? You're restless, distracted, not sleeping. I'm worried about you."

My first instinct for this was to shut this conversation down. I wasn't used to sharing my feelings with anyone, especially the negative shit. But she was looking at me with so much tender care, I couldn't push her away, not this time.

"With me getting this job, I'm worried about how you'll cope if I'm not home."

Damn. She was too perceptive. I hadn't wanted her to know how dependent I was on her right now. I wanted to be her strong man. I felt like I was letting her down and wasn't that just typical.

"I don't know if I can do that," I told her at last, after thinking about it for a few minutes. She looked away, trying to hide her hurt, but I saw it. "I'm not just rejecting the idea outright, but I just don't think that I'm the type to talk to a stranger. Hell, just look at how hard it has been to open up to you. I don't know if I'm built for it."

"Then what should we do? You can't keep going like this. It's not healthy."

It's not healthy. Hadn't Jim said something similar about my obsession with Burke? And he was right.

"I'll figure something out. I promise," I told Lilly. It was time to let go of the things that haunted me and find a new purpose in life.

Settling into my lap, Lilly tucked her head into my shoulder and we lapsed into a comfortable silence until my phone rang, breaking the moment. I glanced at the screen and saw it was Jim.

"Hello?"

"Hey." It was just one word, but the way Jim said it sent a chill down my spine.

"You found him?"

"We think so. We found two bodies tied to cinder blocks. But they've been thirteen years underwater. They're unrecognizable. We'll have to wait for dental records to confirm."

"What's your gut tell you?"

Jim hesitated. Just when I thought he wasn't going to answer, he said, "It's him."

***

Three months later I found myself in the gym with Lilly, doing yoga. I thought it was ridiculous when she brought it up. I worked out nearly every day, lifting weights, aerobics and strength training. Yoga would be boring compared to that high impact stuff and I was already in such good shape that it couldn't possibly benefit me.

I was wrong. Not only did yoga utilize muscles in my body that my regular workouts didn't touch, but it also helped me relax. It cleared my mind. Jim liked to make fun of me for doing something that he considered girly, but I didn't give a shit.

"Okay, now downward dog," Lilly said.

I started to move into position when I glanced up and caught sight of Lilly. The curve of her ass was all I could see from here. So much for relaxing. The lower part of my body was coming to life as I watched her. Her long legs were wrapped in skin-tight black yoga pants and I could see the lean muscles of her thighs flex as she stretched.

I was still crouched, bent halfway, but otherwise not following her instructions at all, when she looked over her shoulder and caught me ogling. Standing straight, she frowned and put her hands on her hips.

"I thought you were taking this seriously?"

"I'm feeling very serious right now," I said, standing and taking a step toward her. She gulped, but her eyes started to darken.

"What's on your mind, then?" she asked, a sultry smile forming on her lips.

"How about I show you?"

Without further discussion, she closed the distance between us and leaped into my arms, wrapping her legs around my waist. I caught her easily as our mouths collided. I walked forward until her back was pressed against the wall, holding her in place. Pulling her sports bra over her head with a rough jerk, I lavished her nipples while she moaned loudly. I went at her with a frenzy, feeling the drive to dominate her body.

"Grant!" she cried as I reached between us and slipped my hand into those tight pants. I found her to be wet and ready for me, with no panties on, making a groan rise up in the back of my throat.

Not wasting another second, I pushed my basketball shorts and boxers down just far enough to spring my erection. I could feel the heat coming from her sex on the head as it pressed against her pants.

Frustrated with the fabric separating us, I grasped each side of her pants and ripped them down the seam in the middle until she was exposed to me. I drove my hips forward, slamming into her with a fierce thrust that made her cry out and dig her nails into my back.

The sting of pain mixed with the pleasure of our joining, heightening my experience as her sex gripped me tightly. The friction between us raged as I took her roughly and she had her legs wrapped around my waist, keeping me pulled in tight.

It was wild and fast, but just what I needed. My orgasm came upon me quickly, but she was right there with me, mewling in my ear as she drew closer and closer to it.

"Do it, Temptress, come with me. Now," I growled as the sensations overwhelmed me, heat spreading through my body just before I filled her with my seed. The pulses of her core made me come even harder until my eyes rolled to the back of my head.

We collapsed against each other, with her still pinned between my body and the wall, aftershocks of her orgasm causing my entire body to tremble as we stayed that way for a moment. Finally, I pulled back and she slid down my body until her feet touched the ground.

"You're amazing," I told her sincerely, tucking myself away in my boxers.

"And you owe me a new pair of pants," she said teasingly. I smiled sheepishly.

"Yeah, sorry about that."

"I'm not," she winked. "I think that's quite enough exercise for today, though. I've got to take a quick shower before work."

"I'll join you shortly," I promised with a wicked grin. She just laughed and left me alone in the gym.

I had also taken up meditation in the last few months. Lilly was the only person that knew about it. I had been working to move past the traumas in my life and my old way of suppressing everything hadn't been working for a long time. I made a promise to Lilly that I would try to conquer my demons once and for all.

I was still a work in progress, but I had found a way to handle my pain that was far healthier than my maddening quest for vengeance had ever been.

I started a non-profit organization for young people that were victims of violent crime, whether they themselves had been hurt in some way or if they had lost a family member, like me. We provided grief counseling, group support, and even a safe place to hide if needed. That last one was part of a team-up with Tyler's security firm. He had been livid to find out about Dwight's betrayal and volunteered to help me out with this project to make up for it.

The organization, which I called Leigh's Place, had been the purpose that I was craving. It turned out that listening to other people's stories, while offering advice and support, was my own form of therapy.

Now, life was good. D-Tech was thriving, with stock prices on the rise and Jumpstart, the small company in Oklahoma that we had almost had to close, was coming back strong from their scandal.

Leigh's Place was my pride and my sanctuary.

Then, there was Lilly. She was still my light, helping me to extinguish the darkness that had dwelled in my heart all these years. It was sickening to think that I had almost lost her, mostly due to my own terrible decisions.

But she was here, and she was mine.

Things had been buttoned up on the Burke end of things. Dwight got his infuriatingly short sentence for the part he played in Lilly's abduction, but she was a free woman because of that plea agreement, so I was letting it go. The last thing I needed was another toxic obsession.

Burke was facing multiple charges and was never expected to be a free man again for the rest of his life. Now, that was justice.

The man that actually murdered Mark Lewis in cold blood, Clint, had been found dead a few months back. He had overdosed on heroin. Lilly successfully identified him as the shooter from a picture that Jim showed her. I wouldn't have wished death on the man, jail time sure, but not death. However, I had to admit that I was glad he wouldn't be able to hurt anyone else ever again.

As I finished up my brief session of meditation, I hurried up the stairs. I could hear the shower still running and I wanted to get in there before she finished. Despite our hot session in the gym, I could feel my body getting ready to take her once again. I couldn't get enough. But this time, I was going to take it nice and slow.

***

The sun was setting as I walked along the narrow dirt path. Lilly had offered to come, but I wanted to do this by myself. A metal urn was tucked under my arm, surprisingly heavy. Once the bodies in the lake had been confirmed as Leigh Harris and Victor Costa, my brother's body had been released to me. On Jim's recommendation, I had him transferred to a funeral home and cremated without seeing the body. According to Jim, it wasn't a pretty sight.

I decided it was better to remember him as he had been, alive and lighthearted with a crooked smile and curly hair. That was the picture I had in my head of my big brother, and it was the one I wanted to keep.

When the ashes had been returned to me, eight weeks ago, I had said that I was going to scatter them in the same place I scattered my mother's, so they could be together. But instead, I sat the urn on the mantle in the living room, looking at it every time I walked by, but being unable to bring myself to scatter the ashes.

I didn't want to say goodbye yet.

But the time to let go had come. I was walking a path along a pond that I remembered visiting as a kid. There were campgrounds in the woods here and we would come every summer, as camping was the only vacation we could afford at the time. Mom taught Leigh and me how to swim in this pond and we taught ourselves how to fish, with poles we borrowed from my best friend's dad. Those were good memories and the ones I had in mind when I scattered mom's ashes here.

I came to the spot, easily identifiable by the large oak tree nearby, and stopped walking. The day was cool and clear, with the sunset painting the sky in shades of purple, blue, red, and yellow. It was breathtaking and complemented the leaves, which were changing color before falling off the trees for winter.

I had chosen a perfect fall day to do this. Looking around to ensure I was alone, I took the lid off the urn and spoke as if I were talking to Leigh.

"Here we are. Back at the old pond, as we used to call it. I brought mom here when the cancer took her. I promised her back then that I'd find you, dead or alive. I think we both knew that you'd been killed, but it was hell not knowing what had happened for sure, not knowing if you'd suffered…"

I trailed off, my voice cracking. I never had allowed myself to cry for Leigh, it didn't seem right, not knowing for sure what had happened to him. But I did know now. The coroner found a bullet lodged in his skull. Burke had killed him with a gunshot.

I tried to be relieved that it was a quick death, but I just felt sadness. He was so young.

"You know," I started again. "I still think of you as my big brother, even though I'm damn near ten years older than you ever got to be. I think I'll always think of you that way. My big bro' that taught me what second base was when I got my first girlfriend and tied my tie for grandpa's funeral. I looked up to you so much and when you were gone… I got lost."

I wasn't sure what I was doing here or if I even believed that there was an afterlife at all, but it made me feel better to talk to Leigh again. I felt a loosening in my chest, as if a muscle that I'd never realized was clenched had finally released, allowing for relief I didn't know I needed. So, I continued.

"But I was found. My girl, Lilly, she found me. I didn't know I was still capable of feeling so good, so capable of loving. But she brings it out of me. I think I'm going to marry her."

The words were like a revelation as they left my mouth. Yes, I was absolutely going to marry that girl.

"Anyway, you guys can rest easy now," I said, talking to mom and Leigh as I turned the urn upside down and walked around the edge of the pond, allowing the ashes to pour into the water. "I love you both."

With it done, I stayed for a few more minutes to watch the sunset, enjoying the beauty of it and hoping that, somewhere, my family members really were together, that they found peace on the other side, just as I had found it here.

Epilogue
Lilly

Some girls dream of their wedding day, planning it all out, down to the last detail, when they are young, long before they even meet the groom. I wasn't like that. Perhaps it was because I had no close family to celebrate the day with, but for whatever reason, I hadn't given it much thought.

So, when the time came to plan my wedding to Grant, I chose a place that I knew he'd love. The Botanical Gardens. Grant loved being outdoors and there was no way that we were having an indoor wedding. Besides, who doesn't love an outdoor wedding in the spring, when everything is green and new? The flowers were all in bloom, creating a gorgeous backdrop for our ceremony.

There weren't a lot of guests at the wedding. There were a few of my new coworkers, including my boss that clearly had a crush on me. He was in the back looking sullen, but he should have just been happy that I made Grant promise not to make a scene by punching him out. I didn't want the guy to steal the spotlight from us today. Some of my old coworkers from The Verve showed up too. That was pretty much it for my side of the aisle.

Grant had Jim, along with his daughter, Macy, who was just about the cutest five-year-old I'd ever seen in my life. Bonnie, his secretary, was there along with a few others from D-Tech. Most of his guests were from Leigh's Place. The non-profit was doing amazing work and Grant, my lovable introvert, had forged such strong connections with many of the people he worked with that many of them had jumped at the chance to attend our wedding.

I had planned everything myself, really enjoying the process, but that was probably because we kept it simple. Grant had all the money in the world, we could have had the party of the century, but we didn't need that. This wedding was a declaration of love, not just a huge party.

I took a deep breath and checked my appearance in the mirror just one more time. My dress was made entirely of lace, with long sleeves and a completely exposed back. I displayed the tattoo that I loved so much, while also being soft and airy. I had curled my hair and pinned it to the side so that it cascaded over my right shoulder. I had kept my make-up simple, adding a little gold to my eyelids and soft pink lipstick to my lips. A bouquet of wildflowers completed my look.

I was bouncing on the balls of my feet anxiously, waiting to hear the wedding march that was my cue. I wasn't nervous, just eager. I had planned this wedding and honeymoon in two months because I wanted to be Mrs. Grant Donovan more than I had ever wanted anything in my entire life.

Finally, I heard the music I'd been waiting for, so I stepped out from behind the trees that were blocking me from view. Everyone stood, but I didn't even look at them. My eyes were glued on the man waiting for me at the end of the aisle. He was positively beaming at me.

Grant could wear the hell out of a suit, but this tuxedo he had on was in a whole new league. It had been tailor-made for him - you could tell by the way the fabric pulled across his shoulders just right, accentuating the muscle underneath. The black color brought out the blue of his eyes and made his smile seem even brighter, if that was possible.

It was hard to even remember what Grant's frown looked like anymore. The grumpy man I had met just last summer no longer existed. Grant had shed that persona and emerged so much happier on the other side.

I liked to think I had a little to do with it, but it was also his own determination to be a better man. I was so damn proud of him for it.

When I reached him, Grant held his hand out to me and I gladly took it, handing my bouquet off to Macy, who had been so eager to be a part of the wedding that we had to find something for her to do.

The officiant began speaking, going through the normal spiel while Grant and I stood there with our hands clasped. We kept it simple. A couple of "I dos", the exchanging of rings and one "kiss the bride"; we were officially married ten minutes later.

I couldn't help throwing myself into Grant's arms when the officiant called for a kiss. We had kissed many times before, but this, our first time as husband and wife, was something else. It was as if the magnitude of what this kiss meant made it even more powerful, like being struck by lightning, but I couldn't get enough.

When we finally pulled away to wolf whistles, the officiant loudly declared us husband and wife. I couldn't help joining in with the cheers that followed.

The happiness of that moment stayed with me during the reception, and it really felt too good to be true. But then I locked eyes with Grant, my husband, and I knew that it was real.

There was champagne and cake, dancing and bouquet tossing. Everything that you expect from a reception. I enjoyed myself, of course, but the longer the night went on, the harder it was to keep my hands to myself. Grant looked sinful in his tux and I was ready to be a bad girl by the time the limo came and picked us up for the airport.

Once we were alone in the limo, I couldn't stand to hold myself back any longer.

Grant was usually the sexually aggressive one, dominating me at every opportunity and I loved it. But now it was my turn.

Straddling him, I slipped my tongue into his mouth, earning a startled gasp from him. All the better, it gave me more access. Snaking my hands into his hair, I tugged lightly at the dark strands while biting gently on his lower lip.

Grant's hands came to rest on my hips as I ground myself against him. The heat between us was palpable and I broke the kiss to catch my breath, feeling him trace the princess neckline of my dress with his tongue.

I sighed in pleasure but didn't let it last long. I was in charge now.

Urging him to remove his jacket, I hiked my dress up until it was around my waist, the light fabric easy to maneuver in the small space. I guided Grant's hand to my core and his eyes darkened as he felt the wet fabric there. Slowly tracing the edge of my panties, he tucked his thumb over the top, pressing against the bundle of nerves there.

"Fuck," I shouted out.

Grant brought his other hand to my mouth, pushing his finger past my lips just as he did the same down below. Using his hands to penetrate both at the same time was shockingly erotic and our eyes locked as I sucked gently on his finger. I gripped his shoulders tightly as he pushed his other finger further into me below, teasing me.

"Do you want more, Mrs. Donovan?" he asked. His use of my new name sent a shiver through me. I pulled his finger free from my mouth and backed off him. I knelt on the floor in front of him staring at the bulge in his pants.

"Take it out," I demanded, my voice not sounding like my own. "I want to see your reaction to me."

I didn't have to tell him twice. In a flurry of movement he shoved his pants down far enough to pull his large erection out. It stood up straight as I watched, so thick and smooth. I felt my core clench almost painfully.

I leaned forward and swirled my tongue around him. I wasn't trying to bring him to climax, just tease him a little. So, I didn't take him into my mouth, instead, I pumped him with my hand and lavished him with my tongue. He clenched his fists tightly as he watched my ministrations.

"Lilly, fuck," he said, squeezing his eyes shut. "Please."

That was what I wanted to hear. In a flash, I was in his lap again, kissing him hard as I reached between us. I pulled my panties to the side and lined him up at my entrance. Slowly lowering myself onto him, I broke our kiss to moan loudly. He stretched me with his thickness, but it was so good.

My dress was too complicated to easily remove, so Grant settled for cupping my breasts through the lace material, still providing enough friction to make my nipples harden.

Once I had lowered myself onto him completely, I held onto the back of his seat and used it as leverage to ride him nice and slow. As I settled into a rhythm, Grant's eyes watched me closely, the passion there taking my breath away and heightening the pleasure.

"Lilly, Temptress, yes." His voice was pleading, and I knew exactly what he wanted.

Bringing my feet up to the seat I angled my hips to take him deeper and bucked against him wildly, crying out his name with every slamming together of our hips. The heat, the pleasure, it was too much. I couldn't last any longer.

With a desperate cry, I fell over the edge, my orgasm taking me as I screamed soundlessly. I didn't seem to have the breath to make a sound.

"Oh my God," Grant cried out as my pulsing pussy seemed to pull the orgasm out of him. As I came down from my own ecstasy, he was still in the throes of his passion. I couldn't keep my eyes off his face, it was so raw, so open. The moment was perfect. And timely, because we had just reached the airport.

We were flying straight to Hawaii for the honeymoon - on Grant's private plane, of course. Make that our private plane.

Though that seemed unreal as I stepped onto the thing. Everything that's his is now mine? I was worried about paying thirty thousand dollars in student loans last year and now I'm a billionaire.

Life could really spin you around sometimes.

The money really didn't matter to me though. As we took our seats on the plane, I turned to look at Grant. My sweet husband. The man that protected me. Saved me.

The man that woke me up singing "Happy Birthday" and holding a cupcake that he had made himself, despite knowing nothing about cooking, on my twenty-third birthday. The man that took my virginity and fell in love with me. This was the man that would be the father of my children.

Those were the things that mattered.

"I love you," I said softly.

"I could listen to you say that for the rest of my life," he responded. I smiled.

"It's a deal."

~The End~

A NOTE FROM THE AUTHOR

Thank-you for reading His Desire. I hope you enjoyed reading it as much as I enjoyed writing it! Can I ask you a favor? If you're happy with the book, could you please leave a review? Reviews help get the word out and they allow me to keep writing the books that you love to read.

Thanks so much,
Ashlee

COPYRIGHT

Printed in Great
Britain
by Amazon